Bridge to Tomorrow

Cold Victory

A Novel of the Berlin Airlift

Part III

Helena P. Schrader

Cold Victory: A Novel of the Berlin Airlift

Cross Seas Press
91 Pleasant Street
Blue Hill, Maine 04614
www.crossseaspress.com

ISBN: 979-898-7177-044 (paperback)
ISBN: 979-898-7177-051 (ebook)
LCCN: 2025902348

Praise for the "Bridge to Tomorrow" Series

"Schrader is well on her way to writing the 'War and Peace' of the Berlin Airlift." —BookTrib

Praise for *Cold Peace*

"Sharp research meets vivid storytelling in an absorbing novel of the postwar period." **Kirkus Reviews**

"...utterly transporting." **The Book Commentary**

"...a wonderful mixture of hard historical facts...[and] raw portrayals of the human condition." **Historical Fiction Company**

"...a spellbinding work of historical fiction that brings a unique pocket of history to life with extraordinary detail and heart." **Readers' Favorites**

"...a very fast-paced, suspenseful, emotional, and riveting story that any reader will find almost impossible to put down."
Feathered Quill

Praise for *Cold War*

A "tour-de-force" **IndieReader**

"...any fan of historical fiction (or well-crafted literary fiction) will find *Cold War* immensely rewarding—and eagerly await the sequel."
BlueInk Starred Review

"Schrader creates a conflict and captures the human condition... with cleverness and clarity. ... It delights from the descriptive prose and the complex characters to the vividly drawn setting." **The Book Commentary**

"This is a trilogy worth the reader's time, attention and emotional investment." **BookTrib**

"...an epic novel that delves into the human experience and belongs in the same conversation with classics like *Casablanca* and *Das Boot*."
Readers Views

"... the power of the book is in how a true sense of humanity prevails."
Kirkus Review

"... intricate and multilayered storylines, relatable characters as well as ... harrowing descriptions of the circumstances of that time period."
Historical Fiction Company

"... a deeply moving and educational novel ..."
K.C. Finn for Readers Views

Contents

Foreword

Cold Victory is the third book in the Bridge to Tomorrow Series, a trilogy which explores how the West stopped Russian aggression without war during the Berlin Crisis of 1948/1949. This series goes beyond the political chess game and logistical achievements that dominate most historical accounts to reveal the human face of history. As a diplomat and long-time resident of Berlin, I was drawn to the topic because of the rise of tyranny and aggression in the world today.

The first book in the series, *Cold Peace*, introduces the bulk of the characters, all of whom are survivors of a traumatic world war. In early 1948, they find themselves in Berlin largely by chance but soon discover that the former German capital has become a vortex of international tension. From their various positions, they witness the deterioration of relations between the Soviet Union and its wartime allies, culminating in a Soviet blockade of the Western Sectors of Berlin. *Cold War* continues their stories as they and others attempt to keep Berlin alive and free through a massive, humanitarian airlift. It also exposes the intimidation tactics of the Soviets, depicts the deplorable state of Berlin's hospitals, and describes the hardships faced by ordinary Berliners.

Cold Victory picks up where *Cold War* ended, taking the reader into the hearts and minds of RAF commanders and controllers, British and American aircrew, and German politicians, policemen and prostitutes. *Cold Victory* opens in December 1948 when, after nearly a month of fog, the Airlift is on the brink of collapse.

Maps are provided before the text, a rank table for readers unfamiliar with the Royal Air Force, a list of acronyms, and a glossary of some common German terms used in the book are included in the appendices. A historical note highlights some of the more extraordinary true events depicted in this volume, as well as identifying deviations from the historical record taken for literary purposes. One note on terminology: I have chosen to refer to the Soviet political police, which permeated Soviet society and operated more ruthlessly than the Gestapo both domestically and in Soviet-occupied territories, as the "Soviet Secret Police." This is because it underwent seven name changes between its inception and the end of the Soviet Union including Cheka, GPU, NKVD, MGB and KGB.

I wish to thank my editor, David Imrie, my cover designer, Anna Dahlberg, and all my test readers. Without their help, this book would not have seen the light of day nor offered readers as much as it does now.

Background on *Cold Peace* and *Cold War*

Synopsis of *Cold Peace*

Cold Peace opens with the appointment of Wing Commander Robert "Robin" Priestman to the post of station commander at the RAF's sleepy, grass airfield in the British Sector of Berlin, RAF Gatow. Priestman, a former Battle of Britain ace, and his wife Emily, a former ATA pilot, are fundamentally hostile to Germans and uncomfortable with their new assignment, although anxious to make the most of it professionally. Also moving to RAF Gatow is the WAAF air traffic controller Kathleen Hart, the widowed mother of a six-year-old girl.

Meanwhile, former Lancaster skipper Kit Moran, disabled after the loss of half his leg in a crash at the end of the war, is finishing his engineering degree, awaiting the birth of his first child, and looking for work. The German-born, Canadian Jew David Goldman, on the other hand, has just inherited a fortune from his estranged father with the mandate to find out what happened to the properties abandoned in Germany when the family fled to Canada before the war. In Berlin, Charlotte Graefin Walmsdorf, a young woman who was gang-raped by the Russian soldiers after losing her entire family in the war, struggles to make a living as a journalist while coping with severe depression and PSTD. Meanwhile, the Social Democratic city councilman, Jakob Lieberr, struggles against the increasing overreach by the Soviet occupation forces.

On arrival, Robin gets a crash course in post-war politics. While sitting in for a more senior officer at a session of the Allied Control Council, he witnesses Soviet intransigence, irrationality, and provocation. He recognizes that the Soviets are intentionally making joint government of Berlin and Germany impossible. Unknown to him, his RAF translator Galyna, a young woman of Ukrainian birth, meets Mila, a female member of Marshal Sokolovsky's staff, during the lunch break. They share views and experiences and soon become friends, meeting privately whenever possible.

Emily hires Charlotte to help her improve her German. David comes to

Berlin to find out what happened to family property and while staying with the Priestmans meets Charlotte. Through her, he learns about the appalling state of Berlin's hospitals and conceives the idea of launching an air ambulance service to evacuate patients to better facilities in the West. He hires Charlotte, Emily and a wartime friend now down on his luck, Kiwi Murray, to help him build and run the company, Air Ambulance International.

Meanwhile, Kathleen encounters a dashing British Army major, who appears keen to help her and her daughter Hope adjust to Berlin, including introducing Kathleen to Berlin's notorious nightlife. In England, Kit's wife almost dies giving birth to a daughter, and his job search is going nowhere. Although Kiwi locates an old Wellington and hires ground crew, the financial pressures inherent in starting up a new company are gnawing at David. Relations between the partners fray even as David finds himself increasingly attracted to Charlotte — and she to him.

On 1 April 1948, the Soviets impose restrictions on Western Allied trains and vehicles bound for Berlin; for five days, the Western garrisons are dependent exclusively on supplies brought in by air. Robin, recognizing the inadequacies of Gatow's facilities, advocates the construction of a concrete runway. International tensions further escalate when a Soviet fighter collides with a British airliner on approach to Gatow.

While attending a dance performance in the Soviet Sector, Galyna overhears Soviet officers bragging about plans to blockade the Western Sectors of Berlin. She reports what she heard to her superiors, and Robin passes the intelligence on, but there is no Western response. In England, discouraged about his prospects of finding work as an engineer, Kit considers taking work as an aircraft mechanic, but his wife Georgina convinces him to keep looking. Sadly, Robin must inform Kathleen that the dashing officer she was seeing socially has been arrested for art theft — and is a married man.

With Soviet kidnappings and interference increasing, Jakob senses that a political confrontation is approaching. His son, an active member of the Soviet-controlled Socialist Unity Party (SED), warns Jakob not to attend an impending meeting of the Berlin City Assembly. Jakob goes anyway, but a Soviet-controlled mob attempts to disrupt the proceedings. Despite the violence, the Berlin City Assembly meets and rejects Soviet demands.

On 26 June 1948, the Soviets cut off the Western Sectors of Berlin by rail, road and canal. They also cut off the electricity, which is generated in the East. The roughly 2.2 million people in the Western half of the city must be supplied by air to survive. An airlift of this magnitude has never been attempted before. None of the senior commanders believe it is possible. However, the RAF liaison officer to the Allied Control Council, Air Commodore Waite, has done some quick calculations that suggest an airlift might work. He enlists Robin's support in convincing the British and American Commandants to try it. The US Commandant, General Clay, insists on consulting Berlin's civilian representatives before committing to a policy that will cause Berliners much hardship. Mayor Reuter takes Jakob with him when he meets General Clay. They assure the American general that the Berliners prefer hardship to surrender.

Cold Peace ends with Robin warning the staff of RAF Gatow that they are in a new kind of war requiring tenacity, creativity, and ingenuity. Kathleen is determined to contribute to this exciting endeavour. However, AAI's ground crew refuses to remain in the besieged city, and David must suspend medical evacuations just when they are needed most. In England, the former bomber pilot Kit Moran wishes he could be part of this humanitarian operation to a city he helped destroy.

Synopsis of *Cold War*

Cold War opens with a reporter describing the hectic, chaotic and improvised character of the Airlift, but Robin and Waite assess the situation more soberly. The Allies lack the necessary aircraft and aircrew as well as departure and receiving airfields for a successful operation. They also lack the construction equipment needed to complete the concrete runway at Gatow, much less build new airports. Furthermore, air traffic control in the congested skies over Berlin is an accident waiting to happen. Robin warns that Britain cannot succeed in supplying Berlin on its own; without the resources of the United States, the Airlift is doomed to failure.

The situation soon turns into a crisis when power supplies to Gatow are cut. Fortunately, Lt. Col. Graham Russell of the Royal Corps of Engineers discovers that power for a nearby Soviet Airfield is generated in the British Sector. In a risky tit-for-tat, Robin orders the power cut to the Soviet field and minutes later Gatow is back 'on the grid.' Russell also recycles materials and parts to complete the concrete runway. Cutting equipment into pieces small enough to be transported by plane and then welding the pieces back together on arrival in Berlin also proves an effective means to later build a new airfield at Tegel in the French Sector.

Unaware of the drama at Gatow, Charlotte is mentally reliving the horrors of her rape. She is terrified that the Western Allies — and with them David — will withdraw, leaving her at the mercy of the Soviets again. Her cousin Christian convinces her not to give up hope just yet.

His advice is good. Kiwi has convinced the ground crew to work from airfields in the West, and David is preparing to resume operations. Unfortunately, the newly appointed RAF Airlift commander won't allow civilian aircraft to operate from RAF airfields, so AAI remains grounded — until Robin informs David that the RAF will be chartering civilian carriers to help transport goods into Berlin.

David seizes the opportunity. With Emily and Kiwi, he returns to the UK to establish a holding company (Emergency Air Services) to cover both freight and ambulance services. They then find and lease two more aircraft and recruit additional air and ground crews to expand the company. One of the skippers hired is Kit Moran, who is given three weeks to recruit a full crew. Meanwhile, the Soviets seek to interdict the Airlift by a variety of tactics, including jamming radio communications, blinding searchlights, and military "manoeuvres" which include shooting artillery and flak in the air corridors.

On the other side of the Atlantic, President Truman had called up the USAF reserves. J.B. Baronowsky, a former B-17 captain who has just finished college, gets orders to report for duty. Just three weeks before his wedding to the rich and beautiful Patty, J.B. finds himself back in uniform and headed for Rhein-Main. On arrival, he is horrified by the destruction caused and the living conditions of the Germans. He meets and becomes the co-pilot of a conscientious, Mormon pilot, Lt. Gail Halvorsen. Flying into Gatow, J.B. hears over his earphones the same voice that once talked him down safely after a nightmare mission to Germany during the war. He tries to find the owner of the voice and eventually tracks down Kathleen — but he is engaged to be married, and she's still smarting from the humiliation of her last relationship; nothing comes of the encounter but unspoken regret.

The Soviets seek to dislodge the elected government by using paid thugs to prevent the City Assembly from meeting. Two attempts by the City Assembly to meet at the historical Town Hall located in the Soviet Sector are thwarted by violent mobs. Reluctantly, the elected representatives recognise that they must meet in the West and surrender their control over the one-third of Berlin's population living in the East.

Meanwhile, a new threat to Berlin's elected government emerges. The Western Powers are negotiating with Stalin. Afraid that a deal will be struck behind their backs and to their detriment, Mayor Reuter calls for a public rally. Before roughly 300,000 Berliners, he demands that Berlin's wishes for freedom be heard. The Allied negotiations with the Soviets break down.

Yet while the political threats are averted, the technical problems are mounting, particularly with regard to air traffic control. The crews of Emergency Air Services experience several dangerous near collisions, and Robin copes with accidents at Gatow. After three crashes in short succession close Tempelhof, the new US Airlift Commander, General Tunner, institutes major changes to Airlift operations and procedures which increase efficiency and safety.

However, the Soviets have many methods to attack the Allies. After twelve years of silence, Galyna receives a call from her mother and is talked into a rendezvous. At their second meeting, she is kidnapped by her stepfather. He tells her that her father is a prisoner in a Gulag and very ill. He suggests she can save his life if she agrees to spy for the Soviets. Galyna agrees to cooperate but informs the intelligence officer at Gatow and offers to act as a double agent.

After a chance encounter with a score of children in Berlin, J.B.'s pilot Gail Halvorsen decides to drop candy to the kids using miniature parachutes made from handkerchiefs. J.B. agrees to help, although he expects they will get in trouble with Tunner. Instead, Tunner sees the public relations value of the candy drops and helps to scale up the spontaneous gesture into a full-scale air force operation.

The main Airlift also continues to expand. Emergency Air Services hires a former Women Airforce Service Pilot (WASP) and her flight engineer husband to fly with Emily in the ambulance, thereby freeing Kiwi to fly freight. In addition, with the company finally cash flow positive, David approves the purchase of a second Halifax, hires more aircrew and relocates Kit's Halifax to Berlin to facilitate back-loading cargoes. Kit's wife Georgina joins him in Berlin and takes a position as a teacher at the British School. Through it all, David and Charlotte are shyly taking steps towards a commitment to one another — until Charlotte's fiancé, who has been MIA since Stalingrad, appears on her doorstep. Although he is a wreck of a man, Charlotte feels she must honour her promise and breaks off with David.

And then the fog comes.

With zero visibility, airfields across Germany close, and most flights into Berlin are cancelled. Deliveries fall to a trickle. The situation is particularly dire for malnourished children, the elderly, and chronically ill patients. The Berlin City Council requests the evacuation of 17,000 vulnerable Berliners before the winter cold sets in and conditions become unbearable. Tunner refuses to carry either freight or passengers out of Berlin because back-loading aircraft increases turn-around times and reduces the volume of supplies flown into the city. The City Commandants, who have given their word to the City Council about the evacuation, appeal to the RAF (via Robin) to do what the USAF will not do. Robin agrees to organise and instigate the evacuation — despite knowing that he will be disciplined for his independent action.

Cold War ends with J.B. receiving orders to return to the US, Robin being relieved of his command at Gatow, and Jakob listening to the sounds of silence. The Airlift has broken down.

Maps

Germany, 1948
Showing occupation zones
and Berlin air corridors
Schleswig-Land
Kiel
Lübeck
Rostock
Lübeck
Finkenwerder
Flensburg
Hamburg
Oldenberg
Bremen
Fassberg
Hannover
Celle
Hannover
Bückeburg
Bielefeld
Magdeburg
Berlin
Dortmund
Kassel
Dresden
Dusseldorf
Cologne
Rhein-Main
Frankfurt
Wiesbaden
Wurzburg
Nurnberg
Stuttgart
Oberpfaffenhofen
Munich
Key
Occupation Zones
British
American
French
Soviet
Map features
1945 border
of Germany
Countries
Airfield
(flag denotes control)
Air corridor
0 miles
50

Berlin, 1948
Key
Occupation Zones
British
American
French
Soviet
Map features
District
Railway
Road
Water
Airfield
Station
0 miles
5
Frohnau
Tegel
Spandau
Charlottenberg
Mitte
Schöneberg
Kreuzberg
Karlshorst
Gatow
Gatow
(British)
Grunewald
Dahlem
Templehof
(American)
Kladow
Zehlendorf
Schonefeld
(Soviet)
Wannsee
Staaken
(British)

Character Overview

(names marked with an * are historical figures)

British Forces of Occupation	**American Forces of Occupation**
General Sir Brian Robertson* British Military Governor in Germany Air Commodore Reginald "Rex" Waite* British Air Attache to the Allied Control Council Generals Herbert* and Bourne*, British Berlin Commandant respectively up to 31. December 1948 and thereafter	General Lucius D. Clay* US Military Governor in Germany Colonel Frank Howley* US Berlin Commandant Edith, Colonel Howley's wife*
British Airlift Personnel	**USAF Airlift Personnel**
Air Commodore J.W. F. Merer*, AOC RAF Transport Command (46 Group) Group Captain Noel Hyde*, Senior RAF Officer on General Tunner's Staff, based in Wiesbaden Lt. Colonel Graham Russell, RCE, responsible for airfield expansion and improvement	General William Tunner*, US Airlift Commander, later Commander of the Combined Airlift Taskforce Lt. Colonels Bettinger* and Foreman*, two of his staff officers Captain J.B. Baronowsky, USAF Reserve pilot
RAF Gatow Personnel	**Members of the Berlin City Government**
Wing Commander Robert "Robin" Priestman Station Commander RAF Gatow S/L Garth, Senior Flying Control Officer Captain Bateman* (RASC) commander of the Forward Airfield Supply Organisation (FASO) Fl/Lt Oliver Boyd, Station Intelligence Officer Fl/Lt Reginald Tucker, CO of the RAF Regiment detachment F/O "Stan" Stanley, Station Adjutant Assistant Section Leader Kathleen Hart, Air Traffic Controller Corporal Galyna Nicolaevna Borisenko, Translator	Ernst Reuter*, Lord Mayor of Berlin Jakob Liebherr, City Councilman from Kreuzberg
	German Residents of Berlin
	Charlotte Graefin Walmsdorf, formerly head of Customer Relations at AAI Christian Freiherr von Feldburg, Charlotte Walmsdorf's cousin, former Luftwaffe fighter pilot Fritz von Bredow, Charlotte's fiancé Alexandra "Alix" Freifrau von Feldburg, widow of Christian's brother Philip, German attorney Anton Sperl, a police inspector

Employees of Emergency Air Services (EAS) Ltd.

David Goldman, founder/owner-manager of EAS

Emily Priestman, Goldman's partner and wife of W/C Priestman, Head of Facilities and Personnel, Wellington (ambulance) pilot

Charles "Kiwi" Murray, Goldman's partner, COO, Wellington and Dakota pilot

Fl/Lt Christopher "Kit" Moran, Halifax pilot

His crew: Bruce Forrester, Nigel Osgood, Richard Scott-Ross, Terry Tibble

Anna Savage, former US Army nurse, hired by EAS as a flight nurse for the ambulance

Jan and Rick Orloff, pilot and flight engineer on the ambulance.

Gordon MacDonald, former flight engineer, crew chief in Berlin

Axel Voigt, Ludwig Winterfeld and Helmut Gries, German ground-crew based in Berlin

Other Characters

Jasha, the Priestman's cook and fiancé of Graham Russell

Soviet Characters

Mila Mikhailivna Levchenkova, Heroine of the Soviet Union, Colonel in the Red Army serving on Marshal Sokolovsky's staff

Anastasia Sergeiovna, Galyna Borisenko's mother

Maxim Dmitrivich Ratanov, Galyna's stepfather

British and German School Staff and Students

Mr Peden. Headmaster of British School

Georgina Moran, Kit Moran's wife, employed as a teacher at the British School;

Dr Altenheyn and Dr Michaelis, Headmaster and Music/English teacher at a German Secondary School

Georgina's girls (sewing class attendees): Sylvie, Dietlinde, Gertrud, Gisela, Hannah, Petra, Ulrike

Bridge to Tomorrow
Book III: Cold Victory

Detailed Contents

Bridge to Tomorrow

Book III: Cold Victory

December 1948 – July 1949

Prologue
Situation Briefing

Headquarters RAF Transport Command, UK

(46. Group)
Monday, 29 November 1948
(Day 157 of the Berlin Airlift)

Preventing 2.2 million civilians from starving and freezing to death was not a task Air Commodore Merer had ever expected to get. Certainly, after fighting two wars against the Germans, he had not imagined that His Majesty's Government might require the Royal Air Force to keep Germans supplied with food, coal and clothing indefinitely. Yet effective two days hence, keeping more than two million Berliners fed and warm was going to be his job.

Merer had a smooth, round face, bushy eyebrows, a moustache and watery blue eyes. He wore wings earned in the First World War, but the ribbons below them were sparse. Although a sober and diligent airman with an impressive portfolio of qualifications on everything from fighters to flying boats, he was not a combat pilot. He had spent his career in the background — transporting aircraft to the ends of the Empire. He'd flown to Cape Town and Cairo, Karachi and Khartoum, Sidney and Singapore. Everywhere his contribution had been essential, but never spectacular or glamorous. That didn't bother Merer, and he hoped it was not about to change, either.

Sleet splattered down from the overcast sky this Monday morning 29 November as Merer arrived at the Cedars, Hatch End, in Middlesex, the HQ of 46 Group. He entered the anteroom to his office muttering to himself about how pleasant it would be to be in Aden or some other desert outpost of the Commonwealth. He removed his damp greatcoat and hung it on the coat rack near the door. As he turned to face the room, Group Captain Noel Hyde got to his feet and saluted. Hyde was the most senior RAF officer on the staff of the Combined Airlift Task Force, the joint US-British command that for the last five months had been trying desperately to keep the blockaded city of Berlin supplied by air. Hyde was stationed in Wiesbaden, Germany, where he worked directly under the American Task Force commander, General William H. Tunner.

"Ah! Noel!" Merer exclaimed, holding out his hand. "Good to see you! I wasn't sure you'd make it in this abominable weather! It must be playing havoc with the Airlift. Did you slip out before this latest low-pressure front hit?"

"I took off just before they closed the airfield, but the weather has seriously disrupted operations all around."

"Well, come in and give me the full briefing," Merer suggested, gesturing toward the open door to his office. As Hyde preceded him inside, he asked his WAAF clerk to bring tea for both of them and closed the door firmly behind himself.

The two officers settled at the coffee table. Beside them, the radiator emitted a musty odour, while the sleet tapped like a thousand fingernails on the window before dissolving into drops that slid down the glass in melancholy listlessness like tears.

"I can't tell you how pleased I am with your appointment, sir," Group Captain Hyde opened. "The Americans sent over their most acclaimed transport expert in August, while we have been muddling through under the command of an officer with no transport experience whatsoever. It's a relief to finally have you fully on board — even if only as Tunner's deputy."

"You might be a little biased, Noel," Merer answered with a smile for his old friend.

"Maybe a little, but it's high time we had a more professional and coordinated command for the British side of this operation."

"It sounds as though you're champing at the bit to give me the gen. Let me have it."

Although the Group Captain opened his battered leather briefcase, removed a thick manila folder stamped "SECRET" in large red ink, and laid it on the coffee table, he spoke mostly from memory and with obvious dedication. "Today," he opened, "is the 157th day of the Airlift. To date, the US and Britain together have flown a total of 83,104 sorties of which 31,101 or 37.4% were made by British carriers, either RAF or civilian contractors. Altogether, British aircraft delivered 116,505 tons or 19.8% of the total of 586,932 tons of supplies sent to the beleaguered city since the start of the Blockade. The difference between our share of sorties and our share of tonnage is due to the composition of our fleet, which — as you know — has fewer heavy transports than the USAF."

Merer nodded. As C-in-C of RAF Transport Command, he knew that the RAF relied more heavily on the twin-engine Dakotas than did the USAF. The Americans had enough four-engine Skymasters, or C-54s in USAF terms, to take their Dakotas off the Airlift entirely; the RAF did not have an equivalent number of heavy transport machines.

Hyde continued his briefing. "On average, our combined efforts deliver 3,715 tons of goods to Berlin each day."

"Wait! I thought the minimum daily requirement was 5,000 tons?" Merer instantly picked up on the discrepancy.

"It is 5,620 tons, to be precise," Hyde agreed. "And that's not the worst of it. Due to heavy fog, which has closed airfields almost 50% of the time this month, the number of sorties has dropped from 18,082 in October to just 13,351 so far in November. In tonnage terms, that represents a decline of about 1,000 tons per day."

Stunned, Merer exclaimed bluntly, "We're failing!" Because all his transport squadrons were committed to the Airlift and his crews were flying around the clock, he'd assumed they were successful. After all, the operation was given a lot of positive attention in the press and touted as a great British achievement in Parliament on an almost daily basis. How could it be falling this short?

"Failure is not a word General Tunner allows anyone to use out loud," Hyde spoke into his thoughts. "Nevertheless, the Airlift has undeniably reached a critical juncture. Coal deliveries are less than two-thirds of what is necessary, and liquid fuel deliveries — which are entirely in our hands because the Americans have no tankers — are at half the necessary volume. Rations for ordinary Berliners — that is essentially anyone not working on off-loading cargoes or constructing airlift facilities — have been cut to 1,600 calories a day, or half what we view as a healthy. Yet even at that level, the food reserves in the city will only sustain the population for another month. Coal reserves are even lower — probably no more than a week, and that's assuming temperatures don't drop."

Merer shook his head in disbelief and concluded he'd been too focused on making things run smoothly, when "smooth" was not good enough. "This is a disaster."

"That's another word Tunner doesn't want to hear," Hyde replied.

"Whether our American colleague likes the terms 'disaster' and 'failure' or not, I believe in facing facts — even when they are unpleasant." Merer retorted in a sharp tone unexpected from such a soft-looking man. "We've committed all 21 UK-based transport squadrons. Does the USAF have any additional capacity to make up the deficit?"

"The USAF has dedicated 225 of their heavy freighters."

That was a lot, Merer conceded mentally. It was unlikely they could find many more. Which left only the civilians. "What is the size of the civilian component these days?"

"Twenty-four British civilian companies are contributing from as little as two Dakotas to as much as a dozen four-engine Halton freighters or twelve Lancastrian fuel tankers. The serviceability of the civilian aircraft varies erratically from day to day, so I can't give you an exact figure, but they contribute roughly one hundred additional aircraft to the overall effort."

Merer did some rough calculations in his head and concluded, "It sounds to me as though we have enough *assets* to meet demand, so why are we falling short?"

"One factor is that the civilian airlift is nowhere near as efficient as it should be. Another is that we still have only two receiving airfields, Gatow and Tempelhof."

"Wait a minute! I attended an opening ceremony — complete with brass bands and press! — at a new airport in the French Sector. What's it called?"

"Tegel," Hyde provided the name, adding, "but although it has officially opened, there still aren't any crew facilities, ATC operates from a caravan, and a Soviet radio tower in the flight path poses a severe hazard, especially at night or in poor visibility. The French have been promising to solve the latter problem since before construction started, but as of today, it's still there and severely inhibiting utilization of the field. Without doubt, however, the weather," he glanced significantly in the direction of the sleet lashing the window, "is the single most important factor interfering with the Airlift."

"And *that* is something over which we have absolutely no control!" Merer concluded in a vexed voice. "At what point will HM government suspend operations and abandon Berlin?"

"The Secretary of State for Air, Sir Arthur Henderson, toured the Airlift bases last month, and we had the opportunity to chat privately. Henderson impressed upon me that the entire government, and indeed the opposition, is determined to stay in Berlin regardless. There is only one factor that might change that."

Merer raised his eyebrows and waited.

"A city election has been called for December 5. The election is viewed by everyone from Moscow to Washington as a referendum on the current mayor Ernst Reuter and his policy of defying Russian demands for the integration of West Berlin into the Soviet Zone."

Merer nodded.

Hyde continued, "You may remember that when the Blockade started, the issue was our right — or rather the right of the British, Americans and French — to maintain garrisons in Berlin. In the past five months, however, British and American policy has shifted. We are no longer defending *our* rights so much as the freedom of the Berliners themselves. This means that we will stay as long — but *only* as long — as the *Berliners* want us to stay. Mayor Reuter has pursued a policy of defying the Soviets despite the misery this brings to the average Berliner. An eloquent speaker, he has held several large rallies that suggest he and his policy are popular. Yet most people don't attend political rallies. We don't know what the little old ladies, the young mothers, the shopkeepers, bookkeepers and other less politically active people of Berlin think about what is going on."

"I take your point," Merer agreed.

"This upcoming election is a referendum on the anti-Soviet position of the current city government. The Russian-backed Socialist Unity Party, known by its German acronym SED, is not taking part in the election because they know they'll lose. Instead, they have called for a boycott. They are attempting to characterize mere participation as a 'vote for division and slavery.' They are warning Berliners to stay away from the polls, and intelligence reports indicate they are arming political activists. We believe they may use violence to disrupt the election or at a minimum, intimidate voters into staying at home."

Merer grimaced as Hyde explained further, "If these tactics work and the turnout is low, then HM government's support for the Airlift will waver. If, on the other hand, the Berliners defy Soviet threats and turn out in droves to vote for Reuter's Social Democratic Party or the equally anti-Communist Christian Democratic Union, then we will have a credible indication that the Berliners want to keep fighting the Russians. In that case, HM government will almost certainly maintain the Airlift — until the Berliners concede defeat and ask us to stop."

"And the Americans?" Merer asked.

"I have no insider information regarding American policy. However, President Truman has been very firm — almost fanatical — about the US not withdrawing from Berlin. Following his surprise election victory last month, he is facing almost no internal opposition for the first time since the Blockade started."

Merer nodded thoughtfully. "I'd lost track of how important this upcoming election is. I've been too focused on the nuts and bolts, I suppose. I'd planned to summon squadron and station commanders to a joint meeting on my first day as Deputy Commander, but it sounds as though I ought to wait until after the election. It would entail only a week's delay in meeting."

"That might be wise," Hyde agreed.

"If the Berliners vote for submission, we'll need to wind operations down quickly and pull out gracefully. If, on the other hand, the Berliners vote for freedom, then we must operate at maximum capacity and see how we can increase efficiency. Either way, I want input and suggestions from the squadron and station commanders. I know the squadron leaders well, but Bagshot's proprietary attitude towards the airfields has denied me access to the station commanders." Group Captain Bagshot had commanded the RAF stations in Germany, but he would be surrendering that control to Merer when the latter's appointment became effective in two days' time.

"I think you'll find they're first-rate," Hyde assured him, but then tilted his head to one side to add, "Although, as of yesterday, we don't have a station commander at Gatow anymore."

"Gatow?" Merer asked alarmed. "That's the most important airfield of the entire Airlift — and the one airfield I *wasn't* worried about. What's happened?"

"I don't have the details. I was simply informed that Bagshot and Priestman clashed and Bagshot posted Priestman effective immediately."

"Odd," Merer mused. Up to now, he'd had a positive impression of Priestman and wondered what had happened. Then he shrugged and remarked, "I suppose it's all moot. If the Berliners vote against the Airlift at this election, we'll be pulling out and won't need any station commander at Gatow."

Chapter One
Limbo

Political Opera
Berlin-Schoeneberg
Tuesday 30 November 1948
(Day 158 of the Berlin Airlift)

The mayor's office was cold. So little coal was getting into Berlin these days that Mayor Ernst Reuter had ordered increased restrictions. Coal went first to the few operating power plants generating electricity, secondly to hospitals and schools with generators, and third to public warming spaces run by churches and other charities with coal-fired warming ovens. Government offices weren't important enough to rate a coal ration.

As a result, Reuter and the city councilmen Jakob Liebherr and Jeannette Wolfe were still wearing their overcoats. Liebherr and Wolfe were both on the committee responsible for providing the Allied representatives with the City Council's list of priorities. From the start of the Airlift, the Allies had refused to decide what goods would be flown into the city; it was the City Council's responsibility to make the trade-offs between coal for heat and electricity vs food, clothing, toiletries and a thousand and one other necessities. The fact that less and less was getting to Berlin made the calculations all the more difficult — or pointless. Other, less tenacious politicians might well have concluded that the task was impossible. Based on last week's figures for delivered goods, the people of Berlin didn't have a choice of dying of cold or hunger since they were most likely to die of both.

But both Liebherr and Wolfe had spent time in Nazi concentration camps and that had left them jaded about the human capacity for suffering.

They were also stubborn. "Anyone who thinks Berlin is cold," Wolfe noted, "ought to try Siberia. I think—"

She didn't get a chance to finish. The door flew open and Mayor Reuter's assistant Willy Brandt burst in. "There's been a coup d'etat!" he gasped out. "The SED — they held an assembly in the Berlin Opera. Thousands of delegates from the collectivized factories and farms voted to elect a new city government!"

"Calm down, Brandt," Reuter countered in a firm and unflustered tone. "Now, tell me exactly what happened."

Still breathless from running up the stairs, Brandt answered by reminding him, "We *knew* that the SED was organizing extraordinary assemblies at the factories and farms—"

"And that they were arming 'readiness troops,'" Liebherr threw in.

"They didn't need them!" Brandt countered, agitated. "They bussed in 500,000 people from across the Soviet Zone, including 1,500 people elected by one of these factory or farm assemblies or by other bodies controlled by the Soviets, and in what they called an 'extraordinary Assembly' they voted unanimously to dismiss the existing City Council."

"Did they give a reason for this high-handed dismissal?" Reuter asked, sounding more amused than alarmed.

"They said by moving out of the Rote Rathaus the existing City Council had 'abandoned its post'," Brandt answered.

"Ah! First, they chase us out by force and then complain that we didn't remain to have our brains bashed in!" Wolfe commented caustically.

"Was there any opposition?" Reuter wanted to know.

"The vote was by show of hands and no one bothered to ask how many were opposed. It passed unanimously at the first vote," Brandt explained.

"Typical Communist Party!" Liebherr snorted eloquently. "The whole charade was designed to discourage and disguise any kind of dissent!"

"Do the procedures matter?" Brandt asked the others in exasperation. "The point is they've done it! They've set up a rival City Council under Friedrich Ebert the Younger." That was the son of the revered first president of the Weimar Republic. "Ebert spoke to the crowd after his election—"

"He was *not* elected, Willie," Reuter reproached his aide. "He is a puppet of the Soviet Military Administration."

"I know, but many ordinary people are going to see this as an election!" Brandt insisted.

"Then we will have to educate them otherwise," Reuter countered calmly but firmly. "Now, tell me about Ebert's speech?"

"His main topic was how he would improve the provisioning of the city—"

"Brilliant!" Wolfe snapped sarcastically. "Anyone sleeping with the bear holding back our food can promise that!"

With a slightly reproving look, Reuter admonished his elder colleague to let Brandt finish, than addressed Brandt, "Did he say anything else?"

"Well, he talked of the economic necessity of being integrated into the surrounding countryside."

"Which is the Soviet Zone, so he openly embraced a Soviet take-over," Reuter concluded.

Brandt equivocated, "He couched it in economic rather than political terms."

Wolfe cursed colourfully, something one didn't expect of a lady over sixty, but Liebherr was less outraged than discouraged. It would take very little for the Soviets to improve the provisioning of the city since all they had to do was end the blockade that they had started in the first place. As for complete integration into the Soviet Zone, that might be the solution to the economic catastrophe, but the price would be Soviet political rule, their worthless currency and their murderous police. From Liebherr's perspective, the problem was that "life" under Stalin was like being a man condemned to death; you knew your life would end abruptly and unnaturally, you just didn't know exactly *when* his terror troops would put you up against a wall.

Reuter remained calm. "Thank you for bringing us the news, Brandt. In a way, it is a relief. The Soviet-controlled media has been whining about 'administrative chaos' and howling for 'action' against us for weeks. I'd feared they might use violence against voters at the elections rather than to put together a farcical 'counter government.'"

"There's nothing to say they *won't* still use violence," Liebherr reminded Reuter, alarmed by the mayor's apparent complacency. "By artificially forming a new city government, they have manufactured a plausible justification for calling the real elections 'superfluous.'"

"Tell that to all the people who *weren't* allowed to vote!" Wolfe snapped.

"I don't care how many puppets from the factories and SED-controlled organisations in the Soviet Zone obeyed orders to vote for the single slate of candidates, no one in the Western Sectors of the city had that opportunity! Certainly not the women! They aren't going to accept this kind of theatrics! An Opera Government indeed!"

"Opera or not, it is dangerous," Liebherr warned his colleagues. "It's because they know they would lose in a free and fair election that they felt compelled to stage this coup. Only by controlling who voted and offering no alternatives could they be sure of winning. But they didn't need armed 'readiness troops' to carry out this staged 'election' of their hand-picked delegates." He paused to let his words sink in before adding, "That can only mean one thing: they created those readiness troops for *another* purpose."

Wolfe caught her breath and Reuter frowned while Liebherr pressed his case, "The most obvious and likely reason to create bands of armed thugs is to disrupt *our* election. They may even dress their bullies in police uniforms and have their Opera Council give them orders to 'disperse counter-revolutionary demonstrations,'" he warned.

"I concur with your analysis, Jakob," Reuter answered, nodding seriously. "We must expect attempts by armed groups to disrupt the election on the 5th, but if we're prepared we should be able to handle them. The Western Powers have agreed to provide military police protection at all polling stations, and we'll mobilize our own activists."

Liebherr frowned but decided it was unnecessary to remind his colleagues that up to now the Western Allies had been alarmingly lax about providing the elected city government with any kind of protection. Reuter, meanwhile, was expounding on his priorities. "First, we must respond to this opera *putsch*. We need to broadcast a statement in which we vigorously condemn this *attempted* coup. We must be careful never to refer to it as a 'coup' because that suggests it was successful. Furthermore, we must stress that actors in the Opera Council possess no democratic mandate and therefore have no legitimacy. We must warn people — especially city employees — not to follow any edicts or orders they issue. We must urge civil servants to resign rather than carry out their policies. We must underline in every way that only those elected in the city-wide election of October 1946 have the right to speak for Berlin — until such time as *they* are replaced in another city-wide election."

"Ernst, there won't *be* a city-wide election on Dec. 5," Liebherr countered. Much as he admired Reuter's determination to fight the Soviets, he worried that he was underestimating the threats. "The Soviets have forbidden the election," he reminded the mayor. "There will be no polling stations anywhere in the Soviet Sector!"

"Which does not prevent the citizens living in the Soviet Sector from crossing into any of the Western Sectors and voting here. We agreed with the Western powers that any Berlin resident can vote at any polling station."

"Only if they have the courage to walk through a cordon of Red Army soldiers frisking them and demanding their business," Liebherr reminded him. "Be realistic, Ernst! The SED is openly warning that those who vote 'will be noted.' Most East Berliners are not going to risk a confrontation with those who control their housing, their rations, their jobs, the education of the children and their very lives. Tens of thousands of Berliners have already been deported to Gulags and camps. The people in the East are not going to risk crossing the sector boundary to vote. What we *can* expect is that SED operatives—who can move freely across the city — will increase their tactics of intimidation here *in the West*. They will probably send their armed 'readiness troops' to harass anyone standing in line to vote on election day. The Soviets control both the guns and the butter. After this *putsch*, I fear many Berliners will lose heart and decide it is pointless to vote at all."

"Then we must re-double our efforts to convince them otherwise!" Reuter insisted. Then he paused and considered his old friend with concern. "Don't tell me you are ready to capitulate?" Reuter asked.

"No," Liebherr replied vigorously, adding with a faint but sad smile, "As a famous opponent of ours once said: I will *never* surrender — but I am afraid."

Time to Say Goodbye
RAF Gatow
Wednesday 1 December 1948
(Day 159 of the Berlin Airlift)

The drizzling rain from the low overcast sky suited Wing Commander Robin Priestman's mood. Although somewhat better than the dense fog of the previous few days, the ceiling was still too low to allow a return to full operations. The tower was landing aircraft with ground-controlled approach (GCA) once every five instead of once every three minutes, and due to worse weather at the departure fields, there were intermittent gaps in the incoming traffic.

Hearing the silence, Robin left his desk and went to gaze into the gloom. Spread out directly before his window were the hangars and hardstandings where the aircraft off-loaded inbound cargoes and a couple of the civilian charter aircraft loaded outbound freight. Further in the distance were the parallel runways, one surfaced with pierced-steel-plate or PSP for take-offs and one made of concrete and surfaced with tarmac for landings. Roughly two dozen Yorks were being unloaded just below his window, while a squadron of Dakotas was drawn up beyond the farthest runway preparing to embark children bound for the West. But no aircraft were moving.

Robin sighed. He was no longer the station commander, merely the "acting station commander" until his replacement arrived. He could not allow that subtle change to alter his efficiency or his outward appearance and behaviour. He had been careful to arrive sharply at 7:30 am as usual. He had dressed in his best blues with his shoes polished to a shine and the creases of his trousers smartly pressed. He attempted to look and sound cheerful whenever he interacted with other personnel.

In the privacy of his office, however, it was hard to maintain that façade of normality. Although he had accepted the assignment to Berlin reluctantly, in the eleven months since his arrival, his lingering wartime hostility toward the Germans had melted away. In its place, first mistrust and then gradually hatred of the Russians had taken root. He had come to see Stalin as every bit as bad as Hitler — if not worse. Stalin had institutionalised inhumanity and was actively trying to spread his reign of terror to the whole of Germany and ultimately the rest of Europe. He had to be stopped. As a result, with each day of the Airlift, Robin's commitment to aiding the besieged Berliners had grown. It had long since reached the point where his work here was not a job but a mission. Only, as of Sunday, it was not *his* mission any more.

There was a knock on the door, and he called "Come in" over his shoulder. Flight Lieutenant Boyd, the intelligence officer, entered. "I've got today's papers for you, sir."

Robin returned to his desk but remained standing as Boyd spread the press clippings out in front of him. Most of the headlines declared "SED *Putsch!*" or "Attempted Communist Coup!" He also noticed an article headed with the words: "Mayor Reuter requests Allied protection." According to the translations tacked to the Soviet-controlled newspapers, the tone in the Eastern media was triumphant: "Workers and Farmers End Tyrannical Government," "Capitalist Puppets Thrown Out!" "Democratically Elected Council Boots Out Reuter Terror-Clique!"

"I'd like to draw your attention to the following item," Boyd continued his briefing by pointing to one of the clippings. "In this article, the Soviet Military Administration promises to increase coal rations and to provide 250 grams of chocolate per household per month to those registered in the East."

Robin snorted, then with a glance at his intelligence officer, he asked, "Do you think many West Berliners will take the bait and register in the East for the sake of a little more coal?"

"It's hard to know," Boyd admitted. "Everyone I've been able to talk to scoffs at the idea — pointing out that it highlights Soviet stinginess and contempt. But it's the people I *can't* talk to who may be inclined to take up the offer."

"Not that it hurts us in any way," Robin reflected. "The more coal the Berliners get from the Soviets, the less we need to fly in. As for the chocolate...." He shrugged. "Why would any child want Russian chocolate when American chocolate rains down on them from the skies?"

"My view exactly. You may be more interested in this piece." Boyd indicated an article he had circled. "The SED's counter-mayor has promised to give workers a 30% pay rise while declaring his intention to expropriate all factories and businesses employing more than five people."

"At least he's honest and open about it. Anything else I need to know?"

"Not just now, sir," Boyd replied. Robin thanked him and the flight lieutenant withdrew.

Before Robin could settle into his work, however, there was another knock. This time the head that looked in was that of Lt. Colonel Graham Russell of the Corps of Royal Engineers. Graham was not his subordinate; he was a friend.

"Got a minute, Robin?" Graham asked.

"For you, yes," Robin answered.

Graham closed the door behind him and advanced across the room to stand just in front of Robin's desk. "I had to talk to you because I've heard a terrible rumour at Army HQ."

Robin raised his eyebrows.

"Herbert made an off-hand remark that you were on our way out. Surely that isn't true?"

"Unfortunately, yes."

"But why?" Graham sounded stunned.

"Because I went ahead with the evacuation of the children and other vulnerable citizens without clearing it through Group Captain Bagshot."

"But the Berlin City Government *requested* the evacuations?"

"Correct."

"I must be missing something," Graham admitted and looked at Robin expectantly.

"General Herbert is Commandant of the British Sector of Berlin. He has no authority over the Airlift. He asked General Tunner to handle the evacuations and Tunner said 'no,' but gave explicit permission for the RAF to do whatever it liked. Herbert asked me for RAF action, bypassing Bagshot, and I agreed without clearing it. Bagshot, unsurprisingly, was livid about my breach of military protocol and sacked me on the spot."

"Did he order the evacuations halted?"

"Even he recognised that I'd made that impossible by my promise to the City Council and by starting the evacuations on a large scale before running cameras. Which is why, no doubt, he was so determined to have my head."

"I can't say how sorry I am about this. Your friendship, Emily's hospitality — it has meant the world to me," Graham stammered out.

Robin nodded his thanks. "The feelings are mutual — not to mention that your gardening skills have improved the menu immeasurably. I hope we'll stay in touch."

"Do you know anything about your replacement and when he might arrive?" Graham asked anxiously.

"The only thing I know is that Air Commodore Merer wants me to report to his HQ next Monday morning before a more general conference of RAF Airlift commanders. I presume that is to facilitate a formal handover to my successor. My replacement may fly back with me at the end of the day."

"Monday of next week? December 6th?"

"That's right."

Graham drew a deep breath. "Well, that doesn't give us much time."

"For what?"

"Jasha and I want you and Emily at our wedding."

"We would be very happy to attend," Robin assured him, "but I don't see how you can manage something in less than a week."

"Neither of us wants anything large. I think we can arrange a small ceremony and dinner this coming weekend."

"If you do, we'll be there."

"Thank you," Graham responded, but then he returned to the initial topic to stress, "I can't believe you're being cashiered for doing what General Herbert asked you to do. Does this mean you could face additional unpleasantness?"

Robin drew a deep breath, "It could. The Air Ministry doesn't like 'insubordinate officers' and I may be handed a bowler hat instead of a new assignment." Robin tried to keep his voice as neutral as possible, but Graham saw through him. They were alike in this; the service was their life.

Graham asked in a low voice, "Do you regret it, Robin?"

"Not for a moment. Look out there, Graham." He pointed toward the row of Dakotas and the dilapidated Berlin buses disgorging children beside them. "Every child that gets out of Berlin today is one who will *not* be subject to Stalin's terror tomorrow. Every child boarding those Daks will have a chance to grow up without the fear of famine or arrest or a trip to the Gulag."

Graham nodded grimly. Eleven days in Soviet detention had convinced him that the worst rumours of brainwashing, slave labour and mass murders were true. Graham had learned to fear the Russian bear.

Robin was watching the invariably chaotic embarkation of the children.

Despite efforts by teachers and parents to keep the kids quiet and still, they were too excited to do as they were told. Even from this distance, Robin could see children drifting off to look at the planes and saw frantic adults trying to herd them back to the side as a Lancastrian tanker on approach fell out of the cloud and plonked down hard on the runway.

"Do you think the kids appreciate what we're doing for them?" Graham asked from behind him.

"They understand, Graham," Robin answered seriously, "they understand more profoundly than you could imagine." He turned to look back at Graham and asked, "Haven't you noticed anything unusual on my desk?"

Graham looked blank and then directed his attention to the station commander's desk. It took him a moment before he exclaimed, "The Teddy Bear!"

Robin reached over and took the ragged, threadbare and lopsided stuffed animal from his desk. He looked down into the beady eyes of the toy for a few moments before turning it around and holding it up to face Graham. "Meet Bertie the Bear, a wise veteran of — I'm told — 62 air raids, including one that destroyed the house in which he lived. Bertie, his friend Liesl explained, kept his beloved friend safe day and night, even when the Ivans broke into her apartment and did terrible things to her mummy. Bertie, she said, was the only thing of any value that she could give to me. I tried to convince her that he wanted to stay with her, but she said 'no.' She said, 'You are keeping us safe from the Ivans. I want Bertie to help you, so you can make sure my mummy will not be hurt like that ever again.'"

In the silence following his words, the sound of the rain seemed stronger.

"If I were still station commander, Graham, I would ask permission to increase, not reduce, these evacuations. I would seek to get not just the children and chronically ill people out of Berlin, but the single mothers and some of the youths as well. Did you know the Boy Scouts have asked permission to help off-load the aircraft? Not one of them weighs what they should at their age, but they insisted they could double up to carry ten-pound sacks of coal!"

Graham nodded understanding, and Robin concluded with a defeated shrug, "But I am no longer station commander, and God knows how my successor will feel about the evacuations — or the Berliners themselves."

The Reds are Coming
Berlin-Kreuzberg
Thursday 2 December 1948
(Day 160 of the Berlin Airlift)

Waiting in line for rations had taken five hours and forty minutes today. Charlotte was chilled to the bone despite wearing her dead brother's Wehrmacht greatcoat over her mother's thickest jumper and woollen underwear. Her feet were sore from standing so long, too. As she dragged herself back in the direction of the apartment house, she shuffled more like a woman in her sixties than in her thirties, and she did not want to think about the future.

On the blank brick wall exposed by the collapse of the house in an air raid, two young men were busy tearing down the SPD posters that had been put up the day before. Charlotte looked at them warily, prepared to make a run for her apartment building, but they were too thin and shabby to be Russians. She relaxed enough to watch them roll out a new poster and affix it to the wall with their glue-soaked brushes. It was a photo of Berlin burning after an air raid. In large red letters dripping red drops to suggest blood, it read: "Voting strengthens the warmongers! Voting means more night bombing!"

As if Hitler hadn't started the war! As if Stalin hadn't been his friend! As if the Western Allies were bombing them instead of bringing in food, clothing, medicine and coal!

She had watched the youths for too long. One of them noticed her. "Hey! Frau! Do you live around here?"

"What business is that of yours!" She answered, turning to hurry away.

He shouted after her. "This block of houses has already been allocated to the Red Army. They'll move in before the New Year. You'll have plenty of opportunity to make them feel warmly welcome!" He and his companion laughed.

Charlotte fled, trying to tell herself it was just empty threats and intimidation. "Bullying" was the word David would have used.

The thought of David almost made her stumble. David, David, David. He had given her the practical, thick-soled, warm shoes on her feet and the soft woollen gloves on her hands. Most of all he had given her back the will and a reason to live. Charlotte had hoped this Christmas would be filled with thankfulness and joy for the first time in five years, but that dream had shattered with Fritz's return.

She paused before the door of her apartment house and looked up toward the top floor. Fritz was up there now, waiting for her and the rations. She wished she didn't have to go up to him. Even queuing in the cold was better than being with Fritz. He watched her every move and his eyes seemed to take her clothes off and seek to penetrate her soul at the same time. He pressured her to tell him everything that had happened since they parted in the autumn of 1942.

She'd told him what she could: what it had been like in Silesia on her father's estate with only women and prisoners of war as labourers. She'd tried to describe what it was like as the front came closer and the refugees swept through, full of horror stories about Russian atrocities. She informed him of her brothers' deaths and explained her father's decision to flee by horse-cart. She'd forced herself to recount how the strafing Soviet fighter had killed both her parents, her mother's maid and one of the horses. She'd attempted to convey how numb and hopeless she'd felt when she arrived in Berlin. She'd tried to make him understand her relief at being given refuge in her cousin's house. Yet when she admitted that her cousin had been part of the plot against Hitler, Fritz had spat out "treasonous filth!" and she had said no more.

That didn't stop Fritz from trying to drag more information out of her. He'd asked her what happened after the war, but she kept her answers vague. She claimed she'd survived as a freelance journalist, which was partially true, but she hadn't breathed a word about Air Ambulance International — or David, of course.

What was the point? She'd broken off with David, admitting to herself that her hopes for a life with him had been a fantasy. He didn't know about the rapes. He would never have married her after he found out.

Drawing a deep breath, she put down the string bag with the rations, took out her key and unlocked the front door. Once inside, she started wearily up the shallow stairs. In the dark of the unlighted interior (there would be no electricity in this part of the city until six am tomorrow), fear closed around her like a stagnant fog. Those young men had said the Red Army would move in as soon as the Western Allies withdrew. Everyone queuing for rations had been talking about how the Amis and Brits would pull out after the election. Not enough planes were getting through. Food reserves were running out. Rations could not be cut any more. Some people claimed that the announced evacuation of children and chronically ill was a sham. What was *really* happening, they said, was that the Allies were sending their own children home. The Allied troops would be on the last planes out, and then all of Berlin would belong to the Ivans again.

Charlotte stopped on the landing to get hold of herself. Her heart was pounding not from exertion but from fear. She would not let them do it to her again. Her cousin Christian had given her a pistol, one of several he'd bought on the black market. She had a dozen bullets as well. She would kill herself rather than let them touch her again.

Sometimes, she indulged in imagining what it would be like to kill one or two of them first. She would aim for their faces. Once upon a time, when she had been the daughter of a count with a large estate and had gone hunting with her brothers, she had been a good shot. She was not unfamiliar or uncomfortable with guns. If they were trying to come in the front door, she could position herself in the doorway of the corner room, just three or four metres away. From there, with them confined in the hall and silhouetted against the light on the landing, she thought she could hit them in the face. Out of hate. Out of revenge.

But she mustn't think about it, she told herself. It was bad enough that her thoughts rotated around this final moment of her life in the dark of her sleepless nights.

She continued up the stairs to the fourth floor and again put down the bag of rations to let herself into the apartment. The interior was dark, silent and icy cold. They did not have enough coal to heat anything except the kitchen oven, and that for only a couple of hours a day. Charlotte could see her breath.

The sound of the door clunking shut behind her provoked a growl from the far end of the hall. "Is that you, Lotte? Where have you been?" Fritz demanded, adding in a self-pitying tone, "I've been waiting for you for hours!"

"Yes, Fritz, it's me!" Charlotte answered, trying to sound cheerful. "I told you I was going out to get our rations."

"That was hours ago!" Fritz complained, limping to stand in the doorway of the "Berliner Room" that occupied the corner of the house. "Don't you realise I can't do anything without your help!"

It was too dark to see more than his shape, but Charlotte could picture him all too well: the way his left eye couldn't stay focused and drifted off to the side; his mouth with only half his teeth and the others rotting and stinking horribly; the mutilated right hand with only two remaining fingers with perpetually filthy nails. Christian and she had found clothes to replace the rags he'd arrived in, but they had no hot water to give him a proper bath. Although Christian had made him strip down and stand in the tub to be sponged off with water heated in the kettle, the stink of the Gulag clung to him.

"The lines are very long," Charlotte explained. "I had to wait five hours and forty minutes."

"Arrogant bastards," Fritz snarled.

"They're doing the best they can," Charlotte reminded him.

"Really? In that case, they're incompetent fools. Bumbling idiots! We could organise things much better!"

"What do you mean?" The question cracked like a gunshot from Christian, who stepped out of the front salon. He lived there now that Fritz had moved into the second bedroom.

"People never had to wait in long lines for rations in German-occupied territory. Everything was properly organised and went like clockwork!" Fritz bragged.

"Right into the gas chambers!" Christian flung back, adding, "Nobody stood in line for rations because we killed or deported them instead."

"I should have known a traitor like you wouldn't be proud of his country!"

"You're proud of murdering millions?"

"Stop it!" Charlotte shouted. "Stop it!" It was directed at both of them.

"This is my house," Christian answered in a tone of voice his subordinates in the Luftwaffe would have recognised. "I'll say what I please."

"Don't, Christian! Please don't!" Charlotte pleaded, tears forming in her eyes. She dropped the rations and, pushing past Fritz, ran to her room at the far end of the hall, slamming the door. Behind her, the angry voices of Christian and Fritz exchanging insults continued. She flung herself onto the bed, covered her head with her pillow and started sobbing. Part of her wondered if she should bother waiting for the Ivans to come. Maybe she should just shoot herself now?

The Right Side of History
Potsdam
Friday 3 December 1948
(Day 161 of the Berlin Airlift)

WAAF Corporal Galyna Nikolaevna Borisenko was so frightened that her hands were trembling. That made the teacup rattle in the saucer, and her stepfather Maxim Dmitrivich Ratanov smiled faintly in satisfaction.

Seeing that he had noticed, Galyna lashed out at him, "Don't think that betraying my colleagues and my adopted country is easy for me! Say what you like, the British gave me refuge. They gave me an education, training and status. I've been happy in the WAAF." She threw this last remark at her mother, who sat at the head of the low table commanding the samovar. Lovely if mismatched antiques surrounded the trio. The furnishings had been stuffed into the dilapidated and damp rooms of the *Rote Haus am Neuen Garten*, which once upon a time had housed the head gardener of the Prussian kings. In May 1945, it had been taken over by the Soviet Military Administration in Germany and, more recently, assigned to Colonel Maxim Dmitrivich of the Soviet Secret Police. The brick house snuggled under willows on the banks of the Heilegensee in Potsdam, and the windows should have revealed the calm waters of the shallow lake. Instead, they were draped in fog.

In the past, Galyna's mother, Anastasia Sergeyevna, had ridiculed Galyna for her service uniform, saying it made her look fat. Likewise, Anastasia had dismissed the possibility that Galyna could find friends among the 'cold' British. Now, she tried to calm her daughter with a patronizing, "Of course, of course, you had no choice but to make the best of things, but now you can do something truly valuable."

"Don't talk that Communist rot with me!" Galyna shot back. "I'm not a child or an idiot! I saw with my own eyes what collectivisation did! I know the so-called Kulaks had nothing left, and yet you stole every last crumb from them, even their seed grain! And when you had taken everything, you still demanded deliveries of food! You drove them to cannibalism!" Galyna spoke passionately, causing her mother to recoil and her stepfather to raise his eyebrows. Galyna turned on him to declare in a calmer but more contemptuous voice, "I haven't forgotten that Stalin was happy to betray millions to Hitler, either. I don't believe black is white just because Stalin says it is!"

"You can believe whatever you like," Ratanov answered laconically, his eyes half closed. "But Stalin is always right." He paused before adding, "Because he silences anyone who says he is wrong."

"And you are proud to serve a monster like that?" Galyna challenged him.

"You sound just like you did at 15 when I sent you to live with your grandmother in Finland. I'd expected you to have grown up by now." His tone was cold and derisive.

"I'm only here to help my father. You said that if I cooperated, the terms of his arrest would be improved."

Ratanov's eyebrows twitched. Galyna wasn't sure if he approved her spirit or pitied her naivety. He said nothing.

In accordance with the advice given her by the RAF intelligence officer Ft/Lt Boyd at Gatow, Galyna continued to stress her reluctance to cooperate, "Don't think I'm an idiot. I'm not going to help you until I've seen proof that my father is still alive. I demand to see a recent photo of him!"

Ratanov shrugged and dismissed the request with a bald, "I don't have one."

"Then get one."

"Or what?" he sneered.

"I will return to Gatow and get on the next plane back to England."

"You won't get as far as the Glienike Bridge," Ratanov told her with a shrug.

Galyna had been warned to expect this kind of threat, and she had planned her response. She turned to her mother and asked, "Will you just sit there, Anastasia Sergeyevna? Will you let your husband threaten your daughter? Will you let him seize and torture me as you let him torture and deport my father? Is that the value of your motherly love?"

"Don't be foolish and cruel!" Anastasia retorted hotly. "Maxim would never harm you. We only want you to understand the importance of being on the right side of history. The forces of Imperialism are doomed. Progress is unstoppable. The Socialist Motherland has conquered Hitler and humiliated the corrupt imperialist powers. All across Eastern Europe, people have been liberated —"

"Enslaved. Shot. Deported," Galyna shot back in sincere anger.

"Propaganda. Lies and propaganda. Only reactionary elements have been shot, and of course, the Germans had to be deported along with the Poles. We've seen how untrustworthy ethnic minorities are. They stab you in the back as soon as they get the chance."

"Including the Ukrainians?" Galyna asked, lifting her eyebrows.

Her mother frowned. "Ukraine is a Soviet Republic, and it should be the home of all Ukrainians. There is no reason for Ukrainians to live in Poland or White Russia or Russia. Besides, that is not the point. Socialism brings prosperity —"

"Is that the term you use for famine?"

"Stop acting like a stupid fool!" Ratanov interrupted the exchange. "You are here to give us information about Gatow, not talk back to your mother like an impudent teenager."

"Not until I know my father is still alive and that my treason will serve a purpose," Galyna countered, her voice was firm even if her face was red and her hand still trembled.

"Your treason serves the Socialist Motherland and Progressive forces all over the world."

"I don't care. I care only about my father. I will not assist you unless you provide proof that my father is still alive."

"Very well," Ratanov snapped. "I will request a photo from the appropriate authorities. You will see it next time we meet. For now, I would urge you to think more realistically about your situation. We have discarded the German puppets of the Western warmongers who claimed to govern Berlin, and we have replaced them with reliable men loyal to us."

"The Berliners do not recognise your Opera government. They plan to *elect* a government two days from now."

Ratanov snorted and made a dismissive gesture. "The Western warmongers may try to gain legitimisation for their terror tactics by staging these so-called elections, but it will do them no good. We have things under control. Most people will stay at home. What do they have to gain by voting? They now have a competent and reliable city government determined to improve living standards rather than starve them to death! The Berliners want bread, peace and unity — not terror bombers day and night and isolation from their brothers and sisters in the surrounding countryside."

Galyna glared at him. She didn't know any Germans and had no way of knowing what the Berliners wanted, much less if or how they would vote.

"And don't think your employer," (Ratanov turned the word 'employer' into a term of derision) "will be saved by the Amis either. Colonel Howley and General Clay will soon be sent home in disgrace. The American president understands that he must come to terms with Stalin, and he wants hotheads like Clay and Howley to disappear—"

"Although I can't expect someone like you to understand," Galyna interrupted him, "that doesn't happen in America. Texas isn't Siberia. American generals don't get shot or 'disappear'—"

"Believe that if you want to, but they can still be withdrawn from Berlin — and they will be. You can't be so stupid as to believe your bankrupt and weary old Empire will remain here after the Americans have left, can you?" He snorted to show the question was rhetorical.

Galyna got to her feet. "If the Airlift is about to be called off, then Gatow is of no value and you don't need my services, so I think I'll leave now."

"But you only had one piece of cake!" Anastasia protested.

"You keep telling me how fat I look," Galyna countered with a saccharine smile, "It's better if I eat less." To her stepfather, she added. "When you have that photo of my father, let me know. I'm not coming again until I know my father is still alive and my cooperation with you has a purpose that *I* care about." She snatched up her handbag and greatcoat from the chair near the door and disappeared into the fog.

Walking back to the bus stop through the seemingly abandoned Potsdam suburb, she hoped Boyd would approve of how she'd handled things. He'd advised her to stay as close to the truth and to be herself as much as possible. He'd told her to embrace the role of angry victim of extortion. "That's what you are!" he reminded her. "Vent at them and make your actions seem transactional. Let it all play out as it would if you had been forced into this game — and *hadn't* told anyone about it."

Well, she'd certainly spoken her mind! She hoped it hadn't been too provocative. She strained to hear the sound of pursuing footsteps, the portent of the Soviet Secret Police shadowing her or Soviet soldiers coming after her. With a shudder, she realized that was the most likely way she would learn that she'd made a fatal mistake. But even holding her breath she heard no sound but the water dripping from the trees. For today, at least, it appeared she'd gotten away.

Chapter Two
Carrying On

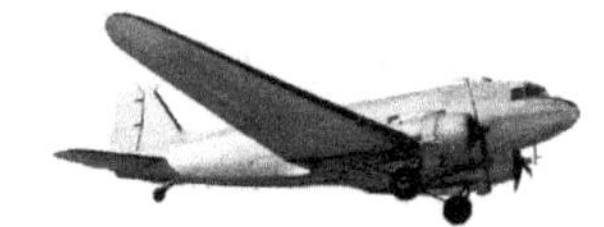

Until They Shoot Us Down
Berlin-Kladow
Saturday 4 December 1948
(Day 162 of the Berlin Airlift)

The residence was cold because Robin disapproved of living in comfort while the native population suffered. Since the Berliners had almost no coal for their homes, Robin thought it was inappropriate to heat anything more than the most essential rooms and he sought to keep their coal consumption at a minimum. In practice, only the kitchen (where the staff ate and relaxed), the breakfast room (where the residents took all their meals), and the den behind the living room, which had an open fireplace, were heated. The rest of the elegant twenty-two-room villa with its grand salon, long library, winter garden etc. was unheated. So were the bedrooms.

Emily had a quick wash and dressed in her Emergency Air Services (EAS) uniform of black trousers, double-breasted, black blazer and red silk ascot. Although she liked this attire and was proud of the golden cloth wings above the left breast pocket and the three golden stripes on her sleeve, she wondered how much longer she would wear it. She could not let Robin return to the UK alone, so his dismissal as station commander meant that her days flying the air ambulance were also coming to an end.

Despite her best efforts to appear calm and resigned about the situation, she was inwardly seething. She found it unfathomable that Robin's dedication and effectiveness at Gatow had gone unnoticed. She also considered it unforgivable that he was being punished for doing the right thing: saving orphans, malnourished children and people with chronic diseases from unnecessary suffering. The fact that he had been requested to organize the evacuation by the senior British officer in Berlin made things even worse. None of it made sense!

Part of her wanted to protest publicly. She'd been briefly tempted to go to the press. What would the public think if they learned that the RAF leadership preferred blind obedience to responding to the needs of innocent children? There was a woman reporter with the *Times* who loved breaking stories of bureaucratic obtuseness and incompetence. Yet Emily held herself in check. Robin didn't want any publicity. He identified too strongly with the RAF to want any criticism of it to be made public.

Coming down the stairs to the ground floor, Emily told herself that rather than pursuing mental fantasies of revenge or protest, she ought to start packing up their personal things in preparation for returning to the UK. Robin's replacement might come with a wife and several children. He would expect to move into the official residence immediately and, according to Robin, that might be as early as next Monday afternoon.

Emily crossed the icy dining room to join their house guests at the breakfast table. Kit Moran was another pilot with EAS, while his wife Georgina worked as a teacher at the British school. "Good morning!" Emily greeted the others as she closed the glass doors behind her to keep as much warmth inside as possible.

Her guests responded with cheerful greetings and then Kit announced, "Georgina and I were just wondering whether the Station might host a Christmas party for some Berlin children. Although the sickest children are being flown out, hundreds of thousands remain, and what sort of Christmas are they going to have? There aren't any Christmas trees or decorations, let alone presents and feasts."

"What I was thinking," Georgina took up the topic enthusiastically, "was to approach some of the nearby German schools. If we work with the teachers and focus on the younger children, we might be able to organise a party for three or four hundred children. We could ask the staff at Gatow to donate presents. I'm sure we'd collect plenty!"

Listening to her, Emily was reminded that Georgina was a vicar's daughter. She was used to both organizing Christmas events —and asking for charity.

Kit, clearly in the spirit of things, pointed out, "I think that a hot meal with turkey, real potatoes and hot chocolate might be more appreciated than gifts. I was thinking, that while we can't take the Halifax off the Airlift, you might be able to sneak in a flight to the UK and back with Moby Dick" (that was what they called the air ambulance). "The Wellington," Kit reminded them, "had a bomb capacity of 4,500 lbs, which means that Moby Dick could carry more than enough turkeys, potatoes and Christmas pudding for several hundred kids."

"We could even bring in oranges!" Georgina enthused.

Her husband, however, had detected Emily's reticence and asked, "Is something wrong?"

"It sounds like a wonderful idea," Emily admitted, "and weather permitting, I think David would be willing to authorise the use of Moby Dick to bring in food. However," she drew a deep breath and then added, "I'm afraid, the station commander will have to approve the use of RAF facilities and access to the station for so many children, their teachers or parents."

"But why wouldn't Robin...." Georgina started confidently only for her words to fade away as her husband flashed her a warning with his eyes.

Emily drew a deep breath and announced, "Robin is no longer station commander, and we have no idea who will replace him, much less if he might be inclined to approve a Christmas party for German children or not."

"But when....why... I don't understand," Georgina admitted, looking from her husband to her hostess and back.

"The evacuations," her husband drew the right conclusion. "I heard rumours that Group Captain Bagshot had not approved them and was furious."

Emily nodded. "Robin won't make a public announcement about his departure until he knows more details, but I should have said something privately. This is RAF housing, you understand, and when we turn it over to Robin's successor, you will have to move out. I'm very sorry."

"Don't worry," Kit assured her. "We can take rooms in the Malcolm Club with the others." The other four members of Kit's crew along with the second pilot and flight engineer of the air ambulance rented rooms at the Malcolm Club at RAF Gatow.

Before Emily could say any more, a voice rang out from behind them. "Hello? Anybody home?"

"That's Kiwi!" Emily exclaimed in astonishment, leaping to her feet to open the glass doors. She called through the dining room towards the front entry, "Kiwi! We're in the breakfast room!"

A moment later the tall, fair-haired New Zealander breezed in. He received welcoming kisses on both cheeks from Emily and handshakes from the Morans. Then he tossed aside his cap and laid his damp greatcoat over the back of an unused chair as he sat down at the table. The sound of his arrival brought one of the housemaids out of the kitchen. She asked politely if she should bring another place setting and more coffee, which Emily welcomed.

"Did you just fly in?" Emily asked eagerly.

"Hitch-hiked with Rafair."

"Which means they're flying?"

"Some flights are getting through — not as many as are needed. They're prioritizing the larger aircraft. Albatross" (the nickname for Moran's Halifax) "ought to be able to get clearance, so I came to find out what's going on. Are we in business or aren't we?"

Silence answered him. Kit and Georgina looked at Emily.

Drawing a deep breath, she explained, "Robin's been relieved of his command—"

"What a flaming cock-up! Excuse me, ladies. That bastard Bagshot!" Kiwi grasped the situation at once. "I should have known!"

"That doesn't in itself close down EAS," Emily hastened to point out. "I will, of course, resign and return to the UK with Robin, but you can take command of Moby Dick, Kiwi."

"That's not the issue," Kiwi replied. "The point is that David's so cracked up over Charlotte dumping him that he's stopping running the company. It's bad enough that Charlotte is no longer handling the customers, but for most of November, David handled them himself and we managed to limp along. Since last Saturday, he's stopped doing even that. I've called the office a dozen times, and all I get is the frightened secretary who doesn't have a clue what's going on. Does David intend to fold or what?"

"I can't answer that, Kiwi," Emily admitted. "I haven't seen David this week either. Robin's dismissal took me by surprise and the weather was an excuse not to probe. It didn't help that Robin thinks the Airlift is on the brink of collapse. If the majority of the Berliners boycott the election or vote outright for the SED on Sunday, then HM government will probably withdraw the British garrison."

Kiwi countered with, "Look, we call ourselves 'Emergency Air Services' and that means we fly precisely where and when things are risky and unstable. We've got two fully serviceable aircraft sitting in a hangar at Gatow, not to mention idle ground and aircrew. We ought to be flying until they shoot us out of the sky."

"Agreed," Kit seconded him. "Albi's had a cargo stowed for eight hours. If Gatow's open, I'll make a run to Hanover with it." He stood as he spoke, bending to give Georgina a quick kiss.

"Emily?" Kiwi asked.

"There's no reason why the Halifax shouldn't be flying whenever visibility allows. Regarding the ambulance, however, we can't fly until we have a flight plan based on what patients need to go where. Either David or Charlotte is going to have to start working again." She hesitated, but it had to be said. "And while I agree that we *ought* to keep flying, David writes the cheques. We have to find out what he wants."

Her remark was met with silence. It wasn't only the people in this room who depended on EAS for their livelihood. The company employed German office staff, eight other aircrew and seven ground crew, including a man paralyzed from the waist down. Closing EAS would be a disaster for all of them. Emily knew that, but David had founded the company, and he was its majority shareholder and chief executive officer.

"I'd better go and talk to him," Emily concluded, knowing that this was much more important than packing up her things.

"Thank you," Kiwi replied, adding "And try to talk some sense into him, would you?"

"I'll do my best."

Echoes of My Mind
Berlin-Nicolassee
Saturday 4 December 1948
(Day 162 of the Berlin Airlift)

Sammy licked David's face to wake him. As the dog's rough tongue brought him back to consciousness, he groaned. His shoulder was killing him from lying on it for too long on the floor. He dragged himself upright and looked around. He was in a small, old-fashioned sitting room with an empty wine bottle beside him and a dirty wineglass on the table. Where was he and what day was it?

Gradually things started to come back to him. After the police had failed to arrest the man living in his uncle's gracious house on the Havel, he'd been slipped the keys with the hint that no one would object to him re-occupying family property while his restitution claim worked its way through the bureaucracy. He'd collected Sammy from the Priestman's home in Kladow, taken all his personal belongings out of the apartment over the company office on Kurfuerstendamm, and moved into the house here on the Schwanenwerder. The main house with its high ceilings and large windows, however, was freezing and lonely. So, he'd set himself up in the housekeeper's old apartment at the back of the house instead. It was small, cosy and could be heated more easily. In addition, the windows were nearly overgrown with vines, making it harder for people to look in. He could also come and go by the back door, avoiding the main entrance that the police had boarded up.

David had made himself quite comfortable, but then the nightmares started. He dreamt of his childhood, fleeing his father's contempt and the ridicule of the other children. He heard again his parents' whispers about bankruptcies, dismissals, terminated contracts and suicides. The memories merged with films of concentration camps and photos of mass graves in the forests east of Warsaw. They mutated into his own melted face, the patchwork of skin, the stitches and swelling, the smell of pus and disinfectant.

"Oh, Sammy," David gasped out and pulled the blond collie mix into his arms. He'd adopted Sammy when his face was at an early stage of reconstruction. The dog had diligently licked his regenerating skin night after night in an obsessive determination to help his new master recover.

Sammy was skinny, he noted with shock, and sat up more completely. How long had he been lying here? Why on the floor rather than the bed? When was the last time he'd fed Sammy? There was a dog door, and Sammy could get out to drink from the lake, but unless he'd managed to catch a bird or a rabbit for himself, David didn't think he'd been fed in several days.

David dragged himself to his feet. He was wearing four layers of jumpers, corduroy trousers, thick socks and fleece slippers. His head ached, his mouth tasted foul, and his stomach rumbled. He hadn't fed himself either. He made his way to the lavatory, relieved himself, and then went into the staff kitchen. He opened cupboards randomly until he found some cans of spam and emptied the contents into Sammy's bowl. While the dog ate ravenously, he returned to the bathroom to strip down and wash himself, brush his teeth and change into clean clothes.

When he was dressed again, he returned to the kitchen, gave Sammy a second can of spam, and cut the contents of a third can into slices that he laid on slabs of stale bread. It was dry and unappetizing but temporarily filling. He washed it down with tap water, left the plate and glass in the sink with a stack of other dirty dishes, and sank onto the chair to stare out of the window.

There was nothing to see but fog and desultory moisture dripping from the eaves. Then he noticed a sparrow clinging to a dead vine. A microcosm of his life perhaps? Sammy leaned against his leg and whimpered, begging for his attention, so he bent to scratch him behind his ears and massage the back of his neck, murmuring apologies. "Sorry, old boy. I didn't mean to neglect you. I promise to improve. I should not have come here. It was a colossal mistake. I should have left the ghosts alone. I don't need anything here. It's a ball and chain around my ankle holding me back, stopping me from flying. We ought to be flying, Sammy. Above the clouds. Soaring again." The thought of a Spitfire on the wing brought the faintest of smiles to his lips, and Sammy reached out with his tongue to express approval.

"At least that Nazi bastard is gone. I can turn the house over to the city and let them relocate homeless people here. Whatever." He shrugged as he registered that most of those homeless people would also have shouted "Heil Hitler," rejected their Jewish neighbours, thought of themselves as 'supermen' and gloried in the conquest of half of Europe. But he couldn't find the energy to be outraged any more. He just wanted to get away. To leave Berlin and Germany behind and start his life over again.

He had a Canadian passport, after all. His mother, one sister and his brother were still there. He could go to the New World and start over again.

But he didn't move. He just stared out of the window and watched the moisture on the tip of a naked vine fatten until it was heavy enough to fall with a soft 'platsch' onto the windowsill. He also heard faint laughter echoing in the rooms overhead. His cousins were giggling as they played some silly game. His uncle called out that he was home, and his aunt urged, "Come girls, your father's home."

"It's so peaceful here," Charlotte said timidly in his brain. "It's as if there never was a war. Are those lilacs? They must be glorious when they bloom. And look! Is that a peacock? Do you think it escaped from the Pfaueninsel?" Charlotte was always so timid and hesitant in his presence. "Is that a stable? Oh, David, could we have horses? I would so love to have horses in my life again."

David put his hands to his face. Desperate to explain why Charlotte had left him, he'd searched his memory a million times for some trace of disdain, contempt, superiority, arrogance, or a hint of antisemitism. Instead, all he heard was Charlotte's shy, breathy voice as she expressed her thanks for every little thing he did for her. His memories revealed only uncertainty when she talked of business matters and diffidence towards every decision he made. He was haunted by the rare tinkling of her laughter and her smiles like rays of sunshine piercing the fog. How could Charlotte, of all people, reject him?

Christian had said it was because of the rapes, but David's brain refused to go there. He simply could not cope with the thought of Charlotte being ravaged — much less six times. He did not believe it. Christian had been trying to manipulate him into forgiving her. Or maybe Christian believed it. But David didn't. Charlotte could not have survived being gang raped. She was too fragile. An experience like that would have destroyed her. She would have gone mad or killed herself. Ergo it could not have happened at all, and that meant she had some other reason for rejecting him. There was something about him that she could not accept....

Sammy abruptly sprang to his feet, lifting his head and straining his ears. Then he burst into loud, wild barking that made David recoil in shock. The dog bounded out of the kitchen, his paws sliding out from under him on the tiles as he scrambled up the stairs. In the silence he left behind, David heard knocking and a female voice calling faintly "David? David? Are you here?"

Emily! Oh, dear God! What could he say to her? Although he asked the question, he made no attempt to escape the confrontation. Sammy was barking at the inside of the boarded-up front door, but David slipped out of the back door and walked around until he could see both the RAF car parked in the street and Emily Priestman on the front porch. She was talking through the door to Sammy, asking him where David was.

David lifted his voice, "I'm here! You'll have to come around to the back."

Emily turned toward the sound of his voice and waved at him. She found her way down from the porch and through the overgrown garden to follow him inside. Only after the door fell shut behind them did she exclaim, "David! We've all been worrying about you! Why haven't you been at work?" Although she sounded concerned, there was also understandable reproach in her words. David looked away ashamed. He should have explained to his partners why he couldn't come to work anymore.

He was spared an answer by the arrival of Sammy. The dog came bounding back to the housekeeper's flat with a wildly wagging tail to demand Emily's attention. Only after the dog had calmed down did Emily redirect her attention to David. "What's going on, David?" she asked seriously and firmly. "Kiwi flew down from Hamburg asking if we are in business or not. It's a valid question."

David drew a deep breath but still avoided looking her in the eye. Instead, he directed his gaze out of a little window as he admitted. "I have no interest in the business any more — or the patients or the profits — nothing. I just want to — I don't even know. I've lost all interest in everything. I'm thinking of going back to Canada."

Emily audibly caught her breath. "Oh, David! Think what that would mean. Not just for the sick and injured Berliners, but for all your employees. I'm not talking about myself. Robin's been dismissed from his post and —"

"What? Why? He's been doing a first-rate job and—"

"He was also insubordinate," Emily pointed out, ending further discussion by insisting, "That's not important at the moment. Emergency Air Services is. Everyone from Kiwi and Kit to the German employees has done outstanding work under extremely stressful conditions, and none of them has ready employment alternatives. Kit and Gordon are both disabled. Jan's a woman pilot, already rejected by the USAF. Unemployment rates in Berlin are astronomical. Kiwi, Bruce, Terry and Nigel were all under-employed before they joined us. Richard faces racism whenever he goes — not to mention that we've made a job offer to an American nurse who sent a telegram just last Friday to tell us that she now has her passport and visa and can come whenever we say. She too has been facing severe hardships, Mrs Howley claims. Do you want me to tell her it was all a joke? That we don't want her when the need has never been greater? And what about the Berliners themselves? You may have lost interest in the ambulance, but the need for one has never been greater."

David closed his eyes ashamed. Emily was right. He had no right to see Emergency Air Services as his personal possession. They had all contributed to making it a success, and the need was, as she said, unquestionable. He nodded and admitted in a whisper, "You're right."

When Emily didn't answer, he opened his eyes to find her gazing at him with an expression that mixed exasperation with concern bordering on pity. He didn't want pity.

Before he could think of how to deflect it, Emily started speaking again. "I know how difficult it has been for you to connect with women since you lost your face." Yes, if anyone understood how hard it had been for him, it was Emily, he conceded mentally. She continued, "I know that Charlotte was the first woman you let into your heart. Her rejection of you at this stage is incomprehensible —"

"You, as a woman, don't understand it either?"

"No, I don't," Emily confirmed firmly.

"That's comforting, I suppose," David remarked, sounding unsure. Then he focused on her and asked intently. "You've been a good friend, Emily, especially when I was going through surgery. I was even a little in love with you, but I knew you had eyes only for Robin. Yet, I want you to be honest with me now. Brutally honest, if necessary. I need to know if there is something about me that women *can't* love."

"Don't be ridiculous! There were plenty of girls who wanted you to pay them more attention over the years, but you always kept your distance. That's why I was so happy that you found Charlotte. From what I saw, she adored you, David. She was always a little afraid that you did not return her feelings and that she was not worthy of you—"

"How not worthy?" He demanded, so anxious to understand that his tone was almost sharp.

"Not pretty enough, not young enough, not bright enough — not to mention that she found the Nazi legacy so difficult. She was mortified by what Germany had done to the Jews generally and to your family in particular. Yet while she expressed her doubts to me several times, she never said anything that would explain what she's done. Then again," Emily admitted, "I haven't spoken to her since she broke off with you and stopped coming to the office."

David sighed. At one level, it was reassuring that Emily had not anticipated this rejection, but it left him just as confused and baffled as before. Then Emily knocked him for a loop by declaring gently, "I will be seeing her tonight."

"Charlotte? Why? Where?"

"Jasha and Lt. Col. Russell are getting married. Graham asked Robin to be his best man, and Jasha asked me to be her witness, but I know she invited Charlotte and Christian as well." She paused, her eyes trying to penetrate David's impassive face. After a moment, she gave up and asked outright. "Is there anything you would like me to say to her?"

David shook his head decisively. "No."

Emily nodded slowly. He couldn't tell if she approved or not. She turned the conversation back to the business. "David, Kit is perfectly capable of running Air Freight International on his own. He receives freight, fuel, flight plans and payment from the RAF. The procedures are clearly laid out and Frl. Klempner knows how to handle the paperwork. The problem is AAI. We need someone to maintain contact with the hospitals, draw up and adjust flight plans based on the priorities and destinations of the patients, and also someone to handle the more complex billing procedures with the USAF."

"Can't you do that?" David asked plaintively.

"No. I'm going back to the UK with Robin," she reminded him. "We need to find another solution. First, do you authorise Kit to keep flying the Halifax at maximum capacity?"

"Of course."

"And, I presume, you're fine with Kiwi resuming command of Moby Dick?"

"Yes, naturally."

"So, would you object to me asking Charlotte if she'd be willing to return to her job? Maybe, if she knows you won't be coming to the office, she'd agree. Jasha claims that the reason she stopped working was because she thinks it is dishonourable to take your money after she disappointed your hopes."

"Jasha has seen and talked to her, then? What else does Jasha say about her?" David wanted to know.

"That Charlotte is miserable, depressed and 'not herself.'"

Was that good news? It suggested she was not greatly in love with Fritz von Bredow. To Emily he replied. "Yes, go ahead and ask her to resume her position. Please, do whatever you need to do to get AAI operating again. Even if it costs money. I can write cheques. I just don't want to have to talk to anyone, meet people, or be around them. I need ...." He didn't know what he needed, so he left the sentence dangling.

"You need to spend time with Mr Bowles," Emily concluded for him. Mr Bowles was the father of a wartime friend who had unofficially adopted David after his son was killed. "Take Sammy and fly the Dakota back to Dorset," Emily suggested.

David flinched in surprise but then felt a flood of relief. "You're right! That's exactly what I need." He looked toward the ceiling beyond which were the empty rooms inhabited by the ghosts of his slaughtered relatives. He had to get away from them. He had to seek out the refuge he had found in the cottage of his best friend Ginger. When he'd needed him after losing his face, Ginger had left the grave to join him there; maybe he would do that again.

"Yes," he repeated out loud. "I'll go home to Mr Bowles and try to sell the Dakota, now that the RAF has banned civilian Daks from the Airlift. Meanwhile, I can draft a cheque for a couple of hundred pounds to keep EAS liquid while I'm gone. You can always cable me if you need more. I don't want the business to fail, Emily," he pleaded for understanding. "I just need a little time for and by myself to sort things out."

In Sickness and In Health
Berlin-Charlottenburg
Saturday 4 December 1948
(Day 162 of the Berlin Airlift)

Jasha looked at herself in the mirror critically. She did not look like a bride. She wore a sleek, three-quarter length gown with matching jacket and hat that while elegant and sophisticated was not bridal. For her first wedding, she'd worn a traditional gown with puffy, white sleeves, and elaborate embroidery on the skirt and bodice that suited her plump and rosy body. But she was not sixteen any more and years as a slave labourer had left her gaunt. Nor was she marrying in a peasant village in White Russia with aunts, uncles and cousins galore. She wasn't wearing white in the English tradition, either. How could she? She was neither pure nor innocent. She'd chosen instead a dress in a dusty rose colour, ashes-of-roses they called it. That seemed appropriate for a forty-five-year-old widow attempting to start over on the rubble of the past.

The only problem with the dress was that she owned no shoes to go with it; she had borrowed a pair of low, grey heels from Emily. Together they had stuffed handkerchiefs into the toes so she could walk in them without falling out. Hopefully, she reflected, she wasn't trying to step into shoes too large for her on an abstract as well as a physical level. A quarter of a century ago, the villagers had whispered and fretted because she was marrying the young schoolteacher Jurek. He was a "stranger" and had gone to university, whereas her parents could hardly read or write. The consensus among her neighbours had been that she was getting "above herself" and no good would come of it.

They had been right, Jasha reflected, but not for the reasons they had imagined. Besides, there had been almost twenty good years before calamity struck. Jurek had taken her away from the hidebound village. He'd found jobs in larger towns and bigger schools until he got his wish of living and working in Minsk. Long before they reached Minsk, she had accepted that she would have no additional children after Alojzy was born. She had started working as a cook outside the home to make extra money. With Alojzy to dote on and worry about, it was easy to ignore that she and Jurek spent little time together anymore. The passion between them had definitely cooled, she admitted, and yet, there was nothing fundamentally wrong between them. If — She slammed a door on her thoughts.

Today she was marrying Graham and starting a new life. She was not going to let the ghosts interfere. She was not going to think about what she had lost. She was not going to ask herself whether Jurek or Alojzy would have approved. Nor did she want to think about what happened to her after Stalin murdered her husband and son. She had survived what she called 'the years of terror' but at a terrible cost. Yet, as she slipped her rosary into her hand-bag, she could not forget that a neighbour in Minsk had been sentenced to ten years in the Gulag just for owning one. The scars were there. They always would be. She was simply determined not to let them cripple her.

Emily Priestman called up the stairs, "Are you ready, Jasha? The car is out the front."

"Yes, I'm coming." Jasha picked up the little wicker suitcase with her change of clothes and toiletries. Graham had booked them a room at the Hotel Olympia. She found she was both nervous and excited by the thought of sleeping with him. It was odd how the act of telling Graham about the rapes had freed her of their spell. They had been pushed into that place in her brain alongside Jurek and Alojzy's murders and her years as a slave, behind that mental door that she kept locked and barred.

She took the stairs slowly, afraid of falling out of her loose shoes, and found Emily waiting impatiently in the front hall. Yet when Jasha reached the last step, Emily broke into a smile and exclaimed, "You look lovely!"

"Yes?" Jasha asked back uncertainly. "I do not want to shame Graham. He is British officer. I do not want to look like peasant or servant."

"You look like neither, Jasha," Emily assured her, meeting her eyes. Then turning around, she pulled a large bouquet of pink roses from the table be-hind her. "Graham sent you these," Emily told her as she handed them over, adding with a wink, "I did tell him the colour of your dress."

They were so big and full that Jasha gasped in wonder. Where had he found roses like these in blockaded Berlin? They could only have come from some royal greenhouse in the West, she thought. Jasha felt tears in her eyes as she buried her nose in the blooms, breathing in their rich scent. Gardening was what had brought them together. Surprising her with a bouquet like this was the perfect gesture.

Emily tapped her watch and Jasha took the hint. She put on her overcoat, and she and Emily went together to the waiting car. They were alone in the back because Wing Commander Priestman had gone directly from the Station to meet Graham at the church. It was already getting dark. The shortest day of the year was just weeks away, and fog had settled over the city again. Jasha could hear no aircraft overhead. "Is Gatow closed again?" She asked.

Emily nodded. "Since about an hour ago."

Jasha knew that was bad, and it reinforced her relief to be getting married today. It meant that even if the British garrison pulled out, she would not be left behind.

Graham had been waiting almost an hour. The church was as cold a tomb. Mass was over and the handful of attendees were shuffling out, except for a woman who was trying to talk the priest into hearing her confession. Father Lucas was explaining that he had a wedding in the next half hour and asked her to come back later, but Graham signalled to the priest to go ahead. The clergyman dipped his head in thanks and led the woman to the confessional.

Graham could be generous because there was still no sign of Jasha, and his nerves were fraying. Fortunately, Robin had joined him half an hour ago and had distracted him with small talk until Charlotte and Christian arrived. Robin was now engaged in a lively conversation with Christian over where they might have encountered each other in the air. Bizarrely, they seemed enjoy the idea they had probably fought one another during the war. Graham shook his head in bafflement, then tuned the pilots' voices out as he morosely wondered if Jasha had changed her mind.

These last months of being 'engaged' had been intoxicating. He'd never had a girl to call his own before, and it filled him with inner pride and self-confidence. He'd felt more charming, more worldly, and more import-ant, all in addition to being blissfully happy in her company. But in the damp and gloom of this December evening, Graham saw himself as a man with a deformed body and an ugly face approaching 50. The parade uniform of a lieutenant colonel of the Corps of Royal Engineers gave him a certain dignity and presence, but it could not disguise that his legs were far too short for his torso and arms. From childhood, people had called him "dwarf," "baboon" or "ape." Single women had either ignored him or pitied him; married women had been kind — unless they had marriageable daughters. Maybe the thought of sleeping with a dwarf had proved too much for Jasha?

Then with a gust of cold air and a loud clunk, the door opened, and Jasha and Emily stepped inside. Jasha anxiously scanned the room until she found Graham. Their eyes met, and her face lit up. No, she had not forsaken him.

Charlotte watched the exchange of glances between Jasha and Graham and felt a pain so intense it was almost physical. With all her heart she wished she were in Jasha's shoes. This ought to be my wedding, she screamed in silence. David and I should be marrying. She didn't mean *instead* of Jasha and Graham; she did not begrudge Jasha her happiness. Yet she wanted to share it so much that she could not bear to watch the way Graham and Jasha kissed. She turned to look the other way as Robin and Christian laughingly protested, "Graham! You're supposed to wait until after the ceremony!"

Robin started ushering Graham toward the front of the Church, while Christian offered his compliments to Jasha. She did look lovely. What a contrast to the slave labourer in faded, work clothes, clogs and a scarf tied under her chin who had arrived at Walmsdorf on the back of a Wehrmacht lorry in the middle of the war!

Charlotte turned her attention to Emily. Her barely formed hopes that Emily might bring David shattered when she saw Emily was alone. Then she told herself that was probably for the best. What could she have said to David?

Yet in the pit of her stomach, she still saw him as her knight in shining armour. She still hoped that he would break the evil spell entrapping her. He would kill the hideous dragon holding her prisoner to her girlhood oath. He would free her from the chains binding her to a selfish, embittered man the way St. George had freed the princess chained to a rock in the sea. David, David, David! Her heart screamed. Rescue me! *Please* rescue me.

Only the silence answered.

Emily was coming towards her, but Charlotte did not want to have to explain herself. She was relieved when the organ started playing Bach's

"Awake!" and the priest gestured for the little wedding party to take their places. Graham already stood at the front of the church with Robin beside him. Emily gestured for Charlotte to follow her, but Charlotte preferred to go to the far aisle so she could slide into the pew from the outside. That way Christian was between them. After they were both seated, she formally offered Emily her hand across Christian with a short "hello." Meanwhile, Father Lucas took up his position and the organ switched to Bach's "Jesu, Joy of Man's Desiring." Every eye turned toward Jasha coming up the aisle alone with the roses in her arms.

"Why not me too?" Charlotte asked the nothingness around her. "She was raped too! She's no better than me! They trampled her and pissed on her no less than me! Why doesn't it matter to her? Or Graham?" She turned to look at the man standing before the altar with a look in his eyes that did not acknowledge that Jasha had been defiled and debased. Yet she knew he knew because Jasha had told him.

Jasha reached the foot of the altar, and the ceremony began. The vows were readily and unhesitatingly exchanged. Robin handed Graham the wedding ring, which he slipped on Jasha's finger. Father Lucas pronounced them 'man and wife,' and they kissed. They took communion kneeling side-by-side, signed the wedding registry, and the priest blessed them again. It was over in no more than twenty minutes.

Emily, Christian and Robin encircled the couple offering congratulations. Emily hugged Jasha and Jasha thanked her. Unfairly, that hurt. Jasha had been Charlotte's best friend through the last years of the war, during their flight from the Red Army and throughout the siege of Berlin. When had she lost Jasha to Emily?

Then she remembered that Jasha was now the wife of a British colonel, just like Emily. They were equals. And Jasha would soon have a British passport, too. If the Ivans threatened to occupy the rest of Berlin, she would be able to leave along with Emily and Robin — and David. But David wouldn't take Charlotte with him when he went. Why should he? She had rejected him for Fritz. So, she would be left to the Ivans. Charlotte shuddered. Mentally, she felt the cold metal of the pistol in her hand. She would kill at least one of them before she took her own life. They would not humiliate her again—

"Are you all right, Charlotte?" Emily asked, touching her elbow.

"I'm just a little chilly," Charlotte answered, pulling away.

"Yes, it's much too cold in here!" Graham announced. "I have a table for six at the Hotel Olympia. Let's go!"

They moved down the aisle in a gaggle and split into two parties. Graham and Jasha climbed into his vehicle, while Emily invited Christian and Charlotte to join Robin and her in the RAF staff car. Robin sat in front beside the driver, while Emily and the two Germans crowded into the backseat.

Leaning across Christian, Emily addressed Charlotte, "I'm so glad we have a moment together. I spoke to David this afternoon...."

Charlotte's heart leapt and she held her breath, unconsciously hoping for the flap of angel wings that would accompany redemption.

"... He has decided to return to the UK for an indefinite period and ...."

Charlotte's misery was so great she didn't listen to what Emily said after that. Something about Dakotas and cottages and people Charlotte didn't know. None of it was important. He was abandoning her....

"Would you think about that?" Emily asked.

"What?"

"Coming back to work and handling the clients again. We really can't keep the ambulance flying without someone in the office fielding requests, developing flight plans, and ensuring a nurse is available — at least until our own arrives. We need you Charlotte."

Long before Emily finished speaking, Charlotte was shaking her head. She couldn't possibly return to the office. She couldn't face the other workers or the hospital administrators. Besides, she had never dared tell Fritz about the job. She knew he'd be furious and jealous and — never mind. He objected to her being away from him for any reason. He felt she owed him her whole life.

"Why not?" Emily asked, baffled.

"I have to look after Fritz. He needs me." Charlotte mumbled. She could feel Christian turn his gaze on her, and his eyes burned into her.

Distressed, Emily remonstrated, "But surely you could —"

"No!" Charlotte snapped. She turned to look out the window, ending the conversation. Besides, with her gaze fixed on the passing street, Emily wouldn't be able to read from her eyes how terrified and miserable she was.

The table at the Hotel Olympia had been decorated with roses spilling out of a large vase and spreading their vines to the edge of the table. Between the roses were crystal glasses, chilled champagne, and candles. The latter were necessary, of course, because there was no electricity. To the delight of the guests, they found that the hotel had the luxury of a wood-burning stove that kept the small dining room moderately warm. Since they all wore jackets, the room wasn't uncomfortable. The champagne, followed by wine donated by Christian, also warmed them.

Yet Emily reflected that Jasha had been right to say Charlotte was 'not herself.' Charlotte's pointed rejection of her overtures would have been wounding, if Emily hadn't sensed they stemmed from deep, internal turmoil. Her first instinct was to try to help Charlotte, but she resisted that impulse. Charlotte appeared psychologically brittle and dangerously unstable, and Emily made no pretence of being a therapist.

She turned her attention to the other guests at the table. This was Jasha and Graham's night, after all. Even amid hardship — as in the darkest hours of the war — people needed to be able to feel joy and celebrate life. Emily was glad that Graham had spared no expense. The meal was fabulous, featuring wild boar in a mushroom and chestnut sauce spiced with cloves and nutmeg. Rather medieval, Emily thought through a veil of champagne, yet the recipe had been dictated more by the fact that all the ingredients could be obtained from the surrounding countryside via the black market. There was even a pudding made with honey — allegedly from bees in the American Sector.

Still, all good things come to an end. At 9 pm, Robin looked at his watch and announced that it was time to go. "The city election is tomorrow," he reminded the others. "The polls open at 6 am, and the RAF Regiment will be assisting the Royal Military Police in trying to ensure the safety of voters in the British Sector. We expect armed attempts to disrupt or intimidate voters. In short, I need a good night's sleep. Not to mention that Graham and Jasha have been waiting for us to leave for the last hour or more." He stood and the others stood with him. Since there was no public transport at this time of night, Christian and Charlotte were dependent on Robin's car to take them home. Congratulations, well-wishes, and thanks were again exchanged all around.

In the lobby, Robin went to get their coats, and Charlotte asked to use the ladies' before the drive back to her apartment. No sooner were both gone, than Christian startled Emily by enquiring, "Mrs Priestman, I deeply regret that Charlotte will not consider returning to a position that did her so much good psychologically. However, since she has made her position clear, would you consider hiring me instead? I ran a squadron in the war, so I understand a bit about organisation, and I'm not going to be intimidated by the *Herr Professor Doctors* at the hospitals either."

"What a splendid idea!" Emily rejoined. She did not doubt that Christian could handle the work — and he was probably correct that the hospital directors would respect him. Thinking quickly, she asked, "I know the election is tomorrow, but do you think you could meet me at the office in the early afternoon? David plans to fly back to Hamburg tomorrow on Rafair, pick up the Dakota there, and fly it back to the UK. Assuming I can get a set of keys from him before he takes off, I could meet you in the office and show you the ropes."

"That would be perfect. It would enable me to start introducing myself to the hospital directors first thing on Monday morning. With luck, we should be able to organise an evacuation that same afternoon — weather permitting, of course."

That was like a breath of fresh air! Emily smiled. "I like the way you think, *Herr Major*."

"I'd rather go by Herr von Feldburg or Christian," he corrected her gently.

"Christian it is then, and I'm Emily, of course."

He clicked his heels and bowed his head with a polite, "At your service." But then he glanced over his shoulder to see if Charlotte was approaching yet. Seeing her emerge from the hallway, he lowered his voice and added in haste, "I have one other favour to ask. If David is returning to the UK indefinitely, do you think he would object to me moving into the apartment over the office? It would enable me to work practically 'round the clock.'"

"But what about Charlotte?" Emily protested. She sensed that Charlotte needed Christian's support now more than ever.

"It would be better for her if I move out," Christian insisted, keeping his voice low and his eyes on Charlotte as she approached them. "I cannot stop myself from quarrelling with Fritz, which only adds to her distress," he explained. "Although I strongly disapprove, Charlotte has made the decision to break off with David and abide by her promise to Fritz — regardless of the consequences. It is time for me to get out of her life and let her and Fritz make their future together."

How terrible, Emily thought, but what could she do? She probably wouldn't even be in Berlin by the end of the week. Nor was it her place to interfere between cousins. Christian had always been protective of Charlotte. She had to trust him to act in her best interests, even if she had her doubts about his actions. She confined herself to saying, "I'll check with David tomorrow and let you know when we meet in the office in the afternoon."

They said no more because Charlotte and Robin rejoined them almost simultaneously. As a group, they went out into the night and the fog.

Chapter Three
Decision in Berlin

Jakob Liebherr limped into the Schoeneberger Rathaus just after five-thirty in the morning. He had not been involved in the election planning because his liaison duties with the Allies could not be interrupted and consumed his attention. Today, however, was different. Nothing was more important than the election results and all other work could wait.

Although it was still pitch dark outside and the streets were deserted, the town hall was teeming with agitated colleagues. A horde of Young Socialists occupied the lobby, blocking the way to the stairs as they milled about exchanging news, speculation and opinions. Jakob pushed his way through the babbling crowd annoyed by their presence until, partway up the stairs, a loud voice called for order and started calling off names and assignments. Ah, Jakob thought, they were being sent to the various polling stations to counter attempts by the SED to intimidate voters. Admittedly, gangs of youth wearing SPD armbands might also be seen as threatening, but he welcomed the action nevertheless.

One flight up, an attentive municipal employee directed him to a conference room. "Mayor Reuter wants all councillors to join him there," she explained.

Jakob nodded and went down the hall to the designated room. Scores of his colleagues already filled it. They formed amorphous groups, chattering almost as wildly as the youth downstairs. A large map of Berlin had pins stuck in it to designate the location of the polling stations, each identified by a numbered paper flag. Like wasps on spilt beer, the pins seemed to cluster in random patterns. There also seemed to be far too many pins. At the sight of Reuter's aide Willy Brandt, Jakob stopped him to ask, "Did we increase the number of polling stations?"

"Yes. That way the vote can continue even if the SED shuts some of them down."

"Good thinking," Jakob conceded, and Brandt went on his way.

Someone had set up four blackboards on which the voting centres were listed by number. Beside each number were four neat boxes, one blank one followed by a box for each of the three participating parties, the Social Democratic Party (SPD), the Christian Democratic Union (CDU), and the Free Democratic Party (FDP). He presumed the results by party would be posted in the latter three boxes but was puzzled by the first box, particularly when a secretary with a clipboard started ticking some of the boxes. Jakob wandered over to her. "What do the checks mean?" he asked.

"That a polling station is open. At least, that's what a white tick means. I have red chalk in case there is violence, and we'll note that with a red X. At the end of the day, we'll record the number of people who voted at each location, as well as the votes by party." Jakob nodded his approval again and lingered behind the efficient woman watching as messengers brought her reports of stations opening. Jakob kept an eye on his watch as he observed the process and noted that by 6 am only a handful of stations had not yet opened; by 6:19 they all were. That wasn't bad. They were off to a running start.

The crowd around Reuter was still impenetrably large, so Jakob joined Jeannette Wolfe instead. She had cracked open one of the windows to shake the ash from her cigarette onto the street below. She forestalled the comment with, "Don't tell me! It's bad for my health and my wallet, but I'm addicted — especially to these American Lucky Strikes."

Jakob just smiled mildly. "At your age, you should be allowed a few vices. Now, tell me—"

"THE SMAD JUST ANNOUNCED A DAY OF RECONSTRUCTION!" a voice shouted across the room. A moment of stunned silence was followed by an explosion of questions. "What the devil is that?" "What does it mean?" "What's happening?"

Reuter called for order and ordered the messenger to explain himself.

"The SMAD has declared today a 'Reconstruction Day.' All workers are required — I repeat, *required* — to report to their place of employment for a day of — I quote — *voluntary* work. Work is to begin at 7:30 and those not attending will be 'noted'."

Jakob glanced at the large wall clock. It was already 6:23.

"How are they getting the message out?" Reuter asked.

"It's all over their radio stations and lorries are out in the streets with loudspeakers, admonishing everyone to show 'solidarity' and 'fight the capitalist warmongers.'"

Reuter nodded and gestured for everyone to resume what they'd been doing, while he took the young man aside and consulted with him earnestly.

Jakob turned back to Jeannette and picked up where he'd left off. "Any sign of the armed 'readiness groups' the SED formed?"

"Oh, yes. They are out in force patrolling the streets along the Sector border. The question is whether they've discovered our tunnel network or not."

"What tunnel network?" Jakob asked back startled.

"Well in places like Wedding and Prenzlauer Berg, you can enter the basement in an apartment house on one side of the Sector border and work your way via air raid shelters, storerooms and coal cellars to a house on the other side of the border. Fortunately, the underground maze spreads across entire blocks so people can enter or leave from several houses along the length of the street. I have no news yet if many people are using the tunnels or not. We couldn't advertise them, or the SED would have closed them. All we could do was try to spread the information by word-of-mouth."

Jakob nodded thoughtfully.

"Comrades!" Reuter called out. "Comrades! The BVG is on strike until 10 AM!"

That caused consternation until the penny dropped. Then someone called out, "Well done, Ernst!" as others started to clap. A public transport strike gave workers who lived in the West but worked in the East an excuse for showing up late for their day of 'voluntary' reconstruction; those who wanted to vote could do so first. A clever response, Jakob conceded, and he glanced towards the blackboard. No red crosses yet. He and Jeannette Wolfe decided to help themselves to the *ersatz* coffee offered at the back of the room.

Around the back table, people discussed the response of the Western

Allies. American, British and French troops were conspicuously patrolling the streets. In fact, the British were holding a parade on Charlottenburger Chaussee, the main east-west axis, from ten am to noon. It was a perfect excuse to have their troops — and tanks — in the very heart of the city close to the border with the Soviet Sector without officially having anything to do with the election. In addition, military police from each respective power supplemented the western police at the polling stations. Yet Jakob worried that even this show of force might not be enough to reassure the Berliners of their safety. Would they come out to vote or prefer to stay at home and be 'victims'?

The first report of trouble came just after eleven am. Armed SED youth crossed into Neukoelln and pushed their way into one of the polling stations where they started singing the *International* while tearing down posters and breaking furniture. Almost at once, SPD youth rushed to the scene and a brawl ensued. The police broke up the fight and made a handful of arrests, but soon afterwards, the station re-opened with more people in the queue than before.

Two similar disruptions occurred in Wedding with the same result, but shortly before three pm, a more serious incident took place when two Red Army soldiers marched into Polling Station 87 and tried to carry off the ballot box. Astonishingly, given that these were Russians in military uniform, the voters didn't wait for the police or the Allies to come to their rescue. They overpowered the soldiers and threw the Russians out of the building hurling bricks and other objects after them.

A little later in the afternoon, reports filtered in that the Americans had prevented a mechanized Red Army patrol from crossing into Kreuzberg by parking some tanks on the bridges and pretending not to understand what the Russians wanted. According to a young man who had witnessed the incident, the American GIs stood around drinking coffee, eating doughnuts and chewing gum as if they were on some harmless exercise. When the Ivans shouted at them to clear the bridges, they smiled and waved back. Eventually, an English-speaking Soviet officer demanded to speak with the American commander. This turned out to be a second lieutenant, who claimed he hadn't a clue why he was where he was. "Just following orders, bud! Just following orders." When the Russian insisted he clear his troops off the bridges, he shook his head. "Can't do that. It would be against my orders. You'll have to take it up with Colonel Howley."

Everyone laughed at that. "Mad Dog" Howley was more anti-Soviet — and more popular with the Berliners — than any other Western officer.

As the day wore on, however, it became clear that the SED had opted not to deploy its armed thugs and probably would continue to refrain from the use of large-scale violence. That question was: why? Were they confident that they could win without it? That is, were they confident that enough Berliners had followed their calls to boycott the elections to make the entire exercise appear meaningless?

Jakob turned his attention more and more to the question of how many people had turned out to vote. No one was reporting long queues or significant gatherings of citizens. The streets looked emptier than ever. Jakob began to fear the Berliners had stayed away. If so, the Allies might decide there was not enough of a mandate for them to continue the Airlift.

Radio in the American Sector Reports
Berlin-Kladow
Sunday 5 December 1948
(Day 163 of the Berlin Airlift)

There was no school on Sunday and the Priestmans' house staff had the day off. Georgina found herself alone at the Priestman residence. Used to boarding schools, she knew how to dress for poorly heated rooms and wore a knitted cardigan over a roll-neck sweater. Under her long, tartan skirt, she wore thick, black stockings and she'd packed her feet into woollen socks and fleece-lined slippers as well. She made herself as comfortable as possible in the partially heated breakfast room, spreading the week's homework assignments in neat piles on the table around her. With a pot of tea in front of her, she set to work correcting maths exercises.

Around 10:30 am, the fog turned into a steady drizzle of fine rain. Almost at once, the first aircraft took off and thereafter the droning of aerial engines provided a steady counterpoint to every thought. Meanwhile, the precipitation slowly swelled the muddy puddles between the naked stakes in the vegetable garden and saturated the grass of the lower lawn until it resembled a rice paddy.

She finished her corrections just after one o'clock and made herself a sandwich. She then wrote a letter to her parents. As always when she turned her thoughts to home, she asked herself if she was a bad mother for leaving her nine-month-old daughter with her parents to take this job in Berlin. Yet she couldn't drum up a guilty conscience. Her parents doted on Donna and the little girl seemed blissfully happy in the cozy Yorkshire vicarage. It made no sense for Georgina to be the fifth wheel in her parental household when she could help so many more children here in Berlin.

The British school in Berlin had been without a maths teacher for two months before she arrived. The headmaster and the other staff members who had been tasked with teaching an extra subject had been elated to have her join them. So much so that she'd been given carte blanche to teach any way she liked "as long as the results meet school standards." For the first time in her career, she had a free hand to try more innovative methods and tailor the exercises to the interests of her pupils. She was enjoying herself, and that was just the start of it.

The school had no choir when she joined, and she'd offered to organise one. The response had been overwhelmingly positive. Although she was a little out of her depth, never having done this before, she'd sung in her school chorus and had helped her father with his church choir. Besides, she had an ulterior motive. The musical traditions of England were closely intertwined with those of Germany. Many of the most beloved composers — Handel, Bach, Beethoven, Schubert, Schumann, Mendelsohn, Brahms, Liszt and more — were German. Favourite Christmas carols like "Silent Night," and "Oh, Christmas Tree" originated in Germany. Georgina saw the choir as a means to offer a hand in friendship to Berlin schools and seek ways to cooperate. She imagined exchanges of soloists and/or joint concerts at Gatow and the British Brigade HQ, and maybe at hospitals as well.

She put her plans and dreams into her letter home, and then donning her wellies and an old sou'wester, she went for a walk in the gentle rain. The dull groan of aircraft engines accompanied her throughout her circular walk through the elegant but grey and soggy suburb. The properties here all had large gardens, and the houses themselves were gracious with decorative facades, large windows, terraces, balconies, and the occasional fountain or statue. Without a doubt, this had been an affluent suburb before the war, and just as in England, the rich did not like living near smelly factories, docks and railway yards which were the targets of the bombers. As a result, they had suffered far less damage than the poor huddled near industrial and government centres.

Yet whether it was just or not, Georgina liked living here. Although living on the Station would be warmer and more convenient for catching the morning school bus, she'd miss the views of the lake and the sound of the trees whispering among themselves at night. Most of all, she reflected, she would miss Emily and the WingCo. Both she and Kit already thought of them as friends.

Returning as dusk sank over the Havel, Georgina went into the kitchen to make dinner. Jasha had the week off after her wedding, so Georgina was doing the cooking. Jasha had conscientiously prepared menus and the necessary ingredients had been dutifully purchased by the housemaids and left on the kitchen table. All Georgina had to do was follow Jasha's hand-written instructions. These were in a unique mixture of languages not always readily comprehensible, but Georgina decided it was rather like codebreaking and enjoyed the challenge.

Just before eight pm, the RAF driver dropped Robin, Emily and Kit back at the house. Kit had flown two round trips, and the Halifax was taking on a return cargo overnight. Emily reported enthusiastically that David had welcomed Christian's offer to take over Charlotte's job and move into the apartment on Kurfuerstendamm. "He sounded really pleased," Emily stressed, "and so am I. Christian and I sat down together and within no time he'd grasped all the essentials. He even started reorganizing things a bit. He's going to be an amazing asset."

The four of them ate in the chilly breakfast room and then, while Emily and Georgina cleared the table, Kit made hot toddies based on Reverend Reddings' 'famous' recipe and Robin got a fire going in the den. Comfortably and informally furnished, the den had become their favourite room now that the rest of the house was so chilly. As soon as they had their drinks and had settled in, Emily tuned the large radio receiver to the RIAS English-language program to get the election results. RIAS was broadcasting big-band music instead. Robin looked at his watch, and remarked, "I suppose they haven't got a count yet."

"Just leave it on," Kit suggested. "I'm sure they'll give the results as soon as they can." Robin complied, while Kit asked, "How good must voter turnout be for His Majesty's Government to remain committed to Berlin?"

"Turnout of 50% or less will be viewed as a major defeat. Turnout of 66% or more, on the other hand, will be seen as a strong showing. Anything in between is ambiguous."

Abruptly the music stopped. A gong struck several times and a self-important voice intoned: "This is RIAS-Berlin! A Free Voice of the Free World! Ladies and gentlemen, we have just now received the first report on the outcome of the Berlin City elections."

Robin reached over and turned up the volume. "Although the votes have not yet been tallied, a count has been made of the total number of valid ballots cast. These came to 1,331,270 votes out of a possible 1,544,752."

Kit calculated fastest, declaring in surprise, "That's more than 85%!"

Robin looked electrified. "That's unbelievable. That's only possible if nearly all the eligible Berliners voted — including residents of the Soviet Zone!"

"I doubt we British would have delivered such a resounding vote for freedom." Georgina risked remarking.

"You're right. We're too spoilt!" Kit agreed, reaching for the jug to refill everyone's glass.

The announcer broke through their chatter, "We have the first projections on winners based on 22% of precincts reporting. The SPD appears to be on track to win an absolute majority in the reconstituted city assembly. The CDU and FDP are running neck-and-neck for second place."

"Well, that's a vote of confidence in Mayor Reuter if I ever heard one!" Emily exclaimed enthusiastically.

Yet as Georgina turned to reach for the fresh toddy Kit was offering, she caught sight of the WingCo. His elation of a moment before had been replaced by an expression of deep regret. This election proved how much the Berliners appreciated the Airlift. The last thing he wanted to do was leave now.

A World Away
Ypsilanti, Michigan
Sunday 5 December 1948
(Day 163 of the Berlin Airlift)

J.B. Baronowsky stood in the living room of his parents' small, single-level house in Ypsilanti, Michigan straining to hear the news crackling over the airwaves. The man speaking was Colonel Howley, the American commandant in Berlin. J.B. knew his voice well because he'd heard it a hundred times over the Armed Forces Network when he was flying the Airlift. Now, although the static made Howley sound like he was a world away, his elation and triumph had survived the trip across the Atlantic. "...a vote for Freedom! Mayor Reuter's party has improved its hold on power by almost 16%. The SPD won an absolute majority with 64.5% of all votes cast."

The reporter asked a question that was garbled by static, but Howley answered clearly. "The SPD is a democratic party, firmly committed to fighting Soviet tyranny and aggression. This is the party, remember, that voted unanimously *against* Hitler in 1933. Mayor Reuter is a courageous leader, and I look forward to working with him more closely than ever in the days and weeks ahead."

Again, the reporter's question was unintelligible, but J.B. hung on Howley's words, "Absolutely, the Airlift will continue! The people of Berlin have made it 100% clear they do not want to be swallowed by the Russian bear. They don't want to become slaves of Stalin. They're willing to go without heat in their houses and live with just two hours of electricity a day and to walk to work and eat powdered potatoes, powdered milk and powdered eggs for as long as it takes to make Stalin loosen his hold. Let me tell you, it isn't easy to live in the cold and the dark on half the food we Americans are used to, but the Berliners prefer that to being prisoners of a system that denies them the right to think for themselves. We could learn a thing or two from these hardy Berliners!"

The reporter thanked Howley and wanted to wrap up the interview, but Howley had a last message. "Don't forget that there are hundreds of thousands of kids here in Berlin that aren't going to have much of a Christmas unless *you* send them something nice. The USAF has promised me they are going to fly in any gifts that make it to our airfields in the West. We're calling it Operation Santa Claus, so if you've got some old toys or kid's clothes you don't need anymore, wrap 'em up and put them in the post addressed to either USAF Rhein-Main or Wiesbaden."

The reporter thanked the colonel and the station cut off the connection with Berlin to turn to the sports news. J.B. reached up to switch off the radio altogether.

"What are you doing here, J.B.?" His father's voice caught him by surprise. "I thought you were out with Patty all day?"

J.B. turned to face his father with a guilty shrug and a sheepish grin. "Yeah, I know, I mean — I don't know. I wanted to hear what had happened in Berlin, and Patty and her folks don't care. Besides, I needed to get away from them all for a bit." He shrugged again uncomfortably and then admitted, "I made up an excuse about your car breaking down and how I had to take you and Mom over to grandma's."

His father nodded slowly, his expression unreadable, but his eyes were fixed hard on his son. J.B. avoided them, turning away to pick up the jacket he'd carelessly tossed on the sofa when he came in. He pulled the sleeves straight and folded it over his arm.

The elder Baronowsky watched him for a moment and then said in a low voice, "Look, Jay, I know you're grown up and you don't have to talk to me about anything. That's fine. I don't want to start running your life. But you ain't been acting like a man who's about to marry the girl of his dreams."

"Dad—"

"Wait!" The older Baronowky held up his hand. "Hear me out, son. It's true that your mom and I never really warmed to Patty, but before you went over to Germany, we agreed that she made you happy. You were pretty hot for her and glowed with pride when she was beside you. Since you came back from Germany, I don't sense that same excitement or passion any more. I don't see much swagger in having such a swanky girl almost in the sack, either. Did something change while you were in Germany?"

"I didn't have an affair, if that's what you're asking!" J.B. snapped back defensively.

"Hadn't even thought of that. I just asked if *anything* had changed."

J.B. couldn't meet his father's penetrating eyes. He looked down and then sank onto the sagging sofa. His eyes were fixed on the old coffee table. Stains of countless cold drinks that had perspired into the wood marred the surface, yet all he saw was Kathleen coming out of the fog towards him. For his father, he shook his head and said slowly, "Nothing specific, Dad."

His father went around to the other side of the coffee table and sat down. "Want to talk about it?"

J.B. drew a deep breath. It would have been easy to brush the old man off, to say it wasn't any of his business or it wasn't important. But it was. He'd hoped that being back with Patty again would make him forget Berlin and Kathleen. Instead, the more he was with Patty, the more he missed what he'd left behind. He tried to put his feelings into words his father would understand. "We were doing something good over there, Dad. I was glad to be part of it. Somehow, choosing drapes for our apartment and selecting the music for the band to play at the wedding just doesn't seem very important."

"No, but if you loved Patty, you'd still find it all kinda cute," his father suggested.

"Are you saying I don't love Patty?" J.B. gasped out.

"Do you?"

J.B. dropped his head in his hands and scratched at his scalp with his fingernails. Without looking up, he muttered, "All she seems to care about is how things *look*. It's all about *appearances*. Does this match that? What's the latest fashion? What colour is in vogue now? What will the neighbours think of this or that? And the bigger the price tag, the better it is. Is that right, Dad? Is life just about money and fashion and prestige?" He looked up to meet his father's eyes.

The elder Baronowsky didn't answer. Instead, he stood, went over to the sideboard, and pulled out a bottle of vodka and two glasses. He filled the glasses, brought them back to the sofa and nudged his son with one hand.

J.B. took the offered glass but didn't drink. Instead, he put it on the table and tried to explain, "I've tried to tell her about Berlin — the conditions people live in, the way the kids went wild when we dropped the candy, the presents they and their mothers gave us — handmade things like knitted socks or old books and lace napkins, anything that had survived the bombing. They didn't have enough to eat, but they kept trying to give *us* presents!"

Although he sounded exasperated, what he wanted was for other people to feel the same amazement and incomprehension that he did. Instead, most people just said something meaningless like: "That was nice of them." Patty, on the other hand, had responded with, "I hope you didn't keep any of that junk! We don't want to clutter up our beautiful house with dirty, old stuff."

His dad's response took him by surprise. "The Poles would have treated you the same way. In Europe, you never take anything without giving a gift in return. If someone invites you to dinner, you bring them flowers or wine. If someone gives you a birthday present, you offer them coffee and cake. Because you are bringing the supplies in, the Berliners want to give you something back. Otherwise, they would feel humiliated."

"That's it! That's just what it is!" J.B. exclaimed. It was a relief to have the mystery solved, and he wondered why he hadn't talked to his dad about this earlier.

"Go on, tell me more about Germany," his father suggested.

It was like opening the floodgates. J.B. had wanted to talk about his experiences ever since he'd returned to the States, but no one else seemed interested. Certainly not Patty and her family.

"I think the biggest thing I learned is that they aren't all Nazis. I don't mean just the kids. There's a woman who takes in laundry, and she had a deaf daughter. The Nazis took her away and put her in a camp — just like the Jews. She died there, her mother thinks from neglect. That woman hates Nazis more than I do!"

His father nodded. "I can believe that, Jay. The way some people talk, all Italians are Romeos, all Irish are drunks, and all Poles are dumb. But we aren't. None of us. I don't think all Germans were Nazis any more than all Russians are Communists or all Americans are good people."

"That's it, Dad. Most of the Germans — just like most Americans — didn't care much about politics until it was too late. They weren't either Nazis or anti-Nazis. They just didn't pay any attention to what was going on in Berlin until they were being conscripted into the army or watching their neighbours get dragged away. Even then, they would have been happier getting on with their lives than going off to conquer somebody. One guy told me that they didn't have any newspapers or radio that weren't controlled by the Nazis, so he grew up thinking the Jews and the French and the Russians were trying to destroy

Germany. He said it wasn't until the war that he found out they'd been lied to for years. It's because of what the Nazis did that the Berliners don't want to bow to Stalin. They know what a dictatorship is, and they've had enough. Helping them is the right thing to do. That's why I'd rather be flying the Airlift than designing trucks for GM."

His father nodded and asked the question J.B. dreaded, "And Patty? Where does Patty fit into all this?"

"I don't know! She certainly doesn't want to hear about Germany or Berlin or what I did there. She doesn't care about any of it." J.B. took a deep breath and admitted, "Sometimes, I get the feeling that she doesn't care all that much about me, either. I'm just part of the furniture. I have the right looks to fit into her living room — yeah, maybe her bedroom too — but is that all I am? A body to put into her perfect home and bring home the bucks so she can live in style?"

"Don't marry her, Jay."

Despite his complaining, the answer shook J.B. "Hey, Dad! That's pretty stiff medicine! She's made wedding plans — a second time now! Her family has spent a fortune on a wedding gown, shoes, flowers, band, catering and all that—"

"No one asked them to," the senior Baronowsky reminded his son. "That was their choice."

"Yeah, I know, but she's been patient while I was away. If I break up with her now, she'll go to pieces!" It was a frightening scenario.

"Listen to me, Jay," his father interrupted his thoughts. "It's the rest of your life you're talking about. If you aren't crazy about her now, you ain't gonna be crazy about her after she's gained forty pounds and is spending your money like it was water."

True, J.B. thought, but if he broke things off he'd trigger a tempest of recriminations.

His father hadn't finished, "I know divorce is becoming fashionable in some circles, but the Church does not recognise it. In the eyes of God, once you give your vows to Patty and take her to your bed, you are bound to her and her alone — forsaking all others — until death takes one or the other of you. You may sin. A lot of men do. But you will never be free of her to find a woman who could make you happy. She will make you miserable, Jay — your whole life long."

J.B. dropped his head in his hands again. Then he noticed the untouched vodka, picked up the glass and threw the alcohol down his gullet with one toss. Shaking his head, he addressed his dad, "If I break off with Patty, that snazzy job at GM goes up in smoke, too."

"I thought you just told me you'd rather be flying the airlift than designing trucks?"

J.B. opened and closed his mouth, swallowed, and then pushed the shot glass across the table, "Can I have some more of that?"

His father got up, poured them both another shot of vodka and handed J.B. his glass. Still standing, he reminded his sitting son, "You never wanted that job, Jay. You wanted the job at the Michigan Aeronautical Research Centre."

"Yeah, but that job's long gone, Dad. They gave it to their next best candidate as soon as I turned them down."

"So, you can go back on active duty with the USAF. I know!" His dad held up both hands as if in surrender. "They pay peanuts! Still, you could volunteer to go back on the Airlift."

J.B. looked down at the table. Kathleen was coming at him out of the fog, and in the background, the kids were waving wildly in happiness.

"That's what you want, isn't it?" his father drummed the message home.

"Yeah," J.B. admitted, looking up at him.

"Then don't let something as inconsequential as a dumb blonde and her temper tantrum get in your way. You've got more important things to do with your life, Jay."

Chapter Four
Lifting Fog

Course Reversal
RAF Gatow
Monday 6 December 1948
(Day 164 of the Berlin Airlift)

Wing Commander Priestman arrived at the station early, just before 7:00 am. Sunrise on this December day was more than an hour away, and no pre-dawn light penetrated the murk of low-hanging cloud. Stepping out of his car, Robin squinted towards the runways, trying to estimate visibility. The fog did not cling to the ground as it had yesterday at this time, and although everything was wet with moisture, none was falling from the sky. A light but bitterly cold breeze swept in from the northeast fretting the canvas covers of the lorries and rattling a metal door somewhere. In short, conditions were good enough for flying as the drone of engines overhead and the screech of tyres on concrete underlined. There would be no reprieve of his execution on account of the weather.

"I'd better get over to the EAS hangar," Emily brought Robin's attention back to the other two passengers in the car. Emily went on tiptoe to give him a rare, public kiss. "Chin up, Robin. You did the right thing, and there *is* life after the RAF. I'll wait in your office."

He nodded absently. She drew back and Kit held out his hand. "Good luck, Robin. Don't let them beat you down. Sometimes, if rarely, it pays to stand up to them."

Robin took Kit's hand grateful both for the good wishes and the reminder that Kit had survived being both publicly insubordinate and publicly humiliated. Still, as he turned to go up the stairs to his office, he felt more like a man facing execution than a self-righteous rebel. He greeted his adjutant and secretary as he passed through the outer office, and Stan jumped up to follow him. "Do you have the latest Met for me?" Robin asked, deflecting other questions.

"Yes, sir. There's a large high-pressure system pushing Arctic air down from the polar circle into Scandinavia. It is forecast to reach Berlin by tomorrow afternoon bringing clear visibility but also freezing temperatures."

Robin looked at Stan, trying to decide if that was good or bad news. Good flying conditions, but at the price of plunging the Berliners into frightful cold at a time when they had almost no means of heating their homes, schools or workplaces. General Winter was definitely a Russian ally. But it wasn't his problem any more.

"Did you want a press briefing before you leave?" Stan asked.

"Not unless there's something else in the news besides the resounding SPD victory in yesterday's election."

"I'd have to check with Fl/Lt Boyd about that, sir."

Robin nodded and while Stan went out Sergeant Andrews entered with a cup of tea. As she put it on his desk, she reported, "The Spitfire is fuelled and ready for you, sir."

"Sorry, I should have told you. I expect to bring someone back with me, so I'll need to take the Anson. Please ask the ground crew to get her fuelled and ready as soon as possible."

"Yes, sir." Andrews hurried out and Robin looked at his watch. It was his mistake. He almost always flew the Spitfire and should have remembered to warn everyone that for today's flight to the UK, he needed the Anson. He hoped it would not cause a serious delay.

He reached for his tea as Fl/Lt Boyd appeared at the door. "I've put together a press folder for you, sir, just in case you have time to read while waiting around for something or someone. The contortions of the Soviet press to turn yesterday's election debacle into a Communist victory are almost comical." He grinned as he laid the folder on the desk. Robin thanked him.

Andrews returned, "The Anson will be ready in twenty minutes, sir."

Robin thanked her and looked at the clock. That was just 7:35 am. He should still be able to reach 46 Group HQ at about 11:30. He checked the telegram from Merer again; it requested that he report 'no later than noon' and noted that a more general meeting was scheduled for 13:30.

Removing his greatcoat, he sat down to remove his shoes. He put them into a paper bag which he stowed inside his flight case along with his folded tunic, the press folder and a file he had prepared the day before. He pulled on heavy woollen socks before shoving his feet into his fleece-lined flying boots. Then he donned a fisherman's roll-neck jumper, wound a scarf around his neck and finally put on his Irvine flight jacket. He checked the pockets for his gloves and then closed the flight case and turned to leave the office.

His eyes fell on Bertie the Bear, and he hesitated. Out of nowhere, he was seized with a silly superstition such as aircrew had been famous for throughout the war. He abruptly believed that Bertie would bring him luck just as Liesl had promised. He hesitated only a fraction of a second and then stuffed the teddy bear inside his flight jacket and clamped him under his left arm.

As he passed through the anteroom, Andrews asked, "What time do you expect to be back, sir?"

"The main meeting doesn't start until 13:30. I'll be lucky to get away by 18:00. So about 10 pm at the earliest. More likely later than that."

"I'll be sure your car and driver are waiting for you, sir."

"Mrs Priestman may want to wait here as well. It's warmer," he added by way of explanation.

Outside the gloom was beginning to lighten enough to reveal cracks of lighter grey in the dense overcast. At the Anson, the groundcrew greeted him cheerfully and assured him the refuelling was nearly finished. Robin clambered up the ladder awkwardly, conscious of the toy under his arm, but no one seemed to notice it. Inside the cockpit, he settled himself down, putting Bertie in the righthand seat. Then he took the clipboard with the checklist and prepared for take-off. By the time he was finished, so was the refuelling.

With both engines purring happily, he pulled on his leather flying helmet, switched on the RT and pressed the microphone to his face. "Gatow Control, this is the WingCo. Ready to taxi."

"Good morning, sir!" It was the low and melodic voice of Assistant Section Leader Hart, their senior female controller. "You'll be taking off to the east on the PSP runway 090. You are cleared to taxi to the head of the queue."

"Roger. I appreciate that." He shoved back the cockpit window and waved the chocks away. At a return wave indicating the chocks and ground crew were clear, he released the brakes and gently pushed the throttles forward to ooze out of his parking position. He had to concentrate more when flying the Anson because at heart he was still a fighter pilot, and the decorous twin-engine aircraft had a totally different feel from a Spitfire. Get used to it, he told himself. If they gave him a bowler hat, his best — if not only — prospect of a flying job was flying Moby Dick with Air Ambulance International.

Robin had mixed feelings about that. It would be awkward taking orders from David, for one thing, and if David wanted him to qualify on the heavies so he could also fly the freighter as well as the ambulance, he'd have to fly second dickie to Moran or his co-pilot Forrester until he had the requisite hours. Better than not flying at all, he reminded himself.

He overtook a dozen aircraft waiting to take off, including the AFI Halifax "Albie." Kit gave Robin a "thumbs up" as he passed, and Robin responded with a salute. He turned onto the runway and ran up the two engines while keeping his feet firmly on the brakes. "Gatow Tower, RAF 995 ready for take-off."

"Cleared for take-off, sir. Climb to two thousand feet and then turn right on 185 and switch to the frequency for the Berlin Air Safety Centre for further instructions. Have a good trip!"

He eased back the throttles a little before releasing the brakes and started down the runway in the direction of the invisible rising sun as he pushed them forward again. After take-off, he was fed into the train of aircraft flying along the central corridor heading for Hannover. He was given clearance to ten thousand feet, however, to enable him to fly above the Airlift traffic at his own speed. At four thousand six hundred feet, he broke free of the cloud cover and was flying over a sea of clouds washed with golden light from the sun rising behind him. The joy of flight transfused him, and the future no longer looked quite so grim. He remarked to Bertie, "Do you understand now, Bertie? This is the closest a man can get to heaven while still alive."

His positive mood stayed with him across the channel and did not dissipate until he re-entered the clouds on approach to his destination. He landed at 11:35 and was met by Merer's adjutant, who took him straight over to HQ. He was able to change out of his flying kit in the back of the car, and the adj promised to leave it at the reception at the officers' mess for his return trip. He'd left Bertie in the copilot's seat of the Anson and wondered how his successor would react to finding him there.

The driver pointed him in the direction of Merer's office, and Robin knocked on the outer office door almost exactly at noon. A moment later he was ushered into the inner office and saluted the Air Commodore. Robin's eyes flitted around the room, looking for the man who would replace him, and was surprised to find they were alone. "It's just the two of us for now, Priestman," Merer told him. "The general briefing doesn't start for another hour and a half."

"Yes, sir. I just presumed you would want me to brief my successor before that."

"Hm. Are you anxious to get out of Berlin, then?" As he spoke, Merer indicated that Robin should take a seat at the coffee table.

"Not at all, sir!" Robin answered forcefully. Perceiving an opportunity, he made a last-ditch attempt to hold onto his job. "After yesterday's election, it's clear the Berliners appreciate our efforts, and frankly, I've been moved and inspired by their stand. There is nothing I'd like more than to remain where I am." Had he made that appeal too strongly?

Merer seemed to take no note of his tension or passion. He responded blandly with, "Would you like some tea and biscuits?"

Robin shook his head. "I'd rather get this over with."

Merer sat down and smiled gently. "You have quite a record."

"Meaning?"

"This isn't the first time you've bent the rules with spectacular effect."

Robin didn't have an answer to that; it was true. The bad part was that with a man like Merer, who had evidently not seen combat, he didn't expect as much understanding as he'd found from Air Marshal Park.

To his surprise, Merer remarked, "I haven't met many good officers who haven't bent King's Regulations now and again. So why don't you tell me in your own words what you did to cause Group Captain Bagshot to lose his wool?"

Robin took a deep breath. A chance to explain was more than he'd expected, so he started with "Thank you for hearing me out, sir." Merer nodded acknowledgement. "In mid-November, the Berlin City government approached Lt. General Herbert and Colonel Howley jointly with the request to evacuate 17,000 vulnerable civilians. They—"

"What did they mean by vulnerable?" Merer requested clarification.

"Orphaned and malnourished children for the most part, but also adults with chronic conditions such as multiple sclerosis, asthma, acute arthritis and so on. Both Howley and Herbert spontaneously assured the City Council that the evacuations could be made — without consulting CALTF."

Merer visibly winced and Robin continued. "Only after committing themselves, did they approach Tunner, and he flat-out refused. He argued that a large-scale evacuation of civilians from Berlin would slow down turn-around times and so reduce the tonnage of supplies delivered."

"Tunner said no, but you went ahead anyway?" Merer's eyebrows had shot up and he sounded shocked.

"Tunner explicitly told General Herbert that he would not stand in the way of the RAF taking passengers. Since I wasn't in the room when that conversation took place, I'm not sure whether Tunner voluntarily made that concession or General Herbert asked about the RAF. Either way, Tunner authorised the RAF to make its own decision. It was at that point that Herbert summoned me and in Colonel Howley's presence asked if I could organise the evacuations. I asked whether they had cleared it with Bagshot." Merer nodded approval. "Herbert bit my head off, saying he was asking me and wanted my answer as a professional and the commander who would be responsible for implementation. In short, they already knew what answer they would get from Bagshot."

"What makes you so sure Bagshot would have turned down a request from the British Commandant of Berlin?"

"Bagshot feels it is humiliating that 'the Colonials' are getting all the glory because they are flying twice as many sorties and delivering four times as much tonnage as we are. He pushed me to increase volumes unremittingly, and he disapproved of any measure that reduced our tonnage totals — even if it reduced risks. Any undertaking that reduced our numbers further was bound to make him blow a gasket."

Merer did not answer at once. Instead, he sat back in his chair and considered his visitor. At length he announced, "Bagshot is a petty-minded bureaucrat. A man lost in his own bumpf. In plain English: he's a twit. His

Majesty's Government is in Berlin to help the Berliners, not to compete with the Americans in some silly cargo-flying contest. If the Berlin government prefers us to fly people *out* of Berlin, rather than more food or coal *in*, then that is exactly what we should be doing."

Robin was astonished by the Merer's unexpected support and asked cautiously. "Does that mean you think I did the right thing?"

"It does. You are re-instated as station commander Gatow forthwith, and I expect you to see that the city's priorities are respected — especially now that the city government has received such a strong and unambiguous mandate from their own population."

Robin hesitated, but then decided this was the time to raise it, "In that case, you should know that the city government has also requested that we fly out manufactured goods produced in Berlin factories to keep them running and people employed."

"Then we'll damn well do that, too!" Merer declared forcefully. "I want you to prioritize good liaison with General Herbert and the city government. Just keep me informed of requests and Tunner's response."

"Yes, sir!" Robin could not keep the grin off his face.

Merer laughed and noted, "This must have been a bad week for you. I'm sorry I didn't get to the bottom of things sooner, but I wanted to see how the election went before bringing people together. Let me buy you lunch to make up for it."

"Thank you, sir." Priestman stood up still beaming and at the back of his mind he promised himself never to fly without Bertie ever again.

Getting Out of Dodge
Washington, DC
Tuesday, 7 December 1948
(Day 165)

Anna Savage ripped open the envelope of the telegram and read:

"A. Savage booked on BOAC flight 97 to London departing Washington National Airport, 10:20 am,

Thursday 9 December, arriving London 7:15 am local
time 10 December and connecting to BEA flight 35 to
Hamburg departing London at 11:50. Ticket must be
collected at BOAC ticket counter no later than two
hours before London flight. On arrival in Hamburg
await AAI rep in lobby. Director of Personnel, Air
Ambulance International, Captain E. Priestman.

Anna's hand started to tremble. It was really happening. She was on her way to Europe. Until this minute it had not seemed possible. She closed her eyes and remembered how it had started in Georgia two months ago.

"Aunt Flora?" Anna called out as the screen door chinked shut behind her. "Aunt Flora? It's me. Anna." The spacious kitchen with its big, wooden counters and endless cupboards stretching along the back of Judge Warren's neo-classical mansion in Eastman, Georgia had been the realm of Aunt Flora for as long as Anna could remember.

Aunt Flora had first brought Anna here when she was eight years old. That was about two years after her mother had left her father because he'd beaten her once too often. Her mother had been trying to make enough money to keep herself and her daughter in clothes and food by working at a diner where truckers stopped. They lived in a shack out back, without electricity or running water. Then, out of the blue, Aunt Flora had arrived and there had been a terrible fight between the sisters. In the end, Aunt Flora stuffed a pathetic pile of worn-out things — all Anna owned — into a cotton sack and brought Anna to Eastman on the bus.

At the time, Anna had never before been in a town with streetlights and rows of pretty houses with big green lawns. Eastman had awed her even before Aunt Flora marched her up to the big, red brick house with towering white pillars and a chandelier hanging over the porch — much less introduced her to a white lady who smelled of flowers. The latter was Miss Josephine, the wife of Judge Warren, and Aunt Flora's employer.

Anna was given her own room above the kitchen. It wasn't so much a room as a walk-in closet, but it had a bed and cupboards in it and it adjoined

Aunt Flora's room, which had two big windows overlooking the back garden. She and Flora had a real bathroom too, with a tub, sink and flush toilet, although they shared this with Mr George, Judge Warren's manservant. Anna felt like a princess to be allowed to live here.

School was almost as exciting. The pupils were divided into classes by age, and each had its own room. The boys and girls had to wash their hands and faces, and they were loaned books for learning. They had to do homework in notebooks that the teachers graded. When Anna turned fourteen, she was one of just three girls allowed to go to the private high school for coloured people. Anna's grades were so good that Aunt Flora wanted to pay the fees out of her own pocket, but Miss Josephine wouldn't let her and made the payments instead. Miss Josephine came to Anna's graduation too, the only white woman in the whole auditorium. After she graduated, Miss Josephine helped her get into nurse's training, too.

The adult Anna was thankful but not beholden to Miss Josephine. She'd worked hard to get those good grades, to qualify as a nurse and to serve her country. The adult Anna also knew that Judge Warren's "mansion" wasn't all that big or all that fancy either. In fact, it was rather run down. But it was still the closest thing Anna had to home.

"That you, Anna?" Aunt Flora called, coming in from the front of the house.

"Yes! Miss Josephine sent for me. Do you know why?"

Flora gave her a look that said she was in big trouble. "Ah don't *know* why Miss Josephine sent for you Anna Elizabeth, but Ah can sure as blazes *guess*! Which is why you are goin' to sit you'self down at that table and get you' ears blistered." Anna might be 26 years old, a qualified nurse and living in her own apartment over on Elm Street, but she respected Aunt Flora too much to talk back. She pulled out a wooden chair and plopped down, but she held herself upright and looked at her aunt with an expression bordering on defiance. She was prepared to defend everything she'd said and done.

Aunt Flora stood with her fists planted on her hips and she glared down at Anna. "Now what Ah heard — and likely what Miss Josephine heard — is that you been meddlin' in this business with the Basey girl, saying she shouldn't have to carry her baby to term—"

"Aunt Flora! Rosie Basey's a *child*. She's just twelve and she's all skin and bones! She's not *strong* enough to carry a baby to term — much less the child of that fat, white—"

"Don't you dare say that bad word in mah kitchen!" Aunt Flora stopped her.

"If somebody doesn't do something soon, she's going to die!" Anna protested furiously.

"Yes and everyone from here to Savannah knows you think that! Which means that if some mornin' that child turns up without a baby in her belly, you goin' to be in such hot water, there ain't nothin' Judge Warren can do to save you!"

"Abortion isn't illegal if it's necessary to save the life of the mother," Anna countered. "I've been reading up—"

"Don't go talkin' legal gobbledegook with me, Anna Elizabeth. This don't have nothin' to do with the law. No one goin' to give you a chance to defend you'self in some court where some fine lawyer paid for by the NAACP might point his finger at Cabe Lawson and demand he stand trial for rape—"

"Which is exactly what he should do!" Anna interrupted. "Why don't people see that and demand it? A helpless twelve-year-old girl was raped by a white —" She bit her tongue, looking for a word she was allowed to use, "— ape, and nobody in this county has the guts to stand up and say so, much less help her!"

"Cabe Lawson's got a rich daddy and people don't want a lot of Yankee newspapermen comin' down here to make fun of them and call them names. Before they let that happen, they will string you up on the nearest tree and use you for target practice like they did you' great-granddaddy."

Anna was blindsided. She'd come here expecting a lecture about being too outspoken. She'd expected Miss Josephine to gently advise her to keep a lower profile and for Aunt Flora to amplify the message more forcefully. She had not anticipated talk of lynching — and no one had ever told her that her great-grandfather had ended that way. The only thing she knew about the man whose photo in Union Army uniform graced Aunt Flora's dresser was that he and all the Washington side of the family were 'respectable' and educated coloured folk — unlike the poor, cotton-pickers on her father's side.

"Great-Granddad Washington was lynched?" Anna asked in a dazed voice.

Aunt Flora nodded, and suddenly the rage that had burned in her was doused as if by a gust of rain. Aunt Flora seemed to shrink before Anna's eyes, her anger replaced with something closer to despair and pain. A chill gripped Anna. "Why?" she whispered, already sensing how terrible the truth might be. "*Why* did they lynch him?"

Aunt Flora sank into the nearest kitchen chair and without looking at Anna she answered in a wooden tone, "They lynched him because he beat to a bloody pulp the boy who done raped me and shot the white boy goin' after you' mother."

That was almost too much to take in. Anna stared at her aunt, her emotions in turmoil and her thoughts careening around her head. After a moment, she forced herself to focus on one fact. "You were raped by a white boy?" Flora nodded slowly. "And my mother?"

"You' mother crawled out the window and ran into the woods screaming. Granddad heard her, saw a man chasin' after her and shot him. Then he rushed into our bedroom and found me crushed on the bed hardly able to breathe, let alone cry for help —" she cut herself off and sat for several seconds with her eyes closed. Then she shook her head sharply as if to clear it of memories, and continued in a more matter-of-fact tone, "Granddad didn't dare shoot in case he hit me, so he used his fists instead. When that boy couldn't fight back no mo', granddad kicked him outside and got me to the hospital. They wanted to keep me overnight, so he went home." She stopped again to gather her strength and drew a deep breath before concluding, "The KKK was waitin' for him. They overwhelmed him, strung him up, and shot him fifteen times."

They stared at one another. Anna had a thousand questions. She drew a breath.

"Befo' you ask," Flora stopped her. "Yes, Ah *did* get pregnant, and that's why Ah had to drop out of school. But Miss Josephine insisted on me comin' and livin' here, and Ah've had a home here ever since. She also found a midwife and a good adoption agency. When Ah gave birth to a little girl almost 28 years ago, Ah held her only for a few moments before she was wrapped up and taken away. Within a week, a nice, respectable couple drove down from Washington, DC, signed all the papers and drove away with her."

"And you've never seen her since?"

"Well, that's what you'd expect, but Miss Josephine took the time to meet Mr and Mrs Hardy when they come down for the adoption. They were elderly when they adopted mah little girl. They called her Coral and kept in touch with Miss Josephine. They even sent photos of her now and again. When Ms Hardy died, Mr Hardy told Coral about me, and she come down to visit. We write regular now."

"That's why you oppose abortion so strongly," Anna whispered in understanding.

"Yes, maybe that's one reason. You see, no matter how horrible that man was, and no matter how horrible it would have been for me to try to raise a child on mah own at 13, the Hardys were good honest people who wanted a child and gave her endless love and as much opportunity as they could. She went to secretarial school, and now she has a job working for the Department of State." Flora was so proud, she looked inches taller.

"But none of that would have been possible without Miss Josephine —"

"And the judge," Aunt Flora added. "Judge Warren was so steamin' mad, he got the governor to offer a reward leadin' to the conviction of the murderers. But no one stepped forward with information that could be used in court. Still, he supported Miss Josephine in everything she did for me, and you, too."

Anna had never been able to warm to Judge Warren. She had always felt he didn't like coloured people, yet she knew that he believed in strict equality before the law and had never stood in the way of his wife's charity. To her aunt she argued, "Kind and powerful white people helped you out, Aunt Flora, but Rosie Basey has no one! Her family's dirt poor, and—

Flora interrupted in a hard and admonishing tone, "Anna Elizabeth, if you dare to lay you' hands on an unborn infant—"

"Now Flora, there's no need to use that tone of voice with our Anna," Miss Josephine swept into the kitchen. Despite her 72 years, she was still elegant, but she was frail too. Anna guessed she weighed no more than 100 pounds, and her pale skin was marred by age marks that no amount of make-up could cover. Yet she was resolute and firm as she declared, "All Anna has been saying is that a mother's life is as important as a baby's and that a doctor ought to look into the matter. She's quite right."

As she spoke she crossed the kitchen to give Anna a hug and then gestured for her to sit down again, taking a seat herself.

"Anna, I didn't send for you because of this business with the Basey girl. You've done nothing wrong, and you are quite right that something must be done to help her." Miss Josephine's bony hand with a large diamond ring reached out and covered Anna's. "Trust me, Anna, the Judge and I will find a way to help. But your aunt is right, too. Some people around here don't see straight, and they might make trouble for you. It's time for you to consider other options for your future."

Anna frowned, feeling patronized and muzzled. She wanted to protest, but she couldn't bring herself to be rude — not knowing the full extent of Miss Josphine's assistance to Aunt Flora. Miss Josephine continued, "I know how frustrated you've been since you returned from the army." No doubt she did, Anna thought; she hadn't made a secret of it. "The work here is monotonous and demoralizing and you're earning donkey's wages." That summarised her life very well, Anna admitted. Her work consisted mostly of futile efforts to counter the effects of acute poverty on coloured women and children. Her daily bread was dealing with malnutrition, dysentery, rickets, TB, abuse, and neglect — with the occasional rape thrown in for variety, she thought bitterly.

Miss Josephine was continuing, "Now, I'm sure you remember Colonel and Mrs Howley, and you must have heard that Colonel Howley is now the US Commandant in Berlin"

"Of course!" Anna replied. How could she not have heard? She was amazed and thrilled to think that a man she had once given physical therapy to was now so important that he was often in the papers or on the radio. His wife had encouraged her to apply to the US Army Nursing Corps, and Anna was certain that the colonel had pulled strings to get her in.

"Well," Miss Josephine continued, "it seems there is a terrible shortage of medical personnel in Berlin and Mrs Howley sent me a cable to ask if you would be interested in working as a nurse on an air ambulance. They thought of you because you speak German from working at that POW camp during the war."

Anna was so astonished she could only stammer. "A flight nurse?" Ever since her army training near some Air Corps bases, she'd longed to fly. "With the army?"

"No, I'm afraid not. Mrs Howley says it's a private British company, but this is still an amazing opportunity for you. It comes at a perfect time, too — when there are so many unkind rumours floating around. Some ignorant folks think you've become uppity and — wrong as they are — they could harm you." Miss Josephine leaned closer to deliver this message. She was, Anna sensed, just as worried as Aunt Flora.

Anna nodded. She had joined the Army Nursing Corps to get away from Georgia. She'd wanted to see more of the country, more of the whole world. She'd dreamed of being sent to a field hospital in Europe. Instead, they'd sent her to a POW camp in Arkansas. Convinced she'd been shunted off to the POW camp because of the colour of her skin, she'd protested. That earned her a reprimand and blotted her record so much that, even when she uncovered an escape plot among some of the prisoners, she'd been given no recognition or reward. Maybe the army was different now that President Truman had ended segregation, but she wasn't sure. So, working for a private company might be better. She'd just never imagined there might be any other way to get to Europe — or to fly. How many hours had she stared up at the sky, watching those bright yellow training planes while she worked at that camp in Arkansas?

Miss Josephine brought her back to the present. "This is a once-in-a-life-time opportunity, Anna. I hope you'll have the courage to seize it."

Anna opened her mouth to agree but stopped herself and looked towards Aunt Flora. The older woman had tears in her eyes, but her voice was firm. "Go, Anna. Go and see the world — not just for you but for me and your mother and all of us stuck here in Dodge County!"

And the day after tomorrow, Anna thought as a chill went down her spine, she was going to start that journey by flying for the first time in her life — all the way to London, Hamburg and on to Berlin. It seemed too good to be true.

ABCs

Berlin-Spandau
Wednesday 8 December 1948
(Day 166 of the Berlin Airlift)

Georgina stood before the Kaiser Wilhelm Gymnasium in Spandau momentarily intimidated. The British School had a loose "association" with this institution, and via her headmaster, she had requested a meeting with the director. The large, grey building in front of her, however, looked more like a military barracks than a school. Furthermore, the roof had been damaged in the war and only provisionally repaired. The upper storey windows were boarded up, and the trees in the school playground had been truncated by people sawing off branches for firewood. Altogether, the visage was harsh and uninviting.

Warily, Georgina climbed the steps and entered a dingy entry hall. The windows were glazed with thick, industrial glass and there was no electricity. An unpleasant smell hung in the air, and it took Georgina several minutes to decide it was a mixture of disinfectant, mould and cooked cabbage from a school canteen. It was also so cold that she could see her breath. As she looked about uncertainly, a door opened on her right and an elderly woman put her head out to ask. *"Wie bitte? Sie wuenschen?"*

"I'm Mrs Moran," she answered in English. "I've come from the British School, and I have an appointment with Herr Dr Altenheyn." (She hoped she'd pronounced his name correctly!)

The demeanour of the woman transformed into one of obsequious welcome. She came out to shake hands and then led Georgina up the first flight of stairs and along a corridor. Just before they reached a door with a sign saying *"Rektor"* on it, a bell started ringing — not an electric bell, but a bell pulled by a cord. The effect was the same. Doors all along the corridor flew open and children between the ages of twelve and eighteen spilled out. Pandemonium ensued with girls and boys running in all directions, chattering to one another, or whistling and shouting to get the attention of friends. Georgina waited in the midst of a confusing torrent until, almost as suddenly as the chaos had erupted, it subsided. The last pupils scurried to their classrooms and disappeared. Silence returned.

"Well, that looked perfectly normal," Georgina thought to herself. She had always imagined German schoolchildren would be more disciplined. Maybe not marching to class singing 'Deutschland Ueber Alles,' but quiet and orderly all the same. She found it comforting to think they were as undisciplined as English children. The other thing that struck her was that while the children were all wearing layers of clothing against the cold, they did not look as though they were starving or listless from lack of nourishment; maybe the Airlift was working better than expected.

Her guide gestured for her to continue into the rector's waiting room. Here Georgina was confronted by straight-backed wooden chairs lining the wall and a lone desk with a secretary behind it. The elderly woman with large, thick glasses got to her feet and bade Georgina follow her through the door to the inner office. She announced Georgina and then withdrew, closing the door behind her.

Georgina faced a tall, slender man who looked at least eighty years old. He was skeletally thin, with wisps of white hair combed over his bald skull, but a bushy white moustache. His pale blue eyes were watery, and a pair of fragile reading glasses perched on the end of his nose. He wore an old-fashioned black frock coat, a striped vest and a bow tie — all of which had seen better days. He stood, offered his hand and then indicated the seat before his desk. When they sat opposite one another, he leaned forward and clasped his hands on the desk to ask. "How may I help you, Mrs Moran?"

"Didn't Mr. Peden explain the purpose of my visit?

The rector shook his head.

Georgina was dismayed but recovered rapidly. "I'm here because I have organised a chorus at the British School and with Christmas approaching we are planning to hold some concerts. I thought it would be fun — and also build better relations — if our schools gave joint concerts." She paused for a response, but the rector just gazed at her as if he did not comprehend what she was suggesting. She tried to explain herself better. "I thought maybe we could give joint concerts singing Christmas carols, or passages from Bach's Christmas oratorio and Handel's Messiah in hospitals and, of course, at the airfields." The rector still looked so sceptical that she fell silent, confused and discouraged.

"You want to do something with a chorus? With our chorus? The school's chorus?"

"Yes," Georgina agreed eagerly, only to be struck by a second thought. Less sure of herself, now, she asked, "Don't you have a school chorus?"

"No, we don't." Herr Dr Altenheyn answered bluntly. Then sensing his guest's dismay, he expanded. "We *used* to have one. A very good one, in fact. You see, this is a private school, devoted to high academic standards. The parents of our students all come from the upper middle class. They are civil servants, officers, doctors, scholars, scientists, lawyers and other professionals. They want their children to have a classical and scientific education. And in the past music was an important and integral part of the curriculum." he assured her. "However, with deepest regret, it is no longer possible to offer musical education."

"May I ask why?"

"Of course, you may ask. It is simple. We do not have the resources. For a start, I do not have enough teachers. At the end of the war, eighty per cent of the staff were members of the NSDAP, who had to be sent away. Most of those who applied for the vacant positions were Communists — sent to us by the SED. I had to beg retired teachers to return to work with the result that the average age of the faculty today is 72. And that is only the start of my problems. How can we teach without textbooks? The library was full of books about the genetic superiority of Aryans, the essence of the "Leadership Principle," the inferior intelligence of women and so on and so forth. Of course, the Soviets sent us crates of free material — filled with Marxist-Leninist rot. So, the teachers have brought what books they had from home, and I have begged friends to lend me books from their personal libraries. We have few duplicates, however, so how can we have reading assignments? In addition, the blackboards are so old they are almost white, and we have very little chalk, while the children have no exercise books or pencils with which to do homework."

Georgina felt smaller by the minute and still the German headmaster continued sternly, "As for music, we have no school instruments any more, not even a piano. How can anyone learn to sing much less sing together in harmony without some accompaniment?" He did not give her a chance to answer before adding, "Yet the biggest problem facing us is this: how can we expect the children to learn anything in the dark and the cold? The sun rises after 8 o'clock and sets before 4 o'clock and some days we have no electricity in all that time. The temperature in this room is currently 12 degrees," he pointed to a thermometer hanging on the wall beside his desk. "As winter sets in, it will get colder. Unless we get a much larger coal allocation, we will have to suspend classes altogether."

He stopped speaking, but Georgina, conscious that she must have sounded foolish and patronizing, concluded for him, "Under the circumstances, Christmas concerts sound frivolous." Herr Altenheyn tilted his head slightly in a gesture of subtle agreement.

That, however, was not the end of the matter. Georgina drew a deep breath and replied, "While I understand your feelings, sir, I do not share them. This may sound naïve, but extracurricular activities often help pupils to forget their problems and enable them to have fun together. During the war, I worked at a school for evacuees from a very poor part of London. They had been sent to rural Lincolnshire to avoid the bombing and were completely separated from their families. We had to keep them amused and keep their minds off the fact that their parents were being blitzed. We too had only limited resources, yet singing was one of the least expensive — and I might add most popular — activities we offered. The children loved singing together whether in operettas, or at church, or just around a campfire. If our schools were to cooperate, Herr Doctor Altenheyn, then the British School could provide the — heated — practice room, and the instrumental accompaniment. We have both a grand piano and an organ in the music room."

The rector looked astonished and then commented, "I see. In that case, maybe..." He reached over and rang a little bell on his desk. His secretary appeared at the door. "*Herr Rektor*?"

"Please send for Herr Dr Michaelis." While his secretary carried out his instructions, Herr Dr Altenheyn explained to Georgina, "Dr Michaelis sang in the chorus of the *Staatsoper*. He now teaches English — or what passes for that in our circumstances, but I think he might like your suggestion."

While they waited, Herr Dr Altenheyn offered Georgina cold tea. She declined and they waited in awkward silence until with a short knock another elderly gentleman entered. He had a head of wild, white hair which reminded Georgina of Albert Einstein. He also walked with a cane and a bad limp. Georgina got to her feet as he entered; he bowed low over her hand, bringing his heels together and addressing her as *"gnaedige Frau,"* gracious lady.

The Rektor spoke to him in rapid-fire German and his face lit up. He turned to Georgina with a wide smile. "A chorus? You would like to form a chorus from our students and let them practice at your school?"

"Yes, that seems best now that I understand—"

"What a wonderful idea! You are an angel from heaven! This is just what we need! When can we start?"

"Well, I'll have to check with the headmaster," Georgina admitted, aware of being out on a limb, "and I haven't thought through the details about transportation etc. I wanted to see if there was any interest first. However, the goal would be to sing carols and other Christmas music at the hospitals and the airfields for the men flying—"

"Could we really do that? Oh, the children would love it! The boys would give anything to meet some of the pilots! But if that is not possible, it would be very exciting just to be at the airfields, close up to planes and see the unloading. To sing for your officers and men would be a great honour."

Georgina was taken aback. She had not dreamed she might receive such an enthusiastic reception and it almost embarrassed her. But then she smiled and declared, "In that case, we better get started straight away! How many of your students do you think will want to participate?"

"All of them!" He answered but waved her protests aside before she could voice them. "I will select no more than forty. Both girls and boys? Or do you have a preference?"

"We have a few more girls, but not enough for it to matter."

"I will make a selection. Tell us when and how we should come to you?"

"I think we should start practising this Sunday. I know the school music room is available then, and I should be able to arrange for one of our school buses to pick up your pupils from here." She knew the school buses were available for extracurricular activities on the weekends and since the distance between the two schools was not great, the consumption of diesel fuel would be minimal. She was confident Mr Peden would approve the proposal.

"If the bus was here at 9.00 o'clock, I could meet you at the front entrance of the British School at half past nine, and we could practice until noon. Would that be agreeable with you?"

"I cannot wait, *gnaedige* Frau!"

"Moran, Mrs Moran," she answered holding out her hand again and feeling elated as he shook it vigorously.

Blurred Impressions
Potsdam
Thursday 9 December 1948
(Day 167 of the Berlin Airlift)

"Don't you recognise your father?" Maxim Dmitrivich Ratanov challenged Galyna. "Your mother recognised him at once!' He glanced towards his wife as he spoke.

Anastasia chimed in. "Yes, I did —although he does look poorly. He must have lost fifty pounds."

"You don't sound upset about it!" Galyna spat out resentfully.

"Of course, it upsets me, lamb, but I am not naïve. I knew what to expect when I was shown images from a gulag."

Gaylna turned her attention back to the photos laid out on the coffee table in front of her. Behind her, the coal-fired oven exuded steady heat as did the radiators. Together they overheated the room. Galyna presumed her stepfather was trying to impress upon her how limitless Russian resources were compared to what the people of West Berlin had, but she found the display childish. The shortages in the West were not due to "failing" capitalism but the result of a callous blockade imposed by the Soviet Union.

Ratanov claimed that the snapshots, one of a gang of men digging a ditch and the other of men hauling logs out of the snow, included her father. The pictures were blurry and the faces tiny. Galyna did not recognise her father in either of them, but she couldn't be sure that it *wasn't* him either. One of the men glared angrily at the camera. He *might* be her father disfigured with wild, unkempt hair and a scraggly beard. Yet in her bones, Galyna thought not.

Her friend Mila had been very insistent that she mustn't fall for the tricks 'they' would play. 'Galyna, from what you've told me, your father was an educated man, articulate and respected. As a teacher, he was in a position of authority. Believe me, Galyna, they don't let men like that live because they might plant doubt in the minds of others. The gulags are for the *completely* innocent —for the family members of the dead, for peasants who hoarded pitiable amounts of their own crops, or workers who spoke their minds too loudly, or priests who won't deny their faith, but not for men like your father who openly protested policies. Even if they didn't shoot him outright,' Mila had insisted, 'almost no one survives the gulag for more than a few years.'

Galyna took one last long look at the photos Ratanov had brought and made up her mind. Mila was right. Her father was long dead. That made it easier for her to play the part she had agreed to when she offered to be a double agent, the role Boyd had coached her to play. She sat back on the sofa and crossed her arms. "All right. What do you want to know?"

Ratanov laughed shortly, shoved the two photos together and pocketed them. Then he also sat back in his armed chair and considered her critically. "Let's start with simple things. How many landings were there at Gatow yesterday?"

"You know that better than I," Galyna countered. "You have men who do nothing but stand around counting. I have work to do."

He laughed and confirmed, "Quite right." Changing the topic he asked, "What about the weather report? Do you know what the British are forecasting?"

"A high-pressure front from the arctic bringing good visibility but bitterly cold winds. Temperatures are expected to drop below freezing tonight and be even colder tomorrow."

"What are people at Gatow saying about that?"

"Due to the good visibility, the airfield will be operating at peak efficiency. We've hired extra stevedores for the weekend."

"Hired? I heard the Boy Scouts had volunteered to help out."

It annoyed Galyna that he was right, but she tried to act indifferent and shrugged. "They volunteered to do the work for nothing, but the Station Commander insisted they receive wages and two hot meals, one at the start and one at the end of their shift."

"The Station Commander. That would be Wing Commander Priestman?"

"Yes, of course. Who else?"

"Who else, indeed? It's just that he was fired ten days ago," Ratanov declared with annoying conviction, and Galyna felt a chill run up her spine. Was that possible? There *had* been whispers. Fl/Lt Boyd had first told her not all rumours were to be believed and then seemed to confirm them by saying they would be told what was happening in due time. But the rumours had faded away.

Meanwhile, Ratanov was talking as he poured himself more tea and demonstratively dropped four cubes of sugar into it. Profligate waste of a substance in short supply in the West, Galyna thought to herself disgusted. "He was sacked very publicly, and I thought he'd be gone within days. Surely you know what's going on?"

His words were a veiled threat. She was supposed to be his informant, but apparently, he knew more than she did about internal RAF affairs. That could only mean that he had another informant inside the RAF. Boyd would be very keen to learn this, and reporting it would do much to justify his faith in her. On the other hand, it also meant that any information she gave Ratanov would be checked against what he learned from this other source. That made the game she was playing doubly dangerous. She felt a sudden need to go to the toilet but crossed her legs and looked Ratanov in the eye. "I think you were misinformed. Wing Commander Priestman is still very much in command."

"Pity! He's too effective and committed to Berlin. We need someone more indifferent to the fate of the Berliners or someone lazier or more sympathetic to progress. Are you sure Priestman isn't on his way out? Maybe he's just awaiting his replacement?" His eyes bore into her.

She made a mental note to mention this intense interest in Priestman in her report to Boyd, but to Ratanov she replied, "Yes, I'm quite sure. Just this past Monday he attended a meeting with other station commanders and Air Commodore Merer—"

"Tunner's new deputy?" Ratanov insisted on confirmation.

"Yes, that's right, and he returned with a slew of new orders."

"Pity. He's quite popular, isn't he? Particularly with the ladies, I hear."

"He's very married," Galyna countered. "He doesn't tolerate any kind of inappropriate behaviour let alone encourage flirting. His wife flies, too, and he's proud of that. The men admire his war record."

Ratanov snorted contemptuously. "What war record? A handful of Messerschmitts shot down, then a holiday in the Mediterranean before spending more than a year in a POW camp. Nothing compared to our heroic pilots."

A tour of duty in Malta in 1942 was hardly a holiday in the Mediterranean Galyna noted. As for the 'handful' of Messerschmitts, while they might not impress the Russian Secret Police colonel (who had seen no combat), what Priestman and his colleagues had torn from the skies in the summer of 1940 had been enough to stop Hitler in his tracks. Maxim Dmitrivich was just trying to provoke her into a more emotional response. She chose to remain silent.

Realizing he had not had the desired effect, Ratanov shrugged and changed tactics. "No matter. There's more than one way to skin a cat. I'm going to have to go soon, so let's meet again on Sunday for dinner. Keep your eyes and ears open and be prepared to give me a more comprehensive report — now that you know your father is alive. Meanwhile, would you like your mother to put some things together for you? Some sugar and chocolate, perhaps? Or Polish sausage and cans of borscht or bottles of pickled herrings?"

Galyna knew he was trying to provoke her again, but she smiled and agreed mildly. "That would be very nice." At the station, they'd set up a large bin to collect Christmas gifts for the Berliners. Anything her mother gave her would go straight into it and, hopefully, make some Berliners happier when Christmas came.

Chapter Five
Once More unto the Breach

Return of the Candy Bomber
USAF Recruiting Station, Ann Arbor, Michigan
Thursday 9 December
(Day 167 of the Berlin Airlift)

"Hey, don't I know you from somewhere?" the sergeant at the Ann Arbor recruiting office greeted J.B.

"Until I graduated last summer, I was enrolled at the University of Michigan, so you may have seen me around campus."

"Nah, it was somewhere else." The sergeant snapped his fingers a couple of times, trying to jog his memory. Then his face lit up. "You're the guy who was all over the papers! The one who dropped candy to the kids of Berlin? Why aren't you in uniform?"

When he was younger, J.B. had imagined that being in the papers would be exciting; now that he was, he found it more like an invasion of privacy. "Yeah, I was on the Airlift most of the fall, but I'm out of uniform because I'm not on active duty, and that's the reason I'm here. I want to talk to someone about going back."

"On the Airlift?" The Sergeant sounded flabbergasted.

"Last I heard, we're still flying 'round the clock," J.B. reminded him.

The sergeant considered him sceptically while scratching the back of his head. "Let me see." Something about the way he said it gave J.B. a sinking feeling. The sergeant started opening and closing the drawers of his filing cabinet until he found what he was looking for. He removed a manila folder, opened it, read something in it, and then excused himself to go into the back office.

J.B. could do nothing but wait, so he looked out the window at the students, hurrying past. Temperatures had dropped to near freezing, and everyone was bundled up in gloves, scarves, and boots. It made him wonder how the Berliners were surviving now that winter had arrived.

"Captain Baronowsky?" A new, firm voice drew his attention.

J.B. jumped to his feet to face a major. Since he wasn't in uniform, he could not salute, but he tried to make a military impression and addressed him as "Sir."

"You'd better step inside my office," the major suggested.

J.B. complied and sat in the chair the major indicated. The major went around to the other side of the heavy wooden desk, sat down and got straight to the point, "I've got a file on you a mile long, Baronowsky. You were yanked off the Airlift less than two weeks ago because of a Congressional request. And now you want to go back? What do you think the USAF is? A travel agency?"

"I didn't ask to be sent home. I wanted to continue flying."

"Then why didn't you?"

"Well, sir, the nature of my orders did not leave me a lot of room for negotiation."

The major snorted in acknowledgement and concluded, "But now you want to negotiate?"

"Not exactly, I just want to go back on active status and deploy on the Airlift again."

"The answer's 'no'."

J.B. hadn't expected anything that definitive and he protested, "Why? From what I've seen in the papers, we're flying more than ever before. The Berliners voted overwhelmingly in favour of continuing the fight, and with winter here, they're in desperate need of coal. We've *got* to keep flying, and we need men with four-engine ratings to do it. It doesn't make any sense for me to be sitting on my ass here in Michigan when I could be helping supply Berlin. The president himself called Berlin his number one priority."

"You think I don't know that?" The major shot back. "But whether it makes sense or not, some congressman doesn't want you flying the Lift, and the USAF isn't going to risk making any congressman unhappy. Period."

"Let me explain about that, sir!" J.B. begged. "The congressman we're talking about doesn't know me from Adam." The major's eyebrows shot up. "I'm serious. He's probably forgotten my name by now if he ever bothered to learn it. He only made the request to pull me off the Airlift as a favour to a senior vice president of General Motors, who I presume, used some sort of persuasive argument to convince the congressmen that doing him a favour was in his interest."

"This 'senior VP at General Motors' wouldn't happen to be your father or something, would he?"

"My dad? Hell, no! My Dad works on the shop floor for two bucks an hour."

"So just what does this VP have to do with you? And if he didn't want you flying two weeks ago, why won't he object to you flying now?"

"As of two days ago, sir, that VP is so pissed with me, he told me to my face that he hopes I crash and burn. If there was some way for him to kill me himself without going to jail, he'd do it."

"Why? What have you done to him?"

"I refused to marry his daughter. Or, more precisely, withdrew a proposal I'd made last spring, and I'm probably about to get sued for the costs of a wedding that isn't going to take place. So, maybe you can understand that all I want to do right now is to get out of Detroit and back to Germany as quickly as possible."

The major laughed and then shook his head in bemusement. "Women troubles, huh? Sometimes I think we'd be better off without the 'fairer sex.'"

"Not really, sir." J.B. thought wistfully of Kathleen. "We just need to stay away from the *wrong* kind of girls."

"Like the daughters of senior corporate executives with the ears of congressmen? You've got an interesting definition of 'the wrong kind of girls,' Baronowsky! Then again, in my experience, it can be pretty hard to tell Miss Right from Miss Wrong. Sounds like you learned the hard way."

J.B. grinned and admitted, "I just had a whole college course in what defines the 'wrong girl' for me."

The major laughed at that and reconsidered J.B. "Can you guarantee me that no congressman is going to be writing General Vandenberg to demand that we release you from active duty?"

"My word of honour, sir." J.B. held up his hand as if to swear an oath.

The major picked up the file on his desk and considered it. "You're a bit of a celebrity too, I see. Flew with Halvorsen, huh?"

"Yes, sir. And I heard Colonel Howley pleading with people to donate to this Operation Santa Claus thing. You know, getting people to donate gifts for the kids in Berlin. Maybe I could put in a big plug for that — even get Hal, that's Lt. Halvorsen, to join for an interview or something like that?"

The major snorted and looked at J.B. with new interest. "What kind of job were you gonna have with GM? Public Relations?"

J.B. laughed. "No, I'm just a dumb engineer."

"Yeah, well, you may be right. It might be good publicity to send you back 'to help the kids' and all that. I'll check with Army public relations and see what they say. Write down a telephone number where I can reach you." He handed J.B. a small notepad and a pen, "I'll call you if I get the green light."

Flights of Fancy
Hamburg
Saturday 11 December 1948
(Day 169 of the Berlin Airlift)

From the time she left Georgia until British European Airways delivered her in Hamburg, Anna had lived in a daze of excitement. First, she'd travelled to the nation's capital, where her cousin Cora had warmly welcomed her into her home and shown her the sights. They'd visited the White House, the Capitol, the Supreme Court, and best of all, the stunning monument to Abraham Lincoln. Cora had also guided Anna through the process of applying for a British visa, an experience that brought Anna in touch with white people who called her "ma'am" for the first time in her life.

Already convinced she was bound for a more tolerant society, she'd boarded the BOAC airliner at Washington National Airport to discover she *wasn't* seated at the back of the plane and that she *was* treated like all the other passengers. Although the flight that followed was long, the excellent service with magazines, food, drinks, blankets and pillows all brought to her seat, combined with the sheer delight in flying, kept her in a state of excitement that vanquished even exhaustion. After the stewardess showed her how to adjust her seat, she even got several good hours of sleep, and she'd been able to freshen up and brush her teeth in the little lavatory — feeling like a veteran flier already.

On arrival in London, her attention was absorbed by making her connecting flight and excitement trumped any latent worries. It was only after completing formalities and collecting her luggage on arrival in Hamburg that Anna suddenly became afraid.

Around her, her fellow passengers were being greeted enthusiastically by wives and squealing children, soberly collected by business partners or scurrying away officiously. Suddenly, Anna found herself completely alone in a strange place. Air Ambulance International had said someone would meet her flight, but no one took the slightest notice of her. Soon the only ones left in the arrivals lounge were a woman sweeping the floor and an airline clerk sorting through some papers at the counter. Too late, Anna realized that the only name she had for AAI was the Chief of Personnel, Mr E Priestman, and she had neither a telephone number nor a business address.

Panic welled up in her chest, but she beat it back. AAI would not have paid for her to fly all the way from Washington to Hamburg just to abandon her. There had to be a mix-up or a delay of some kind. She turned to the BEA representative. "Excuse me, I was supposed to be met by a representative of my employer. Would it be possible to page them?"

The counter agent agreed at once and told Anna to take a seat. A moment later she heard the announcement in English and German and took a deep breath to calm herself. As the minutes ticked by with no response, however, she started wondering what she should do. She had spent what savings she had on the bus to Washington, three nurse's uniforms and an off-duty wardrobe; she didn't want to look like a country bumpkin. She certainly didn't have enough money for a flight home and wasn't even sure if she had enough for a hotel. She opened her purse to see if the telegrams she'd received provided more information or if she had misread something.

"Miss Savage, I presume?" The voice addressing her spoke with such a crisp British accent that Anna assumed it must be a BEA employee. Thinking they were closing the lounge and that she would have to move, she sprang to her feet with an apology on her lips. She was dumbstruck to find herself facing a man as black as she was but wearing a stunningly smart, black uniform with bright red trim.

"Yes," she croaked out after overcoming her astonishment. "I'm Miss Savage."

The apparition held out his hand, "Scott-Ross. Richard Scott-Ross. I'm here on behalf of Air Ambulance International. My apologies for not being here on your arrival; we ran into some delays refuelling. The skipper is now over at ops filing our flight plan for Berlin and the navigator is getting the met — the weather, that is. In short, you'll have to make do with me. I'm the flight engineer."

"A pleasure to meet you, Mr Scott-Ross."

He smiled and assured her with unmistakable amusement, "The pleasure is entirely mine, Miss Savage." Then his expression became more serious as he explained, "Unfortunately, due to the refuelling delay, we're in a bit of a rush. I must ask you to come along with me straight away. Is that all the luggage you have?" He indicated the two bags at her feet, and she nodded. "I'll take those for you. Follow me."

As he led her at a brisk pace down a long corridor lined by windows, Anna managed to ask, "Is AAI entirely run by coloured people?"

Scott-Ross burst out laughing, and then he paused in his stride long enough to explain more fully. "No. I'm the only black, although the skipper on the Halifax is one-quarter Zulu —though you wouldn't know it to look at him. The founder of the company, however, is a German Jew, and his partners are from New Zealand and England. Most of us are ex-RAF, however, and there's not a racist among us. Now, you'd better button up your coat, we have to go outside and it's cold out there."

He led her out of the passenger terminal onto a wet and windy expanse of tarmac with aircraft rolling by in what seemed to Anna like dangerous proximity. Jeeps were also darting around while big fuel tankers and luggage trailers groaned past or stood beside aircraft. Scott-Ross led her to an aircraft smaller than the one in which she'd flown across the Atlantic but larger than the twin-engine plane which had brought her from London to Hamburg. This aircraft had four engines and twin tail fins. It was painted white with red lettering that read: "Air Freight International."

Scott-Ross noticed the way she was gazing at it and with a smile told her, "She's a converted Halifax bomber."

"A bomber?" Anna asked amazed. She'd fallen in love with the majestic bombers she'd seen while in Army basic training in Texas. She'd often stopped to watch the big bombers arching across the sky and wished she could ride in one. Looking again toward the Halifax, Anna felt a thrill run down her spine.

"Come on. I'll introduce you to the rest of the crew." As Richard spoke, she noted that four young men in a uniform like his were smoking near the tail of the aircraft. As she approached, they put out their cigarettes and turned towards her. She hoped she didn't look too bad; at least her overcoat covered the wrinkles in her skirt and blouse. She was greeted first by a tall, slender man with dark hair worn so long a lock fell on his forehead. "Welcome aboard, Miss Savage," he greeted her, adding. "I'm Kit Moran, the first pilot." So, he was the one who had Zulu ancestry, Anna thought with wonder. "This is my second pilot," he directed her attention to a red-headed youth with a wide, friendly face, introducing him as "Bruce Forrester."

Forrester flashed her a smile and held out his hand. "G'day, ma'am. A pleasure to meet you." His accent was different from Scott-Ross and Moran's, but Anna couldn't place it. Next, she was introduced to a young man with thick glasses called Terry Tibble, who welcomed her shyly, and finally came a sullen youth with a guarded smile, Nigel Osgood. Although he was the least friendly, Anna sensed his reticence was not personal.

Moran indicated they needed to go aboard, and Nigel and Terry each took one of her bags, while Scott-Ross showed Anna how to climb up the flimsy-looking ladder into the fuselage. Relieved she was wearing practical shoes but still self-conscious in a skirt, she managed to get inside without tripping and found herself in a metal tube stacked high with crates full of fresh milk. "This is our 'deck cargo,'" Scott-Ross explained, tapping a milk bottle as he squeezed down a very narrow passage between the crates. "Our real cargo is carried in panniers that we winch up into the bomb bay below the floor."

When they reached the cockpit, Moran took over from Scott-Ross. "I apologise for the accommodations on this freighter, Miss Savage. There are no passenger seats, so for take-off and landing, I'm going to ask you to step down into the nose where you can strap into the bomb-aimer's seat. The Perspex has been replaced with aluminium, I'm afraid, so you won't be able to see out from there, but once we're airborne, you can come back into the cockpit until we're ready to land."

"Come with me," Terry told her, and he led Anna down into the nose. He also helped her strap herself onto an old fold-down seat. Shortly afterwards, the engines came to life, the metal frame vibrated, and the crew went through their pre-flight drills. She couldn't get over the fact that she was in a bomber — or that she was being treated like one of the team.

Once airborne, Scott-Ross called her back up into the cockpit, and the co-pilot climbed out of his seat to let her sit down. Was this really happening? She sank down, feeling like a child in a candy store. Only this was better. Scott-Ross and Forrester started pointing things out to her, first in the cockpit and then outside. To her utter amazement, she discovered the sky was full of planes — all going the same way. Half a dozen planes in a string flew a little below them, while ahead of these, another eight planes held position lower still but also in line. Each plane kept the same distance from the plane in front, and all flew at the same speed. Anna watched in amazement for several minutes, and then Moran remarked that they were over the Soviet Zone. Anna looked down at the flat, grey countryside that didn't look all that different from Georgia — at least not at this altitude with the sunlight fading behind heavy clouds to the West.

As they approached Berlin, Anna was sent back into the nose. She caught a glimpse of distant lights and that was all. Then after quarter of an hour or more just listening to the engines and feeling the tipping and sinking of the aircraft, she heard a heavy thud, squealing tyres and creaking metal as they returned to earth. It seemed to take a long time for the heavy plane to come to a halt, and then Terry told her to follow him again. He led her back past the milk bottles which were already being handed out of the fuselage by two men working inside. Terry called for "gangway" and then went down the ladder with her luggage.

She emerged into floodlights and bewildering, frenetic activity. The Halifax's bomb bay doors were open, and huge crates were being winched onto a flatbed truck and then shoved into position by a team of four men. Meanwhile, the boxes of milk were being handed down a chain of men onto the back of a second truck. At the nose, a tank truck had pulled into position and ground crew were preparing to hoist the hose nozzle up to a man on the wing.

"This way!" Tibble called to her, and Anna realized she had stopped to stare at everything.

Anna followed the radio operator blindly, no longer capable of forming expectations, and yet her next encounter still took her by surprise. A figure in the same uniform as the Halifax crew was coming towards her with an outstretched hand — and it was a woman. Not just a woman, but a woman with golden wings on her chest, and a beautiful smile.

"Miss Savage? I'm Emily Priestman, Personnel Chief of Emergency Air Services and the first pilot on the air ambulance. We'll be working very closely together. I'm delighted to meet you."

Anna took her hand in a daze. She'd always assumed that "E Priestman" was a man; it had not once occurred to her that the company Chief of Personnel might be a woman.

She abruptly became conscious of the fact that her stockings were sagging, her gloves were dirty and that she'd slept in the clothes she was wearing without a chance to change or shower in more than 24 hours. She'd expected to have time to dress her best before meeting her new boss! This was no time to express dismay, however, so she accepted Mrs Priestman's hand and stammered out, "I'm very honoured and excited to be here!"

"And utterly exhausted, I'm sure. I've arranged to take you straight home. You'll be staying in one of our guest rooms and will have your own bath for the duration of this assignment. You can settle in, refresh yourself, have a bite to eat and get some sleep. We'll do the introductions to the rest of our crew and staff tomorrow."

Had she heard correctly? She'd be a guest of the Chief of Personnel? She stammered out, "Thank you, I appreciate that very much."

The next thing Anna knew, she was in the back seat of a Mercedes with a uniformed driver that whisked her away to a large mansion. By the time she sank into the large, double bed in her gigantic room, Anna was convinced she was Cinderella — and a little afraid of when the spell would break.

Night Bounce
RAF Gatow
Saturday 11 December 1948
(Day 169 of the Berlin Airlift)

Although Emily took AAI's new employee back to the residence as soon as she arrived, Robin had too much work to do to leave early. His job was never ending, but after his brush with a bowler hat, he was sharply aware of just how much he loved it nevertheless.

Tonight was bitterly cold with visibility of almost ten miles, and Gatow was running at maximum capacity — or the RAF was. As the meeting with Merer at the start of the week had highlighted, the civilian companies were not. They ignored the executive from BEA nominally in charge of their activities and instead did whatever they liked. As a result, they could not be scheduled into operations and had to be squeezed in on an ad hoc basis. In the early days of the Airlift, when everything was improvised, that had not been a problem. More and more, it was becoming one.

The civilians were causing other problems as well. Many of the civilian pilots were either inadequately trained or inadequately disciplined. There had been instances of pilots showing up in the ops room pickled, and more serious incidents (fortunately in the West rather than Berlin) in which civilian aircrew confiscated civilian ground transport, sometimes with threats. Most common were incidents of drunken and disorderly behaviour on the part of civilian crews in the local pubs, nightclubs and hotels, causing severe headaches for the Allied authorities near the departure airfields.

Robin's problem, however, was that the only efficient way to transport liquid fuel was in specially built air tankers of which the RAF had none, so Berlin was dependent on civilian carriers for deliveries of petrol, diesel and aviation fuel. Despite promises from various companies to deploy what should have added up to 35 tankers, only 17 had joined the Airlift. As a result, Berlin had become so short of both diesel and petrol that those few operational tankers were forced to fly around the clock, and that translated into too little time for proper maintenance — or rest for the crews.

More than once, Robin had noticed Donald Bennett, the founder and managing director of the company Airflight and former C-in-C of the Pathfinder force, servicing his own engines with a spanner or an oil can. Furthermore, Kit had confided to Robin that Bennett did not have adequate ground crew in Hamburg either. On top of that, Bennett had been the only pilot in his company qualified to fly at night, meaning he undertook every night flight himself. It was awkward telling a famous flier with a distinguished war record that he was doing something wrong, but Robin had tried to suggest to him that he was "a little over-extended."

Bennett retorted haughtily, "Physical endurance is mental. If you set your mind to do something, you can do it."

To avoid a confrontation with the notoriously thin-skinned and humourless man, Robin had backed off, but he'd been relieved to learn that Airflight finally had a second pilot qualified for night flying. Captain Utting was making his first flight tonight, and Robin wanted to meet him — and discuss the maintenance problem.

The Airflight Tudor landed in pitch dark just after 7 pm and immediately taxied to the fuel dump. Robin went down to the operations room an hour later to intercept Utting before he went home, only to discover that Utting had just left. Exasperated, Robin decided to try to catch him before he took off again.

As he emerged from the admin building, his driver, thinking he was leaving, turned on the headlights and started the engine. Robin paused to explain he had one short errand to run before departing and then chased after Utting.

The night was crystal clear with the pantheon of constellations glittering overhead. Robin turned the collar of his greatcoat up against the bite of the sub-zero air. He could see Utting clearly against the intense lighting on the runway side of the airfield. The Airflight captain was cutting across the grass toward the overflow hardstandings where the Airflight Tudor waited. He was walking fast to keep warm, and Robin wasn't sure he'd catch up with him, so he called out, "Captain Utting?"

The tall figure paused to look over his shoulder, saw Robin's wave and waited. As Robin joined the civilian captain, he introduced himself, "Priestman. Station Commander. I wanted to welcome you to Gatow."

"That's very kind," the man answered with a charming smile and held out his hand. "Clement Utting. But you appear to know that already."

"I'll walk you to your aircraft," Robin offered, and they continued toward the Tudor silhouetted against the brighter lights near the runways. "Have you known AVM Bennett long?"

"I was with him at British South American Airways."

As they spoke, they crossed a vacant hardstanding. Five hundred feet ahead of them Bennett's radio operator and his second pilot were standing under the wing of the tanker flashing a torch up at the number four engine. "You seem a little short on maintenance personnel," Robin remarked, trying to sound casual.

"We could use more, but good aircraft mechanics don't grow on trees," Utting answered.

Just then, Robin felt rather than saw the lights along the perimeter fence blink. It was the same kind of almost imperceptible break in a beam of light that a Messerschmitt made when it fell out of the sun. The sound of a motor groaning reached his ears at the same time. Instinctively, Robin shouted, "Break!" and jumped sideways. A lorry swept by so close that the wind buffeted him, and as he swung about to look at what had almost hit him, he saw the vehicle knock Utting over. Instead of screeching to a halt, the engine groaned more loudly as it clanged into a higher gear and sped away.

Robin rushed to Utting and dropped onto one knee, breathless with shock and horror. Utting was bleeding from his mouth, nose and ears. He groaned when Robin touched him, so at least he was still alive, but from the way he lay limply on the tarmac, Robin suspected he had numerous broken bones. He hesitated to turn him over in case his back was injured. He needed an ambulance and looked around for the lorry that had hit Utting. It had disappeared entirely. If it hadn't been for the man bleeding on the concrete beside him, he would have thought he'd been imagining things.

Panting, Utting's crew arrived asking urgently, "Is he badly injured?" and "Where did that lorry come from?"

"I don't know," Robin answered both questions at once. "We need an ambulance! Stay with him and keep him warm! I'll get help!" One of the men removed his flight jacket and spread it over his injured captain, while Robin sprinted toward the closest hangar. When he thought he was within hailing distance, he shouted and waved, "There's been an accident! Airflight's Tudor! Send the ambulance over immediately!"

The men in the hangar paused to stare, then snapped into action, relaying his orders. Still dazed, Robin returned to the injured man. If only he'd shouted: "Look out!" instead of "Break!" Utting couldn't be expected to understand fighter pilot jargon! Or, better yet, why hadn't he grabbed Utting and *pulled* him aside? If he'd yanked him out of the way, Utting might have escaped injury.

In the distance, the wail of a siren and a flashing red light indicated that the ambulance was on its way. Although Utting appeared to be unconscious, Robin laid a hand on his shoulder and promised, "It won't be long now. You'll be with a doctor soon."

One of the Airflight crew asked a second time, "Where did that lorry come from?"

It was a good question. Robin forced himself to focus on what had just happened, but the questions only multiplied. Where had the lorry come from, and where had it gone? Why had it been driving around without headlights? Why had it been driving so fast? Why hadn't it swerved to avoid them? Why didn't it stop when it hit something? Out loud, he confessed, "I haven't a clue. There will have to be an enquiry."

As he spoke, Robin registered he'd have to ring Air Commodore Merer — and AVM Bennett. The latter call wasn't going to be pleasant, and Bennett might make a stink. The tanker, of course, was grounded until another pilot arrived. He must also alert Fl/Lt Tucker about a possible breach of the perimeter. They must start their own investigation immediately, even before an official enquiry opened.

He felt dazed. The tanker had already unloaded its cargo of diesel and could take neither freight nor passengers back, so no lorry had any business being nearby. The lack of headlights suggested a smuggler, but if someone were trying to steal, wouldn't they have been moving slowly and carefully in order to avoid detection?

As the initial shock dissipated, guilt started to take hold. How was it possible that on his station vehicles were driving around at high speed in unauthorised areas without their headlights? And why hadn't he pulled Utting out of the way? Robin's hands started to tremble. Irrationally, he felt something deeply sinister was at work — or, perhaps more unsettling still, maybe he was just incompetent?

Dicing with the Devil
Potsdam
Sunday 12 December 1948
(Day 170 of the Berlin Airlift)

Galyna could not suppress her inner excitement. For the first time since she had agreed to spy for the Soviets, she had intelligence to divulge to Colonel Ratanov, or rather, information that Boyd sanctioned sharing with him. She felt sure that having something to report to him would increase her credibility, and it made her feel more competent.

She left her greatcoat and cap by the door and followed her mother into the overheated living room with its views of the now-frozen Heiligensee. Half a dozen ducks were waddling out through the limp and naked limbs of the willows to test the thin sheet of ice. Ratanov was reading *Izvestia* in an armchair as she entered. He looked for all the world like a kindly uncle. How appearances could deceive!

At the sight of her, he folded the newspaper and set it aside to level his half-opened, cold eyes at her. Galyna felt strong enough to meet his gaze and even risked sending him a closed, smug smile. She announced confidently, "I have some news that will interest you! Something you won't find in any of the newspapers."

"Ah. What a wonderful surprise!" Was he being sarcastic? It didn't matter.

"Sit down! Sit down!" Anastasia Sergeyevna urged. "The tea is almost ready. I'll just fetch the tarts from the oven." She disappeared, and Galyna took her usual seat on the sofa facing the lake.

Ratanov raised his eyebrows at her.

"There was an accident at Gatow yesterday evening." Galyna had the satisfaction of seeing Ratanov look surprised.

"An accident? An aircraft crashed?"

"No, it was on the ground. A lorry ran over a pilot."

"Oh." Ratanov sounded disappointed. "Doesn't that happen all the time?"

"Of course not! It has never happened before! Besides, it was very peculiar and suspicious," Galyna insisted, annoyed that he showed so little interest in her news.

"In what way?"

Anastasia Sergeyevna chose this moment to arrive, interrupting the conversation to set tarts and whipped cream on the table. Galyna helped herself to the pastries while her mother poured the tea. When everyone was settled again, Ratanov resumed the interrogation. "What was peculiar about this accident?"

"The lorry was driving without headlights at high speed in an area where it had no business to be," Galyna explained.

Ratanov shrugged. "Probably just smugglers. There's quite a bit of leakage from Gatow, you know." She hadn't known and was taken aback. Ratanov exploited her reaction, raising an eyebrow and sneering, "You mean you *didn't* know?"

Galyna told herself he was just trying to make her feel stupid, naïve and incompetent. She brushed off the topic. "That is not the point. This lorry was driving fast enough to cause severe internal injuries; the pilot died in our infirmary early this afternoon."

"Was he anyone important?" Ratanov asked, still sounding only mildly interested.

"No, not particularly. He was a pilot for one of the civilian contractors."

"So, what's the fuss?" Ratanov wanted to know.

Galyna, who had expected him to be keenly interested, was briefly deflated, but Boyd had warned her Ratanov might feign disinterest in precisely the things that interested him most. Boyd had advised her to turn her inexperience into an asset by openly showing disappointment and forcing him to explain his reaction. 'In the best case scenario,' Boyd had explained, 'he'll say he knows all about something already, and you can try to get him to reveal his sources.' Dutifully, she tried to look puzzled as she asked, "Why would a smuggler be driving so fast, and why wouldn't he have swerved to avoid someone?"

Ratanov gazed back at her with as much emotion as a lizard. Then smiling to himself, he shrugged off the question with, "No doubt he was drunk. These German pigs drink self-brewed swill all the time. The more interesting question is what will happen to your Station Commander, don't you think?"

"Why should anything happen to him?" Galyna asked, genuinely baffled.

"He's bound to get into trouble for not controlling the perimeter better and for either not knowing about, or not stopping, the smuggling. I mean it's obvious," Ratanov continued in an exasperated tone. "This whole incident is the direct result of negligence — not to say incompetence on the part of Wing Commander Priestman."

Was it? Galyna asked herself. No one else seemed to see it that way. Yet there was a certain logic to what Ratanov said. Bennett had certainly been upset when he flew in this morning. He had been with Utting when he died and reportedly had been deeply distressed. He had a terrible reputation for being self-righteous and difficult when he thought someone else — whether subordinate or superior — had done something wrong.

"After being in trouble for insubordination so recently, Priestman must be in a precarious position. This accident will do him no good, I'm sure." Ratanov told her confidently, adding, "Was that all you had?"

"Yes," Galyna admitted. "I thought it would interest you."

"Of course, of course," he replied in a patronizing tone. "It is better than nothing — which is what you've delivered up to now," he added with an undertone of contempt. "I would be interested in what the investigation turns up, or if there are other consequences."

"Of course," Galyna answered, reaching for her tea, in a hurry to leave. She wanted to get away from this man and her mother. They made her skin creep.

"Some more of the torte?" Her mother asked.

"No. I'm too fat already, remember?" Galyna shot back as she got to her feet. "Excuse me. I have to get back to Gatow. I'm babysitting for one of the Air Traffic Controllers."

"Oh, how sweet," Anastasia Sergeyevna exclaimed, and they parted.

All the way back to Gatow in the decrepit public bus Galyna repeated the conversation in her head. Something about it troubled her. Was it just that sense of being so completely outclassed by Ratanov? Or was it something else? Maybe an irrational suspicion that he had known about the accident before she told him — indeed known *more* about the accident than she did?

The more she thought about it, the more the suspicion took hold that

Ratanov (or those he worked for) had orchestrated the accident. Although she could not begin to fathom why or how the Soviet Secret Police might have been involved, her instinct said that they were behind the incident. If so, that meant either that they had been able to get a vehicle through the airfield's perimeter security — or that they had coopted or corrupted one of the drivers authorised to work at Gatow. It also meant that they had killed Captain Utting intentionally. But why?

One civilian pilot more or less wasn't going to make much difference to the Airlift. Or did the Soviets think that the violent death would cause enough scandal to have Priestman dismissed? Yet what difference would that make? Priestman might be a good and popular commander, but he was not irreplaceable. If he left, another officer would take his place, and the Airlift would go on as before.

By the end of her journey, Galyna was as confused as ever. Part of her felt instinctively that Ratanov was involved in what she was beginning to see as Utting's "murder". Yet such an accusation would be explosive. Dare she even raise it without evidence of any kind? It was nothing but a gut feeling. Boyd had repeatedly stressed that she had to be 'logical' in this line of work and not give in to 'emotions.' Yet he also said that an agent had to listen to 'intuition.' Was this intuition or feelings?

She supposed the best thing to do was to tell Boyd exactly what Ratanov had said and let him draw his own conclusions. There was no need to tell him what *she* felt or suspected. Yet regardless of how he responded, she could not escape the conviction that the Soviet Secret Police had killed someone inside the perimeter fence of Gatow, and that was a frightening thought.

Chapter Six
Ice on the Spree

Father Frost
RAF Gatow
Tuesday 14 December
(Day 172 of the Berlin Airlift)

Jakob Liebherr stopped to gaze in fascination at the aircraft suspended in the air. The nearest aircraft was wallowing slightly as — with outstretched 'feet' — it sank slowly towards the concrete. Behind it, another York appeared to hover above the runway, also with its undercarriage down. Behind it, higher and smaller, a Tudor descended with its wheels still tucked under its belly, and behind — ever higher and further away — the approaching aircraft formed a line of dark dots against the solid white overcast sky.

Jakob dropped his eyes to scan the hectic activity closer at hand: buses disgorged children on the far side of the runways; men in filthy overalls frantically manhandled sacks and boxes from oil-stained freighters; convoys of lorries dragging trailers plodded in and out of the gate, while Land Rovers and jeeps dashed about self-importantly. It was a scene of fevered yet organised activity that made Jakob nod appreciatively.

Since the election and the lifting of the fog, Jakob's mood had changed. He was starting to believe they might actually succeed in forcing the Soviets to back down. Maybe, just maybe, the blockade would end, and life would return to the pre-blockade 'normal.' However, there were still significant challenges.

Jakob entered the imposing building with the control tower squatting on top, found "Station Commander" on the index board inside the door, and made his way slowly up four flights of stairs. At the top, he paused to catch his breath before following the long corridor to the end and entering the large anteroom. Here he approached a uniformed female clerk and gave her his name.

"Yes, Mr Liebherr. Wing Commander Priestman is expecting you. Take a seat and I'll let him know you're here."

Moments later, Jakob was admitted to the inner office as Wing Commander Priestman came around his desk to shake hands. In greeting, the Englishman recalled the other occasions on which they had met and then invited Jakob to take a seat at the coffee table.

Jakob was pleased to be remembered and gladly accepted the tea offered. Hot tea had become a luxury in a city with only two hours of electricity a day at any one location. He also removed his scarf and gloves to relish the warmth of the air around him. It felt like years since he had been in a room as warm as this, but what made the temperature particularly delightful was the knowledge that it was produced by gas siphoned off from the Soviets rather than from coal that would otherwise have gone to the Berliners themselves.

"Now, what can I do for you?" Priestman asked him attentively.

"Mayor Reuter had a meeting with Colonel Howley yesterday, and the Colonel suggested we approach you directly."

Priestman nodded without emotion, so Jakob launched into his prepared remarks, "As you know, it has been a week since intense cold replaced the fog of November. Mayor Reuter shared with me the latest statistics and I was delighted to see that on two days already, the Allies have delivered more than 6,000 tonnes in a single 24-hour period. In short, the Airlift is back on track in an impressive and reassuring fashion. There are no words to express the immense gratitude of the Berliners for what you and your men are doing, Wing Commander."

"Don't worry. Bertie — that's the Teddy Bear on my desk — is remarkably eloquent for a stuffed animal. Besides, I'm sure you didn't come all the way here just to thank me." Priestman sounded slightly amused but not impatient.

With a faint smile, Jakob admitted, "True, but I was brought up to say thank you when it was appropriate, as it is now, and I wanted to stress that what I have to say next is in no way intended as criticism or reproach. We

Berliners know who is to blame for our misery. We do not blame those who are trying to help us, but the fact remains, I'm sorry to say, that 131 people froze to death last week."

Priestman recoiled visibly. "131? I had no idea."

"There is no reason why you should have known. Their deaths are not your fault. You and all your men," Liebherr gestured again towards the window with a view towards that endless line of approaching aircraft, "are not responsible for these deaths. The Soviet government has them on their hands. Nevertheless, we on the City Council must face facts. We have received confirmed reports of 131 deaths, yet these cases probably represent only a fraction of the actual casualties. Many people who have frozen to death will not yet have been discovered or reported. Elderly people without work are the most vulnerable, and many live alone in small, improvised dwellings. It might be days before anyone notices they have not been seen. Furthermore, temperatures are forecast to continue dropping. The first winter after the war, thousands died of cold, and when the water and sewage pipes froze, people started dying of dysentery as well." Jakob held up his hands to prevent comment.

"We know you have no control over the temperatures and that you are already flying in as much coal as possible. Believe me, I'm *not* here to complain," he reiterated. Priestman nodded acknowledgement and waited for Jakob to continue. "The City Council, however, must prepare for the worst. Perhaps you have heard that we have set up central warming rooms? We have found that if we can keep the waiting rooms of, for example, employment offices or other municipal offices warm, people come, sit down for an hour or two and then return home better able to cope with the cold in their residences. Lately, these warming rooms have been overrun.

"We have also started turning churches and schools into shelters where people can sleep in comparative warmth overnight. While we have identified enough places for these shelters, we're having some trouble finding enough beds. People are asked to bring their own bedding, too. Still, I'm confident that we will soon have shelters all across the city."

Priestman nodded understanding, and Jakob took a deep breath before forging ahead, "Nevertheless, the City Council believes that the evacuation of more people would be beneficial. We aren't talking about sick or vulnerable people, any more, but a wider category of residents, those who do not contribute to the economy or the functioning of the city as a whole."

Priestman, Liebherr noted, did not appear at all surprised. All he asked was: "Have you estimated the total number of people you want to send out of the city?"

"No. We concluded that the best policy would be to make evacuation voluntary. Rather than trying to select whom to send away, we thought people should be told they have the option of leaving if they want to."

For the first time, the Englishman looked sceptical, "Are you sure that's wise?" Before Liebherr could respond, he hastened to explain his reservations. "Don't misunderstand me. I have long felt that it might be wise to evacuate more people from Berlin — particularly young mothers and youths. Without being a defeatist, the outcome of this struggle is far from a foregone conclusion. Yet there is a new threat as well. Since the fog lifted and we proved we can deliver volumes that more than meet demand, I fear the Soviets may decide to escalate. If they fear the Airlift might succeed, they might opt to send in the tanks rather than risk the humiliation of failure. Given that possibility, it seems to me that evacuations should not be random, but rather based on some form of strategic criteria."

Liebherr nodded. "I share your concerns — and so does Mayor Reuter. For that very reason, we refuse to allow the evacuations to be dictated by price."

"Absolutely not," the Station Command agreed emphatically.

"By making evacuation voluntary, a natural self-selection takes place. We believe the people most eager to leave will be those who are most unhappy — and so most likely to undermine morale — and those with family or other ties in the West. The latter factor ensures they do not become a burden to the communities they join. Last but not least, as a general rule, young people are more mobile and flexible than older people. Young men and women seeking a better life in the West are the residents most likely to seize this opportunity."

The Station Commander considered that answer and conceded, "You are probably right. Before we go any further with this discussion, however, let me remind you that flying passengers out will have an impact on the amount of cargo flown in."

"We understand," Jakob assured him.

"Next," Priestman continued, "we're in the midst of evacuating children and vulnerable people, and that operation absorbs the entire capacity of our Dakotas. If any more people were to be flown out of the city at the same time, they could only be carried out by our larger freighters without seats, let alone seatbelts, heating, pressurisation and toilets. The ten-thousand-foot ceiling in the corridors means there's no need for oxygen, but people travelling in cargo holds would be bitterly cold, jostled about by turbulence, subject to drafts, leaks, exhaust fumes and more. Our crews could not be expected to look after them in any way, so they would have to carry their luggage and make themselves as comfortable as possible without facilities of any kind."

Jakob smiled faintly and met his eyes. "Wing Commander, our objective is not to encourage an exodus. However, if people *are* willing to put up with such conditions, then maybe they have good reasons for wanting to leave Berlin sooner rather than later. And let me be clear. The 17,000 vulnerable citizens should and must take precedence."

Priestman nodded. "Thank you for that guidance. I will put this to my superiors as soon as possible and see what they have to say. Please understand I am not promising you anything today, but I'm optimistic that something can be worked out."

Jakob smiled. "Excellent! I'll leave it in your capable hands and hope to hear back from you soon."

"If and when I have the go-ahead, we can meet to discuss the details." The Station Commander stood, ending the interview. "It was a pleasure to see you again, Herr Liebherr. We'll be in touch."

Father Christmas
RAF Gatow
Tuesday 14 December 1948
(Day 172 of the Berlin Airlift)

The weekly staff meeting had been postponed while Priestman met Jakob Liebherr. As soon as the German politician left, the section heads filed into the WingCo's office and seated themselves around his coffee table. Sergeant Andrews arrived with a tray of tea and biscuits.

Because of the delayed start, Robin worked through the agenda at a brisk pace. In less than an hour, he reached the last item and drew a deep breath. "The last topic on the agenda is the investigation into the death of Captain Utting." A rustle of uneasy movement swept over the participants. Robin continued, "Based on the initial and internal investigation led by Flight Lieutenant Tucker," he nodded toward the commander of the RAF Detachment, "the incident last Saturday night appears not to have been an accident but rather a deliberate act. For that reason, I have requested support from the Special Investigations branch of the RAF police. They will be sending a senior inspector over shortly, who will assume control of the investigation." Robin noted that Tucker looked relieved, and the others nodded in agreement. Not wanting to encourage further speculation on the topic, he concluded, "Unless there is something else, let's all get back to work."

To his surprise, the FASO commander Captain Bateman raised his hand and begged, "Just one more thing, sir."

"Captain," Robin acknowledged him.

"I was wondering whether we could discuss Christmas? It is just ten days away tomorrow."

Wary of requests for special leave, Robin responded cautiously, "What aspect of the holiday would you like to address, Bateman?"

"Well, sir. It's going to be a very bleak Christmas for the Berliners. My men and I work closely with the stevedores, as you know, and we know that most of them have no means of making the holidays special — for themselves or their families. It looks as if Christmas is going to be just another day with long hours, hard work, bland, dry food and cold. No Christmas trees, no Christmas candles, no pretty shop displays, no Christmas cards or music, and no extra warmth or food either. My men and I were wondering if we couldn't make Christmas Day a little brighter — at least for those Germans who work with us so hard."

Robin had not expected this initiative, but it pleased him. "Did you have anything in mind?"

"Well, for a start, could the daily meal they get be made a little more sumptuous or festive?"

Robin glanced toward Warrant Officer Pierce, who nodded and announced. "We'd already planned to do that, sir. There'll be turkey, gravy, stuffing, canned red currant jelly, Brussels sprouts and Christmas pudding."

"That sounds excellent, but…"

"Yes?"

"Well, most of the men want something for their families. Might they not also get something that they can take home with them? The men work very hard and, I must stress, the level of smuggling has been remarkably low. We carry out various checks, as you know, and again and again the items most men try to pocket aren't valuables or luxuries — not black market currency items like cigarettes. They're more likely to try to nab a jar of pickles, hot chocolate powder, or a bar of soap — almost always for their wives or children."

Robin nodded acknowledgement; he read the weekly reports on pilfering.

"My question is couldn't we do something special for the families of our workers? You must have heard about this 'Operation Santa Claus' that the Americans are putting on. They're going to fly in presents for the children of Berlin from all over the United States. I know we can't do anything on that scale, but surely there's *something* we could do?"

The others nodded and someone muttered, "Hear, hear." That encouraged Robin to admit, "I'd planned to clear this with Fl/Lt. Tucker first, but since you asked, we've been asked to host a Christmas dinner for several hundred children. We could prioritise the children of our workers, and — once we know how many that would be — invite children from the surrounding area if we have additional capacity." He paused to judge the reaction and saw agreement, so he continued, "Air Ambulance International has offered to fly in up to 4,000 lbs of Christmas food, which it can do without interrupting or delaying Airlift deliveries." The reaction to this news was even more enthusiastic; several people exclaimed, "Good show!" "Jolly good!" or "Well done!"

"Calm down. There are still some challenges. First, Warrant Officer Pierce, it would mean extra work for the catering staff—"

"We can ask for volunteers, sir. I don't think we'll have any problem getting more than enough cooks and stewards. The men are stuck here anyway, and doing something like this would go a long way towards making it *feel* more like Christmas. I think the majority will want to help, and those that don't—" He shrugged eloquently, "There are always a few Scrooges, aren't there?"

The others laughed.

"Where would you propose hosting the dinner? In one of the messes or the Malcolm Club?" Pierce asked.

Priestman looked to Tucker, "What's best from a security point of view?"

"The unused training campus. It's away from all our operations, closer to the south gate, and it has a complete kitchen and dining facilities. We'd have to start heating it a couple of days in advance, but it's on the same gas heating as the rest of the Station, so only the one paying for that will be the Soviets."

"Thanks for raising the issue of cost. Air Ambulance International is prepared to transport everything for the meal, but they can't be expected to pay for it," Priestman pointed out.

"If we put out an appeal for voluntary contributions," the adjutant suggested, "I think we'll collect more than enough."

"We can hang stockings in key places or set up piggy banks." Fl/Lt Boyd added.

"We'll also want to decorate the dining room," Squadron Leader Garth pointed out, and after that, everyone started to throw out suggestions.

"We should have someone dressed up like Father Christmas!"

"And carol singing and Christmas music!"

"Surely we can come up with some small gifts? Toy aeroplanes, or rag dolls or things like that for each child?"

"Isn't there any kind of budget for Christmas, sir?"

"I could plunder the representational funds," Robin proposed. "I have no intention of inviting my Soviet colleagues to dinner as I did last year."

That earned him cheers and applause.

"Come on, chaps," Bateman gestured for calm. "We need to set up a committee and get to work. Sir, would you ask Sergeant Andrews to join us? She's a wizard at organisation."

Preparing for the Messiah
Berlin-Charlottenburg
Wednesday 15 December 1948
(Day 173 of the Berlin Airlift)

Georgina stood beside the piano watching with astonishment as the choir sang the Hallelujah Chorus of Handel's Messiah. She had heard many better performances in her life — even from amateurs, but for a make-shift chorus that had sung together less than a week, this was still creditable. Hr Dr Michaelis, she concluded, was amazing.

From the first day they had come together, Michaelis had instilled enthusiasm and ambition in the pupils. His love of music transcended nationality and language. Rather than frowning and banging his baton in irritation as the English had expected of a German director, he'd shattered their prejudices with smiles and encouragement. "A little higher! A little brighter! This is joy! Let me hear it in the balconies!" He ended each session with praise for everyone.

If some of the German pupils had come initially only for the warmth and the food, they had long since been swept up into the spirit of the endeavour. It helped that Dr Michaelis let the youngsters choose what they wanted to sing. They had chosen the Messiah over Bach's Oratorio largely because it was in English, and they had chosen a dozen Christmas carols from a wider selection. The British pupils had agreed to learn two carols in German, and Georgina had been amazed by how earnestly they had gone about it. She'd seen choir members sitting together in the lunch room practising and correcting each other for three days in a row. This evening, although their pronunciation was questionable, they had learnt the text by heart.

The other thing that struck her was that the pupils were having fun. They laughed, they teased, they flirted and made an effort to look their best. With the British band leader, Mr Edgecomb playing the piano and Dr Michaelis conducting the chorus, Georgina had become superfluous. She was free to just watch and listen and she was fascinated by the group dynamics.

The younger children had been curious about their former enemies from the start and now mingled without regard for nationality. The older boys were more wary of one another, but all the more fascinated by the girls from the other school. The older girls, in turn, appeared to favour the attention of the "exotic" boys from the opposite school. Already, after just five rehearsals, pairs were forming, and she could predict which girl would "randomly" end up standing beside which boy at the snack table during break.

There were, of course, exceptions. A couple of the younger British boys kept to themselves, and a clique of about five German girls formed an island unto themselves, rebuffing the English boys who attempted to be friendly. At first, Georgina dismissed them as the kind of snotty clique found in all girls' schools. Yet as she watched these pupils besiege the refreshment table, she started to have doubts.

Far from being the best dressed of the girls, as was usually the case with snotty cliques at boarding schools, these girls were shabbily attired. Obviously, Berliners hadn't had access to new clothes since capitulation. Since men's fashion changed more slowly and less radically than women's, old clothes stood out more on the girls and all the German girls looked as though they were wearing hand-me-downs from older sisters, mothers or even grandmothers. The girls who didn't mingle were likewise dressed in hand-me-downs, but their high-heeled shoes, bright nail polish and lipstick didn't match their dowdy dresses. Furthermore, Georgina had glimpsed them sharing cigarette butts on the school steps just before practice. Something about their gestures and poses suggested to her that they weren't as innocent as they ought to be. On the other hand, rebuffing boys wasn't the usual behaviour of fast girls. These girls seemed wary of the world around them and uncomfortable in their own skins — let alone their clothes.

One of the girls, Georgina thought her name was Silvie, sensed Georgina's gaze and looked over her shoulder. Embarrassed, Georgina crossed the room to join them at the refreshment table. "I was just wondering," she said to hide her thoughts, "do any of you girls like to sew?"

"Sew?" A girl named Dietlinde asked back as if she'd never heard of it.

"Yes. Make your own clothes?"

They shook their heads, although Gertrud, who was usually very shy, remarked, "My mother has a sewing machine and used to sew for us, but now that we only have two hours of electricity a day, she has to use that time for cooking."

Hannah, one of the girls on the fringe of the clique, admitted, "I had sewing in school before the capitulation, but the Ivans broke all the sewing machines when they overran the school."

"Why would they do that?" Georgina asked baffled. She wished she hadn't.

The girls gazed back at her as if she were an idiot until Gisela explained patronizingly, "Because they wanted to."

Silvie brooked the awkwardness by asking, "Are you married Mrs Moran?"

"Yes, I am," Georgia answered, grateful for the change of subject.

"What does your husband do?"

"He's a pilot," Georgina answered proudly.

Now she had the attention of all the children, English and German, boys as well as girls.

"Does he fly on the Airlift?" One of the boys asked eagerly.

"Yes, he does."

"What kind of aircraft?" Another British boy wanted to know.

"A Halifax."

"I thought that was a bomber?" the boy protested.

"It was, but many have been converted to freighters. Technically they're called Haltons after being modified for cargo just as the freight version of the Lancaster is called a Lincoln and the tanker version a Lancastrian, but my husband says that a Halifax by any other name — and all that."

The boys laughed, but Hannah asked earnestly, "Did he fly Halifaxes in the war too?"

Georgina winced. Why had she started this topic? She was glad she could answer honestly, "No, he didn't."

"You mean he didn't fly in the war?" The British boys looked disappointed.

She would rather not have to answer that question, but it was too late to back down now. "He flew Lancasters during the war."

"Did he bomb Berlin?" one of the German boys asked as silence fell across the little crowd.

Damn, Georgina thought, but she nodded. "Yes, he did."

There was a moment of silence, and then one of the older German boys shrugged demonstratively and announced, "So? We bombed London. It was war."

Dr Michaelis clapped his hands and announced that the break was over. They took their places again and Dr Michaelis raised his baton. The rehearsal continued, but Georgina's thoughts lingered on the exchange. She was impressed by that boy's grasp of responsibility. Throughout the war, the Germans had been presented in the British press as raving madmen, and there had been much talk about the youth being utterly fanaticized. Many had expected that after German surrender, the Hitler Youth would become an underground partisan organization determined to disrupt the Allied occupation. That had not happened. On the contrary, these youths showed a sound understanding of cause and effect. That made her more determined to help, and her thoughts returned to sewing as a means of restoring pride.

During the war, clothing rationing had encouraged her to make her own clothes. She had become innovative at transforming tablecloths, pillowcases and curtains into blouses, skirts and dresses. She knew many tricks that would be valuable in blockaded Berlin, and the British school had a domestic science room with six sewing machines — and longer hours of electricity. The school holidays continued until after New Year, and in the week between Christmas and New Year, she would be able to use that room to offer a crash course in sewing. She decided to see if there was interest.

At the end of the rehearsal, there was the usual chaos as the young people rushed to get their coats, hats and gloves. They were chatting, teasing and making plans. Georgina had to ask Mr Edgecomb to call for silence before they quietened down enough for her to enquire if any of the girls were interested in sewing lessons. She counted ten hands that waved back at her and resolved that it was worth going to the headmaster with the proposal.

As she turned to find her overcoat, she was startled by a soft voice addressing her, "Mrs Moran?"

She looked over to find Silvie standing very close beside her. The other German pupils had already left the room, anxious not to miss their bus back to the Kaiser Wilhelm school. Indeed, they were almost alone in the room as the bus for the British children also waited at the entrance. Only Mr Edgecomb, who was putting away the sheet music and preparing to turn off the lights, remained behind with them.

"Silvie!" Georgina exclaimed. "If this is about the sewing class, we can talk about that tomorrow. You don't want to miss your bus."

Silvie shook her head. "No, Ma'am. I — I —" Suddenly she looked down, her shoulders sagged, and she turned away.

Georgina could have kicked herself. She reached out a hand and stopped her. "What is it?"

Silvie glanced at Mr Edgecomb and shook her head.

Georgina took her by the elbow, and they went together into the hallway. From the stairwell came the sound of young people laughing and chattering, but here they were alone. "What is it?"

"I don't know who else to talk to," Silvie mumbled, looking down.

"About what?"

Silvie looked toward the stairwell, the fading voices of the other pupils and then over her shoulder at Mr Edgecomb who was locking up the music room. As he passed them, he admonished Georgina to turn off the hall light when she came away. Then he too disappeared down the stairs.

"What do you want to talk to me about?" Georgina prompted gently.

Looking down at her hands with chipped red nail polish, Silvie whispered, "About missing my period."

Georgina caught her breath. She saw Silvie wince as if she expected a blow or a tongue-lashing. Georgina reached out and took Silvie's hands in hers. She gripped them firmly until the girl looked up at her uncertainly, biting her lower lip. "How long has it been?" She asked softly.

"Three months," Silvie gasped out and hiccupped as she tried to bite back sobs.

"Have you seen a nurse or a doctor?"

Silvie shook her head vigorously. "If I went to the school nurse, everyone would find out!"

Georgina nodded understanding. "Have you told the baby's father?"

Silvie shook her head as the sobs overpowered her, and she started to cry uncontrollably. A voice shouted up the stairs. "The bus is ready to leave!"

"That's all right!" Georgina called back. "I'll see that Silvie gets home safely." She knew the headmaster was still at the school, and she was prepared to request his assistance. First, however, she had to calm Silvie down. She put her arm around her and let her cry herself out. Then she led her to the headmaster's office, sat her down in the waiting room, and went inside to explain that she had a pupil with a "crisis."

Mr Peden studied her for a moment and then asked stoically. "How long do you intend to stay?"

"Give me another half hour, and then we'll have to find a way to get her safely home."

"Meaning, presumably, that I am to drive both of you to your respective residences. Mrs Moran, if you weren't one of my best teachers, I would be more than a little annoyed."

"I'll try to make it up to you, sir."

He replied with an ambiguous grunt and waved her out of his office.

Georgina went back into the waiting room to sit beside Silvie. First, she just took hold of her hand again, and then she asked softly, "How old are you?"

"Fifteen, Miss."

"Have you told anyone else?"

Silvie shook her head.

"Why haven't you told the father?"

Silvie twitched and then looked down at her hands. "I have no idea who it is. There were ..." She played with her fingers almost counting but not quite. Then she shrugged again. "The cigarettes... Mom trades them... We can get meat that way... My little brother's only nine. Mom says he needs it...."

I'm going to be sick, Georgina thought. She had a hard time getting her emotions under control. Finally, taking a deep breath, she forced herself to ask as calmly as possible, "Are you saying your mother encouraged you to sleep with men for cigarettes?"

"Only Amis. They pay better than the Tommys and the French, never mind the Ivans."

"Have you told her about your missed periods?"

Silvie shook her head in alarm. "She'd kill me! She doesn't want another mouth to feed."

I'll kill *her*! Georgina thought furiously. "Well, what did she expect, if she encouraged you....?"

"She told me to be careful! I'm not supposed to do it unless they have rubbers! But —but —" Silvie started to cry again as she gasped out, "They're bigger and stronger than me and they don't like using rubbers!"

I think I'm in way over my head, Georgina thought, and she drew another deep breath. "Silvie, I'm going to arrange for you to see a nurse. A very nice American nurse, who works for my husband's company. Let's see what she has to say, and then we'll take it from there. Is that fair enough?"

Silvie nodded, wiping the tears from her eyes almost frantically, ashamed of them.

"Silvie, I'll help you in any way I can," Georgina promised.

"Thank you, Miss."

Dynamite
USAF Airfield Tegel
Thursday 16 December 1948
(Day 174 of the Berlin Airlift)

Robin was not amused by an invitation from the French Commandant General Ganeval to a 'morning reception' at Tegel. This appeared to be some sort of French Christmas affair, in which, he presumed, the French intended to praise themselves for their (in Robin's opinion pitiable) contribution to the Airlift. Robin's first instinct was to refuse with the pointed excuse that he was 'too busy.' On second thought, he decided it was a good opportunity to chat informally with Howley, Tunner, and Russell, all of whom would presumably also be attending. So, he put on his dress blues and set off for Tegel.

After the enormous effort the Americans and British had put into laying down runways, building rail and road connections, connecting the airfield to the electricity grid, and constructing a terminal, all using inadequate, re-welded equipment, operations at Tegel remained stymied by the Russian-controlled radio tower 200 feet tall that stood at the end of the runway. This posed such a severe hazard to incoming and departing flights that the French had promised they would 'take care of it' before construction had even begun. Now, five months later, although the airfield had been constructed in record time with the help of thousands of Berliners working practically with their bare hands, it still operated at a fraction of capacity because the tower prevented the use of parallel runways and night flying. To add insult to injury, the tower was used by Soviet-controlled 'Radio Berlin' to blast out insults and disinformation about the Western Allies 24 hours every day.

On arrival, Robin noted that the airfield still looked more like a construction site than an airfield. A couple of forlorn-looking Skymasters stood on the taxiway, but it was unclear if they were loading or unloading. The railway siding looked equally derelict. Meanwhile, beyond the runways, a bulldozer was pushing dirt around in a desultory fashion while scaffolding on the backside of the terminal building suggested it wasn't finished yet. A stand-alone tower built on the model of the two-storey, wartime control towers was under construction but appeared to be weeks away from completion. In the meantime, ATC was being conducted from a couple of caravans. The runways themselves were surrounded by a morass of mud, the windows on the terminal had not been washed since they were installed, and the lack of pavements for walking forced the arriving dignitaries in their dress uniforms to walk on a road which had neither verges nor drainage ditches.

Nevertheless, natty French subalterns in white gloves greeted and directed the dignitaries to the station commander's office. Robin fell in beside his counterpart from Tempelhof, Lt. Colonel Walker. The American remarked half under his breath, "I thank my lucky stars I wasn't assigned *here*." Robin laughed briefly and seconded him. He did not envy whoever got saddled with the task of turning this construction site into an efficient airfield. There wasn't so much as a snack bar, although a Red Cross van offering coffee and doughnuts crouched between the two Skymasters,.

They were ushered into a spacious room with unwashed windows looking out over the runways. The light fixtures were naked and the concrete floor was without either a wood or tile cover, let alone rugs. Nevertheless, General Ganeval, his cap laden with gold braid and wearing white gloves, received them graciously. White-coated stewards circulated through the crowd balancing silver platters with tiny squares of quiche and miniature pies filled with chevre or liver pâté. Other trays floated by on white-gloved hands bearing tall, slender glasses in which the champagne bubbles streamed to the surface.

"At ten o'clock in the morning?" Walker asked with a raised eyebrow to

Priestman. The Englishman laughed in response, but they followed the lead of their more senior officers and helped themselves.

"All very nice," Frank Howley growled in Robin's ear as he passed by, "but I'd be more receptive if there were a hundred planes out there or if this was *after* a long day rather than in the middle of it!" He then continued on his way to join the other city commandants.

Lt Col Graham Russell caught sight of Robin from across the room and waved a greeting before squeezing his way through the crowd. "Good to see you!" He exclaimed as he joined Robin. "I'm so relieved Air Commodore Merer proved a bigger man than Bagshot."

"Me too! How are you doing?" Robin changed the subject. "You look taller than you were last week!"

Graham laughed, "No, I'm not growing, but I feel thirty years younger. I'm not unhappy that I'm finished here at Tegel, either. That bulldozer over there is just doing the final landscaping on the fuel storage tanks."

"Oh!" Robin didn't know if that was good or bad news. It was good that Tegel's fuel dump was complete, but he'd hate to see Graham go. "What is your next assignment?"

"I'm not leaving Berlin any time soon. The powers-that-be were so pleased with the performance of cut-up and re-welded construction equipment that they've decided we can use the same technique to build an entire power plant in our half of Berlin."

"What?" Robin couldn't believe what Graham had just said.

"Yes, it does take a little imagination."

"Doesn't a powerplant require gigantic—"

"Don't ask," Graham stopped him. "It does, and I'm not at all sure it will work, but of more relevance to you, I've also been asked to expand the fuel depot at Gatow."

"Despite what you've put in here?"

"Exactly. We plan to install electric pumps at the fuel depots at the departure airfields, which will cut loading time in half. As a result, we need to build up our capacity to receive liquid fuels in Berlin." Tunner was wielding the whip again, Robin reflected. You had to give him credit for never resting on his laurels. Graham continued, "I'll be returning to Gatow early in the new year, and I'll fill you in on the details —"

A loud bang shook the building as if an earthquake bomb had gone off nearby. Champagne glasses shattered as one of the waiters flinched so violently that he lost his grip on his tray. The guests rushed to the windows. Smoke and dust were billowing up from what appeared to be a major explosion. An instant later, Robin registered that the radio tower was at the centre of the smoke and debris and although it still stood upright it was slowly sinking as if the earth had opened under it.

Ganeval brushed his hands and declared, *"Fini!"*

Robin looked at Graham and then around the room as the guests broke into applause.

Suddenly, a telephone was ringing on the desk. Ganeval signalled for silence as he reached to pick it up. He held the receiver several inches away from his ear so the entire room could hear the furious voice of his Soviet counterpart General Kotikov screaming at him. The Soviet Commandant started in French, found he could not express himself forcefully enough in the strange language and dissolved into what sounded like very colourful Russian before collecting himself enough to shout in accented English, "What have you done? How could you do this?"

Ganeval, evidently enjoying himself and playing to his audience, smiled as he answered: "From the bottom. With dynamite."

Ground Work
RAF Gatow
Friday 17 December 1948
(Day 175 of the Berlin Airlift)

Kit carefully oozed Albie off the taxiway onto the wider apron beside the terminal and then turned off onto the road leading to the older hangars, including their own. They had completed one round-trip so far today, and it was approaching 1 pm. Time for a lunch break, but a light snowfall during the night and temperatures hovering around the freezing mark made the tarmac treacherous. The snow melted in direct sunlight but froze in shadow creating patches of almost invisible sheets of black ice.

After successfully guiding the Halifax onto the apron of the AAI hangar, he turned it around so that the tail pointed toward the open doors, then waved to the waiting ground crew. While two men darted out to put chocks around the wheels, Kit and Bruce shut down the engines and put the aircraft in parked mode.

Kit removed his helmet, but before he could undo his straps, Terry was hanging over his shoulder to announce, "Skipper, it looks like the stevedores that unloaded our last cargo forgot one of the boxes. I found it crammed under the cockpit stairs."

Kit looked suspiciously up at Terry to ask, "You wouldn't by any chance know what is in that box, would you?" Given the amount of temptation, it was surprising that Airlift crews didn't engage in large-scale pilfering, but although the scale of theft was low things did manage to go 'astray' now and again. Kit knew of one American crew that had been so 'outraged' at carrying cheese and pâté for the French garrison that they had felt 'entitled' to half a dozen bottles of cognac. Other crews engaged in more banal trading: a sack of coal for Meissen porcelain, flour for beer steins and powdered milk for antique lace.

"Footwear, skipper, just as they said on the manifest," Terry answered straight-faced.

"Footwear as in surplus flying boots, skip," Nigel added with a grin.

Kit looked from one to the other and then out of the window where the German ground crew was waiting for them to disembark. They looked very cold in their threadbare trousers, ragged tunics, bare hands and battered, old shoes. A couple of them had wound scarves around their necks, and Axel wore a heavy, knitted jumper under his tunic, but they stamped their feet and clutched themselves impatiently, waiting for the Halifax to open its door so loading and routine maintenance checks could begin.

"Just how many pairs of boots are in the box?" Kit asked.

"Ah, twelve, but there are three different sizes and, well, there are the five stevedores that regularly load our return cargoes, too."

Kit looked again toward the hangar where the stevedores were loading up the first trailer of return cargo. They looked even more ragged and frozen than the ground crew.

"Any discrepancy between the loaded manifest and the unloaded manifest will be charged to the company and deducted from our payment," Kit reminded his crew.

They nodded, still grinning, "Understood, skipper."

"All right. Terry, go and tell the ground crew and the stevedores to come inside the aircraft. Have them try the boots on, select which pair they want and put them on *before* they exit. Then put the remaining pairs back in the box and take it into the hangar."

"Thank you!" Terry and Nigel dived out of the cockpit, and a moment later they were waving and signalling to the ground crew and stevedores.

"The RAF will bill us for the missing freight, but what about the company management?" Richard Scott-Ross asked from behind Kit.

"I don't know," Kit admitted. "Mr Goldman tends to do things by the book, and he's very sensitive about our reputation for reliability and honesty. However, I also think he'd like us to reward our ground crew and the stevedores for their good work. He talked about paying a bonus when we turned cash flow positive. Given the fact that there's almost nothing to buy in Berlin, the boots will be more welcome."

The exclamations and excited chatter filtering into the cockpit from the cargo hold underlined Kit's point. Kit and Bruce got out of their seats and with Richard following them, they wormed their way back towards the tail. The eight German workers were shoving their feet into the fleece-lined boots, stamping and strutting as they tried them out. "*Wunderbar!*", "*Ausgezeich-net!*" and other expressions of delight reverberated inside the metal fuselage.

Although wearing just one boot, Ludwig Winterfeld jumped up and caught Kit's arm, exclaiming, "Herr Moran! Herr Moran! MacBoss told me to fetch you! You have a visitor! Important man!"

That surprised Kit. He couldn't imagine who would be seeking him out, but he told Richard and Bruce to go ahead to the Malcolm Club. As he squeezed his way past the Germans, they stuck out their hands and thanked him. Kit nodded towards Terry and Nigel, saying it had been their idea, but the men only shook his hand harder.

As Kit dropped down onto the snowy tarmac, a cold wind hit him. He was grateful for his flying boots and glad Terry and Nigel had discovered and pilfered from the rare cargo. He glanced at the trolley with their next cargo, which consisted of items produced in Berlin's factories. There was no way of knowing what they were because, in place of individual packaging, all factories now shipped their products in standardized crates with a common label:

a white circle in which a black bear stood on his hind legs and tore apart the chains around his fore paws. "Made in Blockaded Berlin" was stamped proudly under the image.

Whoever had thought of this packaging had been wise. It emphasized that every item manufactured in Berlin was equally important. It was the fact that it had been produced, not the product itself, that mattered. Most important of all, each package was a reminder that Berlin was still under siege.

Inside the hangar, Gordon MacDonald was waiting for him, looking annoyed. "What's going on, skip? What's the delay? Why did everyone go inside the aircraft?"

As soon as Kit explained, the Scotsman's tone changed. "Terry and Nigel are good lads! The ground staff have been killing themselves these last two weeks since the fog lifted."

"Ludwig said I have a visitor?" Kit asked looking around and seeing no one else in the hangar.

"He's in the office," Gordon answered, indicating a shed, separated from the rest of the hangar by some plywood walls. "But before you talk to him, I have something to say. It's something I've been meaning to talk to you about anyway. Axel, Ludwig and Helmut don't need me hanging over their shoulders any more. They're good with the engines and they only need my help when something unusual comes up."

"Are you saying you've had enough and want to go home?" Kit asked, astonished.

"Of course not! Hear me out! What I mean is that I have time to train more Germans. Helmut says he knows three more good mechanics. With just two of them, we could take over the maintenance on Albie as well as Moby Dick. It makes sense to do the DI in the same location where you overnight, and that's here, not Hamburg."

Although there was logic in what Gordon was proposing, Kit felt that it would be unfair to the British ground crew who manned their Hamburg maintenance hub. Before he could say anything, however, Gordon urged, "Just keep it in mind when you hear what Captain Peabody wants."

"Who's Captain Peabody?"

"The man waiting for you in the office."

Puzzled, Kit made his way to the makeshift room which housed a drafting table, filing cabinets, a telephone and several chairs. It also contained a small wood-burning, iron stove, which kept the space comparatively warm. The ground crew lived here when the aircraft was out, as stacks of magazines, dirty mugs, a pair of dilapidated and muddy wellies, and other odds and ends testified. To Kit's surprise, the man awaiting him looked about thirty and wore the uniform of Lancashire Aircraft Corporation. He'd been glancing through a magazine and jumped to his feet as Kit walked in "Captain Moran?"

"Yes. That's me."

"I'm Wally Peabody," the other answered and held out his hand as he asked, "Have you got a moment?"

"Of course. We're loading return cargo. But we'd be more comfortable at the Malcolm Club," Kit suggested; he was hungry.

"I'd rather speak to you in private," Peabody answered. So Kit nodded, and they both sat down. Peabody opened with, "I flew with 434 Squadron during the war and demobbed with the rank of Flight Lieutenant."

"Canadian?" Kit asked. 434 had been an RCAF Squadron, known as the 'Bluenose' Squadron, with a reputation as a 'chop' squadron, i.e. with exceptionally high losses

"That's right, but I married an English girl and stayed in England. I've been flying with Lancashire Aircraft Corporation for the last two months, but..." He squirmed uncomfortably, leaned towards Kit and lowered his voice to add, "I'm very unhappy. We're seriously understaffed, and the equipment isn't properly maintained. Last week, I got a strip torn off by the WingCo here because the tanker I flew into Gatow didn't have a hose that was compatible with the storage tanks. That caused a huge delay, of course. A hosepipe had to be improvised. I understand why the WingCo was furious, but no one at the company warned me about that hose issue, and it was the first time I'd flown the tanker."

Kit sympathized.

"The fact that our tanker didn't have a hosepipe suitable for use in Gatow is just typical of the way the outfit is run. The only ground crew we have is located in England, and we aren't authorised to fly back unless we have a major problem. What that means is the aircraft leak hydraulic fluid, there's no such thing as a functional heating system on any of them and half of the engine gauges are u/s. Nor do we have 'luxuries' like windscreen wipers or working intercoms either. The scuttlebutt is that the company now wants to convert entirely to tankers. You know what that means. Even minor defects or a short circuit can end in a ball of flame. I've tried to raise my concerns several times, but nobody takes responsibility for anything. It's always somebody else's job to fix anything. In short, it's a shambles and," he paused to take a deep breath before announcing, "I want out."

"I can imagine," Kit agreed sympathetically.

"It's not just me. I brought my old crew with me when I took the job, and they're as fed up as I am. We were wondering if Emergency Air Services might be interested in hiring a complete spare crew."

Kit sat up straighter. The need for a backup crew had been discussed many times, but Kit doubted whether Mr Goldman would consent to hiring a complete crew all at once. On the other hand, the company had an option on a second Halifax — an option that expired at the end of this year. With a second complete crew, they could operate two Halifaxes as Mr Goldman had originally intended. Out loud he said, "I can't promise anything. I need to talk to my management, but there is a chance we could hire you all. If not, it would be good to have a couple of backup pilots qualified on the Halifax."

"I couldn't leave my crew alone with that outfit," Peabody declared firmly. "Either we all go, or no one does. But if you only want to hire a pilot, I know a flight engineer, also formerly on 434 Squadron, who is now flying with Bond Air Services. He says the chief pilot is blotto half the time and a foul-mouthed bastard when he's sober. He and the second pilot, who he says is a good bloke, would do anything to jump ship."

Kit started to get enthusiastic. At present, they had a pilot (Kiwi), navigator and signaller, all of whom had become 'spare' when the Dakota was taken off the Airlift. A flight engineer and second pilot would give them one complete, new crew. A full backup for two aircraft and crews made sense. The only problem was ground crew — except Gordon had already worked out the solution. They could base the second Halifax in Hamburg, keeping the British ground crew there to service it, and hire more Germans in Berlin to look after Albie. Because Germans were cheaper than Brits, adding German ground personnel would reduce the average cost of ground staff.

To Peabody, he repeated, "I'm going to have to talk to my management. I can't promise anything, but I think there is a reasonable chance we can work something out — for all of you. What I mean is, we might be able to acquire a second Halifax, which you and your crew would take over, while your friend the flight engineer and his second pilot could come on board as part of our backup crew."

Peabody's face lit up. "Seriously?"

"It isn't going to be my decision," Kit warned, "but I'll certainly champion your cause." Kit was 100% invested in EAS. He'd never had a job he liked as much as this, and ever since Georgina had joined him and recovered her enthusiasm for life, he knew that he wanted it to last as long as possible. The problem was he had serious doubts about David Goldman. Ever since he'd left Germany, Kit wondered if he had lost interest in the company altogether.

Chapter Seven
Happy Holidays

Georgia on my Mind
Berlin-Wannsee
Saturday 18 December
(Day 176 of the Berlin Airlift)

A week after she had arrived in Germany, Anna still wondered when the magic spell would shatter. She awoke each morning disoriented not to find herself in the windowless, bed-sitter with a shared toilet that had been her home for three years. Sitting up, she would remember she was no longer fighting windmills to bring health care to dirt-poor coloured families or futilely seeking retribution against the rapists of 12-year-old black girls. Instead, she had a large bedroom with a double bed and a balcony in a manor house on a beautiful lake. Even more incredible, there were three *white* servants who scrubbed her toilet, vacuumed and dusted her room, ironed her clothes, and would have made her bed if she'd let them. Furthermore, she spent her day flying around in a plane looking after patients without any doctor over her. Best of all, she was treated more as a friend than an employee by the ambulance's captain Emily Priestman.

Anna had liked Emily on sight, but in the week since her arrival, she had discovered that Emily was also a highly competent pilot and a warm-hearted hostess. Despite that, Anna couldn't entirely forget that Emily was a partner in the firm employing her, a fact aggravated by Anna's awe of Emily's war hero husband. The other house guests, in contrast, felt more like equals and were friends already. Kit Moran had dispelled any reticence toward a wounded veteran by willingly telling her about his Zulu grandmother, while Anna's friendship with Georgina ignited the moment the school teacher learnt that Anna not only sang beautifully but knew many negro spirituals. Georgina had immediately recruited Anna for her chorus.

The invitation today was different. Anna and the Priestmans were to be guests of Colonel and Mrs Howley. Anna had met the Howleys back in Georgia during the war. However, when Anna had known them in Georgia, Colonel Howley had been just one of thousands of US Army officers in training. His rise to prominence as US Commandant in Berlin left Anna intimidated and unsure of her status.

Her discomfort increased when the Priestmans' car drew up in front of a palace spilling streams of light onto an expansive lawn. Anna knew that electricity rationing left most of the city in darkness after sunset. These bright lights trumpeted the fact that this was the residence of the American Commandant. Next, Anna and the Priestmans were met by a butler, their coats, hats and gloves were taken from them by a uniformed maid, and they were led into an elegant salon with a gilded ceiling. Here Colonel and Mrs Howley sat ensconced before a carved marble mantle framing a booming fire.

The butler announced the guests, and Colonel and Mrs Howley sprang to their feet. As they approached Anna, she offered her hand, saying respectfully, "Mrs Howley."

The latter ignored Anna's hand to give her a warm hug instead, exclaiming as she embraced her, "None of that 'Mrs Howley' talk! I'm Edith, and I'm so happy the ambulance job worked out for you!"

When Edith stepped back, Colonel Howley took Anna's hand and declared in a deep, solemn voice, "It's good to see you again, Anna." Then, shaking his head in disbelief, he added, "Who could have ever thought we'd meet again in circumstances like these?" He gestured to the gracious room around them with the gilded ceiling and antiques and admitted, "I thought I was lucky just to be back on my feet and the only future I could imagine was some shabby desk in a Nissen hut doing boring staff work for General Eisenhower."

Noticing the Priestman's bafflement, Edith Howley explained, "Frank broke his back and pelvis in a motorcycle accident back in '43."

"Crikey!" Robin exclaimed, turning to address the American colonel directly "You don't seem to be at all handicapped."

"Bad enough for the army to throw me out of the cavalry and assign me to 'civil affairs'," Frank growled.

"He was in the Camp Gordon hospital for five months," Edith told her guests. "Most of the doctors thought he would never walk again. Only one young physician thought physical therapy might work. He put Frank on a program run by the Army that was very intensive and rigorous —

"— it was pure torture! The orderlies were a bunch of sadists — or maybe they had worked for the Spanish Inquisition or the Gestapo before enlisting. They certainly made me think death might be preferable."

"Fortunately," Edith ignored the tirade, "we ran into our old friend, Judge Warren, and he invited us to visit him at his home."

"I guess I was pretty vocal about what I thought of Army therapists during the visit," Frank admitted.

"Embarrassingly so, but it turned out to be a good thing," Edith admitted. "The Warrens introduced us to Anna."

"Anna," Frank took over, "isn't just a therapist, she's an absolute miracle worker. After those sadists had convinced me I was doomed to live the rest of my life as a worm, she not only made me believe I would walk again, but she showed me how to do it, too!"

Anna was embarrassed by such high praise and looked down. Edith dissipated the awkwardness by asking Frank to get the drinks. He turned first to Anna, declaring, "We're not in Georgia now. Would you like a cocktail?"

Although raised strictly non-alcoholic, Anna had experimented a little while in the Army. She'd also already observed that drinking was part of the European lifestyle — at least at the Priestman residence. She certainly didn't want to be the only one not drinking alcohol and asked diplomatically, "What are the others having?"

Frank turned to the Priestmans, "Robin? Join me for a bourbon?"

"Delighted."

"Emily?"

"Would a lemon sour be an inconvenience?"

"Not at all. Edith?" Frank turned to his wife.

"I'm drinking rum and coke. Why don't you join me, Anna? If you don't like it, you can have straight coke."

Anna agreed, "That sounds good."

"Coming right up." Frank went to fill their orders at the bar while Edith invited the others to sit down and asked Anna to tell them how she was getting along. "Are you settling in all right?"

"Hardly!" Anna replied with a laugh. "I still feel like I'm in some sort of fairytale."

"More like a nightmare!" Emily countered, adding to Edith, "We've been working her around the clock. After being grounded so much in November, there is a terrible backlog of patients."

"But it's not *hard* work," Anna assured them. "I just sit in the back with the patients, ready to take action *if* something goes wrong. So far nothing has." The one aspect of her new job that disappointed her was that she wasn't doing any serious nursing.

"We had one patient die on an early flight, and I'm certain it wouldn't have happened if we'd had a nurse on board," Emily pointed out as Frank discreetly handed Anna a tall glass with ice and Coca-Cola in it.

Anna thanked him with a nod and a smile as she responded, "Oh, it's absolutely essential to have a nurse on board, but unless there's an emergency, it's not particularly challenging or exhausting work. That's why I'm excited about the German-English choir."

"What choir is this?" Edith asked.

Emily explained, "One of the teachers at the British school, the wife of our senior pilot with the AFI, has formed a choir with students from the British school and a German gymnasium and they are planning to give joint concerts. They asked Anna to teach them some negro spirituals."

"I was amazed by how eager the students were!" Anna reported enthusiastically.

"We must make a point of attending one of the concerts, Frank," Edith suggested.

Her husband nodded, but changed the subject, turning to Emily to ask, "Did I hear a rumour that you were flying back to England tomorrow?"

"We have a chance to hire a second crew and add a second freighter to our fleet, but I need to consult the Managing Director, who is currently in England."

Frank shifted his gaze to Robin, "Does that mean the Airlift is out of the woods?"

"No, but it's holding its own for the moment. I'm particularly pleased that we've flown out almost 11,000 of the vulnerable Berliners that the City Council asked us to evacuate. If the weather holds, we'll have all 17,000 out by the end of the month. In the new year, Merer and I are going to look into the City Council's request for additional evacuations."

"So, this cold snap isn't interfering with operations?"

"Not in the least. Terrible as the cold and snow are for the Berliners, our aircraft were built for it. Fog is far more dangerous, and none is expected for the next five days."

"Let's hope the weathermen got their forecast right!" Frank lifted his glass in a kind of toast to the weathermen, took a drink, and then looked over at Anna. "How do you like that Cuba Libre, by the way?"

"Is that what I'm drinking?" Anna asked surprised. She'd heard about a cocktail named "Cuba Libre," but she hadn't known how it was made. Looking down into her nearly empty glass she reflected that the rum had a pleasant taste and caused a mellow feeling of contentment. She could almost hear calypso music and see palm trees swaying when she breathed in the scent. Looking up at Frank she announced. "I think I'd like another, but I'm inclined to call this drink a Georgia Libre — to celebrate my liberation from Georgia and all its bigotry."

Building Jerusalem
Cheshire, England
Monday 20 December 1948
(Day 178 of the Berlin Airlift)

Emily was not one of those British women who thought nowhere else on earth was as good as England. She'd looked forward to travelling to the Continent, and she shared Robin's dreams of future assignments to Singapore, Delhi or Cape Town. Yet blockaded Berlin didn't exactly qualify as an exotic, tropical paradise. She was thoroughly delighted to be back in England!

She loved the half-timbered, 18th-century tea room where she had arranged to meet David, and the tea, scones and strawberry jam were far more scrumptious than she remembered. Most delightful of all, the room was so warm that she could take off her hat, coat and gloves.

David was a few minutes late, but he arrived wearing his EAS uniform, which encouraged Emily; she'd feared he might have turned his back on the company altogether. She stood to greet him as he joined her, and they touched cheeks. "I'm so glad to see you in uniform, David!" Emily admitted out loud.

He looked down. "I feel positively naked in public without a uniform, although it's been good to walk and laze about in old corduroys and a jumper at the cottage."

"How is Mr Bowles?" Emily asked as they sat down. David was staying with the father of a wartime friend who had unofficially adopted him after his son was killed in action.

"Very well. The barn is a raving success." David and Emily together had conceived of and overseen the transformation of Mr Bowles' 15th-century barn into an up-market bed-and-breakfast. Although Mr Bowles had done much of the work himself, being a skilled carpenter, tiler and thatcher, Emily had ensured that, despite necessary modernisations such as plumbing, the medieval character of the structure was retained. Meanwhile, David had organised the finances; it had been their first joint business venture.

David happily filled her in on recent developments. "At this time of year, the barn is beautifully decorated with wreaths and boughs of yew, holly and mistletoe. It is rented out for one event after another, from wedding receptions to concerts. It helps that Mrs Holden — do you remember her?" Emily shook her head. "Never mind. She had a bakery in the village, but she's taken over the catering for the barn and basically runs the whole show — very competently, I might add. In short, the barn is more popular than ever."

"I'm so glad. *You* look better," she noted.

"I could hardly look worse than the last time you saw me," he noted sourly, picking up the menu from the table. "Have you ordered?"

"No, I was waiting for you, but I'd like tea and scones."

"Excellent," David turned and signalled to the waitress that he was ready to order. When she arrived, David announced, "Cream tea and scones for two." As he closed the menu and the waitress withdrew, Emily noted, "The time with Mr Bowles seems to have done you good."

David faced Emily and declared, "I've been able to put things in better perspective. Ginger died too young to love at all. Mr Bowles lost his beloved wife after only four years. My parents, on the other hand, were married for forty-odd years without ever loving one another. I fell in love with the wrong woman and was rejected. So what? It happens all the time. The entire notion of finding one's 'true love' and living happily ever after is a fairytale. A silly Hollywood illusion."

Although David's tone was reasonable, Emily didn't trust the apparent calm and wasn't sure how to answer. Should she tell him he was wrong to believe Charlotte had rejected him? Or encourage him to move beyond her? Cautiously she suggested, "When I saw Charlotte at Jasha's wedding, she seemed very brittle and defensive. That's not the behaviour of someone comfortable with her choice. I think she deeply regrets what has happened between you."

David responded firmly, "Well, she made her bed, and she has to lie in it. It has nothing to do with me." He avoided Emily's eyes as he insisted, "Whatever happened — whether I misjudged her, or she changed her mind, or Bredow has some strange, secret power over her — doesn't matter any more. Charlotte is dead to me. How is Christian doing?"

Glad to turn to a positive subject, Emily announced, "He has revolutionised our flight planning."

David looked astonished, "How so?"

"Well, you know how short the Wellington's take-off and landing requirements are. There's no need to use large, expensive commercial airports with concrete runways two miles long, and Christian appears to know every single airfield in Germany, regardless of how small or off the beaten track it is, so we've shifted to smaller, cheaper airports. There's also a huge advantage to being a former Luftwaffe officer when dealing with the hospital staff. German academics have a patronising attitude towards women; no matter what Charlotte did, she was never taken completely seriously." She paused to let David comment, but he remained silent.

Emily forged ahead. "Christian, on the other hand, instantly commands respect. Then there's the fact that Charlotte was very conscientious and diligent, but as a woman without any medical background, she never questioned the attending physicians. If the doctor said a patient needed to be transported to Munich, Stuttgart or Augsburg, that's what she organised even when it cost us half a day and a full tank of aviation fuel. Christian, on the other hand, *doesn't* take orders from anyone. Instead, he's knocked some heads together and made the directors concede that, for example, not every patient with an eye injury needs to go to the leading research hospital for ocular surgery on the Continent! For most patients, it's just a matter of getting them to a hospital with adequate morphine, fresh bandages and an operating theatre that can work 24 hours without the lights going off!"

"True," David agreed nodding.

"Christian flatly told the doctors that some hospitals were 'too far away' unless they could fill the aircraft and insisted they find alternatives. It turns out there is a cluster of smaller but fully functional hospitals in Osnabrueck, Gutersloh, Minden, and Detmold — all near the end of the central corridor we have to fly out on anyway. Christian arranged for us to land at a regional airport in Bielefeld — a former Luftwaffe fighter station — which is roughly equidistant from these hospitals. They send land ambulances there to collect the patients, while Moby Dick can fly from there directly to Hamburg, less than an hour's flying time away. The result is that with lower fuel consumption, we're now regularly flying three times a day and evacuating roughly 50% more patients every week."

"Well done," David praised. "We should have brought Christian on board earlier. He's one of those golden boys who'll succeed at anything he touches. He's intelligent, industrious and charming."

"Yes, he's an asset, but he can't replace you," Emily countered, unsettled by David's apparent detachment.

David turned to look at her sharply. "Why do you say that?"

"Christian is good at getting things done, but you're the man with the vision."

David prevaricated, "Moran seems to have a good head on his shoulders."

"He does," Emily agreed. "Which reminds me, he gave me some calculations on how the second Halifax and additional crew would pay off. Do you want to see them?"

David smiled faintly. "I did my own as soon as you called me about Kit's talk with Peabody, but, yes, I would like to see what he came up with."

Emily reached for her handbag and pulled out two sheets of paper folded together. She passed them to David. As he scanned the neat, upright writing on the ruled exercise paper, Emily watched him intently. She saw him smile as he turned the first page over. Shortly afterwards, he exclaimed, "Good man!" without taking his eyes off the notes. "He's quantified the savings from back-loading cargoes in wear-and-tear and replacement parts. That will be very useful when I talk to the bank about loans."

"Then you agree it is a good idea?" she asked hopefully.

"Of course, it's a good idea." David seemed to register for the first time how uncertain she was. He reassured her, "I've already been in touch with the RAF to say we want to exercise our option, and I've arranged to test-fly two of the available Halifaxes tomorrow. You're welcome to join me if you like."

He paused before admitting, "The new aircrew sounds a bit more dubious. They've been working for companies without sterling reputations, to say the least. Then again, that's why they're dissatisfied, I suppose. Besides, we need to move forward on this sooner rather than later. Each day the Airlift lasts is a day closer to when it ends. We want to be flying with two aircraft at the earliest possible date. After we've selected an aircraft, I'll finalise the transfer with the RAF. Then I want Moran to turn Albie over to the new crew and get them settled in Hamburg as rapidly as possible so he can bring his crew over to pick up the new Halifax. While he's here, he can collect the items for the Gatow Christmas party to save disruption to the ambulance service."

"That makes sense," Emily agreed, nodding, and then asked, "But what about you, David? Won't you be coming back?"

"What for?" David shot back. "You've convinced me that Christian is managing the office splendidly. You are in charge of the ambulance. Kiwi has a good grip on the ground crews, and Moran seems to understand the freight side of the business superbly."

"But we're all very busy doing our jobs. We need someone who has an overview of everything that's happening and is planning beyond the next day or two. Not to mention the fact that I need someone I can talk to about problems and ideas."

"Such as...?" David's tone softened slightly.

"Well, there's the question of whether we shouldn't have a second ambulance — assuming we could afford it. I know it may sound premature, but when the Airlift ends, as it must eventually, the need for freighters will disappear overnight, but not the need for ambulances."

"Good point," David agreed and for the first time, Emily thought she saw a spark of real interest in his eye. "I've been thinking along those lines too."

"You have?"

"Yes. Just because I don't want to return to Berlin, doesn't mean I've lost interest in the idea of an air ambulance. On the contrary, getting away from the spotlight on the Airlift enabled me to see that freight is just a short-term windfall. It's lucrative at the moment, but in the longer term, it's a cut-throat business with very low margins. The future — and my heart — are in the ambulance business. We have to be realistic, however. An air ambulance has the best chance of success in places where good hospitals are far apart. Australia and Canada come to mind, but I've also been thinking about India and the Far East, either of which might be a better location for our business."

Emily was startled by such a radical reorientation of their work and showed it. David hastened to explain, "I want to be where we can do the most good, not just make the most money. I'm sure we could make a fortune in America, for example, but it's the last place I want to operate. As I see it, our primary goal should never be maximisation of profit but rather making this a better world. If we don't do that, then we will have betrayed those — like Ginger — who died to stop Hitler."

"Well said," Emily responded earnestly.

"I had hoped that Charlotte would be beside me, but the fact that she has chosen a different path must not divert me from mine. I will continue, in my own way, to strive to build a new Jerusalem."

Emily had never wanted to be part of his endeavour more than she did at this moment — when the chances seemed dimmer than ever before.

Santa Claus is Coming to Town
RAF Gatow
Thursday 23 December 1948
(Day 181 of the Berlin Airlift)

RIAS and the newspapers could talk about nothing but the American 'Operation Santa Claus.' As an American military spokesman explained, since the start of December, five to ten aircraft every day had been devoted to this 'crucial' operation. Rather than flying in coal, powdered potatoes and dehydrated pea soup, they had been flying in boxes of 'special cargoes' met by security guards and escorted to a dedicated warehouse. A hundred pounds at a time, the US spokesman now revealed, the USAF had flown in three and a half tons of chocolate, candy bars, and gum. On top of that, from all across America, private American citizens had donated more than 100,000 gifts for Berlin's children. These, too, had been brought by the USAF to Berlin. The radio and newspapers announced that the children of Berlin could collect their share of the sweets and one present each at one of the 400 parties that the US military government would be hosting throughout the Western Sectors on Christmas Eve.

The sheer scope of the American 'operation' dwarfed and almost mocked the RAF's heartfelt but comparatively modest plans for a Christmas party. Kathleen wished that her daughter Hope wouldn't hear about the American parties and generosity, but she inevitably would. She'd then wonder why she wasn't included, and Kathleen was getting tired of explaining.

Or maybe she was just plain tired, she reflected. She'd been a ground approach controller at Gatow almost from the first day of the Airlift, and she hadn't had a day of leave since. Yes, they had increased the number of controllers, gone on a three-watch system, and had regular days off. But since the aircraft flew around the clock, weather permitting, that meant that like all shift-workers, she spent at least one week in three working through the hours of darkness. The shift changes always left her exhausted. Much as she liked her job, she was burnt out. She needed to get away from aircraft, uniforms, and Berlin itself.

At least today her watch ended before Hope got out of Day Care. She'd have a couple of hours of peace and quiet for herself. Collecting her hat and greatcoat from the stand by the door, she started down the stairs from the tower only to run into Squadron Leader Garth coming the other way.

"Hart," he stopped her, "Did you see the latest article about Operation Santa Claus in *Stars and Stripes*?" He held up a copy of the American military newspaper. "It's got a big picture of Captain Baronowsky and Lt. Halvorsen in it. Do you want to borrow it?"

"Yes, I'd love to," Kathleen agreed, "thank you, sir."

Garth handed the paper to her and carried on up the stairs. Rather than risk a fall by walking and reading at the same time, Kathleen paused at the next landing and stood beside the windows to look more closely at the article. She was surprised to see J.B. posing next to Halvorsen in front of a C-54 disgorging crates of sweets because someone had told her that J.B. had gone back to the States. She'd also never seen a picture of Halvorsen before and was surprised by how slight, pale, bald and shy he looked. J.B. looked like the more forceful character — handsome, wholesome, and attractive. Her eyes caressed his face with longing. Had she been foolish to brush him off that day in the fog? Was it possible that he really had fallen in love with her? Was it possible to fall in love so fast? Or had that encounter been a dream? She was no longer sure.

Turning to the text, the article explained that the Confectioners Association of America had donated three tons of sweets for the children of Berlin. The pilots said they were flying 'round the clock.' They insisted they would be working right through Christmas, although they hinted they might show up at one or another of the parties for the kids. "The USAF is going to try to have pilots at all the parties," the article explained.

Kathleen finished reading and looked up the stairs, wondering if she should return the newspaper to Garth. She didn't want to. She wanted to keep it and the picture of J.B. as a memento. Even if she never saw him again, he was a good man, and she wanted to remember him. Maybe she could buy a copy of *Stars and Stripes* at the NAAFI? For now, she folded the newspaper until it fitted into the pocket of her greatcoat, pulled on her gloves, turned her coat collar up, and went out into the cold. She found her bicycle in the stand and pedalled her way back to her quarters.

The shift she was working this week was the best, 8 am to 4 pm. It enabled her to return to the Waafery when women working in other trades were still on duty. The bicycle stand in front was almost empty as a result, and no one else was coming or going. She unlocked the front door and pushed the button that controlled the stairwell light, timed for just 60 seconds. Although light still lingered in the sky outside, the sun had set, and it was dark in the stairwell and hallway.

As she reached the top of the stairs, she looked down to find her key in her leather handbag, which hung from a strap cutting diagonally across her chest. When she looked up again, she saw a man sitting in front of her door. She gasped and then registered that the man was wearing a bright red Santa Claus outfit complete with a curly white moustache, beard and a floppy, pointed cap with a white pom-pom on the end. Ashamed to be afraid of Santa Claus, she giggled in embarrassment and exclaimed, "I'm sorry, Santa! You startled me."

Santa responded by opening his arms wide and singing in a deep, cheerful voice, *"You better watch out, You better not cry, Better not pout, I'm telling you why: Santa Claus is comin' to town."*

The moment sound came out of his mouth, Kathleen recognized J.B.'s voice. When he fell silent, she burst out, "J.B.! I mean, Captain Baronowsky! Where did you come from? How did you get here? I mean, *in* here? Unescorted." She looked around confused; an American officer had no business inside the WAAF quarters.

"With the Station Commander's permission of course," J.B. answered, getting to his feet.

"The WingCo allowed you to —"

"He approved my offer to bring some candy for the children at the daycare centre and when I said I wanted to stop by to say hello to a friend afterwards, he had his adjutant bring me over. I think his name was Stan."

"Flying Officer Stanley; we all call him Stan."

"Well, Stan, being a true English gentleman, grasped the unspoken delicacy of the situation and — after convincing himself I was not a threat to British National Security or Gatow personnel — he agreed to withdraw discreetly." J.B. paused and his tone changed from jocular to serious as he tore his hat and beard off with one sweep of his hand. "I'm grateful I could come, but I wish I weren't dressed up in this silly costume." He stopped and added with evident feeling, "It's good to see you, Kathleen."

"I was told you'd gone back to the States to get married."

"Yeah. I went home. My fiancé's father got his congressman to request my recall."

"Oh, my!" Kathleen was impressed and intimidated by connections like that. Unconsciously she took a step backwards.

J.B. hastened to explain, "Only, when I got there, I realised that I couldn't marry Patty."

"You *didn't* marry her?" Kathleen asked astonished. Then she had a second thought and added in alarm, "I hope that wasn't because of me. I didn't mean—"

He gestured for her to relax. "You didn't mislead me. When I made my decision, I honestly didn't think we'd ever see each other again. But Patty wasn't the right girl for me. I couldn't face spending the rest of my life with her."

"But — what about her father? And the congressman? There must have been a terrible scene!"

"Yeah, it was pretty bad," he admitted, shaking his head. "Worst drama I've ever seen. Patty found more ways to insult me than I'd ever heard before — and I grew up on the *wrong* side of the tracks. She raged a lot about how much money she'd wasted on the wedding, but what really made her hysterical was being humiliated in front of her friends." He paused, looking off into the distance rather than at Kathleen as he remembered. When he resumed the narrative the slightly humorous, entertaining tone he had used up until now was gone. "It was odd — at least I thought it was odd — that she never once tried to talk me out of leaving her. She never said she'd be willing to move to Willow Run so I could have the job I wanted or anything like that." He stopped again and lowered his voice before adding, "And not once did she say, 'I love you, Jay.' Not once."

"Oh, Jay," Kathleen responded with instinctive sympathy. "I'm so sorry for you! It always hurts when we discover we've given our affection to someone who doesn't return it — or deserve it. It's not just the lack of reciprocity that hurts, it's the realisation that we have misjudged someone so completely." She was thinking of her humiliating 'affair' with Lionel.

J.B. looked over at her in surprise, and then his eyes looked deeper. After a moment, he simply said, "Thank you." Pulling himself together, he put a smile back on his face, and tried to find again a light and witty tone as he concluded, "Given the fact that she didn't love me in the least, I must have done the right thing. And while I didn't leave her *because* of you, I do hope you'll let me see more of you."

For a second time, he dropped the façade of jocularity to plead, "That's all I ask, Kathleen, that you give me a chance to show you who I really am." By the way he looked at her, he was far from certain of her response.

Yet Kathleen wanted exactly what he did: to get to know him better. With a smile, she answered, "Why don't you start by coming in out of this chilly hallway." She stepped toward the door and inserted her key as she warned, "My daughter will be home in less than an hour, but you have time to change out of your Santa suit while I make a pot of tea."

"Tea," he echoed with a faint smile.

"Oh, sorry. Did you want something stronger?" Kathleen looked over her shoulder.

"No. After all the melodrama of the past two weeks, there is nothing in the world I'd like more than a calming cup of English tea."

The Lion and the Lamb
RAF Gatow
Saturday 25 December 1948
(Day 182 of the Berlin Airlift)

Robin had no way of comparing Gatow's Christmas party to the events hosted by the Americans, but he was proud of what his staff had put together. While it was still light, the arriving children had a choice between a tour of a Dakota or a pony ride. The former triggered more interest and enthusiasm than Robin had expected and resulted in an endless line of wide-eyed, delighted little boys waiting for the chance to walk up the aisle and into the tiny cockpit of one of their unserviceable Dakotas. Here, they were shown the dials by a pilot. Meanwhile, the girls gravitated more towards the stables, where pony and cart rides were offered until it became too dark and cold.

As darkness fell, the children, carefully escorted by parents or teachers from the local schools, were herded to the training facility and into the large entry hall. They left their outdoor garments on a table to one side and then entered a large room decorated in traditional English style with boughs of holly and other evergreens garnished with red ribbons, and gold and silver bells. A large Christmas tree bedecked with lights and wooden and paper ornaments stood against the back wall and beside it sat a fat and jolly Santa Claus. On his other side was a transport crate wrapped in Christmas paper and ribbon. The children lined up to approach him one at a time and each received a little gift out of the box.

At the front of the room, a chorus of teenagers sang Christmas carols in English and German. The choir was extraordinarily good, given how little practice they had had together, and Robin found himself watching them almost as much as the children receiving their gifts from Santa. As he turned to leave, he touched his finger to his cap to signal his approval to Georgina and Anna, who beamed back at him.

After receiving a wrapped package each, the children were escorted into the dining room. They were seated at a long table with an adult in every fifth place. At each place setting, a paper angel standing on an orange waited beside a pair of paper RAF wings. Robin watched as the children gasped, squealed, and clapped or reached out to inspect their presents. The boys often grabbed the wings first and put them up against their chests. The girls focused more on the angels, comparing their faces and examining how they had been made. The oranges proved to be a dubious surprise, however, since many of the children appeared not to know what they were. Several of the smaller children thought they were balls and tried to bounce them. Adults or siblings had to show them how to peel them open, accompanied by exclamations of surprise, impatience or shrieks as juice squirted out.

When all the children were seated, the kitchen staff emerged in a long line wearing their white uniforms to an appropriate drum roll from the RAF band. The children were awed for a moment and then broke into wild applause. The decibels rose to an almost intolerable level — except that seeing the excitement and the happiness of children made it tolerable.

As for the food, Gatow's kitchen staff had put together a mouth-watering dinner of turkey, stuffing, gravy, fresh mashed potatoes, brussels sprouts and carrots smothered in melted butter. The meal was accompanied by jugs of hot chocolate and finished off with Christmas pudding. All items had been purchased with money donated by Gatow personnel and flown to Berlin from England in Emergency Air Services' new Halifax.

As the meal ended, the chorus emerged from the kitchen, where they had been served the same meal. They now led the children in singing carols together, ending with 'Silent Night.' As the chorus bowed and filed out, the adult escorts started to herd the children together towards their outdoor clothing and the exit.

Waiting for the event to wind up, Robin formulated in his head the circular he would send out to his staff the following morning praising them for a hugely successful event. His thoughts were interrupted by an elderly gentleman, one of the escorting teachers. "*Herr Oberst?*" The German made a stab at interpreting the three stripes on Robin's sleeve.

"Yes?"

The man thrust out his bony and gnarled hand. Robin took it and winced as the man grasped his hand fiercely and pumped it up and down vigorously. In a tear-choked voice, he exclaimed, "*Vielen, vielen Dank! Das war die schoenste Weihnachten in Jahren! Ihr habt uns alle so geehrt!*"

Robin understood the sentiment rather than the words and responded with, "It was our pleasure." He meant it.

But no sooner had the first man gone than the woman behind him also stopped and the next and the one after. It was like a reception line only at the end of the event rather than the beginning, and that made it very different. These people were not introducing themselves to him but thanking him with embarrassing sincerity. Robin understood that he was nothing more than the most obvious and convenient representative of everyone who had made this evening possible, yet he felt overwhelmed all the same.

"They will always remember this," one of the women said in good English, indicating the wide-eyed children clustered around her, before adding, "We will never forget who our friends are."

And that, Robin realised, was the most remarkable thing of all. A year ago, this feast would have been inconceivable — on his own part, on the part of his staff, or the part of the Berliners. A year ago, although not outright enemies, they had still been victors and vanquished. Tangible hatred might have faded, but in its place, wariness tinged with mutual dislike had taken root. That was now gone. They had overcome their suspicions and put aside their grudges to find the humanity in one another. The lion had lain down with the lamb and they had become friends.

Chapter Eight
Happy New Year?

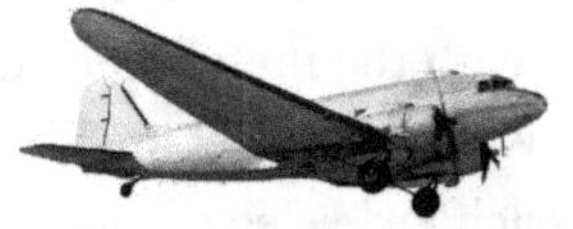

Headmaster Peden approved Georgina's plan to offer sewing classes to the German girls over the school holidays and gave her permission to use the domestic science room at the British School. Because she had seen what a miserable collection of ragged, thread-bare and ill-fitting overcoats the German girls wore, Georgina set herself the goal of ensuring that each girl left the class with a serviceable winter coat.

To that end, she'd brought back in AFI's second Halifax (along with the Christmas dinners and gifts for 400 children) six bolts of fabric purchased in Yorkshire. The investment hadn't been large because she'd bought surplus army, navy and air force serge. This was going for a song because the military was shrinking, and the civilian population wanted any material *other* than that associated with six long years of war. While khaki and navy or air force blue serge were hardly any girl's idea of elegant, feminine clothing, they were durable and warm.

At the first sewing class on 27 December, Georgina faced disappointment bordering on resentment when she showed the ten girls the fabric she'd brought, but she'd anticipated their reaction. In addition to the material, she'd brought a collection of fashion magazines and two books with patterns for winter coats. After passing the magazines around and listening to the reactions and comments of the pupils, she selected three model designs from the pattern books. On the blackboard, she demonstrated how with contrasting collars, cuffs, belts, kick-pleats and other tricks it would be possible to transform the mundane-looking basic pattern into something unique. She showed how khaki and navy blue made a chic combination, while the use of light-blue accents on navy or vice-versa produced a sophisticated look. By the end of the session, she had convinced the girls that with the material available they would be able to make a warm coat that they wouldn't be ashamed to wear.

In the second session, each girl selected one of the three models and got to work designing her individual coat. They dithered at first but were soon whispering amongst themselves and excitement started to build. By the end of the session, they were chattering, laughing and collaborating. The following sessions were devoted to measuring each other and cutting patterns in paper, then arranging them on the cloth to minimize waste. Cutting didn't start until Georgina had reviewed each girl's work.

It wasn't until the seventh session that the actual sewing started. Since the domestic science class had only six sewing machines, these had to be shared and at any one time, four girls were waiting. This provided the perfect opportunity for Anna to offer them a short physical exam, and Georgina secured permission from the British nurse for Anna to use the infirmary. Officially, she was doing a routine check-up — recording height, weight, blood pressure and pulse, as well as conducting a basic vision and a hearing test. The real purpose of the tests was to disguise the fact that Anna had come to examine Silvie for pregnancy.

Over the week, the girls' ease with each other had grown and by this session their chatter was loud, cacophonic, and frequently punctuated with laughter. Georgina was pleased to note that as the coats took shape, the girls became increasingly excited about wearing them.

Towards the end of the session, Gisela, one of the older and bolder girls, returned from her medical exam and somewhat provocatively sat herself on the teacher's table at the front of the class. Georgina decided to ignore her and concentrate on helping Petra get a seam straight. "Hold the material more firmly," Georgina suggested, reaching out and showing the teenager how it was done.

"Mrs Moran?" Gisela called from the front of the classroom. "Doesn't your husband mind you spending Sunday afternoon with us rather than looking after him?" Georgina was too busy to respond at once, so Gisela continued, "My father always expected the whole family to dance around him on Sunday afternoons. My mother had to make a special meal, and we children weren't allowed to be with friends or go out to the cinema or anything else. We had to be together 'as a family,' he said. Isn't your husband like that, Mrs Moran?"

Georgina, having finished helping Petra, stood straight and replied pointedly, "My husband is flying supplies into Berlin. He won't be home until half past seven or eight. So no, he doesn't mind me being here."

"How did you meet your husband, Mrs Moran?" Gertrud asked. She was the youngest of the girls and noticeably more childlike. As she waited to use a sewing machine, she sat on one of the tables swinging her legs and gazing at Georgina with undisguised admiration.

Georgina hesitated, yet she could sense that the girls longed to know more about her. "We met at a dance," Georgina answered cautiously, unconsciously smiling at the memory.

"A dance? What sort of dance?" Ulrike looked up from her sewing to ask. "Was it a fancy ball or a nightclub with jazz music or a tea dance?"

"It was a formal dance in the Assembly Rooms at Lincoln, a fund-raiser for the Red Cross, if I remember rightly."

"Did you fall in love at first sight?" Gertrud asked dreamily, harvesting a chorus of hisses, jeers and rolled eyes from the faster girls in the group. Gertrud looked down blushing.

Georgina came to her rescue by admitting, "I did, actually, but not with my husband. I fell in love with one of his crewmates first, but later he was killed in action."

"Oh, how sad!" Gertrud exclaimed.

"It was," Georgina admitted. "But after I lost Don, I came to know Kit better and we fell in love and decided to get married."

"What about you, Miss Savage?" They turned their attention to Anna, who had just returned to the classroom. "Are you married?"

"No," Anna answered calmly.

"Don't you have a fiancé or boyfriend?"

"No," Anna answered again.

"Don't you want to get married?"

"Not any time soon." She told them and the German girls gaped in astonishment. "My mother was sixteen when she had me, and she had to drop out of school," Anna told them bluntly. "She never had a chance to make anything of herself, and I didn't want to end the same way. I wanted to finish school, get a good job, and see a little of the world before settling down."

"But what if you didn't have a choice?" Petra asked in a strained voice that made Georgina look over at her in concern. Petra rarely spoke up. Usually, she just trailed unhappily in Dietlinde, Gisela and Ulrike's wake.

"A choice about what?" Anna asked, having lost the thread of the conversation.

"About having sex," Petra burst out, her face flushing.

A hush fell over the whole room, and Georgina's instinct was to change the subject. Anna chose to confront the question head-on. "*Especially* when you didn't have a choice, Petra. A man can force you to have sex with him, but he can't force you not to go to school, or not to get job training, or not to work."

"The f**king bastards don't care what our names are, much less give a f**king damn what we do with our lives after they've got what they paid for!" Gisela erupted with an explosion of unexpected fury, adding bitterly, "It's the *rest* of society that won't give us a chance!"

Dietlinde said something to her in German which triggered an even more violent reaction. With a sharp push, Gisela thrust Dietlinde away and screamed at her in German.

Ulrike and Hannah tried to intervene, but that only made things worse. Gisela shouted and screamed in German, eliciting equally vociferous answers from Ulrike, Dietlinde and Hannah. Like a mini cyclone, emotions spiralled out of control.

After recovering from their shock, Georgina and Anna tried to intervene, but Gisela swung on them, shouting in English, "My father wanted me to shoot myself! He gave me his pistol — butt-first. He didn't even give me time to pull up my panties! I was trembling and bleeding and I wanted to be sick, and he just jabbed a pistol butt in my face!"

Georgina stopped breathing and Anna froze.

Gisela continued, "My mother shoved him aside and bundled me out of the house — but he shouted after me not to come back. He said I was dead to him — whether I had the 'decency' to kill myself or not!" She turned and focused on Anna, who had had the temerity to suggest she had control over her fate. "I live with my aunt now, but she has three children and no job. She'd have nothing if I didn't earn enough cigarettes and chocolate for her to trade on the black market. At least she's thankful for it."

Like puss pouring from a punctured boil, the other stories followed.

"My mother says I don't belong in school," Ulrike announced, her teeth clamped. "She says I'd earn more money working all week rather than just on the weekends. But why should I put out for four or five GIs every day so she can buy herself gin? She steals half the nylons they give me anyway, and the cigarettes, of course. But she's a 'lady,' and I'm just a whore!" She grabbed a cigarette and lit up, a grim expression on her face.

"After the Ivans had me, the concierge cornered me and forced himself on me as well. He said since no decent man would ever marry me, I had no right to 'put on airs' and 'pretend to be a nice girl,'" Beate lashed out.

"German men are the worst bastards of all!" Hannah concurred bitterly. "First, they let the Ivans do what they liked with us, and then they call us traitors for sleeping with 'the enemy'!"

"They didn't *all* abandon us!" Petra protested, surprising the others. "My father tried to stop the Ivans. He stood up to them, but they shot him three times in the stomach. Then they raped me while he writhed in pain and bled to death." Petra burst into tears as she cried out with raw guilt, "Maybe if I hadn't resisted, he'd still be alive!"

Georgina recoiled in horror; she could identify with this story more than the others because she could easily imagine her father trying to protect her. The horror of his pain and death on top of the violence of gang rape was unfathomable. She took Petra into her arms and tried to comfort her.

But Dietlinde wasn't finished, "All *good* German men are dead!" she declared. "The ones left alive either surrendered or ran away!"

"*They* surrendered to the Ivans but still think they have a *right* to our bodies for free because the victors have already had them," Ulrike spat out contemptuously, and her words provoked a flurry of agreement that tapered off into silence. Petra gently pulled herself out of Georgina's arms, wiping the tears away from her face with her hands.

The short but intense outburst of confessions, like a violent thunderstorm, ended as suddenly as it started. But instead of clearing the air, Georgina felt the tension simmering. She knew that her nerves were too frayed to cope with any more revelations. She was going to need to reflect on what she'd learnt today for many hours and days to come, and she wanted her father's advice too. She looked toward the clock and announced in relief, "Look at the time! We must pack away our things and lock up."

With exaggerated alacrity to cover their embarrassment, the girls busied themselves putting their unfinished sewing into the lockers at the back of the class and donning their old over-clothes. Meanwhile, Georgina rubbed out the blackboard, and Anna wrapped herself in her cape. When the last of the girls had filed out, Georgina switched off the lights and followed them down the stairs. Outside they waved goodbye "until tomorrow," and the girls walked in a group toward the nearest underground station, while Georgina and Anna climbed into the headmaster's car, which he had put at Georgina's disposal.

After a few moments of silence, Georgina remarked, "Well, that was educational."

"And sobering," Anna agreed. She paused before adding, "There's something else you ought to know." Georgina waited, warned by Anna's tone to expect something unpleasant. "First, Silvie is more than four months pregnant. Second, Gertrud, who was nine when the city fell to the Reds, is the only virgin, and finally, seven of the girls have VD."

Georgina caught her breath. She thought back to when she had been their age, attending an Anglican boarding school for girls. If even one of them had not been a virgin, it would have been a scandal, and she'd never heard of VD. She thought back, too, to her first encounter with Herr Dr Altenheyn. He'd emphasised that the Kaiser Wilhelm School was an 'elite' school. The parents of these pupils, he'd claimed, were bureaucrats, professionals and academics. Perhaps that was the reason they were so incapable of coping with their daughters' fall from grace?

She shook her head and admitted, "I heard about the Russian rapes before I came, but everyone talked about them as though they were history. It was something terrible that had happened 'in the war,' rather like the bombing and the concentration camps. No one seemed to understand that those rapes are *still* warping lives. It must be the same all across the city."

"We shouldn't jump to conclusions," Anna warned. "These girls came from your chorus which was recruited from the advanced English class. The girls have good English because they've been picking it up from their customers over the last three years. We might find that the school as a whole has lower levels of VD."

"Maybe," Georgina conceded, but the shock had turned to indignation, "but those girls aren't out there selling themselves for fun! Every single encounter, whether it's transactional or not, is an act of violence!"

"For a white woman, you understand more than I expected," Anna remarked, giving Georgina an approving look.

"Anna! What does race have to do with this?"

"Just that blacks are more likely to be victims. I don't imagine you knew many girls like these where you grew up."

"No," Georgina admitted, "but I'm not deaf and blind! Those girls said their fathers have rejected them, their mothers are exploiting them, and the young men who *ought* to be protecting and loving them, despise them instead. When I was briefed about the rapes, they were depicted as an example of *Russian* brutality — which they certainly were. Yet it's the *Germans* callousness towards their girls that has turned victims into whores! Not to mention that it's *our* troops who are now taking advantage of them day after day!" Georgina was livid with indignation.

"*Now* you sound like a vicar's daughter!" Anna quipped. "No power on earth can stop cocky young men with money in their pockets from preying on poor women with nothing to sell but their bodies. There's no point bemoaning how they got into this situation. We need to focus on what we can do to help them."

"You and me? But what on earth can we possibly do?" Georgina protested.

"You took the first step by encouraging them to become part of the chorus. That made them part of something respectable. This sewing course is important, too, because it gives them skills useful for a lifetime. Provided I can get access to antibiotics, I can treat their infections, and I was thinking about offering a first aid course. Maybe we could ask Jasha to give cooking lessons, too. What do you think?"

"Frankly," Georgina replied sharply, still too incensed to be positive, "that all sounds frivolous! After the horrors they have endured and considering the situation they're in, sewing and cooking classes are almost insulting. They need to recover their self-respect!"

"But the best way to regain that is for them to stop selling themselves,"

Anna countered. "My aunt was raped when she was 13, but she was rescued from a life on the streets by a kind woman who took her in, helped her put her baby up for adoption, and gave her a job for life — yes, a job as a servant, but a servant who is very much a part of the family. She's had a good and fulfilling life, and the child of that rape was adopted and has done even better. We can't give all these girls a new home, but we can help them find other ways to make a living."

"Anna!" Georgina protested, "They can earn more in a weekend than a German teacher earns in a month. The same is doubly true for nurse's aides and household staff."

"I know that, but girls addicted to the money they can earn on the streets don't bother to go to school. The girls who crave luxuries don't take time off trawling for customers to sing in a chorus — and they don't sign up for sewing lessons. The girls in the class aren't a representative sample of Berlin's streetwalkers. They are a self-selected subset of those girls engaged in transactional sex, who take an interest in other things and *want* a different future. Silvie doesn't want that baby, and she doesn't want to keep living this life. Hannah and Petra are the same. Although I'm not sure about Dietlinde, I believe Gisela and Ulrike, despite seeming brash and cynical, haven't accepted that they are as worthless as society tells them they are — which is why they are embittered and cynical. If we can show them a way to get back on the respectable side of the street, I think they'll take it."

"But what they want most is a young man to love them and cherish them as they had every reason to expect," Georgina reflected sadly. "They want to be respectable wives and mothers."

"Of course," Anna agreed gently, "but we can't bring back the dead or undo the damage that has been done to them. All we can do is try to offer them a different future."

"And you think cooking and sewing and first aid can help?"

"Well, it's all we've got," Anna reasoned, "and it doesn't hurt to try, does it?"

The only possible answer for a woman like Georgina was "No."

Same Song, Second Verse
Headquarters RAF Transport Command, UK
(46 Group)
Tuesday 4 January 1949
(Day 192 of the Berlin Airlift)

Priestman had no reason to think that this summons to 46 Group HQ portended bad news, but he took Bertie along for good luck just the same. As he did not anticipate return passengers, however, he flew the Spitfire, and the stuffed bear joined him in the narrow cockpit, riding on his lap.

The English weather was wetter, darker and warmer than Berlin's. Robin landed in drizzling rain and was met again by Merer's adjutant, who drove him to the HQ building. Here the station commanders from Wunstorf, Celle, Flossberg, Fuhlsbuettel, Luebeck and Schleswig Land were gathered, along with the commanders of all squadrons flying on the Airlift. Coffee, tea, buns and other light refreshments were provided at a buffet in the anteroom while they waited for the last stragglers to arrive.

Although overall command of the British airlift had been transferred to Merer, Group Captain Bagshot remained station commander at Wunstorf. Robin and Bagshot exchanged stiff nods and then avoided each other. They mingled with the other officers, all of whom were easily exchanging news and gossip.

Eventually, Merer asked them into the conference room, and they entered to find a long table set with folders, notepads and pencils at each place. Jugs of water and glasses were also provided. The commanders seated themselves and Merer took his place at the head of the table. He opened the meeting with, "Congratulations, gentlemen. The Airlift has passed the 100,000 sortie mark and delivered more than 700,000 tons of vitally needed supplies to the people of Berlin. In addition, we have evacuated 17,000 vulnerable Berliners. In the month of December alone, the Combined Airlift Task Force flew 141,456 tons of material into Berlin, a volume exceeded only in October of last year. Given the fact that we were grounded for the first week, that's a remarkable achievement. The final week of the month, ending at midnight on the 31st of December, saw the highest weekly tonnage flown into Berlin since the start of the Airlift."

Someone started clapping and they all broke into applause.

Merer waited for the clapping to die down before adding, "Obviously, we can't rest on our laurels. We're still trying to catch up after the disastrous month of November, but with Tegel now fully operational and still more C-54s arriving from the US almost daily, it looks as though we can sustain the Airlift almost indefinitely."

With what Robin thought was a little too much self-satisfaction, the men around the table applauded again. He was pleased when someone mentioned the weather. Merer responded by turning to the senior meteorologist at Transport Command. He drew their attention to the long-range weather maps for central Europe contained in the folders provided, summarising the content, "Temperatures are expected to be moderate, climbing above zero by the second week of January. They are forecast to stay above freezing until the end of the month, although February could see another cold spell. We expect clear skies to predominate throughout January and February, and it is not until March that we might see a return of the low cloud and poor visibility that made life so difficult last month." That was good news, Robin conceded.

The meteorologist took his seat again and Merer resumed, "Now, the main reason I've summoned you is to discuss the problem of the civilian contractors. As we all know, the RAF is operating close to peak efficiency, but the civilians are not. In fact, they are getting in our way. Their equipment serviceability —

"— and that of their pilots!" someone threw in, harvesting chuckles around the table.

"— varies wildly from day to day, playing havoc with our planning. They are fussy about cargoes and won't necessarily take what is waiting to go. Most refuse to fly during hours of darkness. In short, they are cherry-picking the best slots and freight while disrupting our operations significantly."

"Do we really need them?" A young squadron leader asked.

"Unfortunately, yes," Merer replied succinctly. "First and foremost, neither the RAF nor the USAF have tanker aircraft. This means Berlin is completely dependent on the civilian fleet for deliveries of liquid fuel. Diesel, in particular, has become the Achilles' heel of the entire effort with supplies falling dangerously short of demand. Furthermore, civilian carriers account for a quarter of the overall British contribution. Grounding the civilian fleet is not an option. Rather than eliminating them, we need to find a way to get them fully integrated into the operation so we can start using their assets to capacity."

"Nine-tenths of them were RAF in the war," Group Captain Bagshot reminded them. "If we put them back into RAF uniform and under military discipline, we'd soon sort them out. I know what *I'd* do with anyone who didn't do what he was ordered to do!" Bagshot ended bluntly, receiving nods from around the table.

Given his history of clashing with Bagshot, Robin held his tongue, but he was relieved that the station commander from Luebeck countered sharply, "Having a lot of pilots and navigators on charges in some brig is not going to improve overall Airlift performance! We'd be far better off dismissing the unreliable buggers, requisitioning their aircraft and putting service crews into the cockpits!"

Merer dispatched the suggestion by reminding them, "Since we are not technically at war with the Soviet Union, we do not have the legal authority to requisition private property."

"Have you spoken to the BEA manager, Mr Whitfield?" An exasperated voice asked. "Isn't he supposed to be in charge of the whole lot?"

"Poor Mr Whitfield has been tearing his hair out! He was told he was in charge but was given no authority to enforce his instructions. The civilians thumb their noses at him."

Robin raised his index finger and Merer acknowledged him. "I'm not sure everyone at this table is aware that the contracts under which the civilian contractors operate were drafted by civil servants from the Foreign Office." The alarmed flutter around the table confirmed his suspicions.

Bagshot, however, asked dismissively, "Is there any reason why that's at all relevant?"

Robin faced his nemesis and answered in a clipped, forceful voice, "First of all, only the Foreign Office can terminate them, which means BEA's manager is without any means of sanctioning bad behaviour. Second, the gentlemen from the Foreign Office drafted a contract that omitted minimum requirements for aircrew qualifications, did not mandate backup crews, set no minimum or maximum flying time, and did not establish guidelines — let alone minimum standards — for aircraft maintenance."

The entire table was in an uproar. Everyone seemed to be asking how this was possible and who was responsible. Yet while the others expressed their astonishment and outrage, Bagshot leaned across the table to ask Robin in a low voice, "You know all that because your wife works for one of these civilian contractors, doesn't she?"

"No, I know about the contracts because I made it my business to find out about them."

Merer called for everyone to calm down and stop chattering among themselves. "Wing Commander Priestman has put his finger on the main problem. As currently drafted, contracts neither ensure quality nor provide a mechanism to sanction bad practices."

"Can't the contracts be terminated?" Someone asked.

"Just terminating companies doesn't solve the problem," Merer reminded them. "We need to modify the contracts and before we can do that, we need to transfer responsibility from the Foreign Office to the Air Ministry. I've been assured that is finally in the works, and I called this meeting so we could jointly discuss exactly what we want the Air Ministry contracts to look like. Now," Merer stopped himself and looked around the table for something which he didn't find. "Excuse me, I need to find where my legal expert has got to." He stood and left the room.

In his absence, the discussion broke up into individual conversations around the table. Bagshot took advantage of the situation to lean across the table towards Robin again. "Just what outfit *does* your wife fly for?" Bagshot needled. "No first-rate operator would have to resort to hiring women, so it must be one of these dodgy, half-bankrupt outfits with a beaten-up Dakota and drunk first pilot."

"Emergency Air Services operates two Halifaxes and a Wellington. The senior captains are both veterans of Bomber Command, including one from 617 Squadron."

Bagshot didn't care. "AVM Bennett hired first-rate captains — only to have his senior pilot run over by a lorry on *your* airfield. Either you don't have proper control over your personnel, or you don't have proper control over your perimeter."

Robin recoiled. Because he acknowledged his overall responsibility for security at his airfield, he found it difficult to respond. He was spared an answer by the return of Merer with a frazzled-looking civilian who had gone astray. Merer called everyone to order again.

The discussion soon got into the weeds about what requirements for aircrew and aircraft should be included in the new contracts. By the time they finished, it was almost 2 pm and the participants were ready for a lunch break, but Merer did not release them. "Sorry, gentlemen, but we have one last issue to discuss. Now that the evacuation of the vulnerable Berliners has been completed, the question has been raised whether we could — and should — continue to offer passenger service to those desiring to leave Berlin."

"Oh, that must be the latest idea out of Gatow!" Bagshot sneered.

"No," Merer corrected him pointedly. "The request came from the Berlin City Council."

"What difference does that make? It's patently absurd. They'll all want to leave!"

"I doubt it," Robin observed dryly.

"We need to nip this nascent capitulation in the bud! We must make it very clear we won't allow — and certainly won't facilitate — a mass exodus of healthy Berliners. Why should we go to all the trouble of an Airlift, if they don't want our help?" Bagshot asked in exasperation.

"The last election made it quite clear that the vast majority of Berliners *do* want our help," Robin pointed out, bristling at Bagshot's provocations.

Conscious of both the impatience of the other officers and the tension between Priestman and Bagshot, Merer cut off the discussion. "The decision whether further evacuations take place or not is not ours to make. Our job is solely to consider the technical aspects. Have you assessed the feasibility of implementing these evacuations, Wing Commander?" Merer directed his question to Priestman.

"My staff and I see two main alternatives. Either we simply maintain the same schedule with the same assets that were used for the successful evacuation of the orphans, the sick and the elderly, or we increase the numbers evacuated by allowing civilians to fly at their own risk in the empty cargo holds of the larger freighters as well. That is, without seats, seatbelts, heating etc."

"Both alternatives sound feasible to me," Merer declared. "Does anyone else have any thoughts on the matter?" He looked around the table, but the other officers were more interested in lunch. Merer gave up trying to hold them back. He turned to Priestman, "If you haven't already done so, draft a memo outlining the number of evacuees that could be handled using each model and the impact on the volume of supplies delivered. I'd appreciate having it in hand by the start of business on Friday, since I'll be meeting the Secretary of State for Air later in the day and can discuss this request with him then."

"I'll leave a memo with you before I fly back later today," Robin promised. He had anticipated the request, and his staff had prepared a paper in advance.

"Excellent, then if there are no objections, I suggest we break for lunch."

To the scraping of chairs and the banter of conversation, the officers got to their feet and left the conference room. Robin trailed them. Merer's reaction to the proposal for more civilian evacuations had been better than expected, but Bagshot's comments about Utting's death undermined his sense of satisfaction. A man had died on his watch and no amount of good staff work could paper over that fact.

Greetings from the Gulag
Potsdam
Saturday 8 January 1949
(Day 197 of the Berlin Airlift)

Galyna sensed that things had changed the moment a strange young man opened the door to her mother's house.

"Who are you?" Galyna asked, unnerved. She looked past the stranger into the house, searching for her mother. All she saw was Maxim Dmitrivich coming towards her down the hallway. His bulk blocked out more and more light as he approached. When he stood over her, he announced, "Lev Ilyich will be joining us today."

"Where's my mother?"

"She's out. Busy. You're late. Let's get to business." With this, he turned and walked back down the hall. Lev Ilyich gestured for her to follow, but Galyna made a point of unwinding her long woollen scarf and taking off her hat, gloves and coat, before entering the hall. Lev Ilyich followed so closely that she felt his breath on the back of her neck. There was something creepy about him, and to avoid him touching her, she moved faster.

Entering the salon, she noticed that the samovar had not been set up, nor were plates, forks or napkins on the table. Instead, the blinds had been pulled down, cutting off the view of the lake. Rather than having tea in a gracious villa on the banks of a lake, she was in a darkened interrogation chamber.

The two men took their places flanking her. Maxim Dmitrivich sat as he always did in a heavy armchair at one end of the table, and his younger colleague sank into the chair usually occupied by her mother at the opposite end. Galyna took her place on the sofa, but she was too nervous to relax. She perched on the edge of her seat, both feet on the floor, her back straight. Lev, she noticed, was very thin and pale with a pinched face. He squinted, his sharp nose dripped, and he pressed his colourless lips together. He managed to look both nervous and aggressive at the same time.

"What have you got for us?" Ratanov opened without a prelude.

In a hurry to get this over with, Galyna hastened to report, "The most important news is that an inspector from the Special Branch of the RAF Police has arrived to investigate what is now being viewed as the murder of Captain Utting."

Ratanov grunted and dismissed her intelligence with "So what? He'll find nothing. The real issue is that this so-called 'airbridge' has been maintained for almost 200 days. It is no longer amusing. It's time you delivered something that will help us shut it down!" Gone was any trace of geniality or indulgence. Ratanov's voice was gruff and angry.

Galyna drew back a little and reminded him primly, "When you engaged me, you said it was not my job to decide what was important. You said you would be the judge of that. Well, I am telling you what I know. I can do no more."

"Really?" He leaned forward and then abruptly slapped his hand on the table, making Galyna jump. "I think you can do better than that! Comrade Stalin is furious that the Western Allies still occupy half of Berlin! They have no business here, and he wants them out yesterday! We have orders to break this airbridge, and we will." He paused and glared at her with eyes that seemed to burn right through her, before adding ominously, "It is not good when Comrade Stalin is furious."

Unconsciously, Galyna shook her head.

"Show her!" Ratanov snapped and his subordinate reached inside his jacket and removed something from his inside pocket. He held it up by one corner, dangling it in front of her face. It appeared to be a dirty envelope made of poor-quality paper to which partially unstuck stamps had been glued. Circles of red and black ink smudged the face. It was an envelope sent from somewhere deep inside the Soviet Union. Galyna frowned and glanced at Ratanov in confusion. He only stared back. She looked more closely at the envelope and recoiled. Her name was on the front of the envelope. "That's a letter for me!" She gasped out.

"Yes. It is."

"But it's been opened!" She protested.

"Of course. Do you think we'd let a prisoner communicate with the outside world without first ensuring he is not slandering the Soviet state?"

"A prisoner? You mean….? Is it from my father?" She felt an irrational flutter of hope. Maybe Mila had been wrong? If he could write to her, maybe he was still alive?

"Yes."

Galyna reached for the letter, but Lev Ilyich pulled it out of her reach. He shook his head with a mocking "Um um." His smile had the warmth of a snake.

"Not until you have given us information or performed services justifying such a reward," Ratanov explained from the other end of the table.

As soon as he said that, Galyna knew the letter was a sham, a trick. They would never give it to her because her father had not written it. But she also knew she must not give them an inkling that she knew what he was doing. She faced Ratanov and tried to sound injured and confused, "But I've told you all I know! I warned you from the beginning that I did not have access to secrets."

"Then you'd better start thinking about ways to *gain* access to them," Ratanov recommended.

"I don't know how," Galyna protested.

Ratanov slapped the table a second time. "We are not idiots! You have been stringing us along, trying to play us for fools!" Galyna felt as if the floor had just dissolved under her feet. "Either you start delivering, or your father dies — very painfully."

Then they started firing questions at her from both sides.

"Is the RAF flying into Tegel?"

"Where does Gatow get its heat?"

"What company does Mrs Priestman work for?

"How many people did you feed at your Christmas party?"

"How many people went without food so you could have your party for a few chosen children?"

"What did the Americans give the French to make them blow up the radio tower at Tempelhof?"

"How many female air traffic controllers are there at Gatow?"

"Is it true the Americans want to build a new power plant?"

"Why don't you pay your stevedores overtime?"

"How much do parents have to pay to get their children evacuated?"

"Where do the children disappear to?"

"Did a stevedore lose his hand in a loading accident last Wednesday?"

"Isn't it true all the girls flown out are put straight into brothels for British soldiers?"

"Just how many Germans have been injured while working like slaves?

The two interrogators alternated firing the questions at her, and they steadily raised their voices until they were shouting. The questions hit her like gunfire, and she tried to ward them off with rapid answers. To the most egregious allegations, she insisted, "No, it's not true!" But mostly, she just said again and again, "I don't know," while providing a harmless answer or two in between.

Abruptly, Maxim Dmitrivich flung a heavy book on the table, making such a loud noise that Galyna visibly winced. In the silence that followed, Galyna heard the grandfather clock in the hall ticking. Her hands had also started trembling, and she tried to stop them by clenching them together, but she was afraid, and they knew it. That was not a good thing.

She straightened her back and faced her stepfather.

"Now you know what our questions are. I suggest you find the answers and be ready to deliver them to me one week from today. And don't be late!"

"All right," she managed only a whisper.

"Lev Ilyich will drive you to the bus stop," he announced.

"Give me my father's letter," Galyna countered, her voice barely more than a whisper.

"Not until you deliver better information or help us sabotage this shameful mockery of our heroic armed forces!"

She hadn't expected a different answer, so she got to her feet. She felt weak, almost dizzy. To avoid stumbling, she moved with deliberate slowness, trying to convey calm. At the door, she woodenly donned her coat, hat and scarf and then went out into the cold. Lev unlocked the doors of the black Mercedes parked in the drive, and with a mocking bow, invited her into the back seat. She didn't want to get into the car, but she didn't see how she could avoid it. She slipped inside, and he slammed the door shut after her, then climbed into the driver's seat.

They did not speak as he drove along the shore of the Heilegensee, past another small villa and through a cultivated forest planted to create privacy for royalty. She knew that behind the trees stood the manor of Cecilienhof, where the Potsdam Conference had taken place. They came to the narrow canal that allowed water to flow from the Heilegensee into the larger Jungfernsee. A one-lane bridge led across the canal to a once fashionable suburb of Potsdam. The far bank was dotted with bourgeois villas, but they looked run down after years of neglect.

Lev Ilyich stopped the car at the start of the bridge and leered over the back seat at her. Sensing danger, Galyna grabbed the door handle, flung open the door and threw herself out of the car. Before she could make a dash for the bridge, however, Lev grabbed her and crushed her against the bonnet with the full weight of his body. While Galyna struggled to free herself, he grabbed her chin in a vicelike grip and lowered his mouth over hers. She clamped her teeth closed, but his tongue wandered all over the outside of her mouth, making her gag. Meanwhile, his right hand undid the lower buttons of her greatcoat, pulled up her tunic and thrust down the inside front of her skirt. He started to drag her underpants down with his thumbs while his fingers searched deeper.

Desperation made Galyna strong. She jerked her knee up as his fingertips reached her crotch. Her kneecap connected with his testicles, and he let out a bellow as he loosened his grip enough for her to duck away. She ran for her life. She had reached the other side of the bridge before she realised he wasn't following her. When she paused to catch her breath and glanced back, she saw him standing with his fly open and his penis out. "Next time, pussy! Next time!" he shouted and then pissed in her direction.

She fled, running until she was so out of breath she had to stop for a few seconds. When she tried to run again, a cramp in her side crippled her. She could only limp along, holding her ribcage. Since her underpants weren't in place, each step reminded her of that hand with the ragged, torn-off fingernails scratching her flesh and groping for the lips of her vagina. She would never be able to blot out that memory, she thought.

The quiet suburb seemed deserted. There were no parked cars. No dogs. No cats. She didn't see another living soul until she reached the wide, busy Berliner Strasse that led to the Glienicker Bridge. She left the eerily lifeless side streets behind and turned onto the busy thoroughfare where trams rang their bells, buses belched diesel-laden smoke, mothers paraded with prams, and Soviet soldiers loitered in groups.

Galyna dashed across the street so rashly that she provoked an angry protest from the tram driver, who had to brake to avoid hitting her. He shouted after her in German. She didn't care. She reached the bus stop completely out of breath and grabbed the pole to hold herself upright. An old man lectured her, shaking his index finger; a woman complained to the others in the queue. Both spoke German, but Galyna understood the woman's reference to "*imperialistische Schweine!*" (imperialist pigs.)

Fortunately, Galyna did not have to wait long for the bus. She climbed aboard and found a space at the back. At the Sector border, Soviet soldiers boarded to check passengers' papers, and she froze in terror. When they stood over her inspecting her ID and comparing the photo to her face, she felt mounting terror. What if Ratanov had sent them and they dragged her off the bus? Instead, they turned away making jokes about how ugly English women were.

After crossing into the American Sector, she felt safer, but the hour-long trip to Gatow was torture of a different kind. Not only did she feel filthy and humiliated, she struggled to understand what had just happened. She had to find an explanation on her own because she could never, ever bring herself to tell Flight Lieutenant Boyd what had happened — at least not what had happened after she got in the car. Yet it was that part that puzzled her most.

Lev Ilyich's assault had been deliberate and planned. Ratanov had brought him to the meeting and ordered him to drive her to the bus stop. Ratanov had orchestrated the incident, ensuring she was alone in the car with his 'assistant.'

But why? What did Ratanov hope to achieve by humiliating her sexually? Was he trying to remind her of how vulnerable she was each time she ventured into the Soviet Zone? But surely he knew that he risked scaring her away? Didn't he care if she never returned? He'd talked about "next time," and so had Lev Ilyich, but maybe they had already written her off?

Or did they believe that sexual humiliation would make her more pliable, docile and submissive? Had they hoped to rob her of her self-respect, so they could manipulate her more easily? Did they suspect she had been reporting back to a British intelligence officer and count on her being too ashamed to share the details of Lev Ilyich's groping? Was that the point of it all? To make her start hiding things from Boyd?

When she reached her quarters, she flung off her greatcoat, tore off the rest of her uniform and plunged into the shower without running the water to warm it first. She turned her face toward the shower head so the stream of water could wash away Lev Ilyich's slobber. When steam filled the bathroom, she took a bar of soap and worked it between her hands until she had plenty of lather. She applied it between her legs again and again. Only after she was clean did she let herself sink down in a corner of the shower. With the water raining gently down on her, she surrendered to her sobs.

She had failed. She did not dare return. She would rather die than face Lev Ilyich again, but worst of all, she had failed to deceive Ratanov. He had seen through her. Her dreams of being an agent for MI6 were dead. She had been a fool to think she could take on Soviet professionals. She was a stupid girl. She would never be a secret agent.

Chapter Nine
Dangerous Liaisons

Unwanted Children
British School, Spandau
Sunday 9 January 1949
(Day 198 of the Berlin Airlift)

Although school resumed after the holidays, the sewing lessons continued — on a weekly rather than a daily basis. Two girls had dropped out, leaving just eight in the class. Of these, the girls who hadn't finished with their overcoats continued working on them, while those like Hannah and Ulrike, who had been quick, chose new projects using material they brought themselves. The sessions were no longer so much about sewing as about getting together as a group — away from their German teachers and the other students.

Although she didn't know where this would lead, Georgina sensed it was a good thing, and Anna agreed. She had come this Sunday to discuss doing a first aid course and to talk about career opportunities as nurse's aides. When it was time for the girls to pack their things and leave, Anna clapped for attention and made her pitch. All the girls raised their hands when she asked if they'd be interested in a first aid course. She then described the situation in Berlin's hospitals based on information she had from Emily. While flying together, she and Emily had plenty of time to talk, and Emily had talked extensively about her visits to Berlin's hospitals. Anna passed on what Emily said about the acute shortage of medical personnel and the consequences this had for patients. She ended with, "So you see, there are plenty of jobs for those who want to learn about nursing, but I must warn you that the work is very hard. It's not for everyone."

"Do you see a lot of blood?" Beate asked timidly.

"You see much more pus, urine and shit," Anna answered candidly, harvesting embarrassed giggles. "Nursing isn't glamorous," she told them, "But it is a vital and rewarding profession. Helping to ease someone's pain, taking away someone's fears, and maybe saving a life now and again is a wonderful thing."

"Isn't the training very long and difficult?" Petra asked, frowning. She was not the brightest light in the class.

"To be a registered nurse takes years of training, yes, but the hospitals in Berlin are so short-staffed they are looking for aides as well as qualified nurses. The training would be on the job more than in the classroom. Rather like an apprenticeship."

"Could we apprentice with you?" Gertrud asked with a giggle.

"Oh, you wouldn't learn much from me. I'm just flying in an ambulance to keep an eye on patients. The real work is in hospitals."

"But I'd like to fly!" Gisela declared brashly. "All those pilots!"

"I'd like to fly *away*!" Dietlinde topped her, and they all laughed.

Anna ignored the implication and insisted, "I'm in contact with the Head Nurse at the Hospital am Urban. She told me she would be happy to interview any of you who want to start training. Think about it, and we can talk again next week."

The girls started to pack their things together and put on their outdoor clothes. Meanwhile, Georgina went to stand beside Silvie and asked in a low voice. "Can you stay a moment longer? I'll see you get home safely."

The mixture of alarm and hope in Silvie's eyes spoke volumes. She knew what this was about and nodded solemnly.

The other girls waved goodbye as they filed out of the room, except for Hannah. Seeing that Silvie wasn't coming, she stopped and asked, "Should I wait for you on the front steps?"

Silvie looked to Georgina, "Is that all right?"

"Yes, of course. I'll see you both get to a U-Bahn stop," Georgina agreed. Then turning to Hannah she said, "You don't have to wait outside. Wait in the front hall."

Hannah nodded, raised her hands to show she was holding her thumbs, a German way of wishing someone good luck, and then slipped out of the door.

Georgina gestured for Silvie to sit down, then she and Anna pulled up chairs and sat opposite her. Silvie looked from one to the other. "Can you help me?" she asked.

"Yes," Anna answered. "The Head Nurse from the Hospital am Urban says that in the aftermath of the Soviet rapes, many German doctors recognised that exceptional circumstances required exceptional action and agreed to perform abortions. A number of them are still willing to do so, provided they are convinced of the need. As you know, the legal situation is less clear, so no one likes to advertise or talk too loudly about these services. Nevertheless, Frau Liebherr knows of two reputable clinics that will perform an abortion, if that is what you decide."

Silvie brightened visibly, but then bit her lip and asked anxiously, "Do you know what they charge?"

"You don't need to worry about the cost, Silvie," Georgina told her. "We'll take care of that if necessary, but—"

Silvie was so relieved that she didn't let Georgina finish, interrupting to ask, "How soon can I get it over with?"

"Silvie, wait. We want you to think about an alternative," Georgina urged.

Silvie's look turned resentful as she shook her head firmly and complained, "I already told you my mother will kill me if she finds out! It's going to start showing soon, and then the GIs won't want me either. Then I'll have nothing! How can I look after a baby? I don't want a baby!"

"Wait, Silvie. Slow down. What if I told you someone else wanted your baby so much that they were willing to look after you until you give birth?"

"But I don't want to give birth! I just want it out of me!" A whine had crept into her raised voice, reminding Georgina that she was still half-child at 15.

Georgina glanced at Anna, and the nurse took over. "Silvie, an abortion isn't as simple as you seem to think. It is surgery, and even good doctors in good clinics can't guarantee that all will go well. Given the current conditions in Berlin, the risks are greater than normal. I know you said you don't want to have to give birth, but please hear me out." Silvie held her tongue but her look was sullen.

Anna continued, "Before I came out to Berlin, I spent time with my cousin, my Aunt Flora's daughter. She's sharp as a nail and went to secretarial college, where she did so well that she got hired by the Department of State, our Foreign Ministry. Her job is amazing. She types up very sensitive documents and she has a chance to meet foreign dignitaries, members of Congress and even cabinet ministers." Anna's tone betrayed just how impressed she was, but then she paused, and her voice became more sober, "but her Daddy was a cruel, worthless, drunk, who raped my aunt when she was just 13."

Silvie gasped; Anna continued. "My Aunt was just like you, Silvie. She was too young to raise a child, and she didn't have a husband or anyone to look after her and the baby. But there was a couple who couldn't have children of their own and they desperately wanted my aunt's little girl. They adopted her and they raised her like she was their own, and they helped her to become the fine, successful young woman that I met. You see what I'm saying, don't you? That the child you're carrying might be a wonderful person one day."

"Yes, but I don't know anyone who wants it!" Silvie replied. "Berlin is full of unwanted children! There are thousands of war orphans and thousands of babies born of rape that no one wants!"

Georgina reached out a hand to soothe her. "We know, Silvie, but there is a couple in England that desperately want a child, and my parents would be happy to have you come and live with them until after the birth and the adoption."

Silvie looked from Anna to Georgina stunned and asked rhetorically, "In England? What good is that? I can't leave Berlin. There's a blockade!"

"RAF Dakotas fly people out every day, and I can get your name on the passenger list. Once you reach Hanover, you cross to the civil airport and board a commercial flight to London. There my father will meet the plane and take you by train to our home."

"In England?" Silvie asked again, still unable to grasp what was being offered.

"My father is a vicar in Yorkshire, and he knows a wonderful couple who are desperate to adopt a child. He and my mother have offered to look after you until the birth in their own house, the house where I grew up, and where my own little girl is — "

"You have a child?" Silvie interrupted to ask.

"Yes, I have a ten-month-old daughter that my husband and I did not feel should be brought to Berlin the way things are here at the moment," Georgina explained. Silvie's eyes widened, and Georgina continued. "You would be with my parents until your time, and they would see that you get into a good hospital for the birth. They would handle the paperwork for putting the baby up for adoption."

"Why? Why would they do that?" Silvie gasped.

"Because I told them about you," Georgina explained softly.

Silvie frowned. "Did you tell them I was a whore?"

"No," Georgina answered steadily, "I told them you were being forced to have sex with strange men by a mother who needs the income. They would like you to get out of that situation — at least until your child is born."

"In England... Won't I be — be the enemy?"

"Silvie, I can't promise that no one will look at you that way, but I can guarantee that my parents won't."

"But how is it possible for me to go?'

"Officially, you would go as a 'nanny' to help my parents look after my little girl. That way you can get a 'nanny visa,' which is valid only as long as you remain with my parents. In exchange for looking after my daughter, you receive bed and board, but no salary. After your baby has been adopted, you would have the option to continue as my little girl's nanny or return to Berlin."

Silvie shook her head, and admitted in a dazed voice, "I just can't believe this is real."

Georgina reached out and pulled Silvie into her arms. "Yes, Silvie, it's real," she assured her as the teenager broke down in sobs.

Change of Heart
RAF Gatow
Monday 10 January 1949
(Day 199 of the Berlin Airlift)

Corporal Borisenko's salute was not perfunctory, and Robin sensed her earnestness not only in the gesture but in the polish of her shoes and buttons. She was short and plump, but she was proud of the uniform she wore and that inclined him in her favour. After returning her salute, he explained why he had sent for her. "Flying Officer Boyd brought your situation to my attention, corporal, and I wanted to speak to you personally."

"Yes, sir." She wasn't looking at him but at some point over his left shoulder.

"There's nothing to be worried about. I didn't call you in here to give you a ticking off. On the contrary, your translation work has been exemplary, and Fl/Lt Boyd says your efforts to gain intelligence these last months, while not successful, were nevertheless courageous."

Borisenko looked down and swallowed. She appeared to be flushing but she said nothing.

"Fl/Lt Boyd said your Soviet contacts hinted that they knew what game you were playing and threatened you with unpleasant consequences if you did not start to provide them with the information they requested." Borisenko was turning redder by the minute, but she made no attempt to speak. "He and I fully support your decision not to put yourself at risk again." She shifted her eyes just enough to search his face and then looked away again.

"The question is," Robin continued, "whether it wouldn't be better for you to leave Berlin altogether. I can arrange for you to be posted to one of our airfields in Bizonia, or you can return to England, whichever you prefer."

"If I may, sir?" she squeaked out.

"Please."

"I don't want to leave Berlin."

Robin lifted his eyebrows. "Why is that?"

"Well, sir. I like it here. I like the work. I feel it is important. I like being part of this operation. We are fighting back against Soviet aggression — for the first time, when you think about it. I mean, the Finns tried to stop the Soviets in the Winter War, but they lost. The only setback Stalin ever suffered came from Hitler — and then the Germans lost, too. The Airlift is a slap in his face, and I want to support it any way I can."

"You can do that from Bizonia," Robin pointed out gently.

"It wouldn't be the same."

Robin considered that answer and didn't believe her. "Corporal, your life is in danger if you fall into Soviet hands."

"I know, sir."

"So? What's the real reason you want to stay in Berlin?"

Borisenko looked down. She was flushed, and she kept swallowing.

"Do you have a relationship with someone here?" Robin put the question softly, and when she did not respond, he added, "There's nothing wrong with that, Corporal. There is nothing more natural than for a young woman to become attached to a young man. Of course, such a relationship becomes problematic if the object of your affection is a Soviet citizen."

"No, sir," Borisenko lifted her face and looked him in the eye. "I haven't fallen in love with a Soviet man, but I have forged a friendship with a Ukrainian woman. It is a very special relationship, sir — I don't mean anything dirty or unnatural!" She hastened to add, flushing more violently than ever at the mere thought of it. "It's more like finding a sister after being an orphan most of my life. If I leave Berlin, I'll never see her again."

"If the Soviet Secret Police arrest you, you'll never see her again either," Robin countered

"If I never cross over into the East again, they won't be able to."

"Can your friend come to the West?" Robin asked, astonished.

"Yes. We usually meet in Charlottenburg, near the Reichstag, but Mila said she could come to Wannsee or Kladow if I didn't feel safe anywhere else."

"A Soviet with that much freedom of movement isn't an ordinary soldier," Robin concluded.

"No, sir. She's a Hero of the Soviet Union on Marshal Sokolovsky's staff with the rank of major. She has managed to win for herself an exceptional degree of freedom — and it was through her that I found out in advance about the blockade. You remember about that, don't you?"

"Of course I remember, but you crossed the Sector border to get that intelligence."

"I know I've been a great disappointment to you, sir," Galyna told him in a voice on the brink of tears. "I know I proved too transparent and incompetent in dealing with Ratanov." Robin noticed that her hands were shaking. "But Mila is different. She is not part of the Soviet Secret Police. In her heart, she is still a simple Ukrainian peasant, the daughter of Kulaks. She doesn't want to hurt me, and she might just learn something from Sokolovsky that would be useful to us — to Gatow, to HM government or the West generally."

"And she'd tell us about it if she did?"

"Not you or Ft/Lt Boyd, no, but she'd tell me."

"Why?"

"Because she trusts me, and —" Galyna hesitated but then came out with it, "and she hates them. She saw what they did to the Kulaks, to Ukraine."

"A Hero of the Soviet Union who hates the Soviet Union?" Robin asked back sceptically.

Galyna nodded solemnly.

Robin tried to imagine it and to his surprise discovered that it wasn't difficult to imagine at all. He'd sometimes seen flickers of that kind of hate in the eyes of his counterpart at the Red Air Force base in Staaken. If he'd learned anything about the Soviets over the last year, it was that the fighting men lived in fear of the Soviet Secret Police. Their relationship with the regime was ambiguous at best. After thinking about that a moment longer, he made a decision. "Borisenko, I'm not going to judge your friend. I'm willing to let you remain at your post for the time being on the condition that you give me your word of honour that you will not set foot outside the Western Sectors of Berlin without my explicit permission."

Borisenko pulled herself smartly to attention and delivered a parade-ground salute. "Sir!" She stamped her foot as on parade and then added, formally, "I hereby swear I will not leave the Western Sectors of Berlin without your explicit permission."

"Very well, then. Carry on," he concluded, giving her a small smile of respect.

She answered with a broad smile of her own. "Thank you, sir! You won't regret it." Priestman had no way of knowing how prophetic her words would turn out to be.

Murder on the Landwehr Canal

Berlin-Kreuzberg
Monday, 10 January 1949
(Day 199 of the Berlin Airlift)

The outside temperatures had moderated from the sub-freezing range that had gripped the city at the turn of the year, but the cold had settled into the brickwork and plaster of the houses. When Christian went to brush his teeth in the morning, he found a trickle of frozen water in the bathroom sink. At least the pipes hadn't frozen, he comforted himself, as water flowed from the tap. Cold water, of course, because there was no coal to heat the water heater. Christian had long since learned to shave with cold water, and he performed this daily ritual with resignation, but he hated bathing in cold water. Instead, he had fallen into the deplorable habit of bathing only once a week. Since starting work with EAS five weeks earlier, he bathed every Sunday night to be as clean as possible at the start of each work week. He was in good company. Very few Berliners bathed much in the winter of '48-'49.

After shaving and dressing, Christian spread peanut butter on two slices of bread. The Americans made great claims for the calorie and vitamin values of this gooey food, but most Germans remained unconvinced. As a result, it was one of the last items to be sold out in the shops, and Christian had discovered that it was relatively filling.

Since the electricity wasn't on at the moment, he could not make fresh coffee. When the light came on, he would mass-produce both tea and coffee and store it in the four thermos flasks he had managed to beg, borrow or buy on the black market. He didn't like to think about the ridiculous price he'd paid for such a mundane item.

No matter. The sun was shining, and the water dripping off the gutters proved that the temperature on the roof was above freezing. Best of all, the sound of aircraft engines droning towards Tempelhof was constant. The Allies were still flying, and that meant Berlin was still free.

As usual, Christian was the first to arrive at the EAS office because he only lived two flights above. He unlocked the door and continued through the outer office where the office staff, Frl Dorsch and Frl Klempner, had their desks. He went to the office at the back of the room behind a door saying "Director." He left this door open so he could see what was happening in the anteroom and to encourage the ladies to consult him if they had questions.

As he sat down at his desk, he pulled the weekly schedule out of the wooden box where he kept important papers and checked where the ambulance was due to fly today. Moby Dick was taking three passengers with acute stomach cancer to a speciality clinic near Ulm in southern Germany and would not be back in Berlin before 1 pm. It would then take six patients with diverse conditions to Bielefeld and repeat that flight in the late afternoon for another five. A total of 14 patients would be evacuated today. That was a little less than usual, but justified because the cancer patients had been waiting almost a week while they tried to fill that Ulm flight. They could not wait any longer.

From the front office came the cheerful voice of *Fraulein* Dorsch as she called, "*Guten Morgen, Freiherr von Feldburg!*" Christian answered with "*Guten Morgen, Fraulein Dorsch!*"

Christian put aside this week's schedule and pulled the schedule for the next week onto his desk. This was only three-quarters full, and his most pressing task today was to fill in the gaps.

The telephone on his desk rang. Ah, the first 'emergency' of the day, he thought to himself and picked up the receiver. "Emergency Air Services, Feldburg speaking."

"Feldburg?" The voice on the other end of the line was familiar, but Christian could not immediately place it. It did not belong to one of the hospital directors. Before Christian had worked it out, the speaker identified himself, "Sperl here."

"Ah, *Polizei Inspector Sperl!*" Christian answered in a jesting tone. He and Sperl had gone to first names and the familiar form of address long ago, but since Christian had moved out of the family house on the Maybach Ufer, he'd seen little of the policeman. He missed the occasional trips to the *kneipe* for a drink and a good chat that they'd had while he still lived in Kreuzberg.

"Christian," despite using his first name, Sperl's tone remained ominously serious, and Christian's mood sobered even before Sperl announced, "I'm afraid I have some very bad news."

"Something to do with the apartment house?" Christian guessed.

"In a way," Sperl answered ambiguously, then he drew a deep breath and added, "Last night at roughly 11:30 pm I heard a shot followed by two more."

"Shots? Gunshots?" Christian asked, tensing all over.

"Yes, pistol shots."

"On the street in front of the house?"

"No, inside."

"You mean in the stairwell?"

"No, from upstairs."

"In Charlotte's apartment?"

"Yes."

"My God!" Christian felt a wave of guilt sweep over him. He should not have left her alone in the apartment with Fritz! Into the telephone, he asked urgently, "Is she injured?" When Sperl did not instantly reply, he gasped out, "Don't tell me she's dead!" He would never forgive himself if she was dead.

"Neither. She is in custody."

"What?"

"I ran up the stairs and knocked. When no one answered, I shot off the lock with my sidearm. I entered the apartment. It was completely dark and still. Everything seemed in place in the rooms on the street. I turned down the hall leading to the bedrooms and continued to the back. There I almost tripped over the body of Fritz von Bredow. He was gushing blood from bullet wounds in the face, neck and arm."

"Charlotte? What happened to Charlotte?" Christian demanded.

"She was standing in her nightdress, still holding a pistol in both hands and staring at what she had done. Just staring."

"It was self-defence!" Christian burst out.

"Bredow was not armed."

"What did she say?"

"Nothing."

"What do you mean nothing? She must have given you some explanation."

"No. She did not speak one word to me, to the police summoned to the scene, or during registration at the police station. She did not even respond when asked for her name and address. I provided that."

"Where is she?"

"She is being detained at the police station on Friesienstrasse 16."

"Can I visit her?"

"You can try. It's no longer in my hands. A state prosecutor will be assigned, probably today."

"But there is no question that Fritz von Bredow is dead?"

"He was shot in the forehead. The bullet blew off the back of his head. The neck wound would have been fatal, too, just not as quickly. In any case, he was very dead before I arrived." He paused and then added, "Christian, I'm very sorry. I hate being the bearer of such shocking news."

"Thank you for calling me, Anton. I prefer to hear this from you than the public prosecutor."

"You are her next of kin, aren't you?"

"Alive and in Berlin, yes. All her immediate family are dead."

"Good. That's what I told the police at the station. That means you should be able to visit. Regarding the apartment, we removed the corpse but otherwise, the crime scene was left intact, and the apartment has been sealed. You will not have access to it until the prosecutor releases it."

"I understand."

"And Christian, one more thing."

"Yes?"

"She's going to need a top-notch lawyer. Bredow was handicapped, unarmed and wearing only his pyjamas. The bedclothes were all twisted about and half off the bed, but there was nothing to suggest he'd attacked her with an improvised club or something of that kind."

"I understand."

"That's all I can tell you for now. Again, don't hesitate to get in touch with me."

"I won't. Thank you, Anton." They hung up.

Christian sat staring at his desk. Despite Fritz von Bredow's despicable treatment of her, Charlotte had consistently defended him, taken his side in arguments, and waited on him hand and foot. Her continued failure to recognize that David Goldman was the better man had angered him. Yes, he'd used layman's pseudo-psychoanalysis to try to explain her behaviour to David, but he knew he was no psychiatrist. Deep down he had always believed Charlotte would wake up to Fritz's transformed character and realise he didn't deserve her. Never in his wildest dreams had he imagined she might kill him. The only possible explanation was that Fritz had pushed her too far in some way. In which case, Fritz had got what he deserved.

Christian stopped himself. What had he just thought? That a man deserved to be killed because of his attitude or the things he said? That was immoral. He shuddered. Fritz wasn't the only one who had been brutalised by the Nazis and the war. Christian mentally held up a mirror and admitted to himself that he had killed good men simply because they wore a different uniform. Germany was now trying to restore the rule of law, and surely the first law ought to be: Thou shalt not kill.

Yet, his sympathy was with Charlotte. She was so battered and broken. Maybe she shouldn't have killed Fritz, but she must have been driven over the edge. She had been out of her mind. Wasn't 'temporary insanity' a legal term used to describe human behaviour triggered by exceptional circumstances? Charlotte had surely been temporarily insane. They had to convince the court of that. He had to talk to her, hear her side of the story. And he needed to find a good lawyer. The best.

Christian already knew who that was. Philip's widow Alix was an outstanding lawyer. In fact, she'd been recommended to serve as a judge in the new German state that was currently being hammered out at a constitutional convention. Christian was confident Alix would not leave Charlotte in the lurch.

He looked at the phone, unsure if he should call Alix or go to see Charlotte first. Instead, the phone started ringing, reminding him that he had a job and work to do. Damn! He reached for the phone, "Feldburg. Emergency Air Services."

It was one of the hospitals. Although his mind was only partially focused on the conversation, he recorded the request for evacuation, jotting the details in his pre-prepared form and, with a glance at the schedule, allocated a slot. "Thursday midday might be possible, but I'll have my secretary confirm later." He hung up and stared at his desk. He couldn't do his job today. He had to visit Charlotte and get in touch with Alix. Raising his voice, he called Fraulein Dorsch into the office and told her she was going to have to man the phones and take requests while he conducted urgent business. Then he wrapped himself in his greatcoat and scarf and set off to the police station on Friesienstrasse 16.

Chapter Ten
Friends in Need and Deed

The Call
Devon, England
Tuesday 11 January 1949
(Day 200 of the Berlin Airlift)

The snow flurries started when David was still half an hour from the cottage and within minutes they turned into thick flakes of wet snow. At first, Sammy's tail wagged happily as he chased after the flakes, jumping up and trying to catch them in his mouth. After a few minutes, however, the snow started to cling to his fur and turn the winter heath into a morass. With the sun shrouded in heavy clouds, the light drained rapidly from what was left of the day. A wind sprang up, and both David and Sammy started to feel the cold and wet. Sammy's tail drooped and he lowered his nose as they plodded home together across the moors. David was relieved when he saw warm, yellow light reaching out to them from beneath the thatch of Mr Bowles' cottage.

Inside the back door, David shook the snow off his tweed cap and hung it on a wooden peg. Sammy tried to shake caked snow off his back, but it was too heavy. David dropped to his heels to wrap a heavy towel around the dog and rubbed him vigorously. Wiggling his whole body in appreciation, Sammy gave David quick kisses with his tongue to express his thanks. David pulled the dog into his arms and buried his face in the still-wet fur. For a moment, man and dog were alone in the world and completely happy.

The door to the kitchen cracked open, and George Bowles peered out into the hall. The smell of shepherd's pie baking in the oven escaped through the open door. That meant Mrs Holden was here. She claimed the cottage's old, wood-fired range worked better than her modern gas oven, but David thought she liked spoiling Mr Bowles with fresh-baked pies.

"AH!" George exclaimed. "I thought I'd heard something. Do you need another towel for Sammy?"

"No thanks, just let him into the kitchen to warm up," David answered getting to his feet and brushing dirty snow off his wet knees.

George opened the kitchen door wider to allow Sammy to dash inside. David heard Mrs Holden greet Sammy cheerfully but then order him to calm down and go to his bed. "You'll get your share soon enough!" she promised firmly.

"Emily rang," George announced as David leaned against the wall to pull his boots off. "She said it was urgent and asked you to ring back."

"Right," David answered, slipping his cold feet into the waiting slippers. In his mind, he ran through a variety of crises from crashes and engine failures to ground crew strikes and drunken aircrew. Or had there been some political development that ended the Airlift overnight? Whatever it was, he felt a surge of energy, that spark of excitement that came with a challenge. Maybe it was time to go back to work — at least here in the UK. "I'll ring her straight away," he promised.

"Don't be long. Dinner's almost ready," George urged as he disappeared back inside the kitchen.

David went to the front of the house where a telephone had been ensconced with great reverence on an old sideboard. It had been installed only months before and was still viewed as a novelty and a luxury by George. In the older man's rough handwriting, a number had been scrawled on a notepad. David put a call through to the international operator and requested a connection to the number provided. When he finally got through, Jasha answered, but anxiously told him to wait. Shortly afterwards Emily's voice came across the distance, "David? Is that you?"

"Yes. What's happened? Has there been a crash?"

"No. The company is fine. All aircraft are operational. Kiwi and Jan are flying Moby Dick today. I took the day off to try to help Christian —"

"I thought he was doing an outstanding job?"

"This isn't about the company, David. It's a personal problem."

David waited a moment for her to continue and when she didn't he nudged her by speculating, "Is his wife making difficulties?"

"No. It's much more serious than that." She paused again but this time David didn't try to rush her. He waited until she came out with: "Charlotte has been arrested."

"Arrested? Why? What has she been accused of?" David couldn't imagine Charlotte getting involved in any kind of criminal activity. It was probably just a misunderstanding or an innocent mistake. Maybe she'd bought an item that turned out to be stolen or had done something equally harmless.

He was still thinking along these lines when Emily's voice came across the telephone wires saying into his ear: "Murder."

David thought he'd misheard. "What did you just say?"

"She's been detained for the murder of Fritz von Bredow."

Emily's tone told him this was no joke, but he presumed she was being melodramatic or exaggerating. "Has Bredow gone missing or something?"

"No. His body has been found and has undergone a complete autopsy."

"Why do they think Charlotte had anything to do with it?"

"Because police inspector Sperl found her holding the murder weapon in her hands when he broke into the apartment after hearing three shots. The police report says that three shots were fired by the same weapon all in the same direction, eliminating the possibility that Bredow shot first and she then wrested the weapon from him to return fire."

David could hardly find his breath to ask, "Where? When? Why? Why did she want to kill him?"

"The incident occurred on the night of the 12-13 of January, shortly before midnight. She was in her apartment on the Maybach Ufer. In her bedroom to be precise. As to why she did it, I don't know. She has not spoken a word to anyone since she was found. Sperl provided the police with her details and vouched for Christian as her next of kin. Christian was able to visit her in detention. He found her curled up on the bed in the foetal position with her back to the room. When he tried to touch her, she flinched and pulled away as though he'd burnt her. He pleaded with her to talk to him, but she shook her head, closed her eyes firmly and covered her head with her arms."

"I still can't quite grasp what you're saying. Charlotte *shot* Bredow? Intentionally?"

"The preliminary police investigation, which they shared with Christian, suggested that her first shot grazed Bredow's arm, the second found his neck and the third bullet penetrated his skull between the eyes. It blew off the back of his head. Christian was allowed to see the corpse. There is no question about how he died, and there can be no doubt it was intentional. Accidental shots aren't that accurate." Emily was right, David admitted to himself, as she concluded with the words, "Charlotte aimed to kill."

Still, David was stunned. He could not picture Charlotte with a gun in her hand — much less aiming it at someone with the intent to kill. The Charlotte of his memories and dreams was timid and gentle and in need of protection, not a cold-blooded murderer. First, he'd discovered that her apparent affection for him had been an illusion. Now, it appeared, her entire personality had been a façade.

"David," Emily was still on the other end of the line. "Sperl warned us she'll need a first-rate lawyer."

"I can imagine," he paused and then asked cynically, "Do you want me to pay for one?"

"No, that won't be necessary," Emily assured him. "Christian's sister-in-law has spent the last three years working for the prosecution at the Nuremberg War Crimes trials—"

"Charlotte needs a first-rate *defence* attorney, not a prosecutor," David pointed out dryly.

"*Freifrau* von Feldburg's name has been put forward as a judge in the German judiciary, which will be established after a new German constitution has been approved. We can assume she is an outstanding legal expert."

That wasn't the same thing as being an effective barrister for the defence, David thought. He inherently mistrusted appointments made because of family connections rather than objective qualifications, but before he could argue Emily continued, "She agreed to help immediately, and she is not asking for any compensation. She's getting herself to the airfield at Bielefield next Monday, and I'll fly her to Berlin in Moby Dick. She did have one request, however, and that is the reason I'm calling."

David tensed. What could a woman he'd never met want from him?

"She doesn't want to live in the apartment house on Maybach Ufer because it's where her husband killed himself — and where Charlotte has now also killed her fiancé. Christian wondered if you'd mind her moving into your house on Schwanenwerder."

"Of course not." That was such an insignificant request in the face of this crisis, that David hardly thought it needed to be raised. "Christian has the keys. Tell him she is welcome to use whatever rooms she likes. According to Christian, half the furniture belongs to her anyway."

"Thank you, David. Then, I suppose, that's all."

Except it wasn't. David knew it and Emily knew it too. "Emily?"

"Yes?" She sounded hopeful but did not press him.

"I need a little time to think. I'll call you back."

"I'll be waiting."

They hung up, and David stood in the hall trying to collect his thoughts. A light went on in the hallway behind him. "David? We're ready to sit down," George told him respectfully, worried about interrupting something important.

David made his way to the kitchen. The table was laid for three, and George sat down while Mrs Holden wrestled with removing a large pie from the oven. David washed his hands hastily at the sink and then joined them at the table.

"Not bad news, I hope?" Mrs Holden asked as she set a steaming crock filled with perfectly browned shepherd's pie in front of him.

David shook his head, in his imagination, he told her: 'Oh, nothing serious. Only the woman I was desperately in love with has just shot a man between the eyes." But he didn't say that out loud, so George and Mrs Holden continued looking at him expectantly. He drew a breath and decided on, "One of my former employees...is in trouble. I may have to return to Berlin."

"Oh, that's a pity," Mrs Holden exclaimed with apparent sincerity. "We've enjoyed having you — and Sammy —" she tossed the dog a smile.

George, however, was frowning slightly with concentration and nodded more earnestly as he said, "Yes, I think you need to get back to work, David. Young men have to have a purpose in life." Their eyes met, and David felt a wave of affection for this simple, barely literate man who nevertheless understood him so well — and loved him just the way he was.

After dinner, he said he needed to be alone for a bit and went up to his bedroom. This had been the boyhood room of his dead friend Ginger. With the door closed and the light off, he sat on the narrow bed and looked out of the dormer. The moors were smothered in fresh snow, but the clouds were already tearing apart and here and there sharp, intense stars blinked at him knowingly. David drew the chilly air into his lungs and waited for his thoughts to sort themselves out.

Charlotte had killed Fritz von Bredow with a remarkably accurate shot. That was not the act of a hysterical or frightened woman. It was a deliberate and rational act performed by a steady hand and unwavering will. In short, Charlotte had killed Fritz von Bredow because she wanted to. That fact proved that — at least at the moment when she killed him — she had not loved him. The question was: had she ever loved him? As a young girl in a different Germany, probably. But what about last year, when he had been falling in love with her? And what about last November when Fritz returned? And what about the day she had told him they could not have a future together?

David reviewed his memories again, searching once more for clues to her feelings. What if he had been wrong and Christian and Emily had been right? What if Charlotte had not rejected him because she did not love him or because she loved Fritz more but for some other reason? What might have induced her to choose Fritz, if she did not love him? Could it have been a warped sense of duty, perhaps? Or pity? Or had it been a feeling of worthlessness and shame, as Christian had suggested?

David returned mentally to the discussion he had had with Christian. Christian had told him Charlotte had been raped by six Russian soldiers, and he had not been able to believe it. No, he corrected himself. He had *refused* to believe it because he couldn't *bear* to picture it. Not Charlotte! Not his delicate, fragile, sensitive Charlotte brutally humiliated and abused!

But she wasn't as delicate or fragile as he'd thought. Otherwise, she wouldn't have been able to survive the rapes, start a new life — and put a bullet between Fritz von Bredow's eyes.

And that was the crux of the matter. He had misjudged her.

Charlotte was not made of sugar. She was the daughter of a Prussian junker. She might have been battered and bent, but deep inside there was steel. And she had found it again.

David stood up so suddenly that he set the paper aeroplanes of the mobile over the bed in motion. "I have to go to her, Ginger," he said into the darkness.

Just as he slipped out the door, he heard Ginger speak for the first time in years. His friend called out after him in a cheerful, youthful voice, "Good luck!"

Prosecutor for the Defence
Berlin
Monday 17 January 1949
(Day 206 of the Berlin Airlift)

Alexandra *Freifrau* von Feldburg, known to friends and family as Alix, was late for the rendezvous in Bielefield. It had been easy to wrap up her work in Nuremberg because the trials were winding down anyway. Of the twelve secondary trials, only the Ministries Trial was still going on, and her area of expertise had been the judiciary and the military, trials that had ended in December 1947 and the previous October respectively. She'd given notice at that time but had been retained on an ad hoc basis because the process of re-establishing a sovereign German state was incomplete, preventing her anticipated appointment to the restructured German judiciary. Her request to leave so that she could represent a defendant in a criminal case in Berlin was granted instantly with best wishes from her colleagues.

For the last three years, she had lived frugally in a one-room, furnished apartment in Nuremberg. She had no difficulty packing her personal possessions into two suitcases and a rucksack. Then she set off by train. The trip proved arduous due to many changes and because of waits of up to seven hours between connections along the way. It took her two full days to reach Essen, where she had spent a night in a hotel so she could bathe and sleep before the final leg of the journey. The train from Essen to Bielefield, however, had been delayed two hours due to work on the tracks. Then she had difficulty finding a taxi to take her to the airport.

She was relieved to see that a white aircraft with red crosses identifying it as an ambulance was still waiting on the tarmac when the taxi finally reached the airfield. Leaving the taxi driver to unload her luggage, she rushed inside the little terminal to find Christian's colleagues. Her entrance attracted the attention of a man and a woman in smart black uniforms with red trim. They stood as Alix approached them with an outstretched hand. "Are you from Air Ambulance International? I'm Alexandra von Feldburg."

They smiled and shook her hand, introducing themselves as "Emily Priestman" and "David Goldman."

"I'm sorry I'm late. They were doing work on the rails, and the train was held up."

"We're glad you made it. We were just about to give up," Mrs Priestman admitted. "We have two more flights today and couldn't afford to delay our departure much longer, but all's well that ends well. Do you have much luggage?"

"Just those things over there," Alix pointed.

"I'll see they get on the aircraft," David offered, telling Emily to help their passenger board the aircraft.

The next thing Alix knew she was going up a metal ladder into the small white aircraft. Although she'd been warned she would be flown to Berlin in an air ambulance, she had unthinkingly dressed for a business trip. This meant she wore a hat, gloves, a tailored suit with a skirt to mid-calf, and high-heeled shoes. She felt ridiculous as she precariously mounted the ladder and scrambled into the cockpit in her tight skirt where, to her embarrassment, three people were already waiting. They were introduced as "Rick" and "Jan," both clearly Americans and in flying kit, and a black woman in a smart white nurse's uniform called "Anna." Most surprising, however, was a dog, introduced to her as Sammy.

She was told to follow Anna into the sick bay, where Anna pointed to a fold-down seat facing aft. On this perch, she was flanked by three bunk beds on either side of the fuselage and just a yard beyond her feet yawned a huge trap door. Suddenly, her suitcases and backpack flew through those doors to land in the sickbay, followed by David, who nimbly hauled himself inside. Anna at once called forward to the cockpit, "Close bomb bay doors!"

It wasn't until that moment that Alix realised she was in a converted bomber, a thought that made her almost queasy. Fortunately, she didn't have time to ruminate on her feelings because Anna was pointing out the seatbelt hanging down from her bucket seat and telling her to strap in. Anna went aft to sit down in a similar seat facing forward.

Alix found the take-off terrifying and was starting to feel queasy, but fortunately, David invited her into the cockpit. She was astonished to discover the two women were at the controls, while David, Rick and the dog appeared to be only passengers. David drew her attention to the spectacular view outside the cockpit and identified the landmarks they were flying over. Less than an hour later, they banked hard into a right-hand turn, and David explained they had entered the northern corridor to Berlin.

Spread out before her was the astonishing sight of aircraft flying nose-to-tail in independent yet well-regulated streams. A flock of eight two-engine aircraft at one height followed a gaggle of six four-engine aircraft at another, and behind them came nine even larger machines higher than either. The air ambulance flew at the lowest altitude, and they had a spectacular view of the countryside passing below them. No one had to tell her when they crossed from British into Soviet airspace. Suddenly, the cars vanished from the roads, replaced by only occasional horse-drawn carts. All evidence of reconstruction ended. Houses were not scaffolded for repairs, and no concrete mixers clustered around cleared plots ready to create a new factory or office building. The contrast brought home how much the Western Zones were booming these days. Looking down at the Soviet Zone was like going back in time.

That feeling was reinforced as they approached Berlin. Alix had lived through Bomber Harris' 'Battle of Berlin' — on the ground. For the second half of 1944, when she was on the run from the Gestapo after the failed coup attempt of 20 July, she had spent much of her time hiding in closets and behind false walls, cowering in cupboards and lying under beds sometimes for hours. She was wanted for treason and had been given refuge by courageous men and women who allowed her to hide in their apartments, sometimes for only a few days, sometimes for a couple of weeks. Yet she had to keep moving, and without being registered at any residence, she could not appear in the air raid shelter without arousing suspicion. Staying above ground during air raids, on the other hand, became so dangerous that she decided to leave Berlin. She went first to a pig farm near Dessau, where she had disguised herself as a slave labourer for almost four months. From there, she made her way to Braunschweig where she had been able to turn herself over to American troops in the closing days of the war.

Her last memories of Berlin were of a city in flames. She had intentionally planned her escape from the city during an air raid because the raid disrupted normal traffic patterns and distracted the attention of the authorities. She had hidden herself aboard a supply train bound for the Western Front. The Allies targeted railheads, and the *Reichsbahn* did not want their precious cargo of munitions to be found by the RAF bombers. So, the train had crawled out of the city at a pace intended to be too slow for detection from the air. That had enabled her to climb aboard unseen — and prolonged the agony of uncertainty as the bombs rained down.

Yet for all the destruction she had witnessed on the ground, she was not prepared for the carpet of destruction spread out before her as they flew toward the city centre. Before they had reached the worst-hit areas, however, they banked to the right and started to follow the Havel. David shouted above the engines that it was time for her to return to her seat and put her seatbelt on. Alix obeyed in a daze. When she'd agreed to defend Charlotte, she had underestimated how traumatic a return to Berlin would be.

Now she found herself wondering if she could cope. She had told Christian from the start that she would not set foot in the apartment house where she had lived with Philip and where he had killed himself. Christian had arranged for her to live somewhere else. But if she was in Berlin, didn't she have an obligation to find out what had happened to her parent's home? Both her parents were dead; her mother had died of heart failure while working in a munitions factory early in 1945, and her father had been shot for desertion during the assault on Berlin. However, her sister Grete was living with relatives in Marburg and her brother Rudi had returned from Soviet imprisonment without his legs; he was in a rehabilitation centre near Kassel. They might want to live in the family home in the future or they might want to sell or rent it — if it was still standing. To find out if it had survived, she would have to visit her childhood neighbourhood and face the memories....

And then there was the Bendlerblock where she had worked so many long, hard and yet rewarding hours. There she had met and forged friendships with the most determined and unwavering opponents of Hitler's criminal regime — *Generaloberst* Beck, General Olbricht, General von Treschow — and

Philip. Someone said there was a small memorial in the courtyard, marking where Olbricht, Stauffenberg and the others had been executed. She felt she ought to lay a wreath or at least a rose on that spot — yet dreaded the thought of treading the cobbles where such honourable men had been shot without trial. How could she stand where their blood had flowed, cooled and then been scrubbed away by some indignant and ardent supporter of Hitler?

Or what if she had business with subsidiary organs of the Allied Control Council and had to visit the building where the so-called "People's Court" had held kangaroo trials of those involved in the coup attempt? Where Roland Freisler and his fellow Nationalist Socialist 'judges' and lawyers had taunted, ridiculed and condemned her beloved Uncle Erich and so many others because they wanted to restore the rule of law and protect human dignity and rights?

As the tyres squealed under her feet at landing, Alix had a moment of panic. She didn't want to be here!

But here she was. The air ambulance was slowing down, turning, waddling slightly. They came to a halt and the terrible howling of the engines died away. Anna smiled at her as she undid her seatbelt and stood up. David returned to the sick bay as the bomb bay doors swung open. While Anna gestured for Alix to go to the cockpit and down the metal stairs, David jumped down onto the tarmac and dragged her suitcases out after him.

Her feet had hardly hit the concrete before Christian wrapped her in his arms. "Thank you for coming, Alix!" She hugged him back and drew strength from the intensity of his gratitude. He pulled back a little and searched her face. "Are you all right?"

"I don't know yet," she admitted.

Christian's charm was undiminished, and he warmed her with a flattering and encouraging. "You look more than all right! Did I ever tell you that if Philip—"

"A hundred times, Christian!" It was an old joke. Philip had feared she would fall for his more glamorous younger brother, but she had never felt the same attraction for him. She appreciated Christian as a brother, but she did not want him as a lover — and Christian knew it. Teasing her was just his way of saying that he still thought she was attractive.

Christian pointed toward a cart drawn by two horses and driven by a coachman with a proper top hat, cape and a Kaiser Wilhelm moustache. "That," Christian announced, "is Horst, Grandfather Walmsdorf's coachman. He's been helping haul cargoes from Gatow to Kladow for transhipment, but he's agreed to take us to David's home on Schwanenwerder, where you will be quartered."

Only then did Alix make the connection between the man who had met her at Bielefeld and the owner of the house where she was to be staying. Alix turned to David. "Mr Goldman! I'm sorry! I didn't realise who you were before!"

"No reason why you should, *Freifrau* von Feldburg. I hope you don't mind that we will be sharing the house. And I hope you don't mind dogs." He indicated Sammy.

"I'm much happier not to be alone! And please call me Alix."

David smiled at that and reciprocated with "Gladly. Shall we go? The patients are waiting to board," David indicated two land ambulances standing off to one side. Anna had already gone over to consult with the orderlies accompanying them.

Christian and David loaded Alix's luggage on the back of the wagon, and then Alix was given a hand up onto the seat. The coachman bundled her in blankets, one for her feet, one over her lap and one over her shoulders. He sat on one side of her and Christian on the other. David rode in the back with the luggage and his dog. They set off at a brisk trot and wound their way up the west shore of the Havel across the bridge on the Heerstrasse and then back down the east shore. Except for passing through the suburbs of Pichelsdorf and Wilhelmstadt, the trip was a bucolic "coach" ride through a wintry landscape complete with a forest and a partially frozen lake. Perhaps because of Horst's presence, or the cold, they said very little during the long trip.

Finally, they reached the Schwanenwerder peninsula and stopped before a beautiful house in an overgrown garden. The front door was boarded up, but David led them around to the back where he unlocked a door almost hidden behind a trellis with vines. From here, he led them through the house back up to the main rooms. These were so cold that they could see their breath, but David spread his arms and remarked, "Welcome!" His gesture took in not only the semi-circular room with four French windows offering splendid views of the Havel but the rest of the house as well.

Alix's gaze was first drawn to the lake, but when she turned to look at the room she gasped. Hanging over a sideboard at the back of the room was a large oil painting. It had a bad tear in the centre which had been provisionally repaired. "Max Lieberman's painting!"

Christian had told her about finding this painting in the house of a suspicious character and together they had pieced together his identity: the Nazi scientist, Franz von Aggstein. The Berlin police suspected him of manufacturing and dealing in illegal drugs and had tried to arrest him, but he had escaped. That was how David came into possession of this property once owned by his uncle. After lovingly considering the precious image of her husband, Alix turned around and realised that half the furniture in the room had once been in their apartment on the Maybach Ufer. That was unsettling, but she decided she was glad something had survived.

Christian was in a more practical mood. "Are there any rooms we can heat in this house?"

"Of course," David answered. "I propose that Horst moves into the housekeeper's flat and keeps the horses in the stables so he can act as Alix's dedicated transport. Otherwise, she'll have a terrible time getting to the police station and courthouse. I can compensate him for lost income from the Airlift, and I'll ensure that he has hay and feed for the horses. We can bring enough in on one return flight to keep them happy for months."

"Horst will be delighted. He's quite devoted to Charlotte and has already asked me several times how he can help."

"Good. You, Christian, can spend tonight here, but in the future I want you to remain in the apartment on the Kurfuerstendamm and run the business."

Christian nodded in agreement, "That's exactly what I planned."

"I propose housing you, Alix, in the master bedroom suite one flight up. It has a bathroom, sitting room and bedroom, all in a compact space. It also has tile ovens in both the bedroom and sitting room and a water heater in the bathroom. We'll get them all working, and I'll see that we have enough coal to run them. You'll need a warm place to work, so the oven in the sitting room will take priority. I'll sleep in one of the other rooms, and we'll take our meals with Horst in the housekeeper's flat."

"That sounds very generous, David," Alix told him.

Christian was more practical. "We'd better get to work. It will be dark in a couple of hours. I'll go and inform Horst of the arrangements so he can see to the horses while you take Alix up to her rooms so she can unpack and settle in. Then we need to start heating the ovens, find some candles or oil lamps and make a supper of some kind."

It wasn't until she retired to bed that evening that Alix had time to contemplate her fate. They hadn't bothered to heat her suite this evening, and the room was bitterly cold. Fortunately, the bed had a heavy eiderdown and a thick bedspread. As soon as she crawled under the covers, she started to warm up. She was too wound up to sleep, however, so she sat with her back against the headboard and tried to take stock of things.

The room itself, although exquisitely furnished, felt sterile and deserted. A layer of dust covered everything and there was nothing even remotely personal here. She might as well have been in a hotel -- which was perhaps best. Charlotte might be Philip's cousin, but Alix had never met her. To Alix, she was a client — nothing more or less. There was no reason, Alix told herself, that this case should be more personal or emotional than the work she had done these past three years. Alix had been keen to see Nazi war criminals brought to justice, but she had known none of the defendants personally and had been able to retain a degree of professional distance and objectivity. It had served her well.

Yet this *was* different. Downstairs was the secretaire at which Philip had so often sat to write letters. In her imagination, she opened the little drawers on the right-hand side where he had kept his pens, pencils and rubbers and found them all just as he had left them. But that was silly, the Gestapo or the Soviets or Herr von Aggstein would have used or discarded them long ago.

But she *could* move the secretaire into this room where she would be working most of the time. If she did, it would be like having Philip close to her — something she had avoided for almost four years.

On the night of 20 July, Philip had persuaded her to flee — head over heels only moments after Renate Moldenauer knocked on the door and offered to find them refuge. She had been given no time to think or feel. Philip had insisted she go, and Renate had rushed her away. For nine months she had lived one step ahead of the Gestapo, constantly at risk of discovery, unremittingly aware of the fact that her mere presence put the lives of those helping her at risk. She had spent many hours alone and in silence, and yet she had not had a moment to think, much less grieve because she was constantly listening for the arrival of a car in the street below, an unexpected footfall in the hall, or an ominous knock on the door.

She had told herself there would be time to think and grieve when the war was over. Yet the moment she walked into the American headquarters in Braunschweig, she'd been pulled into a new vortex. All she had asked about was how she might get to Altdorf to start tracking down her family, but the American captain asked where she'd learned to speak such fluent English. When she said she'd gone to school in America for five years, he'd hired her as a translator on the spot.

Days later they discovered she'd worked as a secretary and overnight she was put to work in the office responsible for denazification, which at that time was mostly just trying to figure out who was a likely war criminal, who was an 'ordinary' Nazi sympathiser, and who might be trustworthy. She'd been there almost a month doing routine typing and translating before an officer familiar with Germany arrived. He recognised her name, knew Philip had been a key member of the conspiracy, and rapidly uncovered the fact that she'd been wanted by the Gestapo for working closely with leading members of the Resistance on the German General Staff. When two days later he discovered she also had a law degree, he put her on a train to Nuremberg.

It had been difficult to get away from that work even to see her mother-in-law, track down her son, who had been put out for adoption with an SS family, or find her sister Greta. The job always came first because it was important, demanding, and an essential source of income. It also kept her from remembering or feeling. It was easier to leave Greta with her aunt and uncle, easier to let her son grow up with his grandmother in Altdorf, easier to get lost in her 'important' work than to face the fact that she was a widow and that Philip was gone forever.

But tonight, as had happened only at irregular intervals over the last four years, she broke down. Tonight, it did not matter that she had weathered the shipwreck of Germany remarkably well. It did not matter that she had excellent prospects, an adoring son, a loving mother-in-law and a steady friend in Christian. It did not matter that she would soon be able to integrate her son into her life and finally be a mother to him. Tonight, none of that mattered because tonight she felt too acutely what she had lost. The light of Philip's intellect, the warmth of his compassion, the excitement of his energy, and the comfort of his love had been taken from her, his son and the whole world. Nothing could ever bring him back. Surrounded by loneliness, she cried herself to sleep.

Mind of a Murderer
Berlin-Tempelhof
Tuesday 18 January 1949
(Day 207 of the Berlin Airlift)

Charlotte pushed the plate of prison food away. The stale bread and the bowl of room-temperature, powdered potato soup were unappetizing, making it easy to resist. She was determined not to eat. If only she could find the strength to refuse water as well, she could end it all sooner. Unfortunately, thirst overpowered her. She'd tried not to drink, but always she broke down and gulped the tap water eventually.

That was the problem. She was too weak. All she'd had to do was put the pistol to her temple and pull the trigger one last time. Despite wasting the first bullet, there had still been two left. Why hadn't she been able to lift her arm? Why had she just stood there and stared?

She didn't understand it. The first shot had missed because she was out of practice. It had taken two shots to get a feel for the gun. It was Soviet. Christian had bought it on the black market and given it to her long ago, but she'd never used it. She hadn't been prepared for the recoil. The second shot was better, but it wasn't until the third that she found the mark.

But how could she fail to lift her hand one last time and finish it? The whole point had been to put an end to everything. Well, and to take the smug, leering smile off Fritz's face. But that had been secondary. The most important thing was to escape.

Instead, she was still here. She opened her eyes to stare at the wall of her cell just to verify she was still here. Then she closed her eyes again.

Behind her there was noise. Footsteps, the key in the door, the creaking of the hinges. She didn't move or open her eyes. They had just come to take away her tray. "Still not eating?" the female warden asked indifferently.

Charlotte shook her head.

"She hasn't eaten since she arrived a week ago. The doctor says if she keeps it up one more week, he'll order forced feeding," the warden said. Charlotte wondered vaguely why the warden was using the third person, but didn't care. "When you want to leave, ring that bell. I'll come let you out."

Charlotte lifted her head slightly. She could leave whenever she wanted just by ringing the bell?

No, there was another person in the cell. An unfamiliar female voice said, "Thank you, I will."

The door clanged shut, and Charlotte waited tensely for what would happen next.

"Graefin Walmsdorf? Or should I call you 'Charlotte'? We've never met, but I'm your cousin by marriage. Philip's wife — widow."

Charlotte turned just enough to look over her shoulder. An attractive young woman in a smart suit and a silk scarf stood inside the door. She had short blond hair, and she wore earrings and lipstick. She looked very chic, very self-possessed and outrageously successful. As she had every right to look, Charlotte thought enviously.

"Christian has engaged me as your defence attorney," Alix explained. When Charlotte said nothing, she asked, "May I sit down?"

Charlotte rolled over to point towards the only chair in the cell, a small wooden chair with a straight back.

Alix sat down with her handbag on her knees and opened it. She removed a letter and held it in Charlotte's direction. Charlotte stared at it trying to see who it was from. "From your Grandmother Walmsdorf," Alix told her.

Charlotte swung her legs down off the bed and sat up to take the letter and open it. Her grandmother appeared to have scribbled the note in a hurry, making her handwriting hardly legible. She assumed "This is all some kind of terrible mistake." She mentioned that "Christian told me that Philip's wife will be representing you," and concluded that "I'm sure she will soon set everything straight." She closed the letter by saying Charlotte should find a way to visit her in England "as soon as the Blockade ends."

None of this was helpful or comforting. First, there seemed to be little chance of the Blockade ending except in Soviet slavery. Second, Alix could not "straighten things out" when there was no confusion. Finally, the invitation appeared to be based on the assumption that Charlotte was innocent, which she was not. How would her grandmother react when she found out the truth? Charlotte did not believe she would welcome a murderer into her house. She folded the letter, put it back in its envelope, and laid it on the bed beside her, already dismissed and forgotten.

Alix considered her from the chair solemnly. "It would be best if you told me what happened, Charlotte. If you're charged with murder, you will be facing the death penalty, and I can't begin to build a defence unless I know what provoked you and why you reacted the way you did."

Charlotte looked down at her hands and broke her silence at last. "I don't want a defence. I *want* to die."

"Why?" Alix asked without a trace of shock or outrage.

Charlotte shrugged. "Because I hate myself."

"Why?"

"I'm weak and disgusting."

"There is nothing weak about shooting a man between the eyes," Alix countered.

Charlotte was confused by her tone; it sounded almost admiring. Then Charlotte realised that she didn't understand and tried to explain. "Perhaps it wouldn't have been weak if I'd done it sooner..." Her voice faded away as she became lost in her thoughts. Why hadn't she done it sooner? She'd had the pistol. She'd envisaged using it against the Soviets many times. Why hadn't she shot Fritz the first time he came into her bedroom? Why had she let him abuse her again and again before she finally had the strength to put a bullet through his head?

"Did Fritz von Bredow try to assault you?" Alix asked into the silence.

Charlotte nodded and looked down.

"Did he succeed?"

Charlotte nodded again.

"On the night you killed him?"

Charlotte shook her head.

"Before that?"

She nodded.

"More than once?"

Charlotte nodded again.

"When was the first time?"

Charlotte closed her eyes and thought back. "About two weeks after Christian moved out, just before Christmas."

"Did he come every night after that?"

"No. Sometimes he was too drunk or — I don't know. Sometimes he just didn't come."

"When did you decide to stop him?"

"I don't know. The pistol was there the whole time. I don't know why I didn't stop him earlier. That's the point. I could have. I should have. But I didn't. I was too weak, helpless, lame." She shook her head. "After the first time, I didn't even scream and plead as I'd done with the Russians. I just lay there and let him do whatever he liked with me because I loathed myself so much."

"You let him do what he liked with you because you loathed yourself or you loathed yourself because you let him do what he liked with you?"

"Yes."

Alix paused to absorb that and then asked her next question, "And then, last Monday night, for no particular reason, you took a pistol that you'd had in your possession the entire time, and you shot Fritz von Bredow dead."

"Yes," Charlotte agreed, impressed by how calm and detached Alix sounded. The police had shouted at her, insulted and berated her because they had been outraged and shocked by what she had done. It wasn't as if Fritz was a stranger, an intruder, they told her. She had allowed him to live in her house. She was engaged to him. She had led him to expect sex, so she had no right to say no. Christian, on the other hand, had been gentle and understanding. He'd pleaded with her to tell him what had happened because he wanted to help her. She understood that, but she couldn't be helped. She didn't want Christian to get dragged down into this nightmare with her.

Alix seemed neutral or at least objective. She continued her interrogation calmly, "Did you give any thought to what would happen afterwards?"

"No, because I planned to shoot myself too. The last bullets were meant to be for me. I wanted to, but — I don't know. I went numb. I couldn't move.

I just stood there and stared. The pistol seemed too heavy to lift. I waited for something to happen. I don't know what I expected or how long I would have stood there. Then Herr Sperl came, he called the police, and they brought me here. But none of that matters because even if I failed to shoot myself I still want to die."

"Why?"

Charlotte felt she had answered that question already and responded testily. "I told you! I hate myself. I don't want to live with myself another day! I'm worthless and disgusting and don't want to go through this all over again when the Russians come!" Without intending to, Charlotte was getting angry.

Alix remained calm, "Christian tells me that this past summer you asked *him* to kill you. Is that correct?."

"Yes, that's true. When the Blockade started, I knew I couldn't face the Russians again. Christian convinced me that the Allies might win — or I might escape. For a while..." She thought back to those months with David. So enchanted. So unreal. She shook her head. "I never imagined that a German, a young man who had once loved and cherished me and treated me like a princess, would treat me like a worthless, soulless and brainless thing that he had the right to hurt and pollute...." Suddenly, Charlotte was so furious she was gritting her teeth and clenching her fists.

"It's a pity your shot put him out of his misery so quickly, but maybe the Church is right and there is a hell," Alix observed.

Charlotte looked at her astonished. She wasn't neutral after all. Or at least she understood how a woman felt about rape.

Alix continued, "Almost the first thing Christian said after telling me you'd been arrested was that Fritz von Bredow got what he deserved. Thankfully, he is dead, and God will be his judge. Meanwhile, you will be judged in a human court, and the question is whether you want to let Fritz von Bredow's judgement of you stand?" She paused to let Charlotte think about her words and then continued. "Or do you want to prove that he was wrong, that you are neither worthless nor unworthy of respect, but rather a courageous and valuable human being entitled to the full measure of human dignity?"

"But standing trial means facing myself in the mirror day after day — knowing what he and the Russians did to me." Charlotte stopped and added in a softer, more frightened voice because it was a confession she had hardly dared make even to herself, "and facing the fact that I wilfully and stupidly let my chance for happiness slip away out of cowardice." There she had admitted it.

But then she realised that Alix had no way of knowing what she was talking about. The sophisticated, rational lawyer would never be able to fathom how silly and foolish she had been. Charlotte felt she had to explain it to her, "The worst thing about living is facing the fact — again and again — that I was too stupid and timid to seize the chance for a better life when it was offered to me. I was too *cowardly* to take a chance with a far, far better man. I let him slip away...." Charlotte fell silent. She was picturing Jasha at her wedding. She'd been so radiant, and Graham had looked at her as if she were as precious as an angel even though he knew....

"Are you referring to David Goldman?"

Charlotte winced at the sound of his name and then hiccupped and nodded. She could not find the strength or courage to open her mouth much less look at Alix.

The lawyer's voice remained clinical as she announced, "David Goldman gave me this letter for you — in the event that you mentioned him."

Charlotte looked up sharply. Alix was holding out another letter. Charlotte stared at it, her heart thundering in her chest. She could hear her pulse. Was it possible? Was she dreaming? She had dreamt of rescue so many times and all that had come was Fritz stumbling into her bedroom and forcing himself on her.

"David flew to Berlin with me, and I am staying at his house. He is very concerned about you."

Charlotte forced herself to reach for the letter. She half expected it to disintegrate when she touched it, but it did not. She took it gently away from Alix and with trembling hands managed to open the envelope. It was written in David's clean, legible script.

Dear Charlotte,

Christian told me about the Russians and Bredow. I am horrified by what you have suffered and ashamed that I failed you. My love was so great that the pain of rejection blinded me to your fears and doubts. If I'd felt less sorry for myself, maybe I could have said or done something to dissuade you from taking Fritz von Bredow back into your life. Maybe I could have prevented the horror and the tragedy that has overtaken you.

But it is too late to change that now. All I can do is try to salvage your future.

I have come to Berlin to help you in any way I can. I will ensure that Freifrau von Feldburg has everything she needs to defend you. Please let me know if there is anything you need or want. Most of all, tell Freifrau von Feldburg if you want me to visit. I very much want to see you again, but I don't want to force my attentions on you if you would rather I stay away.

Whatever happens, trust that I love you. I admire your courage and integrity, and I always will.

Love, David

Charlotte had stopped breathing from the first line. By the time she finished reading, her heart was racing, and tears were streaming down her face. She read the letter again and again. He knew — and yet he loved her. He knew — and he still loved her. He loved her. David loved her. With tears dripping off her chin, she took the letter and pressed it to her heart as she closed her eyes and pictured his face. David loved her.

"Does the letter change anything?" Alix gently broke through her bubble of unworldly bliss. Charlotte had forgotten she was even there. She looked at her as she eased the letter from her breast and held it in her hands in her lap. She noticed that the lawyer's eyes were smiling. "Yes," Charlotte admitted. "It changes everything."

"You want to live?"

Charlotte nodded, "Please tell David I want to see him with all my heart!"

"Good. Do you also want me to defend you?"

"Yes. Very much. Do you think it's possible?" Charlotte asked. Only now, when she did not want to die any more, did she become afraid of the criminal justice system.

"I think we can build a strong case that you were acting in self-defence, but let's start by me ringing for them to bring you something to eat. You are going to need your strength."

Chapter Eleven
Mayday

RAF Gatow
Monday 24 January 1949
(Day 213 of the Berlin Airlift)

"I still can't believe this is real," Silvie admitted. She was bundled up in her new-made winter coat and wearing a big wool hat and rabbit-lined mittens that Georgina had lent her. With Georgina and Hannah, who had come to see her off, she waited at Gatow for the bus out to the Dakotas that carried passengers.

Georgina could see the dilapidated old bus approaching and knew it was time for final goodbyes. She hugged Silvie and then stepped back to look her in the eye. "You have the photograph of my father so you can recognize him?"

Silvie nodded vigorously, but then asked anxiously, "How should I address him, Mrs Moran?"

"Start with Reverend Reddings, but I expect he'll soon suggest an alternative."

"I can't ever thank you enough, Mrs Moran."

"You can thank me by staying healthy and taking care of yourself and your baby."

"I'll help your mother in the house and look after your little girl as best I can," Silvie promised as the bus pulled up with a groan in a cloud of diesel fumes. A corporal dropped out of the cab and demanded the chits given to Dakota passengers. As Georgina handed Silvie's chit to the driver, pointing her out, Hannah and Silvie hugged each other fiercely. "I wish I could go with you!" Hannah cried out.

"I'll write every day!"

"Please! I want to hear all about England!"

The corporal cleared his throat and Georgina touched Silvie's shoulder and nodded for her to board the bus. "Have a good trip and give my love to my parents!"

"Yes, Mrs Moran! I will!" Silvie disappeared into the bus and the corporal climbed back into the cab.

Georgina and Hannah watched the bus crawl around the perimeter track and pull up beside one of the Dakotas lined up on the far side of the runways. In the dark, it was hard to be sure which of the passengers was Silvie, but they could see when the fuselage door closed and the stairs were pulled back.

"Do you want to go over to the Malcolm Club for something warm to drink before going home, or would you like to watch her take off?" Georgina asked Hannah.

"Oh, let's watch her take off," Hannah suggested, still excited.

So, they stayed outside in the cold until the flight of six Dakotas with passengers rolled slowly onto the taxiway and trundled in a group to the start of the runway. They watched as one after the other the twin-engine aircraft filled with people fleeing Berlin took to the air and disappeared into the low clouds overhead.

Chilled through by then, Georgina insisted on going to the Malcolm Club. She bought Hannah and herself a hot chocolate, and they sat together at one of the vacant tables. "Mrs Moran, aren't there other people in England who need a nanny for their children?" Hannah asked hopefully.

"I'm sure there are," Georgina confirmed, but she also cautioned, "but many English girls train to be nannies. It's considered a very respectable position."

Hannah looked down sadly and stirred her chocolate. "I just wish I could get away from here, from the past, and start a whole new life the way Silvie has," she explained wistfully.

Georgina put her hand on Hannah's arm and assured her, "I understand and I'd like to help, but I don't have an answer just yet. All I can do is keep thinking and looking for opportunities. For now, you'd better finish that chocolate, or you'll miss the next bus back to Spandau."

After seeing Hannah safely aboard the workers' shuttle to Spandau,

Georgina went to wait in the station commander's anteroom. Kit was flying tonight and wouldn't be back for about three hours, so she'd brought a novel to read while she waited.

"Are you sure Luebeck can handle us?" Bruce yelled over the engine noise at his skipper as he readjusted himself in his seat and flexed his fingers in preparation for starting their descent toward RAF Luebeck northeast of Hamburg.

"We're carrying light bulbs bound for Sweden. It makes no sense to unload them at Hamburg, where they then need to be shipped all the way around Denmark, when Luebeck is only a few minutes flying time away," Kit shouted back.

"But I thought only the Dakotas operated out of Luebeck?" Bruce protested at the top of his voice. In the interests of efficiency, Tunner had moved all Dakota traffic to Luebeck, which meant that although they flew out of Berlin on the central air corridor, they then turned north and flew along the Zonal border to land at Luebeck, where they off-loaded their cargoes. The four-engine aircraft, in contrast, dispersed at the end of the outbound corridor to unload at Fuhlsbuettel, Fassberg, Celle, Wunstorf, Rhein-Main or Wiesbaden. Bruce's concerns were not entirely unfounded when he suggested, "Maybe they forgot we were a Halifax?"

"It doesn't matter," Kit yelled back. "With this cargo, we don't weigh much more than a loaded Dak. Of course," Kit yelled, "if you're uncomfortable landing on grass, Bruce, I'd be happy to—"

"I'm perfectly happy landing on grass!" Bruce hollered back, frowning, and Richard and Kit burst out laughing. Too late, Bruce realised Kit had been pulling his leg. He growled something that could not be heard over the noise of the engines but probably wasn't polite.

Before he could start their descent, however, Terry's voice cut in anxiously over the intercom. "Skipper, Rafair 491 just put out a Mayday call!"

"Where is he?" Kit answered, instantly alert.

"Right in front of us, Skip. We've been following him ever since we lost the traffic bound for Hamburg."

"Did he indicate the nature of his emergency?"

"He's reporting an engine fire. The extinguisher hasn't been effective, and the fire's spreading."

"It must be that light up there!" Richard pointed at an unusual golden dot suspended in the night sky about two miles ahead of them. Beyond the point of yellow, the sky lightened to a dark grey over the Baltic Sea, but below them, the land was a blanket of unbroken black. Neither a farmhouse light nor a car headlight interrupted the darkness, and no features of the landscape could be detected.

"He's draining excess fuel from his tanks now," Terry reported.

Bruce instinctively pulled back up on the column to put more space between them, although there was little risk of the fuel reaching them since they were flying two thousand feet higher.

"The fire appears to be spreading," Richard reported, echoing Kit's thoughts; the golden spot floating in the sky ahead of them seemed to be growing.

"What's the distance to Luebeck, Nigel?"

"Eighteen miles."

"Too far," Kit judged. "He's going to have to make a forced landing. Which engine is it?"

"Port."

"Damn." Kit commented succinctly; Bruce exclaimed more colourfully, "Bloody hell!"

Turning into a dead engine on a two-engine aircraft resulted in the loss of rudder control and the aircraft would rapidly spin out of control. This meant that the RAF Dakota could not turn to port, which was to the West. To find an emergency landing field it would have to continue on its present course or turn East. Because they were flying just inside the Zonal border, a turn to the East would take the Dakota over the Soviet Zone and any landing, controlled or uncontrolled, would be inside Soviet territory.

"Rafair 491 turning to starboard now," Terry reported.

The station commander's office door flung open so suddenly that it banged against the wall, startling Georgina. She looked up, a smile for Robin ready on her face, but the Wing Commander did not so much as acknowledge her presence — much less greet her as he usually did when he found her waiting here. Instead, he crossed the anteroom at a rapid pace and disappeared into the hall. Georgina looked over questioningly at Sergeant Andrews, the WingCo's clerk. She answered by pointing a finger at the ceiling; the control tower was overhead. Oh dear, Georgina thought automatically.

When nothing happened, however, she went back to reading her book.

The Halifax had been steadily overtaking the stricken Dakota, and the men aboard the AFI freighter could now clearly make out the dark shape of the aircraft with the flames leaping and licking at the side of the fuselage as it banked and lowered its nose toward the East.

"I presume he's empty," Kit said into the intercom.

"No, skip. He reported carrying 22 German passengers, evacuees from Berlin."

"Jesus, Mary and Joseph!" Richard crossed himself.

"Stay with him, Bruce," Kit ordered, and Bruce gently lifted the port wing and throttled back so they would not overshoot. To Terry, Kit ordered, "Report that we have Rafair 491 in sight and will remain with him until he's down."

"Wilco."

The telephone on Sergeant Andrew's desk rang and Georgina looked up to watch as the clerk answered briskly, "Station Commander's office." She nodded several times and then said, "Yes, sir. Right away, sir," and hung up.

Georgina didn't have to ask, Andrews told her: "One of the Dakotas has an engine fire and it's going to have to make a forced landing in the Soviet Zone."

Georgina's first reaction was relief that it was a Dakota and so couldn't be either Kit or Emily since they flew a Halifax and a Wellington respectively. Then she remembered that Silvie was aboard a Dakota. "Not one of the Dakotas with passengers aboard, is it?"

"That's what I'm supposed to find out straight away," Andrews answered.

"That fire's spreading fast," Bruce muttered.

"Skipper, we just crossed into Soviet airspace," Nigel called up from the nose.

"Understood," Kit answered.

"Fifteen hundred feet," Richard reported, adding, "Maybe we could turn on our landing lights to help him see the ground better?"

"Good thinking," Kit answered.

"Won't that attract the attention of the Soviets?" Bruce wondered, sounding a little worried.

"They're going to need fire engines and ambulances down there," Kit reminded his second pilot and then addressed his wireless operator, "Terry, ask Rafair 491 if they want us to turn on our landing lights to help them see the ground better. Bruce, no offence, but I'm taking the controls."

Bruce looked more relieved than annoyed, particularly when Kit took the Halifax down to fly wingtip-to-wingtip with the burning aircraft that was now less than 1,000 feet above the ground.

"Landing lights would be much appreciated, Skip!" Terry called up.

"Lights on, Richard." In the blink of an eye, the earth below was transformed from a featureless black murk into a colourless agricultural landscape. A farmhouse complex was visible to the left. A tree-lined road cut diagonally across their line of flight and on the far side their lights glinted on ice in the ruts of a ploughed field.

"Five hundred feet," Richard reported.

A couple of hedgerows criss-crossed in front of them, but beyond them, a field opened up. It was covered with stubble from some long-harvested crop that stuck up through the shallow snow, but there were no apparent obstacles in it. The Dakota throttled back to near-stalling speed and sank towards the earth. Kit could no longer stay with him, so he throttled forward and pulled the Halifax up in a steep, climbing turn to circle back.

It took them less than a minute, but by the time they were flying towards the Dakota again with their lights illuminating the scene, the Dakota was almost on the ground. It flew with flaps fully extended but no undercarriage. A second later, the Dakota struck the earth and careered through the field, flinging mud and fragments of metal in all directions. It shed the burning port wing almost at once, and the wreck started to swing to the left as the right engine still thrust it forward. A split second later, the fire on the burning engine reached the fuel tanks, and with a loud whoosh — audible even over the engines of the Halifax — the aviation fuel exploded. The pressure wave rocked the Dakota, tearing the tail off just before the rest of the fuselage came skidding to a halt.

By then, the Halifax had flown beyond the crash site and Kit had to circle around again, but the flames of the burning wing enabled his crew to see what was happening on the ground.

"People are scrambling out of the fuselage!" Richard reported, tensely. "They're running away from the fire!"

"Jesus God! There were children on board!" Bruce exclaimed. "A man and a woman are carrying a child as they run away!"

"A woman's hobbling about in circles confused. Someone's leading her away. No, she's resisting. There must be someone she knows still inside the wreck!"

"Nigel, do you have a fix?"

"Yes, skip."

"Have Terry transmit it to Luebeck."

As they lined up again and came in very low to illuminate the scene with their landing lights, Kit could see what looked like a dozen people huddling together upwind from the flames but there was still movement around the wreckage. Near the cockpit, people appeared to be trying to drag someone clear, other people had gone back to the tail section, and in the mid-section, two civilians were struggling to carry a third who was either dead or unconscious.

"Flashing red lights, skipper!" Richard warned and pointed.

Kit lifted his eyes from the crash site to follow Richard's outstretched finger. He found the flashing lights that appeared to be three or four miles away on the ground. That was probably the local police, fire department, or ambulance on the way.

"Has Luebeck acknowledged, Terry?

"Yes, sir."

"All right, we'll make one last pass over the accident and then resume our flight." As he swept over the people huddling together beside the burning wreck, Kit waggled his wings to indicate help was on the way. A couple of the survivors raised their hands to him. He could only hope that the Soviets would arrive soon.

"Do we have the passenger manifest of the aircraft, yet?" Wing Commander Priestman asked as he swept back into the anteroom.

"I'll have it to you shortly, sir," Andrews responded.

Priestman caught sight of Georgina and came over to tell her, "You know one of the Daks is down?"

"Yes. Is it one of the ones carrying children?"

"Unfortunately, yes, but Kit was following it and stayed with it to help light up the landing area; he's reported survivors." Robin paused and then noted, "You had arranged for one of the girls from your sewing class to return to England tonight, hadn't you?"

"Yes," Georgina squeaked out.

"You better come into my office and we'll see what we can find out."

They didn't have long to wait. Within five minutes, Stan arrived with the manifest. "Rafair KN491, P/O E.J. Eddy. Twenty-two passengers, 17 of whom were children."

Priestman sighed and rubbed his forehead. Then he sat up straighter and ordered, "Ask Sergeant Andrews to put a call through to Mayor Reuter."

"Yes, sir."

As Stan turned to leave, Georgina risked asking, "Do you have the names of the passengers? May I have a look?"

"The names are here, but..." Stan glanced toward his CO, and Priestman nodded his approval. Stan handed the manifest over to Georgina.

She scanned down the list of names: Pilot: P/O Eddy, Nav: Flt/Sgt Senior, Signaller: J. Grout, and then the Germans: Grasshoff, Ursula, Kelch, Irmgard and Emanuel, Lercher, Johann and so on down the list alphabetically to Zimmerman, Silvie.

Georgina couldn't stifle a little cry of shock and pain

"Was it the flight your student was on?" Robin asked from his desk as Stan looked back and forth bewildered.

Georgina nodded numbly. There were so few crashes! Why did Silvie's flight to freedom and dignity have to be one of the few?

"Don't assume the worst. We know there were survivors, we just have to find out how many and who."

Three hours later, when Kit returned, he echoed that sentiment. After describing in detail what he'd seen and stressing that several young women had been among the survivors, he urged Georgina, "Just as when I went down, you must keep your hope up until we find out otherwise." And on that note, they went to bed.

Tuesday 25 January 1949
(Day 214 of the Berlin Airlift)

"The Soviet papers are filled with news of the crash," Emily greeted Georgina as she came down for breakfast.

"What are they saying?"

"That the airbridge has become a death bridge."

"Can you read the article to me?"

"Certainly. The title reads: '*Airbridge – Deathbridge: Senseless evacuation of Berlin children claims tragic victims.*' The text goes on to say: '*A British Dakota carrying 22 passengers, including 17 children, and a crew of three, left Gatow airport late yesterday evening and crashed near the Anglo-Russian Zonal border. Search parties led by Russian officers and personnel were sent out immediately and reached the crash site within twenty minutes. Here they came upon a dramatic scene of morbid tragedy. A pitiful handful of stunned survivors huddled together in the darkness, ignored entirely by the RAF crew, while just yards away the corpses of children burned in the wreckage. Altogether six children were killed in this senseless accident, along with one adult escort and a member of the crew. Another seven civilians, including four children, and two RAF airmen were seriously injured.*

This morning many Berlin parents must be wondering if their beloved little ones were among the unlucky victims of British hubris — or will be among the victims tomorrow or the next day?

Rather than risking the lives of the next generation by sending them away on decrepit and dilapidated aircraft manned by drunks and heartless youths, responsible parents should keep their children safe at home and register for food and coal rations in the East."

"But no names?" Georgina asked.

"No names."

"What am I going to say to Hannah and the other girls?" Georgina asked rhetorically.

"The truth," Emily advised. "Silvie's aircraft developed mechanical difficulties and had to crash land in the Soviet Zone." Then she reached out and drew Georgina into her arms. "You were trying to help her. You couldn't possibly know that her flight would end tragically, and she may yet be among the lucky ones. When is the next sewing class?"

"Not until Saturday."

"By then we should know Silvie's fate one way or another, but whatever happens, no one is going to blame you, Georgina."

"If she's dead, I am going to blame myself," Georgina answered.

Yet just as when Kit had failed to return from his last operation over Germany, Georgina kept her emotions in check and focused on her job throughout the school day. Of course, the pupils had all heard the news and there was much talk and speculation. The boys seemed most interested in what had caused the crash, while the girls were more upset that the youngest passenger had been just seven. The staff, on the other hand, focused on whether the Soviets would release the crew or not. At the end of the day, the headmaster announced that a delegation from the school would attend the ecumenical memorial ceremony that the City Government planned for the coming Sunday.

It was not until she got home that Georgina learned from Kit that Silvie was among the casualties. "Dead?" She asked.

"I'm sorry, yes," Kit answered.

Suddenly furious, Georgina burst out, "Why? Why? Why?"

Kit tried to take her into his arms, but she refused his comfort. "It's not fair! She's known nothing but hell from Hitler's regime and the bombing and then the Soviet occupation, the rapes and her mother's exploitation! Now, the very first time something good happens — when she's on the brink of a new start, God kills her! How could He do such a thing?"

"You'll have to ask your father that," Kit suggested gently.

"I will!" Georgina replied and rushed out to the hall to put a call through to her father. She had spoken to him briefly the night before to let him know he no longer needed to meet the BEA flight. He'd told her to call him as soon as she had additional news. No sooner had he answered the phone, however, than Georgina launched into a tirade against God. Again and again, she said, "It's just not fair, Daddy. It's not fair. I was trying to help. I wanted to make her life better. And don't tell me that was hubris and God was punishing me! He didn't have to kill an innocent girl to punish me! How can He be so cruel?"

Reverend Reddings let his daughter rage. He understood her need to curse God. Sometimes he felt the same way, he just kept his emotions a little better hidden. Only after Georgina had stopped raging to cry helplessly did he remind her, "Dearest Georgina, remember what I said about God's attitude towards death?" He paused and then reminded her, "He does not view it as significant and certainly not as punishment. Dead or alive, God loves us. Perhaps he decided that Silvie had suffered enough on earth already and *deserved* heaven? I am sorry I did not get a chance to meet her, and the Baxters will be dreadfully disappointed not to get the child they were already preparing for. Now rage if you like, but whatever you do, don't stop trying to help people. We cannot always succeed, but we mustn't stop trying."

Chapter Twelve
Full Speed Ahead

Limits
RAF Gatow/Berlin-Dahlem
Monday 31 January 1949
(Day 220 of the Berlin Airlift)

Since his reassignment to a C-54 squadron after Christmas, J.B. Baronowsky was based in Fassberg and flying regularly into Gatow. Although he rarely had much time on the ground, he and Kathleen had managed to squeeze in coffee or a quick snack now and again at the Malcolm Club. At the end of the month, however, they succeeded in scheduling overlapping time off so that they could spend a whole evening together.

J.B. booked a room at the Officer Guest Quarters in Dahlem, while Kathleen arranged for her daughter Hope to have an 'overnight' party with her friend Alice. Alice's mother promised to collect both girls from the school bus, while Kathleen, coming off the night shift, fell exhausted into bed and slept five hours before the alarm went off at 4 pm. She washed, dressed and then biked through the cold to the Malcolm Club to meet J.B..

The American broke into a wide grin and waved the moment he saw her. As she joined him at his table, he gave her a peck on the cheek in greeting and then exclaimed excitedly, "Look! They're showing *Johnny Belinda* at the PX movie theatre in Dahlem! Didn't you say you wanted to see it?" Kathleen was impressed that J.B. remembered her casual reference to the film. He checked his watch. "It's showing at 5:30 and again at 8:30. We might just be able to make the matinee, if you like, and could have dinner at the Officer's Club afterwards, or the other way around. What do you think?"

Kathleen found the prospect of a long trip across Berlin daunting, but his enthusiasm was irresistible. Besides, she reminded herself, J.B. didn't like English food. He was undoubtedly looking forward to a steak or something equally high in protein and calories. With an effort, she pretended an eagerness she did not feel and suggested they leave straight away.

The RAF bus to Spandau was jammed with erks eager for a night on the town. They were in high spirits and soon groups competed in singing off-colour songs too loudly for anyone else to have a conversation. At the S-Bahn station in Spandau, Kathleen and J.B. sprinted to catch the train to Bahnhof Zoo. These carriages were also crammed full, this time with weary Berliners. The mood became glum, and although J.B. and Kathleen would have been able to hear one another if they'd talked, so would everyone else. Instead, they sat side-by-side lost in their separate thoughts.

Kathleen closed her eyes to avoid seeing the blacked-out city and haggard residents. The wheels clacked over the joints in the rails and the car swayed. She leaned towards J.B. to avoid being flung against the stranger on her other side. J.B. put his arm around her shoulder, and she snuggled closer into his protective embrace, breathing in the scent of his aftershave.

'Ken,' she talked mentally to her dead husband, 'this is all right with you, isn't it? It's what you said you wanted for me if you went down, remember? You said you hoped I'd find someone who would look after Hope and I and make us happy.' She heard no answer except for the clackity-clack of the wheels, but she felt safe enough to drift off to sleep.

J.B. woke her up gently at the Zoo station, and they boarded a US Military bus to Dahlem. It was full of men returning from leave on a Sunday night, and J.B. had to stand. The journey continued through the unlit city until they arrived at the American military compound. This stood out like a spaceship in outer space. Street lights blazed, and softer light poured from hundreds of office and housing windows. Shoppers crowded the PX, and music blared from somewhere. The large bulbs on the cinema marquee lit up in sequence as if they were moving.

Much as Kathleen wanted to get into the mood of a happy night out with her young man, the loud voices around her in their strange accents gave her a headache. As they queued to buy tickets, J.B. picked up on her mood and asked, "Is something wrong?"

"I'm sorry, J.B., I'm just tired. I didn't sleep very well last night."

"Something bothering you?"

"I can't seem to get over this latest crash. All those children killed and injured. It reminded me of being in the tower when the BEA flight collided with the Soviet fighter—"

"Woah! At Gatow? When was that?" He had to raise his voice to ask the question because a loud crowd was forming behind them.

"It was April last year, and this new crash—" She broke off as a couple cut through the line with loud excuses.

"Look, we don't have to go to the movies," J.B. offered. "Why don't we just have dinner and talk?"

Kathleen felt a wave of relief. "You wouldn't mind missing the film? I'd like to see it another time, but I have a bit of a headache—"

"Scratch the flick," J.B. declared as he pulled her out of line and let the noisy party behind them move forward. He then led the way off the compound and down the street to the nearby "Harnack House," which housed the US Officers' Club. He avoided the larger dining room with a dance floor where a jazz band was already blasting away. Instead, he took Kathleen to the smaller restaurant at the back. Here the lighting was low, and a pianist was gently playing big-band melodies in the background. They were taken to a small table with linen and silver, and Kathleen told J.B., "I feel better already."

He squeezed her hand. "You know what? So do I! We haven't had all that much time to talk, and well, a crash involving an airliner sounds pretty traumatic to me. Do you want to tell me about it?"

Before she could speak, the waiter arrived with a menu long on American favourites like steak, barbequed pork, 'Southern' fried chicken, Hamburgers and 'French fries,' and ice cream, of course. They ordered, and after the waiter faded away, Kathleen told J.B. about the collision — in far more detail than she'd intended. The American pilot was an attentive and sympathetic listener. He understood enough to ask intelligent questions, and when she finished, he reached across the table to take her hand and declare, "You have a tough job, kid."

His remark hit a raw nerve of doubt that had been festering for weeks. Without thinking, Kathleen blurted out, "It is, and frankly, I'm not sure I'm up to it anymore. I was feeling exhausted even before this latest crash, but now.... I'm starting to wonder how much longer I'll be able to cope."

"You always sound so relaxed and cheerful over the radio," J.B. told her with an admiring smile.

Kathleen looked down embarrassed. Then she admitted, "This may sound strange, but when I'm *on* duty, I'm fine. I like chatting with the pilots, particularly teasing and joking with you Americans. That's what breaks up the monotony. Even a tense situation tends to bring a surge of adrenaline that temporarily makes me feel useful and competent. It's not until I get home that my nerves go. I'm getting a 'twitch.' I can't hold a saucer steady anymore. I'm smoking much too much, and if Hope starts whining or she's naughty, I just want to strangle the girl. It never used to be like that."

"You've been on duty since the start of this thing, haven't you?"

"Yes, but it's not as bad as the war. We're not losing aircraft *every* night. The crates aren't limping back with the hydraulics gone, or the rudder shot away, or the pilot blinded by Perspex splinters...." Her voice faded. Why was she talking about this? They were supposed to be having a good time. Why was she whinging?

J.B. rubbed the back of her hand with his thumb. That was all. Just that silent gesture, and she felt calmer. She felt loved. She looked up at him with tears in her eyes. "I'm sorry. You've come all the way from Fassberg and I'm ruining your evening. I don't know what's wrong with me."

"I do. You're burned out. You're tired. You need a break. You need to get away from Berlin and the darkness and the cold and the threat and the Airlift." He paused and smiled. "If you had a month's leave tomorrow, where would you go? Home to your folks?"

"Good heavens no! They spend too much time complaining about the rationing, the inadequate public services, and the neglected ruins of the Blitz — when they're not nagging at me to take a 'proper job'!" Changing her tone from frustration to longing, she told him, "No, when I dream about a break, I think of the times my husband Ken took me sailing. He was a fanatical sailor, you see, and once we chartered an old 26-foot boat and sailed along the Irish coast. It only had a tiny cabin, and we cooked over a tin of Sterno. It was all a bit primitive but utterly peaceful and calming." She smiled at the memory.

"When I was a boy, my dad took the family on a short vacation to a cabin on the shore of Lake Michigan not far from the Sleeping Bear dunes. We were miles from any town. No theatres or cinemas, and the water heater didn't work too well, either, so we only had cold showers. But we saw deer and beavers and had racoons in the cabin that got up to all kinds of mischief. We all loved it and wanted to go back, but somehow it never happened." He paused and then told her solemnly, "I'd like to take *you* there — and Hope. She's the age my sister Barb was on that trip, and Barb loved it."

"Hope would love seeing wild animals," Kathleen admitted, "not to mention meeting racoons!" She smiled at the thought.

After a pause, J.B. asked in a low, serious voice, "What do you plan to do when the Airlift is over? Go wherever the RAF sends you?"

"I used to think that, but..." She shook her head. "I'm beginning to think I'm not cut out for it. What I'd like is to be an air traffic controller at some sleepy hobby flyer's field or some island where there are just one or two flights a day. Then again, I might get bored." She flashed him a self-mocking smile before adding more seriously, "What about you, do you want to stay in the Air Force when the Airlift is over?"

"Doesn't matter what I want, the Air Force isn't taking me. Too many other guys."

"So, what do you want to do afterwards?"

"I want to work at MARC — that's the Michigan Aeronautical Research Centre."

"That sounds fascinating!" Kathleen exclaimed. "Would you be working on innovations to aircraft and engine design and that kind of thing?"

"Exactly." He was pleased that she understood so readily.

"How exciting! Creative and meaningful work with a future in it!" Although she envied him a little, Kathleen did not begrudge him such an opportunity.

"The downside," J.B. continued earnestly, "is it doesn't pay very well, which is why my ex-fiancé nixed the idea."

"You mean the pay is worse than what the Air Force gives you?" Kathleen teased.

J.B. laughed. "No, better, and like the Air Force it comes with free housing. It's located at Willow Run, where they assembled thousands of B-24 Liberators during the war. Because it wasn't near any major town, they built housing for the thousands of workers who came from across the country to work there. My ex thought that living in housing built for factory workers was a fate worse than death."

"What a snob," Kathleen declared without thinking.

"Yeah," he was looking at her with strange intensity. "They even built a school for kids."

"So, you still want to have kids?"

"Yeah," he cocked his head. "I like the idea of three."

"Any particular reason why you like the number three?"

"Well, I'd like a son and a daughter of my own," he told her deliberately.

It took her a second to grasp the significance of that answer, and then she stiffened a little. Was he proposing? Surely not.

Seeing her reaction, J.B. asked, "Don't you want more kids?"

"I do," Kathleen assured him, adding with a teasing smile, "and I think you're right about three being the perfect number. I just can't guarantee a boy and a girl."

J.B. grabbed both of her hands in a fierce grip and asked intently, "Did you just agree to marry me?"

"Did you ask?" Kathleen countered with a raised eyebrow.

J.B. jumped to his feet and seemed on the verge of going down on one knee, so Kathleen stopped him, "I was just teasing, J.B. Sit down, the waiter is bringing our meal."

He glanced over his shoulder and saw she was right. He sat down again, but he looked confused and hurt. He waited impatiently until the waiter withdrew, then asked almost belligerently, "Am I just a joke to you?"

"No! Not at all," Kathleen assured him firmly. "I'm very touched that you would think of including Hope in your family."

"Kathleen! I've known you were the woman for me since the day you saved my life. I may not have accepted that rationally until I broke up with Patty and saw you again, but in my heart I have always known. I don't want to beat around the bush any more. I want to marry you, and I need to know if you can imagine marrying me and moving to America and living in workers' housing while I earn peanuts doing the job I really want to do?"

"I wouldn't want you to work at any job you *didn't* like," she replied earnestly. "And as long as the housing has flushing lavatories, electricity and central heating, I won't object. It's just...." Her voice faded away.

"What? What's holding you back? Don't you think you could ever come to love me?"

"I think I *do* love you, Jay. At least I'm beginning to," Kathleen admitted, surprising herself a little. She hadn't had that much contact with J.B., and yet, she saw in him the same kind of honest reliability she had found in Ken. She'd fallen for Ken in just a day or two, and it was unfair to punish J.B. with artificial caution because she'd been taken in by Lionel Dickenson. "It's not *you* I have doubts about. It's the thought of moving to America that I find intimidating. America's so far away. So bright, bold, loud, fast-paced and, I don't know, *different* from what I've known. I just can't see myself living there and being happy — not even with a man I love."

J.B. considered that soberly and then reached out and squeezed her hand. "OK, Kid. I understand. I'll just have to work on changing your mind about America."

Charged
Berlin-Moabit
Wednesday 2 February 1949
(Day 222 of the Berlin Airlift)

The judicial complex on the Turmstrasse stood five stories high and occupied a large city block. When it had been built just before the First World War, it been seen as a model, modern court facility. In addition to 21 courtrooms and offices for more than 300 judges and an equal number of prosecutors, it had a telephone exchange, goods and passenger lifts, a water tower and a dedicated power station. The latter was one of the few power stations in the blockaded Sectors of Berlin, and the electricity it produced no longer supplied the courthouse alone but much of the surrounding district.

The Baroque revival façade of the large complex might have been attractive -- if it hadn't been coated in coaldust and pockmarked by small-arms fire. The latter reminded visitors of the final struggle for Berlin in 1945. Alix knew the building well. In 1937, she had spent six months working here as a legal intern to one of the hundreds of state prosecutors. They were not pleasant memories, but she shoved them aside to focus on the present.

Charlotte was in a frail state. She had dark circles under her eyes from sleepless nights and was so thin that all her joints stuck out awkwardly. She seemed so fragile that Alix felt her arm might break if she held it too firmly. As they pulled up in front of the massive courthouse, Charlotte quailed.

Alix climbed out of the police van first and looked around for Christian and David, who had promised to come to the arraignment. Unfortunately, they were nowhere in sight. The escorting, policewoman, who Alix thought would have thrived as a concentration camp guard, barked at Charlotte to stop "dithering" and get out of the van. Alix offered her hand to help Charlotte out onto the pavement. Then, with police flanking them, they entered the echoing entrance hall.

Here they waited in line to talk to the concierge, who had a heavy book with the scheduled hearings as well as the index of judges, prosecutors, clerks and other officials. When it was their turn, Alix gave Charlotte's name, and they were directed to Courtroom 14.

This was a standard German courtroom of the early 20th century. A long podium with seats for five judges ran along one side of the room facing banks of seats separated by an aisle. Behind barriers on the left and right were raised benches for the press and the public. In front of the dais for the judges was a row of desks for clerks and other court personnel. When facing the judges, the defence sat on the left-hand side and the prosecution on the right.

Alix led Charlotte to the front row on the left and told her to take the second seat from the aisle. Alix sat on the aisle and a policeman took the seat on Charlotte's other side. The rest of the courtroom was empty except for policemen at the doors. There were neither press nor visitors yet. Charlotte looked close to fainting, so Alix got up and asked one of the policemen standing at the back to bring water for her. As Alix sat down again, she put her hand on Charlotte's arm and murmured in a low voice, "Try to relax and view the arraignment as your first step towards freedom."

Charlotte nodded, and Alix opened her briefcase and removed the indictment that had been sent to them two weeks earlier. She had gone through it with Charlotte paragraph by paragraph, drawing out of her the full extent of the terror she had endured. Alix no longer felt neutral about this case. She sided strongly with Charlotte, but she was a professional and determined to maintain a calm exterior — and not to show her hand too soon.

After a few minutes, a stenographer entered and started setting up her notepads and sharpening her pencils. Still no sign of Christian and David, however, and it was already twenty past twelve. The proceedings were scheduled to begin at 12:30 pm, the last session before the two-hour lunch break at 1 pm.

With a whirlwind of officiousness, the prosecutor arrived. He wore a gown and a cap with an upturned brim, the standard attire of German prosecutors. He was accompanied by three male assistants, presumably junior prosecutors or legal interns. Alix went to introduce herself, and when he turned to face her, her heart missed a beat. It was the very man she had worked for twelve years earlier.

The memories flooded back. Apprenticing with a state prosecutor was one of the mandatory internships required of aspiring lawyers in Germany. By the time she arrived for her six-month stint, it was a year since she'd passed her first exam. She'd already spent six months clerking in a civil court and another six months interning with a commercial law firm. The latter had been active in helping Jews avoid the various laws inhibiting the transfer of property overseas. That work had been uplifting, and she had been inspired by the notion that when she finished her legal training, she would be in a position to help people oppose injustice.

Everything changed after her encounter with the man opposite her. Not only had he been contemptuous of her as a woman, constantly implying that women didn't have the brains necessary for the job, but she also soon discovered that, in collusion with the judges, he determined the verdicts and the sentence of the defendants *before* the trial. The judges took orders from him because he was a high-ranking member of the Nazi Party with good connections to key Nazi leaders.

"Ach!" the prosecutor exclaimed as their eyes met. "If it isn't little Fraulein von Mollwitz! What a surprise! I thought you'd recognised the futility of pursuing a legal career."

"Only for as long as you and your kind controlled the criminal justice system. I have spent the last three years in Nuremberg — with the prosecution."

He flinched but then smiled derisively and sneered, "So you're one of *those* — a fawning sponger, hanging onto the coattails of our occupiers and besmirching our nest. How charming, Fraulein von Mollwitz."

"Bringing murderers to justice," she countered, adding, "And it's not Fraulein von Mollwitz, but Freifrau von Feldburg."

"Feldburg? Surely not any relation to the infamous traitor?"

"His widow, Herr *Staatsanwalt* Steinbrueck. His proud widow." Alexandra held her head high and met his eye.

"Traitor!" Steinbrueck hissed at her, his eyes narrowing.

"In the name and for the sake of humanity."

"Hanging was too good for your husband. He should have been gassed like the other vermin."

Alix was furious, but she knew better than to erupt. She gave Steinbrueck a twisted smile and remarked, "I'll remember you said that." Then she turned away and took her seat next to Charlotte.

Charlotte leaned close to ask in a whisper, "Is something wrong?"

Alix tried to rein in her feelings. "The prosecutor is Herr Dr Steinbrueck, a man with whom I interned before the war. He was — and apparently still is — an ardent National Socialist. I will try to get him removed from your case and debarred, but I'm not sure of the exact procedures or how long that might take. Today, it doesn't matter. All you need to do is enter your plea."

There was no time for further discussion. The police called for everyone to rise as the three judges entered. They moved to stand before the central seats behind the podium and gestured for everyone to sit. The presiding judge lifted a gavel, knocked it on the table once and announced the court was in session. He then turned to look at Charlotte, "The defendant will rise."

Charlotte got unsteadily to her feet, while Alix looked futilely for Christian and David. Charlotte was breathing so heavily that Alix could hear her.

"Are you Charlotte Graefin Walmsdorf, born May 16, 1916, in Walmsdorf, Mecklenburg to Constantine Alexander Heinrich Graf Walmsdorf and his wife Freya Michaela nee von Linstow?"

"Yes," Charlotte whispered and nodded.

"Do you have legal counsel?"

Charlotte nodded, indicated Alix, and managed to say, "Alexandra Freifrau von Feldburg."

"Have you received and read the indictment?"

Charlotte nodded again.

Scowling at her, the judge asked, "You understand that you are charged with murder in the first degree of Friedrich Adelbert von Bredow on the night of 10 January 1949?"

Charlotte took a shallow breath and breathed out, "I understand."

"How do you plead?"

"Not guilty," Charlotte whispered.

"Speak up! I did not hear your response!" The judge barked.

"My client pleads 'not guilty,' your honour," Alix spoke up clearly and distinctly.

"On what grounds?"

The judge's tone did not sound as neutral as Alix thought it ought to. She decided she'd look into *his* biography as well. On her legal pad, she noted his name, Nuss. Meanwhile, she answered his question, "by reason of self-defence."

"Plea: not guilty. Justification: self-defence. The defendant will remain in police custody without bail until the trial. Court adjourned." The judge hit the gavel on the wooden holder and stood, bringing everyone else to their feet again.

"Is that all?" Charlotte whispered.

"For the moment," Alix told her. They slid out of their seats and started for the door.

Behind them, the prosecutor remarked to his assistants. "What a pair those girls make: the widow of a man who wanted to kill our beloved Fuehrer and the murderer of one of our brave disabled heroes."

Alix gripped Charlotte more firmly by the elbow and kept moving without looking back, their police escort trailing them. This was going to be much more emotionally draining than she'd thought.

They navigated the warren of corridors back to the entry hall and exited into the bleak, wintry day. Half a dozen police vans stood parked at the curb, but their police escort recognised which one was theirs and pointed them towards it. Alix nudged Charlotte forward and was surprised by Charlotte's apparent reluctance to move. She kept looking over her shoulder.

Just when they reached the van, the tall, wooden door of the courthouse flew open with a bang, and David burst out. His coat flapped around him as he ran towards them calling, "Charlotte!"

Charlotte tried to step in his direction, reaching out her arms. The policewoman responded as though she were making an escape attempt. She roughly spun Charlotte about and shoved her into the back of the van over Alix's protest. Charlotte did not struggle. She just kept her eyes fixed on David for as long as she could, calling his name the whole time.

The police driver flung himself out of the driver's seat and with outstretched arms he stopped David from stepping off the curb.

A second later, Christian caught up with David and breathlessly explained, "They wouldn't let us in. They said no visitors were allowed."

David tried to use the distraction, to slip past the policeman and reach the back of the van, but the policeman was faster. With a lunge, he physically dragged David back onto the curb as Charlotte called out "David!" The policewoman jumped out of the vehicle and took up a stance with her arms crossed over her chest glowering at David.

"Let me just say three words to her!" David begged.

With her mouth clamped firmly shut, the policewoman shook her head. The policeman barked, "No one but counsel, court officials and law enforcement officers are allowed to speak with the defendant."

"That's absurd!" David protested.

"She is a dangerous felon!" the policewoman retorted.

"Probably less of a one than you are!" David countered, evidently sharing Alix's suspicions about the woman's past.

The situation might have escalated further if the familiar voice of Dr Steinbrueck had not carried across the icy air. To Alix's dismay, the prosecutor and his assistants had just left the building on their way to lunch.

"Ah, what have we here?" Dr Steinbrueck asked coming up to inspect the scene. He looked with apparent amusement from David to the police, and asked Alix contemptuously, "Would this sorry specimen be the motive or the accomplice of the murderess?"

David swung toward Steinbrueck, and God knew what he might have said if Christian had not grabbed him and hissed, "Don't respond! It could damage Charlotte's case."

Alix intervened with, "Allow me to introduce Herr Dr Steinbrueck, a founding member of the *Bund Nationalsozialistischer Deutscher Juristen*" (the League of National Socialist German Legal Professionals) "and an early member of the NSDAP."

"At least I am a proud German, not a traitor!" Steinbrueck retorted.

"Anyone proud of causing a world war is a moron," Christian retorted to the prosecutor before saying to Alix, "We'll talk later." He pulled David away while Alix turned and climbed into the back of the van to accompany Charlotte back to jail.

"He came," Charlotte whispered, her face alight. "David came. He'll save me."

Alix nodded and stroked Charlotte's arm. She needed faith and hope. The reality, however, was that because Steinbrueck had witnessed the emotional reunion between Charlotte and David, he could now build a plausible case of premeditated murder. Steinbrueck would attempt to show that Charlotte had killed Bredow so she would be free to marry David. He had two police witnesses who could testify to the intensity of the feelings David and Charlotte had just shown for one another. It was not a good development.

Targeted
Cranwell, UK
Friday 4 February 1949
(Day 224 of the Berlin Airlift)

Robin had been summoned to a meeting with Squadron Leader Flannel, the officer charged with investigating the death of Captain Clement Utting. The venue was the headquarters of the Special Investigations Branch, bizarrely located at Cranwell. Robin had not been to the Royal Air Force Academy since his graduation as a cadet in 1935. Although he had requested the intervention of the Special Investigations Branch, he found the abrupt summons unsettling.

His unease was not mitigated by the atmosphere in the dingy, cluttered room, where he found Inspector Flannel. The latter was a lean, bespectacled man, with a thin, straight mouth and a receding chin. He did not exude warmth or comradeship as he dryly asked Robin to take a seat in the small, basement room.

Robin tried not to let his disquiet show and scrupulously avoided any show of annoyance or impatience. Robin could picture how an officer like

Bagshot might puff himself up and remonstrate about 'having more important things to do,' or try to demean the inspector by sarcastically reminding him that 'there was an Airlift on,' but Robin sensed he would be a fool to try to bluster his way through this interview. He also suspected any attempt to intimidate the serious man behind the spectacles would be futile. While he might outrank the inspector, who also suffered from a dearth of wings and war ribbons, Flannel still had the power to wreck his career. A man had been killed on his Station. If anything, he had done or not done as station commander had caused that man to die, then he did not belong in his job. It was as simple as that.

Squadron Leader Flannel asked if he wanted tea; Robin declined. Flannel filled up a large mug for himself, leaned back in his chair and divulged, "We are on the brink of closing our investigation into the fatal accident at Gatow on the night of 11 December last year. Before drafting a written protocol of our conclusions and recommendations, we wanted to speak to you one last time." Flannel used 'we' despite being alone in the room; presumably, he spoke for the Special Inspections Branch.

"Let me start by sharing with you what our investigation has turned up. First, the perimeter fence was not breached, at least not at any time near the date of the incident. Flight Lieutenant Tucker of the RAF Regiment maintains a good watch on the perimeter, and we found no vulnerabilities in his procedures." Good, Robin thought; that was one point in his favour.

"Second, based on the tread tracks in the turf around the accident site, we know the vehicle was German, not RAF." Robin was relieved to hear that, too. "This means there was no deficit in the procedures regarding access to RAF vehicles, and no RAF personnel is under suspicion of involvement in the incident." That, too, was good news to Robin.

"As far as we can tell, the vehicle involved in the accident was a three-ton general-purpose lorry of the kind widely used to carry cargo to Kladow for transhipment." Robin nodded. Although he had not gotten a good look at the vehicle in the dark, a three-tonner matched what he remembered.

Flannel continued, "No less than 27 such vehicles have authorised access to Gatow. Although we inspected all of them, we could find no definitive evidence of a collision with a man." Humans, Robin thought cynically, didn't do a lot of damage to three-ton lorries.

"All vehicles log in and out at the gate. Four members of the RAF Detachment and one corporal are on duty at all times, and the gate is manned twenty-four hours a day. We found no glaring deficiencies in how vehicles are logged in and out and no evidence of tampered logs." Again, that sounded good to Robin, but Flannel's tone suggested that he remained dissatisfied.

The inspector continued, "Due to the variation in unloading times, inevitable delays during transhipment, periodic traffic congestion, weather and human nature — stops for food, drink or to urinate — the vehicles follow no set schedule. Thus, although we meticulously reviewed the log at the gate for the night in question, nothing stood out as exceptional." That did not surprise Robin. One of the first things Tucker had done was review the gate log, and he'd come to the same conclusion.

"Naturally," Flannel explained, "we interviewed the drivers of all three-ton vehicles working on the night of the incident, a total of 18 men."

"All Germans?" Robin asked.

"No, four Poles, two Ukrainians, one Hungarian and eleven Germans. All the drivers denied any knowledge of the incident until the ambulance siren went off and rumours started circulating. Furthermore, they all provided coherent descriptions of their activities."

"If they've been working at Gatow for any time, they know the routines and could easily create a fictional itinerary that obscures their activities at the fatal moment," Robin noted.

"Quite right," Flannel agreed. "Based again on the tracks left in the mud beside the hardstanding, we believe that the lorry was empty at the time of the incident. We believe it had delivered cargo to Kladow, returned through the main gate, and then diverted to the darkened space behind the overflow hardstandings to await the moment to strike."

Gatow's own preliminary investigation had come to the same conclusion and in his bones Robin had known it from the moment the lorry struck, yet irrationally he had continued to hope there might be some alternative explanation.

Flannel was still talking, "We believe a smuggler would have attempted to avoid a collision at all costs in order to escape discovery. Based on the tread marks on the concrete, however, the driver made no attempt to swerve. Indeed, he accelerated as he crossed the pavement."

Robin replayed his memories of the incident for the hundredth time and agreed, "That's what it looked like at the time, but why? Why would a German or Displaced Person want to kill Captain Utting — or anyone else flying the Airlift for that matter?"

"That's what we wanted to talk to you about," Flannel answered, looking at him almost accusingly.

Robin shook his head. "I can't image."

"Let's start with worker satisfaction. Have there been any complaints from workers about wages or working conditions at Gatow?"

"You mean from workers themselves rather than in the Soviet-controlled press?"

"Correct."

"No. None."

"Have there been any incidents of tensions between workers?"

"None that I'm aware of. Captain Bateman would be in a better position to answer."

"We already have."

"And?"

"He said there had been squabbles between men engaged in pilfering and those who oppose it. He said there had also been tensions about politics between some of the released German POWs. He admitted these clashes have resulted in blows once or twice, but always between the workers. At no time, he claimed, had the anger been directed against aircrew flying the Airlift or station personnel."

"It's hard to image that the driver of any unloading vehicle would even know who Captain Utting was," Robin pointed out. "That's what I can't understand."

"AVM Bennett firmly believes he was himself the target of the attack. He was the man who for the last six weeks was in roughly that spot at approximately that time each night. This was the first night that Utting took his place. He thinks the driver of the lorry intended to kill him, not Utting."

"That implies Bennett did something that upset one of the local drivers. Did he?"

"What do you think?" Flannel asked back.

Robin knew that Bennett came across as arrogant and abrasive at times, but he was delivering liquid fuel, and the vehicle involved handled dry cargoes; it didn't match up. "If you're certain the vehicle was driven by a civilian, then I can't imagine how Bennett might have made an enemy among them."

"You were with Utting at the time of the incident," Flannel remarked ominously.

"Yes, I was," Robin met Flannel's eyes.

"How is it that you were not hit?"

"The lights on the perimeter fence blinked as though something had come between them and me. At the same instant, I heard the groan of an approaching engine. That combination triggered an alarm signal in my brain because it's similar to what a fighter experiences before being bounced out of the sun. I shouted a warning and jumped aside. Unfortunately, I shouted 'break' — fighter jargon for 'take immediate evasive action.' Utting was a transport pilot. That I did not physically grab him and pull him aside is something I shall have to live with for the rest of my life."

Flannel showed no sympathy. He just nodded and asked, "Do you think it is possible that someone may have been trying to kill you?"

"Me? Personally?" Robin was astonished and then dismissed the suggestion, "Very unlikely. I haven't seduced anyone's wife, thrown anyone out of work, seized anyone's property, killed their dog, or — I don't know. What other motives are there for murder?" Robin asked back astonished and slightly offended.

Flannel shook his head ambivalently.

Robin feeling he was under suspicion of provoking this attack, hastened to point out, "Look, since I'm almost never out on the hardstandings after dark, there's no reason for someone to be lying in wait to attack me there. At that time of night, I'm usually going home in my car."

Flannel perked up. "Ah, that's interesting. Do you travel on the same access road that the lorries use?"

"The lorries use both access roads."

"Meaning you would normally encounter large numbers of returning lorries when travelling home?"

"Yes, of course."

"But on 11 December, rather than driving home, you chased after Utting?"

"Yes, I wanted to talk to him about Airflight's maintenance record — something Bennett was reluctant to discuss with me."

"Where was your car?"

"My driver waited behind the main admin block to take me home as usual. I stopped to tell him I needed to have a word with Utting first, and he stayed where he was."

"Is it possible that the driver of a returning lorry could have spotted your waiting car and then seen you start after Utting?"

"It's possible. The lorries pass by all the time. I take no notice of them. But what difference does it make if a driver saw me follow Utting? No one has a motive to kill me."

"Wing Commander," Flannel told him in a solemn, almost admonishing tone, "we have come to the conclusion that the most likely explanation of this incident is that a Soviet mole, working as a driver, attempted to kill you in order to disrupt operations at Gatow."

Robin stiffened. He had not thought of that, but even after turning it over in his mind, he remained unconvinced. "What could they hope to gain? There's no shortage of RAF officers qualified to command a station."

Flannel looked back at him with a police expression, revealing neither emotion nor thought process. Then he remarked, "Think about the timing. Fog had closed Gatow for most of November and the first six days of December. The accident took place only five days after the weather cleared, when — as I understand it — everyone was frantically trying to get things back on track. The accident caused morale to plunge even though the victim was almost unknown to anyone at Gatow. Imagine how much worse it would have been if the dead man had been you?" He paused only briefly to let Robin think about that and then continued, "Your violent death would have disrupted operations. Maybe not for more than a day or two, but it would have come at a critical time — just when Berlin's fuel reserves were almost gone."

"If they wanted to disrupt fuel deliveries, then killing Bennett would also have had an impact."

"True," Flannel conceded, "but I can't escape the conclusion that you were a more attractive target — if only because you are better known to the Soviets. Maybe you are correct, and your death would have little or no impact on operations. On the other hand, it might have been the final straw that tipped things the other way. The Soviets had no reason not to try and see what happened."

Flannel paused to let that sink in before adding, "Now that I know about your normal schedule and where your vehicle was at the time of the incident, I would class this as a murder of 'opportunity.' Rather than lurking in wait, the driver probably just happened to see you make off into the darkness and realised that if he followed you at a distance, he might get a chance to run you down."

Priestman thought about that and concluded. "If a driver with access to Gatow is a Soviet mole, then he may try other tricks as well."

"I expect so," Flannel agreed emotionlessly.

"Which means," Robin continued, thinking out loud, "we need to increase security around the new fuel island. Liquid fuel remains the Achilles' heel of the entire Airlift, and if the Soviets are going to target anything for sabotage, it will be the fuel off-loading facilities at Gatow." Since the start of the year, Lt. Col. Russell had been working on upgrading these. His design called for a new fuel 'port' built around a central 'island' with off-loading piers for eighteen aircraft. Each pier was equipped with electronic pumps which fed the fuel from the tankers into one of five underground storage chambers. They also planned to install floodlights so operations could continue around the clock. The entire facility was scheduled for completion on 21 February, or just under three weeks from today. Robin could imagine that the Soviets would rather not see it completed.

"Indeed," Flannel agreed succinctly.

Robin expanded, "Even if we don't have enough evidence to charge someone with manslaughter or attempted murder, we must try to identify the mole. At a minimum, we must terminate his contract. Did you take a look at their access applications?"

"Of course, but the questionnaire was designed to spot Nazi criminals, not Soviet sympathisers. That's not unique to Gatow, by the way. I suspect we have been slow to shift our focus from the Nazi to the Soviet threat in many regards. Ultimately, however, it doesn't much matter. Soviet agents lie very effectively. The safest thing for you to do would be to terminate the contracts of all 18 drivers."

Robin didn't like that answer. Seventeen of them were innocent and they probably had families depending on them. He felt particular sympathy for the displaced persons. But could he risk another incident? Could he risk sabotage to the new fuel port — or anything else for that matter? Wasn't there any other way of keeping an eye on them?

Flannel got to his feet. "That was all I wanted to talk to you about, Wing Commander. As it happens, you provided a very valuable piece of the puzzle. That said, I'm afraid, our official report will state that the case remains unresolved because, despite our suspicions, nothing can be proved. We have not identified the driver involved and have no evidence that he works for the Soviets. In your shoes, however, I would walk around as though someone had a gun pointed at my head."

Chapter Thirteen
One of Our Aircraft is Missing

With relief, Kathleen turned over the GCA radar screen to her colleague and stood up. It was eight pm, the middle of the "Evening Watch" that stretched from 4 pm to midnight. To reduce the strain, the controllers alternated between radar-controlled landings and visually controlled take-offs, swapping over at two-hour intervals. As she walked towards the coffee urn to fetch a cup of fresh coffee before taking her seat at the windows, Kathleen rotated her shoulders to ease the stiffness in the back of her neck.

It had been a bad night so far and it was likely to get worse. Snow was sweeping into northern Germany from the northwest. It had reached the departure fields roughly an hour earlier and would hit Berlin at any time now. Although Gatow had a couple of dilapidated, old snow ploughs to clear the taxi- and runways, keeping the slow-moving ploughs from disrupting the arrivals and departures always posed a challenge. Furthermore, with temperatures hovering around the freezing point, accidents with ground transportation, despite the new speed limits imposed since the Utting incident, were more likely than ever.

As if that weren't bad enough, the incoming pilots were reporting exceptionally strong Soviet jamming. Instead of instructions from the Berlin Air Safety Centre, aircraft radios picked up Russian singers, speeches by Stalin, or unnerving undulating sounds reminiscent of an alarm or siren. Soviet interference combined with weather-induced static made it almost impossible for pilots to communicate with the controllers or other aircraft. "We're flying deaf and blind up here!" One of the Americans from Wunstorf complained.

Kathleen took her seat at the table overlooking the runways and peered into the darkness. A flurry of snowflakes swirled above the human activity, but then they faded away again in the darkness. No doubt the snow would be back with a vengeance later, Kathleen thought pessimistically. That cabin on Lake Michigan was sounding more and more appealing, but the thought of moving to America, away from family, friends and colleagues, was a huge commitment that she still wasn't ready to make.

She rolled her head a couple of times, trying to relieve the tension building between her shoulders. The Air Movements Assistant on this watch with her, WAAF Corporal Henderson, handed her a sheet of paper with the list of aircraft off-loading. With a glance at the board beside her, Kathleen could see the filed flight plans of the first dozen aircraft preparing to depart.

Behind her a telephone rang, and she heard the Duty Flying Control Officer, Fl/Lt. Mitchell, take the call, saying "Tower" into the receiver. She didn't listen any further because an aircraft radioed in requesting clearance to taxi. Kathleen provided him with instructions to join the queue for the PSP departure runway.

Behind her, Fl/Lt Mitchell raised his voice. "Has anyone heard anything from Moby Dick? The WingCo's on the line and he says it's overdue."

"I'll just check, sir," Corporal Groom responded, and Kathleen glanced over as he checked the flight plan for incoming aircraft. A moment later, Groom reported, "Scheduled departure from Wunstorf was 17:50. Turn into the northern corridor should have been at 18:25 with an estimated arrival time of 19:20." That was forty-five minutes ago, Kathleen registered with a whiff of alarm. But Groom provided the explanation, "Wunstorf reported snow starting about that time, sir. They may have had to hold all aircraft while they cleared the runway. Should I call Wunstorf and get an updated ETA?"

"Yes, do that," Mitchell agreed and passed the information on to the WingCo on the other end of the line.

Kathleen focused on splicing a tanker from the fuel depot behind a line of Yorks already in the take-off queue and a flight of Dakotas. She was just about to clear a Dakota for push-back when Groom called across the room in controlled but unmistakable alarm. "Fl/Lt Mitchell, sir! Wunstorf is reporting that Moby Dick departed on schedule, or very nearly, at 17:53 — before the snow set in."

"What?" Mitchell snapped back, and everyone in the entire room went silent and still. Kathleen looked again at the clock. It was now 20:15. Moby Dick was fifty-five minutes overdue.

"Contact the Berlin Air Safety Centre and see if they have contact with Moby Dick. If not, ask them to put out a call to all inbound aircraft on the northern corridor for information."

While Groom complied with orders, Kathleen went back to work, but she felt her neck muscles cramping up again. She alternated rotating her shoulders with rolling her head back and forth, but nothing seemed to help. The tension was rising within her. Every crash was bad, but the thought of the air ambulance going down with Mrs Priestman on board was almost unbearable.

"The Berlin Air Safety Centre says Soviet jamming has made it impossible to communicate with most of the inbound traffic, sir," Groom called across the room.

"Meaning they don't know if Moby Dick is on approach or not," Mitchell interpreted.

"Correct, sir."

"What's the Wellington's fuel capacity? Could they have overshot for some reason and be wandering around Polish air space? I heard one USAF Skymaster did that."

Kathleen remembered the incident, too. Everyone had had a good laugh at the time because it turned out the pilots had tuned their radios into the broadcast of an American football game and become so engrossed in the sport that they had flown right over Berlin and continued for almost a hundred miles before they noticed something was wrong. They radioed in confused and sheepish and were told to turn around and fly on a reciprocal course.

"The Wellington has the fuel capacity," Groom answered his superior's question, "but Flying Officer Priestman" (he used her VR rank) "isn't the kind of pilot to get lost — not by far, anyway." Kathleen agreed with that assessment and nodded unconsciously.

From behind her, a voice asked quietly but firmly, "So, what do you have?" Kathleen tensed. It was the WingCo himself. Kathleen risked only a quick glance and then tried to look completely preoccupied while Mitchell reported what they knew.

"Where are Albie and Peggy?" The WingCo asked, referring to the two Halifaxes owned and flown by Emergency Air Services.

"I'll just check, sir," Mitchell replied and crossed the room to the board with incoming flight plans. He returned with the news. "Albie is outbound for Celle with its last cargo of the day. Peggie is inbound from Fassberg and slightly overdue. Most aircraft are running about five minutes late. Peggie was scheduled to land at 20:20." It was now 20:26.

The WingCo walked away from the tables by the windows and entered the radar room. Kathleen could hear low voices and then the WingCo's precise voice talking over the radio. "Kit, Robin here. Moby Dick is overdue. Have you had any contact with it over the last two hours?" Kathleen could not make out the answer that was badly compromised by static, but she heard the WingCo thank Moran and say, "Turning you back over to Control."

Re-entering the main tower, Priestman addressed Mitchell. "We need to put out a call on all our frequencies."

"Yes, sir. Do you want to do that?"

"Yes, I'll do it."

An aircraft was demanding Kathleen's instructions in an annoyed tone, and she realised she had ignored its first attempt to attract her attention. She picked up her microphone and provided the necessary guidance, trying hard to keep her voice relaxed and not think about Moby Dick.

Shortly afterwards, the WingCo's voice came over the airwaves. "This is RAF Gatow. One of our aircraft is missing. Request all inbound aircraft to report any fires or flashing lights observed on the ground. Repeat: report fires or flashing lights seen on the ground below the northern corridor to Gatow Control Tower." The message went out twice on all their frequencies. Kathleen could hear a smattering of "Rogers" and "Wilcos" from the pilots, but no response containing information.

At 20:31 Peggie for Pegasus put down on the concrete runway and flashed by the tower, easily recognizable by its bright white livery. About fifteen minutes later, FL/Lt Moran arrived in the tower and came straight over to the WingCo, asking what had happened.

"We don't know. They took off practically on schedule from Wunstorf at 17:53 and apparently entered the corridor by 18:25 when you say you talked to her."

"That's right."

"That was the last anyone has heard of them. Did you see anything coming in?"

"I flew above the cloud cover — as did all the heavies. There's good visibility up there and we can use celestial navigation. The only aircraft flying below the cloud are the Daks and, of course, Moby Dick. Emily prefers and usually gets a clearance at 3,000 feet or less since she's without a navigator and the stars are no use to her. Both she and Jan learned to follow the landscape as ferry pilots and are more comfortable at a lower altitude."

"What altitude are the Daks flying in this weather?" The WingCo asked.

"Four thousand, four thousand-five," Moran answered.

"Did Emily mention anything about mechanical problems when you spoke?"

"She said the fuel gauge seemed to be acting up. Look, Gordon will be going crazy by now. Let me nip down to the hangar and see if he has any ideas — or do you want me to stop by the Malcolm Club first and see if I can find some Dakota pilots?"

"Go and talk to Gordon. I'll have someone else sort out the Dakota pilots." Moran departed, and Priestman sent his adjutant to the Malcolm Club.

An unnatural calm descended over the tower. No one was chatting among themselves or joking with the pilots as they would normally have been doing. Everyone confined themselves to the minimal communication necessary to get their jobs done. At least the snow was still holding off.

Moran returned to report that EAS' ground chief swore the Wellington was in A1 condition, including the fuel gauge, which he said had been serviced only a couple of days earlier. The WingCo sighed. "I don't doubt him. It's just that I don't know what else to think." He drew a deep breath, audible to Kathleen even as she concentrated on her job. "You might as well go home, Kit. Georgina will be worrying and there's nothing you can do here."

"I've already rung Georgina. She told me to help you in any way I can. What can I do?"

"Would you mind going down to Translation and seeing if the Soviets are reporting anything?"

"I'll go straight away."

Soon afterwards a Dakota pilot emerged from the stairway. He had already landed and been at the Malcolm Club when the WingCo had made his announcement over the radio, but Stan had found him and sent him to the tower. He anxiously and eagerly reported that he'd noticed navigation lights below him that appeared to be straying off course roughly 30 minutes into his flight. He'd tried to raise the aircraft, thinking they might have a navigational error, but got only static in response. Since he'd heard no mayday call and he could see neither flames nor indications of erratic flying, he concluded it was a Soviet aircraft on approach to the Soviet airfield at Parchim.

This report triggered a flurry of activity as the pilot, the WingCo and Fl/Lt Mitchell tried to calculate where the pilot had been at the time he saw the lights and, based on the direction the aircraft had been flying, where it might have been going.

Shortly afterwards another pilot reported that he'd heard a woman's voice on the radio. The tone of voice had been urgent but not panicky. However, he had been unable to understand what she was saying because Russian singing kept bursting in and blotting out her voice. Just something about "fuel" and "can't reach BASC" — which, he pointed out, none of them could. He ended with, "The odd thing, sir, was that the woman sounded American, but the Americans don't have any women pilots."

"Jan!" The WingCo gasped, and only then did Kathleen register that two of J.B.'s best friends were also on the missing aircraft.

"Sir?" the RAF pilot asked bewildered.

"The Second Pilot on the air ambulance, the one everyone knows as Moby Dick, is a former American ferry pilot."

"Oh. Is that the missing aircraft, sir?"

"Yes."

There was an awkward silence as the pilot made the connections and then said in a small voice, "I'm very sorry, sir."

"Understood," Priestman answered, straining to remain professional.

Kathleen's heart went out to him. He had to maintain perfect calm and the neutrality of the station commander. He couldn't allow himself to treat this missing aircraft differently from any other — and yet it was. It was his wife who was missing.

Just after 21:00, the snow arrived. Although it was a fine, light snow and the ploughs could cope with it, air traffic movements needed to be more carefully monitored, taking Kathleen's full attention. There had been no more word on the lost aircraft anyway, and although the WingCo remained in the tower, he had sent Moran home.

It was like the war, again, Kathleen thought. How often had she remained in the tower after one of their aircraft 'failed to return'? Then, too, the squadron leader and station commander would wait long after the other crews dragged themselves off to bed and the intelligence officers had filed their reports. They'd waited just as the WingCo did now, staring out the windows at nothing and listening to the ticking of the clock that recorded the draining petrol and the waning hope.

At 22:00 Kathleen went back on the radar screen and GCA controlling. The jamming had let up and communications were almost back to normal. The snow had also moved eastwards, although the cloud cover remained unbroken. When midnight rolled around, Kathleen was ready for bed twice over. Her neck was feeling stiffer than ever, and a sharp pain ran down under her left shoulder blade. She needed a hot bath and a back massage — the kind J.B. had given her last time they managed to wangle an evening together. The thought of J.B. reminded her that his friends were missing. She would try to get through to him first thing in the morning to share all she knew.

As she left the tower, she paused to look towards the WingCo. He was still there, staring out of the windows into the dark. It reminded her of the night Ken was listed as 'FTR.' The pain, she registered, was only beginning. This was the numb phase. Soon more information would start to come, confirming the worst yet adding horrifying details that caused more acute distress. In her case, it had been 'Berlin,' 'a flamer,' 'no 'chutes.' God alone knew what they would learn about Moby Dick and its crew, but Kathleen feared that it wasn't going to be pretty.

Spies
RAF Gatow
Sunday 13 February 1949
(Day 233 of the Berlin Airlift)

Sometime after midnight, Robin went home. Wallace, his driver, murmured something about being 'very sorry' to hear that Mrs Priestman was missing. Robin thanked him and not another word was exchanged. At the residence, Kit and Georgina were already in bed and Jasha no longer lived in. She had moved in with Graham and would arrive like the other servants at 7:00 am. Anna, of course, was wherever Emily was, whether that was in the realm of the living or the dead, God alone knew. The whole house was dark and echoing.

Robin got himself undressed and climbed into bed. It was gigantic and cold. He found it impossible to get comfortable. Besides, he could not stop his thoughts. If he hadn't talked Merer into letting him stay on as station commander, he and Emily would have been far away and safe. If he'd been better at his job in the Ministry, they would have sent him somewhere more pleasant than Berlin. And why had he encouraged Emily to join AAI? Indeed, why had he supported her ambitions to learn to fly in the first place?

At some point, he drifted into a half-sleep that led him into a confusing nightmare which had nothing to do with Emily being missing, yet everything to do with the fact that he was frightened and helpless. He was yanked awake by his alarm clock unrested and unsure if reality was better than the nightmare. He dressed, shaved and ate breakfast on autopilot.

Kit and Georgina were at the breakfast table and asked him if they could help in any way. He told them honestly, no. Robin couldn't face food, but forced himself to drink some coffee. They left at the usual time, Kit joining him in the car since he rightly planned to keep flying.

Being Sunday, Georgina did not have school, and her sewing class wasn't until the afternoon, so she assumed responsibility for informing Jasha of what had happened and for ringing Christian to advise him that the ambulance was missing. Christian would pass the news to David, the hospitals and the Berlin City government. With the ambulance missing and presumed crashed, all medical evacuations were suspended until further notice.

When Kit and Robin parted in front of the admin building, Kit asked Robin to keep him informed of any developments. Robin nodded and mounted the stairs to his office. Noise levels seemed normal until he reached his anteroom. Here the silence was deafening. His staff greeted him with subdued voices, and he had barely sat down before Sergeant Andrews brought him tea and two scones with raspberry jam, something she knew he liked. He thanked her, adding "I'll need to inform Air Commodores Merer and Waite of what has happened. Merer comes in late on Sundays, so there's no point trying to reach him before 10 am London time, but I'd appreciate it if you could ring Air Commodore Waite at his residence at nine o'clock."

"I'll connect you as soon as I get through, sir." Andrews withdrew.

Robin hoped that Merer would offer to inform Tunner of what had happened as he did not relish the idea of talking with the cold-blooded efficiency expert. He might dismiss the ambulance as a "nuisance" that was better off grounded anyway — without any consideration for the position Robin was in.

A gentle knock on the door interrupted his speculation, and Robin cleared his throat to call, "Come in."

Fl/Lt Boyd entered the office with a manila folder in his hand and a nervous demeanour. "This just arrived, sir," he announced.

Robin felt his heart pounding harder as he reached out his hand, asking "Press clippings? Anything about the crash?"

"It's a press release from SMAD, sir." Boyd's hand shook as he handed over the folder.

Robin opened the cover and stared at the official Soviet Military Government press statement. Under the title was a blurry photo that resolved itself into a white aircraft with a dark cross on its tail lying in the snow. It was unquestionably Moby Dick. Robin studied the picture trying to see some indication of survivors. There was no sign of fire, and although the aircraft looked crumpled, it was not in bits and pieces. It appeared to have skidded or smashed up against a low, stone building almost completely covered in snow. The shed or whatever it was had probably been invisible in the dark and driving snow — until the aircraft hit it. Moby Dick had come to rest with the right engine partially inside the structure and the right side of the cockpit bashed in.

"Sir," Boyd spoke into his thoughts hesitantly, uncomfortable with the time he'd taken to inspect the photo. "I've provided the translation of the text on the second sheet of paper."

Robin turned over the paper with Russian text and found the attached sheet with the typed translation. The headline read: "Spy plane downed!"

"Spy plane!" Robin exploded. "It's got red crosses all over it!"

"Yes, sir," Boyd conceded. "I think it's best for you to read the full text."

Robin looked down again. The text led with "An American spy plane…" He snorted. What made it American? "…disguised as an ambulance went down near Pritzwalk late Saturday night. Although masquerading as an ambulance, it carried no patients and had wandered far outside of the designated corridors in an obvious attempt to gain information about secret Soviet facilities. The crew members, including a negro in nurse's uniform and a female spy, were taken into custody," Robin stopped reading long enough to close his eyes and thank God — until he remembered that they might be referring to Jan or that Emily could have died *after* being found by the Soviets. He forced himself to keep reading. "…where the injured received medical treatment." So, some or several of the crew had sustained injuries, but at least there was no reference to anyone dying. Instead, the statement declared, "The SMAD will protest at the highest levels against this unlawful violation of Soviet airspace and the misappropriation of internationally recognised humanitarian symbols on an aircraft engaged in espionage." Good God! They were going to treat them as spies! That meant Emily and the others still weren't out of danger.

But apparently she *was* alive. He had not lost her. He'd be damned before he'd let the Russians shoot her for spying! If General Robertson wouldn't help, he'd go to Foreign Secretary Bevin, the Prime Minister or the King himself! He'd make them do whatever was necessary to secure her release. That thought energised him. He nodded to Boyd. "Thank you, Boyd. This is good news, even if it means we have a tricky situation on our hands. We need to get more details as soon as possible."

"I've got my whole team working on it already, sir. Both the German and

Russian translators are scouring the press for all references to the crash. I've also asked Corporal Borisenko to contact her friend on Sokolovsky's staff." Robin nodded agreement, remembering that Borisenko had promised he would not regret letting her stay. She'd been right! He thanked Boyd again and the intelligence officer withdrew.

As the door closed behind Boyd, Robin put a call through to the EAS hangar just in time to catch Kit before he took off. He spoke to Gordon Mac-Donald, who let out of hoot of triumph and promised to spread the word.

Robin had barely hung up before he received a phone call from Air Commodore Waite. Waite had already seen the SMAD notice. When he learnt that Moby Dick had gone missing at half past eight the previous evening, he admonished Robin for not ringing him straight away but accepted that there was nothing he could have done at the time. "All right," he concluded, "I'll get in touch with Robertson, and we'll coordinate how to lodge our protests. We'll demand the immediate return of all crew members and access to the wreck. However, don't get your hopes up that Emily could be back in a day or two. Having issued such an aggressive announcement, it won't be easy for the Soviets to back down. Nevertheless, once we start negotiations over the release of the crew, we'll be able to wring more information about injuries out of them and may be able to send a representative to see them."

"Bear in mind, sir, that three of the crew are American. You'll want to get Colonel Howley and possibly General Clay to weigh in."

"Good point. A joint demarche is better than if we do it alone or separately. I'll get on that straight away."

Robin thanked him, feeling stronger already. He wasn't as alone as he'd felt last night. That feeling was reinforced by the next call he received. Frank Howley was on the line. "Jesus Christ, Robin! Why didn't you call me last night?"

"I didn't have a clue about what had happened last night," Robin answered, although inwardly he admitted he had not reacted well. He'd been too shocked to think straight.

"Look, this is crap about treating an ambulance as a spy plane, and I don't have any problem telling the bastards that. In fact, I'm going to make a stink about this publicly. I plan to go on RIAS and call the bastards out for their stupidity and inhumanity. At a wild stretch, military cargo crates carrying coal, food and clothing might somehow be viewed as a military operation, but nobody can say that about a private ambulance carrying German civilians. I'm going to make them look so foolish, they'll send the crew back like they were hot potatoes."

Robin managed a faint smile as he responded, "Thank you for your support, Frank, but be careful too. Maybe I'm losing my wool, but I'd rather the Ivans didn't discover that one of the crew members is my wife. They might try to extract extra concessions for her release, if they find that out."

"Good point. I'll keep my remarks generic. A private ambulance with an international crew including medical personnel. That kind of stuff. No names whatsoever."

"Thank you."

"Robin, call me if there is anything — and I mean anything — I can do to help."

"I will, and thank you again, Frank."

"Oh, one more thing. I'm not going to ask General Clay for permission to make this statement on RIAS. He'd probably say 'no.' But feel free to contact him directly. He's expressed admiration for Emily more than once, and the other three crew members are Americans. I think we can persuade him to lend his weight to our efforts to resolve this as fast as possible."

Robin was pleased to have that confirmation and decided that it wouldn't hurt for him to reinforce any appeal Waite made to the American general. He asked Sergeant Andrews to see if she could get him a connection to the American Military Governor and in the meantime contacted Georgina at home. She let her emotions show and her expressions of relief were moving. He heard her pause to call, "Jasha! Stop crying! Emily's alive! She's in Soviet custody." A flood of excited Polish in response also made Robin feel better. It was good to know that others cared so much for Emily.

Within the hour, Clay called Robin back. "Wing Commander, I want you to know that you have my unstinting support. We will get them all back as soon as possible. Please bear in mind, however, that if we make it too obvious that something is particularly important to us, the Reds usually up the ante. We're going to have to play our cards carefully. I'm going to put a call through to Sokolovsky shortly, and I'll try to shame him a bit about trying to depict an ambulance as a spy plane."

Robin repeated his concerns that the Soviets might become more intransigent if they knew his wife was among the crew, and Clay agreed not to mention names. "Much as I am concerned about Mrs Priestman, the other three crew members are Americans. Naturally, they must be the focus of my official attention."

"Yes, sir. I understand. I can't tell you how much I appreciate whatever support you can give."

"Wing Commander, your wife is an exceptionally fine woman. I don't want anything bad to happen to her — not to mention that you are one of the bedrocks of this whole operation and Tunner knows it. Now, buck up, and I'll get back to you if I have anything concrete to report."

That affirmation of support and respect cheered Robin up enough for him to attempt some of his routine work. There were three airmen up on charges, for example, but he quickly concluded he could not deal with them fairly. One of them might start with something like, "Before you say anything, sir, I just want to tell you how very sorry I am about what's happened to your wife." He would not be able to be judicial after that. He reached instead for the daily statistics, but he found he could not concentrate on the columns of figures. Maybe he could try calling Merer? He rang Sergeant Andrews, who successfully connected him with the British Airlift Commander.

Robin summarised for the Air Commodore what they knew so far about Moby Dick and added that Howley and Clay as well as Waite and Robertson were already working on the Soviets. "Excellent," Merer responded. "Do you want me to handle Tunner?"

"That would be greatly appreciated, sir."

"That's fine. I'll speak to him straight away."

"Thank you, sir."

Robin had barely hung up when the phone rang again. This time it was his direct line, not the line via Sergeant Andrews. Very few people had the direct number, Emily being one of them. Jasha and Graham were the only others he could think of. He picked up the receiver expecting the RCE lieutenant colonel. "Hello?"

"Wing Commander Priestman?" The voice was utterly unfamiliar and something about it sent a shiver down Robin's spine.

"Who's speaking?" Robin asked sharply.

"My name is unimportant," the voice replied, but a Russian accent was detectable. "It is enough that you should know that we have your wife."

"Where do you have her?" Robin demanded. "Is she all right?"

"That is not relevant. The only thing you need to know is that you will not see her again alive unless you cooperate with us."

"What do you mean by cooperate?" Robin asked in alarm.

"Blow up the new fuel facility at Gatow before it becomes operational."

"That's absurd—"

"You have one week to comply. If you fail, we will deliver your wife's body on the Glienicker Bridge exactly seven days from now." There was a loud click, and the connection was replaced by the dialling tone. Robin spun about to look at his wall clock. It was exactly noon on Sunday, 13 February.

Treason
RAF Gatow
Sunday 13 February 1949
(Day 233 of the Berlin Airlift)

"Graham, I need to talk to you—"

Recognising Robin's voice, Graham broke in to say, "Robin! Jasha just rang to say Emily's OK. Thank God for that, although the crash is still terrible. Any word on when she will be released?"

"That's what I need to talk to you about. In private. Could you meet me out at Number 1 hangar? I'll take you up in the Anson. Officially, it will be so you can assess progress on the new fuel depot from the air."

Graham could tell that Robin was in acute distress and suspected that the news about Emily's situation was not as good as Jasha had made it sound. Possibly she was badly injured. Graham replied simply, "I'm on my way now."

Half an hour later, Graham found himself in the right-hand seat of the small RAF passenger transport as Robin received clearance from the tower. By now, it was brilliantly sunny with temperatures above freezing. Puddles of water formed on the hardstandings as melting snow dripped off the roofs. The Airlift itself appeared to be in high gear. "It looks like we're on the way to setting new records," Graham remarked absently, watching the aircraft landing beside them as they lifted off the PSP and swayed noticeably in a cross breeze.

"We might be," Robin sounded indifferent and exuded tension. Graham decided it would be best to let Robin guide the conversation and was relieved when he didn't waste time. "You know the Soviets are referring to Moby Dick as a spy plane?"

"Yes, I saw that, but that's standard practice. They treated me as a spy, too, remember." Graham's voice faltered. "Surely you don't think they'd treat Emily the same way...." The thought was horrifying, and Graham recognised that a female prisoner faced the added threat of sexual abuse. He looked over at Robin in alarm.

Robin was banking the aircraft around hard, his eyes focused on the ground. "You can see the airfield very well from here," he remarked, and Graham dutifully looked back at Gatow spread out below them.

"Out of curiosity," Robin continued, the words conversational but the tone almost electric with tension, "what would happen to the airfield if your new fuel island were blown up?"

"Blown up? You mean if someone bombed it?"

"No, let's say some idiot dropped a cigarette into it or something of that kind."

"That's not as simple as it sounds," Graham assured him. "It would take deliberate sabotage to blow the whole thing up. I made sure that the five individual storage tanks weren't interconnected. We also took precautions to prevent a fire at any pier from spreading to the others. To destroy the whole depot, each of the five subterranean concrete chambers would have to be set alight separately. Short of sabotage, that's not likely."

"Setting aside the issue of probability, what would the damage to the airfield be?" Robin persisted as he continued to circle the field, carefully remaining at an altitude above the glide path of the incoming and outgoing freighters.

"It would be similar to a Grand Slam — the famous earthquake bomb — hitting the runway. The concrete would crack in many places and the surface would be displaced and deformed. Both runways would become unusable, and it would take days, maybe even a week or more, to remove the broken bits and to level and compact the base before repaving the surface. The airfield would be closed to operations for about a fortnight, I suspect."

"A fortnight? That's all?"

"About that. Of course, rebuilding the fuel depot would take a month or so. Why?"

"I've been told that blowing up the fuel dump is the price for Emily's life."

Graham grabbed his seat and gaped at Robin. "Who told you that?"

"An anonymous caller with a Russian accent who reached me on the direct line to my office at noon today." Graham continued to stare at him as the memories of his week in Soviet detainment flooded back. He could hear the voices shouting insults one moment and reasonably 'suggesting' treason or painting lurid pictures of the horrors that awaited him the next. All the Soviet interrogators had been fluent English speakers, but they had also spoken with heavy accents. He felt nauseous and wished they were not flying.

Robin continued, "He gave me one week to blow up the fuel facilities — or, he said, Emily's body will be delivered on the Glienicker Bridge at noon next Sunday."

"They're bluffing," Graham declared, but his mouth was dry.

"Can you be sure?" Robin turned to look him in the eye.

"It would cause an international incident."

"They don't care about that! Besides, they could claim she was injured in the crash and died in hospital, couldn't they? They could display her bruised and broken body draped in flowers and make speeches about how we're responsible for her death because we sent her out to conduct espionage in a 'decrepit' old aircraft."

"They could do that — no matter what you do. Listen to me!" Graham admonished. "If you blew up the fuel depot, the worst damage wouldn't be to the runways or the airfield, but to you. There would be an enquiry, and it would inevitably identify you as the perpetrator. You'd be tried for treason and possibly hanged — certainly sentenced to a long prison term. Emily would come home to a ruined man."

"At least she'd come home."

"You don't know that. That's the point, Robin! When have the Russians ever kept their word about anything? They never keep their part of any bargain. Doing what the Ivans want only makes them bolder and more aggressive. The more we give, the more they take."

Robin didn't answer. The engines droned beside them. The propellors caught the light of the afternoon sun and looked like flickering golden disks. Robin again banked the aircraft around hard, and Graham clung to the seat. He wished he knew what Robin was thinking. Or maybe it was better not to know.

"What would you do if it were Jasha?" Robin asked as he levelled the aircraft.

"I came close to breaking even before I knew Jasha loved me. Any threat to her now would unman me. I'd grovel and do whatever they asked of me. But you're a better man than I am, Robin. That's why you're wearing those ribbons and have command at Gatow. So, stop thinking about this! It'll achieve nothing but your own destruction."

Robin didn't answer. Instead, he became completely absorbed in flying, and with mounting discomfort, Graham realised that the nose of the aircraft was lifting more and more. As the upward tilt became alarmingly pronounced, Graham clung to the base of his seat in growing fear. They were almost vertical. The speed fell off. The aircraft shuddered and then the right wing fell away. The Anson started to rotate around its axis. Graham tightened his hold on his seat in terror. The lazy turning accelerated. They were spinning faster and faster, heading straight towards the earth. The rotating made Graham feel dizzy. Unable to contain himself any longer, Graham screamed, "Are you trying to kill us both?"

Instantly the aircraft straightened and levelled off. A little ashamed, Graham realised that Robin was still in complete control.

Robin looked over at him apologetically, "I'm sorry. I didn't mean to frighten you. I just needed — I do aerobatics to dissipate tension. I should have warned you first. I'm sorry."

"It's all right, as long as you aren't trying to kill us," Graham grumbled, only partially mollified.

"I'm not going to kill either of us as long as we have a fraction of a chance of saving Emily."

"Robin, don't trust them!" Graham urged again. Robin looked over and their eyes met. "You don't even know for certain that Emily is alive," Graham pointed out. "All you have is their word for it — and they might be lying in order to trap you."

"I could demand proof."

"You could, and let's suppose they provide it. What then? You blow up the fuel island disrupting the Airlift, delivering the Soviets a huge propaganda victory, destroying your reputation and your future —"

"And they'd still have Emily."

"Exactly."

Robin didn't answer this time. He turned his attention back to flying, and in less than ten minutes they were back on the ground at Gatow. Only after turning off the engines did Robin speak again. Turning to Graham he said, "Thank you." He paused and then elaborated, "Thank you for coming. Thank you for listening, and thank you for your advice."

Graham assured him that he'd be glad to help in any way he could, but he refrained from asking what Robin had decided. What he didn't know, he did not have to report.

Chapter Fourteen
In Search of Truth

Opposing Truths
Berlin-Moabit
Monday, 14 February 1949
(Day 234 of the Berlin Airlift)

The news about *Moby Dick* shook David Goldman to the core. Not only had he lost his 'flagship' aircraft, his most cherished asset, but a close friend and three additional crew had gone down with it. While the Soviet reports suggested no one had been killed, David knew how dangerous forced landings could be and that injuries could be horrific. Worst of all, David knew that even if the entire crew had walked away from the crash, Emily, Anna and Jan were still at the mercy of the Soviets — and he knew what they'd done to Charlotte.

Yet he could take no action! A private company had no leverage with the Soviets whatsoever. If the British and American military governors had not been prepared to intercede on the part of his employees, he would have had no hope at all. Yet while the governors' intervention was his best hope, it also left him helpless. The timing and tactics of all dealings with the Soviets were entirely in their hands.

David was particularly distressed that the Americans appeared to be prioritizing Anna over the other three crew members. Howley had gone on RIAS raking the Soviets over the coals for treating an ambulance like a spy plane. He'd pointed out that all aboard had been civilians, but he had placed particular emphasis on the nurse. He'd highlighted the fact that she was a trained medical professional. Howley stressed that even uniformed military medical personnel were treated as non-combatants. "If you start treating medical personnel as political pawns," he warned ominously, "you risk ending the age-old custom of medical *treatment* being apolitical as well." David feared that by singling Anna out, the Americans might gain special treatment for her, whereas he wanted all four of his employees to be treated respectfully — and returned forthwith

As for the material side of the disaster, he didn't want to think about it just yet. With the aircraft down in Soviet territory and the Soviets treating it as a 'military object,' there was no way to conduct any kind of crash investigation, which meant his insurance company might weasel out of any kind of payment. A complete write-off would cause havoc to EAS's balance sheet, but David consoled himself with the fact that as long as the Halifaxes kept flying the Airlift, cash flow and liquidity would not pose a problem. In short, the business was not in immediate danger. With the fate of his downed crew in the hands of the military governors and the business on autopilot, he felt justified in focusing on his other priority: Charlotte.

Charlotte's trial opened today, and Alix had spent the entire weekend writing and re-writing her opening remarks. She warned David, however, that the prosecutor would speak first. "Depending on what tack he takes, I may have to ad-lib the entire speech."

First thing Monday morning, Horst drove David and Alix to the office building on the Kurfuerstendamm to pick up Christian and then left Christian and David at the courthouse in Moabit, before continuing with Alix to the police station where Charlotte was detained. Alix would travel with her in the police van to the courthouse. Meanwhile, David and Christian had a meagre breakfast together at a nearby café and then found their way to Courtroom # 6, where the "Walmsdorf trial" was scheduled to open. They took seats in the visitor's gallery and waited nervously.

David was displeased when first one and then three more reporters showed up. They were all from the local press and looked like junior journalists cutting their teeth. Wearing threadbare clothes and scuffed shoes, they exuded disrespectful eagerness for the "action" to begin. Based on the banter among them, David surmised that these young newsmen viewed Charlotte's ordeal as a chance to advance their careers. A female murderer was rare enough to attract reader interest, but a murdering countess was in a league by herself. If a murdering countess weren't attention-getting enough, a countess who blew a man's head off with a shot between the eyes was sensational. The young journalists agreed that this case was going to be followed by half the housewives in Berlin, most of whom were desperate for any news *other* than Airlift sorties and tonnages.

Roughly a quarter of an hour before the trial was due to start, the prosecutor swept in with his entourage of assistants and interns. He cast David a sneering smile and then settled himself in his seat, fretting with his robes. Next, the clerks took their places primly. Only minutes before the trial was due to start did Alix and Charlotte arrive.

Alix had explained that people associated female murderers either with jealous women obsessed with revenge or with heartless, calculating she-devils interested in wealth and power. She stressed that to win the sympathy of the court, Charlotte must avoid these stereotypes and instead look 'normal' and 'respectable,' but not privileged. Alix had forbidden any make-up or jewellery and dressed Charlotte in a sober, dark skirt, a plain, white blouse and a dark cardigan.

Yet there was no way Charlotte could look 'normal' to David. He saw how thin she was, how her bones stuck out, making her face angular and her hands skeletal. Objectively, she was anything but beautiful, yet David couldn't imagine how anyone could look at her and not see how vulnerable, frail and deserving of protection she was.

The three judges arrived supported by two lay assessors. The latter sat on the outer ends of the bench. In short order, the formalities were concluded, and the prosecution was invited to make opening remarks.

Herr Dr Steinbrueck rose to his feet. "Your Honours. Before addressing the shocking events which have led to this trial, I wish to talk to you about the brave young man who cannot be here today: the victim. Let me tell you about Friedrich Adelbert von Bredow, known to his family and friends as 'Fritz.'

"Fritz was born on a large but far from prosperous estate in Pomerania, the second son and third child of Alfred Berthold von Bredow and his wife Clarita. Just weeks after he was born, his father left to join his regiment at the outbreak of the Great War. While his father did his patriotic duty, Fritz's mother carried the burden of raising her family, running the farm, and keeping her children safe from deserters and Polish terrorists attempting to expel Germans from the region. Although she succeeded, her eldest boy developed polio and was soon confined to a wheelchair. As if that weren't bad enough, her husband returned an invalid, gassed by the British." The prosecutor cast an accusing look over his shoulder at David as he made this announcement. Christian rolled his eyes.

Steinbrueck continued, "At the age of eight, little Fritz was sent away to a cadet school in Stettin. He landed in an environment that was Spartan in its lack of comfort and luxury and ruthless in its dedication to turning little boys into men. Yet Fritz thrived in the school. He was not a scholar, but he was good at sports. He excelled at fencing and running and above all at riding. That was important because, on his school holidays, he had no time to play and have fun. No, Fritz worked hardest during the holidays because, with his brother and father both physically handicapped, it fell to little Fritz to help his mother hold things together.

"These were terrible times," Steinbrueck intoned. "They were years of lawlessness and failed government. Years of crippling reparations, astronomical inflation, and unprecedented unemployment." David and Christian exchanged a look of disgust.

Alix sprang to her feet with an objection, "The Weimar Republic is not on trial here, your honours. The defendant was an infant when the Republic was established and thirteen when it ended. She was not responsible for conditions."

"Sustained."

"The point, your honours, is that at a very tender age, Fritz von Bredow became the 'man' that his mother leaned upon. Although still a youth, she turned to him with her problems as her husband's health deteriorated and her eldest son, unable to cope with his handicap, turned increasingly to drugs."

"How does he know that?" David wrote on a slip of paper that he passed Christian.

Christian scribbled back, "I suspect they've found Fritz's sister. She was always jealous of Fritz and detested Charlotte."

Steinbrueck continued, "It was because his parents needed him that Fritz was not one of those who volunteered for service. He waited until he was conscripted before proudly donning the uniform of our heroic army. Yet although a late-comer, Fritz soon proved his worth. His skill in the saddle attracted attention and honours — all the way to the German Olympic team. During the 1936 endurance event, Fritz von Bredow captured the hearts of all Germany. At the water jump which brought so many riders to disaster, Fritz's horse also refused and lost his footing; Fritz tumbled into the pond. To the shock of the spectators, Fritz seemed in no hurry to recapture his mount, regain the saddle and continue the ride. His delay ran up increasing penalty points. Eventually, however, he did remount and continue the parcourse. Only at the end, did we learn that Fritz had broken his collarbone in the fall. Despite his injury, in pain and with just one hand to control his mount, he not only mastered the remaining obstacles but also secured for Germany the Olympic Gold medal in team eventing."

David pushed Christian another note. "Is that true?"

"Yes," Christian confirmed in writing.

David had not dreamed that his rival was such a hero. He looked intensely at Charlotte, but she was staring straight ahead.

Steinbrueck continued in an indulgent tone, "As you can imagine, Fritz was quite admired by the ladies after that! But he was a shy young man, not attracted by flashy ladies of the night, glamorous socialites or alluring actresses. He didn't want a city girl at all. He wanted a girl who shared his love of nature, horses, hunting, and the great open landscapes of his homeland."

David saw Charlotte stiffen and then recoil when the prosecutor spun and pointed at her as he declared in a loud accusing voice: "He fell in love with that — that woman there." David thought he heard Charlotte gasp. Alix certainly laid a hand on her arm to calm her.

Meanwhile, Steinbrueck explained, "Fritz met her at a ball hosted by a distant cousin. She *seemed* to be the woman of his dreams. She came from a good but rural family. She had grown up, like him, helping out on the estate. She loved horses and she could hunt too. Fritz in his innocence taught her how to use a gun — and how to shoot to kill."

Charlotte's hands balled into fists and Alix stroked her arm and wrote something down. Christian murmured in David's ear, "Nonsense. Her brothers taught her to shoot long before Fritz entered the picture."

"Fritz was bedazzled, and — to be fair — so was everyone else," Steinbrueck conceded. "Just six weeks after that fateful meeting, they became engaged. The letters of congratulation flooded in from far and wide. It was the perfect match. The perfect pair. Fritz and Lotte, as they called her then. The pictures show two young people who can hardly take their eyes off one another. A young couple in love." He paused dramatically and then continued.

"But Germany was at war. Fritz had to return to his unit. Lotte promised him she would wait forever. No matter how long the war lasted, she told him, Fritz would find her waiting longingly for his return."

Christian pressed down on David's arm and wrote out: "She was twenty-two years old and until then very sheltered."

David nodded back. He didn't blame her for falling in love with such a dashing young man. Indeed, hearing this story which made no mention of Fritz in the Hitler Youth or any other Nazi association helped him understand Charlotte a little better. She had not fallen in love with a Nazi or a military man but with a modern-day knight.

"Fritz went back to war. To his panzer regiment. He fought at Minsk and Moscow and the Second Battle of Kharkiv and with his comrades of the IV Panzer Corps he advanced toward Stalingrad." Steinbrueck paused dramatically and continued in a sombre tone of voice. "I'm sure I do not need to remind this court what happened. The weather turned against us. The tanks became bogged down in mud."

Scowling, David started to scribble another indignant note to Christian: "What does this have to do with Charlotte?" Yet as he went to pass the scrap of paper to Christian he caught sight of the judges' faces. All three had pulled themselves erect, eyes misted. He realised that Steinbrueck knew exactly what he was doing by appealing to the patriotism of the judges. The question was what did Alix have to counter it? He was getting increasingly worried.

Steinbrueck continued his narrative, "Heavy cloud and snow grounded our heroic Luftwaffe, while the Soviet counter-offensive encircled our troops. Little by little the supplies ran out. The gallant efforts of the Luftwaffe and the brilliant tactics of the great Feldmarshall von Manstein were not enough. The 6th Army was starved into submission. And Fritz?

"Fritz's last letter to his mother was dated 5 November, but his last *letter* was to his beloved Lotte on 17 November. Two days later, in the fury of the Soviet counter-offensive, Fritz went missing. That was the last anyone in Germany heard from him for six years." Steinbrueck paused and in the silence, Charlotte squirmed and wrote something to Alix.

"But Fritz was not dead," Steinbrueck resumed his narrative. "Fritz had become a prisoner of the Ivans. He was treated with unfathomable cruelty because he was not one of those worms who pretended to embrace Communism to better his lot."

Steinbrueck continued with great pathos, "Without adequate food or clothes, he was forced to labour in the sub-zero temperatures of Siberia. He was beaten — so badly that one eyeball was partially dislodged and could no longer focus. Yet he never broke down. He never became a *traitor*!" He spat the word in Alix's direction. "He never abetted the Soviets. He remained a true German focused on only one thing: escape and return to his Lotte."

"It took him six years. Six years during which his parents died and his family properties were handed over to the Polacks. Six years in which he lost his toes to frostbite and many of his teeth to malnutrition. Over six horrible years in Soviet slavery, one thought kept him alive: that his Lotte was waiting for him.

"And then the day came. Fritz managed to drag himself out of Siberia one step at a time. He managed on his crippled feet, dressed in rags, to cross a continent. Motivated and strengthened by love alone he made it to Berlin, to the very apartment where his Lotte lived." He stopped and cast David a hateful look before readdressing the judges. "Only to discover that his Lotte wasn't waiting for him. The inconstant, disloyal, faithless hussy had decided that she didn't want to wait for a German hero. No, she preferred the luxury and lifestyle our occupation forces could offer."

"Objection! The defendant welcomed Bredow into her apartment—"

"Oh, yes. She pretended to take him in. She let him sleep in her apartment — in the guest room. But she did not take him back into her arms, her heart, or her bed. No. Instead, she waited until she had the perfect opportunity to point a pistol at his face and BLOW HIS BRAINS OUT!" He raised his voice to shout out the last phrase making everyone in the courtroom recoil.

Dropping his voice again to sound like a rational man again, he declared, "Your Honours. I will prove without a doubt that Charlotte Graefin Walmsdorf murdered Fritz von Bredow in cold blood — not out of 'self-defence,' as the defence attorney will attempt to make you believe! Anyone with a brain can see that a man who could hardly walk and had only half of his hand could not harm her. The defendant wasn't *threatened* in any way. She had simply found herself a wealthier and more attractive provider. The defendant does not know the meaning of loyalty or love. Her only interest is her personal advantage. Rather than wait for Fritz, she flung herself into the arms of a wealthy, foreign *Jew*."

"Objection!" Alix sprang to her feet.

"Sustained."

Steinbrueck just smirked as he sat down. David understood. Whether the term was struck from the record or not, the judges and press had heard it. Steinbrueck had ripped the scab off their festering antisemitism in the same way that scratching an old mosquito bite will make it itch again. David felt a chill run down his spine. He could feel the hostility around him.

"That concludes my opening remarks," Steinbrueck announced.

David and Christian exchanged a glance, and David saw his own concerns reflected in Christian's eyes. Alix, he noted, pushed her notes aside. She was improvising.

"Your honours, my colleague Hr Dr Steinbrueck has done an excellent job of introducing Fritz von Bredow to this court. The boy, the youth, the young officer — beautifully described. I know from my husband's letters that Hr Dr Steinbrueck has captured Fritz von Bredow's nature brilliantly. That shy, modest, nature- and horse-loving Fritz was exactly the man Charlotte fell in love with. They shared a love of not only horses but dogs as well." She turned to talk across the aisle to the prosecutor. "I'm surprised you failed to mention the dogs, Herr Dr Steinbrueck. How could you forget to mention the poor little puppy that Charlotte and Fritz rescued together?" The sarcasm made David wince, and he saw Dr Steinbrueck squirm despite his smirk. One of the judges drummed his pencil on his notepad impatiently.

"Yes, Fritz was a kind, loving, loyal, dependable and gentle young man," Alix continued in a normal tone. "And Charlotte loved him with all her heart. I know because she was part of my husband's family. She wrote directly to my husband expressing her boundless joy when Fritz proposed, and we learned of her dreadful grief when he went missing from her mother. Her mother's letters to my mother-in-law also described her mood swings from hope to despair as time passed without any word. I know, too, that when the Red Army forced Charlotte to flee by horse cart during the bitterly cold winter of 1945, she dispensed with a second sweater to make room for Fritz's letters. I've read those letters, your honours, and I would be happy to submit them to this court as evidence that Charlotte loved Fritz with all the passion of a young, warm-hearted and innocent girl."

Christian glanced at David, but he shook his head slightly to indicate he was not upset. On the contrary, he was grateful that he had learned more about the young man Charlotte had been in love with before they met. He now understood better why Charlotte had been moved to pity by what had become of that wonderful young man. Maybe she had even hoped that with her love she might bring him back to life.

To the court, Alix continued, "I will also call as a witness, Christian Freiherr von Feldburg," she turned slightly to nod to him, "Charlotte's first cousin. He joined Charlotte in Berlin in January 1948. He will testify under oath that although Charlotte had lost hope of Fritz's return, she still loved the young man who had courted and won her heart.

"Your Honours, Hr Dr Steinbrueck has eloquently described the physical wounds that the war and the Soviets inflicted on Fritz von Bredow. These are well recorded and have already been filed with the court as part of the autopsy, I believe."

The judges nodded confirmation.

"What Hr Dr Steinbrueck *failed* to do," Alix continued, "was to describe the *other* wounds — the psychological scars — that Fritz sustained. No one who knows just how brutal, heartless and insidious the Communists are, should doubt that they can bend men's minds to evil."

David stiffened as he grasped what Alix was doing. She too was appealing to the prejudices of the court. She was exploiting their deep-seated hatred of Communism just as Steinbrueck had sought to tap into their patriotism and Antisemitism.

"By the time Fritz so unexpectedly returned from presumed death, Charlotte had indeed formed a romantic attachment to a wealthy and successful man. Yet, she nevertheless took Fritz back without hesitation. Full of pity, she let him into her apartment and into her life. She cleaned him up. She gave him new clothes. She assumed the burden of feeding and caring for him. She completely broke off her relationship with the man she had come to love and resigned from her well-paid and responsible position with the air ambulance company that he owned to avoid any further contact.

"Yet as the days passed, she discovered that the man she had let into her home on 31 October 1948 was *not* the same man with whom she had fallen in love in 1940. The man whom the Soviets had sent back to her had a completely different character from the man so meticulously described by my colleague.

"The man who returned to Berlin in 1948 was selfish, grasping, self-pitying, vindictive, and cruel. He showed no gratitude for Charlotte's support, help or care. He demanded constant attention; he complained about everything she did; he mocked and ridiculed her; he isolated her from others. Those six years in Soviet hands, subjected to the worst torments of the gulag, had warped and transformed Fritz von Bredow from that charming, shy, modest and loving young man into a cruel, heartless and sadistic monster. He made her life a living hell. And then he raped her."

"Objection! A dead man can't—"

"He raped her, Hr Dr Steinbrueck, before the night in which she finally defended herself."

"Objection overruled."

"Charlotte Walmsdorf was driven to violence by the sustained and repeated assaults of the man to whom she had given succour. She only resorted to violence after he had expunged the very last traces of affection that she had carried in her heart like a torch for six years. She took a weapon in her hand only when, quite simply, she could take no more. She was not planning or hoping for a future with someone else. How could she? She had broken off with her new admirer definitively. Furthermore, she knew she would be arrested and charged. Indeed, she was so desperate to end the torture that Fritz von Bredow had inflicted upon her that she intended to kill herself. That is the reality, as I shall prove to this court." She paused dramatically and then said in a neutral voice. "That concludes my remarks."

There was a moment of stunned silence before Judge Nuss moved to adjourn the court and set the next trial date. The journalists stood and hurried out to write and file their articles. The prosecutor's entourage clustered around him, lavishing praise on their boss and excitedly discussing the next steps.

As the police escorted Charlotte out of the courtroom, she tossed David one small, pleading look. He nodded and smiled gently back at her, but he no longer felt strong or confident. This was going to be a tough and tricky fight, and while David liked and respected Alix, he couldn't help wondering if a woman lawyer was the best choice to win over this court.

Elusive Truths
RAF Gatow
Tuesday 15 February 1949
(Day 235 of the Berlin Airlift)

The thought hit Galyna in the middle of the night.

She had spent the previous two days trawling through the Soviet press for information about the air ambulance, but on the day of the crash, she'd been too shocked to be efficient. The white Wellington was more than just one of hundreds of Airlift aircraft, it was Gatow's unofficial mascot. Everyone recognised and loved that Wellington in its white and red livery. The notion that the former bomber was now an angel of mercy appealed to their imagination, and it had come to symbolise the humanitarian nature of their mission. Besides, everyone knew that Mrs Priestman flew Moby Dick, and Priestman was a popular station commander.

Undoubtedly, there were those who thought he was too strict or not strict enough or too chummy or too distant. You could never please everyone. Yet when the news spread that Moby Dick was down, Galyna heard dozens of people express sympathy for their WingCo. They said things like, "The Wing-Co must be devastated!" or "The poor WingCo!" or "What a nightmare for the WingCo!" Among the WAAF there was an additional tendency to ask if there wasn't something they could do to help him.

Galyna knew that the best thing she could do to help was to glean as much information as possible from Soviet sources. Unfortunately, Mila had not answered any of her phone calls until late on Monday, almost two days after the crash. As usual, Mila pretended she had the wrong number, but Galyna knew that her friend would get back to her as soon as she could. Meanwhile, all Galyna could do was analyse the official news media yet again.

The Soviets released crumbs of information about the crash in dribs and dabs. After the blurry picture of the downed aircraft on Sunday, they released a second photo the following morning showing the crew disembarking from an ambulance. This showed a stretcher being removed by two Russian orderlies, while a woman in flight gear sat on the floor of the ambulance with one of her legs in an improvised splint. She stared dazed at the camera, her jaw hanging slack. In the foreground, turning away from the camera, was a short, black woman in a nurse's uniform.

Later Monday, a slightly different photo appeared in *Neues Deutschland*. In this image, the woman pilot sat as before, but the stretcher had been completely removed from the ambulance and the nurse now stood behind it, facing the camera. White dressings obscured the stretcher-patient's face, making recognition impossible. The caption identified the subjects as "the alleged nurse, woman spy and pilot." But something didn't make sense, Galyna just couldn't put her finger on what it was.

Then in the middle of the night, she had an epiphany. She sat up in shock, but her discovery seemed so obvious that she doubted herself. She got up, dressed, and went back to her office. She took out the file, found that second photo, and examined it with a magnifying glass. Then she re-read all the articles on the crash once again. Confident that she was onto something, she returned to her quarters to wash and change into her best uniform before, first thing in the morning, seeking out Ft/Lt Boyd.

When the WingCo arrived as usual at 7:30 am, he found Galyna and Boyd waiting in the anteroom of his office. Priestman looked terrible. His eyes were sunken in their sockets, and he hadn't shaved well — as if he didn't care about looking smart any more. The look he gave them made Galyna quail. He was terrified of bad news, and Boyd's request for a meeting only intensified those fears.

Nevertheless, he replied, "Of course," and continued into his office, leaving the door open for them to follow. Galyna closed the door behind her and joined Boyd in front of the station commander's desk. Priestman gestured for them to sit, and they sank into the visitor's chairs. Priestman gave them no encouragement but waited stoically for the blow.

"Corporal Borisenko has been reading and re-reading the press releases about the crash, sir. She has brought something to my attention which, I'm ashamed to admit, I should have noticed myself."

"Please come to the point," Priestman urged in a stiff tone that suggested he was at great pains to retain his composure.

"Based on Corporal Borisenko's analysis, we believe that the Soviets only have three people in custody."

The WingCo shook his head. "There were four people in the aircraft."

Galyna sat tensely on the edge of her seat, bursting with the information she wanted to share, while Boyd patiently explained, "We know that, sir, but the Soviets have no reason to know it. Civilian Wellingtons usually fly with a crew of just two, pilot and co-pilot; there is no *requirement* for a flight engineer. An analysis of the Soviet press confirms that they have consistently talked about a nurse, a female spy and a pilot, and no one else. There is no mention of a flight engineer or a second pilot."

"Presumably because they are referring to the second pilot as a 'spy,'" Priestman replied, exasperation creeping into his voice despite his efforts to retain his self-control.

"Maybe, but none of the photos show more than three people: the nurse is easily identified by her uniform and race, then there is a woman in flight gear —"

"The woman in flight gear with the broken leg is Jan Orloff, the second pilot," Priestman told them brusquely.

Boyd and Galyna exchanged a startled look. They had not been sure about that. Boyd took the lead in answering, saying a little dubiously, "If you are confident of that, sir, then there is good reason to believe they do not have Mrs Priestman."

"She is most likely the one on the stretcher with her entire head in bandages!" The WingCo snapped, his emotions getting the better of him.

The second photo revealing the injured person on the stretcher had not been released until late yesterday afternoon, and Galyna instantly understood that this was what had ruined the WingCo's night. "Please hear me out, sir," Galyna pleaded, and the WingCo visibly drew a deep breath to get a grip on his emotions as he shifted his attention from Boyd to Galyna.

"In all the articles the Russians refer only to three crew members: the nurse, the woman spy, and the pilot. In the caption to the most recent photo, the person on the stretcher is specifically identified as the pilot, but in Russian nouns have gender. The pilot is always referred to in the masculine. I went back and checked all the Soviet texts, and they are consistent. The pilot is masculine."

This information sparked a reaction. The WingCo eyes instantly became alert as he drew the conclusion, "You're suggesting that the Russians think the flight engineer was the pilot." He glanced at Boyd for confirmation.

The Intelligence officer confirmed, "Yes, sir. The pilot is always referred to in the masculine, the 'spy' and the nurse in the feminine, and there has been no mention of a fourth crew member whatsoever. If, as you say, Mrs Orloff is the woman in the photos, then that might explain why they have persisted in referring to Moby Dick as an 'American' spy plane, dismissing the British registration of the aircraft as a red herring. Mr and Mrs Orloff and Miss Savage are all US citizens."

"Then where's my wife?" Priestman countered in a tense voice. "She was in command of the aircraft at take-off and presumably still at the controls when it made a forced landing in the Soviet Zone. Could she have died in the crash without the Russians mentioning it?"

"Very unlikely. They have always been quick to report casualties."

"Which means she's probably alive but has been sequestered away and is being treated differently from the others," Priestman concluded.

"Why would they do that?" Boyd asked, baffled.

The WingCo looked Boyd straight in the eye and answered in a slow, measured voice heavy with implications, "To blackmail me."

Boyd flinched visibly, and Galyna felt a shudder go down her spine. No wonder he looked so tortured!

Priestman seemed to get a hold of himself. He took a deep breath and told his subordinates in a heavy but sincere tone, "Even if I don't like the implications, this is extremely valuable information. I am grateful to both of you for ferreting it out and telling me. I shall pass the information on to the Americans, who have the lead in the negotiations with the Soviets. Maybe they can use it in some way."

Twisted Truths
Berlin-Kladow
Saturday – Tuesday 12 – 15 February 1949
(Days 232 – 235 of the Berlin Airlift)

The crash itself had come too quickly for Anna to feel much fear in advance. In the immediate aftermath, the medical crisis with Rick had kept her from thinking about herself. Even after the East German police arrived, she focused on pointing out Rick and Jan's injuries and helping them get safely aboard the ambulance. The trip to the hospital had been a rough, swaying journey through the bitter cold and darkened countryside. Throughout, she'd held her hand on Rick's pulse, begging God not to let him die.

At the hospital, she had been separated from Rick and Jan. She was taken to what appeared to be a prison, where she was given water and a blanket and confined alone to a cell. Although this was hardly hospitable treatment, she was worrying too much about the others to think about herself. She understood she was in Soviet hands. She knew that as an American she was viewed with suspicion and hostility, but she did not seriously fear for her life or freedom. She was a nurse, a non-combatant, and they were not at war with the Soviet Union anyway. She was sure that she would be turned over to the American authorities in due time. This detention was just a precaution to keep her from seeing something she shouldn't.

The following morning, a gruff woman in Red Army uniform barked at her and gestured for her to leave the cell. She was offended by the rude tone but assumed that she was about to be handed over to the American military. Instead, she was taken to a small, windowless room where another Red Army Officer sat behind a large, wooden desk. She was told to sit on a narrow, uncomfortable, metal chair. The chair was too small for her, and the sharp edges cut into her bottom. She didn't like this, or the fact that she had been given nothing to eat.

"What is your name? And what were you doing in the aircraft that crashed last night inside the Soviet Zone?"

Anna remembered her wartime training. The only information a prisoner was required to give to an enemy interrogator were name, rank, and serial number. Since she didn't have a rank or serial number, she answered with: "Anna Elizabeth Savage, Registered Nurse."

"Are you an American citizen?"

"Yes," she answered quickly. Not only was she proud to be an American, but she also believed that her release would be quicker if there were no question of her citizenship.

"But you aren't really a nurse, are you?" the interrogator sneered.

"Of course, I'm a nurse!" Anna responded indignantly.

"Don't treat us like idiots! Everyone knows the Americans don't have coloured nurses — at least not for white people."

"You're wrong. I am a registered nurse, and all the patients I've treated on the air ambulance have been white," Anna insisted.

The interrogator shook his head and got to his feet to come around in front of his desk. Standing directly in front of her, he looked down and warned in a low growl, "Don't lie to me, or things will be worse for you. That uniform," he nodded with his head at her now dirty and crushed uniform, "is a disguise. A stupid attempt to mislead us. Juvenile really. We know perfectly well that coloured women aren't allowed to hold responsible positions in America. Certainly nothing as important as a flight nurse on an ambulance."

Anna bit her tongue to stop her angry retort, but she felt the bitter irony of him being essentially right. Yes, she was a flight nurse, but only because she worked for a civilian, British company; the US Army Nurse Corps did not allow coloured women to be flight nurses. The Russian officer tried a new question. "What did you do before you started spying?"

Anna recoiled. Spying? The first tentacles of fear reached up to take hold of her insides. She knew that spies were treated differently from soldiers, never mind nurses. Spies could be shot. The need to dismiss the allegation outweighed the risk of giving information to the enemy. "I have nothing to do with espionage! I am a registered nurse, and I have been since 1943! I served in the US Army Nurse Corps!"

The Russian leaned forward so his face was just inches from hers before he abruptly shouted at her. "YOU ARE LYING! Coloured girls aren't allowed to train or work as nurses!" Straightening, he spoke at normal volume but contempt dripped from his lips as he asked, "What did you do before they recruited you as a spy? Clean up bedpans in a hospital?"

"I am a registered nurse, and I have worked as a registered nurse since 1943," Anna insisted, meeting his eyes.

The interrogation went on without any significant change in theme for some time. The worst moment came when the interrogator sneered, "If you're a real nurse, why didn't you help the other crew members rather than letting them bleed half to death?"

That stabbed her to the quick because she had done the best she could, but she didn't know if it had been good enough. She didn't know whether Emily or Rick had made it or not.

After a long time, he changed tactics and tried to get her to talk about the other people in the aircraft with her. Anna feared that anything she said might be used against them and that any show of concern on her part might be used to manipulate her. She decided to answer every question with a stubborn "No comment!" Privately, she was least worried about Emily because her husband was a senior officer, and Robin would not rest until he had her home. Jan and Rick, on the other hand, were civilians with no friends in important places, which made her worry about them most. To her interrogators, however, she presented an indifferent face and a monotonous refusal to speak.

Eventually, her bladder was so full that her discomfort could not be ignored. Before something ruptured, she asked permission to go to the toilet. To her surprise, her request was granted, although a woman soldier stood in the open stall door watching her. Anna was furious and asked the woman what she wanted to see, but of course, Anna spoke in English and her guard didn't — or pretended not to — understand her.

To her surprise, rather than going back to the interrogation cell, she was returned to a different cell and locked in. Moments later, she received black bread, white lard, and some cooked carrots. She gobbled them down, ravenous.

Later they came for her again. This time she knew what to expect — or she thought she did. She was surprised to be taken to a different room with a different interrogator. The chair here was larger, wooden and more comfortable. The interrogator indicated the pitcher of water and glass on the front of his desk and said she was welcome to help herself whenever she wanted. He also offered her a cigarette. His tone, when he started asking questions, was chatty rather than confrontational. Anna remembered hearing about this tactic. It was called "Good cop, bad cop."

"Miss Savage," he opened, "I'm very curious about you. Based on your last interview, you are very loyal to the United States." She was glad they had got that message. "But why?"

"Because I am an American," Anna told him and risked asking, "Aren't you proud to be Russian?"

"Of course! But I am a citizen of the most progressive country in the world! A country dedicated to bringing justice and prosperity to all people regardless of nationality or race. I am especially honoured to wear the uniform of the army that liberated the world from fascism. You, on the other hand, are what? A second class citizen! You're exploited, segregated, denied justice and opportunities."

Anna glared at him. She knew about discrimination and racism in the United States better than this Russian, and she didn't appreciate his meddling.

His tone turned flattering, "You must have shown remarkable skill and perseverance to overcome the American barriers of race and gender. It is truly admirable. I can't help but wonder what someone with your skill and determination could achieve in our great nation where racism plays no role. You do know that if you request asylum, you could become a Soviet citizen?"

Anna glared back at him but gave no answer.

"If you were to request asylum in the Soviet Union," he continued, smiling, "I could arrange for you to attend one of our prestigious colleges. You could *really* study nursing or even train as a doctor. We have many women doctors in the Soviet Union. More than half of our doctors are women. Or you could learn another skill if you prefer. Anything at all! And once you finish training, you would have a chance to work in the most modern facilities in the world."

That wasn't what Anna had heard. She'd been told that Soviet hospital facilities were very poor and backward.

"I've prepared a statement for you to sign, explaining that you prefer to stay under the protection of the Soviet Union rather than return to being a slave in America."

"I am not a slave."

"But your grandparents were, weren't they? Surely, you know that most Americans wish you were slaves again?"

Anna shook her head, "I wish to return to the American Sector. You have no right to hold me in custody. I insist that you return me to American jurisdiction immediately."

Her interrogator shrugged and managed to look sad. "That's a pity," he told her. "You see, the American authorities have shown no interest in you whatsoever. They are howling for the return of the pilot. They are desperate for the return of the other woman spy, but they have made no mention of you in any of their demarches, press releases or verbal communications. It appears that to them you don't exist — or you aren't in the least important. General Clay couldn't care less about what happens to some coloured girl who blew her cover and exposed the whole shabby ruse."

Was that possible? Anna asked herself, shaken. The tenacles of fear gripped harder.

The interrogator sensed he had scored. "Come now! You didn't seriously think that a man from Georgia like General Clay would give a damn about a coloured girl, did you? Why would a son of the Confederacy care what happened to the granddaughter of slaves — especially when your inadequate treatment of the casualties exposed the fact that the ambulance markings were nothing but a disguise for an espionage flight."

Her treatment of Rick had been "inadequate"? That must mean he had died, Anna registered with horror. She had failed. The knowledge lamed her.

The interrogator was talking again, "General Clay doesn't care what happens to you, Miss Savage. He sees you as a liability. So much so, that he hasn't even asked if you were injured."

Anna pulled herself together. Why should General Clay take an interest in her? He was the American Military Governor with almost 100,000 troops under his command and she wasn't even in the US military. She was working for a civilian company and a British one at that. She could not expect General Clay to take an interest in her fate, but she couldn't stop herself from asking, "And Colonel Howley?"

"Mad Dog Howley?" The interrogator asked back surprised and then shrugged. "What about him? He is screaming and shouting insults as usual, but he's made no mention of you. He's all riled up about the pilot and the spy. You mean nothing to any of them. Nothing." He emphasized the word, and doubts started to take root in her belly.

During the second night in her cell, the fear was like an octopus attacking her from all sides. On the one hand, the fear of being charged with espionage was growing. Anna knew too little about it to know what might happen, but that very ignorance made it doubly frightening.

More visceral was the feeling of being as helpless as she had been when, as a small child, a gang of drunks had pounded on the door of the shed where she lived with her mother. They had wanted to rape her mother and shouted insults and smashed their beer cans against the door and the walls. While Anna cowered in the closet, her mother had barricaded furniture before the door.

She was tormented, too, by the thought that she had failed Rick. She'd tried to staunch the bleeding as rapidly as possible, but his skull was soft and perhaps she had done more harm than good? Or had she missed some other, more serious injury in the darkness and confusion? Had the doctors at the hospital concluded that only an amateur could have handled the case so incompetently? That thought undermined her self-confidence and her very identity as a nurse and a healer.

Nagging at her in a different way was the thought that the Howleys' friendship might have been an illusion. They had always seemed so kind and sincere. For her, the Howleys, like the Warrens, were 'good whites,' people who were not racists and who were prepared to accept, encourage and even fight for her. If they abandoned her now, then she lost more than two friends, she lost her faith in the 'other America,' the America that would one day live up to its promise of being a place of equal opportunity and justice for all.

Worst of all, the seed had been planted that she would be treated differently from the whites. The British appeared to be negotiating for Emily separately, while Anna's fate depended on the American authorities. If they treated her differently from the two whites, then not only might she never see home again, but there would also be no point in it. A country that abandoned her when she needed it most just because of the colour of her skin wasn't worth returning to.

When she was next taken to an interrogation cell, she was astonished to be met by yet another Soviet officer. This man affected a bored disinterest in her as he handed her a document and announced, "You will be released as soon as you sign there." He pointed to a line at the foot of a page of tightly spaced Cyrillic text.

Anna shook her head. "I can't sign that."

"Why not?"

"I don't know what it says," she replied.

"It is merely a formality, saying that you were treated well and have no complaints against the Soviet Union."

"I don't believe you," Anna told him flatly.

"This is ridiculous! Haven't we treated you with more courtesy and respect than your American superiors?" As he spoke, the Soviet officer frowned and glanced at the clock. Anna suspected that he was under some kind of pressure. That made her more stubborn. She reiterated her refusal to sign until she had a complete translation.

The Russian officer became increasingly agitated by her intransigence. He pretended to read the document to her out loud, but Anna shook her head. "I want an independent translator," she insisted.

After a tenacious back-and-forth during which he made frequent glances at the clock, he finally shouted at one of the guards, who hastened away. Minutes later, the guard returned with a dishevelled-looking civilian. This bewildered man was handed the document with a flood of orders in Russian. His hands shook as he started to read out loud. "I, Anna Savage, hereby swear that I served aboard an American spy plane—"

The interrogator exploded and brutally slapped the civilian three times and then kicked him, literally, out of the room. As soon as he turned to face her, Anna reiterated firmly, "I'm not signing that!"

The Russian officer glowered at her, and her heart thumped in terror. She braced herself for a blow. To her surprise, the Russian reined himself in and confined himself to threatening ominously, "If you do not cooperate, we will be compelled to use more unpleasant measures to obtain your confession."

Anna felt her stomach cramping up, but she shook her head. He ordered her taken back to her cell.

By this point, her imagination was on the brink of running away with her. It took an effort to force herself to think rationally. She had to resist cooperation because if she broke, they would treat them *all* as spies. She wondered if she could weasel out of a confession by offering to defect. If she defected without implicating the others, she might be able to save them, but what would happen to her? The thought of spending the rest of her life in the Soviet Union was horrifying. She supposed she would learn Russian and make friends, but she would never see Aunt Flora or Miss Josephine, Emily or the Howleys, ever again. She felt the chill of the Siberian steppes entering her cell and freezing her hopes for a better world.

The banging on the cell door startled her. Anna had fallen asleep and was bewildered, unsure how long it had been since the last interrogation. She pulled herself together, sitting up before the door crashed open.

The woman guard barked at her as usual, and Anna got to her feet. She was placed between two Russian soldiers with rifles at their sides. They marched her along the corridor at a quick pace. Anna was terrified, convinced she was about to be tortured. Her legs started to give way. From behind her the Russian woman soldier pushed her in the small of her back and shouted. Anna forced herself to keep moving.

They burst out into a courtyard lit by bright lights. She saw barbed wire and watch towers, so it was a prison. A car stood at the exit, and she was shoved inside. Soviet flags flapped on the fenders as they sped along the deserted streets. It appeared to be the middle of the night, but then nights were more than sixteen hours long at this time of year in Northern Europe. All Anna knew for sure was that she was being moved, and she suspected the timing was meant to make it less likely someone would find out about it. Maybe they were taking her out of Berlin altogether. She might be put on a train for Siberia, where no one would ever hear from her again — much less find her.

Then she noticed that the broad avenues had given way to city streets. These were often cobbled, and the rumble of the tyres on the stones sounded almost like rapid machine-gun fire. No one was on the sidewalks. None of the shops were open. They twisted and turned through the bowels of a city still in ruins. Dogs, cats, and the occasional human darted out of the headlights, seeking the safety of darkness. Wherever she was being taken, it was somewhere no one wanted to be.

Suddenly the car screeched to a halt, and Anna was pushed out of the door. A barricade blocked the road in front of her. Beyond it, other cars were drawn up facing towards them with their headlights trained straight at Anna. They almost blinded her, but she could just make out something dark and rectangular looming behind the cars. Was it a tank? What did that mean? Were they about to shoot her?

"Go!" Her Russian escort ordered.

"Where?"

"Through the barriers!"

"Where am I?"

"Check-Point Charlie."

Anna had never heard of it, but she started forward hesitantly, expecting to be shot at any moment. Suddenly she heard Frank Howley calling to her, "It's all right, Anna! Keep coming! Just keep walking towards the lights!"

Anna started praying her thanks to Jesus in a way she hadn't done since that night when those drunks had tried to break into her mother's shed. She tried to focus beyond the bright beams. Gradually, she deciphered figures. Men stood beside the cars. As she got closer, she recognised the distinctive figure and face of General Clay. Had the American Military Governor of Germany come to see her, Anna Savage, the granddaughter of slaves, released by the Soviets? The thought so moved her that she couldn't take another step. Then in a gesture that she hoped expressed the depth of her respect, she lifted her right hand and saluted him.

Clay returned the gesture. Then he smiled and advised in a voice soaked with the sun of Georgia, "Just a few more steps, Miss Savage."

She was so close to tears, she couldn't move. Frank came forward and put his arm through hers. He led her to General Clay, and the military governor offered her his hand. "I'm pleased to meet you, Miss Savage. Frank hasn't given me a moment's peace since your plane went down. Now, we could all use a good night's sleep, so Frank's going to take you home with him, and we can talk sometime tomorrow or the next day."

"And the others, sir? Are they safe?"

"We're still working on their release, but don't worry about them. It's my job to get them back. You go home with Colonel and Mrs Howley and let them look after you for a bit. There will be plenty of time to talk later."

"Thank you again, sir," Anna managed as she let Frank guide her to his waiting car.

As she slipped inside, Edith Howley took her into her arms. At that point, Anna's nerves gave way completely, and she started crying with relief and gratitude.

Edith held her close, muttering. "It's all right, Anna. Have a good cry, but everything is going to be fine. You can stay with us as long as you want."

Chapter Fifteen
Dancing in the Dark

Shades of Darkness
Berlin-Zehlendorf
Wednesday, 16 February 1949
(Day 236 of the Berlin Airlift)

Frank Howley called Robin first thing in the morning to let him know Anna was back safely. He added that Robin was welcome to call on her to see what she knew about Emily. Robin arranged for Jasha to pack Anna's things and then swung by to pick them up before driving to the Howleys' for lunch. The suitcase was gratefully received, and Anna went to change before joining Edith and Robin at the lunch table. Frank was at the Kommandatura.

"I'm afraid I can't tell you very much," Anna opened in a subdued voice as she sank in the seat opposite Robin. Despite her best efforts to make herself look smart in her clean clothes, traces of her ordeal clung to her: her hair had been hastily combed, the skin around her eyes sagged, and her fingers trembled as she reached for her glass of water. Edith looked concerned and prepared to protect her from further stress.

Robin did not want to add to her trauma, but it had been three days since the Soviets had threatened to kill Emily, and he still didn't know if she was dead or alive. He needed to learn everything Anna knew in case it could help him find and rescue Emily. Speaking as gently as he could, he suggested, "Would you mind telling me what led to the crash?"

"There was something wrong with the fuel," Anna replied readily. "I remember that Rick became concerned shortly before entering the corridor. He said the gauge registered far less fuel than we should have, given that we had refuelled at Wunstorf. Not long afterwards, Rick concluded we must have sprung a leak in one of the starboard fuel tanks. He said the fuel was draining rapidly. I don't know what Emily and Jan did exactly, but they tried various things, and then the starboard engine coughed and went dead." Robin nodded, reflecting on what a difficult landing it had been. If the starboard engine was dead and the port engine still working, the torque would be almost unmanageable, particularly on snow.

Anna continued her narrative, "Jan tried to send a distress call, but there was too much static and jamming. Not long afterwards, Rick reported that the port tanks were also draining abnormally fast—"

"That doesn't make sense!" Robin interrupted irritated. "The probability of the tanks on both wings developing leaks simultaneously without enemy action is....." Robin went ice cold. In his mind, he heard Squadron Leader Flannel warning him to 'walk around as if someone had a gun pointed at him.' Suddenly, he understood that the leaks had not developed by chance. The Soviets had sabotaged Moby Dick's fuel tanks, and they had done so *because* they had known that Emily flew it. The significance of Moby Dick refuelling at Wunstorf immediately became clear. At Gatow and Fuhlsbuettel, Emily knew the ground staff. At Wunstorf they were all strangers. Somehow the Soviet Secret Police had managed to get a sympathiser, or someone who they'd blackmailed or bribed, near Moby Dick's fuel tanks during their fuel stop.

Anna's voice broke through his thoughts. She was saying, "I'm sorry. I don't understand much about planes. I can only tell you what I overheard —"

"Yes, of course! I'm sorry," Robin replied. "I've only just realised that the crash was not an accident."

Anna frowned in confusion and Edith asked in alarm, "What are you saying?"

"There was no mechanical failure. The crash was caused by sabotage," Robin replied confidently.

"But why target the ambulance of all things? It's not even military!" Edith protested.

"No, but they knew it was the aircraft Emily flies."

"Good God, Robin! What have they got against her?" Edith asked horrified.

"Nothing personal, but the RAF Special Branch believes they were targeting me the night Captain Utting was killed. They warned me they would try to attack me again."

"I don't understand," Anna admitted.

"They want to use Emily to blackmail me into disrupting operations at Gatow."

"Have you told Frank about this?" Edith asked alarmed.

"No, because I've only just worked it out," Robin admitted, adding, "but we should." With just four more days until the deadline, he finally admitted to himself that he could no longer cope with the situation on his own.

"I'll call him right now and ask him to join us." Edith stood and left the room.

Robin turned to Anna, who was looking stunned. "Tell me what happened next."

Anna visibly collected herself and explained, "Emily, Rick and Jan agreed that they could not reach Berlin and that they had to look for a field where they could make a forced landing. Emily told me to go back into the fuselage and sit on the floor with my back braced against the main spar. She told me to put blankets behind my back and to clutch my legs in my arms with my head on my knees. She said that as soon as the aircraft came to a stop, I was to get out as quickly as possible. She told me not to worry about anyone else."

Robin just nodded. Anna drew a deep breath. "I went back and took the crash position, but only after I'd pulled down the big first aid kit. I clutched that in my lap so I'd have it ready and wouldn't have to look for it. Meanwhile, things were happening very fast. Jan was shouting instructions to Emily. Then I heard Rick call, "Look out!" just before the belly of the plane hit the ground. But the landing was surprisingly soft — until suddenly we ran into something. There was a terrible crashing sound followed by tearing metal and loud clattering until we shuddered to a halt.

"Even before we came to a standstill, I heard Jan screaming. I scrambled forward into the cockpit. Emily appeared to be stunned. She just sat there staring out of the unbroken window. In fact, for a moment, I thought she was dead, but when I called her name, she came out of shock. She turned to look at me and then looked over and saw Jan and Rick and told me to look after them first.

"I don't think Rick had been strapped in properly because he'd been flung head-first against the engineer's panel. His face was smashed up and bleeding profusely. I got him stretched out on the floor and did what I could to staunch the bleeding, but while I was doing that, I realised his skull was soft on the righthand side. That meant it had broken in several places, shattered. I had to be careful not to cause more damage, and it was dark. I — I—" Her voice faded out as her mind transported her back to the crash site.

"...did the best you could," Robin supplied the words softly, bringing her back to the present.

Anna nodded and drew a deep breath to steady her nerves. "I managed to slow the bleeding and give him a shot of morphine. Then I turned my attention to Jan. She was in terrible pain because her leg had broken in two places: at the ankle and again above the knee. She was semi-hysterical because of the pain and because of Rick, I think. I gave her a dose of morphine for the pain and to sedate her.

"Only then did I look Emily over. She told me she was experiencing intense heart pain and thought she was having a heart attack, but I believe she had only broken her breastbone when she was flung against her straps. In addition, her left wrist had snapped. She seemed dazed, but she was calm, and her injuries weren't life-threatening."

Anna clearly found it painful to relive the experience, but she was also anxious to reassure Robin that Emily's life hadn't been in danger.

"Thank you," he murmured.

"Emily said we had to get help before we froze to death and since I was the only one who wasn't injured, I offered to go. Emily wouldn't let me. She claimed she could not help Rick or Jan and reminded me that her German was better than mine, too. Before she set off, I splinted and bandaged her wrist as best I could, but there was nothing I could do for the breastbone. So, after I'd done up her wrist, I shoved open the cockpit window and helped her to climb out onto the wing."

Anna fell silent and Robin knew this had been difficult. He asked, "Was that the last you saw of her?"

"Yes. The last thing she said was that I must get back into the cockpit and close the windows to keep the snow and cold out. She feared it might be some time before anyone found us. I promised to spread the blankets over Rick and Jan, and then she set off into the night and snowstorm. When the East German police arrived about an hour later, I assumed she had sent them. I thought the Germans had already sent her to a hospital before coming to find us." She hesitated and then asked timidly, "Isn't that what happened?"

"We don't know. We've heard nothing about her since the crash," Robin explained.

Anna's eyes filled with tears, and she murmured as much to herself as to Robin, "I shouldn't have let her go out into the snow."

"You weren't given a choice," Robin reminded her firmly. "Emily was captain of the aircraft, and she ordered you to remain behind with the injured. It was her command decision, and that's an end to it. Now, can you tell me a little more about what happened after the East German police arrived?"

"I was allowed to ride in the ambulance with Rick and Jan, but I wasn't allowed in the hospital with them. I was taken to a prison instead and put in a cell by myself. I haven't seen Jan or Rick since, but Frank said they were OK, although still in Soviet hands."

"Anna, you deserve a medal for what you did!" Edith declared. Unseen by Robin, she had returned. As she sat down again, she told him, "Frank is on his way now. He'll be here any minute."

By the time he'd finished telling Frank about the conclusions of the Special Branch, the threat he had received on Sunday, and Corporal Borisenko's suspicions that the Soviets only had three people in custody, Robin was relieved he'd confided in the American colonel. Frank might have a reputation as a hothead, but he was far from it.

He listened intently to Robin and then concluded. "There are essentially three possibilities, and," he interrupted himself to warn, "I'm going to be blunt."

Robin nodded his agreement.

"Emily may have become lost and disoriented in the dark and the snow resulting in her freezing to death. Temperatures were well below freezing the night of the crash and it's been snowing on and off ever since. For all we know, her body is buried in a drift somewhere, undiscovered by either the Soviets or the locals." Robin nodded acknowledgement. It was a possibility, but somehow he didn't believe it.

"Alternatively, she may have reached a house, contacted the East German authorities and is being held separately from the others, possibly as a hostage to force you to commit treason." That was the scenario Robin thought most likely, and he nodded grimly.

"But there is a third possibility," Frank pointed out. "She *might* have reached a house but been too weak to explain who she was or what had happened. Alternatively, she might have found people who were anti-Soviet. In short, she might have been taken in and helped, without the authorities being informed about her whereabouts."

"But if they targeted Moby Dick because she was aboard it, then they will be looking for her," Robin pointed out.

"Unless they think that Jan is Mrs Priestman."

"She's American."

"Do the Soviets know that you don't have an American wife? A lot of Englishmen do. Jan would otherwise fit a description of Emily — tall, slender, dark, early thirties, a former ferry pilot."

"But she will have identified herself as Janet Orloff."

"Why would the Soviets believe her? They didn't want to believe Anna was a nurse. They might think that 'Janet Orloff' is a fake identity assumed explicitly to disguise who she really is — namely Mrs Emily Priestman."

"Do you honestly think that's credible?" Robin asked sceptically.

"Well, I've been in on all the negotiations for the release of the crew. The Soviets have consistently treated Jan differently from Rick and Anna. They dismissed Anna as a 'red herring,' only there to disguise the real purpose of the flight. They also returned her rapidly because they thought we didn't care much about her." He tossed her an apologetic smile, but Anna nodded understanding.

"Rick, on the other hand, appears to have been critically injured. The Soviets insist he can neither be moved nor visited. Given what Anna has said about the nature of his injuries, he may be comatose, heavily sedated or both. He almost certainly cannot be interrogated. Notably, however, the Soviets seem to assume we don't care much about him either. They treat him as if he is just one of thousands of dispensable pilots.

"In contrast, they have consistently treated Jan as something special. Almost as if she were a particular 'prize.' She is the one described as a spy, whereas Anna was quickly pegged as window-dressing, and Rick has been treated merely as 'crew.' I think the best way to explain that is that Jan appears to fit the description they have of Emily —"

"They must have photos of Emily! We've been here more than a year. She flew in the Air Show we had last spring." In Robin's eyes, Emily was lovely while Jan was plain. He found it impossible to believe that they could be confused.

"True, but Emily was never the centre of attention. At the airshow, she was wearing flying kit and helmet, wasn't she? The photos might not be good enough to enable them to distinguish between Emily and Jan."

Robin thought about that, remembering that Galyna and Ft/Lt Boyd had also not seemed 100% sure of the identity of the woman pilot in the newspaper pictures; he had been the one to identify her to them. But then he remembered, "Emily danced with Sokolovsky at the Victory Day ball!" Robin protested, remembering Sokolovsky's almost amorous interest in Emily and how closely he'd held her on the dance floor.

"Look, Robin, if the Soviet Secret Police wants to use Emily to manipulate you, they might not have told Sokolovsky what they are up to. They may not have told him that they sabotaged the plane or that they believe they have captured your wife. What they undoubtedly *have* told him, however, is that the woman on the plane is a spy and therefore *their* property. Sokolovsky is a figurehead, Robin. The people behind this operation — if it is one — are in the Soviet Secret Police, and as far as we know none of them has ever met, much less danced with, Emily. Yet even supposing they know they have the wrong woman, they may not dare admit to *their* superiors that they messed up and failed to get their target."

"Which leaves me with a new dilemma," Robin pointed out in obvious frustration. "Not only do I still not know if Emily is alive or where she is, but now I also have to fear that Jan might be murdered pointlessly in an attempt to influence me."

"A dead Jan is of no use to them. As soon as the deadline passes and they realise you didn't cave into their demands, they won't have any use for her anymore. I think they'll release her and Rick. In fact, in light of what you've told me, I believe the Soviets have been so intransigent only because they're holding out until Sunday noon just to see if you will break — which we both know you won't."

"You think Jan and Rick might be returned next week?"

"I think it's almost certain they will be."

"But if they don't *have* Emily, then they can't return her," Robin underlined.

"Correct."

"And if they don't know there was a fourth person on the Wellington, how do we find out what's happened to Emily and where she is without alerting them to the possibility that their actual prize is still somewhere inside the Soviet Zone where they could still lay hands on her?"

Frank scratched behind one of his big ears and grimaced almost comically although he was deadly serious. "Frankly, Robin. I haven't got a clue on that one, but if I think of something I'll let you know."

Robin nodded and thanked him numbly, then he took his leave of Frank, Edith and Anna and returned to Gatow.

On arrival in his outer office, Sergeant Andrews met him with the words, "If you'll pardon my French, sir, you look like death warmed up. Why don't you go home and try to get some rest? You aren't needed here just now, and you wouldn't be much use in the state you're in anyway."

That was a very blunt speech from a sergeant to a wing commander and Robin had a vague memory that the RAF took a dim view of such behaviour — except that she was absolutely correct. Somebody probably should have said this to him days ago. Without protest, he turned around and left the office. On his way down the hall, he put his head into Fl/Lt Boyd's office and asked, "Anything from Borisenko and her contact yet?"

"Yes and no, sir," Boyd replied, springing up from his chair and coming around his desk to speak in a softer voice. "Her contact has at last responded, and they have scheduled a meeting this evening at the usual venue near the Reichstag."

"You always provide a car for her, don't you?"

"Yes, sir. We keep a car standing by at Lehrter Bahnhof since no public transport will be running after 6:30 pm and we want to be sure she gets home safely."

"Would you have the driver bring her directly to my residence as soon as the meeting is over? I'm going home to try to get some rest, but I want to know what she learns as soon as possible."

"Very well, sir. Not a problem at all. I hope you can get some sleep. With the release of the nurse, I think we're moving towards a resolution."

"Except that it now appears the aircraft was sabotaged, and it is 100 per cent certain that Mrs Priestman was not with the others," Robin told him.

Boyd deflated, and Robin continued out of the building. He had his driver swing past the AAI hangar so he could report to MacDonald what he'd learned from Anna about both fuel tanks springing leaks. The Scotsman indignantly confirmed his previous assessment. "That's not possible, sir! The wings were in first-rate condition, and they were built to handle far more strain than what we've been putting on them. There is no way that they could have just sprung leaks without some kind of collision or accident. Wellington tanks don't just spring leaks without cause!"

"I never thought they did, Chiefy, but what if someone *intentionally* left the caps off the tanks? Or how difficult would it be to puncture a wing tank while doing a quick 'walk around' in the dark?"

MacDonald blanched. "It would be child's play! But why would anyone do that?"

"If someone was willing to drive a lorry over Captain Utting, why wouldn't they lose a couple of gas caps or puncture a hole in the wing — or both wings — of a Wellington?"

"But it's an ambulance, sir!"

Robin just gazed at him, and MacDonald started shaking his head and grumbling. Robin put a hand on his shoulder. "I didn't want you blaming yourself for some oversight. There's no question that fuel starvation caused the crew to make a forced landing, and that was almost certainly the result of deliberate sabotage during a re-fuelling stop in Wunstorf."

MacDonald nodded solemnly. Meanwhile, one of the German mechanics had been translating the whole exchange in a low voice for the others. One after another, the mechanics offered Robin their hand and expressed their hopes that Mrs Priestman would be returned safely soon. Robin thanked them and returned to his car.

At his residence, exhaustion overcame him. He just managed to drag himself up the stairs, taking off his tie as he went. He pulled his shoes off, lay down, rolled himself into the bedcovers, and fell into a deep and dreamless sleep.

A Dim Light in the Dark
Soviet Zone
Saturday 12 February – Wednesday 16 February 1949
(Day 232-236 of the Berlin Airlift)

Nothing prepares you for a prang. Emily remembered Robin telling her that once, and he should know; he'd had plenty. Yet precisely because her record had been perfect until now, the shock was all the greater. Until the engine cut out, she had not fully believed Rick was right about the fuel leak. The Wellington was comparatively young and meticulously maintained. They had refuelled at Wunstorf. She had doubted they were low on fuel, suspecting a problem with the gauge instead. After the starboard engine cut out, she could no longer deny they were in trouble, but she had still been in a state of denial when Rick reported the port fuel tanks were also draining at an alarming rate. Still, she clung to the conviction that there must be another explanation for the readings; they couldn't be out of fuel.

But they were.

They didn't have a lot of altitude, either; only a little over 3,000 feet. Jan could not break through the jamming to get any response from BASC, and none of the other aircraft seemed to be taking any notice of their mayday call either. They were on their own, sinking down toward the snowy landscape of the Soviet zone as the weather worsened. Soon, the blowing snow was so thick that it overwhelmed the windscreen wipers. Their landing lights did nothing but highlight the snow, reflecting the light back at them.

Jan spotted what looked like a flat, broad field, and Emily adjusted course to take advantage of the longest stretch. She hoped it wasn't a lake under the layer of snow because until two days earlier, temperatures had been above freezing during the day. It was unlikely that surface ice on a deep lake would be strong enough to support the weight of a Wellington.

The initial touchdown was surprisingly soft. The wet snow both softened the impact and provided sufficient friction to slow them down. However, the torque from the functioning engine caused them to veer. Emily tried to apply opposite rudder while calling Rick and Jan to shut down the port engine. It was no good. Rick saw the low, stone shed and yelled at her to avoid it, but the aircraft was out of control. It careered into the structure with a terrible crash and the howl of tortured metal. Bricks and stones hammered against the fuselage and broke through the canvas as the engine smashed the structure open. Then with a shudder, the whole airframe came to a halt and the port engine shut itself off.

In the moment of silence that followed, Emily felt intense pain spreading out from her heart. Her brain shouted at her to escape the wreck before a fire ignited, but her body was lamed. Only gradually did she register that Jan was screaming and Anna was hanging over her shoulder, asking if she was all right.

"See to the others," Emily told Anna. When she went to release her straps, acute pain shot up from her left wrist causing her to gasp. She must have broken it. She would have to get out of her seat without using it. Yet all movement was so painful that she could hardly breathe. Glancing to the right for help, she caught a glimpse of Rick's crushed face streaming with blood and instantly felt queasy. She closed her eyes to regain her composure.

She must have lost consciousness briefly because the next thing she knew, Anna was between her and Jan, trying to calm Jan down. She registered that Rick was now stretched out on the floor of the cockpit with his head wrapped in bandages. To get out of the aircraft, she would have to stand on her seat and climb out of the cockpit window.

She looked up. It was half-covered with snow already and beyond all was dark. That meant there was no fire. On the other hand, if the snow covered them, no one would be able to find them, and they would freeze to death. The Wellington's skin consisted only of canvas glued to the geodetic metal frame. Already, bitterly cold drafts of wind whistled through rips torn in the fabric by bricks from the building they'd hit. She had to get out and go for help. But she didn't have the strength.

Anna had been working by torchlight and now directed her torch at her pilot. "Emily? Are you all right?"

"I think I'm having a heart attack. I have terrible pain all across the front of my chest."

"More likely the straps have broken your breast bone," Anna replied with admirable professionalism. "Anything else?"

"My wrist has snapped." Emily lifted her left arm a little to draw attention to it. She couldn't move or feel her fingers which were already swelling.

"I'll get that splinted," Anna replied and started to rummage through her first-aid kit.

"We have to get help," Emily told her. "We'll freeze to death in here if they don't find us soon."

"I'll go as soon as I've finished stabilizing your wrist."

"No. You have to stay with Jan and Rick. I'm completely useless when it comes to first aid. Just do what you can to splint and ease the pain in my wrist and chest, then help me out of the cockpit window. Once I've gone, bring every blanket from the sick bay up to the cockpit and wrap yourself up."

Anna nodded and set to work splinting Emily's wrist. The pain was terrible, and Emily almost passed out in the process. Anna stopped to give her a small dose of morphine. When Anna finished, Emily sat breathing heavily for a minute or two, collecting her strength and courage. Then she announced, "I want you to push the cockpit window open and help me get out."

That was easier said than done. Anna got the window open easily enough, and Emily managed to stand on her seat by sheer willpower. It was a matter of ignoring the pain, she found. Yet her efforts left her feeling faint and sick. Eventually, moving very slowly and holding her torso as rigidly as possible, she clambered out onto the wing. This was already half covered in snow and slippery. She lost her footing, fell and slid down the slope of the wing to land in a heap in the snow. In the process, she lost consciousness. When she came to, Anna was calling down to her in an almost hysterical voice.

Emily pulled herself together enough to right herself and sit on the edge of the wing while she struggled to regain her breath and still her panic. The pain was so pervasive that she was sick in the snow. After that, she washed her mouth with snow, then took deep breaths and waited for the pain to subside or for the morphine to start working better. Maybe the dose had been too small? No, she couldn't risk falling asleep.

Eventually, she forced herself to her feet and looked around to get her bearings. She couldn't face tramping into the blizzard, so she turned her back to it and let it push her. As she walked, she tried to remember the map, but she rarely paid attention to what was outside the corridor. Tonight, they had been especially preoccupied with the fuel problem. But this was Germany, she reminded herself, a densely populated country in the heart of Europe. There had to be a village or a farmhouse nearby.

She stopped again, this time looking for some sign of settlement. It was hard to see far in the darkness and the blizzard, but she could decipher a line of trees off to her left, possibly a forest. To her right, on the other hand, the land fell away somewhat and seemed less hostile. She decided to veer more in that direction.

Aware of the danger of walking in circles, she looked for some landmark to help her hold her course. If only it had been a clear night, she could have navigated by the stars, but the cloud cover blotted them out. The only distinctive feature she could find was a clump of trees that rose up higher than the rest and she decided to make for them.

Walking was difficult. Although she could ease the pain in her wrist by holding it against her stomach, the pain in her chest was constant and nearly overpowering. She had to stop frequently just to gather her strength and fight back the nausea. The morphine didn't seem to be working, but how could she know how much worse the pain would have been without it?

As she struggled forward, the snow gradually became finer and the flakes drier. Emily started to believe she was making progress. As the clump of trees grew closer, she began to discern a light at the base of them. Then suddenly a patch of tall, dense reeds blocked her way. After staring at them bewildered, she realised that they marked the edge of a snow-covered lake. This expanse of ice lay between her and that clump of trees with the light. Should she try to cross it? It looked as though it was frozen hard — or was there a darker patch in the centre, suggesting flowing water? She couldn't risk falling through the ice. If she died, no one would know about the others, and they would die too.

She turned to follow the reeds marking the edge of the lake, hoping that she could skirt around it and resume her course towards the yellow light glowing under the clump of trees. However, the reeds made walking almost impossible because they were surrounded by ice. Emily slipped again and again, each fall causing intense pain in her wrist and chest. She had to back away from the reeds, extending her detour. Gradually, her goal moved from ahead of her to beside her and then off her quarter. All the while, her strength was fading, and she started to doubt she would make it. She gritted her teeth, put her head down and slogged on through the snow.

When she couldn't take another step, she stopped and looked around. The lake was still to her left, and to her right, the trees of another forest were closing in. As far as she could see, there was not a house or a barn or even a shepherd's hut. How was it possible that in the heart of Germany there was not one single dwelling or living soul?

Emily felt utterly alone, cut off not only from civilisation but from all humanity. For a surreal moment, she wondered if she was already dead. Maybe she was in hell. She seemed to remember hearing that the outer rings of hell were cold and icy rather than hot and fiery.

"Oh, Robin," she cried out mentally, "how did it come to this? Why?" She had never considered the possibility that she might die before him. Throughout the war, she had mentally prepared herself for losing him. She had dreaded and hated the thought of his death yet acknowledged that it was her most likely fate. Not once had she imagined she might be killed, leaving him behind. "I'm sorry," she whispered.

But then she remembered Anna, Jan and Rick. She couldn't abandon them! She was responsible for them. She had to keep going, keep trying. She forced herself to resume her journey, doggedly, stubbornly. She focused on her footing, just following the edge of the lake.

It was impossible to know how long she struggled to keep moving. Anna had removed Emily's watch when she splinted her wrist. Meanwhile, the cold had numbed her to the point where she no longer felt her arm so intensely. Then, quite unexpectedly, she saw wooden planking jutting out into the frozen lake. It was a pier of some sort. She turned in the opposite direction and saw a sunken path between the snow banks leading up an incline to that clump of trees. At this distance, it was obvious that the trees were huge and ancient and towered above a tall, narrow, brick building with vertical slits for windows. These emitted a warm but weak light.

Hope gave Emily the strength to drag herself up the incline to the towering wooden door. It felt ancient, medieval. She stared up, and from the depth of her brain her apparently useless degree in medieval history provided recognition: this was a gothic structure, and its dimensions and isolated location suggested it was — or had been — a monastery. The Reformation in northern Germany had eradicated all the monasteries, but the buildings had remained and been turned over to other uses.

Emily tried knocking on the heavy door, but the sound she could produce with her knuckles was pitiable. She looked for a knocker and found a cord instead. Following it upwards with her eyes, she saw it was attached to a bell. She pulled it with her good hand and almost jumped out of her skin at the loud clang that it emitted. She pulled it again and again until the door cracked open, and light escaped onto the snow.

"*Hilfe!*" She gasped. "*Hilfe!*"

The silhouetted figure answered in a frail, female voice "*Natuerlich! Herein!*" She also gestured for Emily to come in, repeating, "*Herein!*"

Emily shook her head, wracking her brain for the German word for crash. All she remembered was accident, "*Unfall! Unfall!*" Her brain could not construct a whole sentence; that required grammar. Instead, she gasped out, "*Drei Leute! Noch im Flugzeug.*" Three people. Still in the aircraft.

A commotion ensued. First, another woman joined the door opener, and they consulted in agitated voices. When two more women joined the first pair, Emily repeated her litany of "Accident. Three people. Still in aeroplane." Meanwhile, Emily had registered that all the women were wearing long dark robes and white caps. Not nuns, but almost certainly the inhabitants of one of the Protestant institutions established for pious noblewomen that replaced convents after the Reformation. Finally, a fifth woman with an almost regal presence arrived on the scene. She was tall and upright, if skeletal. In the faint light cast by the oil lamps, she was ghostly white, yet her eyes were sharp. Emily made her appeal in her broken German one more time.

"Are you English?" The woman asked without a trace of German accent.

"Yes! Yes, I am. I'm the pilot of an air ambulance that crash-landed on the other side of the lake. I've been walking an hour or more to find help. Three people are still in the aircraft and two of the crew are injured. They could not leave the aircraft. You must get help to them before they freeze to death."

The woman's face clouded with concern, and she nodded solemnly. Yet rather than sending someone to call an ambulance, she remarked, "You look nearly frozen, my dear, and must be exhausted. Are you injured?"

"My chest," Emily gestured. "The nurse thinks I may have broken my breastbone. And my wrist snapped, but that's not important. Two of the crew left in the aircraft were more badly hurt. The engineer has head injuries. Please! You must send help to the others!" Emily insisted.

The German woman gave orders to one of the women who hurried off, and Emily heaved a sigh of relief. Meanwhile, the older woman inspected Emily's splint. She then gave orders to another woman, who also scurried off. Finally, she told Emily come with her.

Emily discovered she was in the nave of a towering church. Although it was empty and bitterly cold, oil lamps had been lit in the windows beside the door and flanking the screens to the choir. Beyond the screens, candles burned on the altar. Emily registered that the inhabitants had been reading the last service of the day when she'd rung the bell. If not for that, the lights might not have been lit and she would have never found it.

She was led through the screens and told to sit down in one of the choir stalls. "Rest here a moment. Sister Annelise will bring you some hot, mulled wine to help warm you, then we'll get you out of those snow-caked clothes, give you a hot bath, and make up a bed for you. You will stay the night with us."

"Have you sent someone to get help for my colleagues?" Emily asked, anxious for confirmation that this had been the first orders issued.

To her horror, the old woman shook her head. "How? We are five old women. We have an old car, but no petrol. We have a cart, but no horses. We are all over seventy. What can we do?"

"Phone for an ambulance!" Emily urged, desperately.

The old woman sadly shook her head. "We have neither telephone nor electricity here. There is nothing we can do for your friends. All we can do is give you food, warmth and rest."

The news overwhelmed Emily. She was in pain, exhausted, numb with cold and drained of all strength. The thought of Anna, Jan and Rick freezing to death because she had failed them was too much for her. She broke down in tears, but the sobbing increased the pain in her chest to an almost unbearable degree and she cried out.

The frail, old woman gently took her into her arms and stroked her shoulders. "Hush, child, hush. You did the best you could. It is not your fault. It is the will of God."

They took her to a large, institutional kitchen complex with an adjoining lavatory block. They removed her snow-caked clothes and coaxed her into a bath filled with water hand-pumped from a well and heated over a wooden stove. They gave her food and mulled wine in addition to a flannel nightgown and slippers before they led her up a stone stairway and along a corridor to a vacant cell. They helped her into an old wooden cupboard bed and heaped thick eiderdowns over her. By then, Emily had lost all power to resist or protest and fell into a drugged sleep.

Emily had no way of knowing how long she slept. She was woken by whispers on the other side of the wooden doors to her bed. Stirring, she gasped with pain; she had lain so long in one position that her body was completely stiff. The wooden doors swung open and two of her benefactors beamed down at her. One was carrying a tray with food and something hot to drink. Her companion reached in to fluff up the pillows and help Emily sit up before the tray was placed over her hips. In German, they asked her how she was feeling, and she did her best to convey 'rested but stiff.' They nodded and told her to eat, then disappeared.

Before she had finished her meal of bread, butter, honey, and (very welcome!) hot tea, the English speaker swept into the little cell and settled onto the only chair. She smiled at Emily and opened the conversation cheerfully, "Are you feeling better, my dear?"

"Better than last night, thank you, but the pain in my chest and wrist—"

"I'll see that you get some more painkillers," the woman promised.

That was kind, Emily thought, but a doctor would be more helpful. She knew that Anna had done the best she could, but the first-aid kit contained only essentials. By the throbbing in her wrist, she feared the break needed to be reset. It certainly needed to be examined. She wasn't sure she hadn't jolted it out of place in her slide down the wing or in one of her subsequent falls on the ice. It would cause permanent trouble if the bones mended misaligned. The thought had barely formed, however, before she chided herself for worrying about her wrist when Anna, Jan and Rick were probably dead.

Her hostess broke into her thoughts. "Before we go through the normal polite formalities such as introductions, I want to tell you that your friends have been found and taken to hospital."

"Oh, that's wonderful news! That makes me feel much, much better. How were they found? Who rescued them?"

"They were found by the authorities. We heard this from the miller who runs the sawmill at the tip of the lake. He and his wife bring us fresh eels and firewood every Sunday. He heard the news over his radio and eagerly told us that an American plane had crashed nearby. We made no mention of you, of course."

The reference to an American plane confused Emily for a moment, but then she realised that since the three crew members picked up were all Americans, the assumption was logical. So, they were safe, now all she needed was to get medical help. Turning to her benefactress she started, "I don't mean to sound ungrateful, but shouldn't I also go to a hospital?"

"Hospitals are in the hands of the Soviet occupation forces, which means you will receive medical attention but also be detained for espionage."

"Espionage? But I was flying an ambulance! My company has been transporting sick and injured patients out of Berlin for almost a year!"

Her hostess gestured for her to calm down. "I don't doubt you, my dear, but the Ivans are alleging a deliberate violation of their air space and have levelled espionage charges at your colleagues. They were not simply taken to a hospital, they were taken into custody. I thought under the circumstances that we should not reveal your presence — at least not until you have had time to consider your situation and to discuss alternatives."

Emily took a moment to digest that, and then she nodded and murmured, "Thank you. I'm sorry if I—"

"I quite understand, my dear. Things have been happening very fast. You are in pain and still a little groggy from the poppyseed I gave you last night. I think it is time we slowed down enough to learn a little more about one another. After that, we can discuss what to do next."

"Very sensible," Emily agreed, chastened.

"Good. My name is Victoria Louise, and I am the abbess, or Domina, of this establishment, the *Evangelische Damenstift* St. Elizabeth. This was founded in 1582 on the premises of a Cistercian convent dating back to 1248.

When I joined 52 years ago, there were 74 ladies here, not counting the staff, but we have been shrinking ever since. The Nazis took advantage of that to expropriate the buildings for their *"Lebensborn"* program, which — as you may know — facilitated the industrial mass-production of parentless babies. They installed plumbing and electricity in a new wing beyond the old kitchen, which contains an institutional kitchen, lavatories, shower and delivery rooms. As the Red Army approached, however, the Nazis packed up and left. Since then, we have had no diesel to run the generator and so no electricity. We have no telephone or radio, either, as I explained last night.

"Yet while the five of us who chose to remain adhere to our old-fashioned lifestyle and values, we are not completely uninformed about current events. We know the Western Allies are blockaded in their half of Berlin by the Godless Soviets and that the British and Americans are attempting to keep the city supplied by air. Because you were part of that effort, you are *persona non grata* with the barbarian Ivans, and welcome in our community. Would you mind telling me a little more about yourself?" She ended with a gentle but slightly reproachful smile.

Emily nodded and drew a deep breath, only to gasp in pain. Unsteadily, she let the air out of her lungs again and then started cautiously, "My name is Emily Priestman. I learned to fly in the war. I came to Berlin with my husband, who is in the RAF." She thought it better not to mention the fact that he was station commander at Gatow. "When Air Ambulance International started flying sick and injured civilians out of Berlin last April, I joined the company as a pilot and have worked for them ever since. On average we have flown between two and three flights a day, and this was our first crash."

"Is your husband still in Berlin? Do you have children there as well?"

"No, we have no children, but yes, my husband is still in Berlin, at Gatow. There must be a way for me to get back to him."

"In your condition without the authorities finding out?" Victoria Louise asked back with raised eyebrows before answering her own question with a tart, "Not very likely!"

Then in a gentler voice she urged, "For the moment, you need to stay still and warm. Bones will heal themselves if given a chance, but your body needs to rest so it can channel its strength to the broken bits. As for getting you back to Berlin, first, you need to understand that we're more than 160 kilometres away. Second, I do not know how you could possibly move by road or rail without encountering either Russian troops or Communist police. They swarm around the railway stations, and everything that moves on the roads is stopped and checked for papers and plunder. The best we can do is get word to your husband that you are alive and safe. Maybe your government can find a way to rescue you."

That sounded as if the worthy nuns expected the SAS to parachute in to spirit her away! Emily was too much of a realist to think that was a possibility. To London, she was a woman of no consequence, while Robin's resources were limited.

Still, Victoria Louise was correct; he must be told of her situation. Maybe he could persuade General Robertson or someone in Whitehall to do something. She nodded feebly, and the older woman patted her hand, told her to get more rest, and withdrew.

Shadow Cabinet
Berlin-Kladow
Wednesday 16 February 1949
(Day 236 of the Berlin Airlift)

Cannon shells smashing into the armour plating behind his seat jolted Robin awake, and he reared up bewildered. He didn't know where he was. It was completely dark and cold. Then the banging sound came again. He realised he was in his bed in Kladow, and someone was knocking at the bedroom door. He looked toward the sound and heard Jasha's timid voice. "Mr Robin! Wake up! Christian is here! With news about Emily!"

Christian? How could he know anything about Emily?

Robin threw the covers off and staggered to his feet. Jasha knocked and called again, prompting him to shout, "I'm coming!" He stumbled over his shoes on the way to the door and yanked it open. A smiling Jasha excitedly explained, "Horst brought Christian with a message from Emily! Come!"

Robin followed her down the stairs in his stockinged feet to find Christian in the den, where Kit, Georgina and Graham had already gathered. "Graham came to take me home," Jasha explained the latter's presence.

"What time is it?" Robin asked generally.

"Almost nine pm," Kit answered.

Robin drew a deep breath. That meant he'd slept almost seven hours. It had done him good. "What's this about news from Emily?"

"I received a letter today," Christian held up an envelope, which was already torn open.

"From Emily?"

"Not directly. Let me read it to you. It's in German, of course, but I'll translate:

Dear Christian,

It seems like ages since we have heard from you. How time flies. We worry about you and wonder if you are OK. We don't understand why you refuse to register for rations in the East.

Christian interrupted himself to explain, "They threw that in to sound like loyal supporters of the SMAD just in case the letter fell into the wrong hands." Then he continued reading:

We're doing well. We have enough wood for the fire, and we aren't starving. Things could be better, but they could be a lot worse. I just hope there won't be another war.

Anyway, I'm writing because I thought you'd be interested to hear that Mimi Preis —

"Pryce was Emily's maiden name. You think they are referring to her?"

"Listen," Christian urged.

You remember her, don't you? Her parents were good, loyal communists even in the thirties when everyone else was crazy about Herr Hitler, but Mimi fell head-over-heels for a Fliegerhauptman—

Again, Christian interrupted himself to explain, "I don't know how to translate that exactly. It's a play on the phrase *'Raeuberhauptman'* meaning bandit leader or highwayman, but the writer of the letter has substituted flier, or pilot if you like, for bandit —"

"And Hauptman — or Flight Lieutenant — was my rank when Emily and I met. You've convinced me they are talking about Emily, but where is she?"

"This is what he says:

She was on her way to Berlin, but her petrol didn't quite stretch far enough, so she landed with us. Or, maybe, stranded is a better word because she broke her wrist when she fell on the ice. She was wondering if you might be able to give her a lift to Berlin. If you can get here that is. We'd love to see you and will keep Mimi warm and safe in the meantime.

"That is the best news I've heard in four days," Robin admitted. "But where is she? Who sent the letter?"

"That's the problem," Christian admitted. "There was no return address on the envelope." He showed the envelope to Robin, "The letter is signed 'Karsten Damien Stift Schenk zu Schwerin.' It must be a code for something because I don't know any Karsten Damien Stift and Schenk zu Schwerin is not a legitimate title. In short, I'm sure this isn't the sender's real name, but I believe the name is supposed to tell us something. I just haven't worked out what."

Robin turned to Georgina who as a teacher used the library in the house more than anyone else. "Do you know if there's a good atlas of Germany in the library?"

"Yes! I'll fetch it!"

A moment later the heavy Atlas had been opened on the table and they all stared down at it. Robin drew with his finger the route of the northern corridor into Berlin. "We know that the starboard engine packed in first, which means Emily had to turn to port to attempt a landing, that put her north of the corridor."

"Didn't the Soviets claim the crash was near Pritzwalk?" Georgina asked, finding it on the map.

"They will have lied," Graham declared, cynically. "If they mentioned Pritzwalk, we can be sure that is the *one* place it is *not*."

Robin nodded in agreement, but added, "The Dakota pilot thought he saw the navigation lights of an aircraft below him heading in the direction of the old Luftwaffe base at Parchim, presumably now used by the Red Air Force." He located this on the map.

"But that's way beyond Schwerin," Georgina pointed out.

"But more than half the way to *Alt* Schwerin," Christian noted with intensity. "If she continued on that course, she might have put down near to Alt-Schwerin, which is why whoever wrote that letter added the 'Schenk' to the title — to denote something old-fashioned."

They stared at the map.

"What's the countryside like up there?" Robin asked.

"It's a flat region dotted with shallow glacial lakes known as the Mecklenburg Lake District. It is only sparsely populated because marshes and swamps make it poor agricultural land. There are no major cities, and the infrastructure is poorly developed."

"Makes you wonder how the East German police found the wreck so rapidly," Robin mused, adding for the benefit of the others, "Anna said the ambulance arrived in roughly an hour."

"That's astonishing!" Christian exclaimed, explaining, "Rural ambulance service is practically non-existent in most of the Soviet Zone. No one can get access to petrol and most ambulances are horse drawn. Such a rapid response suggests the crash site may be close to Schwerin after all."

"Or that the ambulance wasn't a civilian ambulance at all. Maybe it came from the Red Air Force base at Parchim," Robin pointed this out on the map. Parchim lay south and east of Schwerin.

"Yes, that might explain things," Christian concluded, perking up. "If they flew over Parchim, the Red Air Force would have had them on radar, and they'll have both a serviceable ambulance and petrol."

Graham leaned closer to the map to check the scale and measured 40 kilometres between his thumb and forefinger as he hypothesized, "Assuming the ambulance came from Parchim, that the ambulance could cover forty kilometres in an hour, and that Moby Dick maintained a straight course after leaving the corridor, that would put the crash site about here." With his thumb fixed on Parchim, he swung his index finger through an arch forty miles away. "Practically on top of Alt Schwerin," he concluded.

"I don't think even a Red Air Force ambulance could have travelled 40 kilometres in an hour," Christian countered. "It was snowing, remember, and even if they had a radar fix, the roads up there are in poor condition and unlikely to lead in the right direction. I estimate the crash site is closer to 20 kilometres northeast of Parchim, or at most halfway to Alt Schwerin," Christian tapped his finger on the map at a spot between the two towns. "That's where we should start looking."

Graham nodded, but Robin asked, "How? I can't send recce aircraft that far out of the corridor without risking them being shot down and also drawing attention to what we are doing. Furthermore, while we might find the wreck from the air, Emily is in hiding, so the only way to find her is on the ground."

"Exactly," Christian agreed. "I think I could—"

The ringing of the doorbell interrupted the discussion, and they looked around startled until Robin remembered, "It must be Corporal Borisenko. I asked her to stop by when she finished her meeting with her Soviet contact."

Jasha went to answer the bell and returned with Galyna in tow. The latter was startled to find such a crowd collected. The sight of her WingCo in stockings and without a hat or tie also disconcerted her. Robin tried to put her at ease. "Would you like a drink, Borisenko? I think we could all use one."

Kit took the hint and turned toward the drinks cabinet, while the WAAF corporal answered, "I'm reporting as ordered, sir, but if this isn't a good time...." She looked nervously at the others.

"There isn't anyone in this room that I wouldn't trust with my life, Borisenko. What you have to say, you can say to all of us. Are you sure you don't want a drink?"

Borisenko shook her head and seemed uncomfortable, but she accepted the situation. "My friend on Marshal Sokolovsky's staff was hunting last weekend in the Thuringer Forest and didn't return to Berlin until Monday morning, which was why she didn't receive any of my calls on Sunday. She heard nothing about the downed aircraft until Monday afternoon. However, she has since managed to confirm that the Soviets found three people in the wreck. According to her, the first pilot's seat was vacant, but a man was lying on the floor, seriously injured, so he was assumed to be the pilot. Still in the second pilot's seat was an injured woman, who had been sedated but not moved by the nurse. There was no indication that there had been a fourth crew member. All three Americans were taken into custody. The two pilots are still being held and the nurse was released last night."

Robin nodded. None of this was news any more, but then Borisenko ambushed him by adding, "Mila offered to go to the crash site and see what she could find. She was a partisan, remember, and is very good at tracking."

"You told her we were looking for someone?" Robin asked horrified. He had not authorised that.

"Because she can help us, sir," Borisenko explained with tense urgency.

"Why would she be willing to help?" Robin asked sharply. He was furious. The corporal had vastly overstepped her orders. Her actions amounted to betraying sensitive information to the enemy, and in the circumstances, that came dangerously close to treason. Robin drew a deep breath to deliver a severe rebuke.

Borisenko forestalled him and took the wind from his sails by declaring, "Because she wants to defect, sir, to get away to the West. She wants us to give her asylum in exchange for her help."

Robin froze. The defection of a "Hero of the Soviet Union" from Sokolovsky's personal staff would be a sensational propaganda coup. MI6 would be delighted. The press would certainly love it, and the Foreign Office, too. But after the Utting murder and the call this past Sunday threatening Emily's life, Robin found it difficult to trust any Soviet citizen. Since he couldn't admit that outright, he waffled by asking, "What makes her think she can find Emily?"

"Mila says the aircraft went down near one of her favourite hunting grounds. She hunts on the weekends to refresh her sharp-shooter skills. She used to have friends that went with her, but one by one they were all sent back to the Soviet Union. Recently, she has been going alone with just a batwoman to carry things, clean and cook. She said she could go to Mecklenburg this weekend without arousing suspicion."

"And then what?"

"Under the guise of hunting, she can start systematically scouring the countryside in a radius around the wreck until she finds some trace of Mrs Priestman. She suggested I go with her disguised as her batwoman. She says no one would notice because her batwoman doesn't like hunting, so she often borrows a servant from another officer." Borisenko's eagerness was evident in the excited way she explained the plan, but Robin knew that it would be extremely dangerous for her. If she were caught, she would be turned over to the Soviet Secret Police as a double agent. In his desperation to get Emily out of the Soviet Zone before the Soviet authorities discovered her, he was tempted, nevertheless.

Fortunately, Graham burst the bubble by pointing out, "Emily doesn't know you, corporal. If she's in hiding and she sees or hears that a Hero of the Soviet Union and her batwoman are looking for her, she is not going to reveal herself. Furthermore, you would be putting yourself at unconscionable risk. It would make more sense for Christian to accompany your friend."

Borisenko looked bewildered until Christian introduced himself. "I'm a colleague of Mrs Priestman's. I run AAI's office."

"Do you speak Russian?" Borisenko asked.

"No, but—"

"Then you can't disguise yourself as Mila's servant," Borisenko argued.

Christian countered, "I don't have to disguise myself as her servant. There's no need for us to travel together. We could meet up in Alt Schwer-in —"

"Not good! I go," Jasha spoke up.

"No!" Graham countered instantly in alarm.

Jasha looked him straight in the eye and shook her head. "Must help Emily! No British passport yet. Just DP — worthless Polack! Speak Russian and German. I make good slave to Russian officer. No one pay attention to me. No danger. Russian woman officer protect me from Russian men."

"I don't want you to go," Graham insisted.

Jasha went on tiptoe and kissed him. Her hand lingered on his face as she pulled away, but she insisted firmly. "Want to help, Graham. Let me go."

Graham threw up his hands and looked at Robin.

Robin turned to address the WAAF corporal, "Would your friend accept Jasha in your place, do you think?"

Borisenko answered by addressing Jasha in Russian which sparked a lively exchange. Borisenko fired off questions in an almost aggressive tone, but Jasha answered them unintimidated and defiant. The initial tension between the two women gradually eased. Then suddenly the WAAF corporal laughed at something Jasha had said, and Jasha joined in. They nodded to one another, and Borisenko turned to address Robin. "I will take Jasha to my rendezvous with Mila tomorrow. It will be up to her if she agrees or not."

"Fair enough," Robin agreed. He knew it was too soon, but he felt his hopes rising. For the first time since the Russians had made their threat to kill her, Robin believed that he might see Emily again — alive.

Chapter Sixteen
Encounters with the Dark Side

Hunting Expedition
Mecklenburg-Vorpommern
Friday 18 – Saturday 19 February 1949
(Days 238 – 239 of the Berlin Airlift)

Jasha was not happy. Mila treated her with the thoughtless indifference and routine rudeness that Soviet officers cultivated in their dealings with soldiers and servants. Mila never made requests; she gave orders. Nothing was ever done fast enough. Nothing was ever done right. Since Mila was never satisfied, she never said thank you. And she never smiled.

Jasha knew that this treatment was part of her 'disguise.' Because she dressed in the uniform of a simple Soviet soldier, it would have aroused suspicion if Mila had been considerate, polite or friendly. Precisely because Mila took so little notice of Jasha, no one else did either. At least Mila didn't carry things to the extreme of cuffing her, something which would have been quite normal behaviour for Russian officers. Yet her tone left Jasha tense, and the entire situation reminded Jasha of the early days of the Soviet occupation of Poland.

Part of her rebelled. It was almost ten years since the war had started with the joint Soviet-German invasion of Poland; she was no longer the woman she had been in 1939. Then she had still been dazed and frantic with fear after the state murder of her husband and son. She had preferred to play the obedient slave and the humble 'sub-human' rather than attract the attention of either dictator's uniformed thugs. She had placed survival at the top of her priority list.

Since then, the years of good treatment — from the Walmsdorfs, her American employers, and the Priestmans — had made her more sensitive to the indignity that Mila's behaviour constituted. Her marriage to Graham had made her proud, too. She was not a peasant or a pawn, much less a slave. She had also come to believe that even a person doing a menial or simple job deserved respect and courtesy. Her Christian beliefs were starting to colour her politics. Christ taught that all souls were equal. There were no rich or poor souls. There were no ruler souls or slave souls. Christ dwelt not with kings, bankers and policemen but with the poor, the sick, the imprisoned and abused.

Jasha's inner outrage made her dislike Mila, yet her enforced proximity to the Soviet organs of occupation reminded her of what was at stake, too. She could not bear the thought of Emily falling into the hands of these cruel and cynical haters of humanity. She had to find Emily so that her friends could rescue her.

Mila had given her a Russian uniform at their first meeting. It had been selected to fit Borisenko and was too wide and too short for Jasha. That was good, Mila said, because the Russians didn't care if the uniforms fitted common soldiers and most walked around in ill-fitting clothes. Fortunately, Galyna and Jasha shared the same shoe size, so the worn-down and sagging boots were comfortable and functional.

Jasha put on the Soviet uniform in the ladies' room at Spandau station before dawn and took the first train of the day to her rendezvous with Mila at the Ostbahnhof. From there, she trailed behind Mila, carrying all five pieces of luggage. Although she was much weaker than Mila, Jasha alone dragged the baggage aboard the train and put it in the overhead racks. Thereafter, she sat or stood in the aisle with the ordinary soldiers. Only officers were allowed to use the compartments.

After roughly two hours, Mila shouted to her to get the luggage off the train "Fast, fast!" It was only a short stop at a small station and Jasha had so much trouble with everything she barely managed to read the sign: Mestlin.

Across the street from the station a German owned some horses. Mila did not hire them, she expropriated them for her use, saying only she would return them. She told Jasha this was what she always did. The luggage was loaded on one of the horses and Jasha unhappily mounted the most docile nag. She had not ridden in years and felt insecure in the saddle.

Mila got directions to the crash site from the Russian unit billeted in the town. They said it wasn't very interesting and warned that 'everything useful' had already been 'collected.' Mila shrugged and said she was just curious. She'd seen lots of German aircraft wrecks, she told the soldiers conversationally, but not a British Wellington.

The soldiers shrugged. "Cheap construction," they commented dismissively. "Flimsy crap. Not strong and durable like our planes."

Mila and Jasha reached the crash site around noon and dismounted to get a closer look. A couple of bored Russian sentries wandered over to shoo them away, but when they saw Mila's rank and medals, they withdrew. Mila ensured their cooperation and silence by handing over some "officer-grade" cigarettes. That was when Jasha learned that Soviet soldiers were not allowed the same type of cigarettes as their officers.

Approaching the wreck, Jasha felt uncomfortable. She had seen much destruction in the war, but mostly buildings and trains. To Jasha, the downed aircraft looked like a big bird lying on its side with one wing broken and its nose poking out of the snow as if straining for a last breath of air. In her imagination, it was a benign and gentle beast that had been trying to rescue sick people from a besieged city, only to be murdered by the forces of darkness.

While Jasha hung back, Mila climbed inside the wreck and crawled about looking things over. When she came out, she remarked. "Picked clean. Take all gadgets, wires and rubber fittings, too." Then she unhobbled her horse, mounted and led Jasha away from the crash site at a trot.

Jasha hated trotting. The bouncing was uncomfortable and made her feel as though she were going to fall off. She gripped the pommel, and the horse, realising she was not in control, saw no reason to exert himself and fell into a walk. Jasha called ahead to Mila, who returned and took Jasha's reins over the horse's head to lead him. Since they were out of earshot of the Russian soldiers, Jasha risked asking, "How do you know which way to go?"

"Snow drifts show how wind blew. Walk away from wind. Let it push. Also, land slopes down. People walk up only if must."

That made sense to Jasha, and they rode until they came to a lake. Here Mila stopped and looked around, frowning.

"Could she have crossed the lake?" Jasha asked.

Mila shook her head. "Deep lake, strong current. Water flows too fast for ice to build. Runs out under sawmill." She pointed. "I think she go right, west, follow trail to village."

"What village?" Jasha asked looking around at a landscape devoid of any human structure.

"Three kilometres," Mila answered.

They turned to the right, leaving the lake behind, and followed an almost imperceptible indentation in the deep snow. Before long, they came to the village Mila had promised. A handful of low houses with thatched roofs clustered around a brick church with a stocky, square tower. There was no evidence of bombing or fire, but the buildings looked rundown and poor. Mila led straight to the village "*Krug*" or tavern. This looked no different from the other houses except that there was a sign at the front depicting a pewter tankard. The door opened into a low-ceilinged room with a bar at the back and barrels of beer along one side. There were four tables, and one table was occupied by what looked like farmers with straw sticking to the manure on their rubber boots. At another, two policemen sat together with a postman. All were middle-aged and misshapen, in the way of men who had once been fat but were now sagging sacks of skin.

Mila strode towards the policemen and shouted, "No one teach you show respect for Hero of the Soviet Union?"

Belatedly, and Jasha thought a little resentfully, the men stood and knuckled their foreheads. "You know about plane crash?"

"What about it?"

"Someone escaped. See stranger here?"

They all shook their heads.

Mila turned to the other table and shouted. "You! Peasants! See stranger around?"

They shook their heads.

She turned on the innkeeper. "Innkeeper, you have strange customers?"

"They're all strange, Madam Major. These are strange times."

"Anyone you not know? Speak English? Wear funny clothes?"

Everyone was shaking their heads.

Mila frowned and threatened, "You lie, soldiers come!"

But they just shook their heads, and Mila turned and stormed back outside.

As soon as they were out of hearing of the people in the Krug, Jasha pointed out that it was past noon and she had not eaten since before dawn. "Why don't we at least eat something?"

"Know better place," Mila replied. They remounted their horses and retraced their steps to the turning point beside the lake. Here they followed the north shore of the lake until they came to the sawmill Mila had mentioned. It turned out that the mill served cooked eels with boiled potatoes. While they gorged themselves on the fresh fish, Mila asked the staff and other customers if they had heard about someone escaping from the crash. Jasha was surprised to note that her tone was much friendlier here for some reason — and she paid for the eels.

After the meal they continued their search south of the sawmill in a large village called Goldberg, but with no success. It was rapidly becoming darker and colder, and Jasha felt increasingly miserable. She was saddle sore and stiff all over, meanwhile the wind had become colder and sharper. Fed up, she finally declared, "We need to find a place for the night. I saw a sign saying they rent rooms in the window of that house over there."

"No, going somewhere special," Mila answered. "Not far. You like it," she promised with a rare smile. Jasha did not believe her, especially as they turned back towards the lake and rode this time into a gusting wind laced with snow flurries.

To her surprise, however, after a half hour or so, they came to an old convent and were warmly welcomed by five old nuns. After stabling the horses, they were led to a large kitchen heated by a booming fire. They settled down and were given bread, cheese, and hot, mulled wine. Most surprising of all, Mila introduced Jasha by her name and treated her like a companion rather than a servant. As they sat together at the kitchen table, Mila explained to Jasha that she liked to stay here when hunting in the vicinity because the nuns had no politics. Naturally, she also asked the nuns about the crash and if they'd heard about any survivors, but the nuns said they knew nothing. They lived reclusive lives, the Mother Superior stressed. Jasha believed them.

After their meal, Mila announced she would go hunting at the crack of dawn. She had to have something to take back to Berlin with her, otherwise her colleagues might wonder what she had been doing. Her last words to Jasha were, "You can sleep late and rest a bit. We'll continue our search in the afternoon before catching a train to Berlin in time for you to reach the West before public transport stops."

They were each given their own cell for the night. Each was furnished with a prie-dieu, a crucifix, and a cupboard bed, the kind you could climb right into. Although the rooms were unheated, the nuns made sure they had plenty of eiderdowns. Jasha felt warm and safe and contented for the first time all day. She was also utterly exhausted and fell asleep almost instantly.

Along with her evening meal that night, Victoria Louise brought Emily word that a Russian officer had arrived and planned to spend the night. Reading the alarm in Emily's eyes, she hastened to explain, "She has come several times before. She likes hunting in the surrounding forests, and she shares the meat of her kills with us. She rarely stays more than one night, but you must assume she is still here until we tell you otherwise. Meanwhile, be especially careful. We'll put her in a cell on the opposite side of the cloister, but do not use a candle when you go to the lavatory and listen carefully before opening your door for any reason."

The news upset Emily. Victoria Louise's manner reassured her that she was not at risk of immediate discovery, yet the situation reminded her that she was a helpless quarry. She was too weak to flee and had nowhere else to hide in any case. She retreated into her box bed and curled up at the foot, trying to sleep.

Instead, her mind kept her awake with futile speculation about whether she ought to have surrendered to the Soviets earlier. Too late she realised that with each day that she remained hidden, the consequences of her discovery for the nuns became worse. It was effectively already too late to turn herself in.

All she could do was hope the letter to Christian reached him and he was able to decode it. Then again, even if he managed to make sense of it, what could he possibly do? Yes, he would share it with Robin, and Robin would want to act. But what could he realistically undertake? Where could he turn? She couldn't imagine the timid General Robertson approving any kind of rescue, and London would at most send a diplomatic note of enquiry, which the Russians would honestly answer with 'whereabouts unknown.'

She feared that Robin's helplessness would eat away at him, making him angry and bitter or possibly foolhardy and reckless. She didn't like the thought of him trying to find her himself and getting arrested. But she didn't like the thought of him giving up, forgetting her and marrying again, either.

She slept fitfully. She started to imagine herself twenty or thirty years from now, thin and bent, dressed like the sisters, and sharing their routine of prayers, cooking and cleaning. To the outside world, she would be simply lost behind the iron curtain, MIA.

The ringing of the bells woke Jasha. Such a lovely sound! The Soviets had silenced the bells when she was still very little. She had only faint memories of them, but they were good memories. She associated them with incense and candles, cinnamon and sugar sweets, and playing games with other children. She rose and dressed and followed the bells.

She found the church and the five nuns in the choir reading the mass together without a priest. Jasha sat at the back and let the service wash over her. The nuns' voices were frail and wobbly and slightly off-key anyway, so she tuned them out. She prayed simply, first the Lord's Prayer, and then naively: "Dear Mother Mary, help me to find Emily. Help me to bring her home to those who love her, away from the forces of evil that have been unleashed upon the world. She is a good person, and so is her husband. They don't deserve to suffer for trying to help others."

The nuns had stopped singing, and Jasha opened her eyes. The nuns were standing around her. "You aren't really a Russian soldier, are you?" The abbess asked in a suspicious voice.

Jasha shook her head.

"Why are you here? What do you want?"

"I'm trying to find a friend."

"A friend? A nun?"

"No, a man. Karsten Damien Stift Schenk zu Schwerin."

"Karsten? You know Karsten?" The Domina sounded astonished, and Jasha's heart began to hope. Maybe Karsten Stift actually existed? In answer to the question, Jasha explained, "Not directly. He is a friend of my friend Christian, but Christian could not come."

"Does Mila know about Karsten?" The Domina sounded alarmed.

Jasha shook her head vigorously. "No, no, but I told her a friend had been lost in the snowstorm, and she offered to help because she knows the region."

The nuns were frowning and ill at ease. Jasha was afraid they would not help her because of Mila, so she made a new appeal. "Please help me! My friend is a good person. She was helping sick people and children get out of Berlin before Russians take over."

"Then it is a woman you are looking for."

"Yes — Mimi Preis. She was injured, and I must find her and let her know that her husband is searching for a way to help her."

The knocking at the door made Emily retreat to the deepest, darkest corner of the bed. Frozen in place, she held her breath to listen. The door opened. "Mrs Priestman?" It was the voice of Victoria Louise.

"Yes," Emily squeaked out, relaxing only enough to move closer to the still-closed door of the cupboard bed. The door opened from the outside and Victoria Louise looked down at her. "My dear child, there is a woman here claiming to be the wife of a British army officer, but I'm not sure. She doesn't speak English very well. I think she is Polish."

"Polish? Jasha? Jasha is here?" Emily could hardly believe it. Of all the people she had imagined rescuing her — Robin, Christian, David or Kiwi — Jasha had never crossed her mind.

"She gave her name as Jasha Russell. Is that correct?"

"Yes, yes, yes! Where is she?" Emily started scrambling to get out of her bed, ignoring the pain in her chest, only to gasp and cringe when she accidentally hit her wrist against the side of the cupboard door.

"Careful!" Victoria Louise urged too late. "There is no rush. The Russian officer is out hunting. Jasha is in the kitchen. Come slowly." She offered her hand to help.

Emily clambered out of the bed and would have gone into the hall in her night clothes if Victoria Louise had not, with an exasperated exclamation, grabbed a dressing gown and wrapped it around her.

When Emily reached the kitchen, Jasha leapt to her feet with a cry of joy and ran to her. They embraced, Jasha sobbing with relief and Emily gasping in pain until she eased Jasha's arms gently. They talked over one another as Jasha asked Emily how badly she was hurt, and Emily asked how Jasha had found her. Around them, the nuns smiled and shooed them to the table, set hot tea in front of them and brought Emily slippers for her feet.

Eventually, they calmed down enough to discuss what would happen next. "You stay here. Safe. Not safe on roads."

Emily nodded; she knew that.

Jasha continued, "I go back to Berlin. Tell Mr Robin. He not leave you here!" She declared emphatically. "He think of something." Jasha's conviction was reassuring — at first.

Later, long after Jasha and Mila were gone, Emily perceived a new danger. What if Robin thought of 'something' that was entirely too foolhardy and risky for them both? Or worse, what if his rescue efforts set off a chain reaction that escalated into a diplomatic incident or even a new war? She did not want to go down in history as the woman who had ignited a nuclear catastrophe in the heart of Europe.

Life's Lessons
Berlin-Charlottenburg
Sunday, 20 February 1949
(Day 240 of the Berlin Airlift)

It was the afternoon of the day on which the Russians had threatened to deliver Emily's body on the Glienicker Bridge. Although Robin had allowed himself to be convinced that they were bluffing, there could be no certainty until the day was over. The letter to Christian might have been a ruse of some sort or an outright trap. Alternatively, Emily might have been arrested since it had been sent. Jasha could not possibly return until tonight. Meanwhile, Robin was understandably as restless as a caged tiger, and the Howleys had considerately suggested he join them and Anna for lunch. The idea was to spend the afternoon together and so keep their worst fears at bay.

With Kit flying, Georgina would have been alone in the residence. Robin suggested she come to the Howley's with him, promising to lend her his car to go to her sewing class. When after lunch Georgina excused herself, Anna asked if she could join her.

"Are you sure you feel up to this?" Georgina asked Anna solicitously. "The girls are bound to ask you all sorts of questions. It could become awkward."

"I have to start doing something," Anna countered. "I can't just sit around worrying. I need to think about something else."

Georgina could understand that, so they set off together and unlocked the domestic science room at the British school a little early. Within half an hour, the four girls who remained of the original ten arrived. After finishing their overcoats, half the girls had drifted away. Then Dietlinde and Gisela had clashed so violently at the session following Silvie's death that they were no longer on speaking terms. Georgina was not surprised when Dietlinde did not show up today. Remaining were Gisela, Ulrike, Petra and Hannah.

It was two weeks since they had last met because Georgina had cancelled the last class due to the loss of Moby Dick. On arrival, it was apparent the girls had followed the news about the 'spy plane' closely, and the sight of Anna set off an explosion of excited exclamations. They crowded around, asking her if she was all right and requesting details of what had happened.

Anna provided a sanitised version of her 'adventures,' which made no mention of Emily whatsoever. She spoke only about 'the pilot' and the 'woman co-pilot.' Georgina watched the way the girls listened, enthralled and full of sympathy. More than once, one of them asked for assurances that the Russians hadn't 'touched' Anna. Emily was struck by how these young girls assumed a protective attitude towards the chaste Anna when they feared she had faced the sexual abuse they had endured at a far younger age.

"The situation was different," Anna assured them. "The Soviets must have suspected that General Clay would take a personal interest in the incident."

The girls nodded with cynical understanding; they were the defeated, while Anna was one of the victors. The victors might now be at each other's throats, but they still treated each other with wary respect.

Ulrike changed the subject slightly, noting with evident excitement, "In the papers, they said you worked for the same company as that woman murderer."

Anna recoiled shocked and confused. "Woman murderer?" How could anyone suggest Emily or Jan were murderers?

"That countess who shot a man between the eyes with a pistol," Gisela explained, sounding almost approving.

"She's referring to Charlotte Graefin Walmsdorf, who worked for Air Ambulance International before you joined the company," Georgina explained to Anna. "You never met her."

"She shot her fiancé three times," Gisela expanded. "Once in the arm, once in the neck and then right between the eyes!" She sounded downright gleeful.

"I wish I had been able to do that to at least one of the men who raped me!" Hannah admitted, adding, "...without getting caught, of course."

"I don't know," Petra replied in a dubious tone, "he *was* her fiancé, not some Ivan or Ami soldier. Since she'd consented to marry him, she'd agreed to have sex. I'm not sure she had the right to kill him."

"Maybe you should hear *her* side of the story before you pass judgment," Georgina cautioned, and Anna nodded in agreement.

"Oh, could we? Could we go to the trial?" Gisela asked cheekily.

"I believe it is public, otherwise the press would not be able to report, but the next session is tomorrow during school hours," Georgina reminded them.

Suddenly, Anna remembered something. "Is this the woman Mr Goldman returned from England to assist?"

"Yes, and her lawyer is Christian von Feldburg's sister-in-law," Georgina added.

"A woman? There is a woman lawyer?" Ulrike asked, amazed.

"Oh, we must go and watch the trial!" Hannah declared eagerly. "No one is going to care if we miss school! One day won't make much difference anyway."

Georgina shook her head. "I'm teaching all day tomorrow. I cannot possibly get away, but I agree that it would be educational for you to see justice in action."

"With the air ambulance service suspended, I'm not doing anything right now," Anna started cautiously, "and I'd be very interested in attending this trial. It is so difficult for rape victims to get justice. Most rapists walk away free. I find it hard to believe a court would recognise the right of a woman to kill a man to prevent rape. Then again, my German is probably not good enough for me to understand court proceedings."

"But we can translate for you!" Hannah offered eagerly, seconded by the others. In minutes, their enthusiasm produced a collective commitment to play truant from school the next day and attend the trial with Anna.

Testimony for the Prosecution
Berlin-Moabit
Monday 21 February 1949
(Day 241 of the Berlin Airlift)

Alix warned Charlotte that this was going to be a difficult week. The prosecution, Alix explained, was going to engage in 'character murder.' The goal was to establish that Charlotte was a wicked and evil person undeserving of even the slightest respect, much less mercy. Alix told Charlotte to brace for the worst and if possible to ignore what was being said. "You do not have to listen or answer. That's my job."

Still, Charlotte was unnerved to discover the visitors' gallery was nearly full. In addition to the growing crowd of journalists, there was a black woman and several teenage girls. "What are all those girls doing here?" She asked Alix in an undertone, looking over her shoulder as she sat down.

"I'll see if I can find out," Alix agreed, "but try not to worry about them. They will not influence the court."

At least David and Christian were already present, sitting in the first row behind the railing. They nodded and smiled at Charlotte, and she nodded back. Alix had told her that Moby Dick had crashed, but that the crew had been found and taken to hospital. The loss of Moby Dick seemed like a terrible omen as if everything that had been good in her life last year was disappearing. How and why would David remain in Berlin if the ambulance was lost? But here he was, she reminded herself, turning again to look at him over her shoulder. His eyes were fixed on her reassuringly, and he nodded a second time.

After settling in their places, Alix went over to the visitors' gallery, spoke briefly to the black woman and returned with the surprising news that she was AAI's flight nurse, Miss Savage. "She was released from Soviet custody last week."

Charlotte twisted around to get a better look at her. She was surrounded by the younger women, who were chatting with her and each other. "But who are all those girls?"

"They were taking sewing lessons from the wife of another employee, Georgina Moran, and they are very much on your side. They were all rape victims like you."

"Oh," Charlotte was stunned by this revelation. Before she had time to digest it and decide what it meant, her attention was distracted by the arrival of the judges.

The first witness called by the prosecution was Frau Vanessa Meissner, Fritz von Bredow's sister. Charlotte had not seen her in eight years. She was, Charlotte calculated, 41 or 42 years old, and her hair, which she wore in a bun, had streaks of grey in it. She wore no make-up or jewellery and dressed in blacks and greys, thick stockings and low, solid shoes. She looked bleak and hostile. After being sworn in, Steinbrueck asked her how long she had known "the defendant."

"Oh, almost ten years," Frau Meissner exaggerated.

"You knew the defendant before she became engaged to your brother?"

Recognizing her mistake, she modified her answer. "No, but it *seems* like a decade! They made such a fuss about the engagement and threw lots of silly, expensive parties although it was the middle of the war! That was typical of Lotte! She always had to be at the centre of attention. Fritz wasn't like that at all. He was very shy, but Lotte bewitched him! Seriously! It was as though he wasn't himself when he was with her! She could do no wrong in his eyes, and he did anything she asked of him."

"Would you say that they adored each other?"

"What nonsense! He adored her, but she was just using him. You could see that. She was quite plain, really — you only have to look at her." Frau Meissner cast a derisive look in Charlotte's direction. "She didn't have any other suitors. Plain to look at and boring to talk to. So provincial and simple. No one could understand what Fritz saw in her — unless she was sleeping with him, of course."

Charlotte gasped loud enough to be heard on the bench and protested vigorously. Alix stood to protest, "Unless the witness has proof, that is pure speculation."

Judge Nuss addressed Frau Meissner. "Confine your comments to what you know, not what you suspect."

"What I *know* is that any decent woman, any virgin, would have killed herself rather than live with the shame of being raped by six Russians!"

"Then Berlin wouldn't have any women left!" A young woman's voice shouted from the visitors' gallery. The judges called for order, and everyone else turned to see who had called out this remark. Charlotte could not tell, but she saw Miss Savage trying to calm the agitated girls surrounding her.

Steinbrueck resumed his questioning, "Did you see any evidence that she was upset when Fritz went missing?"

"None whatsoever."

"Did she ever try to find out what happened to him?"

"Not that I saw!"

Charlotte started to protest, but Alix hushed her.

"Did your brother have trouble finding her after he was released by the Reds?"

"A terrible time! She left Walmsdorf without telling anyone where she was going. I'm sure she was trying to ensure that Fritz would never find her—"

"Objection. That is speculation."

"The witness will refrain from speculation," Nuss admonished again.

"Well, Fritz had no letter from her after she reached Berlin, so he had no idea where she lived!" Frau Meissner answered the judge directly. "If that's not proof she was trying to hide from him, what is?"

Steinbrueck thanked her for her testimony and turned her over to Alix.

"Frau Meissner, you are seven years older than your brother, are you not?"

"Yes."

"And you married at 21 when Fritz was just 14."

"Yes."

"Where did you live after your marriage?"

"With my husband, of course!"

"Was that in the same household as your brother?"

"Of course, not! My husband was first stationed in Breslau and later in Krakow."

"So, when, again, did you first meet Charlotte Walmsdorf?"

"As I said, at her engagement party."

"Which was in what year?"

Frowning, Frau Meissner admitted, "1941."

"And how often did you see her after that?"

"Oh, a half-dozen times at least." Then hearing how little that sounded, she improved it to, "Twenty or more."

"All in 1941?"

"No, in once or twice in 1942."

"When was the last time you actually saw her?"

"I don't remember exactly."

"Was it before or after Fritz went missing?"

Frau Meissner didn't answer.

"Was it before or after your brother went missing, Frau Meissner?"

"I can't remember."

"You can't remember the date your brother went missing? His loss did not distress you enough for you to place your last encounter with his fiancé in context?"

"I was a married woman with growing children and heavy responsibilities. My husband held a very important post."

"If you did not see Graefin Walmsdorf after your brother went missing, how can you know if she was upset or not?"

"I heard it from others."

"That is hearsay, not evidence. How do you know she didn't try to find him after the end of the war?"

"Because she would have found him if she tried!"

"I see!" Alix sounded pleased. "When exactly did you learn Fritz was alive and what was your source?"

Frau Meissner squirmed. "I — I — Well, as I said, I have children. After the war. There was so much confusion."

"But you must have made enquiries about your brother?"

"I thought he was dead."

"So, you didn't make enquiries?"

"I did — I'm sure I did — but— I can't remember when exactly."

"But they confirmed he was alive?"

"No, there was so much confusion. No one seemed to know..." Her voice trailed off.

"Exactly," Alix commented. "As this court knows, to this day millions of German soldiers and civilians remain unaccounted for. Although hundreds of thousands of Wehrmacht soldiers are presumed killed, rumours persist of tens of thousands still alive in Siberia. Millions of Germans have no concrete information about the fate of their loved ones. Frau Meissner, I would advise you not to make obviously stupid and verifiably false statements while under oath."

Frau Meissner glowered at her furiously.

Turning to Nuss, Alix declared, "I have no further questions for this un-reliable and untrustworthy witness."

Inspector Anton Sperl was called next. Charlotte thought that Sperl looked very serious and handsome. Gone were the days when he slunk about in the corridor, avoiding contact with others and wearing his hat pulled low to shade his eyes. Now he stood ramrod straight and he swore the oath in a voice at ease with command. The prosecutor asked him to describe what he had found on the night of January 10, which he did in sober but not lurid detail.

Charlotte was surprised when Alix stood for cross-examination. She did not think Sperl had said anything but the truth.

"Herr Inspector Sperl," Alix opened. "Just two questions. First, when you found Graefin Walmsdorf, did she make any attempt to deny what she had done or to hide or escape?"

"No, none whatsoever."

"Did she resist arrest?"

"Not at all."

"Thank you. Now to the second issue. You have lived in the Maybach Ufer 27 for more than three years, is that correct?"

"Yes, it is."

"You moved in after the Western Allies had taken control of Kreuzberg, yes?"

"Correct."

"What were your impressions of your neighbour Graefin Walmsdorf?"

Sperl did not hesitate for a second. "She was very shy, very withdrawn, clearly terrified of venturing out into the streets. I didn't understand why until the concierge explained that she had been brutally gang-raped by half a dozen Soviet soldiers shortly after the capture of the city."

"Did she take male visitors to her apartment?"

"Good God, no! As I said, she was very shy."

"The prosecution has alleged that Graefin Walmsdorf had started a new relationship with Mr David Goldman. Mr Sperl, please tell the court if you ever saw Mr Goldman in the Walmsdorf apartment."

"Once or twice."

"How would you characterize those meetings? Lovers' trysts?"

"Good heavens, no! They occurred only after her cousin Major Freiherr von Feldburg had moved into the flat with her. Goldman always came in the company of a Polish woman, who had formerly worked for Graefin Walmsdorf's parents, and an English officer. They went on one or two group outings together last summer, but Mr Goldman never stayed overnight in the apartment. Indeed, as the weather closed in, he would escort her home but take leave outside the front door."

"Thank you, Inspector Sperl." Alix turned and bowed to Herr Dr Steinbrueck and reseated herself as Sperl was excused.

Steinbrueck called Theo Pfalz next. He echoed Sperl's testimony regarding the events on the night of the murder. Again, Charlotte was surprised that Alix got up to ask additional questions. "Herr Pfalz, would you please tell the court when you joined the National Socialist Party of Germany and the SA."

"Objection!" Steinbrueck sprang to his feet. "What is the relevance of Herr Pfalz's former party affiliations? He is not on trial."

"Absolutely not," Alix replied with a smile and a bow of her head to her rival. "I am merely trying to establish for the court that Herr Pfalz is not a 'Jew-lover,' but rather a great admirer of our heroic armed forces."

There was a rumble of voices, but Nuss told Pfalz he need not answer the question. Alix was asked to proceed. "Herr Pfalz, you have known the defendant since she moved into Maybach Ufer 27 in early 1945. How would you describe her?"

"Describe her?" Pfalz asked back helplessly. "But she's sitting right there."

"Her personality."

"As Herr Inspector Sperl said, she is very shy. When she arrived, she had just witnessed the death of her parents at the hands of a strafing Soviet fighter. She was very traumatised. None of the apartments were vacant, so I arranged for her to sleep in the loft over the stables. She was very grateful. Later when the apartment on the fourth floor became vacant, she moved in there. After the rapes —" He broke off and shook his head. "It was terrible! Such a scandal! And no one could do anything! We were helpless!"

"You might have tried! Any of you bastards might have at least *tried*!" A girl's voice rang out.

"Order!" Judge Nuss called, banging his gavel. "Order or you will be removed from the court!" Then turning to Herr Pfalz he nodded, "You may continue your testimony."

"It's as I said! There was nothing we could do! The Ivans were shooting anything that moved! If it was female, they raped it first and then shot it. If it was male, they just shot it. It was terrible." He fell silent.

Alix resumed her cross-examination, "Graefin Walmsdorf returned to the house with two broken arms and lived with neighbours until the casts were removed. How would you describe her mental condition at that time?"

"She was completely shattered. She tried to stay hidden and looked no one in the eye. She was all hunched up, too." He curled up in his seat to show what he meant.

"Did that change over time?"

"Yes, she got noticeably better after she found a little work as a journalist, but even then she always tried to be as invisible as possible and avoided other people. She got better after her cousin moved in with her, but it was only after she found work with the ambulance company that she started to walk upright and smile now and again."

"And what happened after Fritz von Bredow returned?"

Pfalz gazed up at Alix, glanced at Charlotte, and then said softly. "She went back to the way she'd been after the rapes — well, maybe not quite as bad, but she crumpled inward again, avoided looking at me, and she stopped smiling."

"Thank you, Herr Pfalz."

Dr Steinbrueck next called the office staff of Air Ambulance International, who testified that Charlotte and David Goldman were "clearly in love." Their evidence, as Alix pointed out in cross-examination, was weak. It amounted to "the way they looked at one another," or "they always left the office together so Mr Goldman could see her home." Furthermore, under cross-examination, they admitted they had not seen Charlotte at the office after the first week in November. Within a week of Fritz von Bredow's return, she had left, never to return.

Dr Steinbrueck countered this testimony by calling the police who had been present at the indictment. They described, with evident delight, David's attempt to speak to Charlotte in front of the courthouse. Alix declined to cross-examine, explaining in a low voice to Charlotte, "Their description was accurate. The less said about it, the better."

Finally, Steinbrueck called David Goldman. Charlotte gasped, "What's he doing?"

"Trying to establish your motive for murder," Alix replied bluntly.

After David was sworn in, Steinbrueck opened his interrogation with: "Goldman. Is that a Jewish name?"

"Objection. Mr Goldman's religion is not relevant to the trial."

"Sustained."

"Where were you born, Mr Goldman?"

"Wilhelmshaven."

"In Germany?" Steinbrueck pretended surprise.

"Correct."

"But didn't you fly for the Royal Air Force?"

"You may not have noticed, Mr Steinbrueck, but the National Socialist German Worker's Party stripped Jews of their German citizenship in 1933. My family emigrated in 1934, and I obtained Canadian citizenship in 1939 — prior to joining the Royal Air Force in 1940."

"So, what do you consider yourself? A Jew? A German? A Canadian? A traitor?"

"Objection."

"Sustained. The prosecution will refrain from badgering and insulting the witness."

"Just for the record, after fighting *against* Germany for six years, what brought you back to Berlin?"

David allowed himself a faint smile as he answered firmly and loudly, "I came to establish an air ambulance service that takes critically ill or injured Berliners out of blockaded Berlin to hospitals in the West."

The excitement among the journalists indicated he had scored, and Steinbrueck, recognizing his mistake, hastened to redirect attention to the case by asking, "How would you describe your feelings for the defendant?"

David looked straight at Charlotte and replied in a loud, firm voice, "She is the first and only woman I have ever truly loved."

"My my!" Steinbrueck retorted in mock astonishment. "And do you believe that the defendant returned your feelings?"

"I was indeed under the impression that she returned my feelings — until Fritz von Bredow appeared. Less than a week after his miraculous escape from Siberia, she informed me that she must honour her betrothal to him and that she could not see me anymore. I was heartbroken." He held eye contact with Charlotte. He was speaking to her, and she clung to his words.

"Just like that? She broke off with you? Rather fickle of her, wouldn't you say?"

"No. There is nothing 'fickle' about Charlotte Walmsdorf." David corrected the prosecutor firmly, and Charlotte felt stronger just listening to him. "She appeared deeply tormented by the choice she was forced to make, but she'd been raised in an old-fashioned manner and took her oath to Bredow seriously — like a true Prussian noblewoman."

"I see. But surely you tried to make her change her mind?"

"No, I did not. I cannot say that I admired her decision. It hurt me far too much for that, but I accepted it." Charlotte nodded to him, trying to convey that she understood him.

"Didn't you write to her? Promise to give her a better life in England, if she broke off with Bredow?"

"No, I did not."

"You must have called her once or twice?"

"No, I did not."

"You are under oath, Herr Goldman!" Steinbrueck reminded him sharply.

David turned his eyes from Charlotte long enough to look coldly at the prosecutor. "I know and I repeat: I had no contact with Charlotte Walmsdorf from the sixth of November of last year, when she ended our relationship, until the day she was arraigned in this court."

"But it *was* a relationship?"

"It was an unspoken understanding of mutual affection."

"I see."

Charlotte glanced at Alix, who was frowning.

"Before the defendant ditched you, what were your intentions?"

"I planned to marry her."

"Seriously? A woman who had already had sex with half a dozen strange men?" Steinbrueck asked contemptuously — before a scream from the visitor's gallery tore through the courtroom.

"You f***ing bastard! Rape isn't sex! It's murder! She was murdered six times!"

"Clear that girl out of the court and take her name! She is banned from attending this trial."

Charlotte like everyone else turned to watch as the young woman made a dash for the door, slamming it in the faces of two pursuing policemen. Meanwhile, the rest of the visitors were in an uproar. The journalists were trying to get information from the other girls, and Miss Savage was holding the journalists back while the girls made an escape. Meanwhile, Judge Nuss was beating with his gavel and calling for order, while Steinbrueck was demanding the troublemaker's arrest. It was five minutes before testimony could resume. Long before it was over, Charlotte's attention had returned to David. His gaze had hardly wavered.

At last, Steinbrueck continued in a sneering tone, "So you don't care about the virtue of your bride. Does that extend so far that — if by some strange miscarriage of justice, the defendant is not found guilty —you would consider marrying a murderer?"

"Charlotte is less a murderer than most of the people in this room!" David shot back, causing a new commotion during which David raised his voice to be heard above the babble of voices to declare "*You*, Hr Dr Steinbrueck — along with Herr Nuss — aided, abetted, supported and served a regime founded on hatred and intent on mass slaughter! You committed judicial murder —"

"Objection! Objection!"

"The witness is out of order!"

"The witness is correct!" Alix sprang to her feet. "I have here a list of death sentences served by this court—"

"SILENCE!"

Gradually, order was restored. Judge Nuss was glaring at Alix, and something was playing out that Chalotte did not entirely understand. The judge broke eye contact first and told Steinbrueck to resume his examination of the witness.

"Let me summarise for the court. You have declared your willingness to marry the defendant despite her sexual encounters with half a dozen strange men," he smirked as he made this remark and seemed to expect the audience to titter voyeuristically with him. Instead, hissing started up from somewhere and even the males in the audience reacted coldly and unsympathetically to his slur. Unsettled he hastened to his next point, "You stated you were willing to marry her despite her willingness to commit murder. In short, the defendant *knew* that if she could eliminate Fritz von Bredow, she would find refuge and comfort in your arms and wealth. Thank you very much for clarifying that point." Steinbrueck withdrew triumphantly.

Alix approached David. "Where were you on the night of the murder?"

"In England."

"England? Why?"

"After Charlotte chose Fritz over me, I became despondent and lost interest in my business. I recognised the need to get away from the situation and decided to grant myself some leave to lick my wounds and find my balance again."

"So how could Graefin Walmsdorf know that you were prepared to marry her even if she committed murder?"

"She couldn't have known."

"Could you clarify one more thing? Did you ever actually propose to Graefin Walmsdorf?"

"No, I did not. I hinted, but I — foolishly perhaps — hesitated to be explicit."

"So, in fact, she could not know that you would marry her at all — much less after committing murder and taking no action to hide or disguise what she had done."

"That is correct."

"Thank you, Herr Goldman."

Although the court adjourned and the judges withdrew, the agitation in the room did not immediately dissipate. The prosecutor's team clustered together, arguing among themselves, and the journalists fluttered with excitement. Yet Charlotte floated above it all. Nothing mattered to her but David's testimony. It had been so strong and unambiguous. As they hustled her out of the court, for the first time since her arrest, she started to hope and dream about being free again — and with David.

Good News, Bad News
Berlin-Tempelhof
Tuesday 22 February 1949
(Day 242 of the Berlin Airlift)

"Baronowsky!" A voice shouting over the sound of aircraft engines faintly reached J.B.'s ears.

"Did someone just call my name?" J.B. asked his co-pilot. The kid, another newcomer still wet behind the ears, shrugged and shook his head cluelessly.

"Baronowsky!" The shout came again.

J.B. shoved back the cockpit window and leaned out. A jeep had pulled up beside his nose wheel with a staff officer standing up in it. "You looking for me?" J.B. hollered down.

"You Captain Baronowsky?"

"Yeah, that's me."

"Colonel Howley wants to see you as soon as you get to Berlin. A pilot who'll fly the bird back while you report to Howley is on his way over."

"Colonel Howley?" J.B. enquired, not sure he'd heard right. "As in the US Commandant in Berlin?"

"I ain't heard of no other Colonel Howley in Berlin," the lieutenant in the jeep answered.

"What does he want with me? He's army, not air force."

"Captain, if the US military commandant in Berlin wants you to report to his office as soon as possible, then it really doesn't matter what for or what unit you're from. I suggest you shake a leg!" Then jerking a thumb at J.B.'s C-54, he asked, "What's this bird's ID so I can let BASC know?"

"Ah, Big Easy 1549," J.B. answered.

"1549. Got it. You'll be directed by BASC to Tempelhof rather than Gatow. Howley will have someone waiting for you. Here's your supernumerary now." He indicated an Air Force second lieutenant in flight gear climbing out of a jeep that screeched to a halt beside J.B.'s plane. The extra pilot hauled himself into the cargo door, slammed it shut behind him, and crawled over the freight in the hold to strap himself into the jump seat in the cockpit. Meanwhile, J.B. waved the chocks away and off they went.

Sure enough, as soon as they contacted BASC, they were directed into the landing pattern for Tempelhof. It had been a couple of months since J.B. had landed there, and he was amazed by the changes. The new flight path took them over a graveyard, the church of which no longer had a tower. The runway itself was paved and smooth. Not at all like 'the good ol' crazy days of summer,' he thought almost nostalgically.

They taxied to their parking position and the off-loading began with the usual frenzy, but now in addition to the jeep with the met report, the jeep with the ops officer, and the mobile snack van, another staff jeep, this one with a sergeant, pulled up. The NCO urged J.B. to hurry, so he dropped out of the C-54 and pulled himself into the jeep. With squealing tyres, the driver careened between the aircraft and the off-loading trucks while J.B. held onto the side of the jeep with one hand and onto his cap with the other. "What's the rush?" J.B. shouted over the noise of incoming and outgoing aircraft around them.

"Colonel Howley wants you at the Kommandatura no later than 11:30, sir."

"Why?" J.B. asked.

"Damned if I know, sir. No one pays me to *know* anything, just to drive."

The sergeant raced along Berlin's wide and mostly empty avenues. They sped out of the heart of the city and westward toward the lakes and the suburb where the US military HQ and the Kommandatura stood. In less than 30 minutes, they screeched to a stop at the curb in front of the four flags marking the entrance. The driver yanked up the handbrake and ordered J.B.: "Follow me, sir! Fast!"

They arrived in the anteroom of the American commandant's office just as Colonel Howley came out of his office, putting on his cap. He took one look at J.B. and asked, "You Captain Baronowky?"

"Yes, sir!" J.B. saluted and then, still trying to catch his breath added, "Would you mind telling me what this is all about, sir?"

"Rumour has it, Captain, that you and Richard Orloff are old friends and that you know his wife. Is that correct?"

"Yes, sir. Orloff was my bombardier when I flew with the 8th Air Force. Met his wife after the war, and I saw them now and again after they washed up here. If I may say so, sir, I'm pretty damned upset about them being detained by the Reds. They've been flying sick kids out of Berlin, for Christ's sake! If anyone's been on a humanitarian mission, it's them!"

"Well, in just—" Howley stopped to check his watch "55 minutes, the Reds are supposed to hand them back over to us. I asked you to come along so you can make a positive identification. The Reds have been known to send a decoy back rather than the person we request. So, we're going to the Glienicker Bridge, where I want you to make a positive identification before we disengage."

Given the difference in rank, J.B. held his tongue during the drive down to the rendezvous. Howley was focused on a briefcase that he held on his knees, anyway; it appeared to be filled with classified briefing papers. As they approached the Glienicker Bridge that connected the American-controlled southwestern district of Berlin with Soviet-controlled Potsdam on the other side of the narrow waterway, Howley's car slowed to a crawl. The driver asked for instructions and Howley told him to park. He and J.B. got out to continue on foot. They started up the gentle slope of the bridge toward the barricades in the middle but stopped about fifteen feet short of them.

To J.B. it looked as if half the Red Army was on the other side. There were several tanks and about a battalion of Russian soldiers in their best uniforms with shining boots and all their medals flapping. Howley looked at his watch. It was two minutes to noon.

A moment later, there was some commotion on the far side of the bridge.

The soldiers shuffled around a bit to let a dilapidated German ambulance nose its way toward the first barrier on the opposite side. The ambulance stopped. The back doors swung open and the trolley with the stretcher was pulled out. J.B. felt his stomach tensing up. Images of Rick dragging his dead co-pilot out of the seat and taking the controls of the B-17 long enough for him to bandage his wounds flashed through his mind. How could Rick have made it through the war only to be so badly injured flying an air ambulance?

Behind the stretcher, someone hobbled on a single crutch. As they came closer, J.B. could see that one trouser leg had been roughly ripped off to accommodate a full-leg cast. This made the once smart uniform look almost obscene. In addition, the double-breasted tunic flapped open, revealing a blouse that was not tucked in at the waist. As the figure limped closer, he could see Jan's gaunt face. She looked completely shattered, almost corpse-like. Although she was having trouble managing the crutch, no one offered to help her. She kept glancing at the gurney with the stretcher on it.

J.B. forced himself to look more closely at the man beside her. His face and head were swathed in bandages. All that was visible was the stub of a nose, unshaved cheeks and badly cracked, dry lips. What a lousy bunch of bastards, he thought furiously. To Howley he said in a low voice, "That's Jan Orloff all right. She looks like she's been through hell."

"She probably has," Howley muttered under his breath. "And the man?"

"Sir, with all those bandages, I can't be 100% sure, but I'd put my money on it being Rick because of the way Jan's looking at him."

"I'll buy that. Stay here." Howley left J.B. and advanced right to the barriers. He exchanged words with the senior Soviet on the other side, then turned and gestured to US army medics standing beside an American ambulance that had been waiting since before Howley and J.B. arrived. The American orderlies ran forward, pulling a gurney and a wheelchair. J.B. felt pride just watching the alacrity and professionalism with which they transferred Rick from the Russian stretcher onto their own and helped Jan into the wheelchair. He felt relief and knew it must be magnified a hundredfold in Jan.

Howley and the Russian exchanged salutes. Howley led J.B. off the bridge and over to the American ambulance. Here he pulled J.B. a little to one side. "We're sending them both back to our main medical facility in Wiesbaden. I want you to fly back with them. You know, a friendly face to reassure them they are now safe and will be properly treated. No one is going to interrogate either of them at this point. We want to let them get settled into the hospital, get some rest and all that. But if Mrs Orloff is feeling talkative, let her talk and report back to me anything of interest that you learn."

"Yes, sir. Should I do that in writing?"

"I'd rather you stopped by my office on your next trip to Berlin. I know that is disruptive and Tunner won't like it, but this is important." He drew a deep breath and then came out with it. "There's something else you need to know — and this is for your ears only. Tunner does not — and does not *need* to — know. There was a fourth crew member in that plane."

"I know, sir. Mrs Priestman."

"How do you know that?" Howley asked, exasperated.

"Everyone at Gatow knows, sir. I fly in and out of Gatow." Howley raised an eyebrow. "OK. I'm seeing one of the air traffic controllers socially. She was on duty when the ambulance went down. But it's no secret among Gatow personnel. On the contrary, a lot of the Brits are angry that General Robinson has not been as active as General Clay. The general feeling is that their government has been scandalously negligent and there's huge sympathy for their Station Commander, who they feel has been shabbily treated."

"Hm," Howley commented dryly, before adding, "Well, they're wrong. The reason Robinson and Bourne have kept their mouths shut is that she wasn't in the wreck when the Germans found it, and the Russians have not yet apprehended her. They may not know she exists, much less where she is."

"Holy shit!"

"You can say that again, Captain. If Mrs Orloff can shed any light on her fate or whereabouts, get in touch with me immediately after landing. But don't be stupid about it. This is incredibly sensitive. Do you read me, Captain? The most important piece of the puzzle is whether the Reds know she was aboard that plane — or not. And if they know, do they know where she is?"

J.B. nodded his head slowly as the import of what Howley was saying sank in.

"If you find something out, don't blurt it out or tell anyone else — not even your superiors or the IO in Wiesbaden. He's not in on these negotiations. What you need to do is to get a coded message to me. Then get yourself on the next plane back into Tempelhof to bring me the details. I'll be sure your superiors understand the reasons and urgency of your actions."

"Yes, sir."

"Good luck," Howley offered his hand and J.B. took it.

In the ambulance, Jan acted as if she didn't recognise him. He had to say, "Jan, it's me. J.B."

She stared at him and then said woodenly. "The Russians said Rick may never regain consciousness. They said he's already brain dead."

"Don't believe them! They're just trying to muck you about — hurt you. We're taking both of you to the best military hospital on the continent of Europe. Rick will be in the hands of real professionals by six pm tonight."

"It may be too late."

J.B. looked at the inert figure next to her. What the hell did he know about brain injuries? "Yeah. It might be too late, but it is also too soon to give up hope."

"Emily screwed up the landing," Jan shot out bitterly. "She should have closed down #1 engine. If she had, she could have controlled the aircraft with the rudder. If I'd been flying the plane, Rick wouldn't be in a coma."

Jesus, J.B. thought, what a horrible burden of guilt and bitterness to be carrying around with you at a time like this. Out loud he said. "OK. I'll take your word for it. You were there. I wasn't. But what good does it do, thinking about it?"

Jan turned away from him and didn't say another word until they were in an army DC-3 passenger plane. J.B. had been told it was General Clay's personal transport, which had been put at their disposal to get Rick to the hospital in Wiesbaden as fast as possible. It was certainly better furnished than most army personnel carriers. It still had a dozen rows of comfy seats like in a civilian airliner. Rick's stretcher was fastened in the aisle so it couldn't shift dangerously in flight, while J.B. and Jan sat in the first row just behind the curtain separating them from the flight deck and crew. They sat on opposite sides of the aisle.

After the DC-3 levelled off at altitude, flying below the steady stream of Airlift traffic, J.B. made another attempt to reach his friend's wife. "Jan, is there anything I can do to help you? Should I bring you a change of clothes or something like that? All your stuff must still be at the Malcolm Club in Gatow."

"I don't give a shit about clothes. You know that. Rick is — was — my life."

"And flying," J.B. said softly.

She looked over at him sharply. "Are you trying to say it's my fault we're over here? Flying in this crazy Airlift?"

"I didn't say that. I just meant that you loved flying even before you loved Rick."

Jan looked down at her hands. After a long pause, she murmured, "Yeah. I guess so."

"The Russians treat you bad?"

"The fucking assholes! I was lying in a hospital bed with my leg broken in two pieces and my husband in a coma and they stood around leering at me and making jokes about what it would be like to fuck me. They said they'd have to cover my face before they could do it because otherwise, I was too ugly to get a hard-on!"

J.B. felt his stomach lurch. He didn't have the courage to ask if they carried through.

"A nurse came in and chased the bastards out, but it must have been staged — finding three Russians who speak English isn't easy! They just wanted to make it clear to me that they could do with me whatever they pleased. And you know the worst of it?" She asked, turning to him furiously.

He shook his head helplessly.

"They wouldn't let me see Rick or even tell me how he was doing. They kept saying he wasn't my affair. 'We know who you really are,' they said. 'That pilot isn't your husband. You're Mrs Priestman! The wife of the RAF Station Commander at Gatow.'"

"But didn't they have Mrs Priestman, too?" J.B. asked, trying to sound ignorant.

"How the hell should I know? I haven't seen her since she went for help after the crash. Maybe she was telling them she was Jan Orloff so that they wouldn't hurt her or something."

"How did you convince them you were who you said you were?"

She shrugged, "Something happened a couple of days ago. What day is it today?"

"Tuesday."

"Yeah. It must have been Sunday night."

"But what happened?"

"They changed their tactics. They went from being bullies to being friendly. They let me see Rick and pretended to be so sorry that he was brain-dead and would never recover consciousness. They told me how much they'd tried to help him, but it was too late. They said our flight nurse had done more damage than good with her clumsy attempts to stop the bleeding. They said she'd shoved the broken pieces of his skull into his brains. That was what destroyed his nervous system, they said. Then they watched me as I broke down and cried and cried. Eventually, they wrapped me up in warm blankets and carried me to a parlour — I guess the prison commandant's apartment or something. They brought me some good food and the colonel, or whatever he was, fed me vodka and treated me like a human being. He showed sympathy for my situation. He even apologised for what his soldiers had done without his knowledge or permission. It had all been a mistake he said."

"You know he was lying," J.B. burst out, unable to hold back his indignation.

"Yeah," Jan admitted with a shrug. "Yeah. I know that now, but —" She shook her head. "You don't know what it was like, J.B. They tortured me for a whole week, pretending they were 'fixing' or 'treating' my leg but all with inadequate anaesthetics. I had no contact with Rick. No news about how he was doing. They kept saying the US military had washed their hands of us because we were civilians. Then they told me Anna had signed a document confirming we were spies, and they hinted we might all be shot. I tried to be strong, J.B.. For a whole week, I kept to the litany of name, rank and serial number...." Her voice faded away.

J.B. reached across the aisle and took her hand. "It's OK, Jan. No one can take torture forever."

"When they showed me Rick just lying there — not a flicker of recognition, nothing but a breathing corpse and I realised what that dumb coloured girl had done — not intentionally, of course, but she's just a dumb coloured girl." J.B. flinched inwardly but bit his tongue; this was not the time to call

Jan up on remarks like that. "She doesn't know what she's doing. As long as she was only looking after a bunch of Krauts, what difference did it make? But now ... I've lost Rick."

"We don't know that yet," J.B. insisted. He turned to look out the window, hoping they were getting close to their destination. He was ready for this conversation to end.

"It was the vodka too," Jan admitted. "It loosened my tongue. I don't remember everything I said. I know I talked a lot about Rick and how we met. I told them how we'd flown together all over the States, and how our DC-2 got damaged, and we couldn't afford the repairs. I know I admitted we'd used all our savings to come over and fly the Airlift, but I couldn't get a job because I was a woman. The Russian colonel was very sympathetic about that, saying that the Soviet Union has lots of women pilots and that the Russians respect them greatly. He told me if I wanted to defect, I could be a pilot with the Red Air Force or fly for Aeroflot."

"Great," J.B. remarked sarcastically, but he could understand that Jan had been in an impossible situation. God knew what he would have done in similar circumstances. He added dryly, "I gather you didn't accept."

"I — I said I'd think about it."

"How long did this conversation last?"

"I don't know. Several hours. We went through at least one bottle of vodka. Maybe it was two." She paused frowning. "Like I said, he apologised for my treatment saying it was all a mistake, a case of mistaken identity. He said they had intelligence that Emily Priestman flew on the air ambulance, and it was her they had wanted to intimidate. He asked how it happened that I was in the cockpit instead of her, so I explained that she had made that terrible landing and then gone off in search of help."

"You told him that?" J.B. couldn't keep the alarm out of his voice.

"Yeah. Why shouldn't I? She must have got lost and buried in the snow or something, which is why they kept thinking I must be her. None of it makes sense, does it? But then they lie all the time, and I was so exhausted and the vodka..."

J.B. squeezed her hand. "I think we've just left our cruising altitude. We must be on approach to Wiesbaden. It won't be long now before Rick gets proper medical care — and you get some rest and care too."

After seeing Jan and Rick off in the base ambulance, J.B. found his way to the intelligence section at Wiesbaden. He walked in and announced bluntly, "I need to get a coded message to Colonel Howley as soon as possible, and I mean over a secure line."

"Just who the hell do you think you are, Captain?"

"I know who I am, and I was tasked directly by Colonel Howley to obtain some intelligence that he urgently needs. He asked me to send a coded message."

Eventually, he convinced them to take him seriously and found himself beside a teleprint operator who asked, "What's your message, sir?"

"The bear is hunting the escaped bird."

Chapter Seventeen
Confrontation with Reality

Plan B
RAF Gatow
Tuesday 22 February 1949
(Days 242 of the Berlin Airlift)

Robin received the call from Howley just after 6 pm. "Robin," the American colonel opened. "There is no easy way to say this, and I want you to bear in mind that Mrs Orloff was in one hell of a situation. She was immobilised, in pain but not getting enough painkillers, and her husband was — and still is — in a coma. She held up for more than a week, but Sunday night the Reds pulled out the vodka and violins and did a doozy of a 'good cop' act. Maybe the fact that you'd ignored their threats had aroused their suspicion and made them change tactics. Whatever the reason, it worked. Mrs Orloff let the cat out of the bag about Emily."

"The Soviets know she was aboard Moby Dick?"

"And that she went to get help."

Robin didn't answer at once. Ever since Jasha had returned on Sunday night with the news that she'd found Emily, he'd been trying to get his government to undertake a rescue mission. The people he could talk to — Air Commodores Waite and Merer, Generals Bourne and Robertson — were sympathetic. However, except for Robertson, none of them could authorise a commando raid into the Soviet Zone to extricate Emily. While Robertson technically had the authority, he was reluctant to use it without cabinet approval. Robin had no idea how long something like that could take, and he wasn't inclined to trust His Majesty's government to make the right decision.

Howley, worried by the silence, asked, "Robin? Are you still there?"

"Yes. I've been trying to get action for two days. Robertson is afraid of an international incident. From his point of view, it is better to let the Soviets find her and then to negotiate her release."

"Have you told him about the threats?"

"No, because then I would have had to admit I hadn't informed him at the time."

"Yeah, generals don't like being left in the dark by the likes of us. Your best bet is your dirty tricks boys. You've got some of the best in the world."

"I don't know what other option I have," Robin admitted.

"Let me know if there is anything I can do to help — even if it's just someone to share a bottle of Bourbon with."

"I'll keep that in mind," Robin answered.

Howley rang off and Robin sat at his desk staring out at his airfield. As of this month, Gatow had become the busiest airfield in the world with more air movements than even New York City's La Guardia. That was only possible because things were running like clockwork. Just four days earlier, an RAF York had delivered the one-millionth ton of Airlift supplies to Berlin. This month, for the first time since the start of the operation, enough liquid fuel to meet demand had been flown into the city. His new fuel depot, the one the Soviets had wanted him to blow up, had become operational yesterday and he could count twelve tankers clustered around it at this moment. At this rate, they would soon be building up liquid fuel reserves. Meanwhile, the non-performing and troublemaking civilian carriers were being systematically replaced by good, disciplined outfits as contracts with the bad companies were terminated and the firms retained agreed to and met more rigorous requirements. As a result, the British contribution was steadily increasing — despite the fact British carriers, civilian and RAF, were still taking return cargoes and flying out Berliners in unprecedented numbers. Nearly 30,000 Germans had been evacuated to date, and things were going so smoothly that there was no talk of scaling back. Altogether, the Combined Airlift Task Force was on track to deliver its greatest monthly total ever: probably in excess of 170,000 tons.

The weather could still blow things off course. They'd had a couple of bad days like the one on which Moby Dick had gone down. But it was rare for all airfields to be affected simultaneously, and since the start of the year, Gatow had not closed down for more than a couple of hours at a time. They could make up for a slow day with redoubled efforts the next.

Robin was grateful. With a good conscience, he could focus on getting Emily home safely. He left his desk and sought out his intelligence officer. As soon as the door shut behind him, he asked Boyd, "What have you heard from your superiors?"

The Flight Lieutenant looked distressed, "Nothing yet, I'm afraid. It appears that nobody in London knows what Mila actually does on Sokolovsky's staff. That means they can't assess how valuable she might be to us and as a result, they are downplaying her usefulness. They have to weigh possible negative repercussions against what they assume are marginal intelligence gains. London has also questioned the wisdom of welcoming a former partisan with more than a hundred assassinations to her name. Mila might look like a homely popsy, but she was one hell of a marksman! Unfortunately, London seems to think not all her targets were legitimate."

"Legitimate?" Robin asked incredulously. "In partisan warfare? I didn't know there were any rules in guerrilla fighting."

"Well, certain things are still frowned upon. You know, shooting priests, medical personnel, downed Allied airmen..."

"Mila killed Allied airmen?" Robin was shocked.

"I haven't the foggiest. Her record is above my clearance level and I'm not on the 'need-to-know' list. All I'm saying is that London's dithering. They haven't said no, but they haven't said yes either."

Typical London, Robin thought, fiddling while Rome burned. Fortunately, Mila wasn't inclined to waffle. She'd already stuck out her neck for them, and he was not going to let reservations on the part of some wingless wonder at a desk in Whitehall get in his way. He'd bring her out if he could and damn the consequences, but there was no need for Boyd to know that. Instead, he nodded as if accepting the situation and informed Boyd of what J.B. had told Howley.

"I'll pass that up the chain straight away, sir, and I'll try to light a fire under them. As soon as I hear anything, I'll let you know, day or night."

Robin thanked him and left. He appeared calm and resigned, as in a way he was. He'd given 'them' a chance to act, but Howley's intelligence forced his hand. He couldn't wait any longer. He checked his watch. It was 7:07 pm.

He returned to his office and rang the EAS hangar. MacDonald answered the phone with engine noise in the background.

"Has Pegasus arrived for the night?" Robin asked hopefully.

"Yes, sir!" MacDonald confirmed. "Squadron Leader Murray arrived as supernumerary, too."

"Thank you, Chiefy. Please tell S/L Murray and Fl/Lt Moran that I'm ready to leave as soon as they are."

He then rang Graham in his office. Although the expanded fuel depot was complete, Graham was still assigned to Gatow. His next task was to build a second concrete runway. Robin asked without introduction. "Graham, could you and Jasha join me for dinner this evening? I'd like to discuss something important."

"Of course. What time?"

"As soon as we can get to the residence."

"Right oh. I'll let Jasha know I'm on my way. Will there be more of us? Should I ask her to do something extra for dinner?"

"I think we'll be about ten, and some sort of buffet would be much appreciated." His next call was to David, asking that both he and Christian join him. After that he rang the Howley residence and asked Anna if she could join him 'and others' for a light meal. She said she'd be delighted but had no transport. He assured her Frank Howley would provide it — and called in his first favour from the American.

Last of all, and with a touch of trepidation, he rang through to the translation section and requested Corporal Borisenko. "Corporal, I realise this is an unusual request, but I would appreciate your unique skills for planning an exceptional event and wondered if you could come to my residence this evening to discuss it."

"Of course, sir. What time, and will there be transport?"

"I'm leaving the station shortly. You can join me in my car. I'll have my driver bring you back to the station when we finish. We'll have a bite to eat while we work."

When the "committee" convened in the den at the residence 90 minutes later, they crowded the room. The committee consisted of Robin, Kiwi, David, Kit, Graham, Jasha, Anna, Christian, Borisenko and Georgina. Robin first brought everyone up to date on what they knew about Emily's location and health, adding the information from Howley that since Sunday night the Russians knew she had been aboard Moby Dick and that they must now assume the Soviets were actively searching for her.

"We've got to do something at once!" Kiwi exclaimed horrified.

"We have to act as soon as we have a sensible plan," Robin corrected. "Let's start with where she is and how we might get there and back."

Georgina retrieved the atlas and opened it to Mecklenburg-Vorpommern. Jasha had some difficulty finding Mestlin, but fortunately, the sawmill was identified on the map. From there she located a peninsula stretching into the lake marked by a cross. The crash site was considerably further north and west of their original estimate.

"She was over-compensating for the dead engine, afraid of spinning out of control," Kit diagnosed. "It's easy to do, particularly in the dark." The others nodded in understanding.

"The lake's a huge advantage," Christian argued. "With a boat, we could cross to the north shore and set out from there — in the opposite direction from what the Ivans will be expecting. We could head for the zonal border south of Luebeck. That's rural and not so densely populated —"

"Not so fast," Graham interrupted. "With the weather we've been having, the regional lakes are half frozen. They're too mushy for sledges but too frozen for boats."

"Damn!" Christian exclaimed, but frowning, he continued vigorously, "The Ivans control the roads, the railways and the population centres. We cannot travel by vehicle or train without being checked for IDs and movement permits — probably half a dozen times between there and here. What that means is, boat or not, going cross country—"

"Are you talking about taking Emily out on foot?" Robin asked dubiously.

"Or by horse," Christian added, producing immediate and instantaneous protests from both Jasha and Anna.

Jasha shook her head vigorously and declared, "No, she too sick! Can't ride horse long, long way."

Anna was more forceful still. "She has a broken sternum and wrist! Not only would a long journey on foot and horseback be agony, but it might jeopardise her recovery altogether. She could experience permanent damage to her wrist, and she'd probably break down along the route and get you all arrested."

No one risked contradicting the two women and so stunned silence followed this statement.

Then Kiwi picked up the discussion, "Right then. We've eliminated boats, sledges, motor vehicles, trains, horses and travel on foot, which leaves air transport as the only option — and the mode that we're most comfortable with anyway. An aircraft can get in and out fast. Emily will only have to move a short distance to the chosen landing field, and once she is aboard she can lie still. All we need to do is find a suitable aircraft and identify a nearby field where we can land and take off."

"If only we still had the Dakota!" David exclaimed. It was obvious in this company that the Halifaxes were ill-suited to a mission of this kind. In a hesitant voice, David offered, "I suppose, if I flew back to the UK tomorrow, I might be able to snap up one of the Daks that are now idle because contracts with the poor charter firms have been terminated. Money isn't the problem. Emily is a company partner. She's in acute danger and costs play no role, but I'm not sure how long it would take to do the paperwork, and I also have misgivings about the maintenance on Daks used by companies forced off the Airlift. They were notorious for not keeping the aircraft in good order. We can't risk a mechanical failure that might ground us at the wrong moment or cause a new forced landing." Unspoken but understood by Robin, if not the others, was that Charlotte's trial was ongoing and David wanted to be in Berlin for her.

"What about the station Anson?" Kiwi asked Robin. "It's already here and we know it's in first-rate condition."

Before Robin could answer, Kit spoke up, "Ansons were neither designed nor built for landing and taking off in rough conditions. They're also slow and easily intercepted. Mossies, on the other hand, are rugged, nimble, fast for a piston-engine aircraft, and best of all, being made of wood, they're practically invisible to radar."

"No one is going to challenge you on that, mate," Kiwi responded, "but we haven't got a Mossie." He paused and then looked again to Robin to ask, "Do we?"

Kit answered instead. "Group Captain Cheshire does, and I believe he would lend it to us for this operation. It has the added advantage of not being RAF. If I flew to the UK tomorrow to ask him, I could have it here by tomorrow night. MacDonald and his team can give it a coat of camouflage with new — or no — markings overnight, and we'd be ready to start Thursday morning."

Robin was impressed. "Do you seriously think Group Captain Cheshire would let us use his Mossie for such a risky and unsanctioned mission?"

"I'm almost certain."

"In that case, I think it's the best option."

"I should warn you, we'll have to fly one recce flight. We can't risk going in and then discovering the field is too boggy, rough or short for take-off."

"Have you flown this kind of op?"

"No, but my crew and I trained for them scores of times."

That was reassuring. Robin nodded and reminded them, "We'll need to get word to Emily, too, and someone will have to help her get ready to meet the aircraft."

"She'll need help moving," Jasha warned. "I can go back—"

Borisenko intervened. "You don't need to. Mila can move more easily alone, and Emily has met her. But Mila can't be at the convent until Friday night, and remember, she must be flown out at the same time as Emily."

Robin hesitated. He did not share London's qualms about a former partisan. They'd all done things in the war that were better forgotten. The only thing he cared about was whether she could — and would — rescue Emily. She'd helped them find her in the first place, but it was still possible she had done that only to win their trust. She might still betray them after they were fully committed. He put it to the others. "Are we 100% sure that Mila will not betray us?"

"Absolutely," Borisenko declared firmly.

Robin, however, focused on Jasha. The Polish woman was not Mila's friend. Her opinion was less biased.

Jasha admitted, "Don't like Mila, but I believe she want escape — wants to escape," she corrected her grammar, with a little smile at Graham.

Robin decided, "That's settled then." He turned to Kit. "You are the only one who knows Cheshire, which means it is up to you to talk him into lending us his aircraft. However, once it's here in Germany, someone else could fly the sorties." He glanced at Georgina as he spoke.

"We can discuss that again after I've brought the Mossie to Berlin," Kit replied with a fleeting smile.

"Fair enough," Robin agreed and looked around the room. "Any other thoughts, comments or suggestions?"

David spoke up, "I repeat, I'll cover any expenses incurred — whether it's aviation fuel or bribes." He sounded very serious.

"Thank you," Robin replied, deeply moved.

"If you need someone on the ground to guide you in or turn you around, I'd be happy to go," Christian volunteered.

Robin turned to the German whom he had probably fought in the air during the Battle of Britain. There was a special poignancy in his offering to help, especially considering that he knew Emily only superficially. Robin nodded and thanked him. Then he looked around the room again. The challenges and risks were enormous, but the waiting had been killing him slowly. He was relieved finally to be doing something. He also felt stronger having this team around him.

Witnesses for the Defence
Berlin-Moabit
Wednesday 23 February 1949
(Day 243 of the Berlin Airlift)

Alix decided that her legal calling — if she had one — was on the bench or in the prosecutor's office. The responsibility for defending a client was altogether too nerve-wracking. Charlotte might be special, but she knew herself too well to imagine there would never be another client with whom she identified so strongly. Because she cared so deeply about what would happen to Charlotte if she failed, her self-doubts grew. She was becoming indecisive — a trait she had not exhibited while working with the Americans in Nuremberg. There she had been known and admired for her cool objectivity, as well as her ruthless dedication to facts, evidence and justice.

By contrast, in Charlotte's trial, Alix honestly didn't care about justice; she wanted Charlotte to be given a chance to live and love free of terror and trauma. Her partisanship, however, robbed her of her ability to weigh choices dispassionately. As the trial reopened to hear the witnesses for the defence, Alix honestly didn't know if she should call Charlotte to the stand or not.

The courtroom was packed, every seat in the visitor's gallery was full. The school girl who had been most disruptive last time either hadn't come or hadn't been admitted, but there seemed to be more than a dozen other teenagers of about the same age. They were seated near the back with an attractive woman who somehow looked English to Alix. Miss Savage was also in the visitors' gallery, but today she was sitting in the front row beside David, while Christian sat on David's other side. Christian had warned that a 'special project' might keep him away for a day or two later in the week, so she planned to have him testify today.

She started with less important witnesses in order to build towards the stronger ones. Trude Liebherr testified to the horrible abuse Charlotte had suffered at the hands of the Russians. Jasha reinforced Trude's clinical account with a more emotional, personal rendering of events. Neither witness was cross-examined. Steinbrueck had conceded the point that Charlotte had been a victim of abuse by the invaders, he was holding his fire for the more controversial aspects of her subsequent actions.

Alix called Christian third. She supposed she was biased, but a glance toward the prosecutors and the visitors told her that she was not alone in finding Christian's appearance impressive. He had always looked like something out of one of Goebbels' propaganda posters: tall, tanned, blond, lean and muscular — in short, irresistibly good-looking. Now he also looked mature, weathered, and tested. Most striking, however, was his proud and upright bearing. Alix could feel the way it electrified the court. Here was a German who didn't look defeated or humbled.

He took the oath, and Alix asked the routine questions that established who he was and how he knew the defendant. Then she asked him to describe the day Charlotte had asked him to kill her. This essentially concluded the earlier testimony, underlining the depth of Charlotte's psychological wounds from the Russian rapes. Then Alix shifted the attention of the court to Fritz.

"Were you aware of Charlotte's engagement to Fritz von Bredow?"

"Of course! We're cousins. I attended a couple of the engagement parties because I was still recovering from wounds received in aerial combat against England."

Alix smiled at him for that. She knew that by establishing himself as a Luftwaffe veteran he'd just scored with the court, the press and the public.

"How would you describe the young couple?"

"Ridiculously happy. They were both gaga for one another."

"How did you and the rest of the family feel about that?"

"We were very pleased. Charlotte was shy and had not had any suitors before. My brother was in the cavalry, and several of his closer friends vouched for Fritz, saying he was a good and decent man." Their eyes met. During the Nazi era, 'decent' was a code word for anti-Nazi, but Alix doubted if anyone else in the courtroom beyond Christian and herself knew that. Or did David? She glanced in his direction, and he nodded very slightly. Yes, he understood, and knowing that Fritz had not been a Nazi appeared to have helped him to accept Charlotte's affection for her one-time fiancé.

Alix turned back to Christian and resumed her line of questioning, "Graefin Walmsdorf must have been devastated when Fritz went missing."

"As far as I know she was, but I cannot testify to that as I was then leading a squadron in Rommel's Afrika Korps."

God, he was good, Alix thought gratefully. With this answer, he established himself as a rock-solid witness who would not speculate, while cleverly reminding the court of his service to one of their few remaining heroes. Mentioning Rommel pulled them all subconsciously on his side.

"When you moved into the family apartment after the war, would you say that Graefin Walmsdorf was still grieving for Fritz?"

"No." The rustling among the spectators suggested they thought he had hurt her case, but Alix was pleased with the answer. It increased his credibility. He expanded. "I did not arrive in Berlin until January 1948. By then she had exhausted all the various means of trying to track missing persons and had resigned herself to her fate. Furthermore, as I described when recounting how she pleaded with me to kill her, part of the reason the Russian rapes had wounded her so deeply was her belief that, even if Fritz had miraculously survived, he would reject her because she had been polluted by sexual abuse."

"How did she respond to Fritz's return?"

"She was absolutely horrified by the state he was in — as any human with a heart would have been." For the court, Alix asked Christian to describe Fritz's state, which Christian did in a straightforward, blunt manner. The teenagers in the gallery seemed particularly horrified and started whispering amongst themselves until their teacher hushed them.

"But Graefin Walmsdorf took him in?" Alix pursued her line of questioning.

"Without hesitation, and thereafter she devoted herself solely to looking after him. She left her job. She told Mr Goldman they should not see each other again. She lived only for Fritz."

"Was he grateful?"

"Not in the least! He did nothing but complain and whine and demand more attention and care." The youthful observers grew restless again and had to be reined in.

"Were plans made for Fritz and Charlotte to marry?"

"Not that I heard about."

"You moved out of the apartment roughly a month after Fritz returned. Why was that?"

"Because I couldn't stomach seeing the way Fritz insulted and bullied Charlotte — or the way she submitted to it. Charlotte and I argued a lot because I told her to stand up to Fritz or leave him." More loud whispers reached her from the gallery.

"You suggested she abandon a disabled veteran so utterly dependent on her?"

"Fritz von Bredow has plenty of family, starting with his sister who testified before this court just a few days ago. Fritz did not need Charlotte and was not dependent on her. If his intentions had been honourable and he had intended to make her his wife, then he would have treated her as a lady — not a slave. Fritz von Bredow's behaviour was unworthy of a German nobleman. It was utterly despicable. But Charlotte always made excuses for him, defended him against my outrage and made it clear that she was prepared to sacrifice her happiness and dignity to try to please him. So, I left."

"You left her at the mercies of a man you considered dishonourable and despicable?"

Christian looked sober. "In retrospect, I recognise that I was wrong. At the time, however, I thought it was for the best."

"Why was that?"

"Because Fritz and I did nothing but shout at one another, causing Charlotte more distress."

"Were you surprised to hear she had killed Bredow?"

"I was flabbergasted. When inspector Sperl told me he'd heard shots, my first thought was that Bredow had killed her, not the other way around." He paused to let that sink in and then added. "When Sperl told me Charlotte had killed Fritz, I immediately grasped that he must have done something unfathomably horrible to her to provoke such a response. I shudder to think what it was because she had already accepted and absorbed so much abuse. But one thing was clear: if Charlotte had finally been pushed to the point of self-defence, then whatever Fritz had done, he deserved to die."

Alix allowed the shocked rustle that gripped the courtroom to settle down before turning to Steinbrueck with, "Your witness, *Herr Kollege*."

Collecting his black robes like a fussy priest, Steinbrueck approached the witness stand. "Did I hear you correctly just now? Did you just suggest that a splendid young man, an Olympic rider, a courageous officer, a man who had suffered so long and so hard at the hands of our enemies, *deserved* to die?"

"I concede that for someone like you," Christian replied with an undertone of disdain, "who never served on the front and did not regularly witness the death of friends and comrades--" Hoots of approval erupted from the teenagers, "Such a judgement may sound harsh." Isolated clapping broke out and then died away. "However, I have seen far better men than Fritz von Bredow die." He paused and then added almost flippantly, "Bredow certainly deserved to die more than someone who did nothing more than own copies of Social Democratic newspapers printed in Czechoslovakia, or someone who told jokes about a certain Austrian corporal with a silly moustache. Deaths for which you, Herr Staatsanwalt Dr Steinbrueck, are responsible."

Steinbrueck's face flushed red, and his eyes flashed. "I applied the law! You — in contrast — are nothing but an ordinary citizen and have no right to decide what crimes warrant the death sentence!"

Christian's silent smirk made Steinbrueck turn away furiously, and some of the teenagers giggled at his discomfort. He returned to his table to collect his nerves and thoughts. After covering his agitation by taking a drink of water, he returned to face Christian again. "You said that you and Bredow fought frequently. What did you fight about?"

"How he treated my cousin."

"Really? Is that all? Didn't you fight about politics?"

Alix tensed; Steinbrueck was trying to drag her husband's role in the plot against Hitler into the trial to discredit Christian.

Christian astonished her. "Politics? Why would Fritz and I squabble about politics? We both hated the Ivans and supported the Western Allies."

"Yes, but surely you fought about *wartime* politics? After all—"

In a tone of voice that sounded like nothing more than zeal to respond to questioning, Christian cut the prosecutor off before he could raise the 20th of July. "Why should you think that? You never heard one word exchanged between us! Herr Inspector Sperl testified that although he heard loud shouting between us he couldn't hear what was being said. Frau Liebherr is still here. Recall her if you like." He nodded in her direction.

Horrified at the prospect of being recalled, Frau Liebherr protested loud enough to be heard on the bench "I heard nothing but loud voices."

While she wasn't currently under oath, given Sperl's earlier testimony, this sounded plausible. Steinbrueck chose not to force the issue.

Christian meanwhile continued in a coldly aggressive tone, "In short, Herr Staatsanwalt, there is no one left alive who could have heard what Bredow and I fought about in the confines of my apartment — except Charlotte herself."

Alix almost had heart failure. Charlotte had already told her that Christian and Fritz frequently fought about the Nazis, their inhumane policies and the justification for tyrannicide and regime change that motivated the German Resistance to Hitler. If she was called to testify on this issue, she would either undermine her case — or have to perjure herself.

But Christian's gamble paid off.

Judge Nuss intervened with a stern admonishment, "Herr Dr Steinbrueck! Do not attempt to lead the witness."

Frowning in frustration, Steinbrueck excused the witness. As Christian stepped down from the stand he was met by applause that was not confined to the excited high school girls.

Alix had planned to call Charlotte next, and she looked at Alix expectantly, her hand already gripping the back of the chair to get to her feet. They had rehearsed the dialogue dozens of times, adjusting and refining it until Charlotte sounded confident. Alix knew Charlotte viewed this as her chance to tell her side of the story and vindicate herself. Charlotte, having decided to fight for her life, wanted to testify. Alix, however, was afraid of what Steinbrueck would do to her. She hesitated and then against her instincts, called Charlotte to the witness stand.

Charlotte was dressed conservatively in a grey woollen skirt that came to mid-calf, a long-sleeved, white blouse with a prim collar that buttoned at the base of her throat — no décolleté, no colour, panache or defiance, just a grey mouse. Her hair, cut short to make her look more masculine when she was out on the streets, had been pinned and clipped to look as if she were wearing a bun. The effect was to make her look old-fashioned and docile. Alix knew that her survival depended upon the court believing she was a 'good' woman driven to violence only in extremity.

Charlotte took the oath to tell the truth and waited, her eyes turned trustingly to Alix. Alix silently begged God for help and then asked Charlotte to state who she was and where she had grown up and gone to school. This biographical information was meant to establish that Charlotte had led a simple rural life right to the end of the war. Alix was fighting prejudices against aristocrats by highlighting that Charlotte had not travelled abroad, not gone to university, and not run in fast or glamorous company. Only after she had established this premise did she ask Charlotte to describe in her own words how she had met Fritz von Bredow and what she felt about him. Alix was relieved to see Charlotte's face soften as she spoke of her first love. She delivered a flawless account of young love and devastating loss, providing without prompting examples of how she kept her memories and hopes for his return alive until the evidence of his death seemed overwhelming.

Alix asked the court if it was necessary to make Charlotte reiterate what she had experienced during her escape from the family estate to Berlin or at the hands of the Russians. Since this had been covered by earlier testimony, the judges agreed the defendant need not testify at this time.

Alix turned to the topic of Fritz's return, asking Charlotte to describe Fritz. Charlotte echoed Christian's description of his physical state. "But what about the man inside? Was he still the man you loved?"

Tears welled up in Charlotte's eyes and she shook her head sharply.

"For the record, please answer the question verbally," Alix pressed her gently.

"He was not the same. He was a different man."

"In what way? Can you describe the differences?"

"Fritz — the Fritz I loved had been gentle. He cared about every living thing — the horses, the dogs, the cattle, even the sparrows in the barn!" Charlotte declared with astonishing feeling. "He never used crude language. He never made lewd remarks or jokes. He didn't have a temper. He was easy-going and content with little things. Just the song of a bird or the colours of the sunset would make him happy." She fell silent as if remembering something lovely.

Alix had to prompt her. "And what was he like after six years in Russian hands?"

"He was horrible!" Charlotte lifted her face, her eyes wet and her lips quivering slightly. "He used horrible, rude language, even when speaking directly to me. After Christian left, he hit me too, more and more frequently."

"Why?"

Charlotte shrugged, "Because he was never satisfied with anything I did. He didn't like the food I made, calling it — terrible things, but what can I cook with dehydrated potatoes and powdered eggs and without fat? He complained constantly about the cold, too — it was December. The temperature never rose above freezing, and the Airlift almost collapsed. He said I didn't clean the apartment properly, not like a 'good German woman' — saying I had become 'a Russian slut.' But I cleaned as best as I could without soap or detergent."

Alix could sense that people around the room, even some of the clerks and police, were nodding in understanding. Everyone in this court lived under the Soviet Blockade; they knew it meant bland, monotonous food, cold rooms, cold baths, darned clothes, stinking bodies and only half-cleaned apartments. She could feel that support among the public, if not the bench, was shifting in Charlotte's favour.

"Given these grave personality changes — undeniably induced by the terrible things Fritz von Bredow had endured," Alix stressed, "Why didn't you end the engagement with him and throw him out of your apartment?"

"I thought about it. Once or twice, I hinted to Fritz that if he wasn't satisfied, he could go, but he didn't. More and more, he dragged me down, took away my self-respect, and destroyed my faith in a better future. You see," she raised her head, holding it high, and spoke in a clear, vibrant voice, "after I had lost all hope of Fritz returning to me, I had met another man, a man who treated me with respect, courtesy and concern. He had made me feel human again — more than human. He made me feel like an attractive, young woman. He made me want to live again, and I had begun to hope that we could have a future together. I had started to believe he would propose to me, that we could marry. I even dared to dream of children." She kept her eyes straight ahead. She did not turn to look at David, but with a glance, Alix confirmed that David's eyes were fixed on Charlotte with burning intensity. The teenage girls, meanwhile, seemed to hold their breath, their eyes filled with excitement as if they were sharing Charlotte's dream.

"But when Fritz returned, that illusion shattered. It was as if Fritz were a mirror. I saw clearly how deformed and ugly I had become. I realised that that wonderful man who was so good to me would not marry me when he learned what the Russians had done to me. I realised I had been fooling myself."

One of the girls in the gallery let out a little cry, and one of the others held her hand over her mouth in horror.

Charlotte continued, "I comforted myself with the thought that Fritz was still engaged to me and that he had returned to me. I told myself that because of what he had experienced, he would understand how helpless I had been in the hands of the Russians. I thought that precisely because Fritz, like me, had been degraded and abused by the Ivans, he would not blame me for what they had done, but rather understand my helplessness." She stopped speaking.

"And did he?" Alix prompted.

Charlotte stared straight ahead as she answered leadenly. "No. He did not understand. He called me a whore and then he raped me. Since I'd already 'put out' for six Ivans, he said, I had no right to deny him, my fiancé."

A loud gasp came from one of the teenagers and a flurry of whispers erupted among her friends, but more importantly, an uneasy rustling swept across the rest of the room as well. Alix sensed that they had scored. She let the effect sink in before continuing. "Did you resist?"

"I begged him to understand. I described what had happened, how I was trapped, overwhelmed and my arms were broken by their rifle butts. I swore over and over that I had not been willing. I begged him to understand. I was crying and grovelling at his feet, begging for understanding."

Charlotte was starting to break down as the memories overwhelmed her. Alix tried to intercede, but Steinbrueck cut her off and insisted, "The defendant has not yet answered the question whether she resisted or not."

"That is obvious from her answer," Alix snapped back.

"There is a difference between pleading for understanding and saying 'no.' Resisting."

"Is that how a brown rat like you justified forcing yourself on women sobbing at your feet?" David flung out furiously. "Just how many wives of defendants did you abuse before sending their husbands to their deaths?"

The court was in an uproar, and Alix dropped her head in her hands. She should not have shared all she knew about Steinbrueck with David.

"One more word, Herr Goldman, and I will have you removed from the court!" Judge Nuss warned David and then sternly turned to the prosecutor to admonish, "Herr Dr Steinbrueck, you can put your questions to the witness during cross-examination. You may proceed, Freifrau von Feldburg."

"Graefin, can you tell the court when this first rape occurred?"

"Not exactly. My life had become a monotonous blur of trying to please Fritz and failing again and again. I had no sense of days or dates. I only know it was shortly before Christmas."

"You didn't shoot Fritz von Bredow until 10 January. Roughly three weeks later. What happened in between?"

"He raped me a dozen more times. Not every night, but once he assaulted me twice within about six hours."

Behind her, Alix could hear the outraged and agitated voices of the schoolgirls and their teacher's pleas for them to quieten down. She also heard Christian warn David to remain silent.

"Why didn't you leave? Your cousin was living in an apartment on the Kurfuerstendamm. Or why not turn to the Liebherrs, who had taken you in after the Russian rapes? They lived just across the hall. Why didn't you turn to them for help?"

"I was too ashamed," Charlotte whispered and broke down entirely.

The uproar from the teenagers and shouts from other members of the public caused the judges to call for a half-hour break. They also instructed Alix to get her client under control. Alix took Charlotte to the nearest ladies' room and washed her face in cold water. "Do you want me to end my questioning?"

Charlotte shook her head. "No, ask the last question. I want David to hear the answer."

Alix sighed, understanding more fully why Charlotte insisted on going through with this.

When the court session resumed, the entire courtroom was tense. Many observers sat on the edge of their seats. Those at the front leaned forward on the railing. With internal trepidation, Alix posed the final question. "If Bredow had abused you more than once, what was different about the tenth of January? Why did you decide to shoot him then?"

"My cousin Christian had given me the pistol and bullets so I could defend myself from the Ivans. I kept the loaded pistol under my bed. If the Airlift failed and the Soviets took over Kreuzberg, I planned to shoot the first Ivan who broke in. I also planned to use the last bullet on myself. But Fritz took me by surprise the first time he raped me, and after that, I was stunned and lamed. I hated myself and felt worthless. I had no will of my own anymore." Alix heard what sounded like a gasp of collective pain from the crowd of school girls.

"It wasn't until the night of the tenth," Charlotte continued, "that I realised I didn't have to endure any more. I could end it all. I resolved to kill myself, but only after making sure Fritz would never abuse any other woman. When I heard him coming down the hall, calling out his insulting 'endearments' — 'where's my little Russian pussy?' and saying bluntly, 'I'm coming to fuck you, you ugly, old whore' — I reached under the bed, pulled out the pistol, and stood facing the bedroom door with the pistol cocked and aimed. I steadied my right hand with my left, and I was looking down the barrel when he walked in. When I saw his face, I fired three times in quick succession."

Someone in the audience started to clap slowly. Alix glanced over her shoulder and realised that Anna Savage had come to her feet and was applauding with a powerful, measured beat of her hands. As she watched, the teenage girls and their teacher also stood and clapped in unison. Then Christian, David and some of the journalists joined them. Clap. Clap. Clap.

"Order! Order in the courtroom!" Nuss called, hammering with his gavel. But the clapping only grew louder and faster. "Order! Or I will clear the courtroom!" Still, the clapping went on and on. Nuss shouted to the policemen and with obvious reluctance they started to approach the crowd. This caused some of the audience to sit down again, and gradually the clapping died away. David stopped last of all. The police returned to their stations at the door, and Alix declared, "No more questions," and returned to her seat.

Steinbrueck gathered his robes about him and approached the witness stand. "Very dramatic," he sneered at Alix, "Have you ever considered a film career, *Frau Kollegin*? I'm sure this kind of melodrama would play very well in Hollywood, but this being a *German* court of law, we should drop the theatrics and stick to the naked facts." Turning to glare at Charlotte he demanded, "Did you at any time physically resist your fiancé's advances?"

"I cried bitterly and begged him to stop."

"But did you struggle?"

Charlotte shook her head, tears streaming down her face over her trembling lips.

Steinbrueck turned to the clerk and noted. "The defendant responded in the negative." Then directing his remarks to Charlotte again, he asked, "Did you report Bredow's alleged assaults to the police?"

Charlotte again shook her head, and the clerk was ordered to record a negative answer.

"Did you ever lock your door?"

"The lock was broken," Charlotte whispered.

"For weeks? Why didn't you call a locksmith and get it mended?"

"I don't know..." Her voice faded out, inaudible to the court.

Steinbrueck did not bother to ask her to speak up or repeat her answer, he asked instead, "Did you warn Bredow that you had a gun and would use it if he sought to have intercourse with you again?"

Charlotte completely broke down into sobs. Holding her fists in front of her face, she pressed her eyes shut and swung her head from side to side.

Against a backdrop of hissing and unsettled rustling in the courtroom, Alix jumped to her feet. "This is enough, Your Honours! My coldblooded colleague can make his points in his closing remarks. The witness has said enough for the court to pass judgment." Her remarks were met with isolated cheers and more clapping.

Frowning, Nuss conceded. "Sustained." He slammed his gavel down and announced, "This court is adjourned until Friday 25 February, when closing statements will be heard."

Although the judges filed out promptly and Steinbrueck with his entourage hurried away in an apparent huff, the journalists and visitors lingered longer, watching to see what would happen next. Alix went to the witness stand, handed Charlotte a handkerchief and helped her down. With her arm around Charlotte's waist, she guided her to where David and Christian waited.

Before the police could intervene, David reached across the railing and pulled Charlotte into his arms. He kissed her wet face and stoked her hair, pulling out the hairpins. Despite the railing separating them, he held her defiantly, staring the police down when they approached to separate them. The policeman backed off, and when his female colleague reached out to yank Charlotte away, he told her to leave the couple alone.

David bent his face down to Charlotte and whispered. "I love you. I don't blame you for anything. I should not have abandoned you to that monster. When this is over, I will take you away, and we will have a family, Mrs Goldman." Then he released his grip and pulled back slightly.

Christian took advantage of the police's passivity to give Charlotte a quick hug. "It's all my fault. I should not have left you alone with Fritz. I'll never forgive myself."

Charlotte shook her head ambiguously and started crying again, but Alix realised these were tears of gratitude. After letting her cling to David for another few minutes, she gently pulled Charlotte away and made for the exit with the police escort trailing them.

Recce
RAF Gatow
Thursday 24 February 1949
(Day 244 of the Berlin Airlift)

Wing Commander Priestman summoned Fl/Lt Boyd to his office first thing in the morning. Boyd entered looking uncomfortable and forestalled a question from his commander by saying, "There's still no word back from London, sir. I'm doing all I can—"

Priestman held up his hand. "I'm sure you are, Boyd."

Boyd's surprised reaction reassured Robin that he appeared calm, and he continued. "With your nose in your classified documents, it may have escaped your notice that a civilian Mossie landed here last night. It belongs to Group Captain Cheshire," (Boyd's expression indicated that the name still worked wonders) "and he has lent it to me" (that was a bit of an exaggeration, but it sounded better that way) "to undertake a little operation on my own authority."

Behind his glasses, Boyd's eyes widened like an owl's. "Without approval from London?"

"Correct. Two ex-RAF pilots will fly to the location where my wife is being sheltered and, with the help of someone on the ground, will pick her up and fly her out. No service personnel or assets will be involved, and hence none other than myself will face any consequences — regardless of the outcome." He paused and asked, "I hope this does not bother your conscience, Flight Lieutenant?"

"No, sir. Not at all. I'd like to help if I could, but..."

"All I ask is that you turn a blind eye to what is going on until it is over one way or another — and prepare to process a defector."

Boyd nodded, swallowing hard. "Does that mean Borisenko's contact is assisting?"

"Yes. She'll be on the ground, and we'll bring her back with my wife."

Boyd nodded solemnly, "I'll find out what needs to be done to receive a high-ranking defector — secretly, of course. Anything else, sir?"

"Not at the moment but thank you for your cooperation." Looking dazed, Boyd left the room.

The next person Robin called to his office was the Senior Flying Control officer, Squadron Leader Garth. After asking Garth to sit, he explained, "The Mosquito that arrived last night belongs to Group Captain Chesire." Again, the name had the desired effect. Robin took advantage of this to declare, "It has been loaned to us for a special operation that you do not need to know about. It will be flown by two RAFVR pilots, who will not wear uniform. The aircraft will operate under the following ID." He scribbled the ID on a slip of paper and pushed it across the desk to Garth. "They will observe all instructions from your controllers and can be expected to respect Airlift procedures whenever they are in Berlin airspace. What they do beyond Berlin airspace is not your concern and it would be better for everyone if there were to be no speculation about it. The less said about the aircraft the better."

"Understood, sir. Do you know how long the aircraft might be operating out of Gatow?"

"Nobody has said anything about that to me, but personally, the sooner it does whatever it was sent here to do, the happier I will be."

Garth smiled faintly. "I can imagine. Well, we'll just try to ignore the thing and get on with our job. On an unrelated topic, is there any news about your wife, sir?"

"I'm expecting good news imminently, Garth. I've been told she is injured but being cared for inside the Soviet Zone and that it is only a matter of time before some arrangement is made for her to be returned to us."

"I'm very relieved to hear that, sir. Everyone has been worried and distressed."

Priestman smiled faintly, "I appreciate the support and concern shown by all station personnel. I'm sorry if I haven't expressed my thanks sufficiently. It's been a very difficult time for me, and we aren't out of the woods yet. Much could still go wrong. This may sound superstitious, but I wouldn't want to jinx anything by assuming too much too soon, so I'd rather you keep this under your cap."

"I understand perfectly, sir."

"The time to make a public statement is after Mrs Priestman is back safe and sound."

"I quite agree, sir."

"Good. Then that's all I have for you at the moment — except to say how much I appreciate the way you and your entire section have performed throughout the Blockade. At the start of the Airlift, I viewed ATC as one of our weakest links. Instead, you and your controllers have exceeded all expectations and consistently delivered absolutely first-rate work. I'm proud to say you have been the envy of the Americans, who had to induct civilian air traffic controllers. When this is all over, I intend to acknowledge your contribution officially. Meanwhile, I must rely on your continued professionalism and dedication." He stood, concluding the interview. Garth got to his feet, assured him that ATC would not let him down, and departed.

Robin hoped that the news would rapidly spread that "something" was in the works to bring Emily home. That would hopefully cool the grumbling against Robertson and the government and also prepare the way for Emily's reappearance — God willing. Furthermore, while everything he'd said about the Station's air traffic control was true, he hoped that his praise would also generate sufficient goodwill to encourage the controllers to turn a blind eye to the Mossie.

Meanwhile, Kit and Kiwi had taken over the office of the EAS hangar to plan their recce flight. The smell of aviation paint surrounded them as MacDonald and the ground crew put the finishing touches on the Mosquito's new livery. To blend in with the now dirty snow, a coat of greyish-white paint had been unevenly applied to the top side of the Mosquito. To be less visible against the sky when seen from the ground, the underside of the aircraft was painted a darker grey. The transitional surfaces merged and blended the shades of grey. Finally, bogus tail fin numbers and a French flag had been applied to the rudder. "It's about time the French made a contribution to this operation," Kiwi justified the ruse.

The main challenge of the flight was to get a good overview of the area surrounding Emily's refuge without tipping the Russians off that there was something worth looking for in the region. The pilots agreed they had to fly an erratic course that was unpredictable to reduce the likelihood of interception. They also agreed to circle low and show interest in other locations besides their actual 'target.'

"They must know we are interested in the wreck itself, what if we pretend that's what we're looking for?" Kit suggested.

"In which case, we should fly first to Pritzwalk, the location they gave in their announcements." Together they found the town on the map spread on the table.

"We then fly on a course replicating Moby Dick's last known course for fifty miles," Kiwi recommended.

Kit agreed, adding, "Then we reverse as if we think we've flown too far and fly the reciprocal course, past Pritzwalk and back to the corridor."

Kiwi nodded in agreement and next proposed, "After that, acting frustrated, we turn north and start doing broad sweeps back and forth, making sure to pass over the target before finding our decoy, the wreck."

"Once we see the wreck, we go down to the deck acting excited, before scurrying back the way we came."

"Piece of cake," Kiwi agreed and set to work on a detailed flight plan with what courses to fly for how long and at what speed. Kit, meanwhile, went over to the Met Office for the weather. He was a familiar face from his EAS flights and no one questioned his presence. Checking the weather before departure was routine. The forecast was ideal for a recce flight. Although temperatures hovered around freezing on the ground, no precipitation was expected. The cloud cover was complete, 10/10, and the ceiling was at just over 5,000 feet, but visibility below the clouds was good. They should be able to get a good picture of the region surrounding the St. Elizabeth Stift Alt Schwerin.

Back in the hangar, the camouflage was finished, and Kiwi was already kitted up. After Kit similarly donned flying boots, scarves, flight jacket, gloves and helmet, they climbed up into the cockpit. They conducted the pre-flight checks meticulously, both conscious of their inexperience on this type of aircraft and determined not to mess up in any avoidable way. When both were satisfied, they nodded to one another and Kiwi shoved back the cockpit window to put his arm out and signal to the ground crew.

With both engines purring happily, Kiwi contacted the tower with their bogus ID and requested permission to taxi. This was granted, and they took their place in line as if they were flying on the Airlift. Once in the air, however, they listened to the radio chatter without reporting in to BASC. Instead of receiving instructions, they simply tagged along behind the aircraft directly ahead of them. They could get away with this because the wooden Mossie was practically invisible on the radar screen.

After they had left Berlin airspace and were in the westbound, central corridor, they peeled off from the flying convoys, turning hard to starboard. They heard one pilot report an aircraft "straying" over Soviet airspace but ignored several attempts to contact them. Instead, Kit climbed hard until they slipped into the protective cloud.

They flew through the murk on dead reckoning until Kiwi thought they were near their first destination. When they let down through the cloud, they readily identified Pritzwalk by the five roads leading into it.

"Surprising how much easier it is to find things by daylight and without flak," Kit noted dryly. Kiwi laughed.

They flew a complete circuit around the town, before following their plan by flying southeast for fifty miles. They turned and flew the reciprocal course for 100 miles before they started to weave their way north.

Kiwi, the map spread across his knees, found the navigation comparably easy. There were only a few roads, but these stood out like black lines in the surrounding white landscape. The lakes and forests littered across the plain had unique shapes that made them readily identifiable by comparison to the map. Finally, with the large Plauer Lake on their right, they swung northwest and found the road junction at Goldberg. Dead ahead lay the modest-sized, oblong lake stretching east-to-west with a wide thumb of land jutting up from the south shore. This peninsula almost — but not quite — cut the lake in two. Taking up most of the wide peninsula was an ensemble of brick buildings half obscured by tall trees. It was readily identifiable as a medieval complex around a Gothic church crowned by twin towers.

"Bingo," Kiwi remarked.

The pilots scanned the scene below intently. From four thousand feet it was easy to see that the road running northwest from Goldberg towards Sternberg touched the tip of the lake where a sawmill straddled the stream emptying from the lake. Disturbing was the amount of traffic on this artery: tractors pulling logs, horse carts, pedestrians, and a column of tanks with large red stars on them.

"Bloody hell," Kit muttered as he put the Mossie on a wingtip and scudded back westwards.

"Well," Kiwi observed looking back at the tank column, "that got a lot of Russian boys excited."

"Do you think they saw our flag?"

"Let's say they weren't waving greetings."

A loud crack and a puff of smoke below them underlined Kiwi's assessment. The tank guns could not elevate enough to be any danger to them; the shot was simply a message of hostility.

Flying back over the lake, it was clear that a road connecting a series of hamlets ran east-west about two miles south of the lake before intersecting with the north-south road in Goldberg. Roads meant traffic and people, ruling out a landing to the east or south. Without a word, Kit and Kiwi scanned the territory north of the lake, but this was covered with intermittent forest. It would be impossible to land there. That left only the west, and northwest, the direction from which Emily had come.

Having obtained a good feel for the overall lay of the land, they turned northwest scanning for a good place to land as they approached the crash site. From the air, several possibilities appeared viable, although frequent stone walls, ditches, hedgerows and stands of trees underlined that an actual landing would be tricky.

Quite suddenly, they were over the wreck. The broken Wellington lay exposed and surrounded by dirty, trampled snow. Kit circled down for a closer look with an ache of sadness at the sight of AAI's trusty aircraft looking violated and abused. The air screws had been removed from the engines, along with the Perspex from the cockpit. Souvenir hunters had also cut away some of the canvas including all the red crosses. Less than two weeks after the crash, it looked more like a scrap heap than an aircraft.

Kiwi shook his head sadly, "Poor ol' Moby Dick! She deserved better than this."

Kit twisted his neck to check their surrounding and caught a glimpse of motion on the horizon. "Bandits! 7 o'clock high." He yanked the Mosquito up, pushed the throttles forward, and headed for the clouds in a power climb.

Kiwi twisted in his seat trying to identify their pursuers. "I think they're a pair of Yaks. The tank commander must have reported seeing us and they were scrambled from Parchim."

"Very likely," Kit agreed looking at his airspeed indicator. When flying level, the Mossie was as fast if not faster than the Soviet fighter, but the Yaks had the height advantage and were swooping down, using gravity to increase their speed. He, on the other hand, was climbing.

"They're gaining on us," Kiwi confirmed.

Kit estimated he needed 90 seconds to reach the clouds. They weren't going to make it. Instinctively, he pulled his head down and waited for the cannon fire to hit. Tracer flashed past the cockpit, but either the Russian had missed or had fired a warning shot. A moment later, the Yaks were flanking them. They throttled back to format on the Mossie's wingtips. Both pilots were making gestures to turn and land. Kit ignored them and held course for the clouds. One of the Yaks surged ahead and banked just ahead of his nose. Kit skimmed safely under him and then resumed his climb. The second Yak fired a round, but in the same instant, they smashed into the soft, white oblivion of the cloud. Kit almost immediately changed course, banking sharply towards the east to confuse their pursuers and continued to climb.

They broke out of the cloud at 8,000 feet into brilliant sunshine and an empty sky. They had either shaken off the Yaks, or the Russians had decided not to pursue. Kit banked around onto a southerly course, while Kiwi listened on the BASC frequency. Gradually, the signal became stronger and clearer. Kit risked dropping back below the cloud to make visual contact with the northern air corridor and gently slipped into the incoming stream, provoking some excited chatter from other pilots that they ignored. At 14:51, they landed at Gatow and returned to their hangar. It had been a successful reconnaissance flight since it left them much the wiser than before; it had taught them that they were far from ready for a rescue operation.

Kit explained the situation to Robin later that afternoon after he and Kiwi, with Christian's help, had come up with a plan. "The region may be comparatively thinly populated, but the sound of our engines attracts every eye on the ground for miles around. The Red Air Force base at Parchim is so close that if anyone reports us, hostile fighters can readily intercept within a quarter hour — provided they have visibility. The only way we're going to be able to land and extract Emily is by using the cloak of darkness. Because the Mossie's wood structure gives hardly any echo on radar, flying at night without navigation lights and wearing dark camouflage makes us almost invisible. At night, with only the sound to go by, no one will know we aren't one of theirs."

"Do you honestly believe you can safely land in a field you don't know after dark?" Robin asked sharply.

"Not without a flare path. Just as when SOE dropped or picked up agents or supplies during the war, someone on the ground will have to pace out and mark a runway with improvised flares."

Kiwi jumped in to explain, "Christian and I propose parachuting in tonight—"

"Wait a minute," Robin stopped him, "If you parachute in wearing civilian clothes you'll be shot as spies!"

"We'll drop at night near my grandfather's estate," Christian spoke up in a calming tone.

"I thought that was practically on the Baltic Sea!" Robin protested.

"Yes, but if we go in too close to where Emily is, we'll lead the Russkies right to her. Dropping in that far away will ensure that even if things go wrong, they won't make the connection to Emily. Furthermore, I know the region and the people. There is no Red Air Force unit for a hundred miles. We go in, bury our 'chutes in the snow and travel as German civilians to Schwerin —"

"Kiwi doesn't speak a word German!" Robin snapped, revealing his raw nerves.

"*Guten Morgen. Wie geht's? Ein Bier!*" Kiwi threw back with a grin.

Robin just frowned and pointed out, "You don't have any German papers and there's no time to make forgeries."

"Robin, I made it out of France in 1943, remember?"

"The natives were friendly, and there was a highly organised resistance organisation," Robin countered grimly.

"The natives are still friendly," Christian insisted, "and the Soviets aren't looking for or expecting downed airmen so far outside the corridors. We can do this. I get Kiwi to Schwerin's main railway station and hand him over to Mila, who escorts him the rest of the way to Emily, while I return to Berlin."

Kiwi took over explaining the plan. "Once I reach the convent, we tell Emily what is happening. Then I walk over the potential landing fields, find the most suitable stretch and prepare the flares."

Kit picked up the thread, "The next night, I fly in low and flash my navigation lights spelling EAS. If I see the flare path, I know all is well and I land. Kiwi gets Emily and Mila settled in the bomb bay — which Anna and the ground crew will fix up with blankets, cushions, torches and the like before I set out — and Kiwi will re-join me in the cockpit for the return."

"Piece of cake," Kiwi assured Robin.

Robin looked from one to the other speechlessly. He'd braced himself for a risky flight in and out. He'd counted on the operation being quick and taking the Soviets completely by surprise. The recce flight had already squandered some of that surprise, but he acknowledged it had been necessary. The idea of Kiwi parachuting in and wandering around in the Soviet Zone without papers, disguise, or language ability, however, seemed absolutely mad. Both of his own experiences trying to walk around in Germany after escaping from the prisoner of war camp had ended badly.

"Listen, Mate," Kiwi met his eye. "I have no wife and no kids. I was a failed salesman hitting the bottle when David took pity on me and let me join his company. But David would have thrown me out three times over if it wasn't for Emily. She's held us together and made EAS a success. I'm not going to let her fall into Soviet hands if I can help it. Period."

Robin decided the only way to honour those sentiments was to agree. He nodded and turned to Kit. "Does Georgina know what you're planning and approve?"

"Approve might not be the best choice of words, but she trusts me not to be foolhardy."

Robin thought about that answer and thought Emily would probably have reacted the same way if he volunteered for a risky operation that she considered worth doing. Robin took a deep breath and nodded. "All right then. The op is on."

Chapter Eighteen
On the Brink

Hobos
Soviet Zone
Friday 25 February 1949
(Day 245 of the Berlin Airlift)

The EAS ground crew collectively and enthusiastically outfitted Kiwi for his foray into the Soviet Zone. Winterfeld found a pair of old work shoes big enough for the New Zealander, Voigt offered gloves with the fingertips unravelling, and Greis handed over his Luftwaffe cap with the insignia torn off. Kiwi harvested enthusiastic applause by modelling the cap set at a rakish angle. "You would have looked great in Luftwaffe uniform!" Winterfeld assured him but Kiwi demurred. The rest of his outfit was a mismatched assembly of poorly fitting, stained, patched and threadbare clothes that would not have disgraced a beggar in Belgrade. Kiwi complained that he stank and itched.

"Perfect!" Christian assured him and then asked Axel to fill two water flasks with schnapps.

"What's that for?" Kiwi asked irritated. He had been on the wagon for almost a year.

"At the sight of police or Ivans, we take a swig or two so that our breath stinks and we act like we're blotto."

Kiwi nodded. It made sense, he just hoped he wouldn't have to drink too much.

"Cheer up!" Christian urged, "We may be grateful for something to warm us up!"

It was well after midnight when they boarded the Mossie. Christian took the navigator seat to help Kit find their destination, and with difficulty, Kiwi lay in the bomb bay wrapped in blankets against the cold. All wore helmets with intercom connections so they could communicate.

They docilely queued for take-off but left the traffic pattern immediately after leaving Gatow control area. Rather than join the westbound stream of Airlift traffic, they skirted around Berlin's southern districts heading east almost to the Polish border. About ten miles short of Poland, they turned north and dropped down through the cloud to fly at 2,500 feet under Christian's direction. With the Baltic Sea, dull and leaden grey dead ahead, they turned West. Not long afterwards, Kiwi heard a click as Christian switched on his mic and exclaimed, "There! That's the church where my grandfather is buried." Kiwi could see nothing from where he was, but over the intercom, Christian next reported, "The manor is over there." Finally, Christian said, "Time to swing into the wind and hit the silk."

Kit raised his voice above the engines to warn he was opening the bomb bay doors. Kiwi immediately squeezed himself into the cramped space behind the cockpit but ahead of the doors. He also grabbed his 'chute and pulled it on. He should have been exhausted but he was too keyed up. It was four years since his last jump. He'd put on a lot of weight since then. He hoped he didn't bugger anything up. If he broke an ankle or leg on landing, the whole rescue would be ruined.

Meanwhile, Kit opened the bomb bay doors. Kiwi eased himself down to sit on the edge, dangling his legs in the slipstream. He was struck by how incredibly peaceful it was. All Kiwi's earlier jumps had been in emergencies with flames, smoke, and the aircraft coming apart or spinning wildly. Now, in contrast, although the wind rushed in, up, and around the bomb bay and the Merlins growled fiercely, Kit was holding the Mossie straight and level and had throttled back nearly to stalling speed. It seemed surreal to be sitting here peacefully as though he had all the time in the world.

The moment passed. Kit announced that Christian had jumped. Kiwi looked towards the earth running like a rushing stream between the open bomb bay doors and decided this was like jumping into cold water: the less you thought about it the better. He drew a deep breath, and flung himself out of the open doors, grabbing the ripcord almost immediately.

Kiwi and Christian landed without incident some 600 yards apart. They buried their parachutes under bushes half lost in a drift of old snow. Then Christian took out a compass and verified that he was not disoriented before they started walking across snow-decked fields. Roughly half an hour later, they came to a rutted, dirt road and followed it. This led them to a small, rural railway stop. It was not a town or even a village, just a railway junction with a platform and a small station on one side. The station consisted of a stationmaster's office, which was locked, a ticket booth that was closed, and a waiting room with wooden benches for about six people to sit. Although the latter had a coal stove, this was unlit. Kiwi was too exhausted to care. Christian promised to 'keep watch,' while Kiwi stretched out on a bench and dropped off to sleep almost instantly.

He woke to find Christian in earnest conversation with a bent, old man in an ancient *Reichsbahn* uniform. They sat side by side on the other bench and spoke in low voices, or rather the old man spoke, and Christian kept shaking his head in apparent disbelief or distress. Now and again, Christian would ask a question that would set off a new flood of words from the railwayman.

Unable to sleep on the hard bench any longer, Kiwi got up and sought out the lavatory, which was around the back. When he returned, the stationmaster had disappeared into his office. Christian beckoned Kiwi over and with a nod at the wall clock registering 7:18, told him the next westbound train was due at 8:12. This would take them to Greifswald, where they could change to the D-Zug (a faster train) to Rostock. From there they would take a different D-Zug to Wismar. At Wismar, they would have a longer wait before catching a regional train to Schwerin. Unless something unexpected came up, they would arrive in Schwerin well in advance of their rendezvous with Mila and spend the night in the station there.

"What were you talking to the stationmaster about?" Kiwi asked.

Christian sighed. "He was just telling me what happened when the Red Army came. Charlotte's father had prepared for everyone on the estate to make the journey west, away from the Reds. They had loaded eighteen wagons. On the day they planned to depart, however, the tenant farmers and workers, including the Russian and Polish prisoners, opted to stay. They argued they were just peasants and workers, so the Reds would do them no harm. They stayed while my uncle set off with just two wagons, carrying his wife, daughter, three servants and their personal things.

"You know what happened to them. A strafing Soviet fighter shot up the wagon with Charlotte's parents and her mother's maid, killing them and mortally injuring one of the horses. Charlotte, Jasha and Horst continued to Berlin and never learned what transpired here after their departure." Christian stopped and took a deep breath.

"That bad?" Kiwi asked.

Christian nodded. "I'll spare you the details. The best way to put it is that compared to what happened there, Charlotte was lucky to reach Berlin, where she was raped only six times."

Kiwi couldn't speak.

"It is memories like these that shape the behaviour of people in the Soviet Zone. The hatred and loathing are intense — but the fear and shame are greater. The latter emotions have produced a whole class of eager collaborators. Particularly former Nazis are anxious to become handmaidens to the new masters. Others want to obscure the horrors by telling themselves they are creating a 'Socialist Paradise.' They think that if something positive emerges, it will justify the 'excesses.'"

"Where does that leave us?" Kiwi asked.

Christian smiled wanly, "In great danger."

But they had no trouble on the local train to Greifswald, or indeed on the six-hour trip to Wismar. Christian bought newspapers during their halt in Rostock, and while Christian systematically read them, Kiwi pretended to. Passengers boarded and alighted all along the way. Some nodded a greeting that required no more than "*Tag*" in response; some didn't want even that much contact. Kiwi and Christian, unshaven and shabbily dressed were too unremarkable to arouse curiosity, and the other passengers had their own worries. Throughout the journey, the conductors never asked for more than their tickets, which they produced readily whenever asked. Christian went so far as to engage the conductors in harmless conversation about schedules and other banalities.

During their lengthy wait in Wismar, however, their luck ran out. They managed to get a warm meal in town and had settled in at the station to await the regional train to Schwerin when suddenly there were police on the platform. Kiwi looked over his shoulder for an escape route, and to his horror saw Soviet soldiers blocking the door. He didn't know if they were working with the police or if they were there by chance; either way, they were trapped.

"Schnapps," Christian hissed under his breath and Kiwi fumbled to pull the nearly forgotten flask out of his inside pocket. He saw Christian wiping his lips with the back of his hand to ensure the smell was immediately evident. Kiwi did the same before slouching down and letting his hand hang off the edge of the bench as if he were sound asleep.

A moment later, two policemen stood in front of them and barked in German.

"*Was?*" Christian asked back, slurring the final s.

"*Ausweis!*" the police barked.

Christian sat up straighter and fished around in his pockets, trying first one and then another until he produced his papers. The policeman took them, looked at them, and then read Christian's name with a sneer, adding something that began with "Herr Baron" in a mocking tone. Christian just shrugged in reply. Then one of the policemen kicked Kiwi's foot and he groaned and roused himself as if he'd just been awakened. He squinted up at the policeman.

"*Ausweis, Dummkopf!*" That sounded insulting, but Kiwi ignored the tone like a benign drunk and made obliging gestures to indicate compliance while reaching into his pocket and producing the train ticket.

"*Ihren Ausweis nicht die Fahrkarte!*" the police retorted frowning, and Christian also said something in an annoyed tone.

"Ah!" Kiwi answered as if the penny had just dropped. He started looking in all his pockets. At the end of his search, he shrugged and turned to Christian, saying, "Christian?"

Christian responded indignantly and insultingly as one might expect from a friend confronted with a drunken request. Kiwi turned to the frowning policeman and declared with a shrug and a fake burp, "*Zu Hause.*" 'At home' was another German phrase he had picked up somewhere.

This provoked a new flood of angry German from one of the policemen. Kiwi endured it with the indifference and patience of a cow because he understood too little even to be frightened. He answered with a new shrug, and now

Christian tried to intercede on his behalf, using the exasperated yet conciliatory tone of a man annoyed with his friend's carelessness but trying to shield him from trouble. While Christian engaged the police, Kiwi noticed their train was approaching and he got to his feet.

This drew the attention of the police who barked an angry question at him. He pointed to the train, then pulled out and showed his ticket again before declaring in a loud but slurred voice as he pointed at the train, "*Zu Hause!*"

Christian chimed in with what Kiwi took to be assurances that they were trying to get home, and he would see his stupid friend to his door. The elderly policeman seemed on the brink of giving in, but the younger policeman was more ardent and raised an objection. At that moment, Kiwi just walked away. The police called angrily after him. He turned around unsteadily as the train screeched to a halt beside the platform and passengers spilt out. For a moment, he stared at them with his head cocked to one side then very slowly and deliberately he started to fiddle with his fly as if preparing to piss right there and then.

Christian lunged at him, scolding furiously, and pushed his hand away. With profuse apologies to the police, he grabbed Kiwi and yanked him toward the train. Kiwi played drunkenly resistant as if he preferred to piss in front of the police than board the train. Christian became louder and more forceful, shoving him towards the train. The police meanwhile were squabbling amongst themselves, the younger man indignant and gesturing towards Kiwi, while the older man kept his voice low as he dragged his younger colleague away.

Only after the train was five minutes out of the station did Christian look over at Kiwi and burst out laughing. They had the compartment to themselves, and he declared in English. "I've never seen anything like that in my life! The look on their faces when they realised what you were about to do was priceless!"

"We were lucky it was just some kind of routine check — or we didn't match the description of whoever they were looking for," Kiwi responded. His pulse still hadn't fully normalised.

"True, but your imitation of a drunk was worth an Academy Award!" Christian was evidently both impressed and approving.

Kiwi, on the other hand, felt less pleased with himself. He knew the reason he could play the part so well was because he'd been sozzled all too often.

Closing Statements
Berlin-Moabit
Friday 25 February 1949
(Day 245 of the Berlin Airlift)

David had not slept properly since hearing Charlotte's testimony. Although Alix had shared with him the gist of everything she had endured from Bredow, hearing the horror in her voice and words was more distressing than the lawyer's clinical summary. Indeed, David and Christian had spent the evening following Charlotte's testimony wallowing in guilt as they drank themselves under the table. Yet while Christian's decision to move out of the apartment had exposed Charlotte to Bredow's violence, David felt his actions represented the greater sin. Christian's presence might have restrained Bredow, but it could not have given Charlotte what she needed more: hope for a better future — and sincere love.

In retrospect, David recognised his response to her breaking off their relationship had been childish. He'd reacted like a thin-skinned teenager, focusing only on his personal pain and the imagined insults. He'd closed his ears when Christian had hinted at the complex motives for Charlotte's decision, too wrapped up in his hurt pride to probe deeper. If instead of going to England, he'd stayed in Berlin, he could have provided her with a lifeline. If he'd let her know that he would wait for her if she changed her mind, she might have been spared the worst horrors. At the latest, after the first rape, she might have turned to him — or to Christian. Instead, she'd believed she had no alternative and so had felt trapped in a living hell. That knowledge would haunt him for the rest of his life.

As he and Alix climbed aboard the horse cart to drive to Moabit for the closing statements, Alix warned, "It's going to be hard listening to Steinbrueck insult Charlotte but try to ignore him and, above all, keep your indignation in check. Anything you say now might hurt her. Remember, he and the presiding judge, Nuss, were thick as thieves throughout the NS-regime."

"Why are such Nazi pigs still allowed to practice law? Why haven't they been put in jail — or at least debarred?" David asked outraged.

Alix sighed. "Because there are too many of them and the Americans are in a hurry to cut the apron strings. They want Germany to start functioning as a self-governing state sooner rather than later. That means they can no longer vet every bureaucrat and civil servant for their actions under Hitler. They have replaced their official policy of collective guilt with an unstated policy of collective amnesty. Mark my words, before long they will want Germany to rearm and all the generals they once reviled as war criminals will be courted and honoured for their military competence instead."

"My God," David answered. He was appalled but didn't have the energy or the nerves to think through the consequences. Charlotte required his full attention.

As they were coming to expect, the courtroom was crowded. Some of the journalists had to stand. Anna was saving a place for David, but David was surprised Christian was missing until he remembered that Christian had something to do with Emily's rescue. While he recognised that was important too, he regretted the Luftwaffe officer's absence. David had come to rely on his moral support and his calming influence. As for the rest of the public, young women predominated, and they were not exactly innocent schoolgirls.

Anna leaned towards him. "Georgina's girls have been spreading the word about this trial among their colleagues."

David stiffened. "You mean Berlin's streetwalkers?"

"You could call them that, but most of them lost their innocence to the Reds, and each has suffered a similar fate as Charlotte."

"Charlotte isn't a whore!" David protested.

"Nor were most of these girls," Anna reminded him firmly "— until they encountered their own version of Fritz. Whether German or Allied, men have treated them as tarts simply because the Russians deflowered them."

Anna sat back, leaving David frowning with discomfort. He did not think the presence of these girls would help Charlotte's case.

Eventually, the judges arrived, and Steinbrueck was invited to present his closing remarks. The prosecutor struck a self-confident pose and projected his voice to be sure the press caught every word. "We've heard a lot of melodrama in this trial. All very entertaining and good for selling newspapers, I'm sure, but this is a German court of law. It is time to jettison all the noise and nonsense. It is time to focus on the cold, hard facts.

"Charlotte Graefin Walmsdorf became engaged to Fritz von Bredow in early 1941. By all accounts, she remained true to him, even after he went missing in late 1942, until May 1945, when she was one of hundreds of thousands of innocent German women who were subjected to acts of unspeakable barbarity and unfettered violence by the invading Soviet army. She was not to blame. No one is attempting to suggest she was." David couldn't stop his eyebrows from shooting up as Steinbrueck admitted this, but Alix looked tense as if she didn't like how his statement was shaping up.

"Hundreds of thousands shared her fate and tens of thousands committed suicide from shame. The defendant, we have been told, wanted to kill herself and even asked her cousin to kill her, but allegedly circumstances 'prevented' it. It seems to me that had she truly felt as devastated and shamed as the defence claims, then she would have found a way to take her own life."

A low hissing came from the women spectators as he made these remarks, but he ignored them and continued, "Ultimately, that is immaterial. She chose to live. She found work as a freelance journalist and German teacher and eventually as a secretary for the British firm 'Air Ambulance International.' Here she met and developed a romantic attachment for Mr David Goldman" he nodded in David's direction. "The evidence presented to this court suggests the couple was not formally engaged and the relationship was ended shortly after Bredow returned. Indeed, Mr Goldman left Berlin altogether and had no further contact with the defendant." David frowned in incomprehension. Why was Steinbrueck conceding these points?

"Based on the testimony of Christian Freiherr von Feldburg, roughly a month after Bredow's reappearance, Feldburg moved out of the apartment. He cited constant quarrelling with Bredow. According to Feldburg, the defendant consistently sided with Bredow during these disputes.

"Based on the defendant's testimony, she started sleeping with Bredow two weeks after Feldburg departed. She did not offer resistance." A louder and more sustained hiss emanating from scores of spectators reverberated throughout the courtroom, but again, Steinbrueck ignored it. "She did not go to the police — although a police inspector lived one flight down. She did not flee from her apartment to take refuge with her cousin in his new apartment or move in with friends just across the landing.

"No! None of that! She remained in the apartment with Bredow engaging in repeated sexual acts — sometimes, by her own account, more than once a day." Steinbrueck's tone was sneering and his expression disdainful. David would have liked to hit him, but his words were factual and as Alix's silence showed, there was no grounds for an objection.

Steinbrueck continued, "Despite what honest German folk naturally feel about such lewd behaviour, Graefin Walmsdorf is not on trial here for indecency." David felt his blood boil; this kind of appeal to vague and legally non-existent "folk" wisdom or morality was a favourite tactic of the National Socialist courts. It had been used to marginalise and criminalise people who were handicapped, homosexuals, gypsies, and, of course, Jews. David noted that Alix too was squirming with indignation and jotting something in her notes.

But Steinbrueck still had the floor. "After all the evidence presented here, it should be obvious to any decent German observer that the defendant is one of those less attractive females, never popular enough with men to find adequate sexual satisfaction. We can readily see that far from being forced against her will, she craved the sex Bredow gave her."

"What the hell do you know?" A female voice shouted from the gallery.

Steinbrueck turned toward the heckler who had jumped to her feet and mocked, "Well, we know that *you* know nothing of modesty and decency, don't we?"

"YOU HAVE NO—" A policeman had the heckler by the arm and removed her from the courtroom as she shouted insults at the smugly smirking prosecutor. Only after the door shut and the shouts receded down the hall, did Steinbrueck ask the judges if he should continue. They nodded.

"Returning to the defendant, her graphic description of how she grovelled at Bredow's feet shows she is what psychiatrists call 'masochistic.' That is, she enjoyed the role of victim and was titillated by abuse during the sexual act. Perhaps it was the experience with the Russians which awoke this abnormal and non-German psychosis—"

"Objection! Herr Dr Steinbrueck is not a psychiatrist and not qualified to diagnose psychosis of any kind!"

"Sustained. Herr Dr Steinbrueck, you will refrain from speculation about the defendant's mental state."

Steinbrueck bowed his head. "Fair enough. Then let us instead, for the sake of argument, assume that the defendant *was* raped by Bredow. So what?" He paused dramatically. "He was her *fiancé* — the very man to whom she had promised unlimited sex in early 1941." He shrugged, "In short, all Bredow did was claim his rights — admittedly after a slight delay." Steinbrueck chuckled, evidently pleased with his clever speech, but it provoked only rude shouts of protest from the gallery. Indeed, agitated muttering punctuated by angry exclamations swept through the entire room. The judges had to call for order several times before the audience quieted. Finally, Judge Nuss nodded for Steinbrueck to proceed.

"For some reason, we can never know — because only two people were present, and one is dead while the other told a fairytale while under oath — the defendant turned on her lover and future husband and shot him in cold blood. He was unarmed, in his pyjamas, handicapped, and helpless. The defendant freely confessed that she was not threatened. She did not need to defend herself. She simply turned on the man she had been sleeping with regularly and murdered him with violence rare even among gangsters. Such a creature is not only guilty of murder, she is mentally unstable and as such, a threat to society. She deserves nothing less than the death penalty!" With this dramatic announcement, the prosecutor bowed to the judges and resumed his seat with a smug expression despite the uproar among the spectators his words had provoked.

David's insides had knotted themselves. Despite Alix's warning, he was shocked by this transformation of a helpless victim like Charlotte into a caricature of a sex-crazed psychopathic killer. He was appalled by the heartlessness of it. The reminder that Charlotte's life hung in the balance made everything a hundred times worse. He turned his gaze to Alix, silently begging her to put things right — without a clue as to how she might go about it.

Alix took her time, jotting down notes on her prepared remarks, pulling her papers together, knocking them on the edges to straighten them, and finally advancing with her head high.

"Gentlemen," she opened, "the facts of this case have never been in doubt. No one has questioned or denied the fact that Graefin Walmsdorf shot and killed Fritz von Bredow on the night of Jan 10. What you are being asked to decide is whether or not she was acting in self-defence. According to the German Criminal Code of 1926 — the code which this court is required to uphold— Section 32, paragraph 2, self-defence is defined as followed," Alix turned to her notes and read out loud: "Self-defence is any defensive action that is necessary to avert an imminent unlawful attack on oneself or another."

Alix lowered her notes and stressed: "Please note it says: *any* unlawful attack. Rape is defined as an unlawful act under Section 177, paragraph 1 of the same criminal code.

"Furthermore, the prosecution has made much of the fact that the rapes perpetrated by the Russians were horrendous acts of violence, acts of barbarism so vile that — according to the male prosecutor — they can be viewed as negating the victims' right to life itself. If rape is indeed, as my male colleague insists, a 'fate worse than death' requiring the death of the victim to expunge the shame, then logically defence against sexual assault is at least equally, if not *more* justified, than defence against an assault on human life." This conclusion caused a hubbub in the audience with the journalists scrambling to take notes.

Alix continued, "In short, Graefin Walmsdorf had the legal right to defend herself against rape with the same vigour and means as to defend herself against attempted murder." She paused to collect herself and let that conclusion sink in.

Continuing, she noted, "To negate this clear legal principle, my male colleague has engaged in offensive and unfounded fantasies dressed in pseudo-psychoanalysis, without evidence or professional qualifications. Indeed, in crass contradiction of the sworn testimony of a series of witnesses, he alleges that Graefin Walmdorf was not raped but instead welcomed Bredow's sexual assaults. The male prosecutor," she turned to gesture toward a simmering Steinbrueck, "might voyeuristically have *longed* to be in

Graefin Walmsdorf's bedroom when Bredow assaulted her — but he was not." Cheers broke out from the gallery, and Alix waited until they had been quelled. "Graefin Walmsdorf under oath characterised the attacks as rape, and two objective outsiders, including a police inspector, described her as looking abused and broken — that is victimised — after Bredow had moved into her apartment. There is no legal or psychological reason to question the nature of Bredow's attacks."

Alix paused to take a breath before continuing, "This court must recognise that Bredow committed 'unlawful acts' against Graefin Walmsdorf on several occasions and explicitly threatened to attack her again on the night in question. It is legally immaterial, who Bredow was and whether Graefin Walmdorf had once loved him enough to want to marry him. It is legally immaterial that she had not defended herself in the past. On the night of January 10, Graefin Walmsdorf acted within her legal rights when she took action to defend herself against an unlawful act with consequences 'worse than death.' The only verdict this court can legally reach is 'not guilty.'"

As Alix turned away to re-seat herself, half the audience jumped to their feet to give her a standing ovation. David, along with Anna and many others, clapped as hard as he could. He had been wrong to question whether a skilled prosecutor could provide an effective defence. He had been wrong to wonder whether a woman was up to the job. When Alix reached her seat, Charlotte stood to embrace her. The sight of the two women clinging to each other was a powerful and moving image. Several photojournalists sought to capture it, and flashes went off in rapid succession, while other journalists scrambled out of their seats to file their stories. David simply felt some of his nervousness abate. The young woman lawyer had utterly outclassed the bigoted prosecutor. He felt confident of acquittal.

Strangers in the Wilderness

Soviet Zone
Saturday 26 February 1949
(Day 246 of the Berlin Airlift)

The sound of a woman shouting in German brought Kiwi to his bewildered senses. He'd been out cold, and at first had no idea where he was. Then he remembered that he was in Schwerin train station, where the first traces of daylight were seeping through the dirty windows. But why on earth was a stocky, Russian woman in trousers gesturing wildly while shouting at him in German? He saw Christian nod and knuckle his forehead like some Tsarist peasant and point to Kiwi. That's when it hit him: this must be the Russian partisan, the Hero of the Soviet Union and alleged defector, who was supposed to lead him to Emily.

Following Christian's example, Kiwi touched his Luftwaffe forage cap, trying to act like a cowed doorman. In answer, he received a frown and a flood of orders punctuated with gestures toward five pieces of luggage. Christian picked up two, and Kiwi played the obedient servant, taking the rest. They followed the Russian officer out onto the street, where she imperiously flagged down a horse-drawn taxi into which Kiwi and Christian loaded the suitcases.

Then Christian backed away and in a low voice told Kiwi, "I'll take the train to Berlin and report to Robin all is well so far. Good luck and see you back in Berlin."

Kiwi lifted his right hand to his forehead in a semi-salute to Christian and then turned and climbed into the ancient carriage which, based on the mouldy smell and rotting upholstery, had probably been rotting in someone's barn for generations. Mila gave directions which brought them to a livery stable where they hired three horses, putting the luggage on the oldest of them. Then they took off at a brisk pace, crossing the Schweriner See, and following the road to Sternberg.

Mila set a stiff pace, trotting almost continuously. Although it had been a decade or more since Kiwi had ridden a horse, he'd practically grown up on horseback. As a boy on his father's farm in New Zealand, he'd ridden far more than he'd walked, and he rapidly fell into the rhythm again. The pace eliminated the need to communicate, and by mutual consent, they focused on reaching their destination.

Despite their purposeful pace, however, Kiwi was alarmed that it took them half the day to reach Sternberg. Beyond this town, Mila turned onto a secondary road which was far less travelled, and their pace slowed even more. Meanwhile, because he was wearing ordinary trousers rather than riding breeches, the seams on the inside of his legs had rubbed his skin raw. The series of near-sleepless nights were also catching up with him, and when just after 3 pm, Mila plunged off the road and led Kiwi into a forest he was relieved, believing they must be nearing their destination.

He was bewildered when she stopped just inside the woods. With a wide grin that transformed her face into something lovely, she spoke to him in German.

"Sorry. I don't speak German," Kiwi reminded her annoyed. This was no time to stop. He needed daylight to find a suitable landing strip and create a flarepath.

"Oh! Good," Mila answered with an impish smile, "then I try my English."

"You speak English?" Kiwi asked astonished.

"I study English after meet Galyna. We eat now. Piss. Give horses rest and food. Half hour. Then go."

"But aren't we almost there? Wouldn't it be better to press on?"

"No. Need break." She smiled and gestured for him to dismount.

Kiwi looked warily at the sun. It was well down the afternoon sky. By his estimate, they only had another two to three hours of daylight left. "There is a lot to do to prepare," he reminded her.

She nodded vigorously. "Yes, but first piss and eat. I have food," she assured him.

Kiwi gave in and stood in the stirrups to swing his leg over the cantle. With a groan, he discovered that all the muscles he hadn't used for years were stiff, sore, and almost immobile. He dropped to the ground, hobbled his horse, and followed Mila's example of disappearing into the bushes to relieve himself. When he returned, she had removed bread and sausages from one of her bags, thrown a tarpaulin on the ground, and seated herself cross-legged upon it. Kiwi lowered himself with another groan as all his aches and pains assaulted him. Mila laughed with a knowing look in her eye and commented, "Not ride far for long time?"

"About two decades!" Kiwi exaggerated.

In answer, Mila offered him a chunk of dark bread and a long slice of salami. Ravenous, he took her offering gladly. "Everything arranged for me?" She asked.

"You fly back with us and after that, while I don't know the details, you can trust Wing Commander Priestman. When he gives his word on something, you can bank on it."

Mila seemed to consider that and then she held out a flask from which she'd already drunk. Kiwi sniffed it cautiously, expecting vodka. He was pleasantly surprised to find it was strong, sweet tea. He drank deeply and thanked her as he handed it back. Throughout this exchange, Mila watched him intently. Although her expression was not hostile her staring was making Kiwi nervous. Defensively he asked, "Something wrong?"

"You are English?" She asked with big, molten bronze eyes.

"No, I'm a Kiwi, a New Zealander."

Her lovely eyes widened in amazement. There was, he realised, something strangely childlike about this veteran partisan. Out here in the woods, she looked ten years younger than the officer who had so rudely awakened him this morning in the train station. "You are from bottom of world?"

Kiwi laughed, "Yeah, we do call it 'down under,' but it's right side up for us."

Kiwi suspected she hadn't understood him because she changed the subject. "But you know England?" She asked with strange earnestness.

"Lived there the last eight years of my life."

That answer brought a smile to her face. "Tell me! Tell me!"

"Tell you what?" Kiwi asked back confused yet charmed by her innocent enthusiasm. Maybe it was just that her elementary English made her sound like a child, but her round face glowed with eagerness too.

"True is no famine there?"

"Famine? In England?" Kiwi asked back incredulously. Then with a laugh, he assured her, "Not in a thousand years! People are tired of some things still being rationed, but no one goes hungry."

"Galyna say electricity is everywhere." With her arms, she tried to encompass the whole world.

"Pretty much," Kiwi agreed.

"And bathrooms inside?"

Kiwi laughed and nodded. "That's the norm nowadays."

"Is it pretty? Forests are like this?" She gestured around them.

"Not like this," Kiwi answered, "but there are forests." As he answered it dawned on him that her questions sprang from the fact that she expected to be in England soon. For the first time, he gave a thought to what a huge leap she was taking. This was no sophisticated diplomat with experience in the West, no cynical spy familiar with both sides nor even a scientist or artist with international connections. This tough partisan fighter sounded as if she was still a naive and guileless girl — and she looked so young he found himself asking, "How old are you, Mila?"

"Me?" She drew back startled, pointing to her chest questioningly. He nodded. "Twenty-two," she admitted, flashing her ten fingers at him twice and then holding up two fingers just to be sure she had it right. Then, her eyes twinkling and a teasing smile on her lips, she asked back cheekily, "You?"

"I'm a grizzled old wolf of thirty-two — ten years your senior. But if you're only 22 now, you couldn't have been more than 18 when the war ended — and" he calculated, "only 14 when the Soviet Union was invaded." Christ, he thought, she was only a kid when she went to war. How did a girl-child become a war hero before she was 18? All right, he'd been briefed. He knew she'd killed more than a hundred men, something he could readily believe of the gruff Russian officer who had woken him. Yet it didn't seem so suited to this curious girl.

Mila had looked away and she wrapped her arms around her knees. Sensing his gaze and maybe the direction of his thoughts, she looked over her shoulder at him. "I want new life in England. No famine. No killing. No police. I want to say, 'Prime Minister bad' if I want."

"What about your family? Aren't you sorry to leave them behind?"

"Stalin kill Kulaks. Parents, uncles, aunts, cousins. Starve. Gulag. Shot in head by police. Others killed in war — some by Germans, some by Russians. War end. More famine. Sister dead. Typhus."

"No husband?"

Mila shook her head sharply and looked away, her head on her knees. Then she looked over her shoulder at him and tossed him one of her impish smiles. "And you? Wife?"

"Walked out on me for a richer man."

Mila broke into a smile and declared. "She stupid woman." Then she got to her feet, dusted off the seat of her pants and announced. "Must go. Sun sinking."

Kiwi had forgotten about that and tried to get up, only to have his various muscles protest so rudely that he fell back onto the tarpaulin with a groan. Mila laughed at him like a comrade and held out her hand.

"I weigh a lot more than you do, kid!" Kiwi told her bluntly.

She tossed her head, stamped her foot and demandingly held out her hand again.

"You asked for it," he warned. He laid his hand in hers and was instantly in a vicelike grip as she yanked him upward with astonishing strength. On his feet, he gave her a look of amazement that made her laugh. As she turned away to unhobble her horse, however, Kiwi thought she was flushed.

After their break, Mila took up a trot again, but the horses weren't rested, and they weren't cooperating. They could kick and prod the poor nags they were riding, but the pack horse kept baulking. Kiwi started to get nervous. "Just how much farther is it?" He asked as Mila went back to whack the miserable pack horse into motion again.

"If horses won't trot, two hours, maybe three," Mila admitted.

"Two hours! But the sun will have set by then!" Kiwi protested in horror. "I can't survey the surrounding countryside for a suitable place to land in the dark! I need to see what I'm doing!" He started envisaging the impending disaster. If he overlooked some obstacle and Kit crashed on landing, they'd all be trapped in the Soviet Zone with no way out — not to mention the crash would attract the Soviet and German police from a hundred miles around.

"No problem," Mila answered unperturbed. "Tomorrow you look,"

"Tomorrow is too late! The plane is coming tonight!"

"No," Mila shook her head. "Today Saturday. Plane come Sunday."

A chill of shock pierced to Kiwi's bone marrow. Somewhere along the line, there had been a disconnect. When the RAF said Sunday at 1:50 am, they meant the night from Saturday to Sunday, but Mila and evidently Christian had understood the rescue would occur on Sunday night, meaning Monday at 1:50 am. In retrospect, this misunderstanding explained why Christian had felt they could afford to parachute in so far away. In retrospect, Kiwi should have questioned him earlier, but he'd assumed — stupidly — that he had only a short trip from Schwerin and that he and Mila would cover it in a few hours. Now it was too late. Kit would be over tonight, flying low, drawing attention to the location, and there would be no flarepath and no Emily and no way to tell him what had happened.

Night Flight
RAF Gatow
Sunday 27 February 1949
(Day 247 of the Berlin Airlift)

There was no briefing in a Nissen hut with smoke from a hundred cigarettes swirling under the arched ceiling. There was no map with red yarn marking the route to the "target for tonight." There was no kitting up in the crew room with scores of other airmen making bad jokes and worrying about good luck charms. Nor was there an icy ride in the back of a lorry to dispersal. Yet it still felt like — and was — an "op" all the same.

As Kit stepped inside the EAS hangar, Gordon MacDonald waved to him. The crew chief was supervising the final preparations from his wheelchair. The German mechanics had finished refuelling and Winterfeld was polishing the Perspex surfaces, while the other two took the chocks away in preparation for rolling the Mossie onto the apron.

Kit joined the crew chief and, reverting to MacDonald's wartime nickname, remarked, "Wish you were coming with me, Daddy. It's going to be lonely up there all on my own." Kit had served nearly two tours on Lancasters, and they carried a crew of seven. His relationship with his crewmates had been a major source of strength, and aside from his courtship of Georgina, his best memories of the war were of times with them in the air and on the ground.

Daddy grasped Kit's hand but admitted, "Can't pretend I want to join you, Skip." MacDonald had always hated flying.

Kit thought to ask about the company Halifaxes still fully engaged in flying the Airlift, "No problems with Peggy and Albie, are there?"

"Nothing we can't fix with a screwdriver," MacDonald assured him, adding. "Bruce is bursting his buttons sitting in the lefthand seat now and again." With Kit no longer flying on the Airlift, Bruce was allowed to fly as first pilot whenever Captain Peabody had a day off.

Kit laughed, glad to hear that his second pilot was doing well. Meanwhile, Anna joined them. After exchanging greetings, she begged, "Please remember that Emily has broken bones. The sternum will be painful but is embedded in her chest. I'm more worried about her wrist. She must not put any weight on it, which means she can't use it to pull herself up a ladder or push away from anything, either. Someone is going to have to help her board." Anna sounded very concerned, and Kit reassured her that Kiwi would be there to help.

Meanwhile, the ground crew were pushing the Mossie out. Kit zipped up his fight jacket and took his parachute over his shoulder to follow them. He'd only just put his foot on the first rung of the flimsy metal ladder leading up to the cockpit when Robin arrived. He was in his greatcoat and cap, looking every inch the Station Commander. Like the rest of them, he had not gone to bed this evening.

"What's your flying time tonight, Kit?" Robin asked.

Kit appreciated that the senior officer — and husband with so much at stake — had not attempted to interfere with his planning. He'd scrupulously left the decision-making to Kit. At this stage, however, Kit felt he owed Robin as much detail as possible. "The target is roughly 120 miles north of us as the crow flies. I could be there in 20 minutes if I flew directly at maximum speed, but I might draw attention to myself followed by suspicion. Instead, I've chosen a circuitous route at a normal cruising speed — imitating a night training exercise. I intend to approach from the northwest, where the population density is lowest and lose altitude gradually as I near the target. I'll circle at 150 to 200 feet giving the signal. Once the flares are lit, I'll go in, take the three passengers on board and depart immediately. At that point, unless pursued, I'll fly back fast and low, heading directly for the Frohnau beacon, where I'll join the Airlift traffic. All in all, I expect to be back on the ground no later than two hours from now."

Robin nodded. "That's good. I checked the Met for you and they're still reporting clear skies and good visibility. At the moment, the wind is out of the east at five to ten miles an hour and is expected to remain that way for three to four hours." These were ideal conditions for the attempted landing, and Kit nodded with satisfaction. But Robin warned, "Conditions are predicted to deteriorate later, so try to get back as soon as you can. I'll be waiting for you."

"We'll all be waiting for you," MacDonald corrected, echoed by Anna and the ground crew.

Kit stayed with the stream of Airlift traffic from Gatow into the outbound corridor and turned north only after passing Brandenberg. He switched off his navigation lights before peeling off and was now all but invisible both to the naked eye and to radar. Unlike during the war, there was no blackout on the ground, but the Soviet Zone was too poor to glitter. Headlights on the roads were rare at this time of night, and most of the inhabitants had gone to bed. However, streetlights lit up major road junctures, train stations and military installations, and the very sparseness of the lights, particularly in rural areas, made it easier to identify the major towns. Schwerin was especially easy to locate because of its large lakes, and Sternberg was the first town east of Schwerin large enough to boast of street lights. After passing Sternberg at 5,000 feet, Kit swung onto a southeast course and sank down to two thousand feet.

Below was forest and open countryside; the former was dark grey and the latter light grey. Exactly on time, the waning moon, still 90% full, lifted itself over the horizon and lit up the countryside. The brightness exposed cottages, sheds, and barns as well as an abandoned tractor, a derelict tank, and some unidentifiable ruins. Meanwhile, smaller lakes and ponds reflected the moonlight turning them into puddles of brilliant silver.

Kit followed a narrow, secondary road until he saw the distinctive shape of the lake on which the former convent sat. He throttled back and sank lower to the earth, scanning the ground intently for people, motion, or a cart to transport Emily. Nothing. The night landscape was still and motionless except for the shadow of his Mossie as it galloped across the snow.

He flew to the cloister complex looking for some sign of life, but not a light glimmered. The monastery looked like a deserted, medieval ruin. He circled twice, hoping to arouse some response. A light in a window or a torch flashed from the ground. Still nothing.

He flew back to the northwest, the area he and Kiwi believed was the most suitable for landing. Although he flew practically at stalling speed and at lower than 100 feet, he still could find not a single living soul or, indeed, any evidence of preparations such as footprints or markers in the snow.

Baffled and uneasy, he returned to the cloister a second time. Just when he was about to despair, a pinpoint of light blinked at him from one of the twin steeples. He turned his head to focus on the tower. There! It came again and again, but the light wasn't steady. It flashed irregularly. He banked around trying to keep the light in sight. He concluded it was signalling in Morse.

Tensely concentrating on the sequence of flashing, he started to spell out the letters out loud: R – O — then dot-dash-dash for W. Kit had run out of space. He passed beyond the twin steeples and could no longer see the signal. He banked hard and circled around to approach again. There it was! A dash, pause, three dashes, pause, two dashes —

Suddenly, bright lights went on in the village beyond the cloister. These could only be from military vehicles, a conclusion confirmed when a moment a flare shot into the air and then a beam of light was directed into the sky in his direction. The sound of his engines must have aroused suspicion. Kit pushed the throttle forward and experienced the exhilaration of rapid flight at low altitude. Shooting northeast at just over 400 mph, he sought to confuse and deceive whoever he had wakened. He dared not return to the "target." Instead, he flew by a circuitous route back to Berlin.

He had been gone less than two hours when he landed back at Gatow. As he switched off the engines, an eager, smiling crowd poured out of the hangar to greet the passengers he did not have. Even Georgina and Galyna were here, he noted glumly, as he shoved open the cockpit window to shake his head and turn his thumb down. Then he completed the cockpit procedures for shutting down and dropped onto the tarmac.

Robin was waiting for him. "What happened?" he asked in a raw voice. "Have the Russians found her already?"

"I don't think so," Kit replied. "I think there is just a delay of some sort. Someone flashed a signal in Morse saying 'Tomorrow.'"

Robin nodded woodenly and retorted bitterly, "A low-pressure system is forecast to sweep through shortly before dawn bringing colder temperatures, blustery winds and snow. The chances of our bringing off a rescue tomorrow are almost nil."

Chapter Nineteen
Mosquito Bite

RAF Gatow
Sunday 27 February 1949
(Day 247 of the Berlin Airlift)

The howling of the wind through the ruined arches of the cloisters woke Kiwi. Stumbling out of the box bed into the bitter cold of the cell where he'd slept, he peered out of the window at heavy snow lashed by a strong gale. Kiwi cursed colourfully. What the hell were they going to do now? Kit couldn't possibly fly in this muck, which meant they were all stuck here until the weather cleared — or the Russians found them. Whichever came first.

Cursing again under his breath, he pulled on his filthy clothes. At least he'd been able to bathe and wash his underwear the night before. Still, he longed for clean clothes, decent clothes — and the safety of Gatow.

He was worried about Emily, too. She'd been overjoyed to see him — thankful to the point of tears, and almost giddy at the thought that she would soon be back with Robin at Gatow. Yet there was no denying that she looked poorly. She was obviously in considerable pain, and the lack of medical attention gnawed at her. She'd repeated several times that she 'just wished' she could have her bones X-rayed to be sure everything was healing properly. He had never seen her look so fragile, and he sensed that her emotional state was brittle. Yet last night she had believed she was about to be rescued; today that no longer looked likely.

Kiwi found his way to the lavatory and then joined the others who had collected in the kitchen. Emily's welcoming smile was weak, her disappointment and fears stood naked on her face, and she did not speak. At least the wood-burning stove gave off steady heat and tea had been made for them.

As he sat down, one of the old women gave Kiwi a plate, another brought a cup and saucer, and a third offered him bread. He thanked them but ate in silence, acutely conscious of being the only male in the entire complex. It was an odd feeling.

As he finished, Victoria Louise looked at her watch and reminded them, "Today is Sunday. Father Andreas always comes from Goldberg to celebrate Mass at 11:00 am. People from the surrounding region often join us. We must prepare for them." Turning to her visitors, she added earnestly, "You must stay out of sight and make as little noise as possible." With this, she and her companions stood, cleared away their dishes, and disappeared in the direction of the church.

When they were gone, the silence became oppressive. Kiwi felt the weight of Emily's despondency and wished he could find something encouraging or comforting to say. Instead, the wind howled, and snow started to collect on the windowsills, slowly cutting off the view.

Abruptly, Mila turned to Kiwi, "How many flares we need?"

"Flares? Nothing is flying in this weather!"

"Maybe clear by tonight," Mila countered.

Ashamed of himself, Kiwi realised she was right. He kicked himself out of his blue funk, and answered, "Right. Have you checked if we have the materials we need?" Galyna had been briefed about what they needed and tasked with passing the word to Mila.

"Paraffin in cellar. Victoria Louise give two, old sheets. Old tins outside. Collect for military. I bring tins; we make flares. How many tins you need?"

"For a thousand-foot runway, we need a minimum of ten flares — but twenty would be better."

"Good. We make twenty. Come!" Mila ordered, and Kiwi docilely followed her out of the back door to fetch the tins.

Within minutes they had organised the production: Kiwi ripped the sheets into strips, Mila twisted and tied the strips into knots, and Emily dipped them in a vat of paraffin before laying one each into an old tin can. Kiwi loaded the tins back into a carton, and Mila tied some string around it so she could attach it to the panniers of the pack horse.

By the time they had finished with the flares, the snowfall had let up considerably and the sky also seemed lighter. Mila and Kiwi agreed they should investigate the possible landing area. Over Kiwi's protest, Mila insisted on riding. Kiwi's muscles were still stiff and complaining from the ride the day before, but Mila pointed out they could take the flares with them if they took the pack horse. She clinched the argument by saying it was best to avoid leaving human footprints in the snow that led to what they hoped would be their landing strip.

As they led the horses out of the barn, Kiwi noted nearly a dozen horse carts parked in the drive. That was more than he'd expected, and it made him nervous. He and Mila led the horses to the lake before mounting and riding west along the southern shore. At the tip of the lake, they started up a slight slope away from the frozen water. By now the sun was trying to burn through the cloud cover. Kiwi started to hope the rescue might come off after all. With a surge of optimism, he set to work finding the best possible landing path, but the longest stretches of flat open field were at cross angles to the now north westerly wind. The most promising run facing into the eye of the current gale, on the other hand, was severed about a third of the way along by a low hedge, which had produced a large snowdrift. "Damn it!" Kiwi cursed.

"What?" Mila asked.

He explained it to her.

She shrugged. "How big is plane?"

"The wingspan is 55 feet."

"Then we clear drift for sixty feet."

"We'd need to clear closer to eighty or 100 feet in case the wind veers somewhat."

"Start now," Mila replied. "Need axe and shovels."

Leaving the carton of flares hidden under the hedge, they trotted back to St Elizabeth's. The visitors had left, and smoke was wafting gently from the kitchen chimney, promising a hot midday meal. With a sense of improving prospects, they cheerfully entered the kitchen and ran into a wall of gloom.

"What's happened?" Kiwi asked Emily, who looked like she'd just been kicked in the gut.

"The Soviet Secret Police are nearby and looking for me," Emily answered in a tone of hopelessness.

Victoria Louise took over the explanation in a more forceful tone, "Soviet Secret Police troops have come up from Berlin. They scoured the villages south of us, throwing people out of their houses and turning everything up-side down. They've threatened the residents with terrible consequences for sheltering spies. They are currently in Goldberg and planning to continue to Sternberg, but if anyone mentions the Stift, they could be here in less than an hour."

Kiwi checked his watch. It was just after 2 pm. The original plans had called for Kit to arrive at about 2 am to catch the rising moon, but with the change in the weather they could not count on that. He might try to come earlier, but he could not risk coming in by daylight. That meant the earliest the rescue could take place was after dark, or roughly four from now. That wasn't long, but it would still be dangerous to stay at the convent. Out loud he declared, "No flap. We clear out, removing all evidence of our stay and hide near the landing strip." To Victoria Louise, he advised, "Remove all trace of our presence. Clean the dishes we've used. Strip the beds. Wash the sheets and air the rooms. Everything."

"I leave many things," Mila corrected. "They not look for me. I take guns and what I need for England. They ask about me, you say I hunt, back soon, bring meat."

They nodded and set to work with urgency.

The pain was back with a vengeance. Emily's chest felt as though her heart were cramping up, while the slightest movement of her wrist produced sharp stabs of agony. Emily knew she had overstressed both broken bones, but she'd been unable to sit around watching Kiwi and Mila work. While Kiwi and the remarkably tough Mila attacked the hedgerow, axing the branches into tinder and shovelling the snow away, Emily had paced out the landing strip. With her good arm, she'd collected broken bits of hedge to mark where each flare should be placed in the snow. Later, when the gap in the hedge was complete, she'd joined Kiwi and Mila in trying to stomp down the snow to make it level. They weren't entirely successful because they did not have the time or means to dig up the roots, but Kiwi and she thought (or hoped) it would be OK.

As darkness fell, Mila decided to take the horses back to the barn. That seemed risky to Kiwi, but Mila had a mind of her own. Kiwi warned that when Kit came they could not afford to wait. She nodded and insisted, "Back before dark," and left.

Kiwi set to work pushing their improvised flares into the snow at the places Emily had marked. Emily tried to help, but the pain became unbearable. Kiwi ordered her to sit down and rest. "You're going to need your strength when the Mossie gets here," he reminded her.

But sitting in the shelter of the woods meant she had time to think. She was overcome with guilt for not being more grateful and appreciative to Victoria Louise and the other four ladies. They had sheltered, washed, fed and comforted her for over two weeks, yet she had departed head-over-heels in a sudden panic. If the Soviet Secret Police found out what they had done, there was no telling what would happen to them.

If the Soviet Secret Police followed the path made by the horses in the snow, it would bring them straight here.

The sun set but light still lingered on the Western horizon, which suggested it was about 6 pm. There was no knowing when Kit might come — while the Soviet Secret Police might find them at any time at all....

Kit had haunted the Met office all day, but as darkness fell he reported to Robin, "I can't risk waiting any longer. The wind has fallen off for the moment, but it's forecast to pick up again during the night, becoming gusty and variable. Moonlight would have been helpful, but if Kiwi has a flare path for me, I can make do without. If he doesn't have it ready, I'm going to have to abort anyway."

"Understood," Robin agreed, and their eyes met. Kit would not have swapped places with him for the world. It was much easier having a job to do — and knowing Georgina was safe.

The flares were in place and ready to be lit, and Kiwi had joined Emily in the shelter of the trees as the last remnants of light faded from the Western sky. Suddenly Kiwi grunted in alarm and sprang to his feet. "What is it?" Emily asked instantly frightened.

"Over there," Kiwi whispered as he pointed in the direction of the lake and the towering trees around the convent. "The sky seems to be lit up."

Emily followed his gaze. He was right. They looked at one another. Since the convent had no electricity, the light could only come from vehicles — lots of vehicles. The Soviet Secret Police! And Mila wasn't back yet. Had she betrayed them? Or been trapped? Maybe she could talk herself out of trouble. She was a Hero of the Soviet Union after all. Maybe—

Kiwi tensed again, "Did you hear that?"

"What?"

"Someone's behind us!" Kiwi leapt to his feet and spun around to peer into the forest. They both held their breath, listening intently.

Something cracked, branches rustled, and a low, breathless voice came out of the darkness. "It's me. Mila." A moment later, a shadow separated itself from the trees wearing a thick backpack and carrying a rifle in her right hand. When she reached them, she gasped out. "Soviet Secret Police. Many men. Make search."

"Did they see you?"

"No. I stay in barn. Watched from crack. Men go inside, I leave. Took long way. Try to cover tracks, but ...." She made a gesture that suggested she was not happy.

Although it was what they'd feared, it was still frightening. Emily tried to tell herself that the Soviets would not kill them. They had released Anna, Rick and Jan, after all. Maybe she should just have surrendered to them in the beginning. Then she wouldn't have endangered Victoria Louise and the other women — or Kiwi. But it was too late for that.

Kit opted to fly low, fast and direct. It wasn't just the weather forecast. He felt an irrational urgency about today's flight. The 24-hour delay had stretched their luck. The old sense of dicing with the devil was back.

He peeled away from the outbound corridor almost as soon as he left Berlin airspace. He flew at 1,000 feet to keep below the incoming Airlift traffic as he headed north, acutely aware that they would be alarmed by the sight of a stray aircraft flying against the flow. Then again, they would probably assume he was Soviet. The low altitude reduced his perspective and meant he was navigating by the landmarks directly below him. He followed the Berlin-Hamburg autobahn until it split just before Wittstock. Here he veered right taking the route via Plauen. When he had the lake behind him, he banked northeast along the secondary road that diverged from the autobahn and headed for Goldberg.

Over Goldberg, he sensed that something was wrong. It was nearing 7:30 pm on a wintry, Sunday night. Up to now, all the towns, villages and farms had nestled beneath the light coat of snow like children sleeping under a blanket. Suddenly, an inordinate number of cars clogged the streets and people stood and moved this way and that in apparent confusion or agitation. Kit was flying too fast to get a good look, but he glimpsed red stars on the doors of the heavy lorries, and many of the men wore Russian military uniforms with guns over their shoulders. At the sound of his engines, faces lifted to stare at him.

More unsettling, light lit up the sky ahead of him. Jasha had reported that the St Elizabeth Stift did not have electricity, so any lights had to be external. As he neared, he spotted vehicles crowding the courtyard, their headlights flooding the façade. A black Mercedes probably inherited from the Gestapo stood directly before the entrance with the back door flung open. The Russians had arrived!

Kit's first instinct was to flee back to Berlin with the horrifying news. Robin needed to know what had happened at once. General Robinson had to go into action. But in the time it took to think that the Mossie had crossed over the lake and something was winking at him. Dot. Dot-Dash. Dot-dot-dot. E-A-S in Morse. Kit reached for his navigation lights and flipped them on and off in the same pattern.

Instantly, two people broke out of the trees and ran into the field below. Kit reefed the Mosquito around in a tight turn and watched as the first flickers of light appeared in two gradually lengthening lines.

This was it, he registered, but he also recognised that his very presence alerted the Soviets to what was happening. The lights around the convent complex had become agitated. Vehicles were moving, lights were spreading away from the building.

Emily heard the Merlin engines first and called out, "That must be Kit!"

The others lifted their heads and listened for only a second. Then Kiwi pulled his torch from his inside pocket and moved to where he could aim it at the sound. He flashed the code three times, and the navigation lights returned the code. Instantly, Mila and Kiwi dashed out into the field to start lighting the flares leaving Emily alone to reflect that Kit had arrived at the worst possible moment. If he had not come now, the Soviet Secret Police might have simply departed having found nothing in the Stift. As it was, he was leading the Russians straight towards them. With a horrible knotting in her stomach, she looked towards the trees shrouding the medieval complex. She was sure the lights were getting closer.

Kit turned his attention back to the flarepath and registered that it pierced a hedge. The gap was barely wide enough for the Mossie's wings and the wind was already veering more to the west. This was not going to be easy.

He banked around hard to point the Mossie's nose straight at the gap in the hedge. Then he throttled back to stalling speed. On the Mossie that was 120 mph. He kissed the snow with the undercarriage as close as possible to the first two flickering flares and the Mossie careered forward at a tremendous speed, the brakes virtually useless on the snow. Coming abreast of the hedge, the wheels hit a bump, and the aircraft was flung up, briefly losing contact with the ground altogether. For a moment it soared above the snow, then dropped back down to skid forward, yawing into a flat spin. Kit tried to counter the spin with the rudder and the Mossie slid to a halt just short of the last pair of flares facing 45 degrees to starboard. He was on the ground in one piece, but taking off was going to be trickier.

Emily winced as Kit hit the remnants of the drift and bounced up. She thanked God when he recovered. Yet even as he turned the Mossie around to taxi down the improvised runway in her direction, she heard from the opposite direction lorry engines groaning, gears grinding and men shouting.

Kiwi shouted, "Go! To the cockpit! Mila and I can manage better in the bomb bay."

Emily stepped out of the woods and jogged as best she could towards the start of the runway. Kit stopped the Mossie, and without shutting down the engines, opened the hatch and let down the ladder. With her broken wrist pressed against her belly, she tried to drag herself upwards, but the pain in her chest was overwhelming. It took her breath away. She cried out in frustration and despair as she realised she was helpless. She would doom them all.

Suddenly, Kiwi was behind her shoving and lifting her upwards. She found the strength to pull with her good arm, and Kit grabbed her under her arms to heave her into the cockpit. Breathless and trembling she sank into the navigator's seat.

In the next instant, the cockpit was bathed in brittle light. It was like being coned by searchlights. Squinting and trying to shield her eyes, she looked out to see a Mercedes and three Russian lorries approaching. The Mercedes slithered to a halt and the door opened. A Soviet officer climbed out, waving a pistol over his head.

In the next instant, he crumpled up in the snow dropping his pistol. Shouts penetrated the noise made by the engines and scores of soldiers poured over the sides of the lorries. Beside her, Kit nursed the throttles and rudders to turn the aircraft around in place, ready to race back up the runway.

Kiwi's feet had only just hit the ground after helping Emily when he heard the crack of gunfire and realised Mila was standing between the aircraft and the Russians with her rifle at her shoulder. He saw the lead officer from the Mercedes go down, and then two more men crumpled up before Mila turned and ran towards the aircraft. Behind him, the hydraulics groaned, indicating Kit had pulled the lever to open the bomb bay doors. Just then one of the Russians started firing an automatic weapon, and Mila dropped.

Kiwi didn't think. He sprinted across the snow and caught Mila under one arm. He felt her push herself up onto her knee and start staggering forward. He drew her closer and ran with his arm around her shoulder, half dragging and half carrying her towards the Mossie that trembled and danced in impatience.

Kiwi lifted Mila off the ground and shoved her onto one of the panels of the partially opened bomb bay door. He heard her yelp with pain but could not afford to be gentle as he heaved himself onto the other door. Inside, he pounded with his fist on the fuselage as bullets thunked into the wood, sending splinters flying. A second later, the bomb bay doors clunked shut and the engines howled. The Mossie started to gallop forward.

Kiwi felt them hit the snow drift, stagger, and start to tip forward onto their nose. Instinctively, he covered his head with his arms in anticipation of disaster. Somehow Kit recovered. They were still racing forward but bouncing as well. The wings were starting to lift them up. They swayed, caught by a gust of wind. The aircraft rolled to the right, and Mila cried out in pain and fright as she was flung against the fuselage. For another horrible second, Kiwi thought the Mossie was about to stall and crash, but again Kit recovered. They were in a thirty-degree climbing turn and the engines were howling in fury. Then quite abruptly, Kit righted the aircraft and throttled back from emergency boost and Kiwi knew they had found cloud cover.

He sat up immediately to turn his attention to Mila. She was crumpled up, clutching her side, and shivering. Kiwi grabbed the blankets Anna had spread out and stowed so carefully to bundle them around her. His hands came away wet and sticky. He tried to remove her backpack to make her more comfortable, but she resisted. "No," she gasped. "No. Everything. Here. Need." Her English was fading under the onslaught of pain and fear. Kiwi crawled to the stowed medical kit and removed the morphine. He returned to Mila and showed her the syringe. "Morphine."

She nodded.

He remembered from wartime briefings that it was important to inject the morphine into a fatty muscle like the upper thigh or buttocks, but Mila was dressed in thick layers against the cold. He opted to undo the lowest buttons of her tunic and give her the injection in her stomach fat. She seemed to relax almost at once. As he finished, she caught his hand. "Kiwi?"

"Yes?"

"You came back."

"Of course."

She gazed at him with her big, childlike eyes and said something he couldn't understand, but he sensed it had been an expression of gratitude.

Kit had taken off at 19:12. Robin knew because he had stood at the window of his office and watched as the distinctive twin-engine aircraft in its unique white-grey-black camouflage lifted off his runway. He knew that even in ideal circumstances, Kit would not return within an hour. Yet by 8 o'clock, Robin could not concentrate on anything. He pushed his paperwork aside and paced around his office, thinking about all the things that might go wrong. He dared not plan what he would do if things went well, much less let himself think that Emily might be with him tonight. To anticipate success might jinx the rescue.

Out of the corner of his eye, something moved in the dark sky beyond the glare of the hardstandings and runways. It was as if lightning had momentarily lit up the sky in the middle of nowhere, far away from the flight path, but there was no electrical storm forecast for tonight. He turned to stare into the night. The Airlift freighters receded into the distance like a chain of widely spaced diamonds on the soft black backdrop of the overcast sky. They were all in a clear line, but the motion or light had come out of the deeper darkness over the Soviet Zone. Robin scanned that sector of the sky with intense concentration — and his blood ran cold. Gently arching through the night sky was a red flare. A red flare meant "wounded on board."

Robin left his office at a run and took the stairs up to the control tower two at a time. As he burst in, he heard chatter over the airwaves confirming what he'd seen. Several pilots were reporting seeing a flare. Many former bomber pilots now flew on the Airlift. They reported the flare with: "Wounded on board," or "Priority landing for wounded."

Garth called over his shoulder to the radar room, "Do you have him on radar yet?" He got a negative reply as Hart instructed another aircraft, "Do not leave the taxiway. Repeat, hold in place. We have an inbound emergency."

Garth was talking into a microphone standing up. "We do not have you on radar. What is your altitude?"

Kit's voice crackled over the airwaves, "One-thousand two hundred feet."

"Got him!" a voice shouted from the radar room and immediately began to give instructions.

Robin left the tower and hastened to the ambulance station, but it had already left. He hailed a "Follow Me!" vehicle that had just led a York to its off-loading position and ordered the driver to take him to the end of the PSP runway. Ahead of him, the red lights of the ambulance undulated impatiently. Robin leapt out of the open jeep almost before it came to a halt. He fixed his gaze on the far end of the runway in time to see the Mosquito touch down smoothly and roll calmly towards them. Kit did not appear to be the casualty.

As soon as the Mossie came to a complete halt, Robin was beside it. The bomb bay doors were cranked open manually, evidently to avoid dumping the wounded passengers onto the tarmac. Before they were fully open, Kiwi dropped out and crawled from under the belly of the aircraft shouting to the orderlies. "Hurry but be gentle! She's taken at least two bullets. One may have pierced her lung."

Christ, no! Robin thought, unable to take in all the implications. Then someone took hold of his arm. He spun about prepared to tear a strip off whoever was distracting him at a time like this. Then he realised it was Emily. He threw his arms around her so fiercely that she yelped with pain. He released his hold, only to have her lean against him and murmur, "Hold me, Robin. Just do it gently, please."

Robin complied and they stood like that with no need for words, as the orderlies extracted Mila from the Mossie and loaded her into the ambulance. They watched as Kiwi climbed in the back of the ambulance lugging Mila's backpack over one shoulder. As the ambulance wailed its way through the darkness, Robin and Emily turned to one another to kiss before walking away hand in hand.

Chapter Twenty
Fall Out

Baggage
Berlin-Charlottenburg
Monday 28 February 1949
(Day 248 of the Berlin Airlift)

"Sir?" Someone was shaking him. Kiwi awoke from a deep sleep like a swimmer who has dived deep and is paddling towards the surface. He was filthy and smelling. His face and neck inched from the growth of his beard, and his breath was bad. He was also stiff and aching from riding horses, lying in freezing bomb bays, and sleeping in hard chairs.

"Sir?" The voice demanded his attention, and he focused on a man with thick glasses and a white coat. A doctor? Of course, he had stayed with the ambulance when it proceeded to one of Berlin's hospitals because the infirmary at Gatow was not equipped for surgery.

"It looks like the patient is going to pull through. The operation was a success, and we were able to extract both bullets without causing significant additional trauma. The lung was bruised but not punctured. She's just recovered consciousness, and we are preparing to transfer her back to Gatow as instructed."

Kiwi nodded numbly as the orders he'd been given came back to him. Under no circumstances, Ft/Lt Boyd had said, were the Soviets to be allowed near Mila. Since it was not always easy to tell Soviet sympathisers from other Germans, Kiwi had been told not to let Mila out of his sight except during surgery. Instead, he'd fallen into such a deep sleep that ten Russians could have come and whisked her away without him noticing.

Before he had time to feel too guilty, however, an RAF corporal asked.

"Do you want us to bring the patient down?" With relief, Kiwi registered that the two RAF ambulance orderlies had also stayed with the patient. Fortunately, they sounded more alert than he felt and had apparently kept watch.

"We'll bring her down to the emergency entrance if you'll bring your ambulance around," the doctor answered.

The RAF orderlies nodded, put their caps on and prepared to go. Now that he was awake, however, it struck Kiwi that this might be the perfect opportunity for someone to spirit Mila out of the back door into a waiting Russian ambulance, while the RAF waited docilely out in front. "I'll escort the patient down," he announced firmly, leaving no room for contradiction.

"Very well," the doctor answered and gestured for him to follow.

Just as he was about to leave the waiting room, the nurse at the reception desk called after him, "Sir! You've forgotten your rucksack!"

Remembering how Mila had clung to the backpack on the flight, Kiwi concluded it must contain all she now owned. He told the doctor to wait, collected the bag, and then followed him down a corridor to a recovery room. This was brightly lit, a testimony to the efficiency of the liquid fuel deliveries; Berlin was at last receiving sufficient fuel for Berlin hospitals to operate their diesel generators whenever the citywide electricity was cut off.

In the recovery room, Mila lay on the wheeled stretcher wearing a flimsy and threadbare hospital gown under a single sheet. Her long hair had been stuffed under a surgical cap. Kiwi had never seen her look so small or so vulnerable. He pictured how she'd stood in the open, bathed in light from the Russian headlights and silhouetted against the snow; she'd calmly raised her rifle to her shoulder and shot just three times — killing with each bullet. Only now did he fully grasp what she had done: She'd stopped in the open rather than take cover beside the aircraft to draw fire away from the cockpit. The girl knew her business and had risked her life to help Emily escape.

But what would happen to her now? She had left everything behind. Not only her material possessions but also her identity and status. In the West, she wasn't a hero or an officer. She also had no family, no job, and no property. Everything she owned was in her battered, old backpack. No wonder it was so heavy, dragging down his shoulder.

He stepped closer, coming into her line of vision, and her eyes lit up. "Kiwi! You waited!"

"Of course, I did!" He gave her his hand, and she clutched it.

"Will you stay with me, Kiwi?"

"Yes, I'm here to see you safely back to Gatow."

She seemed to want to answer, but the German orderlies arrived and started to wheel Mila out of the recovery room. Kiwi walked beside the stretcher, holding Mila's hand until they went out into the cold and cloudy morning. The RAF orderlies helped shift Mila onto one of their stretchers and lifted her inside the ambulance. They then climbed into the cab, and Kiwi clambered into the back with Mila. The ambulance trembled as the engine was turned on and swayed its way out of the hospital drive and onto the street.

Kiwi sat opposite Mila, and she reached out her hand. Kiwi thought she looked like a frightened child — so unlike that horrible Russian officer he had first encountered, or even the competent partisan who had made flares and cleared the hedge. Now she was injured and among strangers. He took her hand in his and squeezed it.

A little voice reached him through the darkness, "Thank you. Galyna says get new name. No one know about Soviet partisan..." Her voice trailed away.

The mention of Borisenko reminded Kiwi that Mila wasn't completely alone after all; the WAAF corporal was also a friend. Yet sensing Mila's fear, he assured her, "That's right. No one will know about your past."

Mila rolled her head back and forth. "Good. Only..."

"Is something worrying you?" he asked.

"Never finished school. Don't write good. No job. Only thing I do good is kill. Don't want to kill any more."

Kiwi reached out with his other hand and stroked the side of her face. As he'd suspected, his hand came away wet. Tears were oozing from the corners of her eyes and slowly trickling down the side of her face. "Mila," he said gently, "that part of your life is over. I'm sure you'll get more than a new name. They'll have to give you some kind of training too." He had no idea if it were true.

"You help?" She asked, looking at him with great trusting eyes.

"I'll help any way I can, but I'm not important or influential or a hero like you. My wife left me because I was a failure in civilian life. Then I hit the bottle. I only got this job on the Airlift because of friends, and the Airlift won't last forever. Then I don't know where my next meal will be coming from. I don't have a house or an inheritance—"

Mila silenced him with a squeeze of her hand, and he realised he'd looked away when he started talking about himself. Her hand-squeeze made him look at her again and he was startled to see she was smiling. "You capitalist — house, inheritance. Me good Communist. We stay together. Work. Share."

Kiwi liked the sound of that. He could picture working with Mila. There was something practical, down-to-earth and utterly reliable about her despite her dramatic past. She reminded him of his hard-working mother. But he wasn't going to rush into anything, so he answered cautiously, "You may be on to something. We'll talk about it when you're feeling better."

On arrival at Gatow, the ambulance door opened to reveal Corporal Borisenko. Kiwi nodded a greeting to the WAAF before explaining to Mila that he had to get some sleep, a bath and a change of clothes. He promised to visit her later. As the orderlies transferred the stretcher to a wheeled cart, the two women clasped hands and spoke in emotion-laden Ukrainian. Kiwi, feeling superfluous, stopped one of the orderlies to hand over Mila's rucksack. "These are her things," he explained.

"Crikey! That weighs a ton!" the orderly complained. "What's she got in here? Gold ingots?" He lifted it and pried the canvas apart a little to peer inside — only to exclaim in astonishment, "There's nothing here but a bunch of papers!"

Frowning and disbelieving, Kiwi reached over and undid the buckle to look inside himself. The orderly was right. Baffled, Kiwi pulled a handful of paper out.

"Put those back!" Corporal Borisenko called out in alarm. "They are top secret Soviet documents!"

Stunned, Kiwi handed the rucksack with its sensitive content over to Borisenko and turned to gaze again at Mila. She had brought absolutely nothing for herself, just intelligence to help her new country.

From Potsdam with Love
Berlin-Charlottenburg
Monday 28 February 1949
(Day 248 of the Berlin Airlift)

As soon as she had escorted Mila to her hospital room, Galyna personally carried the backpack full of documents up to Fl/Lt Boyd's office and announced, "Fl/Lt Boyd? This is what Mila managed to bring out with her."

"What is it?" He asked curiously, getting out of his chair to peer over her shoulder as she removed the stash of documents. These had clearly been stuffed in the canvas sack in a hurry. Some were scrunched up or roughly folded; all lay on top of each other every which way. Yet Boyd's eyes widened more with each fistful of documents Galyna extracted. The print was too small to read the contents or even the subject headings, but the level of classification stamped in large red letters across the surface left Boyd agog.

"Where did she get these?" he asked awestruck.

"Mila said Marshal Sokolovsky went away for the weekend, and she exploited an indiscretion on the part of his adjutant to slip into his office and plunder one of his document safes. She admits she hasn't a clue what she stole. She was in a hurry, and this was the first safe she managed to crack."

"Mila knows how to crack safes?"

"She says that was the best way to get funds as a partisan. They weren't paid, of course, but they needed cash for some things. At first, they tried to ambush German money transports, but these were heavily guarded, and they took terrible casualties. Then Mila, who was very small and looked younger than she was, learned how to sneak into banks and hide until everyone went home. She learned how to listen to the dials until she could open safes in just a few minutes. She would take as much cash as they needed. Never all, she says. She didn't take all the documents either; just what fitted in her backpack. She also mentioned that Sokolovsky isn't due back in his office until later today. The Soviets probably don't know that — much less which — documents have gone missing yet."

Boyd gazed at her speechlessly for a second and then turned his attention back to the stacks of paper on his desk. "We'd better get to work sorting through this treasure trove. We need to categorise and organise everything by subject before we attempt to read through the contents. We'll probably want to fly the most sensitive stuff to London to let them do the analysis, but we should do some preliminary filtering here. I'll clear it with your Section Head, but you must drop all other work and concentrate on finding out what we've got and how important it is. Let's see about bringing a second desk in here, so you can work in a secure and quiet place."

He seemed to hesitate, but then came out with it, "I wasn't supposed to tell you this just yet, but you have been accepted for training by MI6. I was awaiting your transfer orders, which will make it official, but this work requires immediate attention, so we can't stand on ceremony."

Galyna wanted to jump for joy. She couldn't wait to tell Mila — or wasn't she allowed to talk about it? "May I tell anyone?" She asked Boyd.

He laughed shortly, enjoying her excitement. "Yes, you can talk about it — discreetly, of course. You haven't been selected as an operative, just an analyst — like me. I hope that isn't too disappointing." He looked at her questioningly.

Galyna beamed. "Not at all! I'm honoured. I'm thrilled!"

"Well then, let's get to work. I'll ring stores for an extra desk and chair."

Galyna ate her lunch at her new desk, unable to tear herself away from the documents Mila had brought. They were thoroughly disorganised and just putting them back into some kind of order had taken most of the morning. Then she had categorised things broadly under "Personnel Matters," "Moscow Directives," and "Field Reporting." The latter category was broken down again into reports about Germans, other occupation forces, and surveillance on Soviet troops and staff. The last category had the largest number of documents.

The telephone on Boyd's desk rang. Since he was out of the room, Galyna answered it smartly: "Intelligence Section. Corporal Borisenko speaking."

"This is the central switchboard," a woman answered. "I have a woman on the line asking for you, Corporal. She said it was urgent."

Assuming it was Mila, Galyna said, "Put her through, please." The operator responded with, "Connecting you now." There was a click and then Galyn asked eagerly, "Mila?"

"Galyna?" her mother gasped back. "Is that you?"

Galyna recoiled inwardly but replied as neutrally as possible. "Yes, Mother, it's me, and no I am not coming to tea. Not ever again." In the two months since her escape from her stepfather, her mother had made several attempts to lure her back to Potsdam. She'd promised that Ratanov would not be there, but Galyna didn't trust her.

"Galyna!" Her mother wailed dramatically. "I don't know what to do! I need help. You're my daughter. Who else should I turn to?" Galyna stiffened her back with resentment; her mother never gave, only took. Meanwhile, her mother burst into sobs and blubbered, "Maxim Dmitrivich is dead!"

That took Galyna by surprise and she gasped, "Dead? How? When?"

"Last night!" her mother sobbed. "He was away, on a business trip, and he was killed! Shot dead — along with two of his closest subordinates!" She sobbed more loudly.

Galyna did not find her performance convincing, and asked hopefully, "Not Lev Ilyich, too, by any chance?"

"Yes! How did you know?"

"I didn't. He's just the only one of Maxim Dmitrivich's subordinates I've ever met. But I still don't understand. Who shot them and why? Who would dare? Or did the Party turn on them for some reason?" She thought of how her loyal and devoted Communist father had from one day to the next been labelled a traitor and murdered.

"It was that witch! That partisan girl Sokolovsky was so fond of. Maxim always suspected she wasn't genuine. He tried to warn Sokolovsky about her, but the old goat couldn't see straight when it came to her. He wasn't even sleeping with her! He just insisted she was 'cute.' He called her 'the youthful soul of Mother Russia.' And now she's killed my Maxim."

"How appropriate," Galyna commented. She liked the image of Mother Russia in the guise of Mila killing a senior officer of the Soviet Secret Police. The symbolism was precious.

"What did you say?" her mother asked irritated.

"Never mind. You wouldn't understand."

"No! *You* are the one who doesn't understand!" Her mother answered, dropping the tone of grief to express her outrage. "Without Maxim Dmitrivich, I have no right to this house or access to the commissary! I have no right to be in Germany at all! They are going to send me back to the Soviet Union, and not to Moscow, either! They will send me to Kharkiv!"

"Is that so terrible?" Galyna asked back indifferently.

"People there have nothing! No undamaged housing. No coal. There's nothing in the shops! People can't get shoes, blankets, or enough to eat! You told me that yourself!"

"You said it was propaganda," Galyna reminded her.

"Of course I did! What else could I say? You know we can't speak about such things!" She sounded frustrated with Galyna's naivety. "But we know the truth. If I go back without Maxim's protection, I'll literally be on the street and left to starve to death!"

"I'm so sorry, Mother," Galyna replied without a trace of emotion.

"Then help me!" Anastasia shrieked at her.

"How?"

"Get me out! I can get myself to the gate at Gatow. Just meet me there and let me in. If that partisan bitch with the blood of hundreds of men on her hands can defect to the West, why not a great artist? I'm sure I'd be successful in the West! I'll make so much money you won't have to be a soldier and wear that horrible uniform."

"You want to go to the West?"

"Of course! I could live with my mother until I start getting lucrative commissions."

"With your mother?" Galyna asked in a low voice.

"Yes! What would be more natural? You lived with her until you joined the British Air Force."

"Do you realise that you have never once — in all the time I've been here — asked how she was?" Anastasia seemed to grasp she had blundered because she did not answer straight away, giving Galyna the chance to remind her. "You've never asked what she was doing, or about her health, or asked to see a photo of her. You did not ask for her address so you could write to her. You never even bothered to send 'greetings from Potsdam' to her. But now you expect her to welcome you into her home with open arms?"

"She's my mother," Anastasia insisted in a whine.

"Mother." Galyna repeated the word ambivalently, thought about it briefly, and replied firmly, "No, absolutely not. Never." She slammed the phone down and only then realised that Fl/Lt Boyd had returned and stood in the door gazing at her.

"Who was that?" Boyd asked.

"My mother."

"Oh. What did she want?"

"To defect to the West."

"And you turned her down just like that?" He was aghast.

"She's not like Mila. She doesn't hate Stalin or his murderous policies! All she cares about is a better lifestyle."

"I hate to disillusion you, Corporal, but few defectors are as idealistic as your friend Mila. Most change sides purely for personal gain."

"But she wouldn't bring anything valuable with her." Galyna gestured to the papers spread across her whole office.

"I understand, but we could maybe, I mean, for your mother—"

"No! She would only be a millstone around my neck, holding me back, making me miserable! I never want to see or speak to her again."

And that was the end of it.

The Reckoning
Air Ministry, London
Friday 4 March 1949
(Day 252 of the Berlin Airlift)

Robin had expected to have a strip torn off, he had not expected to be called to the Air Ministry. He was ordered to report on short notice at a set time without further details. He flew the Spitfire to Northolt and took public transportation into London. At Ad Astra House, he informed the receptionist of his arrival, saw his name checked against a list, and was asked to take a seat. While he waited, he had ample time to reflect on his future — or lack thereof, but he found it too impenetrable to worry him. He had made a decision, and he did not regret it. Emily was safe. She was recovering her strength, mobility, humour and joie de vivre. She made him whole and content again. Whatever came, they would face it together. And that was that.

"Wing Commander Priestman?" A WAAF Sergeant stood in front of him.

"Yes."

"Follow me, please."

She led him along echoing corridors and up several flights of stairs to stop before a blank door. The WAAF sergeant knocked twice, then pushed down on the handle to open the room to him before stepping back out of his way.

Robin entered and the heavy door thudded shut behind him. He was facing three senior officers seated at the head of a gleaming, mahogany table. The most senior officer was an Air Marshal, KBE, CB, and DFC, supported by an Air Vice Marshal with various medals and ribbons, and an Air Commodore likewise highly decorated. Robin saluted them and was invited to sit down. They removed their caps.

The Air Marshal did not introduce himself or his colleagues, but he looked vaguely familiar. It was less than 15 months since Robin had worked in the Ministry, and putting two and two together he concluded he was facing the Assistant Chief of Air Staff for Intelligence, Sir Lawrence Pendred. The others were presumably members of his staff.

"Wing Commander, we've called you here to learn more about this recent incident involving a defector. There are a number of points that require clarifying."

"Yes, sir."

"First, how did you know that the defector, who held no post of importance and appeared largely ornamental and superfluous, had access to information of such immense value to HM government?"

Robin thought about the question carefully. He could lie and concoct some elaborate story entailing observing her at the ACC. However, he was likely to get himself tangled in his web of lies at some point and expose himself as a fraud. He opted for candour. "I didn't. It was sheer luck."

"Meaning, that you undertook this operation not in anticipation of an intelligence coup but for the selfish purpose of extracting your wife from the Soviet Zone before she fell into Soviet hands?"

Robin did not look down in embarrassment, wriggle in discomfort, or bristle defensively. He looked the Assistant Chief of Air Staff straight in the eye and answered in an unruffled and unrushed tone, "I went through channels requesting urgent assistance. You will find many telephone calls and wire messages in your logs. Only after I received no response, one way or another, did I take matters into my own hands. Note, however, that no RAF personnel were involved much less endangered at any time, and no RAF assets were used in the rescue. I see no grounds for the RAF to object to this private initiative."

"Group Captain Cheshire denies lending you his Mossie. So, just where *did* you get it?"

"Group Captain Cheshire didn't lend me the aircraft. It was leased by Emergency Air Services, the company for which my wife works."

"And the aircrew?"

"They were likewise employees of Emergency Air Services, which has a long-term lease on the hangar from which they operate. The company pays airfield dues and for their aviation fuel."

Pendred frowned slightly but opted not to belabour the point. He moved on sternly, "Be that as it may, you risked a serious international incident."

"Did I?" Robin shot back. "Surely, if things had gone wrong, you would have — honestly and credibly — denied all knowledge of Emergency Air Services and left everyone involved to their fate." For the first time, a faint note of bitterness crept into Robin's controlled voice.

"HM government adamantly and repeatedly rejected Soviet claims that your wife was flying a spy plane when it went down. This operation had the potential to completely discredit us by creating the impression that the ambulance was indeed on an espionage operation," one of the two staff officers interjected sharply.

Robin turned to look at the man before asking with open scepticism, "*Is* that what has happened?"

"Bizarrely, no," Pendred admitted, re-entering the exchange. "The Soviets appear so embarrassed by the defection of this Hero of the Soviet Union that they have resorted to their well-worn tactic of simply denying facts."

"What do you mean?"

"They have erased all mention and memory of the defector."

"How can they do that?" Robin asked astonished.

"Seriously, Wing Commander, for a state that eradicated all evidence of

one of their most important founders, Leon Trotsky, it is child's play to remove from the record any reference to an obscure Ukrainian girl partisan.
This makes everything very simple. Since she never existed, she could not
defect, and no British aircraft violated Soviet air space. The entire incident,
including your flight, never happened."

"Have they 'erased' my wife, as well?" Robin wanted to know.

"Apparently. According to our sources, they have ceased looking for any
missing member of the ambulance's crew presumably on the assumption
that the American woman pilot had tossed them a red herring. It helps, of
course, that the senior Soviet Secret Police officer responsible for investigating the air ambulance crash was killed by your defector."

That made sense. The unit of the Soviet Secret Police that had come close
to disrupting the rescue had arrived in the area looking for Emily. When
Mila, being the professional sharpshooter that she was, consciously picked
off the three most senior officers pursuing them, she decapitated the team
involved in tracking down Emily.

Yet even so, Robin was acutely aware that he and Emily had been exceptionally lucky — so lucky, in fact, that he was awed into silence. Luck like this
surpassed any sane definition of mere chance and felt instead like grace — a
rather intimidating thought.

"Regardless of how the Soviets cope with their embarrassment," Pendred took up the conversation in an admonishing tone, "the fact remains that
you have placed us in an impossible position."

"How so?"

"To the outside world, your illicit operation looks like a spectacular intelligence coup. There have even been suggestions that you deserve some sort
of recognition."

Robin had not known that, but he was beginning to grasp what was
happening. The staff at Gatow and his line superiors, starting with Merer,
assumed that he had acted with the approval of MI6. The men sitting in this
room, on the other hand, knew that he had not. If they admitted, however,
that he had acted entirely on his own authority, they could not take any credit
for what had turned out to be a highly successful operation.

Pendred was saying, "While you did not technically misuse RAF assets or personnel, your actions were completely unsanctioned and represent a breach of trust. As a result, doubt has been cast on your loyalty to the crown." That remark caught Robin off-guard, and his blood started to simmer.

Unaware of his visitor's reaction, Pendred continued in a pompous tone, "As I'm sure you understand, even if your actions did not constitute a violation of the Military Code, your irregular behaviour has cost you the confidence of this Ministry. Under the circumstances, the most elegant solution would be for you to resign for personal reasons. We would then—"

Robin did not allow him to finish, "Before you pass judgment on my loyalty to the crown, HM government should consider the fact that the Soviet Secret Police promised to deliver my wife's dead body if I did not sabotage the fuel depot at Gatow — which, you may have noticed, is still functioning splendidly."

A stunned silence settled over the table. The three senior officers looked at one another. Finally, Pendred asked. "When and how was this threat delivered?"

"A call on my direct line less than 12 hours after the ambulance went down."

"Why didn't you report the threat?"

"Because, sir, I would have been immediately relieved of my command and repatriated to England, while some junior diplomat was charged with pleading with the Soviets to be nice to my wife." Robin met Pendred's eyes without flinching.

For an indefinite period, the two men measured one another. Then Pendred stood and extended his hand. "Thank you for clarifying things for us, Wing Commander. You may return to Gatow for now."

Robin stood, replaced his cap and withdrew. He wasn't sure what the outcome of this encounter would be, and he suspected that Pendred hadn't decided what he would do either. Yet he sensed that he'd won a reprieve. By refusing to disappear quietly, he forced Pendred to choose between taking credit for the defection of a particularly valuable Soviet officer or punishing Robin for his initiative. He could not have his cake and eat it too.

Chapter Twenty-One
In Search of Justice

Verdict
Berlin-Moabit
Friday 11 March 1949
(Day 260 of the Berlin Airlift)

"If I'm found not guilty, will I be released at once?" Charlotte asked Alix when the lawyer arrived at the jail to escort her to the courtroom for the verdict.

Such optimism was a measure of how Charlotte's state of mind had improved during the trial, but Alix was a realist. She avoided any euphoria as she replied, "Yes. You'll walk out of the courtroom a free woman."

"Then shouldn't we take my things with me?" Charlotte pointed to a pitiable bundle of clothes and toiletries which she had been allowed to keep in her cell. Charlotte sensed hesitation in Alix's silence. "Don't you think I'm going to be released?" she asked, suddenly frightened.

"I honestly don't know. I don't trust the presiding judge and, call it superstition, but taking your clothes with us might be tempting fate. If you are found not guilty, David plans to take you directly to his house on Schwanenwerder where we've both been living. He hired a maid shortly after I arrived, and she has prepared a room for you and will make sure there is enough hot water for you to bathe. I can lend you something to wear until you can collect your things from the police."

Sobered by Alix's tone, Charlotte left the bundle of belongings behind. It was better this way, she decided. She never wanted to wear any of the things she'd worn in prison again, anyway. They stank of fear and humiliation.

They climbed into the back of the police van. The doors clanged shut and they sat facing each other on the benches as they swayed their way across Berlin. They didn't talk because the sour-faced policewoman had joined them. As they approached the courthouse, the van switched on its siren briefly, something it had never done before. Charlotte could hear shouting from outside and whistles blowing. She frowned at Alix uncomprehending.

The door to the van cracked open and noise flooded in. The policeman who had opened the van from the outside barked at them, "Don't stop to wave or speak to anyone! Don't answer questions! Keep your head down, your eyes on your feet and move rapidly!" Then he backed up to let Charlotte step down onto the street.

The pavement before the courthouse was crammed with people. Many in the crowd were journalists with big cameras pointed at her, and the blitz of flashes temporarily stunned her. The rest of the crowd appeared to consist of young women. Dozens of police had cordoned off a pathway to the front door. The escorting policewoman gripped Charlotte's elbow and marched her forward rapidly, through the front door and then along the polished granite hallways. Their footfalls echoed.

They arrived in a courtroom already overflowing with visitors. There was standing room only, and skirmishes broke out between the photojournalists competing for the best shots of Charlotte. She managed only a short nod and smile to David, and was glad to see that Christian was back. She noticed the black nurse was with him as well. Although they had never met, Charlotte sensed her support and found it comforting. The large number of young women in short skirts, high-heels, nylons and vivid lipstick, on the other hand, unsettled her. She did not understand why they were here or why they identified so strongly with her. She was not one of them.

She turned questioning eyes to Alix, but she was consulting with one of the court officials, nodding now and again. The doors to the courtroom were being closed over the protest of people still trying to squeeze in. Steinbrueck and his entourage of assistants and interns had taken their seats at the adjacent table. They were whispering and chattering among themselves. Their mood was tangibly excited and positive — as if they thought they'd already won the case. That made Charlotte uneasy. She looked around for Alix, who hastened to join her as calls for order rang out.

The side door opened, and the judges filed in to take their places. Every-one sat down. Judge Nuss leaned towards one of the supporting justices, who was speaking to him. He nodded once or twice and then collected his papers and lifted his head to intone, "The defendant will rise to hear the verdict."

Charlotte got to her feet and faced the bench. She discovered she felt a little dizzy.

"The court upholds the argument of the defence that rape is an unlawful act the prevention of which falls under the definition of self-defence as codi-fied." Charlotte let out her breath and unconsciously stood a little straighter. From behind her, several of the girls in the audience called out 'Hooray!' or 'You don't say!' or 'Damn right!'

Nuss scowled at the visitors but continued reading his verdict. "Howev-er, the court rejects a blanket application of the term 'rape' to every sexual encounter in which a woman is reluctant to participate since such an interpre-tation would lead to the ludicrous notion that wives can 'defend' themselves against the legitimate demands of their husbands, something the lawmakers never intended."

This pronouncement triggered new chatter among the spectators without erupting into protests or disorder. Nuss quelled the agitation with a sweep-ing frown and continued, "In this case, the court finds that an engagement made eight years earlier followed by six years of silence and the reasonable presumption of death, did not give the victim the right to sexual intercourse without consent."

Some female spectators verbally applauded the verdict or called out "Yes!" and "Hear! Hear!" Nuss suppressed the vocal celebration with a fierce scowl and continued, "The court majority also rules that the defendant's re-jection of the victim's sexual approaches was sufficiently explicit to make him recognise that his attentions were unwanted and therefore unlawful."

Charlotte felt more of her tension ease, and she lifted her head. But then Nuss said "However," and Charlotte tensed again.

"The law explicitly sanctions only those 'actions that are *necessary* to avert an imminent unlawful act.' The court finds that the unlawful sexual as-sault could have been averted by other means than killing the assailant. The defendant could have moved out of the apartment, could have fitted a lock on her door, or — most importantly, could have aimed her shots to warn or at most wound the victim. It was not necessary to put a bullet through his neck, much less one between his eyes."

Charlotte started to grey out. As if from a great distance, she heard the words "guilty" and then "life imprisonment." She wasn't going to be set free. She wasn't going to go with David to his house, his comfort, his arms.

She was vaguely aware that there was an uproar. Women were shouting angrily, and the judges called for order in vain. Scuffles broke out between observers and police. Her police escort took hold of both her arms and was pushing-pulling her towards a side exit. She was separated from Alix, who tried to call something after her, but she didn't understand what she said. Behind her something smashed and Steinbrueck screamed, "Whores! Ami mattresses! Russian pussy dolls!"

Outside, she was shoved into the back of the nearest police van. The siren wailed as it pulled away from the curb. She was going to spend the rest of her life in jail. In a stinking, lifeless cell, alone...

Emperor in Uniform
US HQ Berlin
Tuesday 22 March 1949
(Day 271 of the Berlin Airlift)

"Your visitors, General," the US Army lieutenant announced, holding the door open for three women. General Clay, a man compared to a Roman Emperor in terms of power and profile, got to his feet and came around his desk to greet them. He offered his hand first to Anna Savage with a smile creasing his weathered face. "It's good to see you looking so rested and relaxed, Miss Savage."

"Thank you, General," Anna responded, feeling anything but relaxed. The appeal to Clay had been Alix's idea, powerfully and passionately supported by David. Emily had also encouraged her to go, arguing that General Clay was a fair and reasonable man. Yet Anna still found it hard to believe that she was standing face-to-face with one of America's most highly decorated generals. This was different from him greeting her on her release from Soviet internment; then he had been showing official concern for an American citizen who had been detained by the Soviets. This meeting was entirely different. Anna fell back on protocol, asking nervously, "May I introduce my companions, sir?"

"I wish you would," Clay answered, teasing her slightly with a twinkle in his eye.

"This is Alexandra Freifrau von Feldburg, the lawyer who defended Countess Walmsdorf in the recent murder trial." Suddenly, Anna had doubts, "you have heard about the trial haven't you, sir?"

"Heard about it, Miss Savage? The trial resulted in the most serious incident of civil unrest in the Western Sectors of Berlin since the last elections! I believe there were five arrests, and the Soviet Press had a field day with choice headlines like 'Ami floozies riot for the right to shoot their lovers,' and 'Berlin's female scum conquer the courtroom.'"

Anna stiffened and reached out to her second companion, who had visibly quailed at Clay's words, "General, I trust that you are not swayed by sensational headlines of that sort."

"No, Miss Savage. The reason I put off this meeting for a week was to have time to read a translation of the trial transcript before hearing what you have to say." He gestured to a thick, three-ringed binder on his desk.

"I'm glad to hear that, General," Anna said firmly, "because this is Hannah Roehringer. She is 17 and in the 11th grade at the Kaiser Wilhelm Gymnasium in Spandau. We attended the trial together — and she was one of the 'rioters.' I wouldn't want you to think of her as 'female scum'."

Clay offered Hannah his hand with a simple, "Miss Roehringer." Then he turned his attention to Alix, offering her his hand with the words, "Mrs Feldburg, you come highly recommended by my senior JAG corps officer. He says you did an outstanding job assisting our prosecution in Nuremberg and played a particularly decisive role in assisting our team to understand German law— and how it had been subverted and corrupted by the Nazis. It's a pleasure to meet you." He then indicated his coffee table and suggested they all sit.

When everyone was settled, Clay looked from Anna to Alix and back to Anna. She sat on the edge of the sofa, her feet side-by-side, her hands folded in her lap and her back stiff. She was wearing not her nurse's uniform but her Sunday best: a smart, peach-coloured suit with a white hat and gloves.

"We're here to plead for mercy, General, for a pardon, a complete pardon, for Countess Walmsdorf."

Clay nodded slowly and admitted. "I understand, that's why I read the trial transcript. Why don't you explain to me what your association with this case is and why you think I should commute or suspend the sentence?"

Anna nodded, "Sir, you may well wonder why the child of a farmhand from rural Georgia cares about the fate of a German countess. Yet for all the differences of station, status, and wealth that separate us, the call for justice unites us. You see, General, my aunt was raped when she was a girl younger than Ms Roehringer here. Not only was she raped, but when her grandfather came to her assistance and beat up the man who had ravaged her, he was lynched and used as target practice."

Clay recoiled visibly.

"That wasn't justice, General, and it would not be justice to punish a woman for killing a serial rapist, either. I'd like you to hear from Miss Roehringer how we women — regardless of our nationality or our race — view this trial." She nodded encouragingly to Hannah for her to speak.

Hannah took a deep breath, sat up straighter and licked her lips nervously. She, too, was dressed in her best. Although her clothes were faded and threadbare, they were pointedly modest: a plaid, shirt-waist dress, with a white collar and cuffs. She wore no lipstick, no make-up and her skirt came to her knees. Her legs were bare and her shoes were scuffed and down at the heel. "Herr General," she started in a voice strengthened by inner passion and burning indignation, "the reason that so many Berlin women attended the trial and were so angry about the verdict is that many of us — tens of thousands of us — identify with Graefin Walmsdorf. I don't mean just her pain and humiliation, but her rage, too. I was just 13 when first three Russians, two days later another four, and a week after that another two Russian soldiers, raped me." Hannah paused, drew a deep breath and added forcefully, "Yet, brutal, painful and cruel as those Ivans were, I do not hate them as much as the Germans and Americans who now call me 'scum' and 'whore' and 'Ami floozy.'" Clay squirmed uncomfortably, but Hannah continued, "I didn't choose to be raped nine times, and I refuse to accept that because I was raped, I no longer have a right to life, dignity, education, and honest employment. That is what the trial was about: the right of sexual victims to life — not suicide — and to a future of their choosing."

Clay nodded slowly and drew a deep breath before answering in a sober voice, "Miss Roehringer, I certainly wouldn't want to contradict your premise that the victims of sexual assault, regardless of the circumstances, are entitled to life and indeed all the rights and privileges of any other citizen. But no citizen, male or female, has the right to take the life of another."

"But it was self-defence!" Hannah protested, her composure shredding, and a slightly shrill tone entering her voice.

Anna stepped in. "General, we aren't asking you to find Countess Walmsdorf innocent. We're asking you to recognise that she was pushed over the edge by the weight of what she had already endured. We're asking you to admit that she has suffered more than any woman deserves to suffer in her lifetime. We're asking you to say: 'Enough is enough.' She is not a threat to society and doesn't need to spend the rest of her life behind bars. Give her a chance to live a normal life."

Clay nodded without agreeing and looked at Alix. "Did you have anything you wanted to add, Mrs Feldburg?"

"General, as the reaction of both the audience and most of the Western press suggests, witnesses to the trial overwhelmingly sided with the defendant. The verdict came as a surprise to most, but unfortunately not to me. Both the prosecutor and two of the professional justices on the bench were ardent Nazis who embraced the misogyny of National Socialism and enthusiastically enforced Nationalist Socialist judicial policies."

Alix interrupted herself to ask Clay, "You know that in the Nazi era, the number of crimes that carried the death penalty increased from one to forty-four?" Clay nodded solemnly, and Alix continued. "You also know, I presume, that Nazi justice upended the fundamental principle of 'innocent until proven guilty.'"

Again, Clay nodded. He had taken an active interest in the trials of Nazi war criminals.

Alix pressed her case, "The prosecutor in this case, Dr Steinbrueck, was known for requesting sexual favours from the wives of defendants facing a possible death sentence. He promised to seek a milder sentence in exchange for sex. Although technically he did as promised, the judges were in collusion with him and decreed the death sentence anyway." This information finally elicited a look of outrage from Clay.

Alix forged ahead. "Throughout the Nazi era, prosecutor Steinbrueck and judges Nuss and Eisenbrecher worked together to corrupt justice and deliver draconian verdicts reflecting Nazi ideology rather than justice. Altogether, this trio of German jurists is responsible for sending 137 men and 18 women to their deaths. The victims included a bombed-out, destitute pensioner who helped himself to a pile of clothes abandoned after an air raid, a factory worker who used old, pre-war SPD pamphlets as insulation in his bomb-damaged apartment, and a father with four school-aged children who told a silly joke about Hitler to a colleague."

Clay shook his head in disgust.

"My point, General, is that these men do not have a sense of *justice*. They do not so much believe they are *above* the law, as that they *are* the law. They had decided Graefin Walmsdorf's fate before she ever set foot in the courtroom."

Alix let that sink in and then remarked in a gentler, sadder tone, "I know, General, that you and your government do not hold my husband and those like him, who tried to overthrow Hitler, in high regard. You believe they were willing accomplices, riding happily on Hitler's coattails so long as he was winning wars. You believe they didn't turn on Hitler until defeat stared them in the face. That is not true. Most resistance leaders opposed Hitler before he became chancellor and all opposed his aggressive policies *because* they were leading us to war. Yet, it is equally true that they were not 'democrats.' They were mostly conservative men, many of them monarchists. Yet they were men of honour and compassion horrified by the brutality, cruelty, inhumanity, corruption and, above all, the arbitrary exercise of power displayed by the Nazi regime. Their single most important objective, after an end to the killing, was the restoration of the rule of law — regardless of what form of government ensured that."

Clay did not visibly react, so Alix drew a deep breath before concluding, "When I decided to try to survive rather than take my own life alongside my husband, I did so out of a desire to help re-establish the rule of law in Germany."

Looking Clay in the eye, she told him bluntly, "Today, we are on the brink of creating a new sovereign German state, but the same men who abused their power and arbitrarily punished — even killed — the poor and vulnerable elements of society are about to be restored to full honours and dignity. I think that's wrong, General. This isn't just about Graefin Walmsdorf. It is about what kind of judiciary Germany will have in the future.

"Will it be a humane and compassionate legal system that attempts to understand the motives and circumstances of defendants? Will it be a judiciary that seeks to rehabilitate criminals? A society that strives to eliminate the causes of crime? Or will it be a corrupt and vindictive legal system designed to frighten, intimidate, and silence the poor and disadvantaged?"

Alix paused to let him absorb what she'd said before adding, "This case may not seem particularly significant to you, but it will set a precedent. Either you allow this vindictive verdict to stand, or you show a way to a more compassionate future."

The German widow and the American general gazed at one another for several seconds, and then Clay nodded solemnly and rose to his feet. "Thank you for taking the time to explain this case in greater detail, ladies. I will consider what you have told me and take your request under consideration."

They had been dismissed, and there was nothing more the women could do than thank the general and take their leave.

Towards Sovereignty
US Military HQ Berlin
Wednesday 23 March 1949
(Day 272 of the Berlin Airlift)

The mayor of Berlin and city councillor Liehbherr passed the sentries at the gates to the US military HQ in Dahlem and were escorted to Clay's anteroom by one of his aides. At 4:45 on the dot, the General received them. Punctuality was one value the Germans and the US military had always held in common.

The German politicians were offered seats in front of the General's desk rather than at the coffee table, an indication that this was an official meeting. Clay thanked his visitors for coming and got straight to the point. "Gentlemen, as you probably know, progress toward the establishment of a sovereign German state is rapid. As envisaged, the Western Powers will retain a degree of control only over defence and foreign affairs, while responsibility for economic, social, educational and judicial affairs will be restored to the new German authorities. The final details of this arrangement are being hammered out in Bonn, and a new German constitution could be ready for ratification as early as the end of next month." Reuter and Liebherr nodded earnestly; they were kept informed of developments by the SPD leadership.

"As I understand it, this new state is both desired and dreaded by most Germans. You long to manage your affairs and be readmitted into the community of nations as an equal rather than a pariah. Yet satisfaction over the restoration of German sovereignty is inhibited by the knowledge that it will apply only to those parts of Germany currently occupied by the Western Allies. Like a hostage, the Russian-occupied zone is excluded and remains in abject subjugation to the Soviet Union. There, the Reds continue to oppress freedom, obstruct progress, steal German goods and labour, and bully the population."

Again, Reuter and Liebherr nodded. The American governor had summed up the situation articulately and succinctly.

"The other blemish on the birth of the new German state," Clay continued, "is the exclusion of Berlin. Germany's proud capital cannot be integrated into the new German state." The Berliners exchanged a glance of dismay. Although they had feared this fate, no one had so forthrightly admitted it before now. Clay leaned forward, his elbows on his desk and his hands clasped. "Berlin must remain nominally under Four-Power government for the indefinite future to justify the continued presence of large Allied garrisons in the city."

Liebherr winced inwardly as he recognised the cogency of the argument. Clay paused long enough to remark with dry humour, "Unless I am mistaken, gentlemen, an Allied military presence in Berlin is in your best interests."

"Absolutely, General," Reuter assured him. "We have become very fond of your garrisons, particularly the air component."

Clay nodded and continued. "Yet while we intend to retain a military presence in keeping with Berlin's status as a city ruled jointly by the four victorious powers, we have no desire to interfere in your day-to-day affairs. Regardless of yet-to-be-determined informal ties to the new German state, de facto the Berlin City Council will be the supreme political body in West Berlin."

Reuter and Liebherr nodded more vigorously as his words sank in.

Clay continued, "I expect all this to occur sometime in the next three months — after which I will be going home." General Clay cracked a small smile at the mention of home.

"We'll be sorry to see you go," Reuter countered sincerely.

"That's kind of you to say," Clay replied, "but these have been trying and challenging times for all of us. I could do with a little more rest and a little less responsibility, and I greatly suspect that you could do with more authority and more freedom of action." They did not contradict him.

Clay drew a deep breath. "In light of the imminent alteration of our respective positions of power, I did not want to take action with regard to two judicial decisions without first consulting you." His guests waited tensely.

"First, I presume you are familiar with the Graefin Walmsdorf case?"

They nodded vigorously, and Jakob felt a spark of hope ignite. Meanwhile, Clay explained, "My initial reaction to the verdict was that it had been harsh but fair. However, I've had my mind changed by some very persuasive women, and I'm now inclined toward mercy. That is, to grant the request filed by the defence for a full pardon for Miss Walmsdorf. Would you have any objections to that?"

Jakob was so relieved that he didn't give Reuter a chance to speak, and declared enthusiastically, "None whatsoever, General! I know Miss Walmsdorff personally and she has truly suffered more than enough already!"

"Not to mention," the mayor added, "popular opinion was very much on her side. Don't forget, women still make up the majority of Berlin's population."

"Good," Clay moved a piece of paper from one side of his desk to the other. Then he leaned forward, his forearms flat on the desktop, and announced more earnestly, "Now the more ticklish issue. Credible allegations have been made against two judges and the prosecutor involved in this case. It is alleged that they were ardent National Socialists, who used their power vindictively, imposing draconian penalties, while shamelessly exploiting their power to extort favours."

"That was not unusual," Jakob pointed out dryly.

Clay looked at him with raised eyebrows. "Are you saying it doesn't offend against your sense of justice, Councillor?"

"On the contrary!" Reuter interceded, "But we can hardly pretend to be surprised."

Clay nodded. "Fair enough. However, I was sent to Germany with a mandate to, among other things, de-nazify this country. I'd be very happy to make the dismissal of these three jurists one of my last acts as governor. On the other hand, if you prefer, I can leave it to your discretion to sort out after I depart."

"The sooner they go the better! Throw the bastards out!" Jakob declared spontaneously,

Reuter responded in a more restrained tone, "They will feel martyred by your dismissal and appeal against the decision as soon as you are gone. I think that would set an excellent precedent for judicial review. It will allow us to highlight the domestic injustice of the National Socialist regime, something less obvious than the war crimes. Finding qualified jurists who can administer the law rationally and impartially will be the greater challenge."

"You may not have to look too far. In your shoes, I would start with the highly articulate and impressive woman who defended Miss Walmsdorf."

"Ah!" Reuter responded enthusiastically. "Freifrau von Feldburg! A remarkable woman indeed. She would be a great asset if we can persuade her not to go to the new Constitutional Court in Bonn."

Clay looked surprised, and Jakob remarked with a faint smile, "It is the women who are rebuilding Germany, General. Whether as lawyers or simply as 'rubble women,' shopkeepers, and nurses."

"And schoolgirls who refuse to accept the role men have assigned to them," Clay added, baffling this audience before rising to his feet and thanking them for their time and advice.

End of the Nightmare
Berlin-Moabit
Friday 25 March 1949
(Day 274 of the Berlin Airlift)

They had moved Charlotte from her detention cell in Kreuzberg to the main women's prison in Moabit. The building was five stories high with metal catwalks that led to the individual cells facing each other across a concrete courtyard. The sound of heavy footsteps clanging on the metal stairs or along platforms echoed day and night as prisoners were admitted, fed, taken down for exercise or out to see visitors. Charlotte ignored the clanging and lay on her bed with her eyes closed. She drifted aimlessly through her thoughts like someone trying to sleep when they were not tired.

She had no hope of release and had abandoned her visions of a future with David, but she felt no remorse about killing Fritz von Bredow. She was glad she had done it, and equally happy that rather than committing suicide, she had defended herself. These last weeks had changed her. Looking back, she regretted much: that she had not thrown Fritz out when she discovered how much he'd changed, that she had not moved out of the apartment herself when he became threatening, that she had not reported him to the police after the first rape, that she had not shot him sooner. The judges, she concluded, had been right, there *had* been other and better ways of dealing with Fritz von Bredow.

What she regretted most, however, and what cut her to the core of her soul was that she had not discovered the depth and beauty of David's love until it was too late. On the other hand, if she had not endured the trial — if she had killed herself instead — she would never have learned what a good person David was. Because of the trial, she would know and remember how he had stood by her in her darkest hour.

"Charlotte," the voice penetrated her thoughts, and she opened her eyes. Alix was standing over her bed smiling. "I've come to take you away."

"Away?" Charlotte sat up so rapidly that she became dizzy; she had not been eating much.

"General Clay signed your pardon yesterday. It was forwarded to the court and passed on to the prison today. Come." She held out her hand.

Charlotte looked down. She was dressed in prison garb: a waistless, long-sleeved, linen shift with broad blue and white vertical stripes. It was the same attire that women had worn in the concentration camps. Indeed, the guard had said it was surplus left over from Ravensbrueck.

"A suitcase with the things you left in the apartment has already been handed over to the prison. You can collect it at the gate. Come." Alix urged again.

Charlotte rose unsteadily to her feet. She still couldn't grasp what was happening. What did the American military governor have to do with her? Could he grant pardons to common criminals? Was that what Alix had tried to tell her? Dazed, she slipped her naked feet into her shoes and followed Alix out of her cell onto the catwalk. The view through the metal grid of the platform to the concrete floor sixty feet below made Charlotte dizzy. She gripped the inside railing and took small steps until they reached the stairs. They descended by the switch-backing steps, and Alix led the way to the exit, manned by a uniformed guard in a sentry box. Alix and Charlotte had to sign out in a registry. The guard then disappeared into a back room and returned with a battered old suitcase. He made Charlotte sign a chit to acknowledge receipt of her belongings. He then told her to remove her prison dress and leave it in a waiting hamper.

"Is there a changing room?" Alix asked.

The guard growled, "This isn't the Hotel Esplanade!"

Charlotte hurriedly pulled the prison dress up over her head and donned the first skirt and blouse she laid her hands on. They were crushed from being crammed rather than folded in the suitcase. Alix helped her pull a cardigan on, warning that it was drizzling outside. Finally, the guard unlocked the heavy, metal door and opened it just wide enough for them to slip out.

Charlotte stopped to look around still confused. Was a pardon like an acquittal? Or were there strings attached? Was she free to go anywhere she liked, or would she have to report to the American military regularly? Then she caught sight of a battered farm wagon with Karl and Donner, her father's last surviving horses, hitched in the traces. Horst with his wonderful moustache sat waiting on the seat. The image could only mean one thing: she was going home.

A moment later, she realised that David and Christian stood in front of the wagon lost in earnest conversation. The sight of them so overwhelmed her that she couldn't take another step.

Horst noticed Charlotte first. He called out, lifting his arm in greeting before scrambling down. His shout alerted the other two men, who turned towards her, startled. Unable to speak, Charlotte reached out her arms towards them.

An instant later, David had hold of her. She clung to him and started crying. "Is it over, David? Am I free? Can we be together always and forever?"

"Yes, yes, yes," David assured her. Then he eased his hold a little so Christian could put his arms around her as well.

"I will never forgive myself for leaving you alone with Bredow," he told her, fighting back tears as he held her.

"It was my fault," Charlotte answered. "I wouldn't listen to your warnings or advice. Of course, you got frustrated." Over Christian's shoulder, she could see Horst wringing his cap, tears streaming down his leathery face. She stepped out of Christian's arms to hug the loyal coachman. "Thank you, Horst, for being so loyal."

"If only I'd been there," he sobbed.

"No, Horst. There was nothing you could have done then, but it means everything to me that you are still my friend." She kissed him on the cheek and then turned to Alix. "How can I ever thank you for saving my life?"

"By living happily ever after," Alix retorted with a smile. Then they embraced firmly until Alix pulled away and suggested they get on their way.

David took charge of Charlotte. He helped her up onto the seat of the wagon — after she finished stroking and hugging each horse in turn. He spread a blanket and then a tarpaulin over her knees and handed her a scarf for her head that Alix had lent him. David and Horst climbed up to flank her, while Christian and Alix climbed in the back. Horst took up the reins and clicked to Karl and Donner.

At first, Charlotte wanted only to cuddle in David's arms, drawing strength and courage from his presence. She let the city plod by, seeing nothing, just listening to the clack of the hooves on the cobblestones and knowing they were taking her away not just from the prison but from the past as well.

As they turned into Gruenewald Forest, she noticed the trees were budding, and she exclaimed excitedly, "It's Spring!" Then she looked up at David and asked. "What happens now? Will you really marry me? A convicted murderer?"

"We have an appointment at the *Standesamt* next Tuesday at 8 o'clock unless you want to wait until—

"No! The sooner the better!" Charlotte declared.

"Christian and Alix will be our witnesses — and Jasha and Emily would like to come too if you don't mind?"

Charlotte nodded vigorously, and then thought to ask, "Is Emily all right? She was in some sort of crash in the Soviet Zone, wasn't she?" Now that she was free, Charlotte was disconcerted to realize how utterly focused on herself she had been these last weeks. She'd been so selfish.

"She was rescued and is recovering now," David assured her. "She is anxious to see you and looking forward to the wedding."

"I can't wait to see her and Jasha again," Charlotte told him; it shamed her to remember how jealous she had been at Jasha's wedding, and how rude she'd been to Emily. She had to make up for that.

Meanwhile, David explained, "The earliest appointment I could get at the Canadian consulate in Hamburg is on 20 April at 3:15. However, they explained that they can issue a temporary passport valid for three months, and with that, we can travel to England. We can collect your proper passport in London when it's ready."

"Are we going to live in London?" Charlotte asked surprised. She had not thought of that. She'd always imagined being with David in his house on the Schwanenwerder.

"Not London, really," David admitted. "I thought maybe we should spend some time together in the country first."

Charlotte's face lit up. "I'd like that! I'd love to live on a farm with dogs and horses and take long walks in the clean air and —oh! It will be April or May, won't it? My grandmother always became homesick for England in April. She says the whole island blooms."

"I'm glad you mentioned your grandmother because I thought that was where we'd stay — at least at first. From there we can go to London for a shopping spree or two—"

"And to Stratford-upon-Avon for a play?"

David dropped a kiss on her nose. "Or two or three."

Overhead a York dropped out of the cloud and the dull droning of aircraft engines that had been a constant backdrop suddenly became impossible to ignore. "What about your business, David? You can't spend all your time just looking after me. What is happening with EAS and are you going to get another ambulance? I can't believe Moby Dick is gone."

"Moby Dick did sterling service and although mortally wounded by sabotage, she brought her humans safely back to earth. Kiwi is in England, where he's overseeing the modification of a new Wellington to turn it into an ambulance. We hope to have it ready to take patients by mid-April. Meanwhile, the Halifaxes are flying around the clock and making solid profits. Finally, Anna Savage is training two young women to look after the patients. They won't be fully qualified nurses like she is, but Anna assures us they will have the skills to look after patients on our short flights. It will also give two girls forced into prostitution a chance to start working towards a new profession."

"Were they some of the girls who came to my trial?"

"Yes, Gerlinde was the one who shouted out insults and got expelled, and Hannah went with Alix and Anna to General Clay to plead your case."

"I had given up all hope," Charlotte admitted.

"I can understand, but that's behind us. We need to talk more about what we want for the future."

"I want to be with you, wherever you are. I'll go anywhere in the world — England or Canada or Timbuctoo — but I don't ever want to be separated from you for more than a day or two." David answered by bending and giving her a kiss.

Charlotte continued, "I've thought a lot about children, too. I always wanted a big family, four or five children. Would you mind that?"

David shook his head, too moved to speak.

"They don't have to be our *own* children," Charlotte explained earnestly, "I don't know for certain if I *can* have children, but whether I can or not, there are so many orphans left by the war or abandoned by abused mothers that I started to think maybe we should help one or two of them. After all, they are innocent victims, too." David clutched her to him, tears streaming down his face, and they said no more the rest of the journey.

Back at the house, Charlotte was shooed into the waiting hot bath, and David disappeared somewhere. Christian and Alix found themselves alone in the grand salon looking out at the lake. David had suggested they help themselves to a drink to warm up from the damp drive. The drizzle had stopped, and the low sun was trying to come out, casting a golden sheen on the surface of the Havel.

As Christian handed Alix a brandy in a cut crystal tumbler, he met her eyes and declared. "Philip would have been so proud of what you did — not just Charlotte's defence and pardon but getting Nuss and Steinbrueck debarred."

Alix felt a stab in her heart at the mention of Philip. Over the last month, she had often thought that success would justify her decision to live. In answer to Christian, she lifted her glass and toasted, "To my better half: Philip."

They drank, held their glasses up again, and then Christian asked, "Have you decided if you are going to accept Reuter's offer yet?"

"I'm tempted, but I've also been recommended as a judge on the Constitutional Court."

"I'd heard rumours," Christian admitted, adding, "Very impressive."

Alix shook her head, "*Jein*. On the Constitutional Court, I'd be the token representative of the German Resistance and the only 'working woman' surrounded by men like Nuss and Eisenbrecher." Christian looked surprised, and Alix explained. "The men who dominate in Bonn detest the Reds more than the Nazis. I fear I'll find myself constantly in the minority and increasingly frustrated. I trust the SPD and Reuter to be more vigilant against a return of fascist ideology. I'm also fundamentally more interested in the fate of individuals than in constitutional theory. The most tempting aspect of the Constitutional Court is that it will probably be established in Bonn or Frankfurt. It would give me a completely new start, without any memories and emotional baggage."

"But surely not all your memories of Berlin are bad?" Christian protested.

"No, that's just it," Alix admitted. "I took a walk in Gruenewald the other day and was reminded of my rides with Philip. If I had a horse, each ride would remind me of those good times. Or when the ferry to Kladow reopens, I could travel back with it to the day I fell in love...."

"I don't know if this would make any difference to your decision," Christian started up cautiously, "but David and I agreed today that I will buy this house from him — just as it stands with all the furnishings in it."

"Can you afford that?" Alix asked astonished.

"Yes and no. David agreed to sell it to me for whatever price I get on the sale of our house on the Maybach Ufer. Of course, that house is half yours...."

"So, I'd own half of this," Alix concluded looking around and letting her eyes linger on the Max Lieberman painting over the buffet. "Are you planning to live here or to rent it?"

"I intend to stay here in Berlin. I will send for Yvette and her daughter and start being a proper husband and father for a change. I hope we'll have one or two children of our own, but there would still be plenty of room for you and your son."

Alix nodded and looked around again. She liked the house and felt comfortable here. If Yvette came with her daughter, her son wouldn't feel as uprooted; he'd been living with his Aunt Yvette, her daughter and his grandmother these last three years, and the cousins were close. "And what will you be doing with your days?" she asked Christian.

"Running Air Ambulance International. David doesn't think Charlotte should have to live in a city where she endured so much horror and gained unjust notoriety. He envisages building an ambulance service in India or Asia, based in Rangoon, Singapore or New Delhi. But as long as Berlin is an island in a Soviet sea, it will need air ambulances, so David offered to let me run it as an independent subsidiary. He says I can expand to as many ambulances as I can man and operate profitably. I'll be free to hire German air and ground crew, he said. I'm excited about the idea because I think there's huge potential here."

Alix nodded agreement and sorted through her thoughts for a few moments more before declaring, "That's settled then. I'll accept Reuter's offer, remain in Berlin and we'll bring Yvette and the children up from Altdorf. Of course, we are taking a risk. The Russians might still send in the tanks."

"After what Clay said about the Allies retaining their status and garrison, I'm not worried. More interesting will be if the Airlift can move from supplying bare necessities to enabling a complete normalisation of life."

"Do you think that might be possible?"

Christian laughed. "I didn't think any of this would be possible."

Chapter Twenty-Two
Resurrection

The BBC technicians were still fussing with the microphones and members of the RAF regiment were cordoning off the public from the official guests when the roar of approaching engines blotted out all other sounds. Slowly, oozing cautiously around the end of the EAS hangar, the nose, then the cockpit, propellors, and finally the fuselage of a Wellington appeared. It was freshly painted a bright, glossy white that gleamed in the April sunshine. The red crosses on the tail fin and abaft the cockpit windows and the elegant, italicised lettering spelling out 'Air Ambulance International' stood out like blood on clean sheets.

The sight of the ambulance set off a cheer loud enough to be heard over the growl of engines. Spectators waved hats, scarves, and hands as they welcomed the Wellington. Virginia Cox-Gordon, nervous about her first live radio broadcast for the BBC, stepped as close as possible to the microphone to make herself heard above the noise.

"The cheering you can hear, ladies and gentlemen, is Berlin's response to the resumption of the air ambulance service. Ambulance flights came to an abrupt halt on the 13th of February when the only aircraft providing this service went down in the Soviet Zone. Fortunately, it was on a return flight and no patients were on board at the time. However, flying in the face of logic, customs and international law, three members of the crew were detained by the Soviets and charged with espionage. It took immense pressure from the American government to secure their release. However, the fourth crew member, former ATA pilot, Mrs Emily Priestman, was able to evade capture for more than two weeks. She was rescued in a dramatic covert operation that no one is willing to talk to us about. Meanwhile, many thought the loss of the aircraft and the Soviet treatment of the crew would seal the fate of the ambulance service. Yet here, before my very eyes, is the new ambulance. I'm told that it is ready to resume medical evacuations from Berlin starting tomorrow."

While she was speaking, the Wellington's engines shut down, and Emily, Kiwi, Richard Scott-Ross and Anna emerged from the aircraft to be met by renewed cheers. At the foot of the ladder, a little girl with flowers greeted them before they mounted a temporary podium to shake hands with a delegation of German and British dignitaries.

Virginia narrated for her radio audience, "The crew is being welcomed by Mr Jakob Liebherr, representing the Berlin City Council, and Prof Dr Albert Rudesheim, representing the medical professionals of Berlin, along with Air Commodore Waite and the RAF Station Commander. I'll provide a summary of their remarks:

"Dr Rudesheim says the ambulance service is vital to the city. He notes that since the closing days of the war, Berlin has suffered from a shortage of hospital beds and a severe deficit in medical personnel. There are several acute and life-threatening medical conditions that Berlin's hospitals are incapable of treating. Until the Blockade started, patients suffering from these conditions were evacuated from the city by train. Since the start of the siege, Berlin has been dependent on evacuations by air. He is now shaking hands with the crew and the managing director of Air Ambulance International and giving them each a small wooden bear, representing Berlin, holding a red cross in his forepaws.

"The next speaker is from the Berlin City Council. Mr Liebherr is thanking the company for resuming service despite the loss of an aircraft and severe injuries to two crew members. He says that between starting service on the 1st of April last year and the crash on the 12th of February, Air Ambulance International flew 589 sorties and removed 2,643 critically ill patients from Berlin.

"Mr Liebherr is inviting the founder and managing director of Air Ambulance International to say a few words. Mr. Goldman is a Canadian citizen," Virginia told her audience, "who flew for the RAF in the war. The company is registered in the UK, and its crews are international. Mr Goldman is assuring the crowd of his commitment to continue ambulance services despite the loss of an aircraft. He says he hopes to add a second ambulance and to recruit German crews in the future. You can hear the response that news is getting." Virginia referred to a surge of applause and cheers.

David introduced Emily and Kiwi as his partners, and a delegation from the public came forward with flowers. The conversation between Emily and the delegation was inaudible over the general noise so Virginia gestured vigorously to Robin, who was standing on the periphery watching. In response to her gesture, he reluctantly approached her, and she pulled him closer to the microphone while announcing, "I am joined now by the RAF Station Commander. Thank you for agreeing to answer a few questions, Wing Commander. The Berliners are certainly enthusiastic about the resumption of ambulance service. Do you share that joy? Doesn't the ambulance interfere with normal Airlift operations?"

"The Airlift has become a highly organised and efficient operation with clear procedures and routines, as the delivery of roughly 200,000 tons of supplies last month shows. That converts to an average of 6,500 tons per day, by the way, and includes more than 350 tons of liquid fuel. The civilian component of the Airlift, particularly, has improved dramatically, contributing 70 sorties per day, an increase of almost 50 per cent. We are on track to break all records this month, and I anticipate that by this summer, the Airlift will be able to deliver 8,000 tons daily. Deliveries of this magnitude mean we can include the raw materials needed for the resumption of manufacturing on a large scale, which will create additional jobs. Last but not least, we have evacuated more than 50,000 Berliners. Believe me, with operations on this scale, no single aircraft, no matter how unique, can disrupt or interfere with the Airlift as a whole."

"Is it true that the loss of the ambulance resulted in a covert operation to recover the missing crew member?"

"I wouldn't know."

"Wing Commander, you're being disingenuous," she said in a teasing tone. "I heard from several sources that your wife went missing after the crash and then suddenly reappeared at Gatow — at the same time as a Soviet officer defected to Britain."

"My wife was severely injured in the crash, which is why I'm pleased to see her flying again today," as he spoke he drew Emily into the circle around the microphone.

"Oh! At last!" Virginia gushed. "The moment I've been waiting for! Ladies and gentlemen, I have just been joined by Captain Emily Priestman, the AAI pilot who evaded capture after the crash in February. She's standing here with — let me count — one, two, three, four bouquets given to her by the grateful Berliners. Mrs Priestman, how are you feeling?"

"A little overwhelmed. I hadn't expected any kind of reception." Emily cast Robin a reproachful look, and he grinned back at her.

"You've had a very harrowing time — crashing into the Soviet Zone, sustaining injuries, evading capture, being rescued. Do you want to tell us about it?"

"No, but I would like to tell you about the 13-year-old boy, who severely injured his eye when his bicycle hit a pothole while returning home after dark; his sight was saved by our timely medevac the next morning. I'd also like to talk about the little girl who was playing on some rubble when it suddenly gave way leaving her partially crushed by falling bricks; despite a collapsed lung and several broken bones, we got her to Hanover in time to save her life. Or let me tell you about the grandmother supporting five orphaned grandchildren with a brain tumour. We flew her to Munich for surgery that could not be performed here in Berlin. She is now back with the children that depend on her. That's what the air ambulance is about. It's not about me, crashes or rescues. I recommend you interview some of the people who came out here today. Now, if you'll excuse me, I'm very tired."

"Of course," Virginia agreed, frustrated and inwardly steaming. As Emily and Robin moved off, she brought the broadcast to an end, signing off brightly, "V. Cox-Gordon, reporting from RAF Gatow — the busiest airfield in the entire world."

Robin took Emily's hand. "Are you all right?"

"You shouldn't have organised this. It's my first day back on the job and

I would have preferred it to be as innocuous as usual so I could get back into the feel of things. This was all very embarrassing."

"Well, the press wasn't my idea. Waite insisted on it."

"Why?"

"Because Tunner is planning one of his publicity stunts tomorrow. From noon on Friday until noon on Saturday, he wants to see just how many tons of cargo the Combined Air Lift Task Force can deliver to Berlin. He wants to get everyone competing against each other by keeping track and posting tonnage totals hourly. He's also planning prizes for the station, squadron and off-loading teams with the highest tonnages. I'm not at all fond of this kind of gimmick. For one thing, everyone will be carrying coal to make on and off-loading homogenous and fast, but that means other vitally needed cargoes get left behind. There will be no tankers, no passengers, and no ambulances either. Furthermore, competition creates unnecessary friction, and all the hectic activity is conducive to accidents. However, he's 'the boss,' as the Americans say."

"What's all that got to do with the reception for the ambulance?" Emily wanted to know.

"Well, Tunner's so-called 'Easter Parade' is all about tonnage. Waite wanted us to get out ahead of Tunner's media frenzy with a story of our own highlighting the human side of the Airlift. Nothing suits that objective better than the ambulance." Before Emily could comment, he announced, "We're stopping in here."

"The Other Ranks Mess?" Emily asked baffled. "Why?"

"Because we were asked to," he answered unhelpfully and hastened up the steps. He left her no choice but to follow, although inwardly she was annoyed. After more than a month spent recovering from her injuries at home, she had gone with Kiwi and David to England to collect the new ambulance. They'd been there almost two weeks overseeing the final modifications and handling other business. David had returned yesterday, leaving Kiwi and her to pick Richard up in Hamburg and continue to Berlin. There was so much she wanted to talk to Robin about that she did not relish any official event.

But then they were in the dining room and the airmen and women were getting to their feet and clapping. Emily looked at Robin in confusion. "Everyone was very worried about you, Emily," he told her just loud enough to be heard over the clapping. "This is the first chance they've had to express how happy they were that you made it." The erks had broken into a chorus of "For she's a jolly good fellow," and Emily wanted to sink through the floor.

When the singing stopped, she stammered out, "Thank you, thank you, but I didn't do anything." Her words were drowned out in a new round of applause, and then individuals started to crowd around: the drivers, the corporals from the Met Office, the WAAF air movements assistants, and others. They were telling her how pleased they were that no harm had come to her.

After about twenty minutes, Robin extricated her and led her to the sergeant's mess, where the scene repeated itself, except that after the last strains of "She's a Jolly Good Fellow" faded, Sergeant Andrews called for attention. "Like the captain of a ship," she opened over the beginnings of chatter, "the station commander has a huge influence on how happy a station is. Given that we're under siege, working around the clock, and most of our food is powdered rubbish—" the audience laughed — "we're a remarkably happy crew — which speaks volumes for our WingCo." A spontaneous round of applause started, but Andrews gestured for silence.

"However, as everyone knows, behind every successful man is a *woman*." Some laughed, and some booed good-naturedly. Andrews held up her hands for silence and continued, "Some station commanders' wives amplify their husband's strengths and failings, while others complement them and smooth the edges. I know many a sergeant who *didn't* lose his stripes because of the good graces of a Groupie or Wingco's wife!" She harvested the laughter she was fishing for.

Then her tone turned more serious. "Yet it is very rare for a station commander's wife to step out of his shadow and have an identity and profile entirely her own. That is what we have had in Flying Officer Priestman. When Moby Dick went down in mid-February, it wasn't just the station commander's wife who went missing, it was *our* favourite woman pilot. It was a blow to our morale." Emily was astonished by the nodding heads and murmur of assent that swept the room.

"So," Andrew's tone turned cheerful again as she turned directly to Emily and insisted, "It was a huge boost to our morale to hear you were safe and sound and even better to see you back in the cockpit and back in the sky. That's why we wanted to offer you a little token of our regard."

A sergeant wearing the insignia of a rigger whom Emily could only vaguely remember stepped forward and handed her a model Wellington. It was painted white with "Moby Dick" in red lettering along the side. Emily exclaimed in delight. "Oh! It's beautiful!" She took it from him carefully and turned it around in her hands as her eyes admired the beautiful craftsmanship and meticulous detail. She knew she had to say something but was at a complete loss. She looked to Robin for help, but he only nodded encouragement. She couldn't let him down. She started with "Thank you! I'm very honoured! Flattered. I'm sorry for causing so much trouble. I do hope the Ministry won't decide I am such a liability to morale that my husband can't be entrusted with a station ever again."

"Just the kind of bloody stupid thing they *would* do!" A deep voice boomed from the back of the room, and everyone laughed.

"I know my husband was extremely appreciative of the support and sympathy he received during those two terrible weeks when I was missing. Let me express my thanks for helping him through such a trying time. I don't know what else to say." She looked again to Robin for guidance. He was so much better than she at this kind of thing.

He finally stepped forward, "I don't doubt that we will all remember this assignment for the rest of our lives, but nothing more perfectly exemplifies our mission than the air ambulance. It is bringing aid to our former enemies, and it was targeted by our current enemies, but it is still flying — just as are we. And Berlin is *not* Red."

The room erupted into cheers again, and Robin and Emily were able to take their leave, Emily shaking many hands along the way.

At last, they reached the officers' mess. Emily was relieved when, after leaving "Moby Dick" and the other gifts she had received in the cloakroom, Robin took her to the lounge. Although their arrival brought the others to their feet clapping, at least they didn't sing. Instead, Robin signalled to one of the mess stewards, and shortly afterwards trays laden with glasses of champagne started to make the rounds. When everyone had a glass, Robin raised a toast "To the resurrection of the air ambulance!"

To shouts of "Hear, hear!" they all drank.

Then Lt. Colonel Graham Russell raised his glass again, "And to Emily Priestman."

"I don't deserve all this attention," Emily protested.

"We'll be the judge of that, madam," Squadron Leader Holt growled, and they all drank.

"Ladies and gentlemen, to the Station Commander," Squadron Leader Garth proposed.

Robin accepted the toast and then called for a toast to the king, which ended the round as most glasses were by then nearly empty. Emily could at last sink down onto a sofa, and Robin offered to bring her a drink and a snack. "Gin and tonic? Or a rare and excellent Franken wine which the mess has acquired at a scandalous discount?"

"Christian's wine?" Emily asked hopefully.

"Six barrels of it on the bomb winches of Peggy. It's excellent."

"I'd love to try it."

Robin disappeared, making way for Section Officer Hart and Squadron Leader Garth to come over for a more personal welcome. They ended up telling Emily what it had been like in the tower the night she'd gone down. After that, the MO stopped to ask if she felt fully recovered and advised her against 'overdoing' things. A stream of other visitors followed, while the stewards kept Emily's glass full, but unintentionally neglected the snacks.

When Fl/Lt Boyd stopped to say he was glad to see her, she insisted he sit for a moment to tell her more about what had happened to Corporal Borisenko.

"Oh, she's gone back to Blighty for training. She'll be promoted soon, provided she passes all her tests, which I'm sure she will."

"And Mila? What happens to her?"

"She'll have a new identity and a new past as soon as they finish processing her."

"That's good," Emily thought, absently looking for Kiwi. He had met up with Mila several times during his sojourn in England, and Emily was keeping her fingers crossed for both of them.

When Boyd withdrew, she was momentarily alone. Robin had been waylaid halfway across the room by the WAAF OC who was giving him an earful about something, while elsewhere the mess had gone back to normal with officers drinking, chatting and laughing in clusters scattered across the entire lounge. Over at the bar Kiwi and Kit were standing side by side each with a foot casually on the footrest while laughing about something together.

Without noticing, Emily had been drinking Christian's wine steadily. Abruptly, it caught up with her, and this whole reception seemed wrong. All she'd ever done was crash, whereas Kiwi and Kit had risked their lives and freedom to rescue her. She got up from the sofa with a little difficulty and unsteadily crossed the room to push herself between the two men, taking each by an elbow as she declared, "I don't know why all this fuss has been made over me. You were the ones who did something! It's not fair that we can't talk about it. It's not fair at all!"

"Emily!" Kiwi exclaimed, freeing his elbow to put his arm over her shoulder before explaining, "Of course, we need to make a fuss over you! You're the fair lady who inspired our brave deeds!" Raising an index finger triumphantly, he told her, "You see! I haven't forgotten your lectures on chivalry! You taught me that it was the ladies who motivated the knights to strive for greater honour and prowess. And so it is still. I wouldn't be the man I am today, if not for you — and the plucky little Mila." At the mention of her name, Kiwi's face shone, confirming Emily's suspicions.

"I want to see Mila again so I can thank her directly," Emily told him earnestly. Turning to Kit she added, "I wish I could thank Group Captain Cheshire for loaning us his Mossie, too."

Kit smiled, "You can write him a letter if you like. I'm sure he'd like to hear from you personally because he genuinely cares about people. You should have seen his smile when I returned and told him the mission had been successful. It made him feel good, he said, to have done something positive in these dark and uncertain times."

"He didn't mind about the bullet holes?"

"He's seen a lot worse," Kit reminded her.

Talk of the rescue, however, was reminding Emily of the encounter she'd had with Jan. She'd wanted to talk to Robin about it, but instead she'd been hijacked to these successive receptions. The wine made her less inhibited about sharing, however, and besides Kit and Kiwi were colleagues and friends. "There's something I need to talk to you about," she told the other two pilots, her sober tone warning them that this was serious. "Jan told me

I'm to blame for Rick and her being so badly injured. She claims if I'd turned off the port engine sooner, we could have avoided crashing into the shed—"

"Whoa!" Kiwi interrupted, taking her shoulders and turning her towards him so he could look her squarely in the face. She closed her eyes to stop the tears from spilling out. Solemnly Kiwi told her, "A good pilot never criticises another pilot's forced landing. That's against the unwritten rules of good conduct."

"More to the point," Kit spoke up, "you had your hands full with the brakes, rudder and control column. It was the flight engineer's job to handle the throttles. If anyone made a mistake, it was Rick."

Coming from a man who had flown both as a flight engineer and as a pilot, that meant a lot. Emily opened her eyes and turned to Kit, "Thank you for saying that, Kit."

"I'm not just 'saying it.' It's true. Don't let Jan's whining undermine your confidence, Emily," he advised her earnestly, "The rest of us would gladly fly with you anywhere."

"I thought Rick had pulled through," Kiwi moved the conversation forward.

"Maybe. He came out of the coma, and he is recovering, but slowly. It's not yet clear whether he'll make a complete recovery, but Jan is very bitter. She blames me for the crash, and she blames Anna for not handling his injuries correctly."

"She'd better not say anything against Anna in Gordon MacDonald's presence!" Kit warned sharply. "In just two months, she's helped Gordan regain partial use of his legs, and he swears she will get him fully back on his feet if they keep working at it. Besides, it doesn't matter. In an emergency, no response can be 100% perfect. Rick would certainly have bled to death without her intervention."

That, too, did Emily good. She went on tiptoe to kiss Kit on the cheek, then turned to give a similar kiss to Kiwi. "I'm so lucky to have friends like you," she told them. "I will never forget that I owe you my life and freedom, even if we're never allowed to talk about it."

"No, but we could have a ruddy good *secret* celebration to mark the anniversary of our adventure once a year," Kiwi suggested.

"Oh, yes!" Emily agreed, "And we'll include Mila and Jasha and Graham and Christian, too!"

"I hope I'm going to be invited," Robin remarked coming up behind her.

She let herself fall backwards to rest on his chest and he automatically put his arms around her waist as she looked up at him and promised, "Of course, my love."

"Emily, are you drunk?"

"Oh, I don't think so. Although, I do feel a bit woozy. Do you think I'm drunk?"

"I'd say you're pickled, my dear. Perhaps I ought to take you home before you become disorderly and discredit to me in some way?"

"Yes, please," she agreed, adding with a giggle, "To bed."

"Definitely blotto," Kiwi diagnosed, and Kit agreed, "Sozzled."

"Excuse me, gentlemen. My damsel is in need of succour." Robin guided Emily gently out of the lounge and took her home.

Easter Parade
Fassberg-Tempelhof
Friday 15 April 1949
(Day 296 of the Berlin Airlift)

"Jeeze, J.B.! Have you seen the 'howgozit' board this morning?" Lt. Pete Drakakis, J.B.'s current copilot, exclaimed. "They've posted a daily quota that's absolutely crazy."

Just then, the loudspeaker squawked: "All duty pilots report to the briefing room! All duty pilots to the briefing room."

They crowded in, too many to sit down, and the Base Commander, Colonel Jack Coulter, sprang onto the raised platform at the front of the room with easy grace. He looked particularly smart this morning, with slicked-back hair and highly polished shoes. The assembled officers came to their feet and attention.

"At ease. Gentlemen, General Tunner has tasked us and all other units of the Combined Air Lift Task Force with delivering an Easter present to the people of Berlin. Between noon today and noon tomorrow we are going to fly our asses off non-stop. To speed things up we aren't carrying any fragile or perishable cargoes. Nothing that requires special handling and no mixed cargoes, which need proper configuration to keep the centre of gravity balanced. Nope. We'll be flying nothing but sacks of coal — so forget about looking smart for the Red Cross girls with the doughnuts and wear your oldest, most beat-up duds." They laughed.

"Every departure base has been given a quota by the old man," he explained, meaning Tunner. "He made a point of telling me this is the *minimum*. Got it? The *minimum* that we are expected to fly into Berlin in the next 24 hours." He turned around and wrote in chalk on the blackboard behind him the figure: 250. He underlined the foot-high figure twice. "That's the number of sorties, not the tons carried," he clarified. Someone whistled. "Yep. It's 50% more than our average. Now, 250 C-54 sorties mean 3,500 tons of coal." He wrote this down on the board too. "That's what we're going to deliver from Fassberg to Berlin in the next 24 hours — *minimum*. Got it?"

A ragged chorus of "Yes, sir!" came back at him.

"Now, what I *really* want isn't any measly 250 sorties, but—" he turned to the blackboard and in even larger chalk numerals wrote: 313. With the chalk, he hit each numeral as he read out loud. "Three-One-Three — just like the number of this Group. Got it?"

"Yes, sir!" They answered more energised, many of them grinning.

"To get there, nobody stops flying after three round trips. For the next 24 hours, you are on twelve-hour shifts. You eat in your planes, and you piss on your tailwheels. Got it?"

Another chorus of "Yes, sir!" answered him.

"I've divided you into two teams. The 28th and 48th Transport Squadrons are Team A and the 47th and 49th Transport Squadrons are Team B."

"Team A flies from noon to midnight — that means, the last *take-off* for Berlin is before midnight; you may be landing later than that and your return to Fassberg will be whenever it is. Meanwhile, Team B takes over and flies from midnight to noon tomorrow. Same rule: even if it's only one minute before noon, you take off and fly the cargo to Berlin. It's deliveries to Berlin that count. Understood?"

The response of "Yes, sir!" was the loudest and most enthusiastic yet.

"Then get the hell out there and start flying!"

They burst out of the ops room chattering and laughing and within seconds some of them were jogging and then running to get a head start. Everyone knew their logs showed exactly who flew when. At the end of the day, there would be a "winning" squadron and crew. Suddenly they all wanted to be "the best."

J.B. was assigned to the 48th Transport Squadron, which meant he was flying the first shift from noon to midnight. He and his copilot went straight from the briefing to the ops centre to find out their aircraft assignment and time slot. They then went down to the flight line and found their C-54, which the stevedores were frantically filling with sacks of coal. The German loaders always worked efficiently and energetically; today they were practically killing themselves.

J.B. and Drakakis had to scramble over the coal in the hold to get into the cockpit. No sooner had their radio operator, Sergeant Alcomb, switched on the radio than the voice of their Squadron Leader, Major Duncan, came out of the earphones. "Hurry up, boys! I intend to be at the head of the runway at 11:58 and I want you in line behind me like cute little duckies! As soon as I accelerate, the pilot behind me goes on the runway. If you aren't cleared, tell them to clear you, but get your butt on the runway and follow me into the air." And so it began.

J.B. and Drakakis got into the spirit of things easily. It was a sunny day with perfect visibility and good radio reception. The two men liked each other. Drakakis was a veteran of the war in the Pacific, and like J.B., he was a college grad, albeit he'd majored in classics and hoped to teach at a college when he returned to civilian life. What J.B. liked best about him was that he'd gone through the special Airlift training at Great Falls, Montana, and was a good pilot. Sergeant Alcomb, their radio operator, was a cheerful youngster who got along with everyone. They soon found themselves playing word games or "I spy" to keep from getting bored as they shuttled back and forth from Fassberg to Gatow.

Once Drakakis entertained them by reporting to Air Traffic Control at Gatow in Greek, but that only stumped the Brits for a couple of seconds. Then one of the British controllers replied in the same language. Meanwhile, other pilots were offering ditties and rhyming couplets. The one J.B. always remembered was: "Here comes a Yankee with a blackened soul, bound for Gatow with a load of coal." He and his crew also got a laugh out of their squadron mate who enquired what kind of aircraft was flying in the block immediately ahead of them. It was one of the civilian carriers and Gatow identified it as a 'Wayfarer.' "What? The Mayflower?" Their colleague gasped in mock shock, "You really have thrown everything into this effort, haven't you?"

At both ends of the route, when the operations officer came around in a jeep with their next flight plan, they asked how things were going. Each time they were amazed by how well they were doing. Success kept them fired up.

The ground staff was working just as hard as the aircrews. The mobile canteens rushed from aircraft to aircraft and the girls just handed out potato chips, sandwiches, doughnuts and candy bars. "You can pay us tomorrow!" the girls told them laughing, then waved as they whooshed away to the next plane. At Fassberg, the base commander's wife Constance Bennett, a minor movie star, got into the act by joining the girls who were distributing the refreshments.

Meanwhile, the stevedores were sweating buckets in the April sunshine, and tables had been set up with jugs of water to keep them hydrated. J.B. noticed that troops of Boy Scouts stood by, ready to spring into action if a team of stevedores signalled they needed a short break. It took eight Boy Scouts to replace five men, but they made up in enthusiasm what they lacked in strength. Somehow, the pace never lagged, and J.B. could only shake his head in wonder.

By the time darkness fell, however, J.B. was starting to feel the fatigue. Sunset was now 8 pm, so he'd been on duty eight hours and had completed three round trips already, with still another four hours to go. By 10 pm, they were weary enough for Drakakis to suggest that they nap in turns. This meant that one pilot slept in the corridor inbound to Berlin and the other in the corridor outbound to Fassberg. They took off for their fifth flight of the day just after 11 pm and landed at Gatow twenty-two minutes after midnight. They were done. Now all they had to do was get back to Fassberg.

Drakakis had nodded off to sleep in his seat, and Alcomb had drunk so much coffee he had to jump down for a quick piss on the grass as the last sack of coal was removed from the hold. J.B. waved away the mobile canteen and was about to contact the tower when a figure emerged out of the dark and called up to him. "Captain, can you give me a lift back to Fassberg?"

The hitchhiker was wearing an old beat-up flight jacket and by his voice, he was an older man. Probably some staff officer, J.B. figured. He shouted out of the window, "Yeah, but only if you shake a leg. They need this bird back in Fassberg ASAP so they can fill her up again."

The hitchhiker just gave him a thumbs-up and headed for the door while J.B. contacted Gatow Tower. When he had clearance to taxi, he nudged Drakakis awake with his elbow and the copilot roused himself as J.B. leaned out to shout "Chocks away!" to the ground crew. While taxiing, Drakakis became aware that someone was standing behind his seat watching his every move. The co-pilot glanced up, then took another look to confirm what he thought he'd seen the first time. No, he had not been dreaming. With a yelp, he tried to get out of his seat. A hand on his shoulder stopped him. "Stay where you are, Lieutenant. I'm just a hitchhiker on this flight. Want to see how things are going at Fassberg before I turn in."

Only then did J.B. steal a look himself and realise that his hitchhiker was General Tunner.

They landed at Fassberg shortly before 2 am, and J.B. reported his passenger to the tower as they landed. By the time they reached their loading position, a jeep with Colonel Coulter was waiting. Coulter saluted Tunner as the latter stepped out of the Skymaster and greeted him with, "Welcome to Fassberg, General."

Tunner replied with, "How are you doing?"

"We're ten per cent over the target already, sir, and the second shift is just starting."

"That's fine," Tunner answered nodding, "but of course, it's not up to what they're doing at Celle. They're really on the ball over there."

J.B. would remember Coulter's face for the rest of his life, but at the time, he was just glad that Tunner disappeared with the colonel in the latter's jeep so he could finally go to bed.

When he woke up the next morning his first question was: "How are we doing?"

"Pretty good, I guess," Drakakis answered, yawning. "There are reporters all over the place."

They showered and went down for breakfast, knowing that they would be back on duty in the afternoon. The cafeteria was filling up rapidly and various claims were being bandied about, but no one knew for sure what the total figure was — or which base and squadron were leading.

After ascertaining he wasn't scheduled to fly again until 4:30 pm, J.B. went back to bed to sleep some more. He was woken by a cheer wafting up from the lobby. Squinting at the clock, he registered it was 2:30 pm. He figured the last aircraft that could have taken off before the noon deadline from Rhein-Main must have just landed. He shoved his feet into his shoes and went down to find out what the score was.

He didn't have to ask. At the sight of him, half a dozen pilots shouted at him: "1,398 sorties for 12,941 tons! That's more than all the trains and the trucks delivered before the Blockade!"

"What about us? What about Fassberg? Did we make 313 sorties?"

"Yeah, we made 314 sorties — and Colonel Coulter's pissed because it's one over the 313 he wanted."

They burst out laughing.

Easter Service
Berlin
Sunday, 17 April 1949
(Day 297 of the Berlin Airlift)

The clanging of the bells woke Jakob Liebherr, reminding him that it was Easter Sunday. Although neither he nor Trude were religious, they had always treated Easter Sunday as a special day. Before the war, they'd had an extra good meal, a fine bottle of wine, and visited with family. They had clung to that tradition as long as possible in an effort to retain a semblance of normality. It wasn't until the horrors of 1945 and the Soviet occupation that they had lost the energy to honour the day.

Yet the bells ringing like a cascade awoke in Jakob a desire to celebrate. There was no chance of putting together a feast, not with the rationing and Trude working such long hours, but he felt they still ought to do something special. "Trude," he gently shook her. "It's Easter Sunday and it's a beautiful, sunny day. Let's go to church."

She turned halfway over to look at him. "Church?"

"Yes. It has been such a gloomy, difficult winter. I could do with some joyful hymns celebrating the rebirth of hope after death and darkness, couldn't you?"

Trude sat up, thought about the suggestion for a moment and then decided, "If we go to church, then we should go to St. Mary's in Spandau. That's where the British-German school chorus will be performing."

"The one that includes the former streetwalkers you are training as flight nurses?"

"Exactly."

They got up, washed themselves, and dressed in their "Easter best." Jakob's suit was shiny from decades of wear, and the buttons on Trude's blouse no longer matched, but they put on hats and Trude found gloves too. They took the S-Bahn to Spandau and arrived just before the 11 am service was due to start.

They were not alone. A large crowd had gathered in front of the church, composed of both Germans and British. There were so many people, in fact, that there was a jam at the door. By the time the Liebherrs shuffled inside, the church was almost full. Jakob and Trude found a place near the organ.

The service started almost on time with a procession, accompanied by the choir singing the first hymn. With the sunlight streaming through the windows, the atmosphere was uplifting; Jakob was glad they'd come. The sermon struck the Socialist as hackneyed, but the choir was very good. He liked the fact that they alternated German with English hymns.

The surprise came after the offering when the pastor announced that Miss Anna Savage would lead the choir in a traditional spiritual. She emerged from behind the choir and with a force and purity that made the church ring with joy, she began to sing. From behind her, the choir answered, echoing and elaborating on her lead. Jakob felt a tingle go down his spine. The song was of freedom and liberation, couched as the freedom from death and sin, yet to the old Socialist it sounded like a political message — one that resonated in his ageing heart. When Anna started to clap, the choir followed her lead, and Jakob was the first in the congregation to join in. Slowly, others in the church timidly started to clap and gradually, a little self-consciously, to sway, too. It was so un-German, Jakob thought gleefully. Adolf Hitler must be rolling over in his grave! When Anna ended the song, quite contrary to 'proper' German behaviour, the congregation broke out into spontaneous applause.

After the service, Jakob would have liked to congratulate her, but she was already surrounded by other admirers. Trude suggested they find something to eat instead. She'd noticed a sign in front of a restaurant near the S-Bahn advertising "Easter Dinner from 1 pm."

They started towards the station, Jakob still humming the spiritual in his head, but their progress was disrupted by children standing on the sidewalk. Although Berliners had to stand in line for practically everything nowadays, there should not have been queues for anything official on a Sunday. The predominance of children suggested that something unusual was afoot. Jakob craned his neck to see what had attracted them and realised that there was a bakery on the corner. As he and Trude came abreast of it, he was stunned to see the window filled with Easter treats. There were coloured Easter eggs, a braided bread wreath with almonds and raisins, and buns with glazed sugar on top!

Jakob stared at the sweets and registered that sugar, raisins, almonds, and fresh eggs were available in Berlin. After gaping for another moment, he craned to look towards the sky. He followed the incessant drone of engines until he found them — spread out in a loose line: the C-54s, Lancastrians, Dakotas, Haltons, Yorks and Tudors on approach to Gatow. They had done it. They had won.

Chapter Twenty-Three
Victory of the Candy Bombers

Stalinist Economics
Berlin-Schoeneberg
5 May 1949
(Day 315 of the Berlin Airlift)

On the drive through the city to the Allied Control Council, Robin noticed the change in atmosphere. It wasn't just the warm, sunny weather or the haze of green that enveloped Berlin's remaining trees. There was a tangible alteration in the behaviour of the inhabitants as well. He saw people joking together at bus stops and arms outstretched to help a young man clamber aboard a moving tram. Flower pots overflowing with pansies suddenly appeared on the balconies of half-ruined buildings, and girls wore summer dresses with bright floral prints and short skirts showing lots of leg. Had they hidden these dresses away for years? Had Georgina's tips on turning old tablecloths and curtains into frocks spread at the speed of rumours? Or had some wise member of the City Council thought to put 'ladies' summer dresses' on the Airlift Priority List? Whatever the cause, the effect was a tangible increase in morale among not only the girls flaunting their finery but the men watching them as well.

The ACC also seemed to have been revived. A large number of cars were parked in front, and while the drivers gossiped beside their vehicles, officers bustled in and out with almost as much vitality as before the crisis. Making his way up the stairs and along the corridors to Air Commodore Waite's office, Robin detected a new purposefulness in the pace and expressions of the men and women he passed. Something was definitely in the air — besides several hundred transport aircraft.

Waite was on the phone when Robin arrived, but the Air Commodore gestured for him to sit down. Shortly afterwards, he concluded his conversation and faced Robin. "Well. If you haven't already guessed, Stalin announced the end of the Blockade."

"I hadn't noticed," Robin replied cynically.

Waite laughed. "I mean, he's agreed to lift all restrictions imposed on Allied movements since 1 March last year."

"In exchange for what?" Robin wanted to know. He did not trust Stalin for a second.

"For holding a Council of Foreign Ministers Meeting to 'discuss' the situation."

"Ah, I see." He paused. "Are we supposed to believe that?" he asked incredulously.

Waite smiled faintly. "It's not for the likes of us to judge. Bevin is sceptical but the Americans, as always, are keen, and the French have jumped on the American bandwagon. We'll just have to see what happens. There is no harm in giving in on that one point since the establishment of both the West German government and the North Atlantic Treaty Organisation will proceed regardless."

"Why would Stalin give in now?"

"Two reasons, I think. For one, the RAF and USAF have outperformed the wildest dreams even of their greatest advocates — meaning me!" he admitted with a laugh. "Tunner's 'Easter Parade' was astounding — and a slap in Stalin's face."

"I confess, I misjudged that. I feared it would simply lead to accidents, exhaustion, and a drop in deliveries on the following days. Instead, it went off without a hitch and was a tremendous boost to the morale not just of aircrews, but also airfield staff and the whole city, it seems. Furthermore, deliveries are still above pre-Easter levels. Lesson learnt on my part, but I still find it hard to imagine that it impressed Stalin."

"I have no access to Stalin's inner circle much less his mind. However, based on what I've been told, the Easter Parade was only the icing on the cake. By the time we proved we could deliver as much by air as previously reached the city by rail, road and canal combined, Stalin had already admitted to himself that he had miscalculated. In short, the Easter Parade rubbed his nose in a mess he was already starting to detest. Evidently, his decision to backtrack had been made earlier. The first overtures to the US via surreptitious channels were made in early February. If we assume that he had expected General Winter to kill the Airlift, the defection of that famous Russian general shattered his optimism. As soon as the Airlift weathered the fog and cold at the turn of the year, Stalin recognised it wasn't going to collapse. According to my sources, he tried to tie the lifting of the Blockade to stopping the establishment of a new sovereign German state."

"Of course," Robin commented cynically, adding in surprise, "And we didn't waffle?"

"No. Not in the least. Nor was the establishment of the North Atlantic Treaty Organisation ever on the bargaining table."

"You're saying Stalin agreed to lift the Blockade without any quid pro quo?"

"Not exactly," Waite's eyes twinkled. "The agreement ends *all* restrictions on the free movement of goods and people imposed since last March. We in Berlin tend to forget that the entire Soviet Zone has also been subjected to a blockade. It hasn't been a total blockade like the one of Berlin. We couldn't and didn't cut off children from milk or sick people from medicine, but the Western powers have prohibited the export of coal, steel, cellulose, and rubber, not to mention key manufactured goods such as conveyor belts, ball bearings, ignition and transmission systems, electric motors, and optical equipment. The sanctions technically only prohibit imports into the Soviet Zone, but the destination of many of those exports was ultimately the Soviet Union itself. My colleagues from the Economic Section tell me our Embassy in Moscow is reporting that the situation has become dire in some sectors. Apparently, some Soviet factories can only operate below capacity or have been forced to close down altogether. The Airlift is a propaganda defeat for Stalin, but exposing the economic dependence of the Soviet Block on Western imports is a political disaster that he can ill afford."

Robin nodded solemnly and reflected sadly, "It always comes down to economics in the end, doesn't it?"

"No. Without the triumph of the Airlift and the determination of the Berliners, there would have been no counterblockade. Furthermore, the decision has already been made that, whether the Blockade ends or not, the Airlift will continue. We'll keep flying non-perishable materials into Berlin until so much is stockpiled that Berlin can thrive for months without imports — just in case the Russians change their mind after we send the air fleets home."

"What date are they talking about?"

"Midnight on the morning of the 12th of May."

When the Lights Come on Again
RAF Gatow
Wednesday 11 May 1949
(Day 321 of the Berlin Airlift)

Preparations for receiving rail, road and canal traffic on 12 May fell primarily to the respective ground forces, the *Reichsbahn*, and the Berlin civil authorities. Air Force orders were to continue flying as if nothing had changed. But the news was out. Reporters from around the world flooded into Berlin and the hotels were overbooked. The tangible excitement of the visitors contrasted with the scepticism of personnel at Gatow and the Berliners themselves. They had come to expect nothing but lies, cheating, and double-dealing from the Soviets.

As the clock ticked down towards midnight on 11 May, Gatow vibrated with invisible tension. On the surface, all operations were 'normal.' Yet, as though a subliminal buzz was in everyone's ear, no one had gone to bed, and no one could quite sit still either. Off-duty staff clustered in the messes and clubs, anywhere there was a radio, and in all public areas, radios were tuned to either RIAS or the BBC with the volume turned up.

Robin was in his office. Emily, he knew, was over at the Malcolm Club with Georgina, Anna and all Berlin-based EAS personnel who weren't currently flying. He would have liked to join them but felt it was inappropriate for the station commander to join civilians in a club. Whatever happened at midnight was a matter of professional, as well as personal, interest. Yet it seemed just as inappropriate to go to the officers' mess since the other ranks would be no less seriously affected. Besides, he did not want to listen to some journalist commenting on events. He wanted to witness them.

Spontaneously, he called down to the flight line and requested his Spitfire be made ready for flight. He kicked off his shoes and donned flying boots. As he reached for his flight jacket, his eye fell on Bertie the Bear. "You have a right to see this," he told the stuffed animal and tucked him under his arm.

At the hangar, his Spitfire was filled with aviation fuel and the ground crew completed the checks with alacrity. The Chiefy asked if he wanted ammunition, and he said 'no'. He scrambled up the wing and into the cockpit, dropping onto the parachute waiting there for him. In just 20 minutes, he was ready to take off.

He called the tower and was cleared to jump the take-off queue on the PSP runway, delaying the return flights of the freighters by barely a minute. At just seven minutes to midnight, he was airborne and steered toward the city centre to avoid the streams of Airlift traffic in the corridors. As he approached the Eastern half of the city, the jagged outline of the Sector border stood out dramatically. To the west of the Sector boundary, everything was black except for three large cones of bright light that marked the airfields at Gatow, Tempelhof and Tegel. To the east, in contrast, dim streetlights sparsely lined the major avenues, headlights moved slowly through the maze of buildings, and here and there yellow squares marked the windows of people still awake. Altogether, there was just enough light to make out the contours of the urban landscape.

Robin banked gently to fly over Karlshorst, where the Soviet Military Administration was headquartered. As expected, lights burned in many windows as though everyone was working overtime — as well they should!

He turned and started back towards the West. The navigation lights of the Airlift freighters converged on the city from two directions, the northwest and the southwest, stretching like loose chains of jewels against the dark backdrop of the dark Soviet Zone.

Abruptly, light flooded the cockpit from below. Robin looked down to see West Berlin transformed into a glittering tangle of streetlights and glowing windows. He had not expected such a sudden and dramatic transformation. All across the West, people must have turned their lights on so they would know if the Soviets had kept their word — or not.

People on the ground must be cheering, clapping, shouting and singing for joy, he thought. No doubt they were hugging one another, slapping each other on the back and drinking toasts as well. He almost regretted his decision to fly — and yet, the beauty of the moment was inexplicably enhanced by being alone in the Spitfire — with Bertie. The bear's sad, brown eyes reminded him of the little girl, her mother, and all the others who had so long and silently endured so much for this moment.

He was grateful, too, not to have to find the right words and the right tone to mark the moment. He didn't have to avoid gloating and self-congratulation. He didn't have to set a good example. He could simply soak in the sense of relief and gratitude that the crisis was over. It had overshadowed his life for almost a year, come close to destroying his future and nearly consumed Emily alive. He was boundlessly grateful to God that he had been allowed to witness this moment first-hand, and not through a newspaper while in disgrace or, far worse, alone.

He climbed to 20,000 feet, 10,000 feet above the Airlift traffic, and flew due West until he could see a line of lights crawling away from the town of Helmstedt, on the border of the British and Soviet zones. He counted over seventy lorries advancing on the autobahn; they would reach Berlin in about two hours' time.

Satisfied, he banked hard and set course for Gatow. Calling into ATC, he was cleared to land on the PSP runway to minimise disruption of the incoming freighters. He swooped down low at the very start of the runway where he was visible in the glare of the floodlights for the taxiways and parking positions. At just 100 feet, he did a slow "victory" roll and then touched down before the runway ran out. No victory of his career had ever felt quite so sweet as this one.

When the Boys Come Home Again
RAF Gatow
Thursday 12 May 1949
(Day 322 of the Berlin Airlift)

It had been declared a public holiday across the city. Public buildings, offices, and schools were closed, but shops were demonstratively open and showing off the wealth of goods available in Berlin again. Since the British School had joined in the holiday spirit and closed, Hope was home and terribly excited. Indeed, everyone seemed to be breathing in excitement with the very air, while the airwaves vibrated with newscasts enthusiastically cataloguing the sights, sounds and smells assaulting the city.

Kathleen had worked the night shift, but she was as affected as everyone else. She managed to sleep only a few hours before waking with the sense that she was "missing history" by staying in her bed. She wanted to do more than listen to the radio, she wanted to see things with her own eyes. She wished she could celebrate with J.B., but he was flying (of course!) so she and Hope were on their own. They dressed up and caught one of the Station buses bound for Spandau with Hope skipping and humming to herself the whole way.

A mood of jubilation embraced them in Spandau where the streets were flooded with people, many of them holding up signs saying things like "The Airlift Wins!" or "We're still alive!" The second message sobered Kathleen a little. She had seen the Airlift as a struggle against a bully, rather like the war against Hitler, but she had never thought of it as an existential crisis. That Berliners felt happy "to be alive" gave her food for thought.

But Spandau was just a suburb, and Kathleen wanted to see what things were like in the heart of the city. So, she and Hope squeezed aboard one of the trains bound for the city centre. Although passengers were packed in like sardines, the crowd was in such a joyous mood that they were friendly and courteous to each other. They also made a fuss over Kathleen and Hope, giving Kathleen a seat so she could take Hope on her lap. So many people waved and smiled that Hope giggled and bounced with delight. Kathleen was embarrassed by the many passengers who thanked her for "British support."

At Zoo Station, they followed the crowd out of the station and let the flow of humanity sweep them toward the Kaiser Wilhelm *Gedaechtnis Kirche* at the start of the Kurfuerstendamm. Kathleen could hardly believe her eyes.

Her first encounter with Germany on the train ride through the devastated Ruhr had left a lasting impression. The level of destruction had shocked her, and she had been torn between pride in what the Allies had achieved and shame that she did not feel more pity and sympathy for the German civilians.

In the year that followed, rather than confront her guilt at not being more compassionate, she'd simply chosen to ignore the Germans as much as possible. It had been easy to wrap herself in the British cocoon at Gatow. As a result, she had a bit of a shock when she now encountered Germans laughing and singing cheerful songs so unlike the Nazi marches she remembered from newsreels. Street musicians were out in force, too, particularly old men or crippled soldiers with fiddles or hurdy-gurdys. Best of all, from Hope's perspective, there were men selling ice cream on seemingly every corner — all besieged by children.

Gradually Kathleen realised that the pavements were choked with people standing in queues. Some led to shops selling fruit and vegetables, others to butchers or bakers. As customers emerged, they wandered back along the length of the queue, proudly showing off their purchases to those still waiting. Their baskets and sacks were laden with oranges, lemons, cucumbers, fresh tomatoes, fresh potatoes and more — all things no one had seen for months. The fresh cuts of meat and strings of sausages produced gasps of awe, and fresh fish displayed on a bed of ice received rapturous applause. Now and then, someone in the queue would call out anxiously. "Is there enough for all of us?"

The answer was always the same: "There's more than enough for everyone!"

Gradually, Kathleen became aware that people were gravitating towards the station at Wittenbergplatz. She and Hope were swept along with them. She asked the people around her what was going on, and they answered "Reuter!" "Reuter will speak!" "At Tempelhof!"

Kathleen remembered what a sensation Reuter's speech the previous September had caused. This speech was sure to be another historical event. Inspired by the thought of watching history, she asked Hope, "Shall we go and see the mayor speak, Hope?"

"Will you buy me an ice cream afterwards?"

"Yes," Kathleen promised.

They joined the masses flooding the U-Bahn at Wittenbergplatz and travelled as far as Mehringdam station and from there followed the crowd down the north-south avenue at a leisurely pace. They took time to admire the shop windows that were not only full but also lovingly arranged to display the sudden riches: bolts of fabric, new shoes, lamps, school and office supplies, ladies' dresses and men's suits, make-up and tobacco products. It impressed Kathleen that although some of the shop windows had no or only partial glass, no one seemed to fear they would be plundered. The shopkeepers simply stood in the doorways grinning at the passers-by or gesturing towards their wares with pride.

The avenue led to the large square at the entrance to Tempelhof Airport. A large crowd had already assembled here, and a platform was being hammered together and microphones set up.

Kathleen started to have second thoughts. The speech was bound to be in German. She wouldn't be able to understand any of it. What was the point of standing around for another hour or so? Then she saw two cars inching their way through the crowd and in one of them sat the unmistakable figure of General Clay. The American general would certainly speak in English, she concluded, as around her the crowd started cheering.

Reuter and Clay mounted the podium together, and a hush of anticipation gripped the crowd. Reuter approached the microphones and spoke first. Although he started in German it sounded as though he was intoning names. Listening closely, she heard: "Major Edwin Diltz, F/O I.R. Donaldson, Tech Sgt Heinig, Fl/Lt Kell, Second Lt Donald Leeman...." Kathleen was stunned to realise he was reading off the names of all 48 men who had given their lives during the Airlift.

Her thoughts drifted back to that first crash in the Handjery Strasse when she had felt Ken's presence so strongly. She remembered the Dakota with 17 children on board, and of course Moby Dick. Those were the worst times. Yet it could have been so much worse. As an air traffic controller, Kathleen was all too aware of the hundreds of close calls, near misses and emergency landings that might have ended in disaster — but had not. They were lucky the list was as short as it was. Yet in a sane world, she reflected, it should not have been necessary for anyone to die.

Reuters had stopped reading the roll of honour and the people standing in the square bowed their heads and stood in silence. The only sound came from the aircraft landing and taking off on the airfield just beyond the terminal building. Kathleen wondered if J.B. was flying in. He'd said something about substituting for a pilot who flew to Tempelhof.

Reuter turned to Clay and said something that triggered cheers and clapping from the crowd. Clay stepped up to the microphones facing the crowd, his eyes as ever sunken in dark circles. "The end of the Blockade," he opened, "does not merely mean the trains and trucks are moving again. It has a deeper meaning. By breaking the physical Blockade, there has also been a breaking of the spiritual and moral blockade that long gripped this city. The people of Berlin have earned their right to freedom and to be accepted by those who love freedom everywhere. The people of Berlin rank alongside the American and British pilots as the heroes of the Berlin Blockade." It took a moment for his words to be translated, but when they were, they were greeted enthusiastically, and it took some time before Clay could conclude his remarks. "I shall not use the English word 'good-bye' but rather say to you *Aufwiedersehen*." The crowd erupted in new cheering and clapping, while Clay got back into his staff car and was whisked away.

When Reuter spoke in German, Hope started squirming and Kathleen decided it was time to slip away. Apologizing left and right, she led Hope out of the crowd and across the street.

"Can I have my ice cream now?" Hope asked hopefully.

"Yes, sweetheart," Kathleen answered and looked around. They had passed a couple of cafés on Mehringdam, but these had been overwhelmed by customers. Then she had another idea. "Hope, let's go around to the back of the field and watch the planes land. Remember how we saw sweets dropped on little parachutes?"

"Do they still drop sweets like that?" Hope asked hopefully.

"No, they don't need to any more because the sweets can come by road and railway, but wouldn't it be fun to watch the planes come in over the apartment houses one last time?"

Hope nodded and they walked hand-in-hand along on the cobbled pavement until they came to the open space where only a chain-link fence separated them from the airfield. Where once only children had gathered, a huge crowd of all ages had collected. They held up hand-made signs saying in English and German: "Candy-Bombers Win!" "Airlift defeats Blockade!" or simply "Thank you!"

The crowd was so thick that Kathleen and Hope couldn't get near the end of the runway, so they sought out a place beside the fence where the runway ran out and the C-54s turned off it to taxi back. It was not as exciting as standing just feet below the lowered wheels of the approaching Skymasters, but at least they were directly beside the fence and could see the pilots moving about in the cockpit. They waved to them and the pilots waved back.

Suddenly a C-54 screeched to a halt. Kathleen frowned. Aircraft were prohibited from stopping on the taxiway. The next plane had already touched down with a squeal of rubber and would soon be turning off onto the same taxiway. To her amazement, the cargo door opened, and a man in a leather flight jacket jumped down onto the tarmac and started running towards her. The door closed behind him and the C-54 continued on its way.

Kathleen recognised J.B., and she waved nervously to him. He shouldn't be doing this.

He shouted to her from ten feet away: "We did it! We beat Stalin!"

A second later, he reached the fence and leaned towards her, turning his head so their lips could meet through the chain links. Their fingers gripped each other around the wires. As he drew back grinning, he told her breathlessly. "It's over, Kathleen. Rumours are flying that my whole squadron will be sent home as early as next week! Not that we're quitting. Another unit is coming out to keep flying, but we die-hards are going to be sent home sooner rather than later." He was gazing into her eyes, imploring her. "Kathleen, you know how I feel about you, but I can't wait forever. It's now or never. Please say you'll marry me!"

Kathleen leaned forward to offer him another kiss through the fence. She didn't know exactly when she'd made up her mind, but she no longer had any doubts; being with J.B. was what she wanted. She was even starting to look forward to going to America. As she ended the kiss she told him simply, "Yes, Jay. I'll marry you."

J.B. let out a hoot of triumph and gave her another kiss through the fence. Then he broke off and went down on his haunches to address Hope. "Hi there, Hope! Remember me?"

She nodded solemnly, "You're the man who dressed up like Father Christmas and brought sweets to my kindergarten and then had tea with my Mummy and me afterwards."

"Yup. That's me. What would you say to coming with me and your Mummy to America?"

"To Texas?" Hope asked, frowning slightly.

J.B. laughed. He had no idea why foreigners were so obsessed with Texas, but everyone he met seemed to think Texas was the next best thing after paradise. To Hope he answered. "No, sweetheart, it's a place called Michigan with great, big lakes."

"Like the Havel?"

"Bigger!" J.B. promised without exaggerating.

Still very sober, Hope asked, "Do you want to be my new Daddy?"

"Yes, do you think you'd like that?"

Hope considered this thought carefully for a moment and finally nodded soberly and declared, "Yes. I think I'd like that, but first, will you buy me some ice cream?"

Chapter Twenty-Four
Tomorrow, When the World is Free

Sing a New Song
EAS Halifax
Wednesday 20 July 1949

The Halifax freighter roared as she surged down the runway at Gatow and lifted into the air, doing her namesake Pegasus proud. Since there were no longer any outbound cargoes, the aircraft was empty and correspondingly light. Furthermore, although the RAF and USAF were still flying supplies into Berlin to build up stockpiles, the contracts with civilian companies were allowed to expire as they came due for renewal. Emergency Air Services had delivered its last cargo to Berlin, and this outbound flight represented the end of the company's service on the Berlin Airlift.

Yet if the cargo hold was empty, the crew compartment was full. Georgina had insisted on being aboard this last flight with Kit, and Anna and Gordon were also 'hitching a lift' with them. Although Air Ambulance International was doing so well that Christian calculated it would be only a few months before they could expand to a second aircraft, Anna had decided that the job of flight nurse was not her calling in life. She had turned the flight nurse duties over to the two German girls she'd helped to train and resigned from AAI. This meant that Anna, like the rest of the passengers and crew on "Peggy," hadn't a clue what the future held.

Just a week earlier, Ethiopian Airlines had finally replied to Kit's job application. They informed him that his disabilities disqualified him from flying for them. That answer seemed acridly ironic as he eased his artificial leg on the left rudder to adjust "Peggy's" course. Instead of a flying job, they had offered him a teaching position at their training academy for flight engineers and engine mechanics. In principle, that was a good job, and although the pay was low, so was the cost of living in Addis Ababa. Georgina had been willing to go, excited at the prospect of teaching in Africa. Yet, Kit resisted the notion of working for a company that viewed him as an invalid. Which meant, he was back to where he'd been a year ago: unemployed with no obvious prospects.

Kit glanced toward Bruce. The young Australian had proved to be a reliable second pilot and had grown into a capable captain as well. His job outlook was slightly better than Kit's because he was young and fully fit. Still Kit doubted Bruce would have an easy time finding a flying job because all civil aviation companies would be flooded with applications from pilots who'd flown on the Berlin Airlift.

Gordon MacDonald sat on the engineer's fold-down seat while Richard Scott-Ross stood behind him. Gordon had managed (with help) to shuffle himself into this position after leaving his wheelchair tied down in the hold. Anna had worked wonders with him over the past few months, but his chances of meaningful employment remained virtually nil. For the moment, he seemed happy just to be going home to Maisy and his girls, but Kit feared that mood would not last long. Gordon wasn't a man who liked being idle.

Kit worried about Nigel and Terry, too. They had been a good team. Since joining Emergency Air Services, Nigel had had only a couple of minor scuffles. Yet the chances of either of them finding flying jobs — much less one together — seemed slim; they were almost certain to split up. Without Terry's good influence, Nigel might revert to his old, resentful and belligerent self. At least for the moment, however, they were making the best of things and singing "It's a Long Way to Tipperary" over the intercom. Kit and the others joined in as they left Berlin airspace for the last time.

Kit's flight plan took them south of Hanover and across Holland south of The Hague. Scattered clouds gave them frequent glimpses of the European countryside below them. It was green and there were many more cars on the roads than a year ago. A lot of construction could be detected as well. The Marshall Plan was having a visible impact everywhere. While his crew competed at recognizing and pointing out points of interest, Kit became aware of a rapid exchange of insults between Anna and Richard that crackled with mutual attraction. He caught Georgina's eye after one exchange of quips, and she winked at him, amused. Kit wished them both well but wondered how much racism they would face in the 'real' world they were returning to after the bubble of tolerance EAS represented.

As Peggy swept majestically out over the North Sea, memories briefly caught up with Kit. He remembered the daylight raids against the Tirpitz, the Kembs barrage, the attack on the U-boat factory and the fateful last flight against U-boat pens that ended in a crash inside Germany. Yet the horror was fading, overshadowed by the mere fact of survival, the sunshine and the joy of flying. If only he hadn't feared this would be the last time he sat at the controls of a powerful aircraft....

Suddenly, Terry's voice was in his ear. "Skip! I just received a request to divert to Stansted."

"Is Northolt closed?" Kit asked astonished. The weather looked good as far as he could see.

"No, Skip. It was directed at us specifically."

"But why?"

"I don't know, Skip."

"All right. Give me the new course and ETA, Nigel." He started calculating what impact the diversion would have on their onward travel. He and Georgina had hoped to catch a train north in time to spend the night in Foster Clough with their daughter Donna and Georgina's parents. He knew his in-laws were eagerly expecting them and had probably planned something special. Georgina was anxious to get back to Donna, now that her 'adventure' in Berlin was over. He hoped this wouldn't ruin everything...

When the English coast came into view, Nigel quipped "Enemy coast ahead!" and they all had a good laugh. Then they sang, as they so often had, "White Cliffs of Dover" as the Halifax sank gently down from its cruising altitude of 10,000 feet and entered British airspace.

Compared to the war and Berlin, the skies seemed empty. London air traffic control handed them off to Stansted, which had no other traffic whatsoever. All too soon they were on the ground where a "Follow Me" vehicle led them to a parking position. Kit swung the Halifax around and cut the engines. In the stunned silence after the four Hercules cut out, Kit and Bruce exchanged a melancholy smile.

Around them, Nigel and Terry scrambled up to the flight deck to help Richard guide and carry Gordon back to the exit. Georgina and Anna squeezed themselves out of the way and then followed. Bruce and Kit completed the cockpit drill for leaving the aircraft parked and then unstrapped and put on their caps. Bruce went out first, giving Kit a chance to linger one last moment in the cockpit, his eyes caressing the familiar panel of instruments and the worn leather seat. Then he took a deep breath and forced himself down the fuselage to drop onto the tarmac.

To his astonishment, the others were clustered together chattering excitedly. Kit registered that David Goldman was in their midst accompanied by an airport official. David's eyes lit on Kit, and he started towards him with his hand extended.

"Good to see you, David," Kit greeted him as they shook hands.

"Wait until you hear what I have to say," David cautioned with a wry smile, and Kit tensed. David drew a breath and announced, "Yesterday, I received a call from the International Red Cross. There have been massive floods across northern Burma. Roads have been washed away. Many villages are cut off and people are running short of drinking water, blankets, first aid supplies and just about everything else. They asked if EAS could make a drop of water purifiers, tents, food, and other emergency supplies."

"In Burma?"

"If we do this, Kit, the Red Cross assures me it won't be our last job. They need a reliable partner to get supplies and people in and out of areas struck by natural disasters — and sometimes into war zones. They are offering us a contract with a retainer—" He didn't get to finish his sentence.

Around him, the others had started cheering. Bruce had leapt clear into the air in his exuberance, Nigel and Terry were each giving Kit the thumbs-up with both hands and saying "Yes, yes, yes!" Richard was nodding vigorously. Gordon was clapping his hands, and Anna was grinning.

Kit turned to Georgina and was astonished to see her smiling broadly. "You wouldn't mind?" He asked, torn between euphoria at the prospect of a job like this and his sense of duty to his family. "What about Donna and you?"

"We'll make a home for ourselves — and you — wherever you're stationed," she assured him, adding with a smile, "Stansted looks fine to me!"

Kit turned to David. "Will we be based here in Stansted?"

"No, too expensive. Furthermore, the Red Cross believes humanitarian crises are more likely to be concentrated in Africa and the Middle East. I've been thinking about Cyprus."

Kit looked once more at Georgina, but she beamed, "It sounds marvellous, Kit! I can't wait to tell my father! He'll be so pleased. It's the kind of work you were *meant* to do. I'm sure of it."

"But what about you and Donna?

"I'm far more likely to find meaningful work in Cyprus than here in Stansted, and Cyprus is warm and safe, so we'll take Donna with us. As she grows up, she will benefit from seeing more of the world."

Kit pulled Georgina into his arms and held her to him as he told David, "Done! We keep flying!"

The others broke into a louder cheer and David grinned with relief.

The Sun is Still in the Sky
RAF Gatow
Sunday 31 July 1949

The clouds hung low, emitting a misty drizzle that chilled and dampened everything. The gloom matched Emily's mood. Aside from apprehension about the future, it was hard to leave Berlin. She remembered vividly how reluctant she had been to come — her ambivalence towards the Germans, her doubts about whether she could adequately perform the quasi-diplomatic duties expected of her, and her fear of being bored. Yet it had not been long before she'd met and come to respect Germans like Charlotte, Christian and Jakob. Berlin had also given birth to Air Ambulance International, which had enabled her to be a part of something meaningful. She felt she had grown and matured into a better person over the past 18 months.

Glancing at Robin as he sat beside her in the back seat of the staff car, she remembered that 18 months ago, she had worried about their marriage, too. They had been drifting apart by the end of 1947. They had both been unhappy with themselves and their careers; they had turned inward. Maybe their love had been cooling. Certainly, they had been communicating less. Now, in contrast, she felt closer and more in love than ever before. Maybe love felt less miraculous and magical than in 1940, but it also seemed more profound. Berlin had been good for them both, she thought. Robin, too, had become more comfortable in his own skin, and as a result, more tolerant and understanding of others.

Yet, while these changes made them strong for the future, they did not ease the pain of departing. As they travelled for the last time from their residence to Gatow, she reflected that over the last 18 months, their life had been enriched by encounters with an array of exceptional characters. She hated the thought that she would never see most of them ever again — certainly not political figures like Jakob Liebherr or General Clay. Yet even friends like the Howleys were unlikely to keep in touch after they returned to the States, and Emily questioned if Christian would maintain personal contact. Meanwhile, David was on the other side of the world trying to bring vitally needed supplies to isolated villages in the Burmese mountain. When that crisis was over, he planned to relocate someplace 'globally central' and with him would be not only Charlotte but the best friends Emily had ever had: Kiwi, Kit and Georgina. At least Graham and Jasha planned to retire to the UK, so she might see them again. Still, she was going to miss Anna and Gordon MacDonald and the German ground crews that had worked day and night, in rain, snow and fog, to keep Moby Dick operational. She was even going to miss the gardener and the housemaids at the residence.

The car turned off the Kladower Damm onto the drive into the Station, and Emily registered that people were lining both sides of the road waving and clapping. "Goodness!" She exclaimed in amazement, "They must be here to say goodbye to you, Robin!"

"No," Robin answered, turning to toss her a bemused smile, "they appear to be here to say goodbye to both of us. Look at the signs!" As he spoke, he rolled down his window to start waving with his gloved hand. Confused, Emily looked at the signs people were holding. Among the thank-you signs to the RAF and England were signs that specifically said, "*Danke schoen, Frau Priestman!*" Or even "*Unsere Retterin mit dem weissen Flugzeug!*" (Our saviour with the white plane.)

Emily hastily rolled down her window so she could wave as well, and she heard people clapping and calling out. Their driver, Wallace, grinning from ear to ear, slowed the Mercedes to a crawl. Emily felt tears in her eyes. Even without this gesture, she had been finding it hard to leave. She was overwhelmed by the sense of something ending before she had properly appreciated it. It was a little bit like dying....

At the Station, there were no formalities or well-wishers. Three days earlier, General Robertson and Air Commodore Waite had organised Robin's official departure ceremonies. These had been jointly hosted by the British Military Government and the Berlin City government and held at the City Hall. Attendees at the official event had included not only Mayor Reuter and other municipal dignitaries but also the Allied Commandants and Governors. Only Clay had been missing because he had already left just three days after the end of the Blockade, sent off by huge crowds of thankful Berliners. The ceremony had consisted of speeches, flowers and a presentation of gifts from the City of Berlin.

The next day, they had been the guests of honour at a formal dinner hosted by the Howleys that included General Tunner, Air Commodore Merer, and Robin's American counterparts at Tempelhof and Tegel. Yesterday, Robin had held his farewell parade at Gatow, followed by an evening of speeches and champagne at the officers' mess.

Today, in contrast, they were supposed simply to disappear up the steps of the BEA airliner. Because they had slowed to wave goodbye to their well-wishers, they were late arriving at Gatow. The other passengers were already boarding as they pulled up in front of the terminal. The BEA representative met them with their tickets and directed Wallace to take their luggage directly out to the cargo door of the aircraft, handing him tags to attach to the suitcases. Robin and Emily were escorted to the foot of the stairs, where Robin stood aside to let Emily board first, giving her no chance to look back over her shoulder.

Emily walked up the aisle to the first row, which had been reserved for them and settled into the window seat. Robin dropped down beside her as the pilot started the number two engine, and the Dakota began to vibrate. Within fifteen minutes of leaving their car, the DC-3 was rushing down the PSP runway with Emily peering out of the window, straining for one last glimpse of Gatow. The cloud ceiling was low, however, and the airfield and Havel disappeared from view almost immediately after take-off. Emily couldn't catch even a glimpse of the residence, and the tears she had been holding back started streaming down her face.

Robin took her hand and held it without speaking.

After a moment, she sobbed, "I'm sorry. I didn't expect to be this emotional."

He wordlessly handed her his handkerchief, and she dried her eyes. After collecting herself, she turned to face him. "Won't you miss any of it? The excitement, the collaboration with so many fascinating people, the cheeky resilience and dry humour of the Berliners, the drive and generosity of the Americans, the logistical achievements, the transformation of Germany into a democracy, the way enemies have become friends, and, well, everything?" She felt frustrated by his apparent indifference to something she thought had been a major chapter in both of their lives.

He laughed but squeezed her hand to assure her he wasn't laughing at her. "I will miss all of that — but I almost lost you, and that weighs heavily, too. Besides, we came very close to disaster several times, and it is never wise to press one's luck too far. I'm glad we came. I'm glad we were allowed to stay. I'm glad I saw it through to the end. But I'm ready to move on."

Something clicked. "You know what your next assignment is!" she declared as the Dakota nosed out of the tops of the clouds into brilliant, blue-skied sunshine.

"I do, yes," Robin admitted, looking rather pleased with himself.

"And when exactly did you intend to tell me about it?" she asked, annoyed that he had been hiding such important information.

He grinned impishly. "Now seems as good a time as any."

"Indeed!" she confirmed and prompted, "and?"

"The job is Wing Commander, Flying — or Operations as they are calling it nowadays, although it will entail training as well as operations, I'm told."

"Is that a demotion?" Emily asked cautiously, noting that after filling the position of station commander, he was being relegated to a subordinate role.

"Not really. Remember, when I was assigned to Gatow it was a sleepy backwater; no one ever intended to appoint a Wing Commander, much less me, in particular, to the busiest airfield in the world; it just turned out that way. Furthermore, since the start of the Airlift, there have been no squadrons stationed at Gatow. In my next assignment, on the other hand, I'll have three squadrons: a Spitfire photo reconnaissance squadron, a Gloster Meteor fighter squadron, and a Hastings recce and transport squadron."

"Meaning you'll be doing much more flying."

"And will be required to qualify on jets," Robin explained, clearly delighted.

"No wonder you're looking so pleased with yourself!" Emily declared with sympathy. "Congratulations! But you still haven't told me *where* we're going. I do hope it's not the north of Scotland! I'm getting rather tired of dark and gloomy places."

"Don't worry. We're going to RAF Nicosia."

"Nicosia? Cyprus?" Emily's heart leapt. Robin nodded confirmation, and Emily could not hold back her enthusiasm. "That's absolutely marvellous! The Egyptians were there, and the Greeks, and the Romans and, good heavens, Richard the Lionheart! The Templars. The Venetians. I've always wanted to visit."

"Well, you should have plenty of opportunity to explore to your heart's content; I've been told the assignment is for three years."

Then she had a second thought. "Wait a minute. How far is Cyprus from Israel?"

"About 240 miles."

"And from the Suez Canal?"

"Just a little over 300."

She nodded. No, he was not being sent to a quiet backwater. This looked like a 'hot assignment,' but it was better that way. Robin thrived on challenges. Then she sat up straighter. "Robin? Didn't David say something about wanting to base EAS in Cyprus after they finished their work in Burma?"

"Did he?"

"I'm sure he did." With the whole EAS team in Burma these last weeks, Emily had not been in close contact, but now that she focused on the issue, she was sure David had mentioned Cyprus. She broke into a wide smile and exclaimed, "What a remarkable coincidence! That means I could continue working with them — assuming you agree." Emily did not defer to Robin; rather she understood that no partnership could thrive if either was left out of decisions.

"I'm not keen on the idea of you flying into war zones," Robin admitted seriously, "The risk of something happening to you are too high, and I don't think I could endure for a second time the emotional strain I felt when Moby Dick went down."

"No, that kind of emotional stress isn't pleasant," Emily replied sympathetically. "I went through more times than I can count."

"Touché," he conceded.

"I believe you told me at the time that we could not build a future on the assumption you were going to die tomorrow. The same goes for me."

"Yes, of course, and no one understands your desire to keep flying better than I. I'm not going to stand in your way, Emily."

"It's not just about the flying, you know. The humanitarian work is a rare opportunity to do something valuable and rewarding."

"I'd say it is more than that," he corrected soberly. "I think that if we are going to have a chance at 'peace ever after,' we need to do more than simply defend ourselves from aggression and oppression. We must strive for a more just and compassionate world. That's where EAS — and you — come in."

"Together, we will make the world a better place," she teased him gently.

"Little by little," he countered.

Emily stretched across the intervening armrests to give him a kiss, and when she settled back in her own seat, she kept hold of his hand. They sat that way for the rest of the flight, content and modestly hopeful for the future.

The End

If you enjoyed *Cold Victory* please leave a review on the online retailer of your choice.

Historical Note

Although the principal characters in this novel are fictional, the main events are historical. The extraordinary Soviet siege of Berlin 1948-1949 and the Allied response are well documented. There are many excellent accounts of the Berlin Blockade and Airlift, some of which are listed under "Recommended Reading." In this short note, I merely wish to highlight some of the facts that may seem most far-fetched and to note conscious deviations from the historical record.

A Word on the Characters in this Novel

- The senior military officers responsible for the Airlift were General Tunner and Air Commodore Merer. Political leadership came from US Military Governor General Clay and British Military Governor Robertson. The Berliners were led by Mayor Ernst Reuter. The public actions of all these men were recorded, and their characterisation in the novel is based to the extent possible on their memoirs, biographies or other historical sources.

- Wing Commander Robert Priestman is a fictional character. The historical station commander of Gatow during the Airlift was Group Captain Brian Yarde, who arrived in July 1947 and departed in November 1949.

- British civilian aviation companies played a critical role in the Berlin Airlift and included some of the most colourful characters of contemporary aviation such as Freddy Laker and AVM Donald Bennett. However, Emergency Air Services and its subsidiaries Air Ambulance International and Air Freight International along with all characters associated with them were invented.

The Events Depicted

- Command of the airfields in the British Zone supporting the Airlift was transferred from British Air Forces of Occupation (BAFO) to No 46 Group (Transport Command) on 1 December 1948. The CO of No 46 Group Air Commodore Merer would have been familiar with the Airlift because his squadrons were flying on it, but the briefing is a convenient device to bring the reader up to speed.

- The story of a girl giving an Airlift pilot the teddy bear she had clung to during wartime air raids is true. It is described in the memoirs of Gail Halvorsen, who was the actual recipient of the well-loved stuffed animal.

- The conditions in Berlin schools and the alarming prevalence of VD among female students depicted in the novel are based on historical evidence.

- The lynching described is based on a real incident which took place in Georgia in May 1919. Although I changed some key facts, I used the real name of the victim to draw attention to his fate. Historically, Berry Washington, 72, was lynched in McRae, Georgia, for killing one of two armed, white men who attempted to sexually assault young black girls. Washington turned himself in to the police chief, who sent him to jail in McRae. He was dragged from jail by a mob (led by a Baptist minister), hanged and shot multiple times.

- Captain Utting of Airflight Inc. died from injuries sustained when hit by a lorry on the tarmac at Gatow on the night of 8 December. Witnesses claim the lorry had no headlights and seemed to shoot out of nowhere and aim directly for Utting. Neither the driver nor the truck were ever identified, and the incident was never officially explained. Since Utting himself was a comparative newcomer, AVM Bennett believed he had been the intended victim. Yet this explanation seems doubtful as his role was not critical to the Airlift. An attempted assassination attempt of the station commander by the Soviets is a plausible thesis.

- The French blew up the Soviet radio tower interfering with operations at Tegel on 16 December. As described, Ganeval invited senior Allied commanders to join him at Tegel, where they witnessed the destruction of the tower and the call from Soviet General Kotikov.

- The problems with the civilian contractors — and the solutions found for controlling them — are part of the historical record.

- The construction of Tegel airfield, a modern power plant, the expansion of liquid fuel depots, adding electric pumps and the laying down of additional concrete runways at both Gatow and Tempelhof were just some of the many improvements to the infrastructure in Berlin made during the later stages of the Blockade.

- While in Georgia in 1943, Colonel Frank Howley had a motorcycle accident in which he broke his back and pelvis. For this reason, he was forced out of the cavalry and into 'civil affairs.' The role of Anna Savage is fictional.

- Operation 'Santa Claus' was historical, as was the donation of sweets from the Confectioners Association of America. Likewise, the Christmas dinner at Gatow for Berlin children was a historical event; the role of EAS is fictional.

- The RAF Dakota KN491 crashed into the Soviet Zone on the night of 24 January 1949. The wireless operator and seven German passengers, including Silvia Zimmerman, were killed in the crash. The cause of the crash is not recorded. Although I have used a real name, the character and her story as depicted in the novel are fictional.

- The German judicial system was in transition during the timeframe of this novel. The Federal Republic of Germany had not yet been established, the new German constitution had not yet been ratified, and Berlin would not gain sovereign status in civil affairs until June 15, 1949. In short, Germany was still under the control of the respective occupation military authorities. Yet, day-to-day criminal and civil proceedings were in the hands of the Germans. The occupying powers retained supervisory functions only. Sources are vague on exactly what laws and procedures were applied in this transitional period, so I have imagined a trial based on West German practice. The codes quoted are anachronistically those of the Federal Republic of Germany, but almost certainly in line with evolving judicial theory at this point in time.

- The stages of Charlotte's trial have been condensed for the purpose of a coherent narrative. For example, the examination of witnesses would have spread over many days and the sentencing might have been separate from the verdict.

- Until power was transferred to the German authorities, the Allied military governors held the power to pardon convicted criminals. General Clay conscientiously read trial transcripts. In some cases, he commuted the death sentence to life imprisonment due to insufficient evidence. It would have been in character for him to respond positively to a plea for mercy in a case such as the fictional trial of Charlotte.

- Clay was sincere in his efforts to "de-nazify" Germany. Hence taking an interest in the removal of judges and prosecutors known to have Nazi sympathies would also have been in character, but the events and dialogues depicted are fictional.

- Air Ambulance International is fictional as is the forced landing described in the novel. However, the Soviets threatened to treat Airlift aircrew as "spies" and detained downed fliers for indeterminate periods. In at least one instance, local residents helped Allied aircrew avoid capture by the Soviet authorities after crash-landing in the Soviet Zone.

- Tunner's "Easter Parade" is famous, and the sorties and tonnages are consistently reported as 1,398 flights for the delivery of 12,941 tons of coal. Curiously, however, sources differ with respect to which 24-hour period was involved. Some sources claim the extra effort began at noon on Good Friday and ended at noon on Easter Saturday. Others suggest the exceptional effort took place all day Easter Saturday. Yet other sources date the "Easter Parade" from noon on Saturday until noon on Sunday. Ultimately, it doesn't matter. I've chosen to use the Friday to Saturday dating because such timing ensured that Easter was a day for celebrating Christ rather than the Airlift.

- Tunner is known to have hitched rides with Airlift pilots wearing his old flight gear with his rank covered up. The exchange between General Tunner and Colonel Coulter at Fassberg is retold in many of the accounts of the Airlift.

- The Soviets lifted the Blockade on May 12 and Reuter and Clay spoke before a large crowd in front of the Schoeneberger Rathaus. While Clay's comments reflect those recorded, I changed the venue to Tempelhof to make the encounter with J.B. possible. In his speech, Reuter proposed calling the square in front of Tempelhof "Air Bridge Place" — as it is to this day.

Recommended Reading

- Auer, Peter. *Ihr Voelker der Welt: Ernst Reuter und die Blockade von Berlin*. Jaron, 1998.

- Cherny, Andrei. *The Candy Bombers: The Untold Story of the Berlin Airlift and America's Finest Hour*. G.P.Putnam's Sons, 2008.

- Clay, Lucius D., *Decision in Germany*. William Heinemann Ltd, 1950.

- Collier, Richard. *Bridge Across the Sky: The Berlin Blockade and Airlift 1948-1949*. MacGraw Hill, 1978.

- Gere, Edwin. *The Unheralded: Men and Women of the Berlin Blockade and Airlift*. Trafford, 2003.

- Halvorsen, Gail. *The Berlin Candy Bomber*. Horizon Publishers. 1997.

- Haydock, Michael D. *City under Siege: The Berlin Blockade and Airlift, 1948-1949*. Brassey's, 1999.

- Jackson, Robert. *The Berlin Airlift*. Patrick Stephens, 1988.

- Keiderling, Gerhard. *Rosinenbomber ueber Berlin: Waehrungsreform. Blockade, Luftbruecke, Teiling*. Dietz Verlag, 1998.

- Koenig, Peter. *Schaut auf diese Stadt! Berlin und die Luftbruecke*. Be.Brag Verlag, 1998.

- Miller, Roger G. *To Save a City: The Berlin Airlift 1948 – 1949*. Univ. Press of the Pacific, 2002

- Milton, Giles. *Checkmate in Berlin*. Henry Holt & Co, 2021.

- Parrish, Thomas. *Berlin in the Balance 1948-1949: The Blockade, The Airlift, The First Major Battle of the Cold War*. Perseus Books, 1998.

- Percy, Arthur. *Berlin Airlift*. Airlife, 1997.

- Prell, Uwe and Lothar Wilker. *Berlin-Blockade und Luftbruecke 1948-1949: Analyse und Dokumentation*. Berlin Verlag, 1987.

- Reeves, Richard. *Daring Young Men: The Heroism and Triumph of the Berlin Airlift, June 1948 - 1949*. Simon and Schuster, 2010.

- Rodrigo, Robert. *Berlin Airlift*. Cassel & Co., 1960.

- Scherff, Klaus. *Luftbruecke Berlin: Die dramatische Geschichte der Versorgung aus der Luft June 1948 – Oktober 1949*. Motorbuch Verlag, 1998.

- Schrader, Helena P. *The Blockade Breakers: The Berlin Airlift*. The History Press, 2008.

- Tunner, William H. *Over the Hump*. Office of Air Force History: USAF Warrior Studies, 1964.

- Tusa, Ann & John. *The Berlin Airlift*. Sarpedon, 1998.

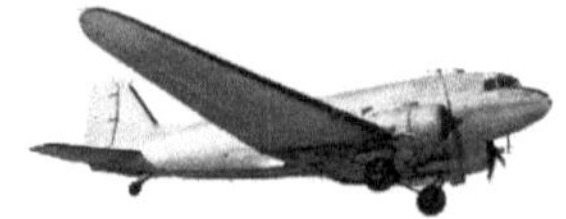

RAF/USAF Rank Table

RAF	USAAF
Marshal of the Airforce	Five Star General
Air Chief Marshal	General (4 Star)
Air Marshal	Lt. General (3 Star)
Air Vice Marshal	Major General (2 Star)
Air Commodore	Brigadier General (1 Star)
Group Captain	Colonel
Wing Commander	Lt. Colonel
Squadron Leader	Major
Flight Lieutenant	Captain
Flying Officer	First Lieutenant
Pilot Officer	Second Lieutenant

Because the USAAF had ten non-commissioned ranks to the RAF's seven, it is not possible to provide exact equivalents, however, the lowest rank in the RAF was "Aircraftman." This is the term from which term "erk" derives in RAF jargon.

The RAF non-commissioned ranks from highest to lowest were:

Warrant Officer

Flight Sergeant

Sergeant

Corporal

Leading Aircraftman — or LAC

Aircraftman (1)

Aircraftman (2)

Key Acronyms

AAI – Air Ambulance International, a subsidiary of Emergency Air Services

ACC – Allied Control Council

AFI — Air Freight International, a subsidiary of Emergency Air Services

ATC — Air Traffic Control

AVM — Air Vice Marshal

BAFO — British Air Forces of Occupation

BAOR — British Army on the Rhine

BVG — Berliner Verkehrs Gesellschaft, the Berlin public transport network

C-47 — The USAF designation for a twin-engine aircraft also known as the "Dakota" or DC3

C-54 — The USAF designation for a four-engine aircraft also known as the "Skymaster" or DC4

CALTF — Combined Air Lift Task Force

CDU — Christian Democratic Union, one of the political parties founded in post-war Germany.

CPSU — Communist Party of the Soviet Union

CRE — Corps of Royal Engineers

DP — Displaced Person

EAS — Emergency Air Services, the holding company for AAI and AFI

FDP — Free Democratic Party

Fl/Lt — Flight Lieutenant

Fl/Sgt — Flight Sergeant

F/O — Flying Officer

GCA — Ground Controlled Approach

KPD — Kommunistischer Partei Deutschlands, the German Communist Party

NSDAP — National Sozialistischer Deutscher Arbeiter Partei, commonly know as the Nazi Party

P/O — Pilot Officer

RAF – Royal Air Force

RAFVR — Royal Air Force Volunteer Reserve

R/T — Radio Telephone, the radio sets used in aircraft at this time

SED – *Sozialistische Einheits Partei* – The Socialist Unity Party, the artificial party created by the Soviet Military Government in an attempt to co-opt the SPD.

S/L — Squadron Leader

SPD – *Sozialdemokratische Partei Deutschlands* – The German Social Democratic Party

SMAD – Soviet Military Administration in Germany

USAF – United States Air Force

USAFE — United States Air Forces Europe

Wg/Cdr or WingCo — Wing Commander

Glossary of German Terms

Frau – Mrs

Fraulein — Miss

Freifrau – Baroness

Freiherr — Baron

Gedaechtnis Kirche — Memorial Church

Gnaedige – Gracious, combined with Frau as in gnaedige Frau, this is a formal form of address to a lady.

Graefin – Countess

Graf – Count

Herr — Mr

Kapitaenleutnant — Lt. Commander/Flight Lieutenant

Kollege — Colleague, used when addressing someone with the same qualifications, eg between lawyers, or members of parliament, or

Kneipe — Urban tavern

Krug — Rural tavern

Kriegsmarine — German Navy

Leutnant — Lieutenant/Pilot Officer

Luftwaffe — German Airforce

Oberleutnant — First Lieutenant/Flying Officer

Oberstleutnant — Lt Colonel/Wing Commander

Polizei — Police

Polizeipraesident — Police Chief

Reichsbahn — German National Railway

S-Bahn — commuter trains

Staatsanwalt — Public Prosecutor

Staatsoper — State Opera

Standesamt — Registry Office, venue of civil marriages

U-Bahn — Underground train network

About Helena P. Schrader

Dr. Helena P. Schrader is the author of six critically acclaimed non-fiction history books and twenty-one historical novels, twelve of which have earned one or more awards. She holds a PhD in history from the University of Hamburg, which she earned with a ground-breaking biography of a leader of the German Resistance to Hitler. She later served as an American diplomat in Europe and Africa.

For readers tired of clichés and cartoons, award-winning novelist Helena P. Schrader offers nuanced insight into historical events and figures based on sound research and an understanding of human nature. Her complex and engaging characters bring history back to life to help us better understand ourselves. Her chief areas of expertise are Aviation, the Second World War, Ancient Sparta, and the Crusader States. For more about all her books, awards, blogs and newsletter visit: https://helenapschrader.net.

Other Aviation and WWII Books
by Helena P. Schrader

Where Eagles Never Flew
A Battle of Britain Novel

Amazon #1 Best Selling book in Aviation,
Military and 20th Century Fiction

Winner of the HEMINGWAY Award for Twentieth Century Military Fiction, SILVER in the Global Book Awards and a MAINCREST Award for Military Fiction, and an Indie BRAG medallion.

Summer 1940: The Battle of France is over; the Battle of Britain is about to begin. If the swastika is not to fly over Buckingham Palace, the RAF must prevent the Luftwaffe from gaining air superiority over Great Britain. Standing on the front line is No 606 (Hurricane) Squadron. As the casualties mount, new pilots find a cold reception from the clique of experienced pilots who resent them for taking the place of their dead friends. Meanwhile, despite credible service in France, former RAF aerobatics pilot Robin Priestman finds himself stuck in Training Command — and falling for a girl from the Salvation Army. On the other side of the Channel, the Luftwaffe is recruiting women as communications specialists — and naïve Klaudia is about to grow up. Buy now on Amazon!

Praise for Best-Selling *Where Eagles Never Flew*

"This is the best book on the life of us fighter pilots in the Battle of Britain that I have ever seen. Refreshingly. it got it smack on the way it was for us. I couldn't put it down!"
Battle of Britain Ace, Wing Commander Bob Doe

"...a tremendously moving tale of human conflict, ... Where Eagles Never Flew is both inspirational and terrifying in its reality and should be required reading for anyone under the illusion that air warfare is in any way glorious."
Steven Robson for **Readers Favorites**

"This is a superb novel about the Battle of Britain and is a must-read for anyone interested in that period in our history. ... So much has been written about the battle ... that it is hard to imagine that a new novel could be written that would make the conflict seem fresh. Yet this is exactly what [Where Eagles Never Flew] has achieved."
Aviation Expert Simon Rodwell

"Its high-octane descriptions of air manoeuvres and daring escapes are breathtaking.... Because of its ambitious scope and phenomenal details, down to the last "Mae West" jacket, the novel is compelling, humanizing a historical event ....."
Foreword Clarion Reviews

Moral Fibre
A Bomber Pilot's Story

Winner of a GOLD in the Global Book Awards for 20th Century Fiction 2024, the HEMINGWAY AWARD for 20th Century Wartime Fiction 2022, SILVER in the 2023 Historical Fiction Company Book Awards for Military Fiction, MAINCREST MEDIA AWARD for Military Fiction and an INDIE BRAG Medallion. In addition, it was a FINALIST for the Book Excellence Awards for Historical Fiction 2023 and a DISTINGUISHED FAVORITE in the Independent Press Awards 2024

Riding the icy, moonlit sky—
They took the war to Hitler.
Their chances of survival were less than fifty percent.
Their average age was 21.
This is the story of just one Lancaster skipper, his crew,
and the woman he loved.
It is intended as a tribute to them all.

Flying Officer Kit Moran has earned his pilot's wings, but the greatest challenges still lie ahead: crewing up and returning to operations. Things aren't made easier by the fact that while still a flight engineer, he was posted LMF (Lacking in Moral Fibre) for refusing to fly after a raid on Berlin that killed his best friend and skipper. Nor does it help that he is in love with his dead friend's fiancé, who is not yet ready to become romantically involved again. Buy on Amazon now!

Praise for *Moral Fibre*

"...a tribute to those who fought for freedom."
Foreign Service Journal

"Meticulously researched and skillfully written, Schrader's Moral Fibre *steps off the pages and comes to life. Her nuanced characters and authentic dialogue also provide a glimpse of Britain›s stratified class-conscious culture during the WWII era. .... A riveting read and highly recommended!"*
Chanticleer Reviews 5-Stars

"Helena P. Schrader ... is a true master at delving into complex psychological dilemmas and emerging with a tantalizing, completely comprehensible tale of human frailty and strengths that blend into a unique experience for her readers."
Tom Gauthier for Readers Favorites

"A richly textured, absorbing war tale that works equally well as a touching love story."
Kirkus Reviews

Grounded Eagles
Three Tales of the RAF in WWII

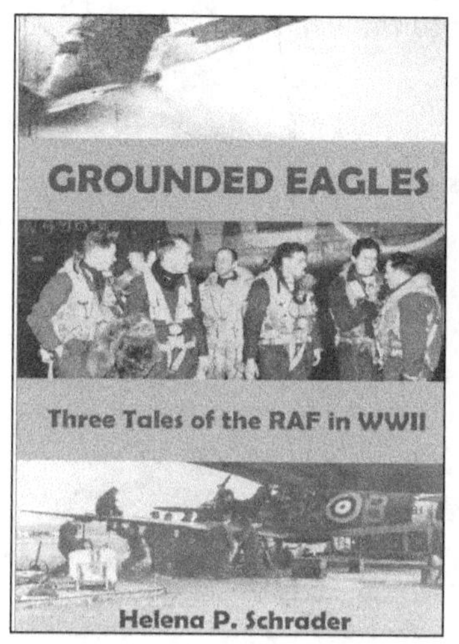

WINNER of a Chanticleer International Book Award for Short Stories, Novellas and Collections, a MAINCREST Media Award and an Indie BRAG Medallion

A Stranger in the Mirror: David Goldman is shot down in flames in September 1940. Not only is his face burned beyond recognition, but he is also told he will never fly again. While a plastic surgeon recreates his face one painful operation at a time, the 22-year-old pilot must discover who he really is.

Lack of Moral Fibre: In late November 1943, Flight Engineer Kit Moran refuses to participate in a raid on Berlin, his 37th 'op.' He is posted off his squadron for "Lacking Moral Fibre" and sent to a mysterious NYDN centre. Here, psychiatrist Dr Grace must determine if he needs psychiatric treatment — or disciplinary action for cowardice.

A Rose in November: Rhys Jenkins, a widower with two teenage children, has finally obtained his dream: "Chiefy" of a Spitfire squadron. But an unexpected attraction for an upperclass woman threatens to upend his life.

Buy now on amazon!

Praise for *Grounded Eagles*

"An impressive and memorable trio of works about the many costs of war."
Kirkus Reviews

"Helena P. Schrader delivers complex plots through the eyes of characters you will wrap your arms around and cheer for to the very end."
Tom Gauthier for **Readers' Favorites**

"Schrader excels at examining the nexus of physical and psychological trauma.... Grounded Eagles will appeal to any fan of WWII fiction."
Blue Ink Reviews

Traitors for the Sake of Humanity
A Novel of the German Resistance to Hitler

Finalist for a Forward INDIES Award 2022

They opposed Hitler's diabolical regime on moral grounds. They sought to defend human dignity and restore the rule of law — at the risk of their own lives. Traitors to Hitler, they were heroes to the oppressed. They remain an inspiration to anyone fighting against immoral and corrupt governments anywhere in the world.

Traitors opens in 1938 when Adolf Hitler seems to have captivated all of Germany. Soon one Nazi victory follows another, yet some individuals with integrity and compassion remain opposed to his regime and all it stands for — people like Philip, Alexandra, and Marianne. They feel isolated and hopeless until they discover each other — and learn that their concerns are shared by men in the very highest places in the German High Command....Buy now on amazon!